PENGUIN ⬤ CLASS

TALES OF ANGRIA

CHARLOTTE BRONTË was born in Thornton, Yorkshire, in 1816, the third of six children of Patrick and Maria Brontë. In 1820 her father was appointed perpetual curate of Haworth, a small town in the rapidly industrializing Pennines, on the edge of the Yorkshire moors. Mrs Brontë died in 1821, and her sister, Elizabeth Branwell, came to take care of the children – Maria, Elizabeth, Charlotte, Emily, Branwell and Anne. In 1824 the four oldest girls were sent to a boarding school for daughters of the clergy (later to be fictionalized as 'Lowood' in *Jane Eyre*). Maria and Elizabeth were taken ill at the school, and returned home to die in 1825; Charlotte and Emily returned home in the summer of that year. For the next six years, the young Brontës were educated at home. They developed a rich fantasy life amongst themselves, constructing together the imaginary world of Glass Town and writing of it in dozens of microscopically printed 'books'. Charlotte and her brother Branwell invented their shared kingdom of Angria in 1834. From 1831 to 1832 Charlotte went as a pupil to Miss Wooler's boarding school for young ladies at Roe Head; she returned there as a teacher from 1835–8. After working for a period as a private governess, in 1842 she went with her sister Emily to study languages at the Pensionnat Heger in Brussels, returning there as a teacher in 1843. She returned to Haworth in 1844. In 1846, at Charlotte's instigation, the Brontë sisters published *Poems by Currer, Ellis, and Acton Bell*. Charlotte's first novel, *The Professor*, was rejected by several publishers, and not published until 1857. *Jane Eyre* appeared, and was an instant success, in 1847. Branwell Brontë died in September 1848, Emily in December of the same year, and Anne in May 1849. Charlotte, the only survivor, continued to live at Haworth Parsonage with her father. *Shirley* was published in 1849 and *Villette* in 1853, both pseudonymously. In 1854 Charlotte married her father's curate, Arthur Bell Nicholls; she died on 31 March 1855.

HEATHER GLEN is a Fellow of New Hall, Cambridge, and Reader in Nineteenth-Century Literature at the University of Cambridge.

She is the editor of the Penguin Classics edition of Charlotte Brontë's *The Professor* (1989), and of *The Cambridge Companion to the Brontës* (2002). Her most recent book is *Charlotte Brontë: the Imagination in History* (Cambridge University Press, 2002).

CHARLOTTE BRONTË

Tales of Angria

Edited with an Introduction and Notes by
HEATHER GLEN

PENGUIN BOOKS

PENGUIN CLASSICS

Published by the Penguin Group
Penguin Books Ltd, 80 Strand, London WC2R 0RL, England
Penguin Group (USA) Inc., 375 Hudson Street, New York, New York 10014, USA
Penguin Group (Canada), 90 Eglinton Avenue East, Suite 700, Toronto, Ontario, Canada M4P 2Y3
(a division of Pearson Penguin Canada Inc.)
Penguin Ireland, 25 St Stephen's Green, Dublin 2, Ireland (a division of Penguin Books Ltd)
Penguin Group (Australia), 250 Camberwell Road,
Camberwell, Victoria 3124, Australia (a division of Pearson Australia Group Pty Ltd)
Penguin Books India Pvt Ltd, 11 Community Centre,
Panchsheel Park, New Delhi – 110 017, India
Penguin Group (NZ), cnr Airborne and Rosedale Roads, Albany,
Auckland 1310, New Zealand (a division of Pearson New Zealand Ltd)
Penguin Books (South Africa) (Pty) Ltd, 24 Sturdee Avenue,
Rosebank, Johannesburg 2196, South Africa

Penguin Books Ltd, Registered Offices: 80 Strand, London WC2R 0RL, England

www.penguin.com

This collection first published 2006
1

Henry Hastings, Harry Elkins Widener Collection, Houghton Library, Harvard
University, HEW 1.4.14 and *Caroline Vernon*, Harry Elkins Widener Collection,
Houghton Library, Harvard University, HEW 1.4.15 published by kind permission of
the Houghton Library, Harvard University. *Mina Laury*, Robert H. Taylor Collection,
Manuscripts Division, Department of Rare Books and Special Collections, Princeton
University Library (Record ID 72190), published by kind permission of the Princeton
University Library. *Stancliffe's Hotel* and *The Duke of Zamorna* and several of the
journal fragments 'All this day I have been in a dream': MS Bon 98 (8) BPM, 'I'm just
going to write because I cannot help it': MS Bon 98 (7) BPM, 'My Compliments to the
weather. I wonder what it': MS Bon 98 (6) BPM, 'About a week since I got a letter from
Branwell': MS Bon 92 (1) BPM, Stancliffe's Hotel ('Amen! such was the sound . . .'):
MS Bon B114 BPM, reproduced courtesy of The Bronte Parsonage Musuem. 'Well,
here I am at Roe Head', 'Now as I have a little bit of time' and 'Two gentlemen in
earnest conversation', autograph ms. diary fragments, Pierpoint Morgan Library MS
MA 2696, published with kind permission of the Pierpoint Morgan Library, New York.

Set in 10.25/12.25 pt PostScript Adobe Sabon
Typeset by Rowland Phototypesetting Ltd, Bury St Edmunds, Suffolk
Printed in England by Clays Ltd, St Ives plc

ISBN-13: 978-0-140-43509-2
ISBN-10: 0-140-43509-3

Contents

Chronology   vii
Introduction   xi
Further Reading   li
Note on the Texts   liii
The Background to Angria   lviii

Tales of Angria

MINA LAURY   3

STANCLIFFE'S HOTEL   63

THE DUKE OF ZAMORNA   125

HENRY HASTINGS   197

CAROLINE VERNON   323

THE ROE HEAD JOURNAL
    FRAGMENTS   441

Abbreviations   467
Notes   469
Glossary   562
Chronology of Angria   576
Principal Characters   580
Places   585

Chronology

(Tales included in this volume are marked by asterisks.)

1816 21 April: Charlotte Brontë, third child of Patrick and Maria Brontë, born at Thornton, Yorkshire.

1817 26 June: Patrick Branwell Brontë born.

1818 30 July: Emily Jane Brontë born.

1820 17 January: Anne Brontë born. April: the Brontë family move to Haworth, where Patrick Brontë becomes perpetual curate.

1821 15 September: Mrs Brontë dies. Her sister, Elizabeth Branwell, joins the household to care for the children.

1824 Charlotte and Emily Brontë, along with their older sisters Maria (b. 1813) and Elizabeth (b. 1815), are sent to the Clergy Daughters' School at Cowan Bridge.

1825 6 May: death of Maria from tuberculosis. 15 June: death of Elizabeth from tuberculosis. Charlotte and Emily are removed from the Clergy Daughters' School.

1826 Inspired by the gift of a box of toy soldiers for Branwell, the children begin their shared 'Young Men's Play', which is to lead to the Glass Town and Angrian sagas.

1831 January: Charlotte goes as a pupil to Miss Wooler's Roe Head school, on the outskirts of Mirfield near Huddersfield, where she meets Mary Taylor and Ellen Nussey, who are to be her lifelong friends and correspondents.

1832 June: Charlotte leaves Roe Head school, and remains at home for the next three years, instructing her sisters and assisting in running the household, as well as contributing prolifically to the Glass Town and Angrian sagas.

1835 July: Charlotte returns to Roe Head as a teacher. Her
sister Emily accompanies her as a pupil. October: Emily
returns home to Haworth and is replaced at Roe Head by
the youngest Brontë sister, Anne.

1836 December: Charlotte writes to Robert Southey, the Poet
Laureate, enclosing some of her poetry, and asking for his
advice about a literary career. Southey replies (March 1837)
to Charlotte's letter, telling her that 'Literature cannot be the
business of a woman's life: and it ought not to be.'

1838 January: Charlotte completes *Mina Laury whilst at
home for the Christmas vacation. June–July: During her
summer holidays she writes *Stancliffe's Hotel (28 June)
and *The Duke of Zamorna (21 July). December: Charlotte
leaves her post at Miss Wooler's school, now moved from
Mirfield to Dewsbury Moor.

1839 February–March: Charlotte writes *Henry Hastings.
March: She refuses a proposal of marriage from her friend
Ellen's brother, Henry Nussey. May–July: she is employed
as a governess with the Sidgwick family at Stonegappe, near
Lothersdale. In July, back at home, she receives and refuses
another proposal of marriage from a visiting young Irish
curate, Mr Pryce. She writes *Caroline Vernon between July
and December.

1841 March–December: Charlotte is employed as a governess
with the White family at Upperwood House, Rawdon.

1842 February: Charlotte and Emily go to Pensionnat Heger
in Brussels to study languages. October: Aunt Elizabeth
Branwell dies at Haworth. November: the sisters return
home.

1843 January: Charlotte returns alone to Brussels as a pupil-
teacher at Pensionnat Heger.

1844 January: Charlotte comes home. Plans to establish a
school with her sisters at Haworth Parsonage come to nothing. She writes a series of passionate letters to Monsieur
Heger, her teacher in Brussels. There is no record of any
response.

1845 May: The Revd. Arthur Bell Nicholls arrives at Haworth
as curate. July: Branwell dismissed from his position as a

tutor in disgrace. Autumn: Charlotte reads Emily's poems and persuades her two sisters to compile a joint selection of their poetry for publication. Emily and Anne agree, on the condition that pseudonyms are used to protect their identity: the gender-ambiguous names of Currer, Ellis and Acton Bell are selected.

1846 April: Charlotte begins to try to interest publishers in the publication of 'three distinct and unconnected tales' – the sisters' respective first novels: *The Professor*, *Wuthering Heights* and *Agnes Grey*. May: *Poems by Currer, Ellis and Acton Bell* is published at the sisters' own expense. Although favourably reviewed by both the *Athenaeum* and the *Critic*, it sells only two copies. August: Charlotte accompanies her father to Manchester for a cataract operation. Whilst there, she begins to write *Jane Eyre*.

1847 July: Thomas Newby agrees to publish *Wuthering Heights* and *Agnes Grey*. Charlotte sends *The Professor* to Smith, Elder & Co. who decline the novel but express interest in other work by its author. September: Smith, Elder & Co. agree to publish *Jane Eyre*. 19 October: *Jane Eyre: An Autobiography* 'edited by Currer Bell' is published and is an immediate success. December: *Wuthering Heights* by Ellis Bell and *Agnes Grey* by Acton Bell are published by Thomas Newby.

1848 June: *The Tenant of Wildfell Hall* by Acton Bell is published by Thomas Newby. July: Charlotte and Anne travel to London in order to confirm to their publishers that Currer, Ellis and Acton Bell are three individual writers – not one, as rumours have suggested. The first volume of Charlotte's *Shirley* is completed by the end of September. 24 September: Branwell dies, probably of tuberculosis aggravated by delirium tremens. 19 December: Emily dies of tuberculosis.

1849 28 May: Anne dies of tuberculosis at Scarborough, 26 October: *Shirley. A Tale* by Currer Bell published by Smith, Elder & Co. November–December: Charlotte visits London as the guest of her publisher, George Smith, and meets William Makepeace Thackeray and Harriet Martineau for the first time.

1850 Charlotte pays visits to the Smiths in London, to the Kay-Shuttleworths in Windermere (where she meets Elizabeth Gaskell) and to Harriet Martineau in Ambleside. 10 December: Charlotte's edition of *Wuthering Heights* and *Agnes Grey* with a 'Biographical Notice' of her sisters is published in one volume by Smith, Elder & Co.

1851 Charlotte visits London, where she goes to the Great Exhibition and Thackeray's lectures, and stays with Elizabeth Gaskell in Manchester. She begins *Villette*, completing the first volume by the end of March. April: Charlotte rejects an offer of marriage from James Taylor of Smith, Elder & Co.

1852 November: Charlotte completes *Villette*, in spite of continuing ill-health. December: Arthur Bell Nicholls proposes marriage, but Patrick Brontë is vehemently opposed.

1853 28 January: *Villette* by Currer Bell published by Smith, Elder & Co.

1854 29 June: Charlotte marries Nicholls.

1855 31 March: Charlotte Brontë Nicholls dies at Haworth, aged 38, from complications during the early stages of pregnancy. 4 April: Charlotte is buried in the family vault at Haworth.

1857 March: Publication of Elizabeth Gaskell's *The Life of Charlotte Brontë*. June: *The Professor, A Tale* by Currer Bell is published for the first time.

1860 'Emma', Charlotte's last, unfinished work, is published in the *Cornhill Magazine*.

1861 7 June: Death of Patrick Brontë.

Introduction

(New readers are advised that this Introduction makes some plot details explicit.)

I

The five tales in this volume were written by Charlotte Brontë when she was in her early twenties. They are witty, racy, ironic, with magnetic, amoral heroes and passionate, daydreaming heroines. Their subject matter is compelling: jealousy, flirtation, political unrest, a criminal on the run, the seduction of a young girl. Yet although they have long been known to Brontë critics and scholars, they have never before appeared together in an easily readable form. This may seem surprising. Charlotte Brontë's later novels have proved enduringly popular. *Jane Eyre* has been a best-seller since its first publication. Why are these earlier fictions not better known?

A large part of the reason seems to lie in the fact that these 'novelettes', as they have come to be called,[1] differ from the novels that their author published in her lifetime in one important respect. They are not quite freestanding, but part of a larger fiction: that voluminous body of writing now known as the 'Angrian saga', in which Charlotte and her brother Branwell had been collaborating since their teens. Angria had its origin in a series of imaginative 'plays' begun by the four young Brontës – Charlotte, Branwell, Emily and Anne – in the late 1820s, when Charlotte was twelve or thirteen, in their home at Haworth Parsonage. The children, casting themselves as four great controlling Genii, had together imagined the establishment of a European colony in Africa by a group of intrepid 'young men'. At first this was called Glass Town and subsequently Verdopolis: Charlotte and Branwell founded the associated kingdom of Angria in 1834.[2] All the young Brontës were voracious readers, of poetry and of fiction, of newspapers and periodicals;[3] and for years they elaborated their increasingly complex 'plays' in dozens of miniature volumes, all purportedly written by the characters they had created, and printed in a distinctive tiny script designed to imitate that of published books.

Early in the 'plays', the two youngest siblings, Emily and Anne, broke off to create their separate world of Gondal; of this, few records remain. But many of Charlotte's and Branwell's youthful manuscripts survive. His are mainly chronicles of military and political affairs, hers romantic tales and sketches of aristocratic life. 'They are the wildest & most incoherent things,' wrote Mrs Gaskell, who saw some of these writings whilst researching her *Life of Charlotte Brontë* in 1856. 'They give one the idea of creative power carried to the verge of insanity.' She provided her readers with a facsimile of a page to demonstrate its 'extreme minuteness', and dismissed it all in her biography as intelligible only to 'the bright little minds for whom it was intended', a 'curious' phenomenon of childhood, hardly to be taken seriously.[4]

A succession of pioneering editors have pieced together, transcribed and published nearly all this 'wild weird writing' It is possible now to make considerably more sense of the Glass Town, Verdopolitan and Angrian 'sagas' than Mrs Gaskell did.[5] But Angria has remained more 'curious' than enticing to readers. Its usual description as 'saga' carries the misleading suggestion of a long and complicated chronicle, intelligible only to those who read the whole. Indeed, the publication of large collected editions of the Brontës' early writings has arguably increased this sense. To the casual reader, it is quickly evident that the fictions they contain are bafflingly different from *Jane Eyre*. It is tempting simply to see them as intriguing relics of a now irrevocably vanished world of childhood fantasy.

Yet Charlotte Brontë's last Angrian writings are much more interesting than this. For the Brontës' 'bright darling dream', as Charlotte called it in some verses written at the age of nineteen,[6] was a peculiarly long-lasting one. Emily and Anne were still

preoccupied by Gondal well into adulthood. Charlotte and
Branwell continued the 'plays' throughout their teens and
beyond. The Roe Head journal fragments reprinted in this
volume, written when Charlotte, aged twenty, was embarking
on her first employment as a teacher, bear striking witness to
the fact that for her that absorbing 'mighty phantasm' continued
long beyond childhood to exert a powerful counterpull to the
demands of adult life. And the pull was not simply that of daydream. For these journal fragments speak also of the writer's
sense of creative powers unexercised, her frustrated longing to
shape her imaginings 'into some narrative better at least than
any thing I ever produced before' (p. 453). For years, the shared
childhood 'plays' had provided her with a space within which
she could develop her skills as a writer, assume the fictional
character of a professional literary man and imitate, parody
and experiment with a variety of literary styles. Indeed, from
the very beginning, her Glass Town and Angrian writings had
been not sections of a single 'saga' but a series of distinct and
generically varied works. Increasingly, to her, they were not an
escapist daydream, but a practical apprenticeship in writing.
Until she was nearly twenty-four she was to continue to work
at them whenever she had time, producing, in her early twenties
a series of more ambitious fictions, which range in length from
15,000 to 40,000 words. The five tales in this volume – *Mina
Laury*, *Stancliffe's Hotel*, *The Duke of Zamorna*, *Henry Hastings* and *Caroline Vernon* – are the last five of these. They were
apparently written between January 1838 and December 1839.[7]

So far as is known, these are Charlotte Brontë's final fictions
of Angria. Shortly after the last of them was finished, she
appears to have decided to bid farewell to that 'burning clime'.[8]
It was to be seven years before she began, unsuccessfully, to
attempt to interest publishers in her first novel, *The Professor*,
and eight before the success of *Jane Eyre* made her famous
beyond her dreams.[9] But these Angrian tales are not juvenilia.
The young woman who wrote them was almost the same age
as the Charles Dickens of *Pickwick Papers* (published in parts,
to enormous acclaim, a couple of years before).[10] For years,
she had been writing for an audience that, if small (probably

consisting only of her brother and her two sisters), was an extraordinarily well-read and sharply critical one. These tales were evidently written in the confidence that the 'reader' or 'readers' frequently addressed within them would be quick to pick up topical allusions and respond to generic cues. They are not, as has often been claimed, artless 'trance-writings',[11] but carefully crafted fictions, in which a highly accomplished writer, alert to the literary, linguistic and cultural life of her time, can be seen playing wittily with contemporary literary fashions and experimenting with an evolving literary form.

The purpose of this edition is to enable these tales to be read with ease and with enjoyment, as their first readers in Haworth Parsonage would have read them, and also with the kind of attention that they deserve. I have included only the last five of Charlotte Brontë's Angrian 'novelettes': few enough to allow a focus on each successive 'book', yet sufficient to enable perception of the interconnections and contrasts between them, the variousness of the writing, their range of allusiveness. Angrian references are explained in the introductory note to each tale and the Notes at the end of the volume. But it is more important for the reader to know something of the other contemporary writings that these tales imitate and parody, the contemporary issues they respond to, the form the writer is using, the generic expectations they invoke. These are not simply tales of Angria, but fictions of the 1830s, flexibly, variously responsive to the world in which they were conceived. If they speak of the scenes and characters of a private fantasy, they were shaped in a sharp witty dialogue with a whole range of other writings of their time.

For the desire to escape a prosaic everyday reality was one that many of the Brontës' contemporaries shared. It was a desire hugely catered to in the late 1830s by a burgeoning publishing industry: writ large in the best-selling annuals, with their exquisite engravings of exotic places and society beauties; in the popularity of narratives of travel beyond the boundaries of Europe, often extensively excerpted in periodicals; in the vogue for 'Newgate novels' featuring criminal heroes and 'flash' slang; in the continuing cult of Lord Byron, the success of the silver

fork novels, the popularity of Sir Walter Scott. In writing of a
'far & bright continent' (p. 447), of fashionable 'high life', of
passion, betrayal and intrigue, Charlotte Brontë was engaging
much more closely with the common cultural currency of her
time than the strangeness of Angria might lead one to suppose.

Most markedly, perhaps, the characters and events of these
tales – love-sick young women, dissolute aristocrats and high-
society courtesans; duelling, drinking, scandal and sexual
licence; adultery and betrayal; 'romantic friendship' between
men – are modelled on those of the fashionable Regency society
known in the 1830s to many sober middle-class readers through
the still hugely popular and controversial writings of Byron.
Charlotte's central male protagonists, the Earl of Northangerland and Zamorna, King of Angria, are in their different ways
Byronic figures: in their pride, daring and ambition, in their
aristocratic disdain for public opinion, above all, perhaps,
in their amorality. Like the charismatic subject of Thomas
Moore's *Life of Byron* (1830), both are 'either strangers, or
rebels to domestic ties'; 'instead of the softer duties and rewards
of being amiable', they have 'reserved for themselves the high,
hazardous chances of being great'.[12] Mary Percy and Mina
Laury, both in love with Zamorna, are adoring, submissive, self-
abnegating, archetypal Byronic heroines, the one a fair vision of
aristocratic elegance, the other a dark-eyed peasant girl. Each,
differently beautiful, bears a close resemblance to an engraving
from *Finden's Illustrations of the Life and Works of Lord Byron*
(1833–4) that the young Charlotte had copied in her teens.[13]

Yet if these tales are Byronic in their depiction of passion and
sentiment, they are perhaps yet more so in their worldliness
and irony. The glorious Marquis of Douro of the earlier Glass
Town writings, intrepid military hero and inspiring political
leader, whose poems were 'better than Byron's',[14] is now
Zamorna, King of Angria, a more disreputable figure, arro-
gantly alienating his subjects and eventually seducing his ward.
The romantic lyric he wrote for his first young love appears in
Mina Laury as a haunting, disconcerting reminder of youthful
passionate idealism; his wife comes upon it inscribed in his

mistress's book, in a half-poignant, half-comic scene of nearly discovered adultery. The faithless King and his Queen, poring over 'a volume of Byron' together at the end of *Mina Laury*, the young Caroline Vernon whose head is 'half turned' by reading Byron (p. 370), her guardian-seducer, whose motto is modelled on Byron's (p. 433), all now inhabit a much more cynical world. Here, romantic feeling is invoked only to be mocked, romantic cliché ridiculed in a recurrent ironic counterpoint to sentiment. 'I began this work with the intention of writing something high and pathetic,' says Charles Townshend, in a typical aside in *The Duke of Zamorna*. 'Let it suffice to say that I found this pitch far too high for me. I could not keep it up. I was forced to descend a peg' (pp. 161, 163).

For the narrator of these tales – more prominent in some than in others – is not, as in *Jane Eyre*, a central, passionate protagonist, but a detached, debunking outsider. Charles Townshend had evolved from the prying, scandal-loving Lord Charles Wellesley, younger brother of Zamorna, who had been Charlotte's favourite narrator since the early days of Glass Town. In both his incarnations he is a figure very different from Branwell's narrators, as he himself half comically confesses in a prose sketch written in 1836:

> [Richton and Hastings] are eagles . . . they are mounted on chargers of the Ukraine. for me I am but a crow, so I must be well content in the rookeries that shade Africa's ancestral Halls. I have but my own shanks to go on, therefore I can travel no further than the groaning park-gates of the magnates.[15]

Unlike Branwell's 'eagles' – Lord Richton, military leader and historian, and Henry Hastings, 'the young hero, the soldier poet of Angria' (p. 284) – Townshend is marginal, ridiculous; a mere cynical purveyor of gossip about the lives of the aristocracy. Branwell's Henry Hastings as narrator evinces an intense, uncritical involvement in the heroics he portrays –

> when I. see. Arthur. or Alexander in person when I hear their living words their sentiments of fire when I know the feeling that

actuates their exertions when I know the vast multitudes who follow them The great forces opposed to them. and above all the Awful struggle they seem about to dash themselves into Then does my spirit most long to partake their destiny to receive some portion of their fame![16]

But Charlotte's Charles Townshend writes of 'Arthur' and 'Alexander' (Zamorna and Northangerland) in a more sardonic style. The world on which he casts a cold eye in these later Angrian fictions is not a place of mighty Byronic passions, but one in which Byron has become a fashionable commodity. When Louisa Vernon affectedly quotes Byron at the opening of *Stancliffe's Hotel* – 'Where do you think my thoughts always stray on a summer night? What image do you think "a cloudless clime and starry skies" always suggests?' – it is less an expression of romantic sensibility than a token of her modishness.

For these are emphatically tales of fashionable life. 'I like high life: I like its manners, its splendours, its luxuries, the beings which move in its enchanted sphere.' Thus had opened Charlotte Brontë's *High Life in Verdopolis*, written in March 1834, shortly after the creation of the kingdom of Angria. The reader of her Angrian writings is never allowed to forget that their protagonists are Earls and Baronets and Duchesses: Byron's casual familiarity with fashionable manners and mores has here been replaced by what might at first appear a naïve fascination with the glamour of 'high life'. Yet even as early as *High Life in Verdopolis*, Charlotte, avid reader of the irreverent satire of *Blackwood's* and *Fraser's*, was more sophisticated than this. 'I like high life' is not the voice of the author. It is, we are told, an extract from an article in 'Tree's *Verdopolitan Magazine*', in which Zamorna polemicizes against the 'cant' of those who disapprove 'the artificial, voluptuous idle existences spun out by dukes, lords, ladies, knights and squires of high degree'. The narrator, Lord Charles Albert Florian Wellesley, quotes it 'not because the tone of feeling which dictated it meets my approval', but as an introduction to his own more ironic portrait of the manners of the aristocracy.[17] And the narrative that follows – as its earliest readers would have recognized with delight – is not merely a satisfying depiction of 'the manners, the splendours, the luxuries' of 'high life', but a witty imitation of a hugely successful contemporary literary genre. *High Life in Verdopolis* tells of an effete young dandy's search for a rich and well-connected wife amongst the 'grace, elegance, fashion and haut-ton of Verdopolis'. In the course of this quest, he meets 'a host of . . . noble and distinguished personages', including the rising politician, Sir Robert Pelham, Bart. The situations, the settings ('sumptuous saloons' and country estates, balls, boudoirs and drawing-rooms), the elaborate descriptions of the 'mingled magnificence and comfort' of the life of the 'beau monde',[18] most tellingly, perhaps, the name of Pelham, are all sharply evocative of one of the most popular fictional genres of these years, the fashionable or 'silver fork' novels, with which in the 1820s and 1830s, as *Blackwood's* was later to recall, 'the shops of publishers teemed, and the shelves of circulating libraries groaned'.[19]

Silver fork novels – sometimes looking back to the dissolute days of the Regency, but more often sharply contemporary romans-à-clef – depicted the exclusive, frivolous world of fashionable society. Their elaborately titled dramatis personae were dandies, rakish young men about town, society hostesses and women of the world, their settings the country estates and town houses of the aristocracy. They offered their readers lavishly detailed descriptions of the manners and mores of a 'high life' that most of them did not share: its luxuries and its pleasures, the 'slang' of the aristocracy, the latest fashions in dress. Indeed, they influenced fashion: the eponymous dandy-narrator of the most famous silver fork novel, Edward Lytton Bulwer's *Pelham* (1828), inspired a seemingly permanent change in the colour of men's evening clothes:[20]

> 'Now,' thought I, as I placed myself before the glass, 'shall I greatly please, or sublimely astonish the "fashionables" of Cheltenham?' . . . Don't put out that chain, Bedos – I wear the black coat, waistcoat, and trousers. Brush my hair as much *out* of curl as you can, and give an air of graceful negligence to my *tout ensemble*.' (ch. 39)

Yct silver fork novels were also much mocked for their glamorizing of 'the artificial, voluptuous idle existences' of the aristocracy.[21] The 'cant' of which Zamorna speaks in *High Life in Verdopolis* would have been quite familiar to his creator: in the early 1830s, such criticism was prominent in *Fraser's Magazine*. Charlotte Brontë can hardly have failed to respond with delight to the satiric pastiche of *Pelham* that appeared there as part of Thomas Carlyle's *Sartor Resartus* in August 1834.[22] Unlike Carlyle, however, she seems to have been acutely aware that silver fork fiction, almost from its beginnings, was itself a highly self-conscious and self-ironic form. 'Careless and indifferent as I seem to all things, nothing ever escapes me,' says Pelham; his coolly watchful intelligence includes a sardonic consciousness of his own ridiculousness as poseur.[23] In this, as in much else, he is like Charlotte's favourite narrator Townshend, with his studiedly languid air and sharp, voyeuristic eye.

For silver fork fiction is a potent presence not merely in *High Life in Verdopolis*, but in all Charlotte Brontë's subsequent Angrian tales. Here, as in silver fork fiction, the reader is given a half-ironic, half-fascinated portrait of a privileged beau monde. There is the same emphasis on talk – scandal, 'fashionable intelligence' (or society news), political rumours, newspaper reports, drawing-room repartee; the same cast of characters – roués, society belles, hard-up younger brothers and sought-after parvenue heiresses; the same aristocratic 'slang' and fashionable sprinkling of French. Here, also, the dandy is a prominent figure. Townshend in *Stancliffe's Hotel* evokes Pelham quite directly (though with his coloured clothes and his hair *in* curl he is not quite in the latest fashion):

> It took me a full half hour to dress, and another half hour to view myself over from head to foot in the splendid full-length mirror with which my chamber was furnished. Really, when I saw the neat figure therein reflected, genteelly attired in a fashionable morning suit, with light soft hair parted on one side and brushed into glossy curls, I thought, 'There are worse men in the world than Charles Townshend.' (p. 91)

Even the heroic Zamorna appears, in *Caroline Vernon*, in a similar attitude:[24]

> Zamorna ... pulled down his brief black silk waistcoat, adjusted his stock, settled himself in his dress-coat, ran his fingers three times through his hair, took his hat and new light lavender kid gloves, turned a moment to a mirror, backed, erected his head, took a survey of his whole longitude from top to toe. (p. 404).

This figure of 'Dandiacal Self-Worship' (to borrow Carlyle's mocking description of the hero óf the silver fork novel) is not the glorious young Apollo of the earlier Glass Town writings. Less heroic agent than fashionable object, he is depicted – as 'Mr Wellesley' – a couple of paragraphs later, creeping into his house 'like a thief', crossing the hall 'like a large tom-cat' and climbing the stairs 'on his toes like a magnified dancing-master' (p. 405) in a vain attempt to evade his jealous wife.

For if 'high life' in these tales is seen through the prism of the irony that surrounded the silver fork genre, so too is the masculine hero. Admiration of great men had been pivotal in the shaping of the Glass Town 'plays', from the moment when Charlotte chose the Duke of Wellington and her brother chose Napoleon to be their favourite protagonists.[25] Such admiration informs all Branwell's writings – mainly 'histories' of military conquest and 'lives' of eminent men. By the mid-1830s, indeed, 'hero worship' was receiving powerful intellectual endorsement in *Fraser's Magazine*.[26] Yet it is emphatically, ironically absent from these last of Charlotte's Angrian tales. Here, Northangerland is a worn-out 'buck' in once-fashionable Regency dress; Zamorna is a farmer, 'all in a muck of sweat', seen through Townshend's deflating eyes as a seedy adulterer. The passionate political speeches of these two founding spirits of Angria, given in full both in Branwell's and Charlotte's earlier Angrian manuscripts,[27] are replaced in *Henry Hastings* by Townshend's cool view of the opening session of the Verdopolitan Parliament:

> My dear reader, when you are inclined to grow enthusiastic about such things, just recall my image, leaning over the gallery with

my hat on, alternately squeezing and sucking a remarkably fine
Madeira orange, and meantime cocking my eye at the honourable
gent. on his legs with an expression sufficiently indicative of the
absorbing interest I take in his speechifications. (p. 210)

The stirring descriptions of battles that are prominent in
Branwell's Angrian 'histories' are mocked in Sir William
Percy's parodic 'quotation' of reports from the front in *Stancliffe's Hotel*. Charles Townshend and Sir William Percy,
impudent young men on the make, here come into focus as they
do not in Branwell's writings. Dandies and dissemblers, shy of
'heroics' and sentiment, these raffish, self-inventing and semi-
serious figures have none of the soaring ambition, the lofty
self-possession, of his iron-willed, grandiloquent Earl of
Northangerland. Pelham's 'self-consequence and absurdity'[28]
are echoed in Townshend's self-ironic awareness of the ridiculous figure he cuts, Sir William's 'sneers of superciliousness or
airs of nonchalance' (p. 283). Here, as in the silver fork novel,
masculinity has become a problematic thing.[29]

Charlotte Brontë's implicit riposte to her brother's heroics
reaches a climax in *Henry Hastings*, where the fall of Hastings,
one of Branwell's hero-narrators, is the pivot upon which the
narrative turns. This, like the other tales, opens in the manner
of a fashionable novel, with Townshend in search of an heiress
to marry, a description of Verdopolis at 'the commencement of
the grand political season' and a society beauty at the opera
quizzed by two dandyish young men. Yet the focus soon shifts
from 'high life' to a remote country mansion and a criminal on
the run. Here, Charlotte Brontë is evidently responding not
merely to silver fork fiction but to another hugely popular
contemporary literary genre: the 'Newgate novel' that portrayed criminal life in a controversially glamorous light. When
Sir William lies down on a sofa and opens *Rookwood's Northern Magazine*, when he and his men arrive at Massinger Hall
with its 'sombre rookery', her readers would immediately
have picked up the allusion to William Harrison Ainsworth's
Rookwood (1834), one of the most famous of these. *Rookwood*, a tale of pursuit featuring the eighteenth-century

highwayman Dick Turpin, set partly in a Gothic mansion surrounded by rookeries, had been reviewed at length, as 'a romance of no ordinary kind' in *Fraser's*.[30] In February 1839, whilst Charlotte Brontë was writing the first part of *Henry Hastings*, Ainsworth's wildly acclaimed *Jack Sheppard*, another 'Newgate' tale of an eighteenth-century thief, had just begun to be serialized in *Bentley's Miscellany* – a periodical specializing in pleasurably exaggerated Gothic and Newgate fictions, like the imaginary *Rookwood's Northern Magazine*.[31]

The hero of a Newgate novel was typically an outsider driven to break the law by the injustices of society. Charlotte Brontë's Henry Hastings may at first seem such a figure. Once the dashing soldier-poet of Angria, he has been goaded into crime by his jealous superior officer, and is, in the tale's first part, on the run from Sir William. Newgate fictions are recalled in the 'strange, blood-thirsty excitement' with which his pursuit is attended (p. 252), the 'flash' slang that is sprinkled through the description of his capture ('lumber', 'babes', 'chickens', 'soap'), even the storm through which his pursuers ride.[32] But the Hastings of this tale is not glamorous, but dissolute, a 'skulking, debauched military miscreant, who dared not own his country, and had blotted out his family name with stains of infamy' (p. 219). He does not, like a Newgate hero, die defiantly on the scaffold, but buys his reprieve by 'peaching' on his associates. His pursuer, Sir William – seen partly through the debunking eyes of his erstwhile friend Charles Townshend, and partly in the dandyish flippancies of his quoted diary extracts – is likewise far from heroic. His own description of himself in hot pursuit, 'pricked up in a saddle, dashing over the bridge of Zamorna like a laundrymaid heading a charge of cavalry' (p. 250), seems an ironic rejoinder to *Rookwood*'s most famous episode, its stirring account of Dick Turpin's ride from London to York. And in the last part of the tale, as Charlotte Brontë dismisses her brother's favourite narrator to his fate, Sir William meets his match in a heroine of a kind unprecedented in Angria: self-determining, self-disciplined, refusing the self-abnegation of a Mary Percy or a Mina Laury, more talented and more passionate than the society belle Jane Moore.

Yet even here irony is prominent. Elizabeth Hastings, 'the little dignified governess', proudly 'dependent on nobody', yet 'burning for warmer, closer attachment' (pp. 287-8), has been pounced upon by later critics as 'a forerunner of Jane Eyre'.[33] Yet *Henry Hastings* is not, like *Jane Eyre*, an intimate first-person narrative, but a series of mockingly observed and ironically juxtaposed scenes. Sir William, casually but purposefully 'ruralizing in a remote nook of the Girnington summerings', Elizabeth, rambling in the fields and 'indulging her morbid propensity for castle-building ... except when now and then scared by hearing the remote and angry low of a great Girnington bull' (p. 292) are portrayed with a knowing cynicism. The romantic encounter between them has an edge of sardonic comedy quite unlike anything in *Jane Eyre*. Elizabeth with her 'dander' raised before the Queen of Angria, is, as she herself feels, a somewhat ridiculous figure. And there is something equally ridiculous in Sir William's failed attempt at seduction, as Charles Townshend portrays it: 'There he remained, where she had left him, for hours ... He must have passed a quiet night – church and graves and tree all mute as death, Lady Rosamund's tomb alone proclaiming in the moonlight "I shall rise!"' (p. 305).

If *Henry Hastings* refuses to glamorize the masculine hero, *Caroline Vernon* portrays a young woman who does. Yet here, still, we are closer, both in subject and in tone, to the ironies of silver fork fiction than to the passionate directness of *Jane Eyre*. Caroline dreams of a splendidly titled lover; she goes, like Pelham, to Paris, to acquire 'the *ton*, the air, the elegance' of those 'on the summit of fashion' (p. 389); her story is informed throughout by its narrator's cynical awareness that an education of this kind might be rather more problematic for a young woman than for a young man. Caroline's 'imprisonment' and flight, her climactic confrontation with her suddenly dreadful guardian in the 'Gothic recesses' of an isolated country mansion, 'far away from the inhabited part of the house', the suggestions of incest that accompany this encounter, are all familiar clichés of an earlier but still very popular fictional genre – that of the Gothic romances which Charlotte had first encountered in childhood in the novels of Mrs Radcliffe and 'the tales of the Ladys Magazine'.[34] Such fictions, characterized by an atmosphere of brooding terror and featuring diabolical villains who threaten sexual violation, focused on the sufferings of a virtuous female protagonist, helpless in face of patriarchal power. In *Caroline Vernon*, however, the clichés of literary Gothic receive a peculiar, ironic inflection. The wild, romantic landscapes which in Gothic romances are evocative of wonder, awe and dread, are here put in their place by Caroline's cross reflection: 'Were those great staring mountains any judge of dress?' (p. 409). This heroine is not terrorized, but bored and frustrated; she is not exactly a figure of innocence in peril, but more than a little complicit in her own eventual fate. As if in riposte to Mrs Radcliffe's practice of prefacing her chapters with poetic extracts expressive of romantic sensibility, here sentiment is counterpointed by a cynical 'coarseness' of tone:[35]

> While Mrs Wellesley sung to herself 'Has sorrow thy young days shaded?', and while the sound of her piano came through closed doors with faint sweet effect, Mr Wellesley Junr and Mr Percy Senior sat staring opposite to each other like two bulls. (p. 356)

The half-comic, half-disturbing irony that pervades this novelette pivots upon the difference between Caroline's thrilling, fearful sense of Zamorna as a Gothic seducer and Townshend's mocking view of him as a 'large tom-cat'. There is certainly something shocking in this heroine's actual powerlessness, in the stark fact of her seduction and in the abruptness of her disappearance after it. But there is also, throughout, a disconcerting sense of the absurdity of rampant masculinity, from the bombast of the 'mad letter' from the drunken, lecherous Quashia at the opening of the tale to the exaggerated braggadocio of the final confrontation between Zamorna and Northangerland, with its ironic reminder that these swaggering heroes are simply puppets of the mighty Genii: 'Blow me up, and I shall live again' (p. 439).

II

The world Charlotte Brontë portrays in these last of her Angrian fictions is emphatically one whose heroic days are gone. By the time of these tales, the dark overreaching of Northangerland, the brilliant triumphs of Zamorna – 'the glories of Westwood and the bloodier triumphs of Leyden' (p. 279) – lie definitively in the past. Just so, in the England of the late 1830s, the mighty battles in which the prototypes for those heroes – Napoleon and the Duke of Wellington – had decided the fate of Europe were becoming a more and more distant memory.[36]

For like all fictional worlds, 'Angria' is partly pure invention, partly a transmutation of a world actually known. Though the names of its characters and places may be odder, its geography, history and politics more elaborately invented, it is in this sense not unlike Thomas Hardy's Wessex or Anthony Trollope's Barsetshire. Much in these tales is redolent of the England of the 1830s, in which manufacturing and commercial interests were becoming increasingly prominent, and economic and political power was beginning to pass to the middle class. When, in *Stancliffe's Hotel*, Charles Townshend and Sir William Percy approach the west end of Zamorna, they come to river banks 'piled with enormous manufactories and bristl[ing] with mill-chimneys', and the air is dense with 'smoke as black as soot' (p. 94): the moment is vividly evocative of the transformations wrought by industry in the England of the early nineteenth century, especially dramatically visible in the Pennines in which the Brontës grew up. The King of Angria's elaborate agricultural improvements and experiments reflect his creator's awareness of the growing sense in the period that the land was not simply the hereditary property of an old aristocracy but a productive commodity. For the English middle classes, this was a time of prosperity and of increasing social mobility – exemplified, in these tales, in the entry into high society of the daughter of a magistrate, without 'one drop of patrician blood in her veins' the nouveau riche Jane Moore (p. 166). The possibility of self-invention – seen comically, here, in Townshend's dandyish posing and also, more seriously, in Elizabeth Hastings's 'acquir[ing] a most impeccable character' (p. 288) – could be a liberating one. But this was also a time, for many, of uprooting and of insecurity, of movement away from known communities into a world of strangers, from accepted social distinctions to instability and uncertainty (figured, here, in the fall of Hastings and Sir William's loneliness). There was a different kind of instability in simmering working-class unrest. 'Britain' itself was not an unproblematically unified nation but, as its language clearly registered, made up of very different social and national groups.[37] There were divisive tensions between metropolitan 'England' and its others – regions, like Yorkshire, Scotland, Wales and Ireland (this latter proportionally far more populous than now); the further-off colonies; its recent enemy, France. The public moral climate was changing: if the success of the silver fork novels suggests that the 'reformation of manners' which had begun in the late eighteenth century was by no means complete, the increasing influence of evangelicalism and dissent had led, by the late 1830s, to a growing moral earnestness amongst the rising middle class.

All these things are reflected, and reflected upon, in Charlotte Brontë's last Angrian tales. Zamorna and his allies, fresh from victory in war but under increasing pressure from domestic discontent, are seeking to raise money to prosecute further colonial wars. The romantic past is being replaced by a modern commercial society. If *Mina Laury*, with its passionate, self-abnegating heroines, its wild northern landscapes and its galloping and duelling heroes, half ironically, half elegiacally evokes the romanticism of Byron and of Scott, *Stancliffe's Hotel* presents the reader with a very different world: vociferous commercial travellers doing deals in imported dyes for the new mass-produced fabrics in a chaotically bustling inn, and a sullenly mutinous populace, whose protest is brutally checked. Here, as in the England of the 1830s, political discontent finds no carthatic expression: it festers, or fizzles out. Here, as there, the military glories of the past are becoming a distant dream; heroic sentiment is domesticated and ironized. In *Stancliffe's*

Hotel, Jane Moore's stirring song of remembered valour in battle is sardonically echoed in Townshend's later description of Lord Stuartville's rather less glorious charge on the 'mad mechanics and desperate operatives of Zamorna': not a battle, but a 'frightful scene' (pp. 115, 116). When in *Henry Hastings* Sir William meets Elizabeth in the 'Girnington summerings', aristocratic flippancy is confounded by a new kind of middle class 'respectability'. But there is an abrupt, ironic challenge to the notion that 'morals ... have improved' (p. 329) in Townshend's sardonic account of Caroline Vernon's 'ruin' in the following tale.

As in the England of the 1830s, the rhetoric of nationhood seeks to overwrite division. Angria is not an old established kingdom, but a newly acquired colony, ruled by incoming 'westerns'; indeed, most of the characters often loosely referred to as Angrian – Northangerland, Zamorna, Mary Percy, Mina Laury, William Percy and Charles Townshend – are Senegambian, not Angrian at all. (Senegambia is closely modelled on Ireland; in an interesting twist, the colonized Irish become here the colonizers.) There are frequent reflections upon the differences beween these 'stranger[s] to the country' (p. 190) and the older Angrian settlers – the Hastings family, Warner Howard Warner, Lord Hartford, Jane Moore. But even the Angrians are not the country's original inhabitants. Like the rest of the Verdopolitan Union, Angria is uneasily founded on bloody imperial conquest, as the reader is reminded, not merely by recurrent references to the ongoing Ashantee wars, but by the 'grinning, capering nigger' depicted in a lithograph (well known in the late 1830s) on the cover of Caroline's music sheet.[38]

These tales, then, are sharply topical, in ways that their readers in Haworth Parsonage would immediately have recognized. They imitate and ironize contemporary literary fashions; they offer vivid glimpses of the manners, the crazes, the controversies of the England of the 1830s; they allude not merely to high literature – Shakespeare, Milton, the Bible, the classics, romantic poetry – but also to popular catchphrases and comic and sentimental songs. They play with different varieties of early nineteenth-century English – thieves' cant, aristocratic 'slang', Yorkshire and northern dialect, the fashionable French of 'high life'. They even display an interest in contemporary non-verbal gestures – putting the thumb to the side of the nose as a sign of contempt or ridicule, extending a forefinger as a mode of shaking hands. And their lively engagement with the world in which they were conceived is evident not simply in their representation of detail, but in their keen analytic sense of the dynamics of the society they depict, their distinctive, ironic take on contemporary issues and debates.

The moral seriousness that critics were increasingly to value in the emerging Victorian novel is notably and, it seems, deliberately, absent here. So, too, is the exploration of individual subjectivity that was to be central to the genre. There is acute psychological observation; there are many memorable protagonists. But again and again, the reader's identification is checked by a distancing external perspective, an ironic narrative voice. For what we see in these Angrian tales is less the intimate revelation of psychologically realistic character than a witty interrogation of the whole idea of 'character', an adroit, sardonic play with different meanings of the term. Thus, in *Caroline Vernon*, the Duke of Zamorna is questioned about his mistress by his ward:

'And what is Miss Laury like?' asked Caroline.
'What is she like? She's rather tall, and pale.'
'But I mean, what is her character? Ought I to visit with her?'
(p. 380)

Here, in a way that she was to develop in her later novels,[39] Charlotte Brontë is playing with the shifting meanings of a key contemporary word, allowing different senses to complicate and ironize one another, exposing telling contradiction and ambiguity. '[S]he had something of an original and peculiar character under all her rubbish of sentiment and inconsequence', we are told of Caroline Vernon (p. 372). But the enlightenment sense of 'character' as essential, individual nature is countered in these tales by other senses of 'character' that were prominent in the England of the 1830s, and of which it seems Charlotte Brontë is provocatively aware.

Angria is a place of gossip, in which 'character' is 'freely canvassed'. 'Madame Lalande and Lady St James are easy about their characters,' Zamorna tells Caroline (p. 380). 'I have never committed an action, or hazarded a word, that would bring my character for a moment under the breath of suspicion,' says Elizabeth Hastings proudly (p. 304); hers, unlike most of the others', is a 'character' formed by self-discipline and the deferral of desire.[40] Such moral construction of character was to be a central theme of the later Victorian novel. Yet it hardly figures in these tales. Even Elizabeth defends her 'character' less as subjective achievement than as the 'good opinion' of others (p. 304), her reputation in the world. Her career as a schoolmistress is founded, as Townshend notes, on her 'most impeccable character for ability, accomplishment, obliging disposition, and most correct and elegant manners' (p. 288). His language is that of the 'character', or testimonial, increasingly required by employers in the early nineteenth century, that he himself has admitted to being unable to produce (pp. 224–5). Such language receives a more comic inflection in the multiple 'etc.'s of his matrimonial advertisement:

> These ladies or any others who may feel disposed to try their luck in this noble lottery are referred for character etc. to the most noble Viscount Macara Lofty, Sir W. Percy, Bart, Mr Steaton Esqu., Rev. G. Bromley, Revd. W. Stephens, Revd M. Chambers, etc., etc. (pp. 201–2)

This, like the England in which the young Brontës were beginning to seek employment, is a world in which 'character' is a valuable commodity.

The primary sense of 'character' was, as Charlotte Brontë was evidently aware, 'a distinctive mark impressed, engraved, or otherwise formed; a brand, stamp'.[41] Thus, in *Mina Laury*, a description of Hartford concludes: 'there was enough seen to stamp his countenance with a character of unpleasantness more easily conceived than described' (p. 41); thus, 'characters' indicative of various vices are 'legibly written in the faces' of the commercial travellers who gather at Stancliffe's Hotel (p. 79). In the rapidly urbanizing society of early nineteenth-century England, people more and more frequently met as strangers, and the reading of character from such signs was a prominent concern. The contemporary pseudo-sciences of phrenology and handwriting analysis, and even 'digitology' (*Henry Hastings*, notes 30 and 163) figure largely in these tales. In *Henry Hastings*, Townshend, on the coach to Verdopolis, tries to 'deduct' the 'character' of the strange young woman he meets. As his narrative unfolds, he encounters a succession of strangers and attempts to make them out: the mysterious 'Mr Wilson'; the young man whose face he recognizes, now unfamiliar in the uniform of a policeman; the magistrate who looks familiar, yet whose name he does not know. The world through which he moves is, as each of these figures suggests, emphatically presented as a place of social mobility, in which men (though perhaps not women) can reinvent themselves.

Encounters such as these foreground another sense of 'character', one with which the four young Brontës had been preoccupied since the earliest days of 'Glass Town'. In her early 'The History of the Year', the thirteen-year-old Charlotte had written both of the heady creation of compelling fictional 'characters' ('This shall be the Duke!') and also of her fascination with the half-fictive public personae of the literary men of the day. The portrayal of the latter in *Fraser's* famous series 'The Gallery of Illustrious Literary Characters' was premised on a sense of the 'character' of a writer as a marketable thing.[42] The self-presentation of the *Fraser's* coterie under a variety of aliases partook of a conscious sense of 'character' as performance: one that the young Charlotte was quick to pick up and imitate in her early Glass Town writings, and one that figures prominently in these final Angrian tales. 'I would not trust the depths of that mind, strong and original though it might be, which thus puts on character and acts a part at will,' says Sir William of Jane Moore (p. 169). But he himself is an adept at such acting; indeed, he is soon to adopt the 'new character of

diplomatist' (p. 181). From the Duchess of Zamorna, masquer-
ading as 'Mrs Irving' (p. 52), 'Messrs Clarke and Gardiner'
playing their ridiculous trick on Jane Moore (pp. 98–9), Henry
Hastings as 'Mr Wilson' (p. 216), Caroline Vernon as 'Lucy
Grenville' (p. 423) to the Duke of Zamorna 'sport[ing] the
Simon Pure' (p. 393), this is a world of aliases, of dissimulation
and disguise. The fixity of 'character' enshrined in the testimonial is countered throughout by a stress on the instability of
personal identity. People are hard to place; social 'character' is
chameleon, difficult to read. 'I could not during the whole night
satisfactorily unravel the puzzle of our heroine's character,' Sir
William confides to Charles Townshend of his attempts to
make out Jane Moore (p. 169). 'You must have a great deal of
cover [i.e. deceitfulness] in your character,' writes Caroline to
Zamorna, adding, with quite unintentional comedy, 'which is
not a good sign' (p. 403). What such passages as these evince
is not simply a lively interest in varieties of character, but an
acutely self-reflexive literary intelligence.

III

If these tales are distinctive in their sophisticated ironies, they
are also distinctive in form. All are markedly shorter than the
average mid nineteenth-century novel, yet none appears to be
part of an unfinished longer whole.[43] They are not straightforward linear narratives, as Branwell Brontë's Angrian 'lives'
and 'histories' are. The reader's interest is held less by an
unfolding plot than by their contrasts of mood and feeling,
their constantly changing views of the same familiar characters,
like the changing patterns produced by a kaleidoscope. Each is
made up of a series of separate vignettes, much of the story
implied in the spaces between. There are sudden changes of
scene, shifts of tone and atmosphere. Yet the feeling is less of
clumsiness than of telling juxtaposition: flexible, witty, assured.
These are not fragments of novels, but quite self-conscious
exercises in a different literary form.

We are so accustomed to thinking of Charlotte Brontë as a

novelist that it is tempting to think of her earlier works as all tending towards that end. Yet in the late 1830s she may well have been less familiar with the novel than with shorter fictional forms. Indeed, a collection of short stories – perhaps the world's most famous such collection – had been pivotal in the shaping of the early Glass Town plays. Like many of their contemporaries, the young Brontës were eager readers of *The Arabian Nights' Entertainments* in one or other of their numerous nineteenth-century versions. The *Arabian Nights* inspired their controlling roles as the Four Chief Genii of Glass Town and many of Charlotte's early stories, descriptions and characters; there are allusions to the *Arabian Nights* throughout her later works.[44] Above all, the *Arabian Nights* were an intimately and early known example of a collection of short prose fictions, discontinuous but connected, contained within a larger narrative frame. By 1838, Charlotte Brontë may also have encountered another such collection, likewise enjoying a resurgence of popularity in early nineteenth-century England. Margaret Wooler, headmistress at Roe Head school, was a noted Italian scholar; if, as Charlotte's journal fragments suggest, she introduced her prize pupil to Italian literature, it is very likely that she included at least some of Boccaccio's *Decameron*.[45]

But there were other, more recent short fictions, which Charlotte Brontë seems to have known. For in the 1820s and 1830s there was a huge amount of interest in and experiment with shorter fictional forms.[46] Such fictions were, prominent amongst the fictional holdings of Keighley Mechanics' Institute Library[47], from which the Brontë family borrowed books. They appeared both in the popular annuals from which the young Brontës copied engravings, and in the periodicals which were their main point of access to the contemporary literary world. *Blackwood's* specialized in 'tales' of sensation and in first-person 'anecdotes' – both of which Charlotte Brontë had imitated in her early contributions to the Glass Town *Blackwood's Young Men's Magazine*.[48] *Fraser's* in the 1830s was also publishing short fictions, amongst them several by the Brontës' childhood favourite, James Hogg. Dickens and Thackeray, who were to be the most famous novelists of the 1840s, were in the late 1830s still primarily seen as writers of 'papers', 'sketches' and 'tales'.[49]

'I consider the story merely as a frame on which to stretch my materials,' writes Washington Irving in 1824, explaining his preference for 'a mode of sketches & short tales rather than long work'. What he aims for, he says, is 'the play of thought, and sentiment and language; the weaving in of characters, lightly yet expressively delineated; the familiar and faithful exhibition of scenes in common life; and the half concealed vein of humour that is often playing through the whole'.[50] The potentialities of short fiction were hardly theorized in the 1830s, but they were certainly exploited in a variety of ways. Some short fictions, like Hogg's tales, had their roots in oral story-telling. Others, like the 'sketch', with its connotations of polite accomplishment, were altogether more urbane.[51] Most, of whatever kind, were written in the first person, with a more or less elaborately characterized narrator – sometimes a central protagonist; sometimes a genial observer; sometimes, like Charlotte Brontë's Charles Townshend, at an ironizing remove from the world that was being described. Dickens's *Pickwick Papers*, which first appeared as a series of comic 'sketches', have a fictionalized 'editor'. Many short fictions were, like these latter, not completely freestanding. In *Blackwood's*, *Fraser's*, the earlier *Lady's Magazine* (all familiar to the young Brontës), and *Bentley's Miscellany* (which they very possibly knew), more or less fictional 'sketches' of place or character, 'tales' and short stories in a variety of styles and tones, loosely connected by setting, theme or narrator, were published as series over a number of months.[52] Such series portrayed the 'scene', the vignette, rather than development over time; they worked by parallel and contrast, rather than by the explicit interconnection of events. Their titles – 'sketches', 'papers', 'tales' – often emphasized their difference from continuous narratives. Many of these series were, like *Pickwick Papers*, collected into volumes, a number of which could be found in Keighley Mechanics' Institute Library.[53] None of the metanarratives which linked such volumes together were as elaborate or as developed as that of Angria. But they may well have suggested to Charlotte Brontë how a series of 'sketches' or 'tales', 'linked together by a chain of interest strong enough to prevent their appearing unconnected', yet each 'to a certain extent, complete in itself', might be developed as an aesthetically serious form.[54]

For it is a form with which, by the time of these Angrian tales, she had been experimenting for a number of years. In sharp contrast to her brother, who throughout the 1830s was producing lengthy chronicles of the history of Angria, she had since her teens been writing short separate tales and vignettes. This may have been partly because she often lacked time and opportunity for more extended composition. As she puts it in one of her Roe Head journal fragments, 'I can't enter into any continued narrative – my mind is not settled enough for that but if I could call up some slight & pleasant sketch, I would amuse myself by jotting it down' (p. 450). But it also appears to have been a matter of deliberate choice. Even before she took up her post as a teacher, her fictions differed from Branwell's not merely in that they were far less ambitious in length. They were explicitly presented to the reader as collections of shorter pieces, their titles like those of other such collections in the period – *Corner Dishes: A Small Collection of Mixed and Unsubstantial Trifles in Prose and Verse* (1835); *Arthuriana or Odds & Ends Being A Miscellaneous Collection of Pieces in Prose & Verse* (1835); *The Scrap Book. A Mingling of Many Things* (1835). The form was one that Charlotte Brontë could be confident her readers would recognize. She was to develop its potentialities to distinctive and striking effect in her final Angrian tales.

Each is short enough to be read in a sitting, or at most (as the division of *Henry Hastings* and *Caroline Vernon* into parts perhaps suggests) in two or three. Their generic signals are those of the 'sketches' and 'papers' of the period: an emphasis on 'scene' rather than narrative connection; shifts of tone and mood; pronounced inconclusiveness. They are more inconclusive, indeed, than many other short fictions of their time. In *Mina Laury*, *Henry Hastings* and *Caroline Vernon*, there are, indeed, climactic moments: a duel is fought, a meeting between wife and mistress takes place; an outlaw is captured; a young woman is seduced, or refuses to be seduced. But such climaxes are momentary; they do not answer the questions or resolve the tensions that have been raised. Each tale ends in impasse or in unresolved dilemma – either with taunting abruptness, like *The Duke of Zamorna* and *Caroline Vernon*; or, like *Stancliffe's Hotel* and *Henry Hastings*, with the lingering after-resonance of a haunting final scene. And if each separate tale works by juxtaposing scenes, so do they as a group, echoing, complicating, counterpointing and ironizing one another, refusing the definitive closure of a single narrative.

Where many later nineteenth-century novels trace cause and effect, making the arbitrary meaningful, here there is no such sense of an authoritative narrative voice. Indeed, the formal properties of these tales – disjunction, indirectness, inconsequentiality – stand at an ironic angle to those of the favoured cultural narratives of early nineteenth-century England – not merely conventional romance (those stories of 'union and a happy succeeding life' invoked and dismissed at the ending of Charlotte Brontë's later *Villette*) but the narratives of battle and politics, of effective, heroic agency, that Branwell, the 'reader' envisaged most directly and intimately here, was writing in these years. The narrating figure of Charles Townshend, cynical younger brother of Zamorna, King of Angria, consciously marginal, mockingly subversive of heroic and romantic pretension, is prominently figured in each as a precise and explicit image of this challenge to narrative authority.

Plot, the vehicle of endeavour, progress, resolution, here appears less important than the atmosphere and tone of the moment: in this, these tales are akin to the contemporary 'sketch'. Yet they are not simply 'sketches'. Each consists of a succession of 'scenes', through which a story unfolds; each is connected to the others not simply by a frame narrator, but by an ongoing narrative. For like other series of short fictions in the period, these would have been read sequentially, not just as separate tales. The 'reader' they address is occasionally reminded of this: 'The last scene in my last book . . .' *Mina Laury* begins. And the careful reader of this volume will notice running through it a number of intertwined narratives: the gradual collapse of the relationship between the Duke of Zamorna and his ailing father-in-law; the declining fortunes of Louisa Vernon; Sir William Percy's development from a frivolous young dandy to a trusted diplomat – to single out just three. Such central narratives are accompanied by suggestions of others, less fully developed (Hartford's increasing embitterment; the developing closeness between Sir William and his sister; Zamorna's growing unpopularity): what Branwell, in a passage that gives a suggestive indication of the sophistication with which the creators of Angria thought about fictional technique, had called in his *Life of Alexander Percy* (1834) 'the by play the under plot that portion which is usually by far the most interesting and important portion of a Novel or tale'.[55]

As in the *Arabian Nights*, the short fictions Charlotte Brontë knew first, 'stories' are in these tales a central concern. Each is full of references to other 'stories' – such as the half-understood anecdotes Townshend recalls hearing in childhood (pp. 131–2), or his involuntary memory of Henry Hastings as a 'bold, handsome, hardy soldier' amongst 'a circle of lovely women' in the heady days of his fame (pp. 218–19). Sometimes there are allusions to events narrated more fully elsewhere, either by Charlotte or by Branwell – such as the story of Rosamund Wellesley, or that of Victoria Delph, or the military history signalled in Townshend's references to 'the campaign of –33, the rebellion of –36' (p. 76). Sometimes a throwaway line points towards a whole untold story: 'I hate that Lord, Townshend' (p. 185) or 'Who can think highly of Lady Stuartville?' (p. 143). The recurrent, emphasized sense is that any 'story' is merely one amongst many; the effect is both to relativize any single version of events and to suggest the inexhaustible multifacetedness of this world.

Yet it is not simply in their emphasis on 'stories' that these tales pose a challenge to unselfconscious linear narrative. There is a different kind of questioning of narrative in that focus on isolated 'scene' that seems to align them with the contemporary 'sketch'. For the 'sketch', as its name suggests, was a distinctively pictorial form. Many collections of literary 'sketches' in the period draw attention to this, bearing subtitles such as 'Pictures' or 'Scenes', and making frequent reference to the visual arts. The advances in mechanical reproduction that made the early nineteenth century a print culture had also made it a highly visual one. Steel engraving, wood engraving and lithography – all of which produced high quality impressions quickly and in vast numbers – meant that visual images were distributed in the England of the 1830s on an unprecedented scale. In serialized fictions such as *Pickwick Papers*, and in drawing-room editions of such poets as Byron, Scott and Thomas Moore, illustrations frequently accompanied text; in the hugely successful annuals, text was usually secondary to the engravings the volume contained.[56] Reviewers often conceived of the writer of fiction as painting a picture in words. Thus, Harrison Ainsworth argues, in 1836, that the novelist's 'representation should address itself . . . vividly to the reader's mental retina'.[57] And Charlotte Brontë, late in 1839, speaks in similar terms of the 'great many books' she has written, in the fragment that has come to be known as her 'Farewell to Angria':

> I have shown my landscapes in every variety of shade & light which morning, noon and evening – the rising, the meridian & the setting sun can bestow upon them . . . My readers have been habituated to one set of features, which they have seen now in profile, now in full face, now in outline, and again in finished painting . . . but we must change, for the eye is tired of the picture so oft recurring and now so familiar.[58]

The young Brontës responded to the bourgeoning visual culture of their day as eagerly as they did to its rapidly expanding print culture. Among Charlotte's earliest surviving manuscripts is a 'List of painters whose works I wish to see', written when she was thirteen; throughout her life, she was passionately interested in the visual arts.[59] For years before she began *Mina Laury* she had been copying engravings in pencil and in watercolour, transmuting their subjects sometimes quite explicitly into the scenes and personae of Angria.[60] As her Roe Head journal fragments make clear, the imaginative process was for her a

distinctively visual one. The 'scenes' she describes as appearing
before her there are full of narrative potential, speaking of that
which has already happened in Angria and suggesting future
events. But they are also simply 'scenes' – sharp visual images:
'the tall man washing his bloody hands in a bason & the dark
beauty standing by with a light remained pictured in my mind's
eye with irksome and alarming distinctness' (p. 455); 'I saw
them stately & handsome, gliding through those saloons where
many other well-known forms crossed my sight' (p. 460). And
the Angrian tales she was to write when at last she had time
and leisure are quite centrally concerned with visuality. It is not
merely that their language of description is often that of the
visual arts: 'The forest of Hawkscliffe was as still as a tomb,
and its black leafless wilds stretched away in the distance and
cut off with a hard serrated line the sky from the country'
(p. 25); 'the moonlight disclosed a clear forehead, pencilled
with soft, dusk curls, dark and touching eyes, and a round,
youthful cheek, smooth in texture and fine in tint as that of
some portrait hung in an Italian palace' (p. 382). Again and
again within them, ongoing narrative is suggestively suspended
by the 'vivid realization' of 'scene'.

'But the scene is no longer vivid. I have forgotten it; its
healthy hues will not stand in the vitiated atmosphere of this
other tableau,' says Charles Townshend in *Henry Hastings*,
looking back from the group of figures before him in 'a room
in the heart of a great town, closed, curtained and lighted
up' to another 'picture' of another group several years before
(pp. 218–19). Charlotte Brontë was clearly aware that the *tableau vivant* – a carefully lit arrangement of silent motionless
figures, designed to tell a story – was a popular entertainment in
the 1830s, both in professional theatre and also in fashionable
drawing-rooms.[61] Indeed, the eloquent tableau, in which a
narrative situation was crystallized and placed on view, was a
prominent feature of much early nineteenth-century verbal,
visual and dramatic art. Such 'pictures' were frequently encountered by readers of fiction in the period, not merely in the
descriptive set-pieces for which Scott, especially, was famous,
but in the actual illustrations that accompanied short stories in

the annuals, and appeared in serialized fictions like *Jack Sheppard* and *Oliver Twist*. The aim, in each case, was to produce

> that instant and vivid flash of conviction, which darts on the mind from seeing the happy and expressive combinations of a single scene, and which gathers from the position, attitude, and countenance of the moment, not only the history of the past lives of the personages represented, and the nature of the business on which they are immediately engaged, but lifts even the veil of futurity, and affords a shrewd guess at their future fortunes.[62]

'Scenes' of this kind recur in Charlotte Brontë's last Angrian tales. The very form of these fictions – neither single, static 'sketch' nor straightforward 'continued narrative' – pivots on the interplay between developing story and the encapsulation of a mood or a situation in visual moments such as these. Indeed, this relation between action and its suspension in a sharply pictured scene is one that they themselves reflect upon in varied and suggestive ways.

'It was in July when affairs reached this climax,' begins the second part of *Caroline Vernon*, looking back to the situation developed in the first. 'It is now November, nearly December, and consequently a period of about four months has lapsed in the interim.' And the narrator goes on, in one of those metafictional jokes beloved of the young Brontës, to mock the contemporary aesthetic fashion for the arrested, expressive image (especially popular in the theatre at the moment when the curtain was going down):

> We are not to suppose that matters have all this while remained *in statu quo*, that Miss Caroline has been standing for upwards of a quarter of a year with her foot on the carriage-step, her hand on the lackey's arm, her eyes pathetically and sentimentally fixed on the windows and chimneys of the convent-like place she is about to leave for good, all in a cataleptic condition of romantic immutability. (p. 388)

Here, the emblematic moment is presented with comic literalism, as the static pose maintained (with difficulty) by a character in a *tableau vivant*. Elsewhere, the eloquent 'tableau' is pregnant with other meanings. As Townshend portrays Zamorna signing state papers with his prime minister, the presentation of narrative as a mute pictorial 'scene' becomes a sardonic pointer to the futility of action: the characters appear as 'performers' without agency, fixed in a timeless moment of perpetual, pointless 'play':

> The scene is a silent one. When you have looked awhile you begin to imagine that both performers are dummies. It reminds you of the mute allegories shown by the Interpreter to Christian, or of the old Dutch groups of ghosts who play dice and nine-pins a hundred years after they are dead. (pp. 305–6)

Elizabeth Hastings's rhythmic, solitary pacing, seen in a lighted window, appears as a more haunting image of movement without progression – less a particular character at a particular point in the narrative than an almost abstract 'figure' of turning and returning, with darkness all around:

> A figure came towards the window, and then paced back again, and was almost lost in the shadow of the opposite end. Again it appeared, drawing near slowly; as slowly, it withdrew to the dusk of distance. To and fro it paced with the same measured step down the whole length of the large old parlour, and there was nothing else visible. A single person walking about there, in that remote mansion embosomed amid boundless fields. (p. 231)[63]

The sense – finely caught in the present participle that replaces the verb in the final sentence – is of a moment suspended both inside and outside time.

Elsewhere, the suspension of narrative in 'scene' enables a more explicit contemplation of the ambiguous timelessness of art. Thus, at a moment of pause in his pursuit of Henry Hastings, Sir William Percy is confronted with a pictured image 'smiling all by itself in [a] frozen dreary room'. Here, the constellation of feeling is not of movement in stasis, but of frozenness and fixity:

> It was an apartment with the chill of a vault on its atmosphere, furnished in drawing-room style, but without fire in its bright steel grate, without light in its icy chandelier, whose drops streamed from the ceiling like a cold crystal stalactite. The mirror between the windows looked as if it had never reflected a human face for ages; the couch, the chairs, the grand piano, all stood like fixtures never to be moved. Over the piano was a large picture, the only one in the room. I could see by the dim candle on the table that it was a portrait, painted by some eminent hand, for the contours were flesh-like and brilliant. It was a girl of about twelve years old, with the lips and the eyes and the soft, shadowy hair that flattering villain Lawrence bestows on all his portraits. The image smiling all by itself in this frozen, dreary room reminded me of that legendary lady who pricked her finger, and having fallen into a trance, was enshrined in a splendid chamber where she sat twenty years, in all the stillness of death and all the beauty of life. (pp. 255–6)

Suggestions of deathly magic play through the passage's images of immutability: the suspended animation figured in the icy chandelier, 'whose drops streamed from the ceiling', the 'flesh-like' unliving portrait, its subject caught forever on the brink of puberty, the Sleeping Beauty of fairy tale, 'enshrined . . . in all the stillness of death and all the beauty of life'. Yet, as if in riposte to this, at the ending of the same tale there is a different kind of image of the ways in which (as Catherine Gallagher has put it, in a suggestive discussion of temporality and fiction) 'form contends against time'.[64] Here, the emphasis is on the fleeting and the transient. The room is emptied, the candles burn down, the 'living figures' disappear. But counterpointing this, as activity becomes stillness, before the implied observer the room becomes a 'scene':

> The candle remained burning on the toilet, the two chairs stood vacant before it, the splendid little room reflected around its fairy

beauty, but the living figures of the scene were gone. Solitude and silence lingered behind them. The candle burnt soon to its socket. The flame flickered, waned, streamed up in a long tongue of light, sank again, trembled a moment, and finally vanished in total darkness. Then a piano was heard playing in the drawing-room below, and, when the first note had stilled the clamour of children, a voice sung:

> ... Merrily, rapidly,
>   Our sunny hours flit by,
>   Then gratefully, cheerily,
>   Enjoy them as they fly. (pp. 321–2)

The past tense of narrative gives way to the timeless present of 'song', as the dwindling, vanishing moment takes on aesthetic form.

The formal self-reflexiveness displayed in such passages as these will come as a surprise to some readers. Perhaps because this was the form she chose for her most famous novel, Charlotte Brontë is still often thought to be an 'autobiographical' writer, whose works are most intimately connected to the story of her life. These tales of her early twenties prompt a rather different view. In their ironizing of 'heroism' and of the clichés of literary Gothic, in their questioning of narrative authority and play with narrative voice, in their extraordinary alertness to the literary, linguistic and cultural life of their time, they point towards much in Charlotte's later novels that an 'autobiographical' reading obscures. In the glimpse they give us of one gifted writer's engagement with the potent, complex legacy of what was to be described in *Jane Eyre* as 'the golden age of modern literature' (ch. 32), they offer a suggestive insight into the relation between the passionate intensities and subversive ironies of 'romanticism' and the social realism of an emerging 'Victorianism'. But they are not simply of interest as a hinterland to those later, more famous novels, or because they illuminate what is still a rather dark corner of literary history. Evocative, irreverent, moving and funny by turns, informed throughout by an acute literary intelligence, they can still be

read with something of the same sophisticated pleasure that
they gave to their first eager readers in Haworth Parsonage.

NOTES

(A list of abbreviations appears on pp. 467–8.)

1. The term is Charlotte Brontë's; she uses it of an apparently
slightly later manuscript in a letter to Hartley Coleridge written in
December 1840 (Margaret Smith (ed.), *The Letters of Charlotte
Brontë* (3 vols.; Oxford: Clarendon Press, 1995–2004), 1,
p. 241). Winifred Gérin adopts it to describe the Angrian fictions
of 1837–9 in *Five Novelettes* (London: Folio Press, 1971).

2. For fuller discussion of this, see The Background to Angria,
p. viii.

3. On the books read by the Brontë children, see Christine Alexander and Margaret Smith, *The Oxford Companion to the
Brontës* (Oxford: Oxford University Press, 2003), pp. 54–6.

4. J. A. V. Chapple and Arthur Pollard (eds.), *The Letters of
Mrs Gaskell* (Manchester: Manchester University Press, 1997),
p. 398; Elizabeth Gaskell, *The Life of Charlotte Brontë*, ed.
Elisabeth Jay (Harmondsworth: Penguin, 1997), pp. 62–70.

5. Gaskell, *Life of Charlotte Brontë*, p. 69. *Mina Laury* and an
'abbreviated' *Caroline Vernon* (omitting 'a few pages not par-
ticularly relevant to the story' (p. 233)) were published in Fannie
E. Ratchford's *Legends of Angria* (1933), and *The Duke of
Zamorna* in *The Miscellaneous and Unpublished Writings of
Charlotte and Patrick Branwell Brontë* (Shakespeare Head
edn, 2 vols., 1936 and 1938), ed. Thomas James Wise and John
Alexander Symington, vol. 2. *Stancliffe's Hotel* (ed. Heather
Glen) was published by Penguin in 2003. Gérin's *Five Novelettes*
includes three of the tales in this volume (*Mina Laury*, *Henry
Hastings* and *Caroline Vernon*) and two earlier ones (there
named *Passing Events* and *Julia*). Two volumes of Christine
Alexander's *An Edition of the Early Writings of Charlotte Brontë*
have so far been published (Oxford: Basil Blackwell, vol. 1,
1987; vol. 2, parts i and ii, 1991); the third and final volume
will contain the last Angrian tales. Victor A. Neufeldt's edition
of *The Works of Patrick Branwell Brontë*, 3 vols. (New York
and London: Garland Publishing, 1999), collected together
Branwell's scattered and disordered writings and made it possible

for scholars to trace the relationship between his and Charlotte's Angrian manuscripts.

   The first extensive discussion of Charlotte Brontë's early writings was Fannie E. Ratchford's *The Brontës' Web of Childhood* (New York: Russell & Russell, 1941). In her detailed and comprehensive *The Early Writings of Charlotte Brontë* Alexander reconstructed the narrative outlines of the Glass Town, Verdopolitan and Angrian fictions, and shed valuable light on the relations between these fictions and Charlotte's later works.

6. 'We wove a web in childhood', in Juliet Barker (ed.), *Charlotte Brontë: Juvenilia 1829–1835* (Harmondsworth: Penguin, 1996), pp. 262–9.

7. The four earlier 'novelettes' that survive were written during Charlotte Brontë's vacations from Roe Head in 1836–7. They are (1) the fragments published in Gérin's *Five Novelettes* as *Passing Events* (April and June 1836); (2) the untitled and undated manuscript published as *The Return of Zamorna* in *SHCBM* Vol. 2 (apparently written in December 1836); (3) the manuscript published in *Five Novelettes* as *Julia* (dated 29 June 1837); and (4) an unpublished, unlocated manuscript known as *Four Years Ago* (21 July 1837), of which there is a transcript in the Brontë Parsonage Museum (Hatfield Transcription 10).

8. See the manuscript fragment beginning 'I have now written a great many books', now known as 'Farewell to Angria', BPM: B125(1).

9. In December 1840, Charlotte Brontë began a full-length realistic novel set in Yorkshire. Of this unfinished, untitled work, now known as *Ashworth*, three opening chapters and a few related fragments survive. See Melodie Monahan (ed.), 'Ashworth: An Unfinished Novel by Charlotte Brontë', *Studies in Philology* 80:4 (Fall, 1983); and Alexander and Smith, *The Oxford Companion to the Brontës*, pp. 24–5. If Charlotte Brontë wrote other fictions in 1840–46, none appears to have been preserved.

10. *Pickwick Papers*, begun when Charles Dickens was 24, appeared April 1836–November 1837.

11. Gérin's suggestion, apparently derived from the Roe Head journal fragments, that the Angrian manuscripts were written in a 'trance-like' state (*Five Novelettes*, p. 16), has been repeated by successive critics. See, for example, Sandra Gilbert and Susan Gubar, *The Madwoman in the Attic: The Woman Writer and the Nineteenth-Century Literary Imagination* (New Haven and London: Yale University Press, 1979), p. 311; Alexander, *Early*

Writings, p. 243; Dianne F. Sadoff, *Monsters of Affection: Dickens, Eliot and Brontë on Fatherhood* (Baltimore and London: Johns Hopkins University Press, 1982), p. 120.

12. Thomas Moore, *Letters and Journals of Lord Byron, with Notices of His Life*, 3rd edn., 3 vols. (London: John Murray, 1833), Vol. 2, p. 113.

13. See Christine Alexander and Jane Sellars, *The Art of the Brontës* (Cambridge: Cambridge University Press, 1995), pp. 236–7.

14. Branwell Brontë, *The Politics of Verdopolis*, in Neufeldt, *Works* 1, pp. 350–51.

15. *Passing Events*, in Gérin, *Five Novelettes*, pp. 35–7. 'Rookeries' were such a staple feature of descriptions of the great country houses of the landed aristocracy in the period as to have become a joke; see, for example, Benjamin Disraeli, *Vivian Grey* (1826), Vol. II, ch. 10.

16. Branwell Brontë, *[Angria and the Angrians] I(e)*, in Neufeldt, *Works*, 2, p. 412.

17. Charlotte Brontë, *High Life in Verdopolis*, in Alexander, *Early Writings*, 2.ii, pp. 4–5.

18. Ibid., pp. 12, 6, 19.

19. [Archibald Alison], 'The Historical Romance', *Blackwood's* 58 (September 1845), p. 341. On silver fork fiction, see Alison Adburgham, *Silver Fork Society: Fashionable Life and Literature from 1814 to 1840* (London: Constable, 1983). The Brontës could have found *Pelham*, probably the most famous novel of the 1830s, along with several other works by Bulwer, in the library of the Keighley Mechanics' Institute. (See Clifford Whone, 'Where the Brontës Borrowed Books: The Keighley Mechanics' Institute', *BST* 11 (1950), pp. 355–8.) They would certainly have read the extensive attacks on Bulwer (including much quotation from *Pelham*) which appeared in the early 1830s in *Fraser's Magazine*. Sir Robert Weaver Pelham, an expatriate Englishman who pays court to Mary Percy, makes his first appearance in Branwell's *The Politics of Verdopolis*, completed in November 1833 (see *Henry Hastings*, n. 103).

20. Adburgham, *Silver Fork Society*, p. 127.

21. *High Life in Verdopolis*, p. 4.

22. Thomas Carlyle's 'The Dandiacal Body' (*Sartor Resartus*, Book III, ch. 10) was first published in *Fraser's* 10 (August 1834), pp. 184–9. William Makepeace Thackeray was to parody the genre in his *Yellowplush Correspondence* (1837–8) and Dickens in *Nicholas Nickleby* (1838–9), ch. 28.

23. Even the earliest of the fashionable novels often themselves half satirized the 'high life' they portrayed. Disraeli's *Vivian Grey* (1826) was puffed on its first appearance as 'a very singular novel of the satirical kind' (Adburgham, *Silver Fork Society*, p. 80); *Pelham* – as its author pointed out in a defensive response to his critics – was less an admiring portrayal of the manners and mores of 'high life' than a witty anatomy of dandyism. (See Winifred Hughes, 'Silver Fork Writers and Readers: Social Contexts of a Best Seller', *Novel* 25.3 (1992), p. 330.)

24. The dandy before his mirror was a favourite image of the period, immortalized in a mocking line drawing of Bulwer in *Fraser's* (see *Stancliffe's Hotel*, n. 43).

25. See Charlotte Brontë, 'The History of the Year' (1829), Barker, *Juvenilia*, p. 3.

26. 'Great men are the inspired (speaking and acting) Texts of . . . HISTORY,' Carlyle, scourge of the fashionable novel, had declared in his *Sartor Resartus* (*Fraser's* 9 (April 1834), pp. 445–6). In his *On Heroes, Hero-Worship and the Heroic in History*, an influential series of lectures delivered in 1840 and published in 1841, he was to urge unqualified admiration of such men.

27. See, for example, Charlotte's 'Address to the Angrians by his Grace the Duke of Zamorna' and 'Speech Of His Grace The Duke of Zamorna At The Opening Of The First Angrian Parliament', in *The Scrap Book. A Mingling of Many Things Compiled by Lord C A F. Wellesley* (1835), in Alexander, *Early Writings*, 2.ii, pp. 296–301, 304–9.

28. Edward Lytton Bulwer, *England and the English* (1833), ed. Standish Meacham (Chicago, 1970), p. 288.

29. 'Are they calculated . . . to brace up manly energy, and promote heroic virtue?' asked an early reviewer of the silver fork novel. 'Or rather, have they not an evident tendency to effeminate and enfeeble the mind?' ('Fashionable Society', *Westminster Review* 10 (January 1829), pp. 173–91); 'A writer of fashionable novels becomes by his very profession an emasculated person in point of excellence,' declared William Maginn ('*The Dominie's Legacy*, or, Fashionable Novels', *Fraser's* 1 (April 1830), pp. 320–21). Charlotte Brontë was evidently aware of such arguments, for the 'slight and effeminate' hero of *High Life in Verdopolis* is taunted as a 'semi-hermaphrodite' (pp. 14, 28).

30. 'Highways and Low-ways; or, Ainsworth's Dictionary, with Notes by Turpin', *Fraser's* 9 (June 1834), pp. 724–8. Ainsworth

was portrayed in July 1834 in that journal's 'Gallery of Literary Characters' as 'THE young Novelist of the Season', and was extensively discussed again there in April 1836 ('Another Caw from the Rookwood', *Fraser's* 13, pp. 488–93).

31. See *Henry Hastings* n. 81.

32. Chapter 6 of *Jack Sheppard*, which appeared in *Bentley's Miscellany* in the month in which the first volume of *Henry Hastings* was completed (February 1839), contained a famous description of a storm.

33. Juliet Barker, *The Brontës* (London: Weidenfeld & Nicolson, 1994), p. 299.

34. In a draft letter to Hartley Coleridge, written in December 1840, Charlotte Brontë describes her early fascination for these tales (Smith, *Letters of Charlotte Brontë*, 1, pp. 236–7). Rose Yorke in *Shirley* (1849), ch. 23, is depicted reading *The Italian*, one of the immensely popular Gothic novels of Ann Radcliffe (1764–1823).

35. On the 'coarseness' that contemporary reviewers were to find in Charlotte Brontë's later novels, see Tom Winnifrith, *The Brontës and their Background: Romance and Reality* (London: Macmillan, 1973), ch. 10.

36. Branwell's Alexander Percy, Earl of Northangerland, was, like his first favourite, Napoleon, a champion of republicanism; Zamorna had evolved from Arthur Wellesley, Marquis of Douro, the Duke of Wellington's son.

37. See Richard W. Bailey, *Nineteenth-Century English* (Ann Arbor: University of Michigan Press, 1996).

38. 'Mr T. Rice as Jim Crow', published by John Fairburn, London (n.d., but clearly during the 'Jim Crow' craze). The print can be seen at http://www.pbs.org/wgbh/aia/part3/3h489b.html

39. See Heather Glen, *Charlotte Brontë: the Imagination in History* (Cambridge: Cambridge University Press, 2002), pp. 3, 43–5, 158–9, 268–74.

40. Such moral construction of character was enshrined, in the following decade, in the cultural myth of the self-made man. See, for example, the chapter entitled 'Character' in Samuel Smiles' best-seller, *Self-Help* (1859).

41. *Oxford English Dictionary* (www.oed.com).

42. This series, which appeared 1830–36, consisted of eighty-one sketches, including three group pictures, and was illustrated with pen-and-ink drawings by Daniel Maclise. It provided a lively, satiric, irreverent counterpoint to Carlyle's much more serious

biographical essays, likewise appearing in the journal in these
years. See Miriam Thrall, *Rebellious Fraser's* (New York:
Columbia University Press, 1934), pp. 19–27.

43. Three of the four tales that survive in manuscript are written on
sheets of paper stacked and folded together to form a rudimentary 'book': the folding of the paper indicates that their
author must from the beginning of each have had a sense of its
overall length. *Stancliffe's Hotel*, the exception, is written on
three separate quires, comprising ms. pp.1–8, 9–24 and 25–34.

44. See Peter L. Caracciolo, *The 'Arabian Nights' in English Literature* (1988), pp. 25–8; Alexander and Smith, *Oxford Companion
to the Brontës*, p. 16.

45. New English translations of the *Decameron* by Giovanni Boccaccio (1313–75) were published in 1802 and 1825. There were
many early nineteenth-century retellings of various of its tales,
and its ten-day frame was employed in a number of early
nineteenth-century works. See Herbert G. Wright, *Boccaccio in
England from Chaucer to Tennyson* (Fair Lawn, NJ: Essential
Books, 1957). See *The Roe Head Journal Fragments*, n. 15.

46. Peter Garside and his co-researchers at the Centre for Editorial
and Intertextual Research at Cardiff University note the 'large
increase' in compilations of various kinds of short fictions in the
years 1830–36 (*The English Novel, 1830–1836: A Bibliographi-
cal Survey of Fiction Published in the British Isles*, compiled by
Peter Garside et al. (http://www.cf.ac.uk/encap/corvey/1830s/).

47. See n. 19 above. The catalogue of the library for 1841 includes
several different kinds of short fictions, ranging from Scott's
innovative 'tales' to Washington Irving's 'sketches', with their
emphasis on atmosphere and tone. Branwell would probably
have been drawn to the library's several collections of tales of
military adventure, such as Matthew Barker's *Tough Yarns: A
Series of Naval Tales and Sketches* (1835) and William Hamilton
Maxwell's *Stories of Waterloo* (1829). Samuel Warren's wildly
popular *Passages from the Diary of a Late Physician* seems
to have spoken more directly to his sisters; it is echoed, indeed,
in Anne Brontë's much later novel, *The Tenant of Wildfell Hall*.
(See Winnifrith, *The Brontës and their Background*, pp. 92–3.)

48. See Robert Morrison and Chris Baldick, (eds.), *Tales of Terror
from Blackwood's Magazine* (Oxford: World's Classics, 1995).
On Charlotte Brontë's early imitations of this genre, see Glen,
Charlotte Brontë, pp. 12–16.

49. Dickens had shot to fame with *Sketches by Boz* (1835–6) and

then *Pickwick Papers*; *Oliver Twist* and *Nicholas Nickleby* were appearing in parts during 1837–9, but their author was still seen as a writer of 'detached tales' (T. H. Lister, 'Dickens's Tales', *Edinburgh Review* 68 (October 1838), pp. 75–97). Many of Thackeray's writings of the 1830s appeared pseudonymously in *Fraser's*: they included *The Yellowplush Correspondence* (1837–8), collected as *The Yellowplush Papers* in his *Comic Tales and Sketches* (1841).

50. Washington Irving to Henry Brevoort, 11 December 1824, quoted in Susan Manning, Introduction to Washington Irving, *The Sketch-Book of Geoffrey Crayon, Gent.* (Oxford: Oxford University Press World's Classics, 1996), p. xxviii.

51. On Hogg, Scott, Irving and the development of the short-fiction form in this period, see R. J. Lyall, 'Intimations of orality: Scotland, America and the early development of the short story in English', *Studies in Short Fiction* 36:3 (Summer 1999), pp. 311–25.

52. In *Blackwood's*, for example, John Wilson, *Lights and Shadows from Scottish Life* (1820–21); John Galt, *My Landlady and her Lodgers* (August–November 1829); Michael Scott, *Tom Cringle's Log* (1829–33); Samuel Warren, *Passages from the Diary of a Late Physician* (eighteen instalments from August 1830 to August 1837). Short fiction series in *Fraser's* in the 1830s included John Galt's sketches and stories of Canada and the West Indies and Andrew Picken's Scottish tales.

53. For example, Irving, *Sketch-Book of Geoffrey Crayon*; Hogg, *The Shepherd's Calendar*; Michael Scott, *Tom Cringle's Log*, Warren *Passages from the Diary of a Late Physician*.

54. From Dickens's Preface to the first complete edition of *Pickwick Papers* (1837). The frequency of this form in the period prompts the speculation that the 'three distinct and unconnected tales' (*Agnes Grey*, *The Professor* and *Wuthering Heights*) that Charlotte Brontë offered to publishers in 1846 (Smith, *Letters of Charlotte Brontë*, 1, p. 461) may have been intended to be juxtaposed, and to reverberate against one another in ways that we now do not see.

55. Branwell Brontë, *Life of Alexander Percy Vol I* (1834), in Neufeldt, *Works* 2, p. 129.

56. One of Charlotte Brontë's earlier Angrian fictions, *A Peep into a Picture Book* (1834), depicts Lord Charles Wellesley turning the pages of such a volume, *Tree's Portrait Gallery of the Aristocracy of Africa*, and enjoying 'the pleasure of hanging over forms

that speak without sound' (Alexander, *Early Writings*, 2.ii, p. 86).

57. W. Harrison Ainsworth, Introduction to *Rookwood: a Romance*, 4th edn. (London, 1836), p. xii.

58. 'I have now written a great many books', see n. 8 above.

59. See Alexander, 'The influence of the visual arts on the Brontës' and 'Charlotte Brontë: the earnest amateur', in Alexander and Sellars, *Art of the Brontës*, pp. 9–64.

60. See ibid., pp. 216–45 for examples of these.

61. On the *tableau vivant* in polite society and its use in stage adaptations of popular novels during the 1830s, see Martin Meise, *Realizations: Narrative, Pictorial and Theatrical Arts in Nineteenth-Century England* (Princeton: Princeton University Press, 1983), pp. 47–9, 247–82.

62. Thus Walter Scott's Tinto, in *The Bride of Lammermoor* (1819), ch. 1, in the course of a discussion of the relation between visual and verbal arts.

63. Cf. Mrs Gaskell's description of the 'household custom' amongst the Brontë sisters in the evening when their domestic duties were done: 'They put away their work, and began to pace the room backwards and forwards, up and down, – as often with the candles extinguished, for economy's sake, as not, – their figures glancing into the fire-light, and out into the shadow, perpetually' (Gaskell, *Life*, p. 111).

64. Catherine Gallagher, 'Formalism and Time', *Modern Language Quarterly* 61:1 (March 2000), p. 231.

Further Reading

Christine Alexander's *The Early Writings of Charlotte Brontë* (Oxford: Basil Blackwell, 1983) remains the definitive account. On the earlier juvenilia and its relations both to early nineteenth-century print culture and to Charlotte Brontë's later work, see Carol Bock, *Charlotte Brontë and the Storyteller's Audience* (Iowa City: University of Iowa Press, 1992) and 'Our Plays: the Brontë juvenilia', in *The Cambridge Companion to the Brontës*, ed. Heather Glen (Cambridge: Cambridge University Press, 2002).

Critical discussion of Charlotte Brontë's later Angrian fictions may be found in:

Firdous Azim, *The Colonial Rise of the Novel* (London and New York: Routledge, 1994).

Susan Anne Carlson, 'Incest and Rage in Charlotte Brontë's Novelettes', in *Creating Safe Space: Violence and Women's Writing*, ed. Tomoko Kuribayashi and Julie Tharp (New York: State University of New York Press, 1998).

Karen Chase, *Eros and Psyche: The Representation of Personality in Charlotte Brontë, Charles Dickens, George Eliot* (New York: Methuen, 1984), pp. 7–24.

Winifred Gérin, ed., *Five Novelettes* (London: The Folio Press, 1971).

John Kucich, *Repression in Victorian Fiction* (Berkeley: University of California Press, 1987), pp. 51–5.

Bette London, *Writing Double: Women's Literary Partnerships* (Ithaca, NY, and London: Cornell University Press, 1999).

John Maynard, *Charlotte Brontë and Sexuality* (Cambridge: Cambridge University Press, 1984), pp. 40–71.

Helene Moglen, *Charlotte Brontë: the Self Conceived* (New York: W. W. Norton & Co., 1976), pp. 47–59.

Carl Plasa, *Charlotte Brontë* (Basingstoke: Palgrave Macmillan, 2004), pp. 14–28.

Dianne F. Sadoff, *Monsters of Affection: Dickens, Eliot and Brontë on Fatherhood* (Baltimore and London: Johns Hopkins University Press, 1982), pp. 120–27.

Sally Shuttleworth, *Charlotte Brontë and Victorian Psychology* (Cambridge: Cambridge University Press, 1996), ch. 6.

Note on the Texts

The tales in this volume were written at Haworth Parsonage between January 1838 and December 1839. The texts are based on my fresh transcription of the manuscripts which survive; and, in the case of *The Duke of Zamorna*, on the typed transcript of the manuscript made in 1926. Details of the location of the manuscripts can be found in the Notes.

The surviving manuscripts of the tales are written in ink on separate sheets of paper, folded to form rudimentary 'books', with pages approximately 18.5 cm × 11 cm in size. The hand is a very small but fairly clear print, quite different from Charlotte Brontë's much larger slanted copperplate as we see it in her correspondence and in her fair copies of *The Professor* and *Jane Eyre*. There is very little punctuation, and that which there is is inconsistent. The manuscripts are interspersed with dashes of varying lengths, often at points at which no punctuation mark would seem to be required. (Long dashes, for example, frequently occur at the end of lines, as though the writer has simply trailed her pen.) Quotation marks are eccentrically used – sometimes omitted altogether (especially at the end of speeches), sometimes inserted inappropriately. Capitalization is erratic, and hyphenation (e.g. bedroom, bed-room) haphazard. Ampersands are used frequently. French accents are often wrong. There are few paragraph divisions, although there are sometimes gaps in the manuscript to indicate changes of scene. *Henry Hastings* and *Caroline Vernon* give evidence of a little more effort to punctuate: here, commas and semi-colons occasionally appear, and there is more division into paragraphs and more accurate use of quotation marks. The exchange between Northangerland and Zamorna at the end of *Caroline Vernon* is spaced out with a new line for each speaker, appearing quite different from earlier dialogues.

Most of Charlotte Brontë's earlier Glass Town writings, with their tiny print, home-made bindings, title pages and advertisements for other publications, are carefully designed to imitate published journals and books. Even in these later manuscripts, where that childish sense of the glamour of print culture seems to have receded somewhat, there is some evidence of this; CHAPTER, for example, is written in capitals to mark the divisions of the last two novelettes. The script is significantly clearer than it is in the same tiny writing in Brontë's private journal fragments; indeed, it was possibly still intended to imitate print. Her first readers in Haworth Parsonage had for years been reading fictions presented in this form. They would have read these tales easily, with excitement and enjoyment, and not found them strange or difficult. This edition aims to enable the present-day reader to have something of the same experience, while remaining as faithful as possible to what Charlotte Brontë wrote.

Reproducing the original, eccentric punctuation, and thereby preserving them as 'quaint' juvenilia, would not have achieved this aim. It seems unlikely, moreover, that Charlotte Brontë would have wished her work to appear in such a form. 'I have to thank you for punctuating the sheets before sending them to me as I found the task very puzzling,' she wrote to her publishers shortly before the publication of *Jane Eyre*, 'and besides I consider your mode of punctuation a great deal mo[re] correct and rational than my own.'[1] The printers had replaced her light pointing with more formal colons, semi-colons and full stops, and corrected her inaccurate use of quotation marks. I have followed this clue to Charlotte Brontë's preferences in editing these tales. Throughout, I have been mindful that the absence of an edition that is both authoritative and readable is a major reason why they have not received the critical attention they deserve.

The manuscripts are untitled: I have given each the title by which it has come to be known. A few apparently omitted words or parts of words have been inserted in square brackets, and the very few uncertain readings have been placed in square brackets with a question mark. I have punctuated and inserted paragraph breaks along the lines of the punctuation and paragraphing of the first edition of *Jane Eyre*. Hyphenation has been regularized, ampersands have been expanded and capitals removed, except for proper names, French accents have been corrected. The spelling of proper names, which varies in the manuscripts, has been regularized to its most frequent form, but some archaic spellings (e.g. 'shewn', 'ancle', 'doat', 'broach') have been preserved.

A pencil note on the typescript of *The Duke of Zamorna* informs us that the manuscript was untitled; as with the other tales, I have given it the title by which it has come to be known. The typescript is fairly heavily punctuated and paragraphed, presumably by the transcriber, since it is unlike any known Angrian manuscript in this respect. It is divided into very short paragraphs, often of only a single sentence, and punctuated somewhat erratically, with a combination of dashes and conventional pointing, sometimes at odds with the sense; odd nouns are erratically capitalized. The typescript is divided into thirteen chapters, each with a chapter title. Chapter divisions appear to have been made by the transcriber. In a letter to Clement Shorter, dated 1 November 1925, C. W. Hatfield, early Brontë collector and editor, writes:

> I have just finished reading [Davidson Cook]'s transcript ... of the Brontë manuscript in the Honresfield [sic] Library. It has no continuity – no plot, – it is just a description of Angrian events and characters at widely different times ... to divide it into chapters is to give it an appearance of continuity which it does not possess. The headings to the different sections might very well remain, but not the word 'Chapter' which precedes each heading.[2]

The 'headings' also appear to have been inserted by the transcriber: a chapter describing the 'western' (or Senegambian)

aristocracy in the days before the establishment of the kingdom of Angria is, for example, titled 'Angrian Aristocrats'.
When Thomas J. Wise and John Alexander Symington published *The Duke of Zamorna* in the second volume of their
edition of *The Miscellaneous and Unpublished Writings of
Charlotte and Patrick Branwell Brontë* (Shakespeare Head,
1938) they preserved the chapter divisions, but dropped the
chapter titles.

In order that *The Duke of Zamorna* should not appear
markedly different from the other tales in this volume, I have
removed capitals, except for proper names and titles; lengthened paragraphs where this seemed appropriate, and replaced
most dashes with conventional punctuation. I have retained
neither chapter divisions nor titles, but have preserved breaks
between 'scenes' where the transcriber made chapter divisions.
Hatfield, who had considerable experience in transcribing
Brontë manuscripts, notes in the letter quoted above that 'there
are many words in Mr Cook's typescript which it is clear are
not correct transcripts. This is most easily seen in the names of
places and persons.' I have silently corrected names of places
and persons to conform with those in the other tales; and in a
few places, where there is obscurity or an apparent typing error
in the transcript, I have followed Wise and Symington: 'myrtle
leaves' for 'mystic leaves' and 'thou wilt' for 'thou wild'
(p. 183).

The text of the Journal Fragments is based on my fresh transcription of the manuscripts. Details of the location of individual manuscripts are given in the Notes. All are written in
tiny, uneven script on unbound sheets of paper folded to form
pages about 18.5 cm × 11.5 cm in size. They were evidently
written in haste. They are even more sparsely and eccentrically
punctuated than the later tales; the lines of script are more
uneven and sometimes run into each other; and the script itself
is much more difficult to read. Unlike the tales, these fragments
were clearly not intended for any kind of publication. Present-
day readers will be more concerned to read them for the insight
they provide into Charlotte Brontë's creative processes than as

finished works of art. For this reason, it seemed appropriate to preserve misspellings and present them in their original, almost unpunctuated form. I have recorded words and phrases deleted in the manuscript. Indecipherable words are indicated by square brackets with a question mark.

For all texts the meanings of foreign, dialect, cant and unfamiliar words are recorded in the Glossary.

NOTES

1. Margaret Smith (ed.), *The Letters of Charlotte Brontë*, 3 vols. (Oxford: Clarendon Press, 1995–2004), 1, p. 542.
2. Hatfield correspondence, BPM.

The Background to Angria

Angrian: Of or pertaining to Angria, an imaginary African empire invented by the Brontë children (Charlotte, Branwell, Emily, and Anne) in stories that they composed. Also as n. (*OED*).

Angria had its roots in the Brontë children's shared 'plays', which began with the gift of a set of twelve toy soldiers to Branwell Brontë in June 1826. These soldiers, named initially after well-known figures of the day, became the original dramatis personae of the imaginary kingdom of 'Glass Town', whose history was elaborated from the late 1820s onwards in dozens of tiny manuscripts which imitated as closely as possible the journals and books the children knew. It seems that at first all four children – who called themselves the 'Four Chief Genii' – collaborated in the Glass Town 'plays'. The changing nature of the plays reflected the children's voracious reading, ranging from Walter Scott to *The Arabian Nights' Entertainments* and *Tales of the Genii* to the accounts of travels to Africa appearing in *Blackwood's Magazine*. Their characters were at first half based on real-life or well-known literary figures, but they became increasingly imaginary. In 1832 Emily and Anne broke away to create their own world of Gondal, but Charlotte and Branwell continued to write about Glass Town, eventually renamed Verdopolis.

The story of Glass Town began with the 'Twelves', a band of adventurers, setting out from England in 1770 to colonize the west coast of a fictionalized Africa. After ferocious battles with the local inhabitants, the Ashantee, they founded the great city of Glass Town as the capital of their colony. The Duke of

Wellington, Charlotte's childhood hero, was originally its head of state, but his two sons, Arthur, Marquis of Douro, and Lord Charles Wellesley, figure far more prominently. Arthur is a charismatic Byronic hero, famed for his military exploits and for his romantic conquests and also for the poetry he writes. Charles, his younger brother, is a snooping, gossipy, rather ridiculous figure who constantly mocks romantic and heroic sentiment; he is a favourite narrator of Charlotte's from the early days of Glass Town. Alexander Percy, often called Rogue (or Rougue), is the hero of Branwell's early writings; like Arthur, he is a Byronic figure, though a darker, more Luciferian one. The two are from their first meeting drawn to one another, but they soon become also enemies. Their love-hate relationship is to be central to the narrative of Angria.

The early history of Glass Town, as recounted by Branwell, was one of war, both against the Ashantees (the country's original inhabitants) and against the French. Charlotte was more concerned with the often dissolute doings of the fashionable beau monde. As the 'plays' developed, Arthur became Duke of Zamorna. He was made monarch of the new kingdom of Angria to the east of Verdopolis in 1834. Alexander Percy married the bluestocking Lady Zenobia Ellrington, and became Earl of Northangerland. His daughter, Mary Percy, became the wife of Zamorna and Queen of Angria. Northangerland was initially Zamorna's Prime Minister, but he soon turned against his son-in-law and mounted a rebellion against him; there ensued a disastrous civil war. According to Branwell's account, Zamorna at this time took revenge on Northangerland by casting aside his wife; this banishment killed her and caused her father dreadful grief. Charlotte, unable to bear this, rewrote this part of the saga: in the novelettes that follow, Mary is alive again. Zamorna, at first defeated and exiled, returned and recaptured his kingdom, only to meet with further war. At the point at which these novelettes open, he has once again, and definitively, defeated Northangerland.

Zamorna has a string of romantic conquests behind him. His first love, the peasant girl Mina Laury, remains his faithful mistress and trusted confidante. He is, however, still married

to the anxious and fading Mary, daughter of Northangerland.
Northangerland, ageing and ill, has been ignominiously
banished to his country estate at Alnwick, where he is allowed
to live as a private individual if he keeps out of politics. He is
still something of a rake, with a string of mistresses in the
background; and his relationship with his wife is stormy. He is
hated in the country, but Zamorna cannot stay away from him.
Northangerland's two surviving sons, rejected by him at birth,
are becoming prominent in Angria. Edward, a wealthy industrialist, is now a member of Parliament. Sir William Percy, at first
a dandyish figure, is becoming closer to his royal sister and
beginning to work for the government. Charles Wellesley, for
his part, has evolved into the cynical Charles Townshend, a
penniless hack writer, and the narrator of these novelettes.

Tales of Angria

MINA LAURY

Introductory Note

Mina Laury was written at Haworth in January 1838, nine months after Charlotte Brontë's twenty-first birthday, during her Christmas holidays from her position as a teacher at Roe Head school. As its opening sentence indicates, it assumes that the reader will be quite familiar not merely with the events and characters and places to which it refers, but also with its narrator and his previous 'books'. This latter is apparently Charles Townshend, a later version of Brontë's early favourite Lord Charles Wellesley, younger brother of Zamorna. Townshend was the 'author' of the Angrian manuscripts immediately preceding this (*Passing Events*, *It is all up!*, *Julia* and *Four Years Ago*). In these 'books' of 1836–7 he appeared as a distinctive character – cynical, dandyish, flippant, counterpointing the romance of Angria with a debunking voice. Here, he is less prominent, presenting a series of scenes 'without note or comment' (p.57), his perspective one of cool, analytic observation rather than of irony.

Mina Laury is set in the aftermath of the disastrous civil war which resulted from the Earl of Northangerland's plotting against Zamorna. Zamorna, who is married to Northangerland's daughter Mary, has returned, victorious, from exile; he is back with his wife, whom he had divorced and discarded in order to punish her father. Partly because of this marriage, but largely because of the enduring fascination between them, he continues to see his former enemy. Northangerland – now a broken-down, querulous, elderly man – is confined to Alnwick, his country estate, where he lives with his wife Zenobia. Here, at the beginning of *Mina Laury*, Zamorna and Mary are visiting her father and his wife. Angria has been devastated and the situation in the country is unstable, largely because of the King's continuing close association with the man who attempted his overthrow.

The war has also had a devastating effect upon Zamorna's marriage. The once spirited Mary Percy, his wife, is now the anxious 'prey to a hundred vague apprehensions' – partly because of her husband's strategic repudiation of her, and partly because of his continuing infidelities. The most serious of these latter is his attachment to Mina Laury, who as a simple peasant girl was the object of his 'first passion' when both were young together in their 'western' homeland, Senegambia. Mina, who has been his trusted confidante in all his political projects and who shared his exile during his temporary defeat, is now a beautiful and intelligent woman, living in retirement at the country house where he has established her.

Mina Laury opens with a conversation between Zenobia and Zamorna, at breakfast in Alnwick House. Zenobia and Zamorna have been friends since youth, and maintained their closeness throughout the months of the civil war; the two are at ease together.

I

The last scene in my last book[1] concluded within the walls of Alnwick House, and the first scene in my present volume opens in the same place. I have a great partiality for morning pictures. There is such a freshness about everybody and everything before the toil of the day has worn them. When you descend from your bedroom, the parlour looks so clean, the fire so bright, the hearth so polished, the furnished breakfast table so tempting. All these attractions are diffused over the oak-panelled room with the glass door to which my readers have before had frequent admission. The cheerfulness within is enhanced by the dreary, wildered look of all without.[2] The air is dimmed, with snow careering through it in wild whirls, the sky is one mass of congealed tempest, heavy, wan and icy; the trees rustle their frozen branches against each other in a blast bitter enough to flay alive the flesh that should be exposed to its sweep. But hush! the people of the house are up. I hear a step on the stairs. Let us watch the order in which they will collect in the breakfast room.

First, by himself, comes an individual in a furred morning-gown of crimson damask, with his shirt-collar open and neck-cloth thrown by; his face fresh and rather rosy than otherwise, partly perhaps with health but chiefly with the cold water in which he has been performing his morning's ablutions, his hair fresh from the toilette, plenty of it, and carefully brushed and curled, his hands clean and white and visibly as cold as icicles. He walks to the fire, rubbing them. He glances towards the window meantime, and whistles as much as to say, 'It's a rum morning.' He then steps to a side-table, takes up a

newspaper,[3] of which there are dozens lying folded and fresh
from the postman's bag, he throws himself into an arm-chair
and begins to read. Meantime, another step and a rustle of
silks. In comes the Countess Zenobia with a white gauze turban over her raven curls and a dress of grey. 'Good morning,
Arthur,' she says in her cheerful tone, such as she uses when
all's right with her.[4] 'Good morning, Zenobia,' answers the
Duke, getting up, and they shake hands and stand together on
the rug.

'What a morning it is!' he continues. 'How the snow drifts!
If it were a little less boisterous I would make you come out
and have a snow-balling match with me, just to whet your
appetite for breakfast.'

'Aye,' said the Countess. 'We look like two people adapted
for such child's-play, don't we?' and she glanced with a smile
first at the 'great blethering King of Angria' (see Harlaw) and
then at her own comely and portly figure.[5]

'You don't mean to insinuate that we are too stout for such
exercise?' said His Majesty.

Zenobia laughed. 'I am, at any rate,' said she, and, 'Your
Grace is in most superb condition – what a chest!'

'This will never do,' returned the Duke, shaking his head.
'Wherever I go they compliment me on my enlarged dimensions.
I must take some measures for reducing them within reasonable
bounds. Exercise and Abstinence, that is my motto.'

'No, Adrian – let it be "Ease and Plenty",' said a much softer
voice, replying to his Grace. A third person had joined the pair
and was standing a little behind, for she could not get her share
of the fire, being completely shut out by the Countess with her
robes and the Duke with his morning-gown. This person
seemed but a little and slight figure when compared with these
two august individuals, and as the Duke drew her in between
them, that she might at least have a sight of the glowing hearth,
she was almost lost in the contrast.

'Ease and Plenty!' exclaimed his Grace. 'So you would have
a man mountain[6] for your husband at once!'

'Yes, I should like to see you really very stout. I call you
nothing now – quite slim, scarcely filled up.'

'That's right!' said Zamorna. 'Mary always takes my side.'

Lady Helen Percy[7] now entered; and shortly after, the Earl, with slow step and in silence, took his place at the breakfast-table. The meal proceeded in silence. Zamorna was reading. Newspaper after newspaper he opened, glanced over and threw on the floor. One of them happened to fall over Lord Northangerland's foot. It was very gently removed as if there was contamination in the contact.

'An Angrian print, I believe,' murmured the Earl. 'Why do they bring such things to the house?'

'They are my papers,' answered his son-in-law, swallowing, at the same moment, more at one mouthful than would have sufficed his father for the whole repast.

'Yours! What do you read them for? To give you an appetite? If so, they seem to have answered their end. Arthur, I wish you would masticate your food better –'

'I have not time. I'm very hungry. I eat but one meal all yesterday.'

'Humph! and now you're making up for it, I suppose. But pray put that newspaper away.'

'No. I wish to learn what my loving subjects are saying about me.'

'And what are they saying, pray?'

'Why, here is a respectable gentleman who announces that he fears his beloved monarch is again under the influence of that baleful star whose ascendancy has already produced such fatal results to Angria – wishing to be witty he calls it the North Star. Another insinuates that their gallant sovereign, though a Hector in war, is but a Paris in peace. He talks something about Sampson and Delilah, Hercules[8] and the distaff, and hints darkly at the evils of petticoat government – a hit at you, Mary. A third mutters threateningly of hoary old ruffians who, worn with age and excess, sit like Bunyan's Giant Pope[9] at the entrances of their dens, and strive by menace or promise to allure passengers within the reach of their bloody talons.'

'Is that me?' asked the Earl quietly.

'I've very little doubt of it,' was the reply. 'And there is a fourth print, the *War Despatch*, noted for the ardour of its sentiments, which growls a threat concerning the power of Angria to elect a new sovereign whenever she is offended with her old one. Zenobia, another cup of coffee, if you please.'

'I suppose you're frightened,' said the Earl.

'I shake in my shoes,' replied the Duke. 'However, there are two old sayings that somewhat cheer me – "More noise than work", "Much cry and little wool".[10] Very applicable when properly considered, for I always called the Angrians hogs, and who am I except the Devil that shears them?'

Breakfast had been over for about a quarter of an hour. The room was perfectly still. The Countess and Duchess were reading those papers Zamorna had dropped, Lady Helen was writing to her son's agent, the Earl was pacing the room in a despondent mood; as for the Duke, no one well knew where he was, or what he was doing. He had taken himself off, however. Ere long, his step was heard descending the staircase, then his voice in the hall giving orders, and then he re-entered the breakfast-room, but no longer in morning costume. He had exchanged his crimson damask robe for a black coat and checked pantaloons; he was wrapped up in a huge blue cloak with a furred collar; a light fur cap rested on his brow; his gloves were held in his hands. In short, he was in full travelling costume.

'Where are you going?' asked the Earl, pausing in his walk.

'To Verdopolis, and from thence to Angria,' was the reply.

'To Verdopolis, and in such weather!' exclaimed the Countess, glancing towards the wild whitened tempest that whirled without. Lady Helen looked up from her writing.

'Absurd, my Lord Duke! You do not mean what you say.'

'I do. I must go; the carriage will be at the door directly. I'm come to bid you all good-bye.'

'And what is all this haste about?' returned Lady Helen, rising.

'There is no haste in the business, madam. I've been here a week. I intended to go today.'

'You never said anything about your intention.'

'No, I did not think of mentioning it. But they are bringing the carriage round. Good morning, madam.'

He took Lady Helen's hand, and saluted her as he always does at meeting and parting. Then he passed to the Countess.

'Good-bye, Zenobia. Come to Ellrington House as soon as you can persuade our friend to accompany you.'

He kissed her, too. The next in succession was the Earl.

'Farewell, sir, and be d—d to you. Will you shake hands?'

'No. You always hurt me so. Good morning. I hope you won't find your masters quite so angry as you expect them to be. But you do right not to delay attending to their mandates. I'm sorry I have been the occasion of your offending them.'

'Are we to part in this way?' asked the Duke. 'And won't you shake hands?'

'No!'

Zamorna coloured highly, but turned away and put on his gloves. The barouche stood at the door. The groom and the valet were waiting, and the Duke, still with a clouded countenance, was proceeding to join them, when his wife came forwards.

'You have forgotten me, Adrian,' she said in a very quiet tone, but her eye meantime flashing expressively. He started, for in truth he had forgotten her. He was thinking about her father.

'Good-bye then, Mary,' he said, giving her a hurried kiss and embrace. She detained his hand.

'Pray how long am I to stay here?' she asked. 'Why do you leave me at all? Why am I not to go with you?'

'It is such weather!' he answered. 'When this storm passes over I will send for you.'

'When will that be?' pursued the Duchess, following his steps as he strode into the hall.

'Soon, soon, my love, perhaps in a day or two. There now, don't be unreasonable. Of course you cannot go to-day.'

'I can and I will,' answered the Duchess quickly. 'I have had enough of Alnwick. You shall not leave me behind you.'

'Go into the room, Mary. The door is open and the wind blows on you far too keenly. Don't you see how it drifts the snow in?'

'I will not go into the room. I'll step into the carriage as I am if you refuse to wait till I can prepare. Perhaps you will be humane enough to let me have a share of your cloak.'

She shivered as she spoke. Her hair and her dress floated in the cold blast that blew in through the open entrance, strewing the hall with snow and dead leaves. His Grace, though he was rather stern, was not quite negligent of her, for he stood so as to screen her in some measure from the draught.

'I shall not let you go, Mary,' he said. 'So there is no use in being perverse.'

The Duchess regarded him with that troubled, anxious glance peculiar to herself.

'I wonder why you wish to leave me behind you,' she said.

'Who told you I wished to do so?' was his answer. 'Look at the weather, and tell me if it is fit for a delicate little woman like you to be exposed to?'

'Then,' murmured the Duchess wistfully, glancing at the January storm, 'you might wait till it is milder. I don't think it will do your Grace any good to be out to-day.'

'But I must go, Mary. The Christmas recess is over, and business presses.'

'Then do take me. I am sure I can bear it.'

'Out of the question. You may well clasp those small, silly hands, so thin I can almost see through them, and you may well shake your curls over your face, to hide its paleness from me, I suppose. What is the matter, crying? Good! what the d—l am I to do with her? Go to your father, Mary. He has spoilt you.'

'Adrian, I cannot live at Alnwick without you,' said the Duchess earnestly. 'It recalls too forcibly the very bitterest days of my life.[11] I'll not be separated from you again except by violence.' She took hold of his arm with one hand, while with the other she was hastily wiping away the tears from her eyes.

'Well, it will not do to keep her any longer in this hall,' said the Duke. He pushed open a side-door which led into a room that during his stay he had appropriated for his study. There was a fire in it, and a sofa drawn to the hearth. There he took the Duchess, and, having shut the door, recommenced the task of persuasion, which was no very easy one, for his own false play, his alienations and his unnumbered treacheries had filled her mind with hideous phantasms of jealousy, had weakened her nerves and made them a prey to a hundred vague apprehensions – fears that never wholly left her, except when she was actually in his arms or at least in his immediate presence.

'I tell you, Mary,' he said, regarding her with a smile half-expressive of fondness, half of vexation, 'I tell you I will send for you in two or three days.'

'And will you be at Wellesley House when I get there? You said you were going from Verdopolis to Angria.'

'I am, and probably I shall be a week in Angria, not more.'

'A week! and your Grace considers that but a short time? To me it will be most wearisome. However, I must submit; I know it is useless to oppose your Grace. But I could go with you, and you should never find me in the way. I am not often intrusive on your Grace.'

'The horses will be frozen if they stand much longer,' returned the Duke, not heeding her last remark. 'Come, wipe your eyes, and be a little philosopher for once. There, let me have one smile before I go. A week will be over directly. This is not like setting out for a campaign.'

'Don't forget to send for me in two days,' pleaded the Duchess, as Zamorna released her from his arms.

'No, no. I'll send for you to-morrow if the weather is settled enough, and,' half mimicking her voice, 'don't be jealous of me, Mary – unless you're afraid that the superior charms of Enara and Warner and Kirkwall and Richton and Thornton[12] will seduce me from my allegiance to a certain fair-complexioned brown-eyed young woman in whom you are considerably interested. Good-bye.'

He was gone. She hurried to the window; he passed it. In three minutes the barouche swept with muffled sound round the lawn, shot down the carriage road and was quickly lost in the thickening whirl of the snow-storm.

Late at night, the Duke of Zamorna reached Wellesley House. His journey had been much delayed by the repeated change of horses which the state of the roads rendered necessary. So heavy and constant had been the falls of snow all day that in many places they were almost blocked up, and he and his valet had more than once been obliged to alight from the carriage and wade through the deep drifts, far above the knee. Under such circumstances any other person would have stopped for the night at some of the numerous excellent hotels which skirt the way, but his Grace is well known to be excessively pig-headed, and the more obstacles are thrown in the way of any scheme he wishes to execute, the more resolute he is in pushing on to the attainment of his end. In the prosecution of this journey he had displayed a particular wilfulness. In vain, when he had alighted at some inn to allow time for a change of horses, Rosier had hinted the propriety of a longer stay, in vain he had recommended some more substantial refreshment than the single glass of Madeira and the half-biscuit wherewith his noble master tantalized rather than satisfied the cravings of a rebellious appetite. At last, leaving him to the enjoyment of obstinacy and starvation in a large saloon of the inn, which his Grace was traversing with strides that derived their alacrity partly from nipping cold and partly from impatience, Eugene himself had sought the traveller's room, and while he devoured a chicken with champagne he had solaced himself with the muttered objurgation, 'Let him starve and be d—d!'

Flinging himself from the barouche, the Duke, in no mild mood, passed through his lighted halls, whose echoes were still prolonging the last stroke of midnight, pealed from the house-bell just as the carriage drew up under the portico. Zamorna seemed not to heed the call to immediate repose which that sound conveyed, for turning as he stood on the first landing-place of the wide white marble stairs, with a bronze lamp pendant above him and a statue standing in calm contrast to his own figure, he called out, 'Rosier, I wish Mr Warner[13] to attend me instantly. See that a messenger is despatched to Warner Hotel.'

'Tonight, does your Grace mean?' said the valet.

'Yes, sir.'

Monsieur Rosier reposed his tongue in his cheek but hastened to obey.

'Hutchinson, send your deputy directly – you heard his

Grace's orders – and, Hutchinson, tell the cook to send a tumbler of hot negus into my room. I want something to thaw me. And tell her to toss me up a nice hot *petit souper* – a *fricandeau de veau* or an omelette. And carry my compliments to Mr Greenwood and say I shall be happy to have the honour of his company in my salon half an hour hence. And, above all things, Hutchinson' – here the young gentleman lowered his tone to a more confidential key – 'give Mademoiselle Harriette a hint that I am returned – very ill, you may say, for I've got a cursed sore throat with being exposed to this night air. Ah! there she is! I'll tell her myself.'

As the omnipotent Eugene spoke, a young lady carrying a china ewer appeared, crossing the gallery which ran round this inner hall. The French *garçon* skipped up the stairs like a flea.

'*Ma belle!*' he exclaimed, '*permettez moi porte cette cruse-là!*'[14]

'No, monsieur, no,' replied the young lady, laughing and throwing back her head which was covered with very handsome dark hair finely curled. 'I will carry it; it is for the Duke.'

'I must assist you,' returned the gallant Rosier, 'and then I shall earn a kiss for my services.'

But the damsel resisted him and, stepping back, shewed to better advantage a pretty foot and ancle, well displayed by a short, full petticoat of pink muslin and a still shorter apron of black silk. She had also a modest handkerchief of thin lace on her neck. She wore no cap, had good eyes, comely features and a plump round figure. A very interesting love scene was commencing in the seclusion of the gallery, when a bell rang very loudly.

'God! it's the Duke!' exclaimed Rosier. He instantly released his mistress, and she shot away like an arrow towards the inner chambers. Eugene followed her very cautiously – somewhat jealously, perhaps. Threading her path through a labyrinth of intermediate rooms, she came at last to the royal chamber and thence a door opened direct to the royal dressing-room. His Grace was seated in an arm-chair by his mirror – an enormous one taking him in from head to foot. He looked cursedly tired and somewhat wan, but the lights and shadows of the fire were playing about him with an animating effect.

'Well, Harriet,' he said, as the housemaid entered his presence. 'I wanted that water before. Put it down and pour me out a glass. What made you so long in bringing it?'

Harriet blushed as she held the refreshing draught to her royal master's parched lips. (He was too lazy to take it himself.) She was going to stammer out some excuse, but meantime the Duke's eye had reverted to the door and caught the dark vivacious aspect of Rosier.

'Ah!' he said. 'I see how it is! Well, Harriet, mind what you're about. No giddiness! You may go now, and tell your swain to come forwards, on pain of having his brains converted into paste.'

Eugene strutted in, humming aloud, in no sort abashed or put to the blush. When Harriet was gone, the Duke proceeded to lecture him, the valet meantime coolly aiding him in the change of his travelling-dress, arrangement of his hair, etc.

'Dog,' began the saintly master, 'take care how you conduct yourself towards that girl; I'll have no improprieties in my house, none.'

'If I do but follow your Grace's example, I cannot be guilty of improprieties,' snivelled the valet, who, being but too well acquainted with many of his master's weaknesses, is sometimes permitted a freedom of speech few others would attempt.

'I'll make you marry her at all risks if you once engage her affections,' pursued Zamorna.

'Well,' replied Rosier, 'if I do marry her and if I don't like her, I can recompense myself for the sacrifice.'

'Keep within your allotted limits, my lad,' remarked the Duke quietly.

'What does your Grace mean? Matrimonial limits or limits of the tongue?'

'Learn to discern for yourself!' returned his master, enforcing the reply by manual application that sent Monsieur to the other side of the room. He speedily gathered himself up and returned to his employment of combing out the Duke's long and soft curls of dark brown hair.

'I have a particular interest in your Harriet,' remarked Zamorna benevolently. 'I can't say that the other handmaids of the house often cross my sight, but now and then I meet that nymph in a gallery or a passage, and she always strikes me as being very modest and correct in her conduct.'

'She was first bar-maid at Stancliffe's Hotel in Zamorna not long since,' insinuated Rosier.

'I know she was, sir. I have reason to remember her in that station. She once gave me a draught of cold water, when there was not another human being in the world who would have lifted a finger to do me even that kindness.'

'I've heard Mademoiselle tell that story,' replied Eugene. 'It was when your Grace was taken prisoner of war before MacTerroglen, and she told how your Grace rewarded her afterwards when you stopped six months ago at Stancliffe's and gave her a certificate of admission to the royal household – and into the bargain, if Mademoiselle speaks truth, your Grace gave her a kiss from your own royal lips.'

'I did and be d—d to you, sir. The draught of water she once gave me and the gush of kind-hearted tears that followed it were cheaply rewarded by a kiss.'

'I should have thought so,' replied Rosier, 'but perhaps she did not. Ladies of title sometimes pull each others' ears for your Grace's kisses, so I don't know how a simple bar-maid would receive them.'

'Eugene, your nation have a penchant for suicide.[15] Go and be heroic,' returned Zamorna.

'If your Grace has done with me, I will obey your wishes and immediately seek my quietus in a plate of ragout of paradise and such delicate claret as the vintages of la belle France yield when they are in a good humour.'

As the illustrious valet withdrew from the presence of his still more illustrious master, a different kind of personage entered by another door – a little man enveloped in a fur cloak. He put it off and, glancing round the room, his eye settled upon Zamorna. Released from the cumbrous costume of his journey, Zamorna was again enveloped in his crimson damask robe, half reclined on the mattress of a low and hard couch, his head of curls preparing to drop on to the pillow and one hand just drawing up the coverlet of furs and velvet. Warner beheld him in the act of seeking his night's repose.

'I thought your Grace wanted me on business!' exclaimed the minister. 'And I find you in bed!'

Zamorna stretched his limbs, folded his arms across his chest, buried his brow, cheek and dark locks in the pillow, and in a faint voice requested Warner to 'arrange that coverlet for he was too tired to do it'. The Premier's lip struggled to repress a smile. This was easily done, for the said lip was unaccustomed to that relaxation.

'Has your Majesty dismissed Monsieur Rosier, and have you sent for me to fulfil the duties of that office he held about your Majesty's person?'

'There, I'm comfortable,' said the Duke, as the drapery fell over him arranged to his satisfaction. 'Pray, Warner, be seated.'

Warner drew close to his Grace's bedside an arm-chair and threw himself into it. 'What', said he, 'have you been doing? You look extremely pale – have you been raking?'[16]

'God forgive you for the supposition! No, I have been fagging myself to death for the good of Angria.'

'For the good of Angria, my lord! Aye, truly, there you come to the point! And it is I suppose for the good of Angria that you go to Alnwick and spend a week in the sick room of Lord Northangerland?'

'How dutiful of me, Howard! I hope my subjects admire me for it.'

'My lord Duke, do not jest. The feeling which has been raised by that ill-advised step is no fit subject for levity. What a strange mind is yours, which teaches you to rush headlong into those very errors which your enemies are always attributing to you! It is in vain that you now and then display a splendid flash of talent, when the interstices, as it were, of your political life are filled up with such horrid bungling as this.'

'Be easy, Howard. What harm have I done?'

'My lord, I will tell you. Has it not ever been the bitterest reproach in the mouth of your foes that you are a weak man, liable to be influenced and controlled. Have not Ardrah and

Montmorency a thousand times affirmed that Northangerland guided, ruled, infatuated you? They have tried to bring that charge home to you – to prove it – but they could not, and you, with all Christian charity, have taken the trouble off their hands. You have proved it beyond dispute or contradiction.'

'As how, my dear Howard?'

'My lord, you see it, you feel it yourself. In what state was Angria last year at this time? You remember it laid in ashes – plague and famine and slaughter, struggling with each other which should sway the sceptre that disastrous war had wrested from your own hand. And I ask, my lord, who had brought Angria to this state?'

'Northangerland!' replied Zamorna promptly.

'Your Grace [h]as spoken truly. And knowing this, was it weakness or was it wickedness which led you to the debauched traitor's couch and taught you to bend over him with the tenderness of a son to a kind father?' Warner paused for an answer but none came. He continued, 'That the man is dying I have very little doubt – dying in that premature decay brought on by excesses such as would have disgraced any nature, aye, even that of an unreasoning beast. But ought you not to have let him meet death alone, in that passion of anguish and desolation which is the just meed for crime, for depravity like his? What call was there for you to go and count his pulses? Can you prolong their beat? Why should you mingle your still pure breath with his last contaminated gasps? Can you purify that breath which debauchery has so sullied? Why should you commit your young hand to the touch of his clammy nerveless fingers? Can the contact infuse vitality into his veins or vigour into his sinews? Had you not the strength of mind to stand aloof and let him who has lived the slave of vice die the victim of disease?'

The Duke of Zamorna raised himself on his elbow.

'Very bad language, this, Howard,' said he. 'And it won't do. I know very well what the reformers and the constitutionalists and my own opinionated and self-complacent Angrians have been saying because I chose to spend my Christmas recess at Alnwick. I knew beforehand what they would say – and above all I knew in particular what you would say. Now, it was not in defiance of either public or private opinion that I went. Neither was it from the working of any uncontrollable impulse. No, the whole matter was the result of mature reflection. My Angrians have certain rights over me. So have my ministers. I also have certain rights independent of them, independent of any living thing under the firmament of heaven. I claim the possession of my reason. I am neither insane nor idiotic, whatever the all-accomplished Harlaw may say to the contrary, and in two or three things I will, whilst I retain that valuable possession, judge for myself.

'One of these is the degree of intimacy which I choose to maintain with Lord Northangerland. In a public sense, I have long done with him. The alienation cost me much, for in two or three particular points his views and mine harmonized, and neither could hope to find a substitute for the other in the whole earth beside. However, though it was like tearing up something whose roots had taken deep hold in my very heart of hearts, the separation was made – and since it was finally completed, by what glance or look or word have I sighed for a reunion? I have not done so and I cannot do so. My path I have struck out, and it sweeps far away out of sight of his. The rivers of blood Angria shed last year, and the hills of cold carnage which she piled up before the shrine of Freedom, effectually, eternally divide Northangerland's spirit from mine. But in the body we may meet – we shall meet – till death interposes. I say, Warner, no sneers of my foes nor threats from my friends, no murmurs from my subjects, shall over-rule me in this matter.

'Howard, you are a different man from Northangerland, but let me whisper to you this secret. You also love to control, and if you could you would extend the energies of that keen haughty mind, till they surrounded me and spell-bound my will and actions within a magic circle of your own creating. It will not do, it will not do. Hate Northangerland if you please – abhor him, loathe him. You have a right to do so. He has more than once treated you brutally, spoken of you grossly. If you feel so inclined, and if an opportunity should offer, you have a right to pistol him. But, sir, do not dare to impose your private feelings on me, to call upon me to avenge them. Do it yourself!

In you the action would be justifiable, in me dastardly. Neither will I bend to Ardrah, or to the defiled cuckold Montmorency. I will not at their bidding give up the best feelings of a very bad nature – I will not crush the only impulses that enable me to be endured by my fellow-men – I will not leave the man who was once my *comrade*, my *friend*, to die in unrelieved agony, because Angria mutinies and Verdopolis sneers. My heart, my hand, my energies belong to the public – my feelings are my own. Talk no more on the subject.'

Warner did not. He sat and gazed in silence on his master, who with closed eyes and averted head seemed composing himself to slumber. At last he said aloud: 'A false step, a false step! I would die on the word!'

Zamorna woke from his momentary doze.

'You have papers for me to sign and look over, I daresay, Howard. Give me them. I wish to despatch arrears to-night, as it is my intention to set off for Angria. I wish to ascertain in person the state of feeling there and to turn it into its legitimate channel.'

Warner produced a green bag well filled. The Duke raised himself on his couch and, collecting his wearied faculties, proceeded to the task. A silence of nearly an hour ensued, broken only by occasional monosyllables from the King and minister as papers were presented and returned. At length Warner locked the padlock with which the bag was secured, and saying, 'I recommend your Majesty to sleep,' rose to reassume his cloak.

'Warner,' said the Duke, with an appearance of nonchalance, 'where is Lord Hartford? I have seen nothing of him for some time.'

'Lord Hartford, my lord! Lord Hartford is a fool and affects delicacy of the lungs. His health, forsooth, is in too precarious a state to allow of any attention to public affairs and he has withdrawn to Hartford Hall there to nurse his maudlin folly in retirement.'

'What, the maudlin folly of being ill? You are very unsparing, Howard.'

'Ill, sir! The man is as strong and sound as you are. All trash! It is the effects of his ruling passion, sir, which will pursue him to hoar age, I suppose. Lord Hartford is love-sick, my lord Duke – the superannuated profligate!'

'Did he tell you so?'

'No, indeed, he dared not – but Lord Richton insinuated as much in his gossipy way. I will cut Lord Hartford, sir. I despise him! He ought to be sent to Coventry.'[17]

'How very bitter you are, Warner! Be more moderate. Meantime, good-night.'

'I wish your Grace a very good night. Take care that you sleep soundly and derive refreshment from your slumbers.'

'I will do my best,' replied the Duke, laughing. Warner, having clasped on his cloak, withdrew. Could he have watched unseen by the couch of his master for two hours longer, he would have repined at the hidden feeling that prevented the lids from closing over those dark and restless eyes. Long Zamorna lay awake. Neither youth nor health nor weariness could woo sleep to his pillow. He saw his lamp expire. He saw the brilliant flame of the hearth settle into ruddy embers, then fade, decay, and at last perish. He felt silence and total darkness close around him. But still the unslumbering eye wandered over images which the fiery imagination pourtrayed upon vacancy. Thought yielded at last, and sleep triumphed. Zamorna lay in dead repose amidst the hollow darkness of his chamber.

Lord Hartford sat by himself after his solitary dinner with a decanter of champagne and a half-filled glass before him. There was also a newspaper spread out on which his elbow leant and his eye rested. The noble lord sat in a large dining-room, the windows of which looked upon a secluded part of his own grounds, a part pleasant enough in summer leafiness and verdure, but dreary now in the cold white clothing of winter. Many a time had this dining-room rung with the merriment of select dinner-parties, chosen by the noble bachelor from his particular friends, and often had the rum physiognomies of Richton, Arundel, Castlereagh and Thornton been reflected in the mirror-like surface of that long dark polished mahogany table, at whose head Edward Hartford now sat alone. Gallant and gay, and bearing on his broad forehead the very brightest and greenest laurels Angria had gathered on the banks of the Cirhala,[18] he had retired with all his blushing honours thick upon him from the council, the court, the salon. He had left Verdopolis in the height of the most dazzling season it had ever known and gone to haunt like a ghost his lonely halls in Angria. Most people thought the noble General's brains had suffered some slight injury amid the hardships of the late campaign. Richton was among the number who found it impossible to account for his friend's conduct upon any other supposition.

As the dusk closed and the room grew more dismal, Hartford threw the newspaper from him, poured out a bumper of amber-coloured wine and quaffed it off to the memory of the vintage that produced it. According to books, men in general soliloquize when they are by themselves, and so did Hartford.

'What the d—l,' he began, 'has brought our lord the King down to Angria? That drunken editor of the *War Despatch* gives a pretty account of his progress – hissed, it seems, in the streets of Zamorna, and then, like himself, instead of getting through the town as quietly as he could, bidding the postillions halt before Stancliffe's and treating them to one of his fire and gunpowder explosions! What a speech, beginning, "My lads what a d—d set you are! Unstable as water! you shall never excel!" It's odd, but that western dandy knows the genius of our land. "Take the bull by the horns":[19] that's his motto. Hitherto his tactics have succeeded, but I think it says some-where, either in Revelation or the Apocrypha, the end is not yet.[20] I wish he'd keep out of Angria.'

Here a pause ensued, and Hartford filled it up with another goblet of the golden wine.

'Now,' he proceeded. 'I know I ought not drink this Gua-nache. It is a kindling sort of draught and I were better take to toast and water.[21] But Lord bless me! I've got a feeling about my heart I can neither stifle nor tear away, and I would fain drown it. They talk of optical delusions – I wonder what twist-ing of the nerves it is that fixes before my eyes that image which neither darkness can hide nor light dissipate? Some demon is certainly making a bonfire of my inwards. The burning thrill struck through all my veins to my heart with that last touch of the little warm soft hand – by heaven, nearly a year ago – and it has never left me since. It wastes me. I'm not half the man I was. But I'm handsome still!'

He looked up at a lofty mirror between the two opposite windows. It reflected his dark, commanding face with the prominent profile, the hard forehead, the deep expressive eye, the mass of raven hair and whisker and mustache, the stately aspect and figure, the breadth of chest and length of limb. In short, it gave back to his sight as fine a realization of soldier and patrician majesty as Angria ever produced from her ardent soil. Hartford sprang up.

'What should I give up hope for?' he said, rapidly pacing the room. 'By G—d, I think I could make her love me! I never yet have told her how I adore her. I've never offered her my title and hand and my half-phrenzied heart. But I will do it. Who says it is impossible she should prefer being my wife to being *his* mistress? The world will laugh at me – I don't care for the world – it's inconsistent with the honour of my house. I've burnt the honour of my house, and drank its ashes in Guanache. It's dastardly to meddle with another man's matters – another man who has been my friend, with whom I have fought and feasted, suffered and enjoyed. By G—d it is, I know it is, and if any man but myself had dared to entertain the same thought I'd have called him out. But Zamorna leaves her and cares no more about her – except when she can be of use to him – than I do for that silly Christmas rose on the lawn shrivelled up by the frost. Besides, every man for himself. I'll try, and if I do not succeed, I'll try again and again. She's worth a struggle. Perhaps, meantime, Warner or Enara will send me an invitation to dine on bullets for two, or perhaps I may forget the rules of the drill, and present and fire not from but at myself. In either case I get comfortably provided for and that torment will be over which now frightens away my sleep by night and my sense by day.'

This was rather wild talk, but his lordship's peculiar glance told that wine had not been without its effect. We will leave him striding about the room and maddening under the influence of his fiery passions. A sweet specimen of an aristocrat!

*

Late one fine, still evening in January the moon arose over a blue summit of the Sydenham Hills and looked down on a quiet road winding from the hamlet of Rivaulx.[22] The earth was bound in frost, hard, mute and glittering. The forest of Hawkscliffe was as still as a tomb, and its black leafless wilds stretched away in the distance and cut off with a hard serrated line the sky from the country. That sky was all silver blue, pierced here and there with a star like a diamond. Only the moon softened it, large, full, golden. The by-road I have spoken of received her ascending beam on a path of perfect solitude. Spectral pines and vast old beech trees guarded the way like sentinels from Hawkscliffe. Farther on the rude track wound deep into the shades of the forest, but here it was open, and the worn causeway bleached with frost ran under an old wall grown over with moss and wild ivy. Over this scene the sun of winter had gone down in cloudless calm, red as fire and kindling with its last beams the windows of a mansion on the verge of Hawkscliffe. To that mansion the road in question was the shortest cut from Rivaulx. And here a moment let us wait, wrapped, it is to be hoped, in furs, for a keener frost never congealed the Olympian.

Almost before you are aware, a figure strays up the causeway at a leisurely pace, musing amid the tranquillity of evening. Doubtless that figure must be an inmate of the before-mentioned mansion, for it is an elegant and pleasing object. Approaching gradually nearer, you can observe more accurately. You see now a lady of distinguished carriage, straight and slender, something inceding and princess-like in her walk, but unconsciously so. Her ancles are so perfect and her feet – if she tried she could scarce tread otherwise than she does, lightly, firmly, erectly. The ermine muff, the silk pelisse, the graceful and ample hat of dark beaver, suit and set off her slight, youthful form. She is deeply veiled; you must guess at her features. But she passes on, and a turn of the road conceals her.

Breaking up the silence, dashing in on the solitude comes a horseman. Fire flashes from under his steed's hoofs out of the flinty road. He rides desperately. Now and then he rises in his stirrups and eagerly looks along the track as if to catch sight of some object that has eluded him. He sees it, and the spurs are struck mercilessly into his horse's flanks. Horse and rider vanish in a whirlwind.

The lady passing through the iron gates had just entered upon the demesne of Hawkscliffe. She paused to gaze at the moon, which now fully risen looked upon her through the boughs of a superb elm. A green lawn lay between her and the house and there its light slumbered in gold. Thundering behind her came the sound of hoofs and, bending low to his saddle to avoid the contact of oversweeping branches, that wild horseman we saw five minutes since rushed upon the scene. Harshly curbing the charger, he brought it almost upon its haunches close to the spot where she stood.

'Miss Laury! Good evening!' he said.

The lady threw back her veil, surveyed him with one glance, and replied, 'Lord Hartford! I am glad to see you, my lord. You have ridden fast; your horse foams. Any bad news?'

'No!'

'Then you are on your way to Adrianopolis, I suppose. You will pass the night here?'

'If you ask me, I will.'

'If I ask you! Yes, this is the proper half-way house between the capitals. The night is cold, let us go in.'

They were now at the door. Hartford flung himself from his saddle. A servant came to lead the over-ridden steed to the stables, and he followed Miss Laury in.

It was her own drawing-room to which she led him, just such a scene as is most welcome after the contrast of a winter's evening's chill: not a large room, simply furnished, with curtains and couches of green silk, a single large mirror, a Grecian lamp dependent from the centre, softly burning now and mingling with the warmer illumination of the fire, whose brilliant glow bore testimony to the keenness of the frost.

Hartford glanced round him. He had been in Miss Laury's drawing-room before, but never as her sole guest. He had, before the troubles broke out, more than once formed one of a high and important trio, whose custom it was to make the lodge of Rivaulx their occasional rendezvous. Warner, Enara and himself had often stood on that hearth in a ring round Miss Laury's sofa, and he recalled, now, her face looking up to them, with its serious, soft intelligence that blent no woman's frivolity with the heartfelt interest of those subjects on which they conversed. He remembered those first kindlings of the flame that now devoured his life, as he watched her beauty and saw the earnest enthusiasm with which she threw her soul into topics of the highest import. She had often done for these great men what they could get no man to do for them. She had kept their secrets and executed their wishes as far as in her lay, for it had never been her part to counsel. With humble feminine devotedness, she always looked up for her task to be set, and then not Warner himself could have bent his energies more resolutely to the fulfilment of that task than did Miss Laury.

Had Mina's lot in life been different, she never would have interfered in such matters. She did not interfere now; she only served. Nothing like intrigue had ever stained her course in politics. She told her directors what she had done, and she asked for more to do, grateful always that they would trust her so far as to employ her, grateful too for the enthusiasm of their loyalty; in short, devoted to them heart and mind, because she believed them to be devoted as unreservedly to the common master of all. The consequences of this species of deeply confidential intercourse between the statesmen and their beautiful lieutenant had been intense and chivalric admiration on the part of Mr Warner, strong fond attachment on that of General Enara, and on Lord Hartford's the burning brand of passion. His Lordship had always been a man of strong and ill-regulated feelings and, in his youth (if report may be credited), of somewhat dissolute habits, but he had his own ideas of honour strongly implanted in his breast, and though he would not have scrupled if the wife of one of his equals or the daughter of one of his tenants had been in the question, yet as it was he stood beset and nonplussed.

Miss Laury belonged to the Duke of Zamorna. She was indisputably his property, as much as the lodge of Rivaulx or the stately woods of Hawkscliffe, and in that light she considered herself. All his dealings with her had been on matters connected with the Duke, and she had ever shown an habitual, rooted, solemn devotedness to his interest, which seemed to leave her hardly a thought for anything else in the world beside. She had but one idea – Zamorna, Zamorna! It had grown up with her, become a part of her nature. Absence, coldness, total neglect for long periods together went for nothing. She could no more feel alienation from him than she could from herself. She did not even repine when he forgot her, any more than the religious devotee does when his deity seems to turn away his face for a time and leave him to the ordeal of temporal afflictions. It seemed as if she could have lived on the remembrance of what he had once been to her without asking for anything more.

All this Hartford knew, and he knew, too, that she valued himself in proportion as she believed him to be loyal to his sovereign. Her friendship for him turned on this hinge: 'We have been fellow-labourers and fellow-sufferers together in the same good cause.' These were her own words, which she had uttered one night as she took leave of her three noble colleagues just before the storm burst over Angria. Hartford had noted the expression of her countenance as she spoke, and thought what a young and beautiful being thus appealed for sympathy with minds scarcely like her own in mould.

However, let us dwell no longer on these topics. Suffice it to say that Lord Hartford, against reason and without hope, had finally delivered himself wholly up to the guidance of his vehement passions, and it was with the resolution to make one desperate effort in the attainment of their end that he now stood before the lady of Rivaulx.

Above two hours had elapsed since Lord Hartford had entered the house. Tea was over, and in the perfect quiet of evening he and Miss Laury were left together. He sat on one side of the hearth, she on the other, her work-table only between them, and on that her little hand rested within his reach. It was embedded on a veil of lace, the embroidering of which she had just relinquished for a moment's thought. Lord Hartford's eye was fascinated by the white soft fingers. His whole heart at the

moment was in a tumult of bliss. To be so near! To be received
so benignly, so kindly! He forgot himself. His own hand closed
half involuntarily upon hers.

Miss Laury looked at him. If the action had left any room
for doubt of its significance, the glance which met hers filled
up all deficiencies – a wild fiery glance as if his feelings were
wrought up almost to delirium. Shocked for a moment, almost
overwhelmed, she yet speedily mastered her emotions, took
her hand away, resumed her work, and with head bent down
seemed endeavouring to conceal embarrassment under the appearance of occupation. The dead silence that followed would
not do, so she broke it, in a very calm, self-possessed tone.

'That ring, Lord Hartford, which you were admiring just
now, belonged once to the Duchess of Wellington.'

'And was it given you by her son?' asked the General bitterly.

'No, my lord. The Duchess herself gave it me[23] a few days
before she died. It has her maiden-name, Catherine Pakenham,
engraved within the stone.'

'But,' pursued Hartford, 'I was not admiring the ring when
I touched your hand. No, the thought struck me, if ever I marry
I should like my wife's hand to be just as white and snowy and
taper as that.'

'I am the daughter of a common soldier,[24] my lord, and it is
said that ladies of high descent have fairer hands than peasant
women.'

Hartford made no reply. He rose restlessly from his seat and
stood leaning against the mantle-piece.

'Miss Laury, shall I tell you what was the happiest hour of
my life?'

'I will guess, my lord. Perhaps when the bill passed which
made Angria an independent kingdom.'[25]

'No,' replied Hartford with an expressive smile.

'Perhaps, then, when Lord Northangerland resigned the
seals[26] – for I know you and the Earl were never on good terms.'

'No. I hated his lordship, but there are moments of deeper
felicity even than those which see the triumph of a fallen
enemy.'

'I will hope then it was at the Restoration.'[27]

'Wrong again. Why, madam, young as you are, your mind is so used to the harness of politics that you can imagine no happiness or misery unconnected with them. You remind me of Warner.'

'I believe I am like him,' returned Miss Laury. 'He often tells me so himself. But I live so with men and statesmen, I almost lose the ideas of a woman.'

'Do you?' muttered Hartford, with the dark, sinister smile peculiar to him. 'I wish you would tell the Duke so next time you see him.'

Miss Laury passed over this equivocal remark and proceeded with the conversation.

'I cannot guess your riddle, my lord, so I think you must explain it.'

'Then, Miss Laury, prepare to be astonished. You are so patriotic, so loyal, that you will scarcely credit me when I say that the happiest hour I have ever known fell on the darkest day in the deadliest crisis of Angria's calamities.'

'How, Lord Hartford?'

'Moreover, Miss Laury, it was at no bright period of your own life. It was to you an hour of the most acute agony, to me one of ecstasy.'

Miss Laury turned aside her head with a disturbed air and trembled. She seemed to know to what he alluded.

'You remember the first of July, —36?' continued Hartford. She bowed.

'You remember that the evening of that day closed in a tremendous storm?'

'Yes, my lord.'

'You recollect how you sat in this very room by this fireside, fearful of retiring for the night lest you should awake in another world in the morning? The country was not then as quiet as it is now. You have not forgotten the deep explosion which roared up at midnight, and told you that your life and liberty hung on a thread, that the enemy had come suddenly upon Rivaulx and that we who lay there to defend the forlorn hope were surprised and routed by a night attack? Then, madam, perhaps you recollect the warning which I brought you at one o'clock in the morning, to fly instantly, unless you chose the alternative of infamous captivity in the hands of Jordan. I found you here, sitting by a black hearth without fire, and Ernest Fitz-Arthur[28] lay on your knee asleep. You told me you had heard the firing, and that you were waiting for some communication from me, determined not to stir without orders lest a precipitate step on your part should embarrass me. I had a carriage already in waiting for you. I put you in and, with the remains of my defeated followers, escorted you as far as Zamorna. What followed after this, Miss Laury?'

Miss Laury covered her eyes with her hand. She seemed as if she could not answer.

'Well,' continued Hartford. 'In the midst of darkness and tempest, and while the whole city of Zamorna seemed changed into a hell peopled with fiends and inspired with madness, my lads were hewed down about you and your carriage was stopped. I very well remember what you did – how frantically you struggled to save Fitz-Arthur, and how you looked at me when he was snatched from you. As to your own preservation – that, I need not repeat – only my arm did it. You acknowledge that, Miss Laury?'

'Hartford, I do. But why do you dwell on that horrible scene?'

'Because I am now approaching the happiest hour of my life. I took you to the house of one of my tenants whom I could depend upon, and just as morning dawned you and I sat together and alone in the little chamber of a farmhouse, and you were in my arms, your head upon my shoulder, and weeping out all your anguish on a breast that longed to bleed for you.'

Miss Laury agitatedly rose. She approached Hartford.

'My lord, you have been very kind to me, and I feel very grateful for that kindness. Perhaps sometime I may be able to repay it. We know not how the chances of fortune may turn. The weak have aided the strong, and I will watch vigilantly for the slightest opportunity to serve you. But do not talk in this way. I scarcely know whither your words tend.'

Lord Hartford paused a moment before he replied. Gazing at her with bended brows and folded arms, he said:

'Miss Laury, what do you think of me?'

'That you are one of the noblest hearts in the world,' she replied unhesitatingly.

She was standing just before Hartford, looking up at him, her hair in the attitude falling back from her brow, shading with exquisite curls her temples and her slender neck, her small sweet features, with that high seriousness deepening their beauty, lit up by eyes so large, so dark, so swimming, so full of pleading benignity, of an expression of alarmed regard, as if she at once feared for and pitied the sinful abstraction of a great mind. Hartford could not stand it. He could have borne female anger or terror, but the look of enthusiastic gratitude softened by compassion nearly unmanned him. He turned his head for a moment aside, but then passion prevailed. Her beauty, when he looked again, struck through him, maddening sensation whetted to acuter power by a feeling like despair.

'You shall love me!' he exclaimed desperately. 'Do I not adore you? Would I not die for you? And must I in return receive only the cold regard of friendship? I am no Platonist,[29] Miss Laury. I am not your friend. I am – hear me, madam – your declared lover! Nay, you shall not leave me, by heaven! I am stronger than you are!'

She had stepped a pace or two back, appalled by his vehemence. He thought she meant to withdraw, and determined not to be so balked. He clasped her at once in both his arms, and kissed her furiously rather than fondly. Miss Laury did not struggle.

'Hartford,' said she, steadying her voice, though it faltered in spite of her effort. 'This must be our parting scene. I will never see you again if you do not restrain yourself.'

Hartford saw that she turned pale, and he felt her tremble violently. His arms relaxed their hold; he allowed her to leave him. She sat down on a chair opposite, and hurriedly wiped her brow, which was damp and marble pale.

'Now, Miss Laury,' said his Lordship. 'No man in the world loves you as I do. Will you accept my title and my coronet? I fling them at your feet.'

'My lord, do you know whose I am?' she replied in a hollow, very suppressed tone. 'Do you know with what a sound those proposals fall on my ear, how impious and blasphemous they seem to be? Do you at all conceive how utterly impossible it is that I should ever love you? The scene I have just witnessed has given a strange wrench to all my accustomed habits of thought. I thought you a true-hearted, faithful man; I find that you are a traitor.'

'And do you despise me?' asked Hartford.

'No, my lord, I do not.'

She paused, and looked down. The colour rose rapidly into her pale face; she sobbed, not in tears, but in the overmastering approach of an impulse born of a warm and western heart.[30] Again she looked up. Her eyes had changed their aspect, burning with a wild bright inspiration truly, divinely Irish.

'Hartford!' she said. 'Had I met you long since, before I left Ellibank and forgot the St Cyprian[31] and dishonoured my father, I would have loved you. Oh, my lord, you know not how truly! I would have married you, and made it the glory of my life to cheer and brighten your hearth. But I cannot do so now, never. I saw my present master when he had scarcely attained manhood. Do you think, Hartford, I will tell you what feelings I had for him? No tongue could express them; they were so fervid, so glowing in their colour that they effaced every thing else. I lost the power of properly appreciating the value of the world's opinion, of discerning the difference between right and wrong. I have never in my life contradicted Zamorna, never delayed obedience to his commands. I could not. He was something more to me than a human being. He superseded all things – all affections, all interests, all fears, or hopes, or principles. Unconnected with him my mind would be a blank – cold, dead, susceptible only of a sense of despair. How I should sicken if I were torn from him and thrown to you! Do not ask it; I would die first. No woman that ever loved my master could consent to leave him. There is nothing like him elsewhere. Hartford, if I were to be your wife, if Zamorna only looked at me, I should creep back like a slave to my former service. I should disgrace you as I have long since disgraced all my kindred. Think of that, my lord, and never say you love me again.'

'You do not frighten me,' replied Lord Hartford hardily. 'I would stand that chance, aye, and every other, if I only might see, at the head of my table in that old dining-room at Hartford Hall, yourself as my wife and lady. I am called proud as it is, but then I would shew Angria to what pitch of pride a man might attain, if I could, coming home at night, find Mina Laury waiting to receive me, if I could sit down and look at you with the consciousness that your exquisite beauty was all my own, that that cheek, those lips, that lovely hand might be claimed arbitrarily and you dare not refuse me. I should then feel happy.'

'Hartford, you would be more likely, when you came home, to find your house vacant and your hearth deserted. I know the extent of my own infatuation. I should go back to Zamorna and entreat him on my knees to let me be his slave again.'

'Madam,' said Hartford, frowning, 'you dared not if you were my wife. I would guard you.'

'Then I should die under your guardianship. But the experiment will never be tried.'

Hartford came near, sat down by her side and leant over her. She did not shrink away.

'Oh!' he said. 'I am happy. There was a time when I dared not have come so near you. One summer evening, two years ago, I was walking in the twilight amongst those trees on the lawn, and at a turn I saw you, sitting at the root of one of them by yourself. You were looking up at a star which was twinkling above the Sydenhams. You were in white. Your hands were folded on your knee, and your hair was resting in still, shining curls on your neck. I stood and watched. The thought struck me – if that image sat now in my own woods, if she were something in which I had an interest, if I could go and press my lips to her brow and expect a smile in answer to the caress, if I could take her in my arms and turn her thoughts from that sky with its single star and from the distant country to which it points (for it hung in the west, and I knew you were thinking about Senegambia), if I could attract those thoughts and centre them all in myself, how like heaven would the world become to me. I heard a window open, and Zamorna's voice called through the silence "Mina!" The next moment I had the pleasure of seeing you standing on the lawn, close under this very casement, where the Duke sat leaning out, and you were allowing his hand to stray through your hair, and his lips –'

'Lord Hartford!' exclaimed Miss Laury, colouring to the eyes. 'This is more than I can bear. I have not been angry yet. I thought it folly to rage at you because you said you loved me, but what you have just said is like touching a nerve; it overpowers all reason. It is like a stinging taunt which I am under no obligation to endure from you. Every one knows what I am. But where is the woman in Africa who would have acted more wisely than I did if under the same circumstances she had been subject to the same temptations?'

'That is,' returned Hartford, whose eye was now glittering with a desperate, reckless expression, 'where is the woman in Africa who would have said no to young Douro, when amongst the romantic hills of Ellibank, he has pressed his suit on some fine moonlight summer night, and the girl and boy have found themselves alone in a green dell, here and there a tree to be their shade, far above, the stars for their sentinels, and around, the night for their wide curtain.'

The wild bounding throb of Miss Laury's heart was visible through her satin bodice. It was even audible, as for a moment Hartford ceased his scoffing to note its effect. He was still close by her, and she did not move from him. She did not speak. The pallid lamplight shewed her lips white, her cheek bloodless.

He continued unrelentingly and bitterly: 'In after times, doubtless, the woods of Hawkscliffe have witnessed many a tender scene, when the King of Angria has retired from the turmoil of business and the teazing of matrimony to love and leisure with his gentle mistress.'

'Now, Hartford, we must part,' interrupted Miss Laury. 'I see what your opinion of me is, and it is very just, but not one which I willingly hear expressed. You have cut me to the heart. Good-bye. I shall try to avoid seeing you for the future.'

She rose. Hartford did not attempt to detain her. She went out. As she closed the door, he heard the bursting, convulsive gush of feelings which his taunts had wrought up to agony.

Her absence left a blank. Suddenly the wish to recall, to

soothe, to propitiate her, rose in his mind. He strode to the door and opened it. There was a little hall, or rather, a wide passage without, in which one large lamp was quietly burning. Nothing appeared there, nor on the staircase of low broad steps in which it terminated. She seemed to have vanished.

Lord Hartford's hat and horseman's cloak lay on the side slab. There remained no further attraction for him at the lodge of Rivaulx. The delirious dream of rapture which had intoxicated his sense broke up and disappeared; his passionate stern nature maddened under disappointment. He strode out into the black and frozen night, burning in flames no ice could quench. He ordered and mounted his steed, and, dashing his spurs with harsh cruelty up to the rowels[32] into the flanks of the noble war-horse which had borne him victoriously through the carnage of Westwood and Leyden, he dashed in furious gallop down the road to Rivaulx.

The frost continued unbroken, and the snow lay cold and cheerless all over Angria. It was a dreary morning. Large flakes were fluttering slowly down from the sky, thickening every moment. The trees around a stately hall, lying up among its grounds at some distance from the road-side, shuddered in the cutting wind that at intervals howled through them. We are now on a broad and public road. A great town lies on our left hand, with a deep river sweeping under the arches of a bridge. This is Zamorna, and that house is Hartford Hall.

The wind increased, the sky darkened, and the bleached whirl of a snow-storm began to fill the air. Dashing at a rapid rate through the tempest, an open travelling carriage swept up the road. Four splendid greys and two mounted postillions gave the equipage an air of aristocratic style. It contained two gentlemen, one a man of between thirty or [?and] forty, having about him a good deal of the air of a nobleman, shawled to the eyes, and buttoned up in at least three surtouts, with a waterproof white beaver hat, an immense mackintosh cape,[33] and beaver gloves. His countenance bore a half-rueful, half-jesting expression. He seemed endeavouring to bear all things as smoothly as he could, but still the cold east wind and driving

snow evidently put his philosophy very much to the test. The
other traveller was a young high-featured gentleman with a pale
face and accurately arched dark eyebrows. His person was
carefully done up in a vast roquelaire of furs. A fur travelling
cap decorated his head, which, however, nature had much more
effectively protected by a profusion of dark chestnut ringlets,
now streaming long and thick in the wind. He presented to the
said wind a case[34] of bared teeth firmly set together and exposed
in a desperate grin. They seemed daring the snow-flakes to a
comparison of whiteness.

'Oh,' groaned the elder traveller, 'I wish your Grace would
be ruled by reason. What could possess you to insist on prose-
cuting the journey in such weather as this?'

'Stuff, Richton, an old campaigner like you ought to make
objections to no weather. It's d—d cold, though. I think all
Greenland's coming down upon us. But you're not going to
faint, are you, Richton? What are you staring at so? Do you
see the d—l?'

'I think I do,' replied Lord Richton. 'And really, if your Grace
will look two yards before you, you will be of the same opinion.'

The carriage was now turning that angle of the park wall
where a lodge on each side, overhung by some magnificent
trees, formed the supporters to the stately iron gates opening
upon the broad carriage-road which wound up through the
park. The gates were open, and just outside, on the causeway
of the high road, stood a tall, well-dressed man in a blue coat
with military pantaloons of grey having a broad stripe of scarlet
down the sides. His distinguished air, his handsome dark face,
and his composed attitude – for he stood perfectly still with
one hand on his side – gave singular effect to the circumstance
of his being without hat. Had it been a summer day one would
not so much have wondered at it, though even in the warmest
weather it is not usual to see gentlemen parading the public
roads uncovered. Now, as the keen wind rushed down upon
him through the boughs of the lofty trees arching the park
portal, and as the snow-flakes settled thick upon the short raven
curls of his hair, he looked strange indeed.

Abruptly stepping forward, he seized the first leader of the chariot by the head and backed it fiercely. The postillions were about to whip on, consigning the hatless and energetic gentleman to that fate which is sought by the worshippers of Juggernaut,[35] when Lord Richton called out to them, 'For God's sake to stop the horses!'

'I think they are stopped with a vengeance,' said his young companion. Then, leaning forward with a most verjuice expression on his pale face, he said,

'Give that gentleman half a minute to get out of the way and then drive on forward like d—ls.'

'My lord Duke,' interposed Richton, 'do you see who it is? Permit me to solicit a few minutes' forbearance. Lord Hartford must be ill. I will alight and speak to him.'

Before Richton could fulfil his purpose, the individual had let go his hold and stood by the side of the chariot. Stretching out his clenched hand with a menacing gesture, he addressed Zamorna thus:

'I've no hat to take off in your Majesty's presence, so you must excuse my rustic breeding. I saw the royal carriage at a distance, and so I came out to meet it something in a hurry. I'm just in time, God be thanked! Will your Grace get out and speak to me? By the Lord, I'll not leave this spot alive without an audience.'

'Your Lordship is cursedly drunk,' replied the Duke, keeping his teeth as close shut as a vice. 'Ask for an audience when you're sober. Drive on, postillions!'

'At the peril of your lives!' cried Hartford, and he drew out a brace of pistols, cocked them, and presented one at each postillion.

'Rosier! my pistols!' shouted Zamorna to his valet, who sat behind, and he threw himself at once from the chariot and stood facing Lord Hartford on the high road.

'It is your Grace that is intoxicated,' retorted the nobleman. 'And I'll tell you with what – with wine of Cyprus or Cythera.[36] Your Majesty is far too amorous; you had better keep a harem!'

'Come, sir,' said Zamorna in lofty scorn, 'this won't do. I see you are mad. Postillions, seize him, and you, Rosier, go up to

the Hall and fetch five or six of his own domestics. Tell them
to bring a strait waistcoat if they have such a thing.'

'Your Grace would like to throw me into a dungeon,' said
Hartford, 'but this is a free country, and we will have no
western despotism. Be so good as to hear me, my lord Duke,
or I will shoot myself.'

'Small loss,' said Zamorna, lifting his lip with a sour sneer.

'Do not aggravate his insanity,' whispered Richton. 'Allow
me to manage him, my lord Duke. You had better return to the
carriage, and I will accompany Hartford home.' Then, turning
to Hartford: 'Take my arm, Edward, and let us return to the
house together. You do not seem well this morning.'

'None of your snivel,' replied the gallant nobleman. 'I'll have
satisfaction, I'm resolved on it. His Grace has injured me
deeply.'

'A good move,' replied Zamorna. 'Then take your pistols,
sir, and come along. Rosier, take the carriage back to the
town. Call at Dr Cooper's, and ask him to ride over to Hartford Hall. D—n you, sir, what are you staring at? Do as I
bid you.'

'He is staring at the propriety of the monarch of a kingdom
fighting a duel with a madman,' replied Richton. 'If your Grace
will allow me to go, I will return with a detachment of police
and put both the sovereign and the subject under safe ward.'

'Have done with that trash!' said Zamorna angrily. 'Come
on, you will be wanted for a second.'

'Well,' said Richton, 'I don't wish to disoblige either your
Grace or my friend Hartford, but it's an absurd and frantic
piece of business. I beseech you to consider a moment. Hartford,
reflect; what are you about to do?'

'To get vengeance for a thousand wrongs and sufferings,'
was the reply. 'His Grace has dashed my happiness for life.'

Richton shook his head. 'I must stop this work,' he muttered
to himself. 'What demon is influencing Edward Hartford? And
Zamorna too, for I never saw such a fiendish glitter as that in
his eyes just now – strange madness!'

The noble Earl buttoned his surtout still closer and then
followed the two other gentlemen, who were already on their

way to the house. The carriage, meantime, drove off according
to orders in the direction of Zamorna.

Lord Hartford was not mad, though his conduct might seem to
betoken such a state of mind. He was only desperate. The
disappointment of the previous night had wrought him up to a
pitch of rage and recklessness whose results, as we have just
seen them, were of such a nature as to convince Lord Richton
that the doubts he had long harboured of his friend's sanity
were correct. So long as his passion for Miss Laury remained
unavowed and consequently unrejected, he had cherished a
dreamy kind of hope that there existed some chance of success.
When wandering through his woods alone, he had fed on
reveries of some future day when she might fill his halls with
the bliss of her presence and the light of her beauty. All day her
image haunted him. It seemed to speak to and look upon him
with that mild friendly aspect he had ever seen her wear, and
then, as imagination prevailed, it brought vividly back that
hour when, in a moment almost of despair, her feminine weakness had thrown itself utterly on him for support, and he had
been permitted to hold her in his arms and take her to his heart.
He remembered how she looked when, torn from danger and
tumult, rescued from hideous captivity, he carried her up the
humble staircase of a farmhouse, all pale and shuddering, with
her long black curls spread dishevelled on his shoulder and her
soft cheek resting there as confidingly as if he had indeed been
her husband. From her trusting gentleness in those moments
he drew blissful omens, now, alas! utterly belied. No web of
self-delusion could now be woven. The truth was too stern.
And besides, he had taunted her, hurt her feelings, and alienated
for ever her grateful friendship.
    Having thus entered more particularly into the state of his
feelings, let me proceed with my narrative.

The apartment into which Lord Hartford shewed his illustrious guest was that very dining-room where I first represented
him sitting alone and maddening under the double influence
of passion and wine. His manner now was more composed,

and he demeaned himself even with lofty courtesy towards his sovereign. There was a particular chair in that room which Zamorna had always been accustomed to occupy when in happier days he had not unfrequently formed one of the splendid dinner-parties given at Hartford Hall. The General asked him to assume that seat now, but he declined, acknowledging the courtesy only by a slight inclination of the head, and planted himself just before the hearth, his elbow leaning on the mantlepiece and his eyes looking down. In that position the eye-lids and the long fringes partly concealed the sweet expression of vindictiveness lurking beneath. But still, aided by the sour curl and pout of the lip, the passionate dishevelment of the hair and flushing of the brow, there was enough seen to stamp his countenance with a character of unpleasantness more easily conceived than described.

Lord Hartford, influenced by his usual habits, would not sit whilst his monarch stood, so he retired with Richton to the deeply embayed recess of a window. That worthy and prudent personage, bent upon settling this matter without coming to the absurd extreme now contemplated,[37] began to reason with his friend on the subject.

'Hartford,' he said, speaking soft and low so that Zamorna could not overhear him, 'let me entreat you to consider well what you are about to do. I know that the scene which we have just witnessed is not the primary cause of the dispute between you and his Grace there, which is now about to terminate so fatally. I know that circumstances previously existed which gave birth to bitter feelings on both sides. I wish, Hartford, you would reconsider the steps you have taken. All is in vain: the lady in question can never be yours.'

'I know that, sir, and that is what makes me frantic. I have no motive left for living, and if Zamorna wants my blood, let him have it.'

'You may kill him,' suggested Richton, 'and what will be the consequences then?'

'Trust me,' returned Hartford. 'I'll not hurt him much, though he deserves it – the double-dyed infernal western profligate! But the fact is he hates me far more than I hate him. Look at his face now reflected in that mirror. God! he longs to see the last drop of blood I have in my heart.'

'Hush! he will hear you,' said Richton. 'He certainly does not look very amiable, but recollect, you are the offender.'

'I know that,' replied Hartford gloomily. 'But it is not out of spite to him that I wish to get his mistress. And how often in the half-year does he see her or think about her? Grasping dog! Another king when he was tired of his mistress would give her up, but he –! I think I'll shoot him straight through the head; I would, if his death would only win me Miss Laury.'

That name, though spoken very low, caught Zamorna's ear, and he at once comprehended the nature of the conversation. It is not often that he had occasion to be jealous, and as it is a rare so also it is a remarkably curious and pretty sight to see him under the influence of that passion. It worked in every fibre of his frame and boiled in every vein. Blush after blush deepened the hue of his cheek; as one ended another of darker crimson followed. (This variation of colour resulting from strong emotion has been his wonted peculiarity from childhood.) His whiskers twined and writhed, and even the very curls seemed to stir on his brow.

Turning to Hartford, he spoke:

'What drivelling folly have you let into your head, sir, to dare to look at anything which belonged to me? Frantic idiot! To dream that I should allow a coarse Angrian squire to possess anything that had ever been mine! As if I knew how to relinquish! G—d d—n your grossness! Richton, you have my pistols? Bring them here directly. I will neither wait for doctors[38] nor anybody else to settle this business.'

'My lord Duke!' began Richton.

'No interference, sir!' exclaimed his Grace. 'Bring the pistols!'

The Earl was not going to stand this arbitrary work.

'I wash my hands of this bloody affair,' he said sternly, placing the pistols on the table, and in silence he left the room.

The demon of Zamorna's nature was now completely roused. Growling out his words in a deep and hoarse tone, almost like the smothered roar of a lion, he savagely told Hartford to measure out his ground in this room, for he would not delay the business a moment.[39] Hartford did so, without remonstrance or reply.

'Take your station!' thundered the barbarian.

'I have done so,' replied his Lordship, 'and my pistol is ready.'

'Then fire!'

The deadly explosion succeeded, the flash and the cloud of smoke.

While the room still shook to the sound, almost before the flash had expired and the smoke burst after it, the door slowly opened and Lord Richton reappeared, wearing upon his face a far more fixed and stern solemnity than I ever saw there before.

'Who is hurt?' he asked.

There was but one erect figure visible through the vapour, and the thought thrilled through him, 'The other may be a corpse.'

Lord Hartford lay across the doorway, still and pale.

'My poor friend!' said Lord Richton and, kneeling on one knee, he propped against the other the wounded nobleman, from whose lips a moan of agony escaped as the Earl moved him.

'Thank God he is not quite dead!' was Richton's involuntary exclamation, for though a man accustomed to scenes of carnage on gory battle-plains, and though of enduring nerves and cool resolution, he felt a pang at this spectacle of fierce manslaughter amid scenes of domestic peace. The renowned and gallant soldier, who had escaped hostile weapons and returned unharmed from fields of terrific strife, lay, as it seemed, dying, under his own roof. Blood began to drop on to Richton's hand, and a large crimson stain appeared on the ruffles of his shirt. The same ominous dye darkened Lord Hartford's lips and oozed through them when he made vain efforts to speak. He had been wounded in the region of the lungs.

A thundering knock and a loud ring at the door-bell now broke up the appalling silence which had fallen. It was Dr Cooper.[40] He speedily entered, followed by a surgeon with instruments etc. Richton silently resigned his friend to their hands, and turned for the first time to the other actor in this horrid scene.

The Duke of Zamorna was standing by a window, coolly buttoning his surtout over the pistols which he had replaced in his breast.

'Is your Majesty hurt?' asked Richton.

'No, sir. May I trouble you to hand me my gloves?'

They lay on a side-board near the Earl. He politely complied with the request, handing over at the same time a large shawl or scarf of crimson silk which the Duke had taken from his neck. In this he proceeded to envelop his throat and a considerable portion of his face, leaving little more visible than the forehead, eyes and high Roman nose. Then, drawing on his gloves, he turned to Dr Cooper.

'Of what nature is the wound, sir? Is there any likelihood of Lord Hartford's recovery?'

'A possibility exists that he may recover, my Lord Duke, but the wound is a severe one. The lungs have only just escaped.'

The Duke drew near the couch on which his general had been raised, looked at the wound then under the operation of the surgeon's probing knife, and transferred his glance from the bloody breast to the pallid face of the sufferer. Hartford, who had borne the extraction of the bullet without a groan, and whose clenched teeth and rigid brow seemed defying pain to do its worst, smiled faintly when he saw his monarch's eye bent near him with searching keenness. In spite of the surgeon's prohibition, he attempted to speak.

'Zamorna,' he said, 'I have got your hate, but you shall not blight me with your contempt. This is but a little matter. Why did you not inflict more upon me, that I might bear it without flinching? You called me a coarse Angrian squire ten minutes since. Angrians are men as well as westerns.'

'Brutes, rather,' replied Zamorna. 'Faithful, gallant, noble brutes.'

He left the room, for his carriage had now returned and waited at the door. Before Lord Richton followed him, he stopped a moment to take leave of his friend.

'Well,' murmured Hartford, as he feebly returned the pressure of the Earl's hand, 'Zamorna has finished me. But I bear him no ill-will. My love for his mistress was involuntary. I am not sorry for it now. I adore her to the last. Flower,[41] if I die give Miss Laury this token of my truth.' He drew the gold ring from his little finger and gave it into Richton's hand. 'Good G—d!' he muttered, turning away. 'I would have endured hell's torments to win her love. My feelings are not changed; they are just the same – passion for her, bitter self-reproach for my treachery to her master. But he has paid himself in blood, the purest coin to a western. Farewell, Richton.'

They parted without another word on either side.[42] Richton joined the Duke, sprung to his place in the carriage, and off it swept like the wind.

II

Miss Laury was sitting after breakfast in a small library. Her desk[43] lay before her, and two large ruled quartos filled with items and figures which she seemed to be comparing. Behind her chair stood a tall, well-made, soldierly young man with light hair. His dress was plain and gentlemanly; the epaulette on one shoulder alone indicated an official capacity. He watched with a fixed look of attention the movements of the small finger which ascended in rapid calculation the long columns of accounts. It was strange to see the absorption of mind expressed in Miss Laury's face, the gravity of her smooth white brow shaded with drooping curls, the scarcely perceptible and unsmiling movement of her lips – though those lips in their rosy sweetness seemed formed only for smiles. Edward Percy at his ledger could not have appeared more completely wrapt in the mysteries of practice[44] and fractions. An hour or more lapsed in this employment, the room meantime continuing in profound silence, broken only by an occasional observation addressed by Miss Laury to the gentleman behind her, concerning the legitimacy of some item or the absence of some stray farthing wanted to complete the accuracy of the sum total. In this balancing of the books she displayed a most business-like sharpness and strictness. The slightest fault was detected and remarked on, in few words, but with a quick searching glance. However, the accountant had evidently been accustomed to her surveillance, for on the whole his books were a specimen of arithmetical correctness.

'Very well,' said Miss Laury as she closed the volumes. 'Your accounts do you credit, Mr O'Neill. You may tell his Grace that all is quite right. Your memoranda tally with my own exactly.'

Mr O'Neill bowed. 'Thank you, madam. This will bear me out against Lord Hartford. His Lordship lectured me severely last time he came to inspect Fort Adrian.'

'What about?' asked Miss Laury, turning aside her face to hide the deepening of colour which overspread it at the mention of Lord Hartford's name.

'I can hardly tell you, madam, but his Lordship was in a savage temper. Nothing could please him; he found fault with everything and everybody. I thought he scarcely appeared himself, and that has been the opinion of many lately.'

Miss Laury gently shook her head. 'You should not say so, Ryan,' she replied in a soft tone of reproof. 'Lord Hartford has a great many things to think about, and he is naturally rather stern. You ought to bear with his tempers.'

'Necessity has no law,[45] madam,' replied Mr O'Neill, with a smile, 'and I must bear with them. But his Lordship is not a popular man in the army. He orders the lash so unsparingly. We like the Earl of Arundel ten times better.'

'Ah!' said Miss Laury, smiling. 'You and I are westerns, Mr O'Neill – Irish – and we favour our countrymen. But Hartford is a gallant commander. His men can always trust him. Do not let us be partial.'

Mr O'Neill bowed in deference to her opinion, but smiled at the same time, as if he doubted its justice. Taking up his books, he seemed about to leave the room. Before he did so, however, he turned and said: 'The Duke wished me to inform you, madam, that he would probably be here about four or five o'clock in the afternoon.'

'To-day?' asked Miss Laury in an accent of surprise.

'Yes, madam.'

She paused a moment, then said quickly, 'Very well, sir.'

Mr O'Neill now took his leave, with another low and respectful obeisance. Miss Laury returned it with a slight abstracted bow. Her thoughts were all caught up and hurried away by that last communication. For a long time after the door had closed she sat with her head on her hand, lost in a tumultuous flush of ideas, anticipations awakened by that simple sentence, 'The Duke will be here to-day.'

The striking of a time-piece roused her. She remembered that twenty tasks awaited her direction. Always active, always employed, it was not her custom to waste many hours in dreaming. She rose, closed her desk, and left the quiet library for busier scenes.

Four o'clock came, and Miss Laury's foot was heard on the staircase, descending from her chamber. She crossed the large, light passage – such an apparition of feminine elegance and beauty! She had dressed herself splendidly. The robe of black satin became at once her slender form, which it enveloped in full and shining folds, and her bright blooming complexion, which it set off by the contrast of colour. Glittering through her curls there was a band of fine diamonds, and drops of the same pure gem trembled from her small, delicate ears. These ornaments, so regal in their nature, had been the gift of royalty, and were worn now chiefly for the associations of soft and happy moments which their gleam might be supposed to convey.

She entered her drawing-room, and stood by the window. From thence appeared one glimpse of the high road visible through the thickening shades of Rivaulx. Even that was now almost concealed by the frozen mist in which the approach of twilight was wrapt. All was very quiet, both in the house and in the wood. A carriage drew near. She heard the sound; she saw it shoot through the fog. But it was not Zamorna. No, the driving was neither the driving of Jehu the son of Nimshi,[46] nor that of Jehu's postillions. She had not gazed a minute before her experienced eye discerned that there was something wrong with the horses. The harness had got entangled, or they were frightened. The coachman had lost command over them; they were plunging violently.

She rang the bell. A servant entered. She ordered immediate assistance to be despatched to that carriage on the road. Two grooms presently[47] hurried down the drive to execute her commands, but before they could reach the spot, one of the horses in its gambols had slipped on the icy road and fallen. The others grew more unmanageable, and presently the carriage lay overturned on the road-side. One of Miss Laury's messengers came back. She threw up the window, that she might communicate with him more readily.

'Any accident?' she asked. 'Anybody hurt?'

'I hope not much, madam.'

'Who is in the carriage?'

'Only one lady, and she seems to have fainted. She looked very white when I opened the door. What is to be done, madam?'

Miss Laury, with Irish frankness, answered directly, 'Bring them all into the house. Let the horses be taken into the stables and the servants – how many are there?'

'Three, madam. Two postillions and a footman – it seems quite a gentleman's turn-out, very plain but quite slap up. Beautiful horses.'

'Do you know the liveries?'

'Can't say, madam. Postillions grey and white, footmen in plain clothes. Horses frightened at a drove of Sydenham oxen, they say. Very spirited nags.'

'Well, you have my orders. Bring the lady in directly, and make the others comfortable.'

'Yes, madam.'

The groom touched his hat and departed. Miss [Laury] shut her window. It was very cold. Not many minutes elapsed before the lady, in the arms of her own servants, was slowly brought up the lawn and ushered into the drawing-room.

'Lay her on the sofa,' said Miss Laury.

She was obeyed. The lady's travelling cloak was carefully removed, and a thin figure became apparent, in a dark silk dress. The cushions of down scarcely sunk under the pressure, it was so light.

Her swoon was now passing off. The genial warmth of the fire, which shone full on her, revived her. Opening her eyes, she looked up at Miss Laury's face, who was bending close over

her and wetting her lips with some cordial. Recognizing a
stranger, she shyly turned her glance aside, and asked for her
servants.

'They are in the house, madam, and perfectly safe. But you
cannot pursue your journey at present. The carriage is much
broken.'

The lady lay silent. She looked keenly round the room, and
seeing the perfect elegance of its arrangement, the cheerful and
tranquil glow of its hearthlight, she appeared to grow more
composed. Turning a little on the cushions which supported
her, and by no means looking at Miss Laury but straight the
other way, she said, 'To whom am I indebted for this kindness?
Where am I?'

'In a hospitable country, madam. The Angrians never turn
their backs on strangers.'

'I know I am in Angria,' she said quietly. 'But where? What
is the name of the house, and who are you?'

Miss Laury coloured slightly. It seemed as if there was some
undefined reluctance to give her real name. That, she knew,
was widely celebrated – too widely. Most likely, the lady would
turn from her in contempt if she heard it, and Miss Laury felt
she could not bear that.

'I am only the housekeeper,' she said. 'This is a shooting
lodge belonging to a great Angrian proprietor.'

'Who?' asked the lady, who was not to be put off by indirect
answers.

Again Miss Laury hesitated. For her life she could not have
said, 'His Grace the Duke of Zamorna.' She replied hastily, 'A
gentleman of western extraction, a distant branch of the great
Pakenhams; so, at least, the family records say, but they have
been long naturalized in the east.'

'I never heard of them,' replied the lady. 'Pakenham; that is
not an Angrian name.'

'Perhaps, madam, you are not particularly acquainted with
this part of the country?'

'I know Hawkscliffe,' said the lady, 'and your house is on
the very borders, within the royal liberties,[48] is it not?'

'Yes, madam. It stood there before the great Duke bought up

the forest manor, and His Majesty allowed my master to retain this lodge and the privilege of sporting in the chase.'

'Well, and you are Mr Pakenham's housekeeper?'

'Yes, madam.'

The lady surveyed Miss Laury with another furtive side-glance of her large, majestic eyes. Those eyes lingered upon the diamond ear-rings, the bandeau of brilliants that flashed from between the clusters of raven curls, then passed over the sweet face, the exquisite figure of the young housekeeper, and finally were reverted to the wall with an expression that spoke volumes. Miss Laury could have torn the dazzling pendants from her ears. She was bitterly stung. 'Every body knows me,' she said to herself. ' "Mistress", I suppose, is branded on my brow.'

In her turn she gazed on her guest. The lady was but a young creature, though so high and commanding in her demeanour. She had very small and feminine features, handsome eyes, a neck of delicate curve and hue, fair, long, graceful little snowy aristocratic hands and sandalled feet to match. It would have been difficult to tell her rank by her dress. None of those dazzling witnesses appeared which had betrayed Miss Laury. Any gentleman's wife might have worn the gown of dark blue silk, the tinted gloves of Parisian kid and the fairy sandals of black satin in which she was attired.

'May I have a room to myself?' she asked, again turning her eyes with something like a smile toward Miss Laury.

'Certainly, madam. I wish to make you comfortable. Can you walk up-stairs?'

'Oh yes!'

She rose from the couch, and, leaning upon Miss Laury's offered arm in a way that shewed she had been used to that sort of support, they both glided from the room. Having seen her fair but somewhat haughty guest carefully laid on a stately crimson bed in a quiet and spacious chamber, having seen her head sink with all its curls onto the pillow of down, her large shy eyes close under their smooth eye-lids, and her little slender hands fold on her breast in an attitude of perfect repose, Miss Laury prepared to leave her. She stirred.

'Come back a moment,' she said. She was obeyed: there was

something in the tone of her voice which exacted obedience. 'I don't know who you are,' she said, 'but I am very much obliged to you for your kindness. If my manners are displeasing, forgive me. I mean no incivility. I suppose you will wish to know my name. It is Mrs Irving; my husband is a minister in the northern kirk; I come from Sneachiesland.⁴⁹ Now you may go.'

Miss Laury did go. Mrs Irving had testified incredulity respecting her story, and now she reciprocated that incredulity. Both ladies were lost in their own mystification.

Five o'clock now struck. It was nearly dark. A servant with a taper was lighting up the chandeliers in the large dining-room, where a table spread for dinner received the kindling lamp-light upon a starry service of silver. It was likewise magnificently flashed back from a splendid side-board, all arranged in readiness to receive the great, the expected guest.

Tolerably punctual in keeping an appointment when he means to keep it at all, Zamorna entered the house as the fairy-like voice of a musical clock in the passage struck out its symphony to the pendulum. The opening of the front door, a bitter rush of the night wind, and then the sudden close and the step advancing forwards were the signals of his arrival. Miss Laury was in the dining-room looking round and giving the last touch to all things. She just met her master as he entered. His cold lip pressed to her forehead and his colder hand clasping hers brought the sensation which it was her custom of weeks and months to wait for, and to consider, when attained, as the ample recompense for all delay, all toil, all suffering.

'I am frozen, Mina,' said he. 'I came on horseback for the last four miles, and the night is like Canada.'

Chafing his icy hand to animation between her own warm supple palms, she answered by the speechless but expressive look of joy, satisfaction, idolatry, which filled and overflowed her eyes.

'What can I do for you, my lord?' were her first words, as he stood by the fire rubbing his hands cheerily over the blaze. He laughed.

'Put your arms round my neck, Mina, and kiss my cheek as warm and blooming as your own.'

If Mina Laury had been Mina Wellesley she would have done so, and it gave her a pang to resist the impulse that urged her to take him at his word. But she put it by, and only diffidently drew near the arm-chair into which he had now thrown himself and began to smooth and separate the curls which were matted on his temples. She noticed, as the first smile of salutation subsided, a gloom succeeded on her master's brow, which, however he spoke or laughed afterwards, remained a settled characteristic of his countenance.

'What visitors are in the house?' he asked. 'I saw the groom rubbing down four black horses before the stables as I came in. They are not of the Hawkscliffe stud, I think?'

'No, my lord. A carriage was overturned at the lawn gates about an hour since, and as the lady who was in it was taken out insensible, I ordered her to be brought up here and her servants accommodated for the night.'

'And do you know who the lady is?' continued his Grace. 'The horses are good – first-rate.'

'She says her name is Mrs Irving, and that she is the wife of a Presbyterian minister in the North, but –'

'You hardly believe her?' interrupted the Duke.

'No,' returned Miss Laury. 'I must say I took her for a lady of rank. She has something highly aristocratic about her manners and aspect, and she appeared to know a good deal about Angria.'

'What is she like?' asked Zamorna. 'Young or old, handsome or ugly?'

'She is young, slender, not so tall as I am, and I should say rather elegant than handsome. Very pale, cold in her demeanour. She has a small mouth and chin, and a very fair neck.'

'Humph! a trifle like Lady Stuartville,' replied His Majesty. 'I should not wonder if it is the Countess. But I'll know. Perhaps you did not say to whom the house belonged, Mina?'

'I said,' replied Mina, smiling, 'the owner of the house was a great Angrian proprietor, a lineal descendant of the western Pakenhams, and that I was his housekeeper.'

'Very good! She would not believe you. You look like an Angrian country gentleman's dolly. Give me your hand, my girl. Are you not as old as I am?'

'Yes, my lord Duke. I was born on the same day, an hour after your Grace.'

'So I have heard, but it must be a mistake. You don't look twenty, and I am twenty-five. My beautiful Western – what eyes! Look at me, Mina, straight, and don't blush.'

Mina tried to look, but she could not do it without blushing. She coloured to the temples.

'Pshaw!' said his Grace, pushing her away. 'Pretending to be modest! My acquaintance of ten years cannot meet my eye unshrinkingly. Have you lost that ring I once gave you, Mina?'

'What ring, my lord? You have given me many.'

'That which I said had the essence of your whole heart and mind engraven in the stone as a motto.'

'FIDELITY?' asked Miss Laury, and she held out her hand with a graven emerald on the forefinger.

'Right!' was the reply. 'Is it your motto still?' And with one of his hungry, jealous glances he seemed trying to read her conscience. Miss Laury at once saw that late transactions were not a secret confined between herself and Lord Hartford. She saw his Grace was unhinged and strongly inclined to be savage. She stood and watched him with a sad, fearful gaze.

'Well,' she said, turning away after a long pause, 'if your Grace is angry with me I've very little to care about in this world.'

The entrance of servants with the dinner prevented Zamorna's answer. As he took his place at the head of the table, he said to the man who stood behind him: 'Give Mr Pakenham's compliments to Mrs Irving, and say that he will be happy to see her at his table, if she will honour him so far as to be present there.'

The footman vanished. He returned in five minutes.

'Mrs Irving is too much tired to avail herself of Mr Pakenham's kind invitation at present, but she will be happy to join him at tea.'

'Very well,' said Zamorna; then, looking round, 'Where is Miss Laury?'

Mina was in the act of gliding from the room, but she stopped mechanically at his call.

'Am I to dine alone?' he asked.

'Does your Grace wish me to attend you?'

He answered by rising and leading her to her seat. He then resumed his own, and dinner commenced. It was not till after the cloth was withdrawn and the servants had retired that the Duke, whilst he sipped his single glass of champagne, recommenced the conversation he had before so unpleasantly entered upon.

'Come here, my girl,' he said, drawing a chair close to his side. Mina never delayed, never hesitated, through bashfulness or any other feeling, to comply with his orders.

'Now,' he continued, leaning his head towards hers and placing his hand on her shoulder, 'are you happy, Mina? Do you want anything?'

'Nothing, my lord.'

She spoke truly. All that was capable of yielding her happiness on this side of eternity was at that moment within her reach. The room was full of calm. The lamps burnt as if they were listening. The fire sent up no flickering flame, but diffused a broad, still, glowing light over all the spacious saloon. Zamorna touched her; his form and features filled her eye, his voice her ear, his presence her whole heart. She was soothed to perfect happiness.

'My Fidelity!' pursued that musical voice. 'If thou hast any favour to ask, now is the time. I'm all concession, as sweet as honey, as yielding as a lady's glove. Come, Esther, what is thy petition and thy request? Even to the half of my kingdom it shall be granted.'[50]

'Nothing,' again murmured Miss Laury. 'Oh, my lord, nothing. What can I want?'

'Nothing!' he repeated. 'What, no reward for ten years' faith and love and devotion; no reward for the companionship in six months' exile; no recompense to the little hand that has so often smoothed my pillow in sickness, to the sweet lips that have

many a time in cool and dewy health been pressed to a brow
of fever; none to the dark Milesian[51] eyes that once grew dim
with watching through endless nights by my couch of delirium?
Need I speak of the sweetness and fortitude that cheered sufferings known only to thee and me, Mina; of the devotion that
gave me bread, when thou wast dying with hunger, and that
scarcely more than a year since? For all this, and much more,
must there be no reward?'

'I have had it,' said Miss Laury. 'I have it now.'

'But,' continued the Duke, 'what if I have devised something
worthy of your acceptance? Look up now and listen to me.'

She did look up, but she speedily looked down again. Her
master's eye was insupportable. It burnt absolutely with infernal fire. 'What is he going to say?' murmured Miss Laury to
herself, and she trembled.

'I say, love,' pursued the individual drawing her a little closer
to him. 'I will give you as a reward a husband – don't start now!
– and that husband shall be a nobleman, and that nobleman is
called Lord Hartford! Now, madam, stand up and let me look
at you.'

He opened his arms, and Miss Laury sprang erect like a
loosened bow.

'Your Grace is anticipated!' she said. 'That offer has been
made me before. Lord Hartford did it himself three days
ago.'

'And what did you say, madam? Speak the truth, now.
Subterfuge won't avail you.'

'What did I say? Zamorna, I don't know. It little signifies.
You have rewarded me, my lord Duke! But I cannot bear this
– I feel sick.'

With a deep, short sob she turned white, and fell close by the
Duke, her head against his foot. This was the first time in her
life that Mina Laury had fainted, but strong health availed
nothing against the deadly struggle which convulsed every feeling of her nature when she heard her master's announcement.
She believed him to be perfectly sincere. She thought he was
tired of her, and she could not stand it.

I suppose Zamorna's first feeling when she fell was horror,

and his next, I am tolerably certain, was intense gratification. People say I am not in earnest when I abuse him, or else I would here insert half a page of deserved vituperation, deserved and heart-felt. As it is, I will merely relate his conduct without note or comment. He took a wax taper from the table and held it over Miss Laury. Here could be no dissimulation. She was white as marble and still as stone. In truth, then, she did intensely love him, with a devotion that left no room in her thoughts for one shadow of an alien image.

Do not think, reader, that Zamorna meant to be so generous as to bestow Miss Laury on Lord Hartford. No, trust him: he was but testing in his usual way the attachment which a thousand proofs, daily given, ought long ago to have convinced him was undying. While he yet gazed, she began to recover. Her eye-lids stirred, and then slowly dawned from beneath the large black orbs that scarcely met his before they filled to over-flowing with sorrow. Not a gleam of anger, not a whisper of reproach. Her lips and eyes spoke together no other language than the simple words, 'I cannot leave you.'

She rose feebly and with effort. The Duke stretched out his hand to assist her. He held to her lips the scarcely tasted wine-glass.

'Mina,' he said, 'are you collected enough to hear me?'

'Yes, my lord.'

'Then listen. I would much sooner give half – aye, the whole – of my estates to Lord Hartford than yourself. What I said just now was only to try you.'

Miss Laury raised her eyes and sighed, like one awaking from some hideous dream, but she could not speak.

'Would I,' continued the Duke, 'would I resign the possession of my first love to any hands but my own? I would far rather see her in her coffin. And I would lay you there as still, as white and much more lifeless than you were stretched just now at my feet, before I would, for threat, for entreaty, for purchase, give to another a glance of your eye or a smile from your lip. I know you adore me now, Mina, for you could not feign that agitation, and therefore I will tell you what proof I gave yesterday of my regard for you. Hartford mentioned your name in my presence, and I revenged the profanation by a shot which sent him to his bed little better than a corpse.'

Miss Laury shuddered. But so dark and profound are the mysteries of human nature, ever allying vice with virtue, that I fear this bloody proof of her master's love brought to her heart more rapture than horror. She said not a word, for now Zamorna's arms were again folded round her, and again he was soothing her to tranquillity by endearments and caresses that far away removed all thought of the world, all past pangs of shame, all cold doubts, all weariness, all heart-sickness resulting from hope long deferred. [He] had told her that she was his first love, and now she felt tempted to believe that she was likewise his only love. Strong-minded beyond her sex, active, energetic and accomplished in all other points of view, here she was as weak as a child. She lost her identity. Her very life was swallowed up in that of another.

There came a knock to the door. Zamorna rose and opened it. His valet stood without.

'Might I speak with your Grace in the ante-room?' asked Monsieur Rosier, in somewhat of a hurried tone. The Duke followed him out.

'What do you want with me, sir? Anything the matter?'

'Ahem!' began Eugene, whose countenance expressed much more embarrassment than is the usual characteristic of his dark sharp physiognomy. 'Ahem! My lord Duke, rather a curious spot of work! A complete conjuror's trick, if your Grace will allow me to say so.'

'What do you mean, sir?'

'*Sacré!* I hardly know. I must confess I felt a trifle stupefied when I saw it.'

'Saw what? Speak plainly, Rosier.'

'How your Grace is to act I can't imagine,' replied the valet, 'though indeed I have seen your Majesty double wonderfully well when the case appeared to me extremely embarrassing. But this I really thought extra – I could not have dreamt –'

'Speak to the point, Rosier or –' Zamorna lifted his hand.

'*Mort de ma vie!*' exclaimed Eugene. 'I will tell your Grace all I know. I was walking carelessly through the passage about ten minutes since when I heard a step on the stairs, a light step, as if of a very small foot. I turned, and there was a lady coming down. My lord, she was a lady!'

'Well, did you know her?'

'I think, if my eyes were not bewitched, I did. I stood in the shade, screened by a pillar, and she passed very near without observing me. I saw her distinctly, and may I be d—d this very moment if it was not –'

'Who, sir?'

'The Duchess!!'

There was a pause, which was closed by [a] clear and remarkably prolonged whistle from the Duke. He put both his hands into his pockets and took a leisurely turn through the room.

'You're sure, Eugene?' he said. 'I know you dare not tell me a lie in such matters, because you have a laudable and natural regard to your proper carcass. Aye, it's true enough, I'll be sworn. Mrs Irving, wife of a minister in the North – a satirical hit at my royal self, by G—d! Pale, fair neck, little mouth and chin! Very good! I wish that same little mouth and chin were about a hundred miles off. What can have brought her? Anxiety about her invaluable husband – could not bear any longer without him – obliged to set off to see what he was doing. It's as well that turnspit Rosier told me, however. If she had entered the room unexpectedly about five minutes since – God! I should have had no resource but to tie her hand and foot. It would have killed her. What the D—l shall I do? Must not be angry; she can't do with that sort of thing just now. Talk softly, reprove her gently, swear black and white to my having no connection with Mr Pakenham's housekeeper.'

Ceasing his soliloquy, the Duke turned again to his valet.

'What room did her Grace go into?'

'The drawing-room, my lord. She's there now.'

'Well, say nothing about it, Rosier, on pain of sudden death. Do you hear, sir?'

Rosier laid his hand on his heart, and Zamorna left the room to commence operations.

*

Softly unclosing the drawing-room door, he perceived a lady
by the hearth. Her back was towards him, but there could be
no mistake. The whole turn of form, the style of dress, the
curled auburn head, all were attributes but of one person – of
his own unique, haughty, jealous little Duchess. He closed the
door as noiselessly as he had opened it, and stole forwards. Her
attention was absorbed in something, a book she had picked
up. As he stood unobserved behind her he could see that her
eye rested on the fly leaf, where was written in his own hand:

> Holy St Cyprian! thy waters stray
>   With still and solemn tone;
> And fast my bright hours pass away,
> And somewhat throws a shadow grey,
> Even as twilight closes day
>   Upon thy waters lone.
>
> Farewell! if I might come again,
>   Young, as I was, and free,
> And feel once more in every vein
> The fire of that first passion reign
> Which sorrow could not quench, nor pain,
>   I'd soon return to thee;
> But while thy billows seek the main
>   That never more may be!

This was dated 'Mornington, 1829'.[52] The Duchess felt a hand
press her shoulder, and she looked up. The force of attraction
had its usual results and she clung to what she saw.

'Adrian! Adrian!' was all her lips would utter.

'Mary! Mary!' replied the Duke, allowing her to hang about
him. 'Pretty doings! What brought you here? Are you running
away, eloping, in my absence?'

'Adrian, why did you leave me? You said you would come
back in a week, and it's eight days since. I could not bear any
longer. I have never slept nor rested since you left me. Do come
home!'

'So you actually have set off in search of a husband,' said

Zamorna, laughing heartily, 'and been overturned and obliged to take shelter in Pakenham's shooting-box!'

'Why are you here, Adrian?' inquired the Duchess, who was far too much in earnest to join in his laugh. 'Who is Pakenham? And who is that person who calls herself his housekeeper? And why do you let anybody live so near Hawkscliffe without ever telling me?'

'I forgot to tell you,' said his Grace. 'I've other things to think about when those bright hazel eyes are looking up to me. As for Pakenham, to tell you the truth, he's a sort of left-hand cousin[53] of your own, being natural son to the old Admiral, my uncle, in the south, and his housekeeper is his sister. *Voilà tout.* Kiss me now.'

The Duchess did kiss him, but it was with a heavy sigh. The cloud of jealous anxiety hung on her brow undissipated.

'Adrian, my heart aches still. Why have you been staying so long in Angria? Oh, you don't care for me! You have never thought how miserably I have been longing for your return. Adrian –'

She stopped and cried.

'Mary, recollect yourself,' said his Grace. 'I cannot be always at your feet. You were not so weak when we were first married. You let me leave you often then, without any jealous remonstrance.'

'I did not know you so well at that time,' said Mary, 'and if my mind is weakened, all its strength has gone away in tears and terrors for you. I am neither so handsome nor so cheerful as I once was, but you ought to forgive my decay because you have caused it.'

'Low spirits!' returned Zamorna. 'Looking on the dark side of matters! God bless me, the wicked is caught in his own net. I wish I could add, "yet shall I withal escape".[54] Mary, never again reproach yourself with loss of beauty till I give the hint first. Believe me now, in that and every other respect you are just what I wish you to be. You cannot fade any more than marble can – at least not to my eyes. And as for your devotion and tenderness, though I chide its excess sometimes, because it wastes and bleaches you almost to a shadow, yet it forms the very firmest chain that binds me to you. Now cheer up! Tonight you shall go to Hawkscliffe; it is only five miles off. I cannot accompany you, because I have some important business to transact with Pakenham which must not be deferred. Tomorrow, I will be at the castle before dawn. The carriage shall be ready. I will put you in, myself beside you; off we go, straight to Verdopolis, and there for the next three months I will tire you of my company morning, noon and night. Now, what can I promise more? If you choose to be jealous of Henri Fernando, Baron of Etrei, or John, Duke of Fidena, or the fair Earl of Richton – who, as God is my witness, has been the only companion of my present peregrination – why, I can't help it. I must then take to soda-water and despair, or have myself petrified and carved into an Apollo[55] for your dressing-room. Lord, I get not credit with my virtue!'

By dint of lies and laughter, the individual at last succeeded in getting all things settled to his mind. The Duchess went to Hawkscliffe that night; and, keeping his promise for once, he accompanied her to Verdopolis next morning.

Lord Hartford lies still between life and death. His passion is neither weakened by pain, piqued by rejection, nor cooled by absence. On the iron nerves of the man are graven an impression which nothing can efface. Warner curses him, Richton deplores.

For a long space of time, good-bye, reader.[56] I have done my best to please you, and though I know that through feebleness, dullness and iteration, my work terminates rather in failure [than] triumph, yet you are bound to forgive, for I have done my best.

C Brontë Jany 7th

Haworth 1838

STANCLIFFE'S HOTEL

Introductory Note

Stancliffe's Hotel was written at Haworth six months after *Mina Laury*, in June 1838, when Charlotte Brontë had returned home, with shattered health and spirits, from her employment as a teacher at Miss Wooler's school. Here, the icy winter landscapes of that earlier novelette, written during one of the coldest months ever recorded in England, have been replaced by the sultry, changeable 'dog-days' of a hot and stormy June. Here, once again, the narrator is Charles Townshend; but here he is much more sharply characterized – as a detached, debunking observer of Angrian life and manners, a dandy who takes 'a full half hour to dress, and another half hour to view myself over from head to foot'.

The action takes place six months after the events described in *Mina Laury*. Hartford, we learn from Sir William Percy, has recovered from the wound he received in his duel with Zamorna and rejoined his regiment; Northangerland, says Zamorna, is a 'feeble invalid'. The underlying political situation is one of instability. Zamorna's continuing friendship with Northangerland has alienated the populace and angered his supporters. The differences between 'west' and 'east' touched on in *Mina Laury* (and highlighted here in the 'western' Townshend's comments about Angrian life and manners, in the Angrian beauty Jane Moore's song about the men of Ardsley) here come more to the fore. When Mary speaks in the final scene of 'their alien senses, their foreign hearts', we are sharply reminded of that which the people cannot forget – that Zamorna ('that western dandy', as Hartford calls him in *Mina Laury*) is not an Angrian, but 'a son of Senegambia'. That contempt for the Angrians

which he expressed in *Mina Laury* – 'I always called the Angrians hogs, and who am I except the Devil that shears them?' –
reaches a bloody climax in the cavalry charge on the people led
by Lord Stuartville. Mary Percy, Duchess of Zamorna, is still
caught helplessly between her husband and her father, and still
watches jealously for Zamorna's infidelities. All these tensions,
personal and political, are unresolved at the end.

Yet *Stancliffe's Hotel* is quite different from *Mina Laury*. It
opens not in an aristocratic breakfast room but in an overheated
Methodist chapel. The tone of the whole is set by the way in
which, in the opening scene, Louisa's romantic rhapsodies are
deflated by Charles Townshend's satiric voice. In *Mina Laury*,
Hartford's hopeless passion devours his life and almost brings
about his death; here, however, two dandies pursue a young
woman, and are smartly cut down to size. Where the earlier
novelette pivoted upon Mary Percy's anxious devotion to, and
Mina Laury's adoration of, the potent, troubling Zamorna, at
the centre of this is Jane Moore's deflating amusement at the
antics of Charles Townshend and Sir William: 'two chits', says
she. Here, even Zamorna is portrayed with a certain irony,
taking snuff in a carriage in the midst of a hostile crowd, sitting
'like any wet Quaker whom the spirit had not moved'. What
should be climactic moments of masculine assertion or triumph
either do not happen or end in discomfiture. The only 'heroes'
described are a 'cavalcade' of manufacturers returning from
dinner on market-day, 'safe in the external shield of waterproof
capes and the internal specific of no less waterproof cognac';
the only 'reveille' that of a 'thrilling voice' in a drawing-room.
Predominant throughout is the deflating perspective of the cynical Charles Townshend, a half-ridiculous figure: watching the
riot from the second storey, 'twenty persons . . . at my back,
pressing one behind another to get a glimpse from the window';
voyeuristically describing the final tableau in the bedroom
where, in the company of her disturbing husband, who is, 'for
aught she knew, faithful', the Duchess tries to find peace.

'Amen!' Such was the sound, given in a short shout, which closed the evening service at Ebenezer Chapel. Mr Bromley rose from his knees. He had wrestled hard, and the sweat of his pious labours shone like oil upon his forehead. Fetching a deep breath and passing his handkerchief over his damp brow, the apostle sank back in his seat. Then, extending both brawny arms and resting them on the sides of the pulpit, with the yellow-spotted handkerchief dependent from one hand, he sat and watched the evacuation of the crowded galleries.

'How oppressively hot the chapel has been to-night,' said a soft voice to me, and a bonnet, bending forward, waved its ribbons against my face.

'Aye, in two senses,' was my answer. 'Literally, as to atmosphere, and figuratively, as to zeal. Our brother has exercised with freedom, madam.'

'Nonsense, Charles! I never can get into this slang![1] But come, the crowd is lessening at the gallery-door. I think we shall be able to make our way through it now, and I do long to get a breath of fresh air. Give me my shawl, Charles.'

The lady rose, and, while I carefully enveloped her in the shawl and boa which were to protect her from the night-air, she said, smiling persuasively, 'You will escort me to my villa and sup with me on a radish and an egg.' I answered by pressing the white hand over which she was just drawing a glove of French kid. She passed that hand through my arm and we left the gallery together.

A perfectly still and starlight night welcomed us as we quitted the steam and torches of the chapel. Threading our way quickly through the dispersing crowd at the door, we entered a well-known and oft-trod way, which in half an hour brought us from among the lighted shops and busy streets of our *quartier* to the deep shade and – at this hour – the unbroken retirement of the vale.

'Charles,' said my fair companion in her usual voice, half a whisper, half a murmur. 'Charles, what a sweet night – a premature summer night! It only wants the moon to make it perfect – then I could see my villa. Those stars are not clear enough to bring out the white front fully from its laurels. And yet I do see a light glittering there. Is it not from my drawing-room window?'

'Probably,' was my answer, and I said no more. Her Ladyship's softness is at times too surfeiting, more especially when she approaches the brink of the sentimental.

'Charles,' she pursued, in no wise abashed by my coolness, 'how many fond recollections come on us at such a time as this! Where do you think my thoughts always stray on a summer night? What image do you think "a cloudless clime and starry skies"[2] always suggests?'

'Perhaps,' said I, 'that of the most noble Richard, Marquis of Wellesley,[3] as you last saw him, reposing in gouty chair and stool,[4] with eye-lids gently closed by the influence of the pious libations in claret with which he has concluded the dinner of rice-currie, devilled turkey and guava.'

Louisa, instead of being offended, laughed with silver sound. 'You are partly right,' said she. 'The figure you have described does indeed form a portion of my recollections. Now, will you finish the picture, or shall I do it in your stead?'

'I resign the pencil into hands better qualified for its management,' rejoined I.

'Well, then, listen,' continued the Marchioness. 'Removed from the easy chair and cushioned foot-stool and from the slumbering occupant thereof, imagine a harp – that very harp which stands now in my boudoir. Imagine a woman, seated by it. I need not describe her: it is myself. She is not playing. She is listening to one who leans on her instrument and whispers as softly as the wind now whispers in my acacias.'

'Hem!' said I. 'Is the figure that of a bald elderly gentleman?'[5]
Louisa sighed her affirmative.

'By the bye,' continued I. 'It is constantly reported that he
has taken to –'

'What?' interrupted the Marchioness. 'Not proof spirits, I
hope! Watered Hollands, I know, scarcely satisfied him.'

'No, madam, repress your fears. I was alluding merely to
his dress. The pantaloons are gone: he sports white tights and
silks.'[6]

Low as the whisper was in which I communicated these
stunning tidings, it thrilled along Louisa's nerves to her heart.
During the pause which followed, I waited in breathless expectation for the effect. It came at last. Tittering faintly, she
exclaimed, 'You don't say so! Lord! how odd! But after all, I
think it's judicious, you know. Nothing can exhibit more
perfect symmetry than his leg, and then he does get older, of
course, and a change of costume was becoming advisable. Yet
I should almost fear there would be too much spindle, he was
very thin, you know – very –'

'Have you heard from his Lordship lately?' I asked.

'Oh no! About six months ago I had indeed one little note,
but I gave it to Macara by mistake, and really, I don't know
what became of it afterwards.'

'Did Macara express hot sentiment of incipient jealousy on
thus accidentally learning that you had not entirely dropped all
correspondence with the noble Earl?'

'Yes. He said he thought the note was very civilly expressed,
and wished me to answer it in terms equally polite.'

'Good! And you did so?'

'Of course. I penned an elegant billet on a sheet of rose-tinted
note-paper, and sealed it with a pretty green seal bearing the
device of twin hearts consumed by the same flame. Some misunderstanding must have occurred, though, for in two or three
days afterwards I received it back unopened and carefully en-
closed in a cover. The direction was not in his Lordship's handwriting: Macara told me he thought it was the Countess's.'[7]

'Do you know Selden House, where his Lordship now
resides?' I asked.

'Ah yes! Soon after I was married I remember passing it while on a bridal excursion to Rossland with the old Marquis. We took lunch there, indeed, for Colonel Selden (at that time the owner of it) was a friend of my venerable bridegroom's. Talking of those times reminds me of a mistake everybody was sure to make at the hotels and private houses, etc. where we stopped. I was universally taken for Lord Wellesley's daughter. Colonel Selden in particular persisted in calling me Lady Julia. He was a fine-looking man, not so old as my illustrious spouse by at least twenty years. I asked Dance,[8] who accompanied us on that tour, why he had not chosen for me such a partner as the gallant Colonel. He answered me by the sourest look I ever saw.'

'Well,' said I, interrupting her Ladyship's reminiscences. 'Here we are at your villa. Good-night. I cannot sup with you this evening: I am engaged.'

'Nay, Charles,' returned she, retaining the hand I would have withdrawn from hers. 'Do come in! It is so long since I have had the pleasure of a quiet tête à tête with you.'[9]

I persisted for some time in my refusal; but at length, yielding to the smile and the soft tone of entreaty, I gave up the point, and followed the Marchioness in.

On entering her Ladyship's parlour, we found the candles lighted and a supper-tray placed ready for us on the table. By the hearth, alone, Lord Macara Lofty was seated. His hand, drooping over the arm-chair, held two open letters: his eyes were fixed on the fire – as seemed, in thought. Louisa roused him. I could not help being struck by the languid gaze with which he turned his eyes upon her as she bent over him. There was vacancy in his aspect, and dreamy stupor.

'Are we late from chapel?' said she. 'Bromley's last prayer seemed interminably long.'

'Rather, I should think,' was the Viscount's answer. 'Rather, a trifle or so. Late, you said? Oh ah! to be sure. I have been sitting with you two hours, have I not, Louisa? Just dusk when I walked up the valley. Late, certainly!'

This not particularly intelligible reply was given in the tone and with the manner of a man just startled from a heavy slumber, and yet the noble Viscount had evidently been wide awake when we entered the room. Having delivered the speech above mentioned, he ceased to notice the Marchioness, and relapsed as if involuntarily into his former position and look.

'Won't you take some supper?' she inquired.

No answer. She repeated the question.

'G—d, no,' he said hastily, as if annoyed at interruption, his countenance at the same time wearing a rapt expression, as if every faculty were spell-bound in some absorbing train of thought. The Marchioness turned from him with a grimace. She nodded at me and whispered,

'Learned men now and then have very strange vagaries.'

Not at all discomposed by his strange conduct, she proceeded quietly to remove her bonnet, shawl and boa; and having thrown them over the back of a sofa, she passed her fingers through her hair, and shaking aside the loose ringlets into which it was thus parted, turned towards the mirror a face by no means youthful, by no means blooming, by no means regularly beautiful – but which yet had been able, by the aid of that long chiselled nose, those soft and sleepy eyes, and that bland smile always hovering round the deceitful lips, to captivate the greatest man of his age.[10]

'Come,' she said, gliding towards the table. 'Take a sandwich, Charles, and give me a wing of that chicken. We can amuse each other till Macara thinks proper to come round and behave like a sensible Christian.'

I did not, reader, ask what was the matter with Macara, for I had a very good guess myself as to the cause and origin of that profound fit of meditation in which his Lordship now sat entranced. I fell forthwith to the discussion of the sandwiches and chicken, which the Marchioness dispensed to me with liberal hand. She also sat, and, as we sipped wine together, her soft eyes looking over the brim of the glass expressed far more easy enjoyment of the good things given her for her use than perplexing concern for the singular quandary in which her *cher ami* sat speechless and motionless by the hearth. Meantime, the ecstatic smiles which had, every now and then, kindled

Macara's eye and passed like sunshine over his countenance began to recur with fainter effect and at longer intervals. The almost sensual look of intense gratification and absorption gave place to an air of fatigue. Our voices seemed recalling him to recollection. He stirred in his seat, then rose, and with an uncertain step began to pace the room. His eye – heavy still, and filmy – caught mine.

'Ho! is that you?' he said in a peculiar voice, which scarcely seemed under the speaker's command. 'Hardly knew you were in the room – and Louisa too I declare! Well, I must have been adipose.[11] And what has Bromley said tonight? You were at chapel, somebody told me a while since – at least I think so, but it may be all fancy! I daresay you'll think me in an extraordinary mood to-night, but I'll explain directly – as soon as I get sufficiently collected.'

With an unsteady hand he poured out a goblet of water, drank part and, dipping his fingers in, cooled with the remainder his forehead and temples.

'My head throbs,' said he. 'I must not try this experiment often.' As he spoke, his hand shook so convulsively that he could hardly replace the glass on the table. Smiling grimly at this evidence of abused nerves, he continued, 'Really, Townshend! Only mark that! And what do you think it is occasioned by?'

'Intoxication,' I said concisely. 'And that of a very heathen kind. You were far better take to dry spirits at once, Macara, than do as you do.'

'Upon my conscience,' replied the Viscount, sitting down and striking the table with that same shaking hand, 'I do believe, Townshend, you are in the right. I begin to find that this system of mine, rational as I thought it, is fraught with the most irresistible temptation.'

Really, reader, it is difficult to deal with a man like Macara, who has candour at will to screen even his weakest points from attack. However infamous may be the position in which he is surprised, he turns round without a blush, and instead of defending himself by denying that matters are as appearances would warrant you to suppose, usually admits all the dis-grace of his situation, and begins with metaphysical profundity to detail all the motives and secret springs of action which brought matters to the state in which you found them. According to this system of tactics the Viscount proceeded with his self-accusation.

'It was a fine evening, as you know,' said he, 'and I thought I would take a stroll up the valley, just to alleviate those low spirits which had been oppressing me all day. Townshend, I daresay you do not know what it is to look at an unclouded sun, at pleasant fields and young woods crowding green and bright to the edge of a river, and from these fair objects to be unable to derive any feeling but such as is tinged with sadness. However, I am familiar with this state of mind; and as I passed through the wicket that shuts in Louisa's lawn and, turning round, paused in the green alley, and saw between the laurels the glittering red sky, clear as fire, which the sun had left far over the hills, I, Townshend, felt that, still and bright as the day was closing, fair as it promised to rise on the morrow, this summer loveliness was nothing to me – no.

'So I walked up to the house; I entered this room, wishing to find Louisa. She was not there, and when I inquired for her I was told she would not return for some hours. I sat down to wait. The dusk approached, and in that mood of mind I watched it slowly veiling every object, clothing every tree of the shrubbery, with such disguises as a haunted, a disturbed, a blackened imagination could suggest. Memory whispered to me that in former years I could have sat at such an hour, in such a scene; and from the rising moon, the darkening landscape on which I looked, the quiet little chamber where I sat, have gathered images all replete with bliss for the present, with softened happiness for the future. Was it so now? No, Mr Townshend; I was in a state of mind which I will not mock you by endeavouring to describe. But the gloom, the despair, became unendurable; dread forebodings rushed upon me, whose power I could not withstand. I felt myself on the brink of some hideous disaster and a vague influence ever and anon pushed me over, till clinging wildly to life and reason, I almost lost consciousness in the faintness of mortal terror.

'Now, Townshend, so suffering, how far did I err when I had

resource to the sovereign specific which a simple narcotic drug offered me? I opened this little box and, sir, I did not hesitate. No, I tasted. The change was wrought quickly. In five minutes I, who had been the most miserable wretch under that heaven, sat a rational, happy man, soothed to peace of mind, to rest of body, capable of creating sweet thoughts, of tasting bliss, of dropping those fetters of anguish which had restrained me, and floating away with light brain and soaring soul into the fairest regions imagination can disclose. Now, Townshend, I injured no fellow-creature by this: I did not even brutalize myself. Probably my life may be shortened by indulgence of this kind[12] – but what of that? The eternal sleep will come sometime, and as well sooner as later.'

'I've no objection,' returned I, coolly. 'Louisa, have you?'

'I can't understand the pleasure of that opium,' said the Marchioness. 'And as to low spirits, I often tell Macara that I think there must be a great deal of fancy in them.'

The Viscount gently sighed and, dropping his hand on hers, said, as he softly pressed it with his wan fingers, 'May you long think so, Louisa!'

Finding that his Lordship was in much too sentimental a mood to serve my turn, I shortly after rose and took my leave. The Marchioness attended me to the hall-door. 'Is he not *frénétique*, Charles?' said she. 'What nonsense to make such a piece of work about low spirits! I declare he reminds me of Ashworth. He, poor man, after a few days of hard preaching and harder drinking used to say that he had a muttering devil at his side. He told Bromley[13] so once, and Bromley believed him. Would you have done, Charles?'

'Implicitly, madam. Good-night.'

I like the city. So long as winter lasts, it would be no easy task to entice me from its warm and crowded precincts. So long even as spring, with lingering chill, scatters her longer showers and fitful blinks of sunshine, I would cling to the theatre at night and the news-room[14] in the morning. But at last, I do confess, as June advances, and ushers in a long series of warm days, of soft sunsets and mellow moonlight evenings, I do begin to feel certain intuitive longings for an excursion, a jaunt out into the country, a sojourn somewhere far off, where there are woods, pastoral hills and bright pebbled becks.

This feeling came strong over me the other day, when, sitting in Grant's Coffee-House, I took up a fashionable paper[15] whose columns teemed with such announcements as the following:

Preparations are making at Roslyn Castle, the seat of Lord St Clair in the North, for the reception of his Lordship's family and a party of illustrious visitors, who are invited to spend the summer quarter amidst the beautiful forest scenery with which that part of the St Clair estate abounds.

Prince Augustus of Fidena set out yesterday, accompanied by his tutor, for Northwood-Zara, whither the Duke and Duchess of Fidena are to follow in a few days.

Lord and Lady Stuartville leave town to-morrow. Their destination is Stuartville Park in Angria.

The Earl of Northangerland is still at Selden House. It is understood that his Lordship expresses little interest in politics.

General Thornton and his lady took their departure for Girnington Hall last week. The General intends adding to the plantations on his already finely wooded property in Angria.

The Earl and Countess of Arundel are at their seat of Summerfield House, in the province of Arundel.

General and Mrs Grenville propose to spend the summer at Warner Hall, the residence of W. H. Warner Esqre, Premier of Angria.

John Bellingham Esqre, banker, is rusticating at Goldthorpe Mowbray. The physicians have advised sea bathing for the perfect restoration of Mr Bellingham's health, which has suffered considerably from a severe attack of influenza.

The Marquis of Harlaw, with a party of friends, J. Billinger Esqre, Mr Macqueen, etc., is enjoying a brief relaxation from state cares at Colonel Luckyman's country house, Catton Lodge.

Lord Charles and the young ladies Flower have joined their noble mother at Mowbray. Sigston's Hotel is engaged entirely for the use of Lady Richton and her household.

Lord Charles Flower, who, as well as his sisters, is just recovering from the measles, continues under the care of Dr Morrison, the family physician. The noble ambassador himself is in the south.

From these paragraphs it was evident that the season was now completely over. No more assemblies at Flower House, no more select dinner-parties at the Fidena Palace. Closed were the saloons of Thornton Hotel, forsaken were the squares round Ellrington Hall and Wellesley House, void were the habitations of Castlereagh, darkened the tabernacles of Arundel! Whereas now, in remote woods, the chimneys of Girnington Hall sent out their blue smoke to give token that the old spot was peopled again; in remoter meads, the broad sashes of Summerfield House were thrown up, to admit the gale sweeping over those wide prairies into rooms with mirrors cleared and carpets spread and couches unswathed in holland. Every blind was withdrawn at Stuartville Park, every shutter opened, and the windows through crimson curtains looked boldly towards the green ascent where Edwardston smiles upon its young plantations. The rooks were cawing at Warner Hall with cheerier sound than ever as, early on a summer morning, the Prime Minister of Angria, standing on his front-door steps, looked at the sun rising over his still grounds and deep woods and over the long, dark moors of Howard.

I could have grown poetical. I could have recalled more distant and softer scenes, touched with the light of other years, hallowed by higher – because older – associations than the campaign of −33, the rebellion of −36.[16] I might have asked how sunrise yet became the elms and the turret of Wood Church. But I restrained myself, and merely put the question, shall I have me out or not? And whither shall I direct my steps? To my old quarters at the Greyhound opposite Mowbray Vicarage? To my friend Tom Ingham's farm at the foot of Boulshill? To some acquaintances I have north, awa' in the vicinity of Fidena? Or

to a snug country lodging I know of in the south not far from
my friend Billinger's paternal home? Time and chance shall
decide me. I've cash sufficient for the excursion; I've just
rounded off my nineteenth year and entered on my twentieth;
I'm a neat figure, a competent scholar, a popular author, a
gentleman and a man of the world. Who then shall restrain
me? Shall I not wander at my own sweet will? *Allons*, reader,
come, and we will pack the carpet-bag. Make out an inventory:
Item – 4 shirts, 6 fronts, 4 pair cotton, 2 pair silk stockings,
1 pair morocco pumps, 1 dress satin waistcoat, 1 dress coat,
2 pair dress[17] pantaloons, 1 pair nankeens, 1 brush and comb,
1 bottle macassar oil, 1 tooth-brush, box vegetable tooth-
powder, 1 pot cream of roses, 1 case of razors (N.B. for show
not use), two cakes of almond soap, 1 bottle *eau de cologne*,
1 bottle *eau de mille fleurs*, 1 pair curling-irons. *C'est tout!* I'm
my own valet now! Reader, if you're ready, so am I. The coach
is coming, hillo! Off at full speed to meet it!

'Well, I think I shall have to stay at Zamorna all night. It's a
delightful June evening.' So I soliloquized to myself, as, standing
in the travellers' room at Stancliffe's Hotel, I from the window
watched the umbrellas, cloaks and mackintoshes which ever
and anon traversed Thornton Street in Zamorna. It had been
market-day, and the gigs of the clothiers, now homeward-
bound, were bowling along the pavement in the teeth of the
driving showers and fitful blasts in which the before-mentioned
delightful June evening had thought proper to veil its close.
Now and then a cavalcade of some half-dozen mounted manufacturers passed the window at full trot. These gentlemen had
doubtless dined *en comité* at the Woolpack or the Stuart Arms,
and the speed and lightness of their progress, the pleasing gaiety
of their aspects, and the frequency of the laugh and jest in their
ranks indicated pretty plainly that they were, one and all – to
speak technically – market-fresh.[18] Many of the gigs, too, shot
past with a vengeable rapidity which warranted that [the] occupants had duly laid in the stock of brandy and water. Wild and
boisterous as the wind swept up the street and drove before it
a heavy constant rain, these heroes, safe in the external shield

of waterproof capes and the internal specific of no less waterproof cognac, dashed away towards the open Edwardston or
Adrianopolitan roads, as if in defiance of the storm which was
to meet them in fuller force when removed from the partial
shelter of the city.

The travellers' room at Stancliffe's Hotel by no means
exhibited the silence and solitude of a hermit's cell. Gentlemen
in the soft and hard line[19] strode in and out incessantly from
the trampled inn-passage, whose wet and miry floor plainly
told the condition of the streets outside. Then there were loud
calls for the waiters, incessant ringings of the weary bell,
orders about sundry carpet-bags and portmanteaus, deliveries
of divers wet great-coats and drenched pea-surtouts to be dried
instantly at the kitchen-fire, expostulations about mysterious
subjects unintelligible except to the affrighted waiter and the
aggrieved complainant. One furious individual, whose gig
drove up to the hotel amidst the pelting of a wilder torrent of
rain than had fallen in the course of the whole afternoon,
entered the room with a dark and ominous aspect. As he was
drawing off his three-caped great-coat, from which the water
dripped in streams, something in the condition of the fire-place
seemed to strike him with conscientious horror. He rushed to
the door.

'Waiter! Waiter!! Waiter!!!' he exclaimed with the voice of
a lion.

The waiter came. The person who had summoned him was
a portly man and an apoplectic; his rage seemed at first to
impede his utterance, but not for long. He opened forth:

'Look at that grate, sir! Do you call that comfort – tawdry
rags of blue and yellow paper instead of a good fire?'

'It's June, sir,' replied the waiter. '18th inst. We never put on
fire in the low-rooms after May goes out.'

'Damn you,' said the bagman. 'Light a fire directly, or I'll
send for your master and give him a jobation to his face about it.
Let me tell you, your people here at Stancliffe's get abominably
careless. Such a blackguard dinner as I had here last circuit!
But I promise you, if you set me down to such another I'll put
up at the Stuart Arms in future. Light a fire, sir, and take my

coat. If you leave a wet thread on it, I'll subtract it from the reckoning. Bring me some hot punch and oysters for supper, and mind the chambermaid airs my bed well. I'd damp sheets last time I slept here, I'll be d—ed if I had not.'

Your Angrian commercial traveller is one of the greatest scamps in existence, much on a par with your Angrian newspaper editor. Anything more systematically unprincipled, more recklessly profligate than these men, taking them as a body, is not easy to conceive. Characters indicative of these vices were legibly written in the faces of the half-dozen gentlemen gathered on this stormy evening in the apartment to which I have introduced my readers. Conversation did not flag amongst them. Amidst the ringing of crushers and tumblers, such sentences were heard as the following:

'Brown, I say, you're lucky to have no further to go to-night!'

'Well, and so are you, an't you?'

'Me! I must push on ten miles further if it rain cats and dogs: I must be in Edwardston by nine to-night to meet one of our partners.'

'Which of them: Culpeper or Hoskins?'

'Culpeper, ac—d cross-grained dog.'

'Pretty weather, this, for June, ain't it?' interpolated a young dandy with red curls and velvet waistcoat.

'Aye, as pretty as your phiz,' replied the furious man who had ordered the fire to be lit, and who was now sitting with both his feet on the fender, full in front of the few smoky coals which, in obedience to his mandates, had been piled together.

'I say, can you change me a bank-note?' asked one man with his chin shrouded in a white shawl.

'Bank of Angria or private bank?' said the person whom he had addressed.

'Private bank – of our own Amos Kirkwall and sons.'

'I can change it with our pound notes – Edward Percy's and Steaton's: I got them at their warehouse this afternoon.'

'I'd prefer these any day to sovereigns – less chance of their being counterfeit.'

'Well, and how go politics to-day?' asked a smart traveller in a gold chain,[20] slapping on the shoulder a studious individual deeply absorbed in the perusal of a newspaper.

'God knows!' was the answer. 'I should not be much astonished to hear of the Prime Minister resigning.'

'And he will if he does his duty,' exclaimed a third person. 'Have you seen the *War Despatch* for this morning? My word, their people do go it!'

'Manly, independent print, the *War Despatch*,' answered the first speaker. 'Delivers the sentiments of the nation at large. Curse it – who's to hinder us from asserting our rights? Aren't we all free-born Angrians?'

'The *Rising Sun* swears that Percy[21] has tendered his resignation, and been solicited to withdraw it. What do you think of that?'

'That he had a capital opportunity of discharging with interest many a long bill of insults he has been storing up against the Czar[22] for these three years at least.'

'But I think it would hardly be like him to let such an opportunity pass, if it be so. Brandy and Water[23] will serve them out next sessions, in style.'

'By G—d, that he will, and *before* next sessions too. *A propos* of that, they say some of the leaders in the *War Despatch* are penned by him.'

'Very likely; he's a real trump-card. Do you deal with him?'

'No, our house is in the cutlery-line.'

'We do, or rather, we did a while since; but he screwed[24] so hard in that last bargain about some casks of madder, and came down so prompt for payment at a time when ready money was rather scarce with us, that our senior partner swore upon the Gospels he'd burn his fingers in that oven no more.'

The furious man, who had hitherto sat silent, here turned from the fire, which he had by this time coaxed into something like a blaze, and growled sotto-voce: 'Shall be happy to supply you, Mr Drake, with madder, indigo, logwood and barilla[25] of all qualities on the most reasonable terms. Shall feel obliged if you will favour me with an order. May I put you down?' He drew out a pocket-book and unsheathed a pencil.

'Of what house?' asked Mr Drake.

'I do for Milnes, Duff & Stephenson, Dyers, Anvale,' answered the fire-eater.

'Humph!' rejoined Drake with a kind of sneer. 'I've seen that firm mentioned somewhere.' He affected to ponder for a moment, then, snapping his fingers: 'I have it! It was in the *Gazette*. Paid a second dividend, I think, a month ago – half-a-crown in the pound.'

The man of choler said nothing: he was flabbergasted. But he leant back in his chair, and, lifting both feet from the fender, he deposited one on each hob. His favourite element, now burning clear and red, seemed to console him for every *contre-temps*.

'Drat it, the weather's clearing!' suddenly ejaculated that gentleman who had declared his obligation to be at Edwardston by nine o'clock. He rushed out of the room and, having peremptorily ordered his gig, rushed back again; and having swallowed the contents of a capacious tumbler besought Dawson to help him on with his d—d mackintosh. Then, as he settled the collar about his neck, he bade an affectionate adieu to the said Dawson in the words:

'Go it, old cock! Good-bye! Judging by thy nose, next circuit will use thee up.'

I saw him from the window mount his gig and flash down the still wet street like a comet.

In truth, the clouds for the first time that day were now beginning to separate. The rain had cease[d]; the wind likewise had subsided; and I think, if I could have seen the west, the sun, within a few minutes of its setting, was just shedding one parting smile over the Olympian. Several of the travellers now rose. There was a general ordering out of gigs and assuming of coats and cloaks. In a few minutes the room was cleared, with the exception of two or three whose intention it was to take up their quarters at Stancliffe's for the night. While these discussed professional subjects, I maintained my station at the window, watching the passengers whom the gleam of sunshine had called out at the close of a rainy day.

In particular, I marked the movements of a pretty woman who seemed waiting for someone at the door of a splendid mercer's shop opposite. Drawing aside the green blind, I tried to catch her eye, displaying a gold snuff-box under pretence of taking a pinch, and by the same action exhibiting two or three flashy rings with which my white aristocratic hand was adorned. Her eye was caught by the glitter. She looked at me from amongst a profusion of curls, glossy and silky though of the genuine Angrian hue.[26] From me her glance reverted to her own green silk frock and pretty sandalled feet. I fancied she smiled. Whether she did or not, I certainly returned the compliment by a most seductive grin. She blushed. Encouraged by this sign of sympathy, I kissed my hand to her. She giggled, and retreated into the shop. While I was vainly endeavouring to trace her figure, of which no more than the dim outline was visible through the gloom of the interior, increased by waving streamers of silk and print pendant to the shop door, someone touched my arm. I turned. It was a waiter.

'Sir, you are wanted, if you please.'

'Who wants me?'

'A gentleman upstairs. Came this afternoon. Dined here. I've just carried in the wine, and he desired me to tell the young gentleman in the travellers' room who wore a dark frock-coat and white jeans that he would be happy to have the pleasure of his company for the evening.'

'Do you know who he is?' I asked.

'I've not heard his name, sir, but he came in his own carriage – a genteel barouche. A military-looking person. I should fancy he may be an officer in the army.'

'Well,' said I, 'show me up to his apartment.' And, as the slippered waiter glided before me, I followed with some little curiosity to see who the owner of the genteel barouche might be. Not that there was anything at all strange in the circumstance, for Stancliffe's, being the head hotel in Zamorna, every day received aristocratic visitants within its walls. The Czar himself usually changed horses here in his journeys to and from his capital.

Traversing the inn-passage – wetter and dirtier than ever, and all in tumult, for the evening Verdopolitan-coach had just come

in and the passengers were calling for supper and beds and
rooms and at the same time rushing wildly after their luggage
– traversing, I say, this rich mêlée, in the course of which transit
I nearly ran over a lady and a little girl and was in requital
called a rude scoundrel by their companion, a big fellow in
mustachios – traversing, I once more repeat, this area wherein
a woman with a child in her arms – dripping wet, for she had
ridden on the outside of the coach – came against me full drive,
I at length, after turning the angle of [a] second long passage
and passing through a pair of large folding doors, found myself
in another region. It was a hall with rooms about it, green mats
at every door, a lamp in the centre, a broad staircase ascending
to a gallery above, which ran round three sides of the hall,
leaving space in the fourth for a great arched window. All here
was clean, quiet, stately. This was the new part of the hotel,
which had been erected since the year of independence. Before
that time, Stancliffe's was but a black-looking old public, whose
best apartment was not more handsomely furnished than its
present travellers' room. As I ascended the staircase, chancing
to look through the window I got a full and noble view of
that new court-house which, rising upon its solid basement, so
majestically fronts the first inn in Zamorna. There it was that,
after the disastrous day of Edwardston, Jeremiah Simpson
opened his court martial; there, on such an evening as this. At
this very hour, when twilight was sealing sunset, a turbaned
figure, with furred robes like a sultan and shawl streaming
from his waist, had mounted those steps, and, while all the
wide and long street beneath him was a sea of heads and a hell
of strange cries, had shouted: 'Soldiers, bring on the prisoner!'
Then, breaking through the crowd, trampling down young and
old, Julian Gordon's troopers burst on amidst the boom of
Quashia's gongs and the yell of Medina's kettle-drums.[27] A gun
mounted on the court-house was discharged down on the heads
of the mob, as was afterwards sworn before the House of Peers.
Through the smoke the prisoner could hardly be seen, but his
head was bare, his hands bound; that court-house received him,
and the door was barred on the mob.
    'This is the room, sir,' said the waiter, throwing open a

door in the middle of the gallery, and admitting me to a large apartment whose style of decoration, had I been a novice in such matters, would have burst upon me with dazzling force. It was as elegant in finish, as splendid in effect, as a saloon in any nobleman's house. The windows were large, lofty and clear; the curtains were of silk that draperied them – of crimson silk, imparting to everything a rosy hue. The carpet was soft and rich, exhibiting groups of brilliant flowers. The mantle-piece was crowned with classical ornaments – small but exquis-ite figures in marble, vases as white as snow, protected from soil by glass bells inverted over them, silver lamps and, in the centre, a foreign time-piece. Above all these sloped a picture, the only one in the room: an Angrian peer in his robes, really a fine fellow. At first I did not recognize the face, as the costume was so unusual; but by degrees I acknowledged a dashing like-ness to the most noble Frederick Stuart, Earl of Stuartville and Viscount Castlereagh, Lord Lieutenant of the Province of Zamorna. 'Really,' thought I, as I took in the *tout ensemble* of the room, 'these Angrians do lavish the blunt – hotels like palaces, palaces like Genii dreams.[28] It's to be hoped there's cash to answer the paper-money, that's all.' At a table covered with decanters and silver fruit-baskets sat my unknown friend, the owner of the genteel conveyance.The waiter having retired, closing the door after him, I advanced.

It being somewhat dusk, and the gentleman's face being turned away from the glow of a ruddy fire, I did not at first glance hit his identity. However, I said,

'How do you do, sir? Glad to see you.'

'Pretty well, thank you,' returned he, and slowly rising, he tenderly took his coat-tails under the protection of his arms and, standing on the rug, presented his back to the before-mentioned ruddy fire.

'Oh, it's you, is it!' I ejaculated, for his face was now obvious enough. 'How the devil did you know that I was here?'

'What the d—l brought you here?' he asked.

'Why the devil do you wish to know?' I rejoined.

'How the devil can I tell?' he replied.

Here, our wits being mutually exhausted by these brilliant sallies, I took a momentary reprieve in laughter. Then my friend began again.

'In God's name, take a chair.'

'In Christ's name, I will.'

'For the love of heaven, let me fill you a bumper.'

'For the fear of hell, leave no heel-tap.'

'I adjure you by the gospels, tell me if it's good wine.'

'I swear upon the Koran, I've tasted better.'

'By the miracle of Cana, you lie.'

'By the miracle of Moses,[29] I do not.'

'According to your oaths, sir, I should take you to be circumcised.'

'According to yours, I should scarce think you were baptized.'

'The Christian ordinance came not upon me.'

'The Mahometan rite I have eschewed.'

'Thou then art an unchristened heathen.'

'And thou an infidel Giaour.'[30]

'Pass the bottle, lad,' said my friend, resuming his seat and grasping the decanter with emphasis. He and I filled our glasses, and then we looked at each other.

A third person, I think, would have observed something similar about us. We were both young, both thin, both sallow and light-haired and blue-eyed, both carefully and somewhat foppishly dressed, with small feet set off by a slender *chaussure* and white hands garnished with massive rings. My friend, however, was considerably taller than I, and had besides more of the air military. His head was differently set upon his shoulders. He had incipient light brown mustaches and some growth of whisker; he threw out his chest, too, and sported a length of limb terminating in boot and spur. His complexion, originally fair almost to delicacy, appeared to have seen service, for it was, like my own, much tan[ned], freckled and yellowed to a bilious hue with the sun. He wore a blue dress-coat with velvet collar, velvet waistcoat and charming white tights: I endued a well-made green frock[31] and light summer jeans. Now, reader, have you got us before you?

The young officer, resting his temples on his hand and

pensively filling a tall champagne glass, renewed the conversation.

'You'll be surprised to see me here, I daresay, aren't you?'

'Why yes; I thought you were at Gazemba or Dongola, or Bonowen or Socatoo, or some such barbarian station, setting slot-hounds on negro-tracks, and sleeping like Moses among the flags on some river-side.'[32]

'Well, Townshend,' said he. 'Your description exactly answers to the sort of life I have led for the last six months.'

'And are you stalled of it?' I asked.

'Stalled, man! think of the honour! Have you not seen in every newspaper: "The exertions of the 10th Hussars in the east under their Colonel Sir William Percy continue unabated. The efforts made by that gallant officer to extirpate the savages[33] are beyond all praise. Scarce a day passes but five or six are hung under the walls of Dongola"? Then again: "A signal instance of vengeance was exhibited at Katagoom last week, by order of Sir William Percy. A soldier had been missing some days from his regiment stationed at that place. His remains were at length found in a neighbouring jungle, hideously mangled, and displaying all the frightful mutilation of negro slaughter. Sir William instantly ordered out two of the fiercest and keenest hounds in his leashes.[34] They tracked up the murderers in a few hours. When seized, the blood-stained wretches were sunk up to the neck in the deep mire of a carr-brake. Sir William had them shot through the head where they stood, and their bodies merged in the filth which afforded them such a suitable sepulchre." Eh, Townshend, is not that the strain?'

'Exactly so. But now, Colonel, since you were so honourably occupied, why do I now find you so far from the seat of your glorious toil?'

'Really, Townshend, how can you be so unreasonable? The 10th Hussars – all gods as they are, or god-like men, which is better – can't stand the sun of those deserts and the malaria of those marshes for ever. It has therefore pleased our gracious monarch to command a recall; that is, not by his own sacred mouth, but through the medium of W. H. Warner Esqre, our trusty and well-beloved councillor, who delivered his instruc-

tions to our General-in-Chief and Commander of the Forts,
Henri Fernando di Enara, by whom they were transmitted to
your humble servant.'

'And with alacrity you jumped at the reprieve.'

'Jumped at it? No; I perused the despatch with, I believe, my
wonted coolness – awed, of course, by the sublime appellation
of our Lord the King, in whose name it was penned – but
otherwise I sweat not, neither did I swoon. It is not for us
poor subalterns to feel either joy or grief, satisfaction or disappointment.'

'Well, Colonel, where are you going now?'

'Lord, Mr Townshend, don't be in such a hurry! Let one
have a minute's time for reflection! I've hardly yet got over the
anguish of soul that came upon me at Gazemba.'

'How? On what account?'

'All a sense of my own insignificance – a humbling to the
dust, as it were. That organ of veneration is so predominent in
my cranium,[35] it will be the death of me some day. You know,
being to go to Adrianapolis, it was needful to pass through
Gazemba, and being at Gazemba, it was onerous to wait upon
our Commander of the Forts at his pretty little villa there. So,
having donned the regimentals over a check shirt for the more
grace (it would have been presumptuous to appear in cambric
while his Highness sported huckaback),[36] I made my way to the
domicile. Signor Fernando must be a man of some nerves to
endure about his person such fellows as form the household of
that garrison. The dirtiest dregs of a convict hulk would scarce
turn out such another muster. Parricides, matricides, fratricides,
sororicides, stabbers in the dark, blackguard bullies of hells,[37]
scoundrel suborners of false testimony: of these materials has
he formed the domestic establishment of his country-seat. A
forger in the disguise of a porter opened the door for me; a
cut-purse wearing a footman's epaulettes shewed me to an
ante-room; there I was received by one bearing a steward's
wand who had been thrice convicted of arson; he gave my name
to a Mr Secretary Gordon, who had visibly been hanged for
murder but unfortunately cut down before the law had done
its perfect work.[38]

'Of course I sweat[ed] profusely by the time I had passed
through this ordeal, and when at length Mr Gordon introduced
me to a dismal little dungeon called a cabinet where sat Enara,
my knees shook under me like aspen leaves. There was the great
man in his usual attire of a gingham jacket and canvas trousers
of more than Dutch capacity.[39] Stock he disdained, and waistcoat: the most fastidious lady might have beheld with admiration that muscular chest and neck bristled with heroic hair.
Between the commander's lips breathed a cigar, and in one
hand he held a smart box of the commodity, fresh as imported
from the spicy islands where springs the fragrant weed. With
head a little declined, and brow contracted in solicitude respecting the important choice, the illustrious General seemed, at the
moment I entered, to be engaged in picking out another of the
same. Mark the noble simplicity of a great mind stooping to
the commonest employment of an ordinary shop-boy! Having
made his election, he handed the Havannah to a person who
stood beside him, and whom till now I had not perceived,
ejaculating as he did so, "Damn it! I think that'll be a good
'un!" "G—d, so it is!" was his companion's answer when, after
a moment's pause, he had tried the sweet Virginian. I looked
now at this second speaker. Townshend, it was too much! At
Enara's chair back there stood a man in a shabby brown surtout, with his hands stuck in the hind pockets thereof, wearing a
stiff stock out of which projected a long and dark dried-vinegar
physiognomy, shaded with grizzly whiskers and overshaded
with still more grizzly hair. The fellow was so ugly, at first sight
I thought it must be a stranger. A second glance assured me
that it was General Lord Hartford. What could I do? The blaze
of patrician dignity quite overpowered me. However, I made
shift to advance.

'"How d'ye do, Sir William?" said Enara. "Recalled, you
find? I regret the necessity, which doubtless will be a great
disappointment to you." I ventured to ask in what respect? He
looked at me as if I had put the question in Greek. "As a man
of honour, sir, I should suppose – but most probably you are
consoling yourself under the disappointment by the prospect of
a speedy return. We shall see, sir; I will speak to the Duke in

your behalf. Your services have given me much satisfaction." I bowed, of course, and then stood to hear what more was coming, but the General seemed to have said his say. Lord Hartford now grunted something unintelligible, though with the most dignified air possible, his under lip being scornfully protruded to support the cigar and his branded brow corrugated over his eyes with the sour malignant look of a fiend. He seemed to breathe asthmatically, I suppose in consequence of that wound[40] he received last winter. Finding that there was no more talk to be had for love or money, I rose to go. In reply to my farewell genuflection Enara nodded sharply, and muttered a word or two about hoping to see me again soon and having a spot of special work cut out purposely for me. Hartford bent his stiff back with a stern, haughty bow that made me feel strongly inclined to walk round behind him and trip up his heels.'

I laughed as Sir William closed his narration.

'Well, you do give it them properly, Colonel!' said I. 'A set of pompous prigs! I like to hear them dished now and then. And how did you get on at Adrianopolis? I suppose you saw the Premier?'

'Yes, I went to the Treasury; and I'd scarcely got within the door of his parlour there before he began in his woman's voice, "Sir William, Sir William, let me hear what you have been doing. Give a clear account, sir, of your proceedings. General Enara's despatches are not sufficiently detailed, sir; they are too brief, too laconic. The government of the country is kept in the dark, sir – comparatively speaking that is – at a time, too, when every facility for obtaining information ought to be afforded it. I wish to know every particular concerning that late affair at Cuttal-Curafee." He stopped a minute, and looked at me. I looked at him, and sat down after settling the cushion on my chair.

'The pause being a rather lengthened one, I remarked that it was a fine morning. "What?" said he, pricking up his ears. "The morning is charmingly cool and dry," was my answer. "Is it possible?" exclaimed Warner. "Sir, I say, is it possible that the trite remarks of the most indolent and vacant time-killer

should be the first and only words on the lips of a man just
returned from the active service of his king, in a country reeking
with rapine and carnage and teeming with the hideous pol-
lutions of pagan savages?" "What do you wish me to say?" I
asked, taking up a pamphlet that lay on the table and glancing at
the title-page. "Sir," said the Premier, very lofty and impressive.
"Sir, my time is valuable. If your business with me is not of so
important a nature as to require immediate attention we will
defer it for the present." Endeavouring to suppress a yawn, and
slightly stretching my limbs – not inelegant, are they, Townshend? – I replied, "Business, sir? Your honour, I hardly know
what I called upon you for. It was merely, I think, to pass away
an idle hour. Can you tell me what the newest fashions are?
I'm quite out just now in dress, for really one sees little in
that line at Cuttal-Curafee." "Sir," replied Warner, "I wish you
a very good morning. Mr Jones will show you the door."
"Good morning, sir," said I, and I left the Treasury as good as
kicked out.'

'Well, and where did you go next?'

'I went to a perfumer's, and bought a few trifles in the
way of gloves and combs. On returning, whom do you think
I met?'

'Can't guess.'

'Why, none other than the President to the Board of Trade.'

'What, Edward Percy?'

'Yes; he stopt [?] in the street and began: "William! I say,
William, who sent for you back? I know it for a fact, sir, that
you sent up a puling memorial[41] soliciting a recall. You did, sir,
don't begin to deny it."

'"Not [I]," I answered. "Good morning, Edward! Charming
seasonable weather! Take care of your lungs, lad – always
phthisically inclined. I would recommend balsam of horehound
– excellent remedy for pulmonary complaints! Good morning,
lad!" And gracefully waving my hand, I passed on.'

Here a waiter came in with wax-lights and a supper-tray.
Sir William invited me to partake of his roast chicken and
oyster-sauce, but I declined, as I had ordered supper on my
own account in a room below. We separated therefore for the

night, after shaking hands in the Colonel's peculiar way – that is, a cool presentation of each individual's fore finger.[42]

The next morning rose as lovely and calm a day as ever ushered in the steps of summer. Wakened by the sunshine – I saw it streaming in through the stately windows of my chamber between the interstices of the carefully drawn curtains – my heart was rejoiced at the sight, and still more so when, on rising and withdrawing that veil, I beheld, in the lofty and dappled arch of a few marbled clouds, in the serenity and freshness of the air, a soft promise of settled summer. The storms, the fitful showers and chilly gusts, to which for the last month we had been subject were all gone. They had swept the sky and left it placid behind them.

It took me a full half hour to dress, and another half hour to view myself over from head to foot in the splendid full-length mirror with which my chamber was furnished. Really, when I saw the neat figure therein reflected,[43] genteelly attired in a fashionable morning suit, with light soft hair parted on one side and brushed into glossy curls, I thought, 'There are worse men in the world than Charles Townshend.'

Having descended from my chamber, I made my way once again into the bustling, dirty inn-passage before described. It was bustling still, but not so dirty as it had been the night before, for a scullion wench was on her knees with a huge pail, scouring away for the bare life.[44] A gentleman's carriage was at the door. Two or three servants were lifting into it some luggage, and a family party stood waiting to enter – a lady, a gentleman and some children. The children, indeed, were already mounted behind, and a stout, rosy Angrian brood they looked. Their mother was receiving the parting civilities of a fine, tall, showy woman, most superbly dressed, who had come sailing out of a side room to see them off. It was Mrs Stancliffe, the hostess of this great house. I went up to her when the carriage had at length driven away, and paid my respects, for I had some little significance with her. She received and answered my attentions much in the tone and with the air of the Countess of Northangerland, only more civilly. Let not the Countess hear me, but it is a fact that she and the landlady bear a strong resemblance to each other, being nearly equal in point of longitude, latitude and circumference. Big women both! awful women! In temper, too, they are somewhat like, as the following anecdote will shew.

A public dinner being given a few months since by the Corporation of Zamorna to their Lord Lieutenant, the Earl of Stuartville, and to Sir Wilson Thornton, in honour of the eminent services rendered by those officers to their country in the war campaign, the whole conduct of culinary matters was of course consigned to the superintendence of Mrs Stancliffe. It so happened that, by some oversight or other, the individual with whom she had contracted for a supply of game failed in his duty. On the great day of the feast, the tables were spread in the court-house. Stancliffe's plate, conveyed over the way in iron chests, shone in tasteful arrangement and more than princely splendour on the ample boards. The gentlemen of the province were collected from far and near. The hour of six struck; the soup and fish were on the table.

The Lord Lieutenant walked in amidst deafening cheers, looking as much the fine gentleman as ever, and smiling and bowing his thanks to his townsmen. General Sir William Thornton followed, and Edward Percy Esqre, M.P. Last, though not least, the proud, bitter owner of Hartford Hall entered, with a face like an unbleached holland sheet (it was after his wound), supported between Sir John Kirkwall and Wm Moore Esqre, an eminent barrister. A blessing being solemnly pronounced by the Right Reverend Dr Kirkwall, primate of Zamorna, and Amen responded by Dr Cook, vicar of Edwardston, all fell to. Fish and soup being despatched, game ought to have entered. But instead of it, in walked Mrs Stancliffe, grandly dressed, with a turban and a plume and a diamond aigrette like any countess in the gallery. She went to the back of Lord Stuartville's chair.

'My lord,' said she, with great dignity of manner and in a voice sufficiently audible to be heard by everyone present. 'I ought to apologize to your Lordship for the delay of the second course, but my servants have failed in their duty and it is not forthcoming. However, I have punished the insult thus offered to your Lordship and the gentlemen of Zamorna. I have revolutionized my household. Before to-morrow night, not an ostler or a chamber-maid of the present set shall remain in my employment.'

The bland Earl, passing his hand over his face to conceal a smile, said something gallant and polite by way of consolation to the indignant lady, and General Thornton assured her that such was the luxurious profusion and exquisite quality of her other provisions, two or three hares and partridges would never be missed. Mrs Stancliffe, however, refused to be comforted. Without at all relaxing the solemn concern of her countenance, she dropped a stately curtsey to the company and sailed away. She did revolutionize her household, and a pretty revolution it was, never such a helter-skelter turn-out of waiters, barmaids, ostlers, boots and coachmen seen in this world before. Ever since this imperial move she has been popularly termed the Duchess of Zamorna! So Lord Stuartville delights to call her, even to her face. This is a liberty, however, taken by none but his gallant lordship. If any other man were to venture so far she'd soon spurt out in his face.

I had scarcely finished my breakfast when a waiter brought me a billet to the following effect: 'Dear Townshend, will you take a walk with me this morning? yours etc. W. Percy'. I scribbled for answer: 'Dear Baronet, with all the xcing. Yours etc. C. Townshend'. We met each other in the passage; and arm in arm, each with a light cane in his hand, started on our jaunt.

Zamorna was all astir. Half her population seemed poured out into the wide new streets. Not a trace remained of last night's storm. Summer was reigning with ardour in the perfectly still air and unclouded sunshine. Ladies in white dresses flitted along the streets and crowded the magnificent and busy shops. Before us rose the new minster, lifting its beautiful front and rich fretted pinnacles almost as radiant as marble against a sky of southern purity. Its bells, sweet-toned as Bochsa's harp,[45] rang out the morning chimes high in air, and young Zamorna seemed wakened to quicker life by the voice of that lofty music.

How had the city so soon sprung to perfect vigour and beauty from the iron crush of Simpson's hoof?[46] Here was no mark of recent tyranny, no trace of grinding exaction, no symptom of a lately repulsed invasion, of a now existing heavy national debt, nothing of squalor or want or suffering. Lovely women, stately mansions, busy mills and gorgeous shops appeared on all sides.

When we first came out, the atmosphere was quite clear. As we left the west end and approached the bridge and river, whose banks were piled with enormous manufactories and bristled with mill-chimneys, tall, stately and steep as slender towers, we breathed a denser air. Columns of smoke as black as soot rose thick and solid from the chimneys of two vast erections – Edward Percy's, I believe, and Mr Sydenham's – and, slowly spreading, darkened the sky above all Zamorna. 'That's Edward's tobacco pipe,' said Sir William, looking up, as we passed close under his brother's mill-chimney, whose cylindrical pillar rose three hundred feet into the air. Having crossed the bridge, we turned into the noble road which leads down to Hartford, and now the full splendour of the June morning began to disclose itself round us.

Immediately before us, the valley of the Olympian opened broad and free; the road, with gentle descent, wound white as milk down among the rich pastures and waving woods of the vale. My heart expanded as I looked at the path we were to tread, edging the feet of the gentle hills whose long sweep subsided to level on the banks of the river – the glorious river! brightly flowing, in broad quiet waves and with a sound of remote seas, through scenery as green as Eden. We were almost at the gates of Hartford Park. The house was visible far away among its sunny grounds, and its beech-woods, extending to the road, lifted high above the causeway a silver shade. This was not a scene of solitude. Carriages smoothly rolled past us every five minutes, and stately cavaliers galloped by on their noble chargers.

We had walked on for a quarter of an hour, almost in silence, when Sir William suddenly exclaimed,

'Townshend, what a pretty girl!'

'Where?' I asked.

He pointed to a figure a little in advance of us: a young lady, mounted on a spirited little pony, and followed by a servant, also mounted. I quickened my pace to get a nearer view. She wore a purple habit, long and sweeping; it disclosed a fine, erect and rounded form, set off to advantage by the grace of her attitude and the ease of all her movements. When I first looked, her face was turned away, and concealed partly by the long curls of her hair and partly by her streaming veil,[47] but she presently changed her position, and then I saw a fine, decided profile, a bright eye and a complexion of exquisite bloom. From the first moment I knew she was not a stranger.

'I've seen that face before,' said I to Sir William. Then, as my recollection cleared, I added, 'It was last night in the mercer's shop opposite Stancliffe's.' For in fact this was the very girl whom I had watched from the window.

'I, too, have seen her before,' returned the Baronet. 'I know her name. It is Miss Moore, the daughter of the noted barrister.'

'What!' I exclaimed. 'Jane – the beautiful Angrian?' Perhaps my readers may recollect a description of this young lady which appeared some time since, in a sort of comparison between eastern and western women.[48]

Sir William proceeded. 'I saw her last autumn at the musical festival which was held in September in the minster at Zamorna. You remember the anecdote concerning her which was told in the papers at that time?'

'Can't say I do.'

'Why, people said that she had particularly attracted the attention of His Majesty, who attended the festival, and that he has bestowed on her the title of the Rose of Zamorna.'

'Was it true?'

'No further than this: she sat full in his sight and he stared at her as everybody else did, for she really was a very imposing figure in her white satin dress and stately plume of snowy ostrich feathers. He asked her name, too, and when somebody told him, he said "By God, she's the Rose of Zamorna! I don't see another woman to come near her." That was all. I daresay he never thought of her afterwards. She's not one of his sort.'

'Well, but,' continued I, 'I should like to see a little more of her. Heigho! I believe I'm in love!'

'So am I,' said Percy, echoing the sigh. 'Head over ears! Look now, did you ever see a better horse-woman? What grace and spirit! But there's that cursed angle in the road, it will hide her. There, she's turned it. I declare, my sun is eclipsed. Is not yours, Townshend?'

'Yes, totally; but can't we follow her, Colonel? Where does she live?'

'Not far off. I really think we might manage it, though I never was introduced to her in my life, nor you either, I daresay.'

'To my sorrow, never.'

'Well then, have you any superfluous modesty? Because if you have, put it into your waistcoat pocket and button your coat over it. Now, man, are you eased of the commodity?'

'Perfectly.'

'Come along, then. Her father is a barrister and attending the assizes at Angria. Consequently, he is not at home. What so natural as for two elegant young men like you and I to be wanting him on business, respecting a mortgage – on a friend's estate, possibly, or probably on our own, or a lawsuit concerning our rich old uncle's contested will? The servants having answered that Mr Moore is not at home, can't we inquire for his daughter (she has no mother, by the bye), to give her some particular charge which we won't entrust to menials? Now, man, have you got your cue?'

I put my thumb to the side of my nose,[49] and we mutually strode on.

Mr Moore's house is a lease-hold on Lord Hartford's property, and he has the character in Zamorna of being a toady of that nobleman's. The barrister, though an able man, is certainly, according to report, but lightly burdened with principle, and it is possible that with his large fortune he may have hopes of one day contesting the election of the city with its present representative – in which case Lord Hartford's influence would be no feather in the scale of success.

'We enter here,' said Percy, pausing at a green gate which opened sweetly beneath an arch of laburnums upon a lawn like velvet. A white-walled villa stood before us, bosomed in a blooming shrubbery, with green walks between the rose trees and a broad carriage-road winding through all to the door. In that bright hour (it was now nearly noon) nothing could be more soothing than its aspect of shade and retirement. One almost preferred it to the wide demesne and princely mansion which it fronted with such modest dignity. Arrived at the door, Sir William knocked. A footman opened it.

'Is Mr Moore within?'

'No, sir; master left home last week for the assizes.'

Sir William affected disappointment. He turned, and made a show of consulting me in a whisper. Then again, addressing the servant:

'Miss Moore is at home, perhaps?'

'Yes, sir.'

'Then be kind enough to give in our names to her – Messrs Clarke and Gardiner – and say we wish to see her for an instant on a matter of some importance.'

The servant bowed, and politely requesting us to walk forward, threw open the door of a small sitting-room.

The apartment was prettily furnished. Its single large window, flung wide open, admitted the faint gale which now and then breathed over the languor of the burning noon. This window looked specially pleasant, for it had a deep recess and a seat pillowed with a white cushion, over which waved the festoons of a muslin curtain. Seating ourselves within this embayment, we leant over the sill, and scented the jessamine whose tendrils were playing in the breeze around the casement.

'This is Miss Moore's own parlour,' said Sir William, pointing to a little work-table with scissors, thimble and lace upon it, and then, reverting his eye to a cabinet piano with an open music book above its key-board. 'I always appropriate when I'm left alone in a lady's boudoir,' he continued; and getting up softly, he was on the point of prigging something from the work-table, when a voice slightly hummed in the passage, and without any other sound, either of footstep or rustling dress, Miss Moore like an apparition dawned upon us. The Colonel turned, and she was there.

He looked at her, or rather through her, before he spoke. Really, she seemed to be haloed – there was something so radiant in her whole appearance. Not the large dark eyes of the west, nor the large even arch of the eye-brow; not the enthusiastic and poetic look, nor the braided or waving locks of solemn shade; but just a girl in white, plump and very tall. Her riding-habit was gone, and her beaver; and golden locks (the word golden[50] I use in courtesy, mind, reader) drooped on the whitest neck in Angria. Her complexion seemed to glow: it was so fair, so blooming. She had very rosy lips and a row of small, even teeth, sparkling like pearls; her nose was prominent and straight and her eyes very spirited. Regularity of feature by no means formed her chief charm: it was the perfection of a lively complexion and handsome figure.

The lady looked very grave; her curtsey was dignified and distant.

'Permit me, madam,' said the Colonel, 'to introduce myself and my friend. I am Mr Clarke, this gentleman, Mr Gardiner. We are both clients of your father. You will have heard him mention the lawsuit now pending between Clarke and Gardiner versus Jowett.'

'I daresay,' returned Miss Moore, 'though I don't recollect just now. Will you be seated, gentlemen?' She took her own seat on a little couch near the work-table and, resting her elbow on the arm, looked very graceful and majestic.

'A warm morning,' observed Sir William, by way of keeping up the conversation.

'Very,' she replied demurely.

'A pretty place Mr Moore has here,' said I.

'Rather,' was Miss Moore's answer; then, carelessly taking up her work, she continued. 'How can I serve you, gentlemen?'

Sir William rubbed his hand. He was obliged to recur to business.

'Why, madam, will you be so good as to say to Mr Moore when he returns that James Cartwright, the witness who was so reluctant to come up, has at length consented to appear, and that consequently the trial may proceed, if he thinks proper, next month.'

'Very well,' said she. Then, still bending her eyes upon the lace, she continued. 'How far have you come to tell my father this? Do you reside in the neighbourhood?'

'No, madam, but we are both on a visit there at present. We came to look after some little mill-property we possess in Zamorna.'

'You must have had a hot walk,' pursued Miss Moore. 'Will you take some refreshment?'

We both declined, but she took no notice of our refusal and, touching a bell, ordered the servant who answered it to bring wine etc. She then quietly returned to her lace-work. We might have been lap-dogs or children for all the discomposure our presence seemed to occasion her. Sir William was a match for her, however. He sat, one leg crossed over the other, regarding her with a hard stare. I believe she knew his eyes were fixed upon her, but she kept her countenance admirably. At last he said,

'I have had the pleasure of seeing you before, madam.'

'Probably, sir; I don't always stay at home.'

'It was in Zamorna Minster last September.'

She did colour a little, and laughed, for she recollected, doubtless, the admiration with which her name had been mentioned at that time in the journals, and the thousand eyes which had been fixed upon her as the centre of attraction as she sat in her white satin robe high placed in the lofty gallery of the minster.

'A great many people saw me at that time,' she answered, 'and talked about me too, for my size gave me wonderful distinction.'

'Nothing but size?' asked Sir William, and his look expressed the rest.

'Will you take some salmagundi, Mr Clarke?' said she, rising and approaching the tray which the servant had just placed on the table. Mr Clarke expressed his willingness; so did Mr Gardiner. She helped both, plentifully, and they fell to.

A knock came to the door. She stepped[?] to the window and looked out. I saw her nod and smile, and her smile was by no means a simper: it showed her front teeth, and made her eyes

shine very pleasantly. She walked into the passage, and opened
the door herself.

'Now, Jane, how are you?' said a masculine voice. Percy
winked at me.

'How are you?' she answered. 'And why are you come here
this hot day?'

'What! you're not glad to see me, I guess,' returned the visitor.

'Yes, I am, because you look so cool! I'm sorry we've no fire
to warm you, but you can step into the kitchen.'

'Come, be steady! Moore's at Angria, varry like?'

'Varry like he is – but you may walk forwards notwithstanding.' Then, in a lower voice, 'I've two chits in my parlour – very
like counting-house clerks or young surgeons or something of
that kind. Just come and look at them.'

Percy and I arrested the victual on the way to our mouths.
We were wroth.

'The jade!' said Percy.

I said nothing. However, a more urgent cause of disturbance
was at hand. That voice which had been speaking sounded but
too familiar, both to Sir William and myself, and now the
speaker was approaching with measured step and the clank of
a spur. He continued talking as he came:

'I've come to dine with you, Jane, and then I've to step
over to Hartford Hall about some business. I'll call again at
six o'clock, and Julia says you've to come back with me to
Girnington.'

'Whether I will or not, I suppose, General?'

'Whether you will or not.' And here Sir Wilson Thornton
paused, for he was in the room, and his glance had encountered
us, seated at the table and tucking in[to] the wines with which
Miss Moore had provided us.

I don't think either Sir William or I changed countenance.
General Thornton's eye always assumes a cold, annoyed
expression when it sees me. I met him freely:

'Ho! General! how d'ye do? My word, you do look warm
with walking! Is your face swelled?'

'Not 'at I know on, Mr Townshend,' he answered coldly,
and, bowing to Sir William, he took his seat.

'My dear General,' I continued. 'Don't on any account drink water in your present state. You seem to me to be running[51] thin! I wish you may not catch your death of cold! Dear, dear – what a pity you should appear such a figure before a beautiful young lady like Miss Moore!'

'If I'm any vex to Miss Moore she'll be good enough to tell me of it without yer interference,' said the General, much disturbed.

'Had you ever the scarlet fever?' I inquired anxiously.

'I cannot see how my health concerns you,' he answered.

'Or the sweating sickness?' I continued.

The General brushed the dust from his coat-sleeve and, turning briskly to Miss Moore, asked her if these were the lads she had taken for two young surgeons.

'Yes,' said she, 'but I begin to think I was in the wrong.'

'I would like to know what nonsense brought 'em here,' said Thornton. 'They're no more surgeons nor I am. Percy, I wonder ye'll go looking abâat t' country wi' such a nout as Townshend.'

'Percy!' exclaimed Miss Moore. 'Oh, it is Sir William Percy! I thought I had seen that gentleman before. It was at a review: he was one of the royal staff.'

The Colonel bowed. 'The greatest compliment I ever had paid me,' said he, 'that Miss Moore should single me out from among thousands and recollect my face.'

'Just because it struck me for its likeness to Lord Northanger-land's,' replied she.

'From whatever cause, madam, the honour is mine, and I am proud of it.'

He searched her countenance with one of those sentimental and sinister glances which, when they flicker in his eyes, do indeed make him strongly resemble his father. I don't think he was pleased with the result of his scrutiny. Miss Moore's aspect remained laughing and open as ever. Had she blushed or shrunk away, Sir William would have triumphed. But hers was no heart to be smitten with sudden, secret and cankering love – the sort of love he often aims to inspire.

'Come, Townshend,' said he, drawing on his gloves. 'We will go.'

'I think you'd better, lad,' observed Thornton. 'Neither you nor Townshend have done yourselves any credit by this spree.'

We both were bold enough to approach Miss Moore; and she was good-natured or thoughtless enough to shake hands with us freely, and say that when her father came home she should be happy to see his clients Messrs Clarke and Gardiner again, either about the lawsuit or to take a friendly cup of tea with them. The girl, to do her justice, seemed to have some tact. I don't think I shall soon forget her very handsome face, or the sound of her voice and the pleasant expression of her eyes.

As we two passed again through the embowered gate and stepped out into the now burning road, I asked Sir William if he was smitten.

'Not I,' said he. 'There's no mind there, and very little heart. If ever I marry, rest satisfied my choice will not fall upon the Rose of Zamorna.'

Yet something had evidently gone wrong with the young Colonel. His vanity was wounded, or he was vexed at the interference of General Thornton. Whatever the cause was, certain it [is] he grew mightily disagreeable, snapping on all sides and snarling sourly at everything. We had not walked above a quarter of a mile, when he said he had business which called him elsewhere, and he must now bid me good-day. The Baronet turned into a retired lane branching from the main road, and I continued my course straight on.

The rumour of invaders through all Zamorna ran.
Then Turner Grey[52] his watch-word gave:
        'Ho! Ardsley to the van!'

Lord Hartford called his yeomen and Warner raised his clan,
But first in fiercest gallop rushed Ardsley to the van!
On came Medina's turbans, Sir Jehu[53] hurled his ban:
'Mid the thousand hearts who scorned it still Ardsley kept the van!

The freshening gales of battle a hundred standards fan,
And doubt not Ardsley's pennon floats foremost in the van!

Cold on the field of carnage they have fallen man for man,
And no more in march or onslaught will Ardsley lead the van!

Loud wail lamenting trumpets for all that gallant clan,
And Angrians shout their signal:
      Ho! Ardsley to the van!

Give them the grave of honour where their native river ran,
Let them rest! They died like heroes
      In the battle's fiery van!

And when their names are uttered, this hope may cheer each man:
That land shall never perish
      Where such true hearts led the van!

The aged halls of Girnington echoed to this heroic song, and a few notes even strayed through the open windows of the drawing-room into the twilight park. It was still evening. A heaven unclouded smiled to the ascent of a moon undimmed. That summer day was gone, and while the burning west closed its gates upon her departure, softer paths opened in the east for the steps of a mild summer night. Is that horseman thinking of the glory which smiles above those trees through which his form glances so fast? Pressing up the avenue, he never turns to look from what source stream those silver rays which fall upon him at every opening of the giant boughs. Yet no heavy care absorbs his thoughts, for he lifts his head to listen when that music comes across his way, and he smiles when at its close a laugh is heard from the mansion at whose door he now dismounts.

General and Lady Thornton sat *vis à vis* in two opposite arm-chair[s] by a window of their saloon. The softening light stole upon Julia and, in Sir Wilson's eyes, made her look like an angel. In the background, and almost lost in the dusk, a third person sat at the piano, playing and talking at the same time. The voice sufficiently indicated her identity. It was Miss Moore of Kirkham Lodge, Hartford, who had accompanied Colonel Thornton according to his invitation.

'General,' she was saying, in answer to some bantering speech of the worthy Baronet's, 'I am afraid I shall die an old maid.'

'I[t]'ll be your own fault if you do, I think, Jane.'

'Well, but nobody ever made me an offer yet, positively.'

'Because you're so proud and saucy,' said Julia. 'You frighten them away.'

'Indeed, you're mistaken! There's one man, at least, whom I've done my very best to win.'

'Who is that?'

'Lord Hartford. Now, I've long been in love with that man. Seriously, there's nobody I should like half so well to be married to – and I've danced with him and smiled at him and sung him all my most triumphant songs in my finest style, without as yet gaining even an outwork of the fortress. Once I thought I had made some little impression. It was after singing that Ardsley song you've heard just now. He came and stood behind me, and asked for it again. The same night, he offered to let me have his carriage to go home, for our own was engaged with my father in one of his circuits; and the next morning he actually walked down to the Lodge to breakfast with me. How I did exert myself to please! I'm sure I was most fascinating! He went home, and I fully expected to receive a proposal in form[54] before night; but no. I'm afraid I had overshot the mark. At any rate, nothing came of it.'

'The Earl of Stuartville,' said a servant, opening the door, and the Earl of Stuartville walked in.

'Good evening, Thornton,' said his Lordship. 'All in shadow, I see – no candles. Perfectly romantic! Is that Lady Julia, covered with moonlight? Good heavens! My heart's gone! Who ever saw anything so perfectly transcendent? Thornton, you'd better challenge me forthwith!'

The Earl threw himself into a chair next to Lady Julia, and, stretching out one elegant leg, leant towards her like an enamoured Frenchman.

'What on earth has brought you here, Castlereagh?' said her Ladyship. 'Excuse me for forgetting the new title – but you know, Castle, that former name must be endeared to me, for with it are connected all our earliest associations.'

'Of the days when your ladyship's pet cognomen for me was man-monkey.'

'Happy days, those, Castlereagh!' sighed Julia. 'You'd nothing then to do but to dress and dance and dine. No Secretary of State, no General of Division business, no county politics to control or court intrigues to counteract.'

'True, Lady Julia; I used to turn out of bed at two o'clock in the afternoon, dress till four, lounge till seven, dine till nine, and dance till six next morning.'

'You did, my dear lord; that was just a chart of your life. Alas! did I ever think the owner of the pretties[t] fancy waistcoat and the best perfumed pair of mustaches in Verdopolis would ever expose his elegance to the rigours of a winter campaign, his eye-glass[55] to the danger of being broken in a field of battle!'

Here the chat was hushed, lost in a solemn burst of music from the piano and the reveille of a thrilling voice:

'Deep the Cirhala flows,
And Evesham[56] o'er it swells,
The last night she shall smile upon
In silence round her dwells!

'All lean upon their spears,
All rest within, around,
But some shall know to-morrow night
A slumber far more sound!

'The summer dew unseen
On fort and turret shines:
What dew shall fall when battle's voice
Is heard along the lines?

'Trump and triumphant drum
The conflict won[57] shall spread:
Who then will turn aside and say
We mourn the noble dead?

'Strong hands, heroic hearts
Shall homeward throng again,
Redeemed from battle's bloody grasp:
Where will they leave the slain?

'Beneath a foreign sod,
Beside an alien wave,
Watched by the martyr's holy God,
Who guards the martyr's grave![58]

Miss Moore rose and came forward as she concluded the song. 'Now, my lord,' said she, addressing the Earl of Stuartville. 'You see, I have forced you to hear, if you will not see me. Don't apologize! I am offended, of course. It will avail you nothing to say you did not observe me, it was dark, etc. You should have perceived my presence by instinct.'

'What!' returned his Lordship. 'I suppose the Rose of Zamorna ought to be known by its fragrance. Miss Jane, sit down. I have something to tell you; something which – I can answer for it – will make your heart beat high with indignation.'

'Does it relate to the reason which has brought you here?' she asked, taking her seat on an ottoman near him.

'Exactly so; and you must needs think it an important circumstance which should bring me ten miles at this time of night.'

'Why then, let's hear it, without any more ado,' interposed Thornton. 'Did aught go wrong at the magistrates' meeting after I left them?'

'No,' returned the Earl, 'except that Edward Percy and I had some sparring about a case of illegitimacy. However, that was all settled; we'd cleared scores, and Edward was just turning down his final glass of brandy and water, when Sydenham, who was standing by the court-house window, remarked that there seemed to be a crowd collecting at the lower end of the street – and as he spoke we heard a yell just for all the world like one of their election cries. I desired Mackay to go immediately and see what there was to do, but before he could get out, five or six gentlemen of Zamorna rushed in a body up the steps of the magistrates' room, and the foremost announced, with more glee than grief, he believed there was going to be a riot. "What about?" I asked. Nobody answered, and some of us turned pale, for all at once a great rush thundered up the street, and in two minutes the whole front of Stancliffe's and the court-house was blocked up by a mass of howling ragamuffins.'

'Did they break t' windows?' asked Thornton.

'Not they; there was not a stone thrown, and indeed, they were not thinking of us. Their faces were all turned the other way, lifted up to the front windows of the hotel. They were yelling terribly, but for my life I could not tell what they said. However, you may be sure we set sharply about the business of swearing in special constables, and a message was despatched to the barracks to have the soldiers ready. Meantime I and Percy went out onto the steps and shouted to the crowd to disperse, but they answered us with a loud roar of "Down with Northangerland! No French! No Ardrahians!"[59] "Well, my lads," I said, "do you call us French? Do you say we're for Northangerland and Ardrah? If that be all, I'll join you in a hearty groan against all three – and then disperse, and go home quietly." And so the groan was given, and a tremendous rumble it was; and Edward, stepping forward and sticking his thumbs in the armholes of his waistcoat, shouted out, "Now, lads, let's have a yell – the highest you can raise – set apart entirely in honour of the old harlot-ridden buck Northangerland! Lift it up, lads! I'll set the time!" He did so, and the very steps he stood on quaked to the hellish sound they raised in unison. "Fellow-countrymen!" said Edward. "I'm proud to see such a spirit amongst you! Now go home. You've done enough for one day." But they did not stir. They only answered by a confused and horrible jabber which it was impossible to comprehend, and still they looked up at the hotel, as if there was something there they could have liked to have gotten out. "Do you think Northangerland is at Stancliffe's?" I asked. "No, no," was the answer. "We'd have had blood if he were!" and a single voice added, "But that dog, his son-in-law,[60] is."'

Castlereagh paused. This announcement included much. Thornton started from his chair, and strode once or twice through the room; Julia looked troubled, and uttered some faint exclamation; as for Miss Moore, she said nothing, but even in the pale moonlight it might be seen that she coloured. The Earl went on.

'When we heard this, Edward Percy just walked back into the court-house, sat down, and said he wished he might die if he lifted a hand to prevent anything that might happen. I stood over him and swore in good earnest, "If what we had heard was true, and if the crowd did not disperse immediately, I'd have three hundred cavalry from the barracks and ride them down like vermin." "By God you shall not," said Edward. "The soldiers have no right to control the people, d—d red[61] tyrants!" I said my measures should be vigorous, and that I would not be restrained by his cursed malignity.

'I got on horseback and dashed through the crowd over the way to Stancliffe's. I went in. They were all in some panic, as you may suppose, but I sent for the mistress and asked her if the Duke was really here. She said no, but that the Earl of Richton's carriage had arrived an hour ago, and that had given rise to the rumour. I asked her if the ambassador were in it, but she said, only his family physician, Dr Morrison, who had brought word that his Grace had left Selden House and would be in Zamorna to-morrow at twelve o'clock. Richton was travelling with him, and Morrison preceded them by a day's journey to prepare the way. Furnished with this information, I went out again, told the people to go now and be sure to come to the same spot at noon to-morrow, when Zamorna would be there to meet them in the body. "And then," I said, "let us see what you'll do. At present he's two hundred miles off." They took the word, and in a few hours the street was clear. Now, Thornton, what think you of the prospect? You and I must be at Stancliffe's betimes in the morning. As for Edward Percy, he says he'll lie in bed all the day to-morrow.'

'Let him lie there and be d—d!' muttered Thornton. 'I care naught about him, and t' Duke deserves what he's like to get. He sudn't vex folk so. What need had he to go three or four hundred mile to see an ow'd worn-out rake?[62] Edward's raight enow abâat that. He's allus brewing bitter drink for hisseln, and now he mun sup it for aught I know. I wish he'd his raight wit. Where's Hartford?'

'Just returned to the Hall from Gazemba. But he'll be of no use. He'll go to bed too.'

'I niver knew sich bother,' continued the worthy General. 'I hate t' thoughts o' folk being ridden down wi' troopers. It's not natural like. But if they mess wi' them they sudn't do, I care n't if t' cannon be pointed at 'em. Hasaiver, ya mun flay[63] 'em first, Castlereagh – flay 'em first, and let's hear what *he* says hisseln when he comes. Happen if he once gets among 'em they'll think better on't.'

'I hope they will,' echoed Julia, wringing her hands. 'I hope they will. Do you think, Thornton, they'll try to do him harm?'

'Who cares?' answered Sir William gruffly.

'I am sure you do,' said she, 'for all you're so cross about it.'

'Julia, be quiet!' returned he.

Julia was quiet; and Miss Moore looked at her from under the dark shadow of her eyelashes with an expression almost of scorn – a momentary expression, which vanished instantly. 'The Duke will pass Girnington gates on his way to the city,' she observed in an indifferent tone.

'Yes,' said Castlereagh. 'But you will hardly distinguish the carriage if you watch for it. It is quite a plain one, like any private gentleman's with six horses and three postillions.'

'Perhaps one might distinguish the Duke himself,' she replied, regarding Castlereagh with the same side-glance out of the corner of her eye.

'Jane, talk sense!' said Thornton testily, and she raised her head and fixed on him a look kindling with sudden astonishment and anger. But she did not speak, and by biting in her under-lip seemed to control the emotion which was darkening her face with crimson. Thornton now asked Lord Stuartville to step with him into his study, and the party broke up.

All business seemed suspended on the morning of the 26th of June. A spirit of excitement pervaded the population of Zamorna, as though at the time of a general election. Few ladies were to be seen in the streets, but groups of gentlemen or mechanics loitered by every lamp-post.[64] Most of the mills were idle, for the men would not come to their work. At ten o'clock the court-house doors were thrown open, and, contrary to Lord Stuartville's prediction, Lord Hartford's carriage was the first that drew up at the steps below. Special constables began to appear, leaving the magistrates' room and crossing the street to Stancliffe's. As noon approached, the crowd thickened. A dense mass began to form in front of the hotel.

It was now that from a window in the second storey I saw the whole. It was a fine day – the sun burning high, the sky of its deepest summer azure – but nobody seemed to feel the scorching heat. Harried expectation appeared in every face. This would have been a capital position for a stranger, for the greatest men of the province crossed the street at every instant. General Thornton, I saw, had arrived, for he was standing on the inner steps, and pointing out to Mr Walker, a principal mill owner, a heavy red flag which hung stirless from a tall banner-staff held by two grimy operatives just opposite. As the flag occasionally deployed its sullen folds, rather to the swaying of its pole than to any breeze felt in the sultry air, it revealed these words: 'Angria scorns traitors – Northangerland to the block'; on the reverse: 'No Percy influence'. Lord Stuartville walked up, and I heard him say distinctly, 'We'll not put down that banner! It has a good motto.' Indeed, it was evident that the nobility and gentry of the town were by no means at war with the lower orders. On the contrary, they were pleased with this demonstration of feeling against the arch-enemy, whose stinging insults were fresh in the memory and keen in the hearts of each. They only wished to keep this feeling within bounds to prevent any unseemly and impolitic ebullition.

Well, time passed on. The tumult swelled and the crowd thickened. The who[le] air seemed hoarse with sound. Impatient expectation was at its height. People looked up to the town-clock, which shewed, in vivid sunlight, its hand on the stroke of twelve: another second, and every ear heard the deep, strong stroke of iron reverberate on the air. From Trinity Church and the minster it pealed more musically. Their chime was hardly hushed when a few flags on the farthest outskirts of

the crowd were seen to wave agitatedly. They crowded forward, and then were hurried back. A wild, deepening sound
arose. One felt a sensation of panic, as it rushed on through
the swaying, agitated ranks, gathering strength in its rapid
approach. At last, close under the hotel windows, 'He is coming
– he is coming!' was shouted from a hundred voices. Within
the house the announcement rose, and footsteps stamped up
the staircase. My chamber door burst open, and twenty persons
were at my back, pressing one behind another to get a glimpse
from the window; I saw, as I leant far out, every sash along the
wide front similarly occupied.

The magistrates were all now out on the court-house steps.
I looked for Edward Percy, but doubtless he was in bed; at any
rate he was not there. Meantime, a dark furrow opened in the
crowded distance – I know not how, for the street had seemed
too densely packed to admit another man. Slowly wading
through, I perceived the heads of horses and the mounted figures
of postillions. At this moment, the groan began – the scornful,
abhorrent, malignant groan of the populace. It filled one with
dread, the sound grew so loud and furious, the people thronged
and swayed with such frantic motion, while above them the
two gigantic standard bearers wildly waved their vast and gory
ensign. All, meantime, stretched to gaze at the approaching
carriage. It delved its way through the solid mass with difficulty,
but still on it came. The horses tossed their heads high as they
backed to the hard curb of the postillions. They were now near.
My strained eyes viewed the whole distinctly. The carriage was
open and large: it contained three figures. There was a deep
interest in watching these three, and trying to discover how
their present situation affected them.

One, in a white hat and blue frogged dress coat,[65] was bending forwards and directing the postillions earnestly. He seemed
anxious, I thought, for the carriage to be drawn up close by
the court-house; he looked towards the gentlemen there, and
glances of intelligence seemed to pass between them and him.
These – I mean the magistrates – had all uncovered. Lord
Stuartville appeared in front; his curls were shining in the sun;
he held his hat in one hand and with the other was motioning

to the people to part their ranks. General Thornton, likewise hat in hand, was hastily giving orders to [a] man whom I knew to be his own attendant; I saw him point to the barracks. As to Lord Hartford, he stood back silent and upright: his deep eye wandered over the people and fixed fiercely on the carriage. Lord Richton (of course, the owner of the blue frogged coat and white hat could be no other) is said not to have the nerves of a lion, yet he can exhibit much self-possession in cases of considerable apparent danger. I was amused by watching the calmness of his face, divested either of smile or frown and expressing in its light eyes, always quick in their motions, a sort of concern wholly unmixed with either fear or anger. He seemed to take upon himself the office of dictator and manager, and very busy he appeared, now telegraphing with the group on the court-house steps, and now checking or urging the postillions as prudence seemed to demand. The other male occupant of the carriage was very still. He leant back in what seemed a very careless posture; a hat with a broad brim and slouched much forwards shaded his face; he said nothing; he looked at nobody. The only token of life I saw him give was taking a gold snuff-box from his waistcoat pocket, tapping it thrice, extracting a pinch of snuff with his finger and thumb, then replacing the box and buttoning his coat well over it.

A more interesting object was presented by the third figure of this group – a lady, and, of course, the Duchess of Zamorna. She was dressed with that sort of stylish simplicity peculiar to herself – a light summer pelisse, gracefully fitted to her figure; a pretty simple bonnet, tyed with a broad ribbon; no veil, no flower, no plume. Her very hair was smoothed out of its native luxuriance of curl and plainly parted on her forehead: this mode, which suits so few, suited her. It seemed to impart additional serenity to her forehead, additional straightness and delicacy to her nose; it reli[e]ved by more striking contrast her fair, transparent complexion, and gave her eyes a touch of something saintly. I cannot tell whether she was afraid, or grieved or mortified; your great people will not reveal their emotions to the eyes of common men; however, she was wholly colourless except a faint tinge in the lips.

'No Percy influence!' shouted and howled the frantic mob. 'Down with Northangerland roll his bloody head in the dirt!' and they shook the insulting banner high over his daughter, involving her figure for a moment in the sullen fiery shade reflected from its folds. Meantime, the person in the broad brim sat like any wet Quaker whom the spirit had not yet moved.[66] His carriage, however, having by dint of Richton's skilful pilotage at length reached the court-house, now cast anchor at the steps. The cessation of motion seemed to remind him that he was in rather a peculiar situation. He gave a look straight before him, then to the right hand, the left, and finally over his shoulder. After a moment's meditation he lifted his forefinger and beckoned to the Earl of Stuartville. I was surprised to see him do anything half so intelligent. A conference of three minutes ensued, in which Stuartville's part seemed to consist in answering a string of running questions, delivered as fast as the lips of the inquirer could move. Broad-brim then drew himself up, lifted his beaver a little, rose all at once to his feet in the carriage and, in so doing, uncovered his head. A breeze passing through his hair waved it from temples and brow. He stood confessed.

A sudden movement, unexpected, generally checks affairs for a moment at least, in whatever channel they may chance to be running. On the present occasion, this rising of the Duke of Zamorna lulled the yell which had given him such hoarse welcome to his kingdom. The hush first dropped on those immediately round him; others caught the feeling that there was something to be seen, something to be heard, and they too were silent. The calm spread, and ere long nothing was to be heard but the dull ocean-murmur of a mighty and expectant multitude. He, meantime, remained erect, the breast of his coat open, one hand resting on his side. The other at first held his hat, till Richton relieved him of it without his apparently being conscious it was gone. He seemed to wait and watch till the living vortex round him sunk into tranquillity. Comparative silence stole over it: every eye sought his. So mute was the pause of expectation, one's heart quaked at the thought of its being broken.

'I wish,' said the Duke of Zamorna, 'I wish, lads, you'd all something to do at home.'

His voice was familiar, and so were his features. The people seemed disposed to hear more, and, after pushing his long fingers through his hair, he spoke again.

'Is there a man among you wise enough to render a reason for the bonny display you're making just now?'

('Yes! Yes!' exclaimed several voices.)

'I say no! Is it because I have been to see an old acquaintance and distant relative of mine who is a feeble invalid?'

('Your Grace has been taking on wi' Northangerland again and we hate him,' replied a single voice in the crowd.)

'What do you say, my lad?' said the Duke, who, it seems, had not distinctly heard the observation. The man repeated it.

'Taking on with Northangerland!' continued his Grace. 'That's a vague sort of expression. I've been to the south, look-ing after my own and my kinsfolk's concerns, and concerning myself no more about politics than most of you do about religion.'

'Have you leagued with Northangerland?' asked one of the bannermen sternly.

The Duke turned upon him with a dark and changed aspect. He eyed his rebellious standard and said coldly, 'Take down that flag.'

'No!' shouted the bannerman. 'This is the flag of the people.'

'Take it down,' replied his Grace in a deepened tone, and he savagely glared at the magistrates. They instantly despatched six special constables to execute the Duke's mandate.

Loud uproar ensued. The huge flag was tossed up and down as its bearers struggled to retain what the constables were resolved to seize; the yelling of the mob redoubled; and all at once, with hideous roar, a rush was made on the royal carriage. A frightful scene ensued. The gentlemen who had crowded the court-house steps and windows sprang into the crowd. A dismal shriek was heard as the startled horses, no longer obedient to the postillions, plunged in terror amongst the densely wedged crowd. Their wild eyes and streaming manes were seen tossed over the sea of human heads, as their iron hoofs, prancing madly, crushed all around them. I looked in agony at the Duchess; she was bending back, and had hid her face in the cushions of the carriage. As for Zamorna, with teeth fast set and the curls of his bare head shadowing his fierce eyes, he looked hellish; he gave not a word either to his wife or Lord Richton; his glance was fixed in one direction. At last, as a thundering beating sound and a dense cloud of dust rose in the quarter where he looked, he got up and, speaking with a very loud, distinct voice, said,

'Men of Zamorna, three hundred horsemen are upon you. I see them; they are here; you will be ridden down in five minutes if you do not bear back instantly from the carriage.'

There was no time: with horse-hair waving and broad sabres glancing, with loud huzza and dint of thunder, the cavalry charged on the mob. Lord Stuartville led the van, waving his hat and mounted on a horse like a devil. Nothing could stand this, not even the mad mechanics and desperate operatives of Zamorna. They flew like chaff; it was the whirlwind chasing the sand of the desert.[67] Causeway and carriage were cleared; the wide street lay bare in the fierce sun behind them. A few wounded men alone were left with shattered limbs, lying on the pavement. These were soon taken off to the infirmary, their blood was washed from the stones, and no sign remained of what had happened. When I looked for the royal carriage, it stood in front of Stancliffe's, empty; a cloak was flung over the seat and two grooms were taking out the horses. *Sic transit* etc.[68]

It was afternoon, and the hotel was somewhat quieter. I had gone out to get a little cool air in the garden, whose bushy shrubs in some measure screened the sun. Two or three gentlemen were walking there, and in an arbour I found Sir William Percy.

'Well, Colonel, where did you put yourself this morning while that dust was kicking up?'

'Oh, I got the snuggest possible corner in the court-house. I witnessed the whole spectacle quite at my ease. Very good sport for winter; rather too active for these dog-days.[69] How

the canaille did run! What will your brother say when he hears
of their rout?'

'Bah – swear himself to the bottomless pit and then call for
a drop of brandy to cool his tongue! But, Townshend, don't I
look very languid? Quite stived up, to use a classical phrase?'

'Can't say but you do. The heat seems to have overpowered
you.'

'Well it may. Ever since noon, I've been in the presence of
the Great Mogul.'[70]

'What, of Zamorna?'

'No other. He sent for a whole lot of us into the great
dining-room; and then, when I and Stuartville and Thornton
and Sydenham and Walker and a dozen more went in, he was
striding up and down from the fire-place to the window with a
face ten times blacker than the smoke from Edward's tobacco-
pipe. He just stood and put his hand on the long table when
we came in, each man doffing his castor and bowing at the
door. He never asked us to sit down, but let us stand at the
lower end, like four and twenty honey-pots all of a row.[71] He
began by asking Lord Stuartville if the troops were gone back
to their quarters. Stuartville stepped forward a pace and made
answer that they were, with the exception of a small detachment
which had been left to keep order in a part of the town which
as yet seemed scarcely settled. "Then," his Grace continued, as
coldly as you please, "I must say, my lord, I have been a good
deal surprised at the state of dissatisfaction in which I have
found the province under your lieutenancy." And without
softening this pretty sentence by another word he stopped for
an answer.

'Stuartville said very plainly "he believed there was a strong
feeling in the minds of the people against the Earl of Northangerland." "Allow me to put your meaning in other words,"
said his Grace. "There seems to me to be a strong feeling in the
minds of the people that they have a right to dictate how, when,
where, to whom and on what subject they will. Let it be your
business, and that of the gentlemen behind you, to subdue this
feeling; to shew those who entertain it the fallacy and danger
of acting upon it." General Thornton remarked that they had

done their best, he thought, that morning. The answer he received proved to him that this idea was all a delusion. "I have not seen your conduct in that light," said the Mogul. "Ordinary vigilance on the part of the city authorities would have prevented the assemblage of such a mass of scum. Ordinary decison would have broken into firewood the staff of that banner which in your town was this day insolently hoisted over my head." He made another of his frozen pauses, and then asked if the Mayor of Zamorna was present. Mr Maude bowed and came forward. "Your police is lax," began his Grace without a word of civility. "Your Corporation is indolent, and ought to be overhauled. Everything indicates disorder, negligence and misrule. If I do not find a speedy change for the better, I shall consider it my duty to set on foot measures for depriving your city of its corporate privileges."

'There fell another pause, in the course of which Mr Sydenham said "he believed his Grace judged the town too hardly. It was his opinion that the feeling manifested that day was no proof of disloyalty, but the contrary." At this speech the Duke scowled like a Saracen. Fixing his eyes on Sydenham he said, "Favour me by keeping that opinion to yourself while you remain in this room. I never yet admitted the value of the loyalty which would dictate the choice of my private friends, or control the course of my private actions. It was not on that condition I accepted the crown of Angria – and how long will it take you to learn that when I became a monarch I did not cease to be a man? Your country put into my hands the splendour and power of royalty, but I did not offer in exchange the freedom and independence of private life."

'Nobody answered him and, after another of his pauses, he began dictating again. "Lord Stuartville, Zamorna has not done well under your lieutenancy. In this capacity you have disappointed my expectations. I must supersede you if you do not act with greater vigour." Stuartville coloured high and said, much moved, "Your Grace shall be anticipated. From this moment I resign my office. Had I been aware before –" And, would you believe it, Townshend, here he broke off with a gulp as if he had been choked. Thornton went red, too, and said he thought all this was far too bad. Our Czar went on: "Your magistracy have disgraced themselves; one was absent; another was perfectly inactive; and the remaining four shewed neither foresight, resolution, nor energy. Gentlemen, you may go."

'And so he turned his back on us, walked up to the window, and we made our exit. Thornton's gone back to Girnington as surly as a bull; Stuartville flung himself on his break-neck horse and set off at a gallop, which must have brought him to the D—l long since; Sydenham and Walker both mounted the Edwardston stage and are doubtless now drinking d—tion to the sovereign in a bumper of Edward's best; as for me, I came here to take the air and get an appetite for some fricandeau I've just ordered.'

'Well,' said I. 'There's a pretty go! And pray, what has become of the Duchess? Do you know whether she's frightened to death?'

'Almost, I daresay. She did look white when the rush began; I heard she turned sick as soon as they got her into Stancliffe's.'

'Then you've not seen her?'

'Yes, for a minute; going up the staircase, leaning on Richton's arm.'

'Did you speak?'

'No. Indeed, she was all but dead then, and neither noticed me nor anybody else. The man is coming to say my fricandeau is ready. Townshend, will you walk in and take a snack?'

Evening drew on at length. Oh, how cool, how balmy its first breeze came sighing, to call away the beams of day-light. Sunset was over; the streets were still and dim; an early moon gazed from heaven on the towers of Zamorna's minster, which fairly lifted its white front and shafted oriel to meet that gaze.[72] The breeze which ushers in evening fluttered the blinds of a large upper saloon at Stancliffe's. Every window was shaded, as if to shut out light and noise and all that could chase repose from that couch in the recess. Sunk among a pile of cushions, a lady lies asleep – pale, with her hair loose, and her figure shewing in its attitude the relaxation of extreme fatigue.

Is that person about to awake her, who is leaning over the

couch?[73] Pity there is not another living soul in the room to bid him stand away, and let her sleep! What is the individual smiling at? He seems to find matter for amusement in the exhaustion of that slender form and marble face, and the saintly folding of those little fairy hands. Villain, don't touch her! But with his long fore-finger he is parting the loose hair farther from her forehead, and then he smiles again at what any other person would worship – the open brow, gleaming fair and serene like that of a sculptured Virgin Mary. He takes his unhallowed hands from her for a moment, and puts them in his pocket. Man, you look no fit guardian for that shrine! You break the harmony of the scene. Why don't you go away? All round is so still and dim, and she is so fair, one might think her a saint and this room a consecrated chapel. But while you stand there, I defy anybody to soothe their mind with so pious a delusion: a fellow with whiskers and something like mustaches, and so much hair – almost black it looks in this light – that you hardly know whether he has any forehead or not, until all at once he pushes the pile away and then there's an expanse underneath, whose smoothness tells you he's not old enough to be a priest.

Fresh from the stern interview with his Lord Lieutenant and the Corporation, from scenes of an equally iron nature which had followed and occupied him all the afternoon, Zamorna had now sought, in the cool of evening, the apartment to which his Duchess had retired. It was an undefined mixture of feelings that brought him there. Half, he wished to know how she had borne the scene of the morning – a scene so unfitted to her nature. Half, he felt an inclination to repose on her softness faculties worried with the bitter and angry contest of the day. Then, in metaphysical indistinctness, existed, scarce known to himself, the consciousness that it was her connection with him which had thus embroiled him with his people; and he was come now partly to please himself with her beauty, partly to dream away an hour in amiable meditations on the sorcery of female charms and the peril of doating on them too fondly, being guided by them too implicitly.

He drew aside the crimson curtain and let the evening sun shine upon her. He walked softly to and fro in the saloon, and every time he passed her couch turned on her his ardent gaze. That man has now loved Mary Percy longer than he ever loved any woman before, and I daresay her face has by this time become to him a familiar and household face. It may be told by the way in which his eye seeks the delicate and pallid features and rests on their lines that he finds settled pleasure in the contemplation. In all moods, at all times, he likes them. Her temper is changeful; she is not continual sunshine; she weeps sometimes, and frets and teazes him not unfrequently with womanish jealousies. I don't think another woman lives on earth in whom he would bear these changes for a moment. From her, they almost please him. He finds an amusement in playing with her fears – piquing or soothing them[74] as caprice directs.

She slept still, but now he stoops[75] to wake her. He separated her clasped hands and took one in his own. Disturbed by the movement, she drew that hand hastily and petulantly away, and turned on her couch with a murmur. He laughed, and the laugh woke her. Rising, she looked at him and smiled. Still she seemed weary, and when he placed himself beside her she dropped her head on his shoulder and would have slept again. But the Duke would not permit this: he was come for his evening's amusement, and his evening's amusement he would have, whether she was fit to yield it or not. In answer to his prohibitory and disturbing movements she said,

'Adrian, I am tired.'

'Too tired to talk to me?' he asked.

'No, Adrian, but let me lean against you.'

Still he held her off.

'Come,' said he. 'Open your eyes and fasten your hair up; it is hanging on your neck like a mermaid's.'

The Duchess raised her hand to her hair; it was indeed all loose and dishevelled over her shoulders. She got up to arrange it, and the occupation roused her. Having smoothed the auburn braids before a mirror, and touched and retouched her loosened dress till it resumed its usual aspect of fastidious neatness, she walked to the window.

'The sun is gone,' said she. 'I am too late to see it set.' And she pensively smiled as her eye lingered on the soft glory which the sun, just departed, had left in its track. 'That is the west!' she exclaimed; and, turning to Zamorna, added quickly, 'What if you had been born a great imaginative Angrian?'

'Well, I should have played the fool as I have done by marrying a little imaginative Senegambian.'

'And,' she continued, talking half to herself and half to him, 'I should have had a very different feeling towards you then to what I have now. I should have fancied you cared nothing about my country so far off, with its wide wild woodlands. I should have thought all your heart was wrapt in this land, so fair and rich, teeming with energy and life, but still, Adrian, not with the romance of the west.'

'And what do you think now, my Sappho?'[76]

'That you are not a grand awful foreigner, absorbed in your kingdom as the grandest land of the earth, looking at me as an exotic, listening to my patriotic rhapsodies as sentimental dreams, but a son of Senegambia as I am a daughter – a thousand times more glorious to me, because you are the most glorious thing my own land ever flung from her fire-fertilized soil! I looked at you when those Angrians were howling round you to-day, and remembered that you were my countryman, not theirs – and all at once their alien senses, their foreign hearts, seemed to have discerned something uncongenial in you, the great stranger, and they rose under your control, yelling rebelliously.'

'Mary!' exclaimed the Duke, laughingly approaching her. 'Mary, what ails you this evening? Let me look – is it the same quiet little winsome face I am accustomed to see?' He raised her face and gazed, but she turned with a quick movement away.

'Don't, Adrian. I have been dreaming about Percy Hall. When will you let me go there?'

'Any time. Set off to-night if you please.'

'That is nonsense, and I am serious. I must go sometime – but you never let [me] do anything I wish.'

'Indeed! You dared not say so, if you were not far too much indulged.'

'Let me go, and come with me in about a month when you have settled matters at Adrianapolis – promise, Adrian.'

'I'll let *you* go willingly enough,' returned Zamorna, sitting down and beginning to look vexatious. 'But as for asking me to leave Angria again for at least a year and a day – none but an over-fondled wife would think of preferring[77] an unreasonable request.'

'It is not unreasonable, and I suppose you want me to leave you? I'd never allow *you* to go fifteen hundred miles if I could help it.'

'No,' returned his Grace. 'Nor fifteen hundred yards either. You'd keep me like a china ornament in your drawing-room. Come, dismiss that pet! What is it all about?'

'Adrian, you look so scornful.'

He took up a book which lay in the window-seat, and began to read. The Duchess stood a while, looking at him and knitting her arched and even brows. He turned over page after page, and by the composure of his brow expressed interest in what he was reading and an intention to proceed. Her Grace is by no means the victim of caprice, though now and then she seems daringly to play with weapons few besides would venture to handle. On this occasion her tact, so nice as to be infallible, informed her that the pet was carried far enough. She sat down, then, by Zamorna's side, leant over and looked at the book. It was poetry – a volume of Byron.[78] Her attention, likewise, was arrested; and she continued to read, turning the page with her slender [finger],[79] after looking into the Duke's face at the conclusion of each leaf to see if he was ready to proceed. She was so quiet, her hair so softly fanned his cheek as she leant her head towards him, the contact of her gentle hand now and then touching his, of her smooth and silken dress, was so endearing, that it quickly appeased the incipient ire her whim of perverseness had raised; and when, in about half an hour, she ventured to close the obnoxious volume and take it from his hand, the action met with no resistance – nothing but a shake of the head, half-reproving, half-indulgent.

Little more was said by either Duke or Duchess, or at least their further conversation was audible to no mortal ear. The shades of dusk were gathering in the room; the very latest beam of sunset was passing from its gilded walls. They sat in the deep recess of the window side by side, a cloudless moon looking down from the sky upon them and lighting their faces with her smile. Mary leant her happy head on a breast she thought she might trust – happy in that belief, even though it were a delusion. Zamorna had been kind, even fond, and, for aught she knew, faithful, ever since their last blissful meeting at Adrianapolis, and she had learnt how to rest in his arms with a feeling of security, not trembling lest when she most needed the support it might all at once be torn away. During their late visit to Northangerland he had shewn her marked attention, conscious that tenderness bestowed on her was the surest method of soothing her father's heart, and words could not express half the rapture of her feelings when, more than once, seated between the Earl and Duke on such an evening as this, she had perceived that both regarded her as the light and hope of their lives. Language had not revealed this to her. Her father is a man of few words on sentimental matters; her husband, of none at all, though very vigorous in his actions; but Northangerland cheered in her presence, and Zamorna watched her from morning till night, following all her movements with a keen and searching glance.

Is that Hannah Rowley tapping at the door? She says tea is [ready],[80] and Mr Surena impatient to get into the shop again. Good-bye, reader.

June 28th 1838

THE DUKE OF ZAMORNA

Introductory Note

The Duke of Zamorna was written shortly after *Stancliffe's Hotel*, in July 1838. 'In a distant retreat . . . I am now forgetting all the worries of the past spring and winter,' Charles Townshend opens his narrative. His creator, too, was still at home in Haworth, on her summer holiday from Roe Head. She was able to immerse herself in Angria and she was, this tale suggests, thinking about the relation between its past as recounted by Branwell and the situations she had begun to develop in *Mina Laury* and *Stancliffe's Hotel*.

Here, once again, the narrator is Townshend, not cocky and ironic as in *Stancliffe's Hotel*, but – at least at the beginning – in a more reflective mood. Now far from the temptations and distractions of the city, he recalls the tales he heard as a child, of the dissolute 'western' aristocracy in the years before the establishment of Angria. Musing over old letters, he presents the reader with a series of vignettes of some of the darkest passages of the past, all of which Branwell had portrayed in his *Life of Alexander Percy*, written in 1834 (Neufeldt 2, pp. 92–190): the murder of Alexander Percy's father, the doom of Augusta di Segovia, the decline of Maria Henrietta Percy, the wild 'extravagance of vice' (p. 144) into which Percy plunged after her death. We hear, too, of the youth of Zamorna, then Marquis of Douro, and his passionate early friendship with Alexander Percy, by then Lord Ellrington. And there is a 'sketch' of these two in the more recent past, discussing Percy's former mistress, Louisa, and her daughter Caroline Vernon, during the visit made by Zamorna to his aged father-in-law.

In the second half of *The Duke of Zamorna*, we move to the

present day, and narrative attention turns from the passionate attachment between Douro and Ellrington to the more ironic friendship glimpsed in *Stancliffe's Hotel* between Sir William Percy and Charles Townshend. In a series of letters, Sir William writes to Townshend of the world of Angrian society: of a county ball, of his audiences at the Foreign Office and the Home Office in Adrianopolis, of his final interview with his sister, before his departure for Paris. The tone of the letters gradually changes from flippancy to seriousness, as the complexities of his character are revealed.

Here, once again, rather like a soap-opera in which a number of different strands are developed, the Angrian saga has moved on. Hartford has not died, but has begun to 'dash out like a good'un' into Angrian society, done up like a dandy, 'with his chest padded and set out with stars and chains and orders, his waist strapped in, and his grizzling locks curled and oiled' (p. 164). Jane Moore reappears, irritating Sir William with her equable good-humour. Sir William's military exploits in Africa have led to his selection to go on a mysterious diplomatic mission. Rumours about Hartford and Mina Laury are circulating in Angria, enraging Zamorna and annoying Sir William, who here begins to hint at a hopeless passion for her.

The Duke of Zamorna seems more like a scrapbook of sketches than a coherently constructed whole. The time of the narrative shifts back and forth between the distant and the more recent past; tangential characters appear and disappear. The tone changes abruptly, from melodramatic darkness to sardonic anti-romanticism. 'Let it suffice to say that I found this pitch far too high for me. I could not keep it up. I was forced to descend a peg,' announces Charles Townshend (p. 163), as he turns from a histrionic depiction of Augusta di Segovia's death to Sir William's mocking account of Colonel Hartford's dandy ball. Yet many of the concerns of preceding tales are brought to the fore and developed in the juxtaposition of these apparently random scenes. The heroics of the past are contrasted here with the irritations of the present, long vanished passions and agonies with the often ridiculous vanities of a sharply seen social world. Questions are left open, tensions left unresolved. Jane Moore's meaningless good-humour is mystifying in its blandness. In a moment of rare directness, soon overlaid by irony, Sir William confesses his loneliness. Through it all, a disturbing undercurrent, runs an awareness of the continuing decline of the once-mighty Northangerland, and of Zamorna's growing unpopularity with the Angrians over whom he rules.

In a distant retreat, very far indeed from the turmoil of cities provincial or metropolitan, I am now forgetting all the worries of the past spring and winter. A plane tree waving its large leaves in the wind is the most life-like object my eyes may now rest on. Yet, when I rise and look out of the narrow window, a long way off on a dim hillside I see herds feeding. Near at hand, however, in my cottage, its garden, and beneath its shadowing tree, this morning sun rises over solitude. There is a woman in the house, but I neither hear nor see her. Two or three closed doors intervene between her kitchen and my parlour, and she does her work quietly. I am in Angria, but in which of her provinces? Ask not. No companion accompanies me; at present, I am dead to the world.

When we think little of the present, when the gay scenes of the immediate past are fading from our memory like rosy clouds, or rather, like the stirring scenes of a theatre where gorgeous gold and scarlet dazzled for a time – the pomp, perhaps, of some oriental city, dreamlike from its very splendour – when, I say, these things leave us, we either sink exhausted into longings for the future, or turn back and recall visions of the far departed past. There is a bench under that plane tree, and all yesterday afternoon I lay stretched upon it in the languor of July heats, just in front of the clean, calm house where I lodge, musing divinely, not much of what I had seen, but of what I had heard: anecdotes, tales, stories, almost legends (not from their antiquity but from their romance), wild and fearful hints never fully explained to me, soft but dim glimpses which had been given to the precocious child – a bliss he could not then appreciate, though when, in the narrators' tales, I was shewn, as through a glass darkly, some scene of love either in splendid saloon or shaded grounds of a hall, what would I have given to cast away the medium and behold the figures face to face![1]

I am not speaking of fiction, nor of the traditions of a wholly departed generation. No, I refer to the far more piquant rumours, news in servants' halls, which in my childhood were rife in every aristocratic house in the west. How often have I been an unmarked auditor of words darkly whispered from butler to housemaid – how, in the drawing-room above, Miss Fanny had been seen sitting as white as death on a sofa, sobbing wildly for some untold mysterious distress; how Mr Dorn had never smiled for days, and would not speak to his daughter; how a lady and gentleman had been seen at dusk, parting with an embrace at the gates of Chatham Grove, how the gentleman was bold and wicked-looking, and said by many to be Mr Arthur O'Connor, and the lady, from her pale face and very black hair, guessed to be Lady Anne Vernon.[2] Then it was related that Mr St John Young was returned from Verdopolis, and with bated breath it was added, some said he had played away more than half his estates this season, and that Mr Jones the great auctioneer was come down to value St John's Grange. Then one would ask after Mrs Young, and with finger on lip, the answer told that she had stayed behind, and was not like to follow the Major soon. He intended to sue for a divorce, and people said young Lord Caversham intended to marry her, but he was not to be trusted. Disquisitions succeeded on Mrs Young's beauty, on the splendour of the diamond ear-rings she had worn at the opera on the very night she ran away with Lord Caversham; then, lamentation about her children – her eldest daughter, who was said to be like herself, very beautiful but too frolicsome for any nurse or governess to manage; her only son, who was at school and whom his father would never allow to come home in the vacations. This, and much more, I have lain awake for hours listening to, while the nurse sat at my bed-foot and, with her companion the chamber-maid, thought I was fast asleep.

*

A bad set were the western aristocracy, terribly bad, and theirs was no giddy flutter of vanity, such as in sunny France keeps the gay Parisians in one ceaseless whirl of glittering dissipation. They rushed with more of uncontrolled impulse into those vortices[3] which the passions open in society, and, excited a moment by the rapid reel of the waters, were presently engulphed at the centre and dragged down to darkness, hurled by boiling eddies upon flinty rocks where at last the shark death found and devoured them.

Women as well as men met a fate like this. So perished the Segovia. In the very prime of her life and the flower of her gorgeous beauty, she among her own groves died a violent death. Like a queen of antiquity, encompassed by more than ancient splendour, she shrieked out life in the agonies of poison, just as one before her, amid his own hills, had moaned and gasped and looked in vain for help, while in his fearful death he howled out her name as a murderess.[4] What else was she? The mandate came out of her saloon in Wellington. She was seen on that fatal night to rise, to leave her seat, and while her three councillors – old Lord Caversham, Mr Simpson and Mr Montmorency – held their breath to gaze, she, beautiful and imperial, laid her hand on Robert King's arm, bent her head to his, and in his ear whispered that instigation which none but herself dared to utter in words.

Whilst I was thinking of these things, I took from my desk a pocket-book. I opened it, and spread its contents on the table before me. They were letters, yellow, many of them, with time, stained and faded with the damp of old drawers and cabinets where they had lain. Ask not how these came into my possession. My eye is quick, my fingers are light; I had sought these autographs in houses long deserted, in receptacles long unopened and, aided by chance, I had found them. How strange it is to look upon this little billet which I now hold in my hand! It is dated 'Jordan Villa, August, 1811.' The hand is that of a lady,[5] small and accurate; the words are few:

> Mr Simpson, I find young Percy has not been supplied as I directed. You will oblige me by advancing the money directly.

He wants it, and he must have it. Are you afraid of not receiving payment? You may help yourself if you choose. There is a way, but none of you possess courage to take it. However, Lord Caversham will not wait much longer. Supply Percy.

  A. di Segovia.

On this paper, then, her hand lay. Her fingers traced these lines, her eye directed them (strange thought!). Seven and twenty years ago this was penned in Jordan Villa in Senegambia. Where is the writer now? Nothing answers. None even of her kindred survive[s]. Here is the answer, much blotted and slurred:

My noble lady, how long do you command me to furnish sinews[6] to the profligate wing of that young debauchee whom you have taken under your care? By G—d, madam, and as my soul liveth, he is my debtor to the tune of 5000£. Lord Caversham can shew a much longer account, and Percy Snr is still in good health. I had your minion here this morning, and in obedience to your message allowed myself to be bled for an additional 400£. Here I stop. The lad shall have no more, though he brings your ladyship's slipper to collect it in. Some new arrangement must be made.

  Yours,
  Jeremiah Simpson.

Here is di Segovia's hand again:

To Mr Wood, Manager of the Queen's Theatre.
Sir,

Your prima donna insulted me last night. I met her at Lord Vernon's private concert and, I repeat it, Miss Hunter insulted me. She turned to a gentleman who was in my suite and, with a look I could not but notice, summoned him from my very side to turn the leaves of her music-book while she sat at her harp.

Sir, you yourself must have seen her conduct to this same gentleman. Last Thursday night, when she appeared on the boards of your theatre in the character of Juliet, did she not, sir, direct her eyes full toward my box; and did she not utter all the amorous speeches meant for Romeo to one young man who was leaning on my chair back? That young man, sir, is in my hands. I am his protectress, and I will not allow his principles to be corrupted by the impudent freedoms of a woman like Hunter.

Sir, you will look to it. I will throw up my box ticket and withdraw my countenance from the Queen's Theatre if you do not instantly dismiss that prima donna from her engagement.

    I am,
        A. di Segovia.

I possess, too, the answer to this note; not, however, from the pen of Mr Wood. It is a female hand; all the words are not quite correctly spelt.

Lady Augusta di Segovia,

    Wood is a gentleman and he gave me your precious billet. So you imagine the manager of the Queen's Theatre really dares to part with his prima donna in the middle of the theatrical season? Wood would as soon dare fling off his skin. You're jealous, are you, about your fine young Adonis?[7] You had need to be. Let me whisper in your Ladyship's ear. After Lord Vernon's concert was over, I had a quiet select little supper at my own house, and your lambkin formed one of my party. The next morning he politely sent me a pair of bracelets clasped with pearls.

If your Ladyship would like to settle this business we can do it convenient in the green room to-morrow night. The Italian Gabriella Cena and I had a turn-up there scarcely a week ago. Her voice never displayed such compass before. Wood and the Earl of Ellrington will be my seconds. You may bring young Montmorency and anybody else you like.

    I am, etc.
        Eliza Hunter.

These, reader, are creditable fragments, are they not? How, you will ask, did they come into my possession? Never mind! Trifles of this nature are scattered up and down the world; a piece of paper is light and may be blown by any breath.

Mementos of disgrace live long to blot the characters of the departed. Besides, 'men's evil actions live in brass – their virtues we write in water.'[8]

Here is another, dated 'Harcourt, June, 1810', addressed to

Major Steighton, Oakwood.

Dear Major,

I have asked out a lot of them to Harcourt here, just to make a row in the old place. The Sultana is coming with her court, and amongst the rest little Harriet.[9] Now this is to give you notice that I wish no one to meddle with that last save myself. You may take to Mary Dorn or whosoever else you like, but Harriet is to be my companion when we ride out in the morning, and my partner when we dance in the evenings.

You'll come, of course. The Sultana forbids cup play,[10] but we'll see if she sticks to it. Mont says her fingers will itch when she sees the dice. 'What's bred in the bone etc.'[11] To speak truth, I never saw a woman so given up to the vice as she is.

> Of course she'll bring under her wing
> The unfledged dove that shares all our love.[12]

You see I am turning poet. Simpson swears he can't leave the shop, but, God willing, he'll look in upon us every other evening. Remember my hints about our mutual friend Harry,[13] and believe me
  Yours truly,
    George Vernon.

Here is another almost illegible scrawl, written as if with a faltering hand, from Lord Caversham to Edward Percy,[14] Esq., Percy Hall.

Dear Percy,

I am sorry to hear that Alexander still continues so wild. I am afraid he has got entangled with a sad set at Wellington. That Lady Augusta, of whom I told you, is one of the most vicious women in the capital. Alexander is with her constantly; she seems to have bewitched him. He receives challenges from her other followers almost daily. Mr King tells me he has fought three duels within the last month. In one of them his antagonist was a Signor di Rossi, an Italian fiddler, formerly a great favourite with her Ladyship.

He is gone now in her company to Lord George Vernon's, who is entertaining a very large party at Harcourt. I have had an invitation, and if you wish it I will accept it, that I may have an opportunity of watching over your son and screening him, if possible, from the arts of that truly infamous woman. King hints darkly about the state of his young master's accounts. He says it is not to tell how he has concerned himself with money-lenders. In spite of all these untoward circumstances, I wish you would take care of your health and dismiss care, if possible, from your thoughts. How is that short troublesome cough with which you were troubled when I saw you last?

> Believe me,
> Yours sincerely,
> Caversham.

What scrap is this, hastily written in a hand scarcely yet formed, almost that of a schoolboy, directed to 'Miss O'Con-nor, O'Connor Hall'?

My dear Harry,

You know I take an interest in you and therefore you will not be surprised at my writing a note the first thing this morning, to ask what made you look so out of spirits last night. I could never raise my eyes but yours were fixed upon me with an aspect of suffering I don't understand.

Has your termagant step-mother been making your home more uncomfortable than ever? Or (I speak as a friend, Harry) are you in love? If this be so, just tell me upon whom you have placed your affections. I hope you do not intend to rival me. I hope you are not lifting ambitious aspirations to my glorious Augusta. Dear Harry, anywhere but there.

If this evening should be fine, as the day seems to promise it will be, just throw your shawl round you, and at sunset run down to your low plantation. I will meet you there and we'll have a friendly talk *au clair de la lune*, during which the topic I have touched on may be discussed more fully.

Keep up your gallant little heart. Set the sex at defiance and believe me

        Your sincere friend and brother,

           Alexander Percy.

Here is a letter written in the most delicate female hand addressed to Robert King Esqre:

Sir,

I want your assistance in settling a little troublesome affair I have now on my hand. The Earl has turned restive and I am now in straits. If you can spare half an hour from the concerns of di Segovia and her handsome new favourite I shall consider myself obliged. Ride over to Ennerdale to-morrow evening at nine o'clock. You will find me in my boudoir alone except [for] Pakenham. The Earl is to attend a levee in town on that day. Pakenham grows very urgent about a final decision. He wishes me to leave all, take up my cross and follow him.[15] You will see there are difficulties in the way of such a step.

I want your advice. Mr Simpson tells me he cannot at present be of service to me. His veins are emptied by Augusta who, I understand, exacts terribly in behalf of her pretty protégé. Seriously, I saw your pupil[16] about a week since at Jordan Villa. He is very young and slim, but in truth exquisitely beautiful. I told him my opinion of his looks. He answered me in my own native tongue in some wild romantic stanza from da Vega. The boy overflows with sentiment. He kindles an ardent flame in these our select circles. All admire him. Augusta, meantime, guards him vigilantly; *she* does not let 'her tassel gentle' slip a little from her hand.

Pakenham's eldest daughter[17] is come home from school. I will never approach Grassmere again if she is suffered to stay there. In compliance with my wish he has sent both his sons to work their passage abroad.

        In haste I am

           Paulina Louisiada Ellrington.

           Ennerdale House, May 1809.

These letters are all unconnected.[18] Here is one of five years' later date:

To Hector Montmorency, Esqure., Derrynane.
Dear Hector,

I went to court yesterday as you told me. I saw the young Duchess you raved about so. She was always pretty; she is now divine. Mr Percy – Alexander, I mean – was at the drawing-room. He swore grievously at the Duke of Wellington, but said nothing about the Duchess. Her Grace seemed to remember me. Anne Vernon said her eye followed me after I had passed her. Mrs Alexander Percy is much admired in the metropolis.

You will come here soon, of course. I feel less feverish, but not so strong as I was. I never hear Augusta's name mentioned now. She is forgotten.

    Good-bye. Yours etc,
     H. Montmorency.[19]

My pocket-book is nearly exhausted. That is the last letter. I will relinquish my pen for a moment, and go and lie down in the shade of that plane-tree. In the whispering of the leaves I will recall the voices of the departed. I will close my eyes and see shapes dawning out of the sunlit air, whose phantom faces shall bear, as they come and go, a mystic semblance to the pictures I have seen in many old houses of the west. *Aura, veni!*[20]

The south wind blew, and they (that is, my visions) were scattered. I return to my pocket-book.

From Dr Sinclair to Mr Bland, Surgeon.
Dear Bland,

I am sorry to say my patient is a great deal worse. I have summoned a consultation to be held at Percy Hall tomorrow. Will you attend? This child too – her third son, a fine boy – is removed. The father disowns them.[21] Judging from his conduct, we might entertain doubts of their paternity. The child only came into the world last Wednesday, and Mr Percy ordered it to be dismissed from the house this morning.

I was summoned in haste today. She was in great agitation, weeping bitterly. 'Why may I not keep my children?' she exclaimed when I entered the room. I muttered something about unnatural barbarity. She was silent directly. She will not hear a word of reproach against her husband. Her temper must be very gentle; no bodily pain extorts complaint from her. She is adored by her servants.

Percy roams about his grounds like a wandering spirit. I hear him open the hall door often after midnight; and then I can see him from my window cross the park to his woods.

Mrs Percy may recover this time, but she cannot last very long. I fear decline;[22] she has all the constitutional mildness and sweetness often inherent in that complaint. These bereavements prey on her mind. Not infrequently she expresses an intense wish that her children had been daughters instead of sons. She talks, however, little on the subject, and always in such a way as to screen her husband. The Duchess of Wellington visited her yesterday. I am informed that her Grace adverted devoutly to the peculiar affliction of her circumstances. She answered calmly, 'Yes, Alexander thinks I am not strong enough to nurse my own children. He sends them out to be fostered.'

The Duchess had brought with her her own son and heir,[23] who is now three years old. She left him in the carriage, for she feared lest his appearance might agitate Mrs Percy. The little Marquis, however, who has a somewhat wilful spirit, tried to give his attendant the slip, and by some means, unfortunately, made his way upstairs to the very apartment where his noble mother was. I came in a few minutes after and found him seated on her knee, laughing at her efforts to hush him, and stretching out his hands to Mrs Percy, who pressed his little fingers with her thin and trembling hand, and tried to smile in answer to his gleeful salutation.

'I will speak to her, Mamma,' he said. 'Why do you want me to hush? Mrs Percy, how are you? Dr Sinclair says you have been poorly.' And bending forward from his mother's arms, he would lay his round rosy cheek on the pillow of her couch, pressing it against Mrs Percy's pallid face.

All at once her eyes gushed over with tears. 'Let him stay,' she said, as his mother drew him back, but the Duchess, with a grieved look, rose, took him in her arms, and carried him herself from the room, after saying to Mrs Percy that she would come and see her again tomorrow, 'without this unconscionable little disturber'.

I could not help remarking the contrast of the two figures, as poor Mary Percy lay white and languid on her couch, looking up with sad eyes at the blooming Duchess, who stood with her son clasped to her breast, a fine lovely woman, and her child one of those bright, picturesque creatures young mothers doat on most intensely. I wish Percy himself could have seen them. Surely he would have relented.

I have written myself into a most pathetic mood, but this old hall with its melancholy scenes would melt an alderman to pathos. Excuse my maudlin thus, and believe me,

Yours,
J. Sinclair.

Well, reader, is it not odd, to think that that rampant thing which flung its round curled head beside young Mrs Percy's, was taken in her feeble arms to her aching heart, kindly tolerated in its wilful clamour, to think that that unthinking animal (all laughing selfishness even then) should be now a big man, riding forth in the middle of a general's staff to review ten thousand troops at Gazemba? Can he remember being carried in a lady's arms down the staircase of Percy Hall? Can he remember that figure[24] that crossed the passage as they entered it, and stopped to speak to his mother – the young man of unusual height and slim mould, with a head conspicuous in its Grecian curls – how he bowed as the graceful Duchess approached and, after assisting her to enter her carriage, bowed again, waved his hand without smiling, but with a sad, dark look that seemed permanently settled on his features?

I have heard his Grace of Angria mutter something about a slight remembrance of Mary Henrietta Percy. How one bright summer afternoon she came to Mornington Court, and he was sent for to his mother's drawing-room, where he saw a lady in a white dress sitting by the open window, how she smiled as he entered and called him to her, and he, never bashful, ran and most willingly assumed the offered seat on her lap. I have heard him say, too, that she talked to him, and that her voice was soft and slow, much slower than his mother's. That he dimly recollected walking with the same lady once, he knew not where, but in some garden, when it was evening and a star was shining above a long grove; that she told him that star was a world, and the sky a wide and lofty sea, more distant than the Atlantic, and which none ever crossed but dead people, that beyond it there was that place which in the Bible is called heaven, and that angels would come out to meet such as were good and lead them to the shore.

He asked her if she were good, and if she would go to heaven. She said she hoped to do so, and then she stopped and sat down on some steps that led up to a terrace.

'She drew me towards her,' said the King of Angria, 'and at this moment I seem to feel her breast heaving beneath my cheek as she gave a sudden sob. I felt dismayed. It seemed strange that a lady like her, whom I had looked up to as one of the angels of whom she told, should all at once cease speaking, sit down and weep.

'Some high bleak trees waved over my head from the terrace. It was growing dark, and the garden was quite lonely. I know not what suggested it to me, but I remember asking if she was afraid to die. She said, "Sometimes," and then she wiped her eyes and added, smiling at me, "but you, love, Augustus, need never fear death if you believe in your Bible, and as you grow up try to act as it directs you." My mother now came to call me. I was glad to leave that pale lady's arms, and run from the dreary garden into the house, which, I recollect, was lit up and filled with company.'

All people have their faults, it is said, reader, and sometimes, when I look over the wicked world, I am tempted to think that all people have nearly the same number of faults, that the shades of difference in individual vice are not so many or so various as people in general suppose. Look, now, at Angria; look at the higher orders there. Carry your mind's eye along the country, pause a moment at the gates of every park-surrounded mansion as you pass it. Who, now, of the whole set is free from the stains of ambition, tyranny, licentiousness, insolence, avarice, blood-thirstiness, bad faith? Perhaps the ingredients vary a little in their proportions, but the deficiency of one vice is made up by the redundancy of another. Mr Warner, for instance, is not lewd as some, but what he wants in looseness of morals, he atones for by preposterous ambition in politics. Lord Hartford professes strict honour in all affairs of state. In private life, he is one of the most dissolute men alive, even now. Then, when a man sets up for decency, like General Thornton, do not trust him. The fact is, all the different qualities I have mentioned exist in such persons' minds, and the seeming moderation of their characters results from the accurate proportion one vice has with another, so that no single gesture of crime stands out conspicuously from the accurately adjusted whole.

'Tis the same with their wives. Who can think highly of Lady Stuartville? What Pope would canonize Lady Julia Thornton? When will Lady Maria Percy be entitled Santa Maria? Is even the Countess of Arundel,[25] with all her pride, equivalent to an angel? Are not these, and others whose names I have not mentioned, fleshly, vain, silly, extravagant, over-bearing, some having a tincture of disreputable gaiety, others selfishly and lavishly prodigal, others imperiously haughty, hot and sudden-tempered?

But, you will say, there are some exceptions. I cannot charge my memory with any living instance of that kind, but one or two dead I have heard of, and of the number of these was undoubtedly Mary Percy. To form a character like hers there must be a combination of qualities and circumstances which rarely indeed meet together. She was intellectual, poetically so; she was constitutionally soft-tempered, and had, indeed, sweet and kindly manners. She had no satire in her disposition, and but little fire. She would not have hurt the feelings of the veriest wretch in nature. She could not be harsh or haughty; she was mild to everything that came near her. Her aspect was benign, her voice was low and peaceful, her deportment very full of the grace of kindness. All this seemed very fascinating in one so young and so very lovely.

You would have expected, on being introduced to the fair and aristocratic Mrs Percy, to see some consciousness of rank, some air of peerless beauty, some frivolity or caprice of youth, but she showed none. She looked kindly at you with her dark eyes, and spoke kindly to you with her sweet voice, and moved with unostentatious though perfect grace, a fair young Christian lady. She was not gay. Even in her smiles she seemed softly sad. She thought much, and all her thoughts were tinged with a high religious melancholy. She really loved to ponder over the glories of a heavenly hereafter far better than to play with the frivolities of the earthly present. This it was which seemed to free her from the selfishness, the vanities, the pride of her station. She had subjects for reflection which suited her system of mind better to dwell on than the magnificence of this world, or its cares, or its vexations.

Percy she loved. How well, how deeply, with what morbid fervency of devotion, no mind but such as her own could fully conceive. But she died, and thousands were sorry for the untimely end of one so wholly beloved. She had no enemies even among the proud and profligate, for there did not breathe the man or woman on earth whom she, by word, look, or action, had insulted.

Her death changed the destiny of Africa. From the close of that August evening when Percy turned away from his Mary's grave and went home a desolate man, he was no more what he had been. Heart and feelings were embittered, life and motives utterly perverted. Perhaps a recollection of his former self may have returned upon him when he has stood alone, looking at the sepulchral tablet, but at all other times, in all other scenes, he has been a torrent turned from its original channel.

The course of things in this world is strange – inscrutable. Seventeen years elapsed after Mary's death, during which her husband gave himself up to the wildest extravagance of vice, partly in obedience to the impulse of his own very bad mind, partly to drown in the ruling rush of debauchery all recollection of that soft spirit which had once charmed him to alienation from his evil genius and communion with his guardian angel.[26]

During those seventeen years, he never spoke of Mrs Percy, never revived by words the remembrance of her features, her voice, her pure life and saintly death.

At last we see him again, spent, almost, with sin, lying down, looking upwards, confiding his long pent-up feelings to an ear which to us seems all unmeet for confession. Who can calculate the probabilities or possibilities of this our changeful life? Percy, who had never referred to his wife, or her actions, or his feelings towards her, since the first spadeful of earth rang hollow upon her coffin-lid, now contradicts every previous habit of his life and chooses a friend. Who is that friend? A young man of rank, with a handsome face, a hot heart, an iron mind, in the first flush of existence, mastered by the wildest passions of youth, intractable and fierce and amorous, eager to have his stake in every desperate game, political or private, of his day, a boy of lawless will and unruly desire, and of mental gifts vigorous enough to overl[e?]ap every boundary which social right or civil law raised against his wild ambition. Such was the confidant to whom Lord Ellrington[27] – the frozen cynic, the man-hater – revealed the tenderest, the holiest feelings his heart had ever known.

It was strange! If young Castlereagh or Frederick Lofty, or poor Arthur O'Connor, had ventured to speak to him as Douro spoke, to come about him, and importune him, and worry him as Douro did, he would have lifted his endless limb[28] and caused them evacuate his presence with more speed than ceremony. But still more, if these or any other had turned on him those glances of feeling – clashing, ardent, enthusiastic – which sometimes glowed in the Marquis's dark eyes when they rested on the rebellious democrat, if, I say, Rogue had discerned anything like attachment to his person in any other man or boy than Arthur Wellesley, the first moment of such a discovery would have been marked by a testimony of his intense and eternal hate. He would have persecuted the unfortunate sentimentalist from that hour with a malignancy to be appeased only by his annihilation. Somehow it was different in the present case. Douro pestered him, thwarted him, opposed his will, counteracted his projects, ridiculed his peculiarities, stormed at his prejudices, hated his adherents, shunned and scorned his mistresses, and still he was endured. Douro sought his society, followed his footsteps, hung spellbound on his persuasive lips, insinuated his way to his confidence, listened with changeful cheek and fettered sympathy to the revealing of his inmost soul, and Douro was not repulsed: he was retained, almost clung to.

True, Ellrington broke upon his young comrade sometimes with fury, and at other times he seemed to freeze and turn away with hollow coldness from his enthusiasm. This the Marquis felt at his heart's core. He could meet Percy's passion with wilder passion, and it so happened that Rogue, even when intoxicated, never inflicted on him the reckless violence by which he certainly shortened the lives of some of his own associates. Once or twice he is known to have held a loaded pistol to Douro's very temples after some mad provocation of the young scoundrel, but he never drew the trigger, though dared to do it by the bold tongue and defying eyes of his prostrate vice-president,[29] who was sure, when Ellrington had relaxed his hold, to spring up and grapple with him again and again, though at that time almost always overmastered by the superior strength of the Drover. However, coldness mortified him in a way he could not conceal. The varying complexion[30] alone was sufficient to reveal it, and Percy had a real pleasure in thus agonizing his proud heart by feigning to check its affections with rooted rocky indifference. Then he would swear that he never could feel anything but detestation for such a depraved, treacherous old debauchee, whose heart was far too cold and false to cherish for an instant one noble or lofty feeling; that he hated, despised him, saw through him, etc. Yet after all, twenty-four hours would hardly elapse before they would be bound again together, perhaps reasoning calmly on things high and sublime like Milton's angels,[31] perhaps sitting almost silent side by side, or, it may be, again in furious contention, ready to drink each other's heart's blood.

All this I have written before, but the subject is a strange one and will bear recurring to. And the fact is, when I once get upon the topic of Douro and Ellrington, I cannot help running on in the old track at a most unconscionable rate.

*

I alluded in my last work[32] to the Duke of Zamorna's visit to
Selden House in Rossland. Here it was that the latest renewal
of Ellrington and Douro's confidences took place. Let me sketch
one if I can:

'Is Arthur here?' asked the Earl of Northangerland, opening
the door of his wife's library.

'No,' said the Countess, looking up from the pages of a book
which the very latest light of evening faintly enabled her to
read.

'Where is he, Zenobia?'

'I don't know. Last time I saw him he was talking to the
Duchess in Lady Helen's drawing-room, but that was just
after tea.'

Northangerland closed the door as quietly as he had opened
it, and went wandering all through the long quiet passage
separating two suites of rooms upstairs.

'Is Arthur here?' he again asked, gently pushing back another
door, which led into his mother's apartment.

'No,' answered a tall, dark-robed figure sitting in the dusk at
the open drawer of a cabinet.

'Where is he, Mother?'

'I don't know, my son. Perhaps Mary can tell you. She is in
her dressing-room.'

Again his Lordship closed the door and followed his quest
with the same slow, silent tread. Entering a large chamber, he
opened a door within.

'Is Arthur here?' he reiterated, precisely in the same patient,
equable tone of inquiry he had used twice before.

'No, Father,' replied a voice of music, and the speaker turned
from the darkening casement at which she stood gazing down
on the quiet grounds.

'Where is he, Mary?'

'Gone out, Father, three hours since, to see what has been
done about the larch plantation which he ordered Wilson to
thin and prune this morning.'

'Damn the larch plantation!' returned the Earl, very quietly.
'And pray, Mary, when did he say he would be back?'

'Before supper, Father.'

'Why can't you keep him in?' continued his Lordship, in a tone slightly expressive of irritation.

'He won't be tied to my apron-string,' answered the Duchess. 'I asked to go with him, but he said he thought I had better not, as the day had been so hot and he thought there would be a heavy dew in the morning.'

Northangerland sat down and was silent.

'What do you want with Adrian?' asked the Duchess, approaching her father, and seating herself on the same sofa.

'Not much, Mary. I only want to tell him he has been long enough here. I can't bear his commotions; he keeps the house in too great a bustle.'

'Will you have some music?' inquired his daughter, smiling to herself.

'No, Mary, not now.'

He put his hand on her head and stroked her ringlets to soften the refusal, which he saw she did not like.

'Father, you don't want Adrian really to go?' she said, looking up at him.

'Is he kind to you?' asked the Earl, not answering her question.

'Yes,' replied her Grace briefly, blushing, though the twilight veiled her blush.

'Have you been out today?' he inquired.

'Yes, I took a ride on horseback this afternoon as far as Alderley Wood.'

'By yourself?'

'No, with Adrian.'

'Are you very well now, Mary?'

'Yes, quite well.'

'You don't feel that tightness on your chest which you complained of some time since?'

'Not at all.'

'Do you ever cough?'

'Never!'

'Well, take care of yourself.'

He got up and slowly loitered out of the room. His footsteps were heard on the carpeted stairs as he descended to the hall below.

'Damn him!' muttered Northangerland, as he paused from his restless pacing through a large, lonely room shrouded all in dusk, without candles or fire, and with a moonless evening looking coldly in at the windows. He threw his worried form on a couch. All was silent. One dreary whisper of a tree in the grounds mocked his impatient ear. There came a sound remote, from the distant kitchens or the upper rooms, a hurried thud, or the sudden closing of a door. He started, listened, and it was hushed. 'Damn him!' he again groaned, and again his listless head dropped on the sofa-cushion.

Something rushed through the grass waving outside a glass door at the other end of the apartment. There was a kind of snort, and a large dog, rooting with its muzzle, appeared through the panes. Percy saw it. He did not stir. He pressed his aching temples more closely to the cushion. A voice was heard remotely, gradually approaching nearer.

'Wilson, when you've finished that job in the plantations, do look after these plants. On the front here they've been sadly neglected. These creepers must be cut and trimmed; they quite darken the windows. And I want some of those rose-trees trans-planting. Hey, Juno, is that a bat you've got? Take it from her, Wilson; she struck it down with her paw. Well, old lass, what do you want? There! there! down now! Well, that's all I have to say to-night, Jem. You'll not forget the grapery? It must be thoroughly repaired.'

'No, my lord. I wish your Grace good-night.'

'Good-night! Call at the porter's lodge as you pass, and ask Crabb if he thinks the flies I sent will make good baits; and tell his eldest lad I shall want him tomorrow at eight o'clock for the fishing.'

'I will, my lord. Good-night!'

'Good-night, Jem. Now, Juno, now you may have your bat – it's killed dead. What? Too thoroughbred to touch it? Down, lass! There, put your head on my foot.'

The voice ceased, and the room was made darker than ever.

A lofty gentleman stood on the lawn, just without the glass door before mentioned, his back to the house and his face to a wide, dim champaign, waving with sombre trees and canopied by a sky of blue. He seemed at his evening meditations. He was silent and motionless, his head a little lifted towards a southern constellation which was slowly kindling star after star out of the cloudless heaven.

Whistling a wild stave, he turned away, unhasped the glass door, and stepped over its threshold into the house.

'Hey, all darkness!' said he, looking around, and his hand was immediately stretched to the bell-rope.

'I desire you won't ring for candles,' murmured a languid voice out of the impenetrable gloom of a recess.

'What for, old codger? What are you doing here by yourself?'

'I shall esteem it a favour,' returned the voice, 'if you would so far do violence to your natural and acquired habits of colloquial coarseness as to give me my right name in my own house.'

'By all that's demure!' exclaimed the intruder. 'I must certainly go to a lady's finishing boarding-school, or I shall never be able to please in this country seat of a prim old beau of the last century. Brummell,[33] where are you?'

'Brummell may be a name, for ought I know,' replied the viewless spirit of some sweet sound,[34] 'but it is certainly not my name. Perhaps you intend it for a sobriquet. Those are vulgar things which only vulgar persons use. I daresay Lord Arundel calls Mr Enara "Bloodsucker", and Signor Fernando designates Chevalier Frederick "Soap-suds". Mr Howard Warner will likewise often in your court be denominated "Nanny-Goat", and the farmer person[35] who lives at Girnington will be familiarly termed "Muck-midden".

'Come, now, my bold buck,' said the tall gardener who had been giving orders about rose-trees. 'Come, now, my primitive peacock,[36] that's very well said. Let us have a little more of the same.'

'Have you been about compost and manure, Arthur?' asked the unseen oracle. 'I don't think you're quite sweet – an odour of the stables, eh?'

'Why, I believe I did go into your stables a few days since,' replied the land-surveyor, 'and I found them in such an Augean condition[37] for want of looking after that really it's not impossible the scent may be haunting me even yet, though I changed my clothes on the instant after coming out, and took a bath besides.'

'What makes you so fond of looking after brute animals?' inquired the voice. 'Is it because Arundel employs you to purchase his dogs and horses, and gives you a go of gin whenever you get him a sound charger or well-bred pointer?'

'Not exactly! It's rather because I find relish in their dumb society when wearied with the innuendoes and back-bitings indulged in by an elderly individual of weak vigour and strong venom.'

The voice was going to reply when it was broken by a harassing cough which, when it passed away, left a short, hurried respiration, audible enough in the silence which succeeded.

'Come now, you're no worse this evening, are you?' said the Duke of Zamorna, taking a chair and placing it alongside the couch where his father-in-law lay reclined.

'I'm worse every evening, Arthur.'

'Pooh! that's hypochondrical. On the contrary, I believe you improve daily. I could not help noticing to Zenobia this morning how buckish you were beginning to look in the silks and smalls.'[38]

'Arthur, your language is unpleasant to me, and there's a jaunty kind of slang in all you say which annoys me extremely.'

'Oh, you get so refined and romantic with living out of the world. I think now, if I could get you off to a fashionable watering-place – Mowbray, for instance – it would do you an incalculable deal of good, especially if you would consent to see company and dine at the ordinary.'

A slight rustle was heard in the recess, as of one feebly rising, and a voice murmured, 'I'll go!' But Zamorna drew his chair to the front of the sofa and held his arm out by way of barrier.

'Be orderly,' he said. 'Let us have no hysterical outbreaks at the thought of eating your dinner in the society of half a score

well-dressed, well-bred persons, one and all of whom would,
I'll be sworn, deem[39] themselves much more rationally than
yourself.'

'Have you entered into a conspiracy to send me to Mowbray?' asked the Earl.

'Don't know. I am thinking about it,' returned his son-in-law,
'especially if you don't shake off these solitary habits.'

'D—n you! None of your hectoring!' ejaculated Northangerland, with sudden alteration of tone; and he sprang erect on
the couch and sat glaring at his son-in-law, with eyes whose
gleam was visible even through the shade of gloaming.

Zamorna laughed.

'Now what new crotchet has come over you?' he asked.
'Why, you remind me of nobody so much as Louisa Vernon.
You've all her ladyship's theatrical starts and trances and
capricious changes of temper.'

After a moment's pause the Earl's wrath seemed gone, and
he sank down to his pillow as quiet as ever.

'Where is Louisa now?' he inquired. 'Is she still in your
custody?'[40]

'Yes, safe enough. I keep her at a little place on the other side
of the Calabar.'

'I thought she was at Fort Adrian.'

'No; she took such a conceit against the place that I thought
she'd fret herself to death out of sheer obstinate wilfulness. I
was obliged to remove her, but it was under threat of being
carried back again if she did not rest satisfied with her new
home.'

'Do you ever see her?'

'I saw her once, about three weeks since, for the first time
since my return from the Cirhala.'

'Are you sure it was the first time, Arthur?'

'Yes, sir. Why do you ask me so particularly? Surely you're
not jealous, old Puritan?'[41]

'I never had occasion to be jealous of you yet, but Louisa is
very pretty, and though I don't care a curl of your royal locks
for her now, I should not like to transfer her, even to your
Majesty.'

'Never fear, sir. I think your tastes and mine very much opposed. I never thought Vernon pretty. She's so dark and fierce.'

'Does she frighten you, Arthur?'

'Almost; especially when she turns sentimental.'

'Then the witch tries that method with you now and then. Now, confess the truth. Has she not made love to you sometimes?'

'Very furiously,' replied his Grace, laughing.

'Damn her!' muttered Northangerland. 'What did she say?'

'That she adored me – not so much, she stipulated, as she had once adored her divine Percy, for that was her first love – and, said the little Grecian-bred actress, laying her hand on her heart, "Your Majesty knows that the sentiments of a first love can be extinguished only with death."'

Zamorna mimicked Lady Vernon's tone and Percy nichered a faint laugh.

'Tell her,' said he, 'I am of the same opinion, and therefore, however frequently I may have been called aside by the songs [of] syren opera-singers, and by ardent eyes and raven hair, I still in the end remain true as steel to my first love, Robert King Esqre.[42] By the way, Arthur, does she ever strike you?'

'Strike *me*!' exclaimed Zamorna, in a tone of great surprise. 'Why, Percy, I never met with such a little coward anywhere. She always begins to tremble if I come near her, and if I lift my hand suddenly or speak sharply, she gives a nervous start and ejaculation.'

'Poor Louisa!' said the Earl, pityingly. 'I daresay she lives in hourly terror lest you should chop off her head some fine morning.'

'I have no doubt of it,' replied Zamorna. 'Once, I recollect, she was singing to me. She always contrives to introduce a song when I go, though I understand she sometimes says that Zamorna has no soul at all for music compared with Northangerland, or else she is certain she would have won her way out of captivity long since. Percy was so soft and gentle when she sang to him; there was nothing he would not grant her for the sake of "Angels ever bright and fair" or "Thou wilt not leave my soul in hell'. But as for Zamorna, he would stand by and hear the divinest harmony, the most heavenly melody, from morning till night, and yet when she turned round and looked at his face, it was as hard and austere as ever, and gave as little hope of freedom. However, as I was saying, on one occasion she had sung me "Hark 'tis the breeze of twilight calling" very exquisitely indeed, and without turning round for applause, which I dislike, she had struck softly into "The soldier's tear".[43] I am fond of ballads of that kind, and I came very near and leant over her. The little sorceress, as she sung, waved her head after her fashion, and in so doing loosened a curl. It escaped over her eyes and annoyed her. She shook it aside again and again, but it still fell back upon her brow. Now don't be jealous, Percy, when I say that I at last put out my hand and gently secured the tress with the comb from which it had escaped. Shall I tell you how she behaved when I did so?'

'Go on,' replied the Earl. 'You can tell me nothing which I cannot guess beforehand.'

'Well, then,' continued Zamorna, with a look which shewed how well he enjoyed the narration, 'as my finger touched her brow the music ceased. She let her hands pause on the piano keys, relax their position and drop silently on to her lap. Her voice died with a kind of falter. She looked down, and then she sobbed. "What's coming?" thought I, but I had not time to think long. By heavens, Percy, she stormed the fortress. My own 19[th][44] couldn't have done it better.'

'What do you mean, Arthur? Don't bring in any coarse metaphors.'

'Why, she jumped up, threw her arms round me, and kissed me to her heart's content.'

His Grace closed the anecdote with his most hearty laugh. If there had been light enough to see, his eyes at that moment were twinkling and flickering with most ineffable mischief, and his complexion coloured high with delight. Percy keckled too, very faintly.

'What did you do?' he asked.

'Why, what would you have done under the same circumstances?' retorted his son-in-law.

'Surrendered at discretion, to be sure,' answered North-angerland.

'But I did not,' replied the virtuous Duke, with emphasis. 'I just extricated my royal person from her grasp as soon and as quietly as I could, and then, making her sit down, I begged her to be composed. But that was out of the question. She flew into a most unimaginable fury, tore her hair from her head and shrieked like a rabid wild cat. I walked about the room, meantime, till she had exhausted herself, and then I made her get up from the carpet, on which she lay all her length, and taking a small Bible from my pocket, which I always carry there, I put it into her hand and told her to read aloud some passages in Paul's epistles[45] which I marked out for her. She shrieked and cried and stamped, but I compelled her to go through with it, and then when she had finished I thought she would have died with vexation. There was no word of reproach which she did not in her frenzy bestow upon me. I was unmanly, brutal, cold as ice, unfeeling as adamant. Then I was harsh, vindictive, barbarous, and after all, the tide turned, and she broke raving out about her adoration, her idolatry of me.

'I said at last I should be obliged to bleed her if she was not quiet, and to confirm my words produced a pen-knife. As soon as she saw the bright blade, and felt that I had got hold of her arm and was loosening her sleeve to commence operations, she sank mute and began to tremble.

'"My lord, my lord," she said, wiping her eyes and looking up as subdued as possible, "I am still now. I'll cry no more. Only don't hurt me! I shall die if you draw my blood. Forgive me, forgive me."

'She was absolutely as white as clay and shook like an aspen leaf. I put away my instrument, though I could not help smiling at her. I still shook my head. "People say you are wild," sobbed she, "but I am sure you are not. I never saw anything like gallantry about you yet. You seem to be impenetrable to love. Neither music, mirth, sentiment, vivacity, nor even an absolute declaration of intense passion can make the least impression on you. Even as you smile at me just now, there is something so scornful about your lips. I do hate you! I abhor you! I could kill you!" she said, grinding her teeth, and then, crying afresh, she added, "But still, still, I love you, too, till my heart aches as if it would break."'

'The accursed fool!' exclaimed Percy. 'The flimsy, witless idiot, throwing herself thus at the feet of a man whom, when I was in power, she was day and night tormenting me to murder.[46] So she has acted all through her wretched life. That D—l Vernon loved her and promised to marry her. She was flattered by a nobleman's homage and swore she loved him. I saw her, and turned her brain. She cut with Vernon and ran after me till, utterly weary, I jilted her and went beyond seas. She crawled back to Vernon, and coaxed the maniac till he married her. I came home in a few years, looked at my lady, and bewitched her again. She could not help herself. She would have gone with me to hell. For about ten years she stuck to me. At last I could endure the leech no longer: it absorbed my blood too greedily. I turned her over to a close jail and a hard jailer. There I thought I had her, for she hated you like death. The silly thing, mad with ambition and vanity, rushes from abhorrence into cupidity. Arthur, I'll hear no more about the person – curse her! If she comes near me, I'll tell Shaver[47] to speak to a druggist. I will, by G—d, and if I hear that you go to see her above once in six months or so, I'll alter my will.'

After a pause, the Duke remarked,

'I wonder, Percy, you never ask me a single question about your daughter – about Caroline.'

'I had forgot there was such an existence,'[48] uttered the Earl, feebly. 'Pray, is anybody taking care of her, or is she running quite wild?'

'She lives with her mother,' answered Zamorna, 'and I have furnished masters to teach her something, but they complain of her extreme volubility and wilfulness.'

'Do you ever look after her at all yourself, Arthur?'

'Now and then. She grows tall. I should think she must now be eleven years old.'

'Thereabouts. Will she be handsome?'

'No, scarcely, I think; that is, according to my ideas. She is like you, but it is such a strange likeness – almost bold and hard for a little girl. But she has pretty eyes and plenty of shining hair. She has, too, a kind of intuitive, perhaps hereditary grace. She likes notice too well, and has very uncurbed and ardent feelings. However, her head is naturally much stronger than her mother's, and her heart has no vice yet, whatever it may acquire.'

'Does she ever speak of me, Arthur? You know I've no genius for male friendships, and therefore I cling most tenaciously to the notion of being loved by a few women and children.'

'She speaks of nothing else,' replied Zamorna. 'At least, not in my hearing. Last time I called, I thought her looking a little pale and delicate, so I asked her if she would like to go with me to Hawkscliffe for a few days. She jumped up from the carpet where she was kneeling and gave a wild scream of delight, more like a liberated falcon than anything else.

'"Yes!" she said. "Yes, and then I can talk to you about Papa all the time, and perhaps if I am with you three or four days, I can persuade you to let me go and see him."'

'Well, she went to Hawkscliffe?' said Northangerland, evidently pleased with the subject and wishing his son-in-law to pursue it.

'Indeed she did; and I never saw any living thing in such a fever of enthusiasm as she was all the time she stayed. All the winter she had been cooped up at Fort Adrian, and this week of freedom seemed to transport her.

'One day, I recollect, she had followed me into the forest, and I took her to a lonely glade where I had great pleasure in wandering myself. It is green and wide, and some splendid trees tower in the midst of its sweep. Towards the centre there is a marble statue on its pedestal, which I ordered to be placed there. It is a female figure, standing as if in meditation, with downcast eyes and long drapery flowing to her feet. The features are not ideal.[49] I had them moulded from a bust now in the west somewhere; and when I look at that face, cold as it is, and mute and vacant of all answering expression, I feel always a revival of thoughts which were once bitter, but are now, from the lapse of time and the utter change of circumstances, mournfully sweet.

'The day was hot and clear and the sky of a deeper blue than is often seen in Angria. Caroline gazed at the statue, glowing in almost Italian sunshine. She placed a finger on her lips, and stood for a moment silent. Gradually, as if at the recollection of some remote idea, the tears swelled into her eyes. I lifted her face and asked what ailed her. "This is like St Cloud," she said, "and the gardens of Fontainbleau where I used to walk with Papa."

'On another occasion, she had been sitting in my study as quiet as a lamb. I was writing, and had told her to go and amuse herself at the window. For above two hours she had been so still that I had forgotten her presence. At last I heard her softly whispering something to herself in a very solemn cadence. It was getting dark, and I laid down my pen and looked at her. The window was open. She sat in the window-seat, her arm on the sill, and her head leaning upon it, intently gazing toward the Sydenham Hills which, at that point of view, look peaked and high. She half sung, half said:

> ' "Beneath Fidena's minster
>   A stranger made her grave,
> She had longed in death to slumber
>   Where trees might o'er her wave.

> ' "An exile from her country
>   She died on mountain ground,
> The Flower of Senegambia[50]
>   A mountain tomb has found.

> ' "Why did he cease to cherish
>   His Harriet when she fell?
> Why did he let her perish
>   Who had loved him all too well?

> ' "She called on Alexander
>   As she sickened, as she died,
> When fever made her wander
>   For him alone she cried.

    ' "But Percy would not listen,
        Would not hear when Harriet wailed,
    Where Europe's icebergs glisten,
        Far, far away he sailed.

    ' "But memory shall discover
        Her woes some future time.
    Ere long that haughty Rover[51]
        Shall darkly mourn his crime."

'Now, sir, what do you think of that?' continued Zamorna, as he finished this fragmentary lay.

'Where had she got it?' asked the Earl with hollow tone.

'She said she had read it in an old magazine, and had learnt it by heart because it had Papa's name in it.'

'Was she at all aware what it referred to?'

'Not in the least. She thought it merely an old song which by some strange chance echoed the name of Percy.'

Just then a chime was heard from another room as it struck eleven. At the same moment, the door opened, and a clear, narrow beam penetrated the almost total darkness in which the saloon was by this time shrouded.

'Will you come to supper?' said a pleasant voice, and the speaker, a young, graceful lady, raised her lamp and looked, smiling, towards the recess.

Zamorna turned to her, and his eye, as it caught her illuminated figure at the door, emitted a gleam of latent, lingering fondness. He got up without answer to her summons and followed her through the hall. As the lamp faded in the distance, a laugh was heard, happy but subdued. Then a door closed, and all was silent.

'They have left me!' moaned Lord Northangerland. A heavy sigh escaped his lips, and thenceforward the saloon was still.

'Arthur, what features were those you spoke of last night?'[52] asked the Earl of Northangerland suddenly, without any preamble, as he and his son-in-law sat by themselves in the afternoon shade of Selden House, the lawn and grounds being calm, and the garden-seat sequestered amidst the leaves of a vine.

His Grace of Zamorna suspended the whistle in which he had been for some time indulging, and looked round at his relative with an expression that seemed to say, 'What whim are you harping on now, old cock?' He made no audible answer, but presently began his whistle again, which he soon changed into a hum and then a song:

> 'Why do you linger and why do you roam?
> I'm feared o' the gude-wife: I dare not go home.
> What will she do, lad, and what will she say?
> She'll send me to hell, man, the Devil to pay.[53]

> 'Just cut her a stick, lad, and give it her well.
> Let *her* pay the Devil, let her go to hell.
> As I've settled my wife, go thee settle thy wife,
> What bother 'twill save thee it is not to tell.

> 'Down from the barracks
>   Came four bold dragoons.
> Every man swore roundly
>   And shouted "Blood and 'oons."[54]

> 'Each had a red coat
>   And each had a helm.
> These are the fellows
>   For holding the helm.'[55]

'What have you had since dinner, Arthur?' asked the Earl, with patient resignation of look and accent.

'Some coffee with Zenobia,' was the answer.

'And rum in it, eh?'

'Go and ask the Countess,' replied the polished monarch, and clearing his organ-pipes,[56] he struck off again:

> 'Your mama's in the dairy, your father's in the field,
> The moon's rising slowly as round as a shield.

Come through the back door, there's no one to see,
'Tis a sweet summer evening for courtship with thee.

'The dusk follows sunset with hush and with hum,
Now I'll tell you my secret tonight if you'll come.
Hidden and wondrous and dark though it be,
You shall know all if you'll hasten to me.

'Wave me no signals and glance me no signs,
Evening is wasting and daylight declines.
'Tis not in laughter or love that I crave,
Hasten, remember the promise you gave.'

One cannot live always in solitude. One cannot continually keep one's feelings wound up to the pitch of romance and reverie. I began this work with the intention of writing something high and pathetic. To the more perfect attainment of such an aim, I had withdrawn myself from the mercantile suburbs of Zamorna to a soft seclusion on the farthest verge of green Arundel. There, amid summer gales and July suns, I strove to lull myself into a sort of dream which should recall all the fair, the wild, the wondrous of the past.

I meant to tell how some had died the victims of strange treacheries and some of unutterable woe. I saw again the close of that fatal night which in Jordan Castle sealed such a doom – the fast pelting rain blown aslant by an autumn wind, the woods groaning through the grey twilight and shaking their heavy and sere boughs over glades all wet and dim; within the house, everything tranquil, quiet fires glowing in the saloons just before the time of lamplight, cheering with serene glimmer the dusk reigning everywhere. I seemed standing at the foot of a great staircase in the midst of profound silence and gathering gloom. The wind roared without. The rain beat upon the castle casements. Within, all lay in apparent peace. I heard a bell sound from a remote chamber above, then a distant but dreadful cry. What could it be?

Voices came, and footsteps; and with dismay, hurrying from

an inner chamber, stepped out an attendant figure, exclaiming, 'She is dying!'

Then awakened imagination painted before me the death-bed of Augusta di Segovia. I saw her struggling with yet unquelled energy against that death which she so hated, but which now so resistlessly overwhelmed. Struck at once in the prime of life and the fullest, deepest tide of voluptuous enjoyment, there her proud, strong form was stretched on the couch. Not still – madly struggling, so that no attendant could hold her, her almost masculine vigour as yet unweakened, but convulsed by mortal pains, one fine round arm flung out, the other across over her head, her noble features livid, her splendid hair, of which she was so proud, loosened, hanging down over the couch, spread wildly over her bosom, all in black masses, silken and sable and streaming. Clytemnestra[57] in every feature, a murderess and now murdered, she cannot die; life is still so full of temptation to her vicious nature, so rich in gratification for her warring appetites.

And where is Alexander, oh where?

There comes a change. Till now she has raved like a fury with blasphemous violence. She has been cursing her murderer, for she knows she is murdered. She has demanded life of God, and has blasphemed him when she felt mortal anguish collapsing all within. Then she has shrieked in superstitious horror as her polluted vices and sanguine crimes crowded black by her dying bed. The frenzy all at once is softened; it dies away in sorrow at one thought of Alexander. There her passions centre. She had loved him long; she is touched. Augusta turns on her bed, on her arms conceals her brow, and gushing tears and stifling sobs lament their eternal bereavement. Where is he? Where?

At last she looks up and commands all to leave her. The pain of the poison is over and with it the mental agony. She has nothing now to do but die. Strong in mind as in sin, she has power to calm herself, and to meet death at last like a martyr. She is by herself, laid straight on the bed, 'chilly, white, and cold',[58] with hair parted from her forehead and hands clasped

THE DUKE OF ZAMORNA

on her breast like the recumbent marble of a tomb. Two or
three lamps watch to see her die.

And now approaches the last scene. One that has ridden far
through a night of awful tempest comes at last; how brought,
by what strange impulse, and by what more than natural intelligence, it is vain to conjecture. All is calm and stately. No shriek
now, no curse or yell of blasphemy.

> The ante-room is hushed and still,
>   The lattice curtained close,
> The tempest sweeping round the hill
>   Awakes not its repose.

And there before him reclined his own Augusta, her beauty and
her splendour as mute as a dream. Her large eyes are open, but
they never move; her cheek ne'er changes, her robes never wave.
He calls upon her:

> AUGUSTA! But the silence round
>   Could give him no reply,
> And straightway did that single sound
>   Without an echo die![59]

But reader, why should I pursue this subject? All this has
been told you before in far higher language than I can use!
Revenons à nos moutons![60] Let it suffice to say that I found this
pitch far too high for me. I could not keep it up. I was forced
to descend a peg.

I grew weary of heroics and longed for some chat with men of
common clay. The following letter, which my landlady brought
in one morning whilst I was at breakfast, let me down easy. I
knew the hand directly. Its clear mercantile strokes and turns
revealed what had once been the calling of the writer,[61] though
now detested and disowned by him.

'Ah, Sir William,' said I half aloud, as I removed the franked
envelope, 'this epistle tells tales of the counting-house.'

Whilst munching my toast and sipping my coffee I read as follows:

Well, Townshend, if I can imagine what you are doing with yourself at a farmhouse in Arundel, may I be carbonadoed! 'Tis such folly going away to those back provinces. You might as well play Alexander Selkirk at once and locate yourself in the Ascension Isle.[62] After all, Zamorna, Adrianopolis and a segment of Arundel, Angria, are the only portions of this our oriental realm which boast other inhabitants than the fowls of the air or the beasts of the field.[63]

I shrewdly suspect you must be in love. Some fair belle of Zamorna has sent the shaft of Cupid through your heart and, like the wounded deer, you have fled away to the shades that you may lie and gasp out your soul in peace.

Can it be our quondam mutual acquaintance,[64] the fair lady of Kirkham Lodge, has done this? We were both, you know, smitten by that first glimpse of her cantering gaily on her palfrey down Hartford Dale. Ah, Townshend! that long purple riding habit, that graceful horsewoman's cap, so piquant, so dashing, set on a fair brow, a trifle on one side to shew the cluster of bright hair; that light whip, too, Townshend, and the hand that held it, lady-like and fairy-like, even through its glove! My poor fellow, I'm afraid you smart.

Do you know, I've seen her again? That remarkable man Hartford, just awaking from a torpidity of twelve months, has begun to shake his ears and dash out like a good'un. Nothing to be heard of but parties at Hartford Hall, horse-races and shooting matches under his lordship's special patronage, new exchange buildings at Zamorna, the first stone whereof is laid by the noble Baron, musterings of the Zamorna yeomanry at the back of their distinguished Commander, splendid county balls got up under Lord Hartford's direction, etc., etc., etc. At all these stirs he appears furbished up like a new brass warming-pan, with his chest padded and set out with stars and chains and orders, his waist strapped in, and his grizzling locks curled[65] and oiled like my Lady Stuartville's.

Some say all this resurrection of youth, casting of the slough, etc., is owing to success in a certain quarter, diddling of one too sublime to be named[66] – he! he! he! Townshend, my buck, how do you like that idea? Shall you and I go and try our fortune some fine day? I think we're every bit as good as the sunburnt, leather-skinned, frowning, poker-backed old dragoon that glorious creature is said to have smiled on.

Oh, there *is* no accounting for the caprice of women. However, I was talking about Miss Moore. It was at Hartford's county ball that I saw her. She came into the room late, being one of my Lady Lieutenant's party, who always, you know, is of the last, hindermost.

Bah – but Jane was in her glory! A murmur through the company warned me of her approach, and when I turned, there she was at the lower end of the long Assembly Room, standing quite erect, looking round on her first entrance to discover the faces of her acquaintance. A smile was ready on her lips and in her eyes. She knew she came to be courted and adored.

A group passed between me and her and I lost sight of her. In a few minutes she was visible again, with shining blue satin dress, her proud neck and falling shoulders as white as snow, half veiled, half revealed by a fall of dazzling yellow curls. She was in the act of being introduced to somebody and was curtseying low and smiling at the same time. The prig with whom my Lady Stuartville was making her acquainted bowed like a Frenchman, far projecting the swallow-tails of his embroidered blue coat; and as he ungloved his right hand and carried it to his breast, a couple of rings glittered on his little finger. This was one of the crack personages of the ball, being no other than the noble Ambassador, the gallant and illustrious Earl of Richton.

As Miss Moore passed him, he lifted up his eye-glass[67] and watched her progress up the whole length of the room. Scores of gentlemen thronged about her, and as she gave her right and left hands to them, she raised her head and nodded over their shoulders to the ladies who stood behind. She seemed to know all, and she would not omit one.

I wonder if she is afraid of female envy, or whether it is simple good humour which makes her so affable to everybody? But what do I talk about affability? The girl is no countess or duchess or queen. She has not even one drop of patrician blood in her veins. Her father is an Angrian lawyer, an understrapper of that profligate Hartford's, wealthy, but so void of all honourable principle that for aught I know he may have so carefully reared and so highly educated his splendid daughter with a view to seeing her one day high in office as Hartford's mistress. I like to take the worst view of human nature.

In a little while Miss Jane, as she passed along, at last reached her chieftan, and I thought I would observe how she conducted herself towards him. His Lordship was leaning against the arm of a sofa where Lady Thornton was sitting, talking to her and watching the play of that discreet young woman's dark ringlets and darker eyes, as she shook about her head and laughed and jested with him as naively and, of course, as innocently as possible.

'Good evening to your Lordship,' says Miss Moore, quite frank and open. Oh, that openness! It's a convenient thing, isn't it, Townshend? So interesting, you know! Such a mark of a pure mind which is not afraid of its thoughts being known to the whole world!

'Good evening, Miss Jane,' groans the magnifico in his profound bass, at the same time changing his posture as if on drill, and folding his stalwart arms afresh.

'Your Lordship will dance with me tonight?' says the beauty, looking sweet and languishingly bending her white neck on one side till the curls reposed gleaming on her shoulder.

'I will waltz with you, Miss Jane. Come.'

'Oh, waltz!' she exclaims with a pretty and certainly most affected scream. 'Not for worlds![68] I would waltz with General Thornton, or with the noble Ambassador there, if he would condescend to ask me, but with your Lordship, never!'

'The exception is flattering,' replied the mulatto.[69] 'You think me too handsome, too attractive. You would get confused.'

'Ah, and then your Lordship is a single man,' interposed Lady Thornton with all due simplicity.

'Yes, and people would say I wanted to marry you,'[70] says Jane, looking, as it appeared to me, ineffably silly.

'I am sworn a bachelor,' replied the haggard fop, trying to

smile but only girning, to use an expressive Angrian word. 'I am bound by the vows taken over sacrament and Bible never to ask a woman's hand again. If a woman asks my hand, it's a different thing; so come, Miss Jane.'

Miss Jane tittered a little bit, and then she says, with what seemed to me a very heartless smile,

'Will your Lordship favour me by being my partner in the next quadrille?'

'I will,' was the answer.

'But,' says she, assuming a tone of playfulness, and it might be all playfulness – for what, I know not; women are such deep dissemblers – 'but remember, if I perform the gentleman's part in asking, I will carry it on all through, and your Lordship shall be the lady.[71] I am a sailor, Captain Arthur Fitz-Arthur, commander of the *Formidable*, one hundred guns. Your Lordship is Miss Jessy Heathcote. I love you and intend to run away with you. You are very little and very slender, and you like me because I am so brave, and such a tall, handsome man – quite young, though not half as old as your Lordship, and not half as dark, and I never frown, at least not at ladies. I believe I am good-tempered. Now, Miss Jessy, will you dance with me? The musicians are beginning.'

I believe Hartford had not had the manners to hear her out. His eye kept wandering as she spoke, and when she had done, he suppressed a yawn and said he really feared, to speak seriously, he could not dance tonight; and then he threw into his demeanour a certain indescribable haughty peculiarity which effectually silenced Miss Jane.

She was not, however, in the least abashed. She threw a sly look out of the corner of her eye to Lady Julia, as much as to say, 'I can't get him. There's no sense in him,' and with her finger on her lip she walked away.

Five minutes after I caught a glimpse of her flashy satin robe, whirling past in a waltz; and there she was, smiling, her head thrown back, reeling round, round – in whose arms, do you think? Why, our sage Lord Lieutenant's.[72]

After the dance was over, I saw her again promenading the rooms with his Lordship, leaning on his arm so confidingly,

Townshend, and listening to his gallantries and replying to all his pretty compliments, evidently so smartly and readily, and with such a sparkle of her deep blue eyes. Oh, it was charming! Then, as she swept up and down the long rooms, waving her plume, dividing from her brow her tresses when they encroached, with a hand as white as – what? why, plaster of Paris, of course – she was all unconscious of the gaze of admiration drawn by her stately height, her perfect form and flushing bloom. Bah, Townshend! You and I know a thing or two!

Stuartville led her to a seat, and instanter up stepped, or rather rushed, two or three aspirants for her hand in the next quadrille. 'No, I am so tired,' says Jane; and she quietly leant back in her chair and looked as unaffected, as unflattered as possible. Her admirers gathered round in a circle, and Jane allowed them to talk, and answered them with all kindness and no coquetry. No, none in the least. She bantered a few, but she snubbed none. They might have been brothers, she was so cordial with them.

Just then another personage approached the group.

'Will Miss Moore admit me to the honour of being her partner in the Lancers?'[73] asked a quiet, high-bred voice, without any of the fluster into which the canaille put themselves upon such an occasion. And Miss Moore looked up; lo, her eyes met the blue embroidered swallow-tailed coat again, with a white silk waistcoat and a gold eye-glass set with brilliants; also, on the breast of the coat, a star and the august Order of the Rising Sun,[74] conferred not long since by royal favour and now sported, with the noble Ambassador's good taste, at an Angrian county ball.

Miss Moore looked. The Earl's aristocratic hand was held out. Don't suppose the Rose of Zamorna could resist this honour – no! She entrusts her fingers to that patrician palm, throws back a quizzical glance on her deserted trail, and my lord bears away his prize in triumph.

Pooh,[75] Townshend, to see the mandarin dancing, eyeing his partner all the while with that lofty, critical look of his, pointing his illustrious toe, laying one hand gently on his side, then on his breast, approaching and receding from Miss Moore, and smirking, meantime, confoundedly! After he had conducted her again to her seat, I saw him sidle away to Lord Hartford, and the two stood at the upper end of the ballroom, conversing in all friendly confidence. The Ambassador, every two minutes, te-he'd his snivelling laugh, and Hartford curled his lips into a half-sour, half-rakish smile.

I could not during the whole night satisfactorily unravel the puzzle of our heroine's character. That is, I could not perfectly ascertain whether she has, beneath her fluttering folly, a grain of sense, or whether it's all empty froth to the far-end.[76] If her apparent good-temper, affability and equanimity is genuine, natural, etc., why, she's a fool; she's one of no heart, no acute perceptions, no powers of intense attachment; she must be destitute of reflection, feeling and passion. If this smiling, pleasing outside, which shines unabashed on the proudest and cannot find [it] in its heart to frown coldly on the very meanest, if *this* be discerned, she's a knave, and I would not trust the depths of that mind, strong and original though it might be, which thus puts on character and acts a part at will.[77] Neither, Townshend, would I step within the influence of passions whose vortex is too deep and rapid to be exposed rapidly to view, but must be concealed by the curtain of an indifferent demeanour. If this view of her character be right, the organ of secretiveness[78] must be too large. A thousand thoughts must be ever passing in her mind which for worlds she would not utter. Nerves must often be acutely touched whose quiver of agony she must most jealously conceal, laughing all away as if she had not heard the jest or seen the look. Feelings warm and quick must be crushed, must be frozen as if they had never existed. Others must be assumed which she is incapable of fully expressing. She must be professing to see life through an unexaggerating but cheerful medium, when perhaps since earliest childhood she has gazed on its reflection in the magic mirror of imagination, seen the bright hues and divine forms that wizard imparts, the dazzling rush, the burst of sunshine, the wild waving of foliage in a glorious landscape, the opening of blue hollows in the sky, of wide moonlight sweeps of heaven pierced with stars; or she has watched clouds dimly close and storms gather and fall, with the dreary sighing of wind and the winter-like desolation which seems to forbid all thoughts of summer returning again.

Has the girl known this? Pooh! what a fool I am! She – butter-
fly, gossamer's web, floating feather of a stray bird of paradise!
She swallow her heart, gulp down her feelings, disown her identity, banish her real self and come as another and different existence before the world? I am dreaming! There never was a woman
who could do this, and there never will be. If there were, I would
be the last man to admire such a woman, or to trust myself to
her distorted, morbid affections.

Jane Moore is a handsome, easy-conditioned creature, who
thinks like a simpleton, as she is, that the whole world is pleasant
and good-tempered, everybody likes her and she likes everybody.
Ain't that the burthen of the song, Townshend?

Hoping you're not yet married to your landlady's serving-
wench, and that you'll take a friend's advice before you determine
on so important a step, I beg to remain,

Yours unalterably, unreservedly and unintentionally,
   William Percy, Baronet.
                        Zamorna, July 16ᵗʰ, —38.
            Charles Townshend Esqre. Mrs Chester's, Hill-foot.

I'm tired of solitude, thought I, as I dropped the letter. I'll go
back to the tents of Kedar. 'Tis but four miles to Beckford
and from thence I can take the coach either to Zamorna or
Adrianopolis. I want to make observations for myself. This
living out of the world[79] is abominable. I want to know how
the Angrians have settled with their King; whether he and they
are on good terms or not. I want to learn the reason of Hartford's sudden burst of gaiety. I want to find out why people
talk so much about Miss Moore. The girl is a fine girl, but I
saw nothing in her to create such an amazing sensation.

'Oh, Mrs Chester, make out your bill, and let me go.'

I had now been a fortnight without seeing the face of any
living creature except those of my landlady and her servant,
and of the half dozen milk fetchers who came morning and
evening to Hill-foot with their cans. Once, indeed, when I was
walking out, a nurse-maid had passed me in the fields, with two
fair little girls running before her – tiny animals in white, having
long flaxen curls hanging down on their necks; and I spoke to

them and gave them each some scarlet hips which I had been gathering from the hedge. And then, as they looked up at me and curtseyed, at the nurse's suggestion, like well-bred little ladies, one of them lisped with a very pure and not at all Angrian accent, 'Please, will you get me that rose?', lifting at the same time her large blue eyes to a briar-spray drooping above.

As I was plucking the flower (I like to humour children) a voice near me said, 'How do you do, Mr Townshend?'

It was a lady's voice, calm and soft; and when I turned in surprise, the speaker was within a yard of me – a young woman of stately mien, with a pale olive face and very black hair separated in two glossy folds on her forehead. Her eyes were grave and deeply set, her features good.

I took off my hat and bowed. I was standing in the presence of a greater personage than I had calculated on meeting.

'A lovely morning! Your Ladyship is wisely availing yourself of it,' said I.

'Yes,' she returned, and after a slight pause: 'Are you staying in the neighbourhood, Mr Townshend?'

'I am, madam, at Hill-foot.'

'Indeed! It will give me pleasure to see you at the Hall any day, though my lord is at present in town. Amelia,' (speaking to her little daughter, who was pulling my coat for another rose), 'don't be troublesome to Mr Townshend. I wish you good-morning, sir.'

And so with serene inclination of her head she glided on.

'Is Summerfield House in this neighbourhood?' I asked of the nurse-maid.

'Yes, sir, about three miles from here by the high road, but only a mile and a half by the private way through the plantations.'

'Does the Countess often walk out so slightly attended?'

'Very often, sir, when she is in the country, though she is considered high in town and keeps up a great deal of state.'

'I know she does,' thought I, 'and more betoken that she never spoke two words with me before. But some of your great folks make a practice of drawing these nice distinctions according to the air they breathe. When the Countess of Arundel sits in the drawing-rooms of Frederick's Place in Adrianopolis, there is not a haughtier woman breathing, nor one more attached to the forms of state. It seems she unbends here.'

And I looked at her again as her figure lessened in the distance. The path was winding, and she slowly traced the mazes, with head gently bent in the perusal of a book. Now and then she looked up, and turned an anxious, yet smiling, eye towards her children. She spoke once or twice with a mild voice of caution. Lord! I could hardly acknowledge her as the same woman whose haughty plume always waves foremost in court drawing-rooms and state dinners, and whose glance, when amongst her equals, ever seems to say, 'I was born a princess; do not approach me.'

I did not avail myself of her Ladyship's invitation, because really I am not at all used to the society of either Arundel or his Countess. They are not of my set. She considers me, no doubt, as a depraved, half-crazed sort of being, and he regards me as just nothing at all. If I pass Lord Richton, now, in any circumstance of pomp or splendour, his Lordship and I always exchange a glance, or a nod at least; but the Chevalier, when mounted on his snow-white charger, perhaps curbing it at his sovereign's side, would as soon think of bowing to a turnspit as to me. His gallant Lordship has no literary turn,[80] and in his eyes I am nothing more than a small, mean man of doubtful rank and eccentric habits, with whom he has not a single idea in common. Well, I care as little about him as he does about me, and so our accounts are even.

I've just asked Mrs Chester if she can get a boy to carry my carpet-bag as far as Beckford. She sent Susan across the fields to fetch one; and then, good-bye to reverie and solitude, and away to life and cities again!

Reader, I will close my present work with another letter from Sir William Percy, which I found lying in the post-office at Beckford, awaiting my arrival there.

Townshend,

I am writing to you in the midst of the most confounded bustle of packing etc., for I am going off somewhere to serve my country in an official capacity. You shall hear how the matter came about.

I was sitting down as quietly as could be to a cup of excellent chocolate, when my morning batch of letters came in. I gave a careless glance towards them, thinking I'd finish reading the newspaper and sipping the beverage before I examined into their contents, which I opined were of no great importance, when lo! my eye caught the glance of a broad red seal, and when I looked a little nearer it was stamped with the arms of Angria!

'The D—l!' I said aloud, and hastily turning it to look at the frank, I saw a strange hieroglyphic, scarcely referable to the characters of any known language, but which I knew by instinct to denote H. F. ENARA!

Now it happened that that morning I was breakfasting at Girnington Hall, having stayed there all night after being present at a party which was given the evening before. Consequently Sir William Thornton sat opposite to me, trifling with a pound or two of ham and some half dozen or so of eggs.

'A grand hay-day!' says the General, turning half round in his chair and staring out with all his eyes through the open window towards the wild clumps of wood waving in that savage park of his, whose shade hardly allowed you to see the morning sunshine or to feel the fresh early breeze which was tossing their antediluvian arms. I fear I was hardly civil enough to answer his remark, for my attention was wholly absorbed in the important letter whose outside I still continued to contemplate.

'There's naught I like to hear as weel as t'craws, first thing of a summer morning,' observed the college-bred[81] Baronet again.

'Very musical sound, sir,' says I.

'I allus thowt so!' replies the General, and rising, he lifts the sash a bit higher and puts out his sandy pate through a screen of the roses about the casement, in order that he may obtain a better view of his favourites wheeling and screaming in the air above their rookery of firs. Coming back to the table, he exclaims,

'What the mischief is Julia doing that she does not come down?

I wonder onybody can fashion to lig i'bed such a morning as this!'

Just then, the door slowly uncloses and in saunters my lady in a stylish undress, scarce awake, looking as slovenly, as lazy and as handsome as possible. The General shakes his head and sets her a chair.

'Well, Thornton,' begins her ladyship, 'it's only nine o'clock.'

'Three hours too lat', replies Sir William. 'I wor up at six.'

'But Percy there has only just come down, I am sure,' says she. I nod assent and inquire if her ladyship has passed a good night.

'No,' says she, 'I had such an odd dream. I thought I was sitting in the drawing-room there one afternoon, and a servant came in and told me a gentleman wanted to speak to me, and so I thought I said he was to shew him into the library, and when I went there, I saw a very tall gentleman sitting at the table writing –'

'Come, come, Julia,' interrupts the General, 'tak yer breakfast. Ne'er heed dreaming and sich nonsense.'

'Well, but I must finish it,' responds madam. 'And so, Sir William, I asked him what he wanted, and he looked up, and I was so frightened! His face was exactly the very picture of Lord Northangerland's. It had just his kind of hair.'

'That must be a wig, madam, I suppose,' says I, 'for I understand his Lordship doesn't sport much natural decoration of that sort.'

'Well, it had his forehead and nose and eyes, and I am sure, whatever people say about him, he is exceedingly handsome.'

'I often think womenfolk hev varry little sense,' remarks the General. 'It may be neither polite nor civil-like to say so, but I am sure they are far away sillier nor men i' many things.'

'Thornton, will you give me an egg?' asks Julia.

'Tak' it, lass, and let's hear no more of your havers about dreams. I know nowt more childish nor telling ower senseless cracks like them.'

'Eh, Colonel! what's that letter?' exclaims Julia, suddenly catching a glimpse of my still unopened despatch. 'May I look at it?' and her little white hand was on it in a moment. She paused, however, and looked at me for consent before she took it.

I don't much admire her Ladyship. I always think she's something of a simpleton. However, at that instant she looked a very pretty one, her Spanish eyes just waking into vivacity and fixed half interestingly, half smilingly on me, her taper fingers fastening on the letter.

'You may read it,' said I, as if it were my death-warrant.

'Is it from the Duke?' she said in a low tone, and the idea evidently struck her childish mind with awe. She paused before she broke that imposing broad seal. She half cracked it, then, with characteristic indecision, 'Nay!' said she, tendering it back. 'I dare not! He'll perhaps get to know that I have been opening his letters.'

'You need not fear, madam. That billet doux has General Enara's frank on it.'

'Oh!' exclaims her ladyship. 'Then away with scruples! The bandit and I are good friends. I've promised that he shall be my second when Thornton goes.'

She broke the seal and read:

'Lieutenant Colonel Sir William Percy is requested to repair to Adrianopolis immediately. General Enara has authority to intimate to Sir W. P. that it is in contemplation to appoint him to some situation where his merits may be fully appreciated. General Enara begs to congratulate Sir William on his flattering prospects. The General is of opinion that Sir William has a chance of being sent further into the interior than any of His Majesty's troops have as yet penetrated. The General considers that in procuring this commission for Sir William he has taken the best and most acceptable means of testifying his approbation of the gallant and gentlemanly manner in which Sir William discharged the duties of his late arduous station at Cuttel-Curafee.

'FOREIGN OFFICE, ADRIANOPOLIS'.

'There, you *are* honoured,' said Lady Julia as she finished the letter. 'But does the General really mean that you are to be sent back again to those horrid regions where it is so hot and where the rivers are haunted by amphibious blacks instead of alligators?'

'I'm afraid his letter will bear no other interpretation, ma'am,' returned I.

'And will you like it? He speaks as if it were a reward.'

'Whisht, Julia!' says the General, who meantime had been

listening to Enara's billet with a sufficiently significant smile.
Then, turning to me, 'Well, Colonel, ya mun set off direct for
t'capital at ony rate. You sall have my horses as far as Zamorna,
and then ya can tak' t'mail.'

'But will he like to go?' says Julia. 'I think the Colonel scarcely
looks strong enough for such a climate. Wouldn't it be best,
Thornton, to write an answer to Enara and say he'll take a few
days to consider it?'

'Julia, my woman,' returns Thornton, 'go thee upstairs, put on
thy hat and shawl, and then come down; and when I've seen Sir
William off I'll tak' thee a drive as far as Cheshunt i' t' phaeton.'

Julia left the room, and Thornton proceeded to bustle me
away with all expedition,[82] for, you know, I'm somewhat dila-
tory, Townshend, especially when other people seem fussy. For
the present, good-bye. I'll write you the result of my journey in
another letter.

Yours, W. Percy.

In a few days I received the continuation of the affair thus:

Townshend, my chuck, you and I ought to be very good
friends. There's no one to whom I write so many letters or
communicate so many secrets as yourself. Perhaps a similarity in
our destitute conditions and vagabond propensities has produced
a sort of sympathy. We do love each other, don't we, Townshend?

Howsumdever, here I am at Adrianopolis, and I've had my
audience at the Foreign Office and another at the Home Office,
and I'm as uplift as a midden-cock upon pattens. You shall hear
how I proceeded.

Having left Girnington with a last look at my fair, pitying
hostess, who came running down the oak staircase into the old
dark hall to bid me good-bye, after a farewell squeeze at her
pretty little hand, and a long romantic gaze on her blooming face
smiling at me from under the brim of the bonnet she had just
donned, after asking for a tress of her raven ringlets as a keepsake
and being refused, after promising to think of her when I should
be lying far away on the soldier's bed of reeds and looking up at
the moon of the desert sailing high above the blue Benguela,

after these things, Townshend, did I mount the good spunkie saddle-horse which your all-but-father[83] proffered to lend me, and away I dashed among the woods, all rushing in the morning wind and glancing in the morning sunshine. In a quarter of an hour I had passed Edwardston Hall at full gallop, with my valet behind me. My spirits were at such an unusual pitch of elevation that I could not resist the impulse of reining up at the grand gates and just doffing my beaver, giving it a walt in the air, and catching it again with a loud huzza of scorn.[84]

Then I broke away again and scarcely ever slackened gallop till I reached the suburbs of Zamorna. I was just thundering in at Adrian Road when behold, a gig just before me, smacking along like a Doverham collier in a brisk gale, one man in it, in browns and stones,[85] all bright, complete and slap-up.

'Ho,' thought I, 'this is the very chap I should like best to meet me at this identical moment.'

It was our Edward. Dashing my spurs into the beast's sides, I came up to him with a spang. There were plenty of people on the causeway, ladies etc., for this is a fashionable street, but I was at such a pitch of effervescence I did not care who saw me. Off again then with my castor! Hurra, my hero! Lift it up! I'm on the high road for promotion! G—d d—n the ledger! Charge for a Field-Marshal's baton! Hip, hip, hip, hurrah!

'Fire and fury! Butter and brimstone! What the devil have we here?' shouts 'Brandy and Water'.[86] 'I'll settle matters!'

Up goes Ned's arm. Whizz! His whip cuts the air, but my bonny bay springs to one side and we both miss it within a straw-breadth. Striking sparks from the stones, I'm off again, rising in my stirrups. Ajax and I vanish, waving a white handkerchief as a parting token of fraternal affection.

I think it was just about sunset when the mail entered Adrianopolis, and without waiting to put myself into any kind of order, but just sweating, puffing, disarranged and travel-stained as I was, having my coat powdered with the white dust of the Adrianopolitan road which, you know, traverses with a broad, bleached line as white as milk the whole region of green fields and heavy dark woodlands through which it runs, just, I say, in this predicament did I spring from the top of the Oriental

Mail in the yard of Westwood Tavern and, instantly hiring and entering a cab, order it to convey me then and there to the Foreign Office.

The room was darkened into which I was shown on my arrival, and two tapers were twinkling through the doubtful dusk which had settled on every object. A pale, undersized man sat at a desk, beside him a hat and gloves.

'Sir William Percy?' said he, rising with a bow.

'Yes, sir. Can I see General Enara?'

'General Enara is not here. General Enara has withdrawn, sir. The regular office hours are over. You call late; you should have been more punctual.'

'I've ridden express since I received General Enara's despatch,' said I, considerably chagrined, and I sat down and began to wipe my forehead with my handkerchief.

'You will do well,' continued the pale, provoking, under-sized man, 'you will do well to come at an earlier hour when you have any business to transact with General Enara. However, I am here. I can probably supply the General's place. What have you to say, Sir William?'

'That it is very warm travelling, sir,' I replied, 'and very dusty roads, but charming weather for the hay, charming. Don't you think so, Mr Warner?'

'Come, come,' replied the busy, interfering little fellow, with more calmness than I had expected. 'Come, come, Sir William, drop that affected strain of yours. You ought by this time to be above it. I am surprised that you should have business with General Enara concerning which I have received no intimation. I thought you were in the country on furlough. Have you been recalled?'

'Not exactly, sir.'

I paused. I was not going to entrust the imperious, all-controlling little Bonaparte with another word. What business had he at this time of night in the Foreign Office? After a few minutes' mutual silence, he rose.

'I was on the point of retiring,' said he, 'when you were announced. Are you provided with apartments in town?'

He said this with a sort of stately politeness.

'No, sir, but I can soon get them.'

'My carriage is at the door,' he continued. 'If you will step into it, I shall be happy to escort you to Warner Place. Mrs Warner will be glad to see you.'

I bowed to him, muttered my acknowledgements for civility, which I had not at all expected, but declined it. He did not seem vexed. He can be very imperturbable when he likes. By this time, he had drawn on his gloves and, taking his hat, he made a slight indication of the head, murmured a good evening, and departed.

I was glad to be rid of him. Now, thought I, I will see my old, grim commander if I can only catch him. I entered my cab again, and ordered it to drive to Calabar Street, where the Tiger[87] had his den.

I reached it, but my difficulties were not yet over. It was with a world of entreaties, threatenings, bullyings, that I got his people to carry my name up. He was dining, they said, and not to be disturbed; the General admitted nobody at that hour; I must call to-morrow, etc. I prevailed at last. A footman went up with my card, and in two minutes returned with an invitation that I was to follow him.

I found him in a rather grand room, with dark walls and five or six pictures, wild Salvator scenes.[88] It was only half lighted, with four large wax candles on the table which served to illuminate the centre but left both sides in obscurity. There were two magnificent chandeliers – royal gifts, both of them, as I afterwards understood – but neither of those were kindled. The General was at his dessert. He had no company except the members of his own family,[89] persons whom I had indeed seen by glimpses before, but never obtained a full view of; four, I think, all girls, with white dresses of gauzy muslin, bronzed skins and dark, brilliant Indian eyes. The three youngest were strange, sunburnt creatures, who seemed to have as much idea of polite manners as the most uncouth little Angrian you could pick up among the Howard moors. The eldest, who might be about thirteen, was of a paler, clearer complexion, less scorched. She restrained the fire of her glances somewhat, and her raven hair, instead of hanging in savage elf-locks,[90] was arranged in long jetty curls. She had been educated a trifle, I think. I should doubt if the others know their letters.

Well, the Tiger got up when I entered and, waving me to a chair which stood vacant at the table, asked if I had dined. I said 'Yes!' which was a lie, for the fact was, I had no appetite for dinner, and so didn't want to be bothered.

'But you'll drink wine,' said he. 'Maria,' (speaking to his eldest girl) 'pass the decanter of Shiraz towards Sir William.'

Maria did so, but a smaller cub, rearing itself upon the bar of its chair, pushed it back, saying with an odd, un-English accent that wine was *sacré* – it was not for heretics.[91]

'Maria, take your sisters to their attendants, and go yourself to the Senora Grey,' said the General.

Maria rose, called, 'Giulietta', 'Francesca,' and 'Gabriella', and with a profound curtsey at the door, and a lingering, solemn gaze at me, vanished with her wild charge[s] from the apartment.

'I see you've lost no time, Colonel,' says my Commander, glancing with approbation at my fair, clean face and elegantly arranged habiliments.

'I was at Girnington Hall when your summons reached me this morning,' says I, 'and I'm here tonight.'

'Hum! Very well. Now, you want to know what irons are in the fire for you, I suppose?'

'Yes, sir.'

'Well, you shall learn all in time. Final arrangements are not yet completed, plans are not fully ripe, for the expedition I hinted at eastward. You must curb your impatience for a month or so yet. Meantime, there is a trifle to be done abroad, a sort of diplomatic affair in which our master wished to make you useful. I know this kind of work will not be so congenial to your disposition as the more honourable service of the field, but still I have that opinion of you, that I think whatever task is to be done, provided it be such as a gentleman may without reproach put his hand to, you will not scruple to bend your back to the burthen. If I thought otherwise, I'd despise you, sir! D—n the fools that stand paltering about their own frivolous inclinations while the King's work is lying at the wall.'[92]

I answered naught to this tirade, but smelt at a vinaigrette and waited for more. He now bid me draw in my chair, pass the bottle, and he would explain matters to me. Thereupon followed sundry revelations of state which it would ill suit my new character of diplomatist to reveal. However, I'll just tell you that in a week's time I shall be in Paris – not with any public splendour and stir, but merely as a private individual. They've trusted me, however, and William Percy will not be such a fool as to betray them, because in so doing he would betray himself.

A third letter from the Baronet shall conclude this work:

Manhood is the best portion of human life after all. My childhood and early youth were poisoned with bitter feelings I shall never forget – no, never! I am unfettered now. I see my steep path clearly, and I have got strength to climb. It is no labour to me; it is a delight to mount up, up, clinging to every projecting stone, grasping at every tough root and wild stem of heath, gazing at the far-above, cloud-piercing summit. When I do reach it, what will strained sinews, weary limbs, dizzy brains be then? I shall forget all when I look down at the unbounded prospect. Once or twice during the ascent I have turned and for an instant seen the green stretch of plains, the grand overclouding of groves, the wide blue flash of waters, but I dared not gaze long. O! what will it be when I see it all?

I knew nothing of this glorious hope six years ago. I thought only of gaining reckless freedom where I might live without the crushing insolence of tyranny. I thought of enlisting as a private soldier and hardly had a wish to rise above the ranks. When Edward and I were in penury, kept chained together by want, and abhorring each other for the very compulsion of our union,[93] I used to endure worse torments than those of hell. Edward overwhelmed by his strength and bulk. He used his power coarsely, for he had a coarse mind, and scenes have taken place between us [of] which remembrance to this day, when it rushes upon my mind, pierces every nerve with a thrill of bitter pain no words can express. I always affected indifference to his savage, hard, calculating barbarity, and I always will affect indifference to it to my dying day. But if there be a power superior to humanity, that power has witnessed feelings wringing my heart in silence which will never find voice in words.

However, I am discovering my own strength now. It reminds me of a higher destiny, and I am leaving the dreary path of my youth far below. If I had died in that midnight desolation, in that cold solitude of feeling – but Fate spared me.

I tell you, Townshend, that I will never marry till I can find a woman who has endured sufferings as poignant as I have done, who has felt them as intensely, who has denied her feelings as absolutely and, in the end, has triumphed over her woes as successfully. A woman so gifted, with youth and refined education, would attract my love far more irresistibly than the beauty of Helen or the majesty of Cleopatra.[94] Beauty is given to dolls, majesty to haughty vixens, but mind, feeling, passion and the crowning grace of fortitude are the attributes of an angel.

Amidst all the vicissitudes of life it has been my lot to see one such woman,[95] and only one. She, indeed, added fine symmetry of form and transcendent beauty of feature to the interest of a noble spirit and disastrous destiny. How often have I looked at her with wonder and absorbing sympathy! Imagination in her had to struggle through no dull intervening obstacle to shew its light divine. That face offered a clear medium; her eyes were large, with dark orbs and long romantic lashes. Sorrow in them was doubly wild. They flashed frenzy when the tears gushed into them, and joy, hope, love, looked in their expressive smiles, so soft and touching. She never smiled on me, however, nor ever wept for my sake, and whether her fair image be still lingering in a world that was not worthy of her, or whether she lies asleep amidst holy bounds which even sacrilege would hardly profane, it imports little to me to know. It is enough for me to have seen her once, and after that to carry the vision of her pale inspired face to my deathbed.

Townshend, you'll never dare to twit me about what I've written above, but if you do, I've an answer ready. How do you know whether the sentimentality is in jest or in earnest? Ain't it very probable that I may be bamming you by doing a bit in the soft line?[96]

Well, to proceed. I'm at Doverham now, as the date of my

letter will shew, and tonight I embark for Calais on board the *Little Vic* steam-packet, so named, let it be remarked *on passant*, after the famous heiress, Miss Victoria Delph, whose half-million is said to have turned more than one peer's coronet, and a great earl's bald head and magnificent monarch's crowned one into the bargain. You heard the story about that royal spree, and the young man of prepossessing appearance being found chanting a serenade one wet night under little Vic's chamber window. Also another tale, still more remarkable, which is very popular in the Adrianopolitan court at the present moment, concerning the discovery made by Miss Delph's maid, who found a poor lunatic of the name of Flower[97] – in other words, a peer of the realm – very much intoxicated, sitting on the top step of a flight of stairs which led direct to little Vic's apartment, and when questioned as to his motives for being there, the noble Lord hiccuped out that his intentions towards Miss Delph were perfectly honourable.

The eve of my departure from Adrianopolis being come, I fell, as I usually do on such occasions, into a melancholy mood. All the excitement of preparation was over. That morning I had taken my last instructions from Enara, and the whole afternoon had been spent in a long interview with the Premier at the Treasury. One step only remained to be taken, and the time was not yet arrived for that. I was alone now in my hotel. It was near sunset. The summer day, after a long flight, was quietly folding its wings of gold and setting like a bright bird on the remote hills which swell to a ridge between Zamorna and Adrianopolis. Some flowers which stood in the casement had closed their petals, and the sun, pausing, as it seemed, before its departure over the purple summit which was soon to conceal it, shed through the myrtle leaves and geranium blossoms a crimson glory which was seen chequered by leaf and stem on the opposite wall.

In evening silence, a three-legged stool, a fatted calf, or even the Marquis of Harlaw[98] might think; and as I walked to and fro in my parlour, now facing the refulgent west window, and now a solemn picture of old times against the wall, I also thought.

'Well, Percy,' suggested the inward voice with which we all converse at times, 'to-morrow thou wilt leave this land for a foreign shore. Thou art bound on a far journey, and hast in thy keeping the mandates of a ministry and the secrets of a king. Bethink thee now, hast thou naught to do before the farewell word is spoken? The farewell word! Percy, to whom wilt *thou* speak it? This is a great city – a capital! Surely, amid all its wide squares, its long streets, its thousand houses, there may be one who will feel heart-touched if thou leave without a token. Is there no fair gentle ladye[99] bound to thee in love who, every night when thou art gone, will send her deepest aspirations after thee?'

'Monitor, there is none!'

'Percy, think again. Surely some one breathes who will wish thee well, clasp hands with thee kindly, when it is known that thou must leave Angria on a dangerous and mysterious mission, it may be for ever.'

I thought and thought, and all seemed vacant. I could not call up to imagination the face of one bound by any ties to love me. At last, the inward voice whispered a single name. I believe I smiled with hollow doubt at the suggestion. Nevertheless, I acted upon it.

However, before that interview could take place, one last act of business remained to be performed, for which the hour appointed was now come. Before I left Mr Warner that afternoon he told me I had now in my hands every necessary document except a single paper which would be delivered to me at eight o'clock that evening at the Zamorna Palace. It was eight now. As I left my hotel the sun just dropped behind the hills. I can't bother myself with describing to you the transit in a dashing barouche through two miles of streets to the Palace, nor the first entrance there, nor the ushering up staircases and through galleries to the vicinity of royalty. Imagine me at last in an ante-room, standing alone, while the usher is gone to announce me. He soon returns and says,

'You will be sent for presently, Sir William,' bows, closes the door, and I am again *solus*.

By this time it was dusk. The great royal pile seemed unusually still, and when I looked from the row of windows at the end of the room, I saw, spreading up to the walls, a wide garden planted with thick shade, and here and there, dimly visible at openings, the pallid gleam of sculpture. It was too dark to see much, and I soon grew weary of the sombre trees.

I walked about the room. I paused and listened. There was nothing to be heard; neither step, voice, nor whisper. Do they make the walls of palaces thick, Townshend, that the ongoings of the royal inmates may be concealed from one another? As yet I had not been informed whether it was from the hands of some minister I was to receive the document in question, or from those of the King himself. What a tantalizing position of alternate expectation and doubt for an ambitious courtier like me!

There was a sound at last – the smooth parting of folding doors. Some one entered.

'You will attend me, Sir William, if you please,' said a treble voice, and I saw before me a silken page with hair parted on his forehead like a girl.

The folding doors led into a long passage, softly carpeted, with lamps shining along the whole length. I followed the jackanapes sent to summons me, and ere long stood at the threshold of another pair of folding doors, whose polished dark panels reflected the lamps so brightly that at first I mistook it for an immense mirror.

'Are you conducting me to his Grace?' I asked the page, stopping him when his hand was on the door-lock.

'I don't know,' said he. 'I was ordered to bring you here.'

'By whom?'

'By Lord Hartford,' was the answer.

'Lord Hartford!' I exclaimed, somewhat astounded, you may be sure. He was the last person[100] one would have expected to have the power of ordering in Zamorna Palace. I hate that Lord, Townshend.

Before I could speak my surprise, the doors had rolled back and poured upon me a flood of light. When the dazzle passed away, I found I was within a large apartment, the entrance of which had immediately closed behind me. It was all shut close: the heavy curtains of deep crimson were dropped over the windows, though it was yet twilight, as if for midnight conclave. Enormous wax lights were blazing upon the table, over the mantle-piece, and in every recess. It might have been lit up for some regal festival. I looked round, expecting to see the flash of diamonds and the waving of plumes. Nothing of the sort.

Four plain figures sat at the centre table, looking into each other's faces with anxious, worrying eyes, and besides them not a living creature was visible. Only, on the rug, slumbered an enormous dog. One, who sat erect in his chair, with his arm thrown over the back and his legs crossed, I recognized as Lord Arundel. Another, who bent over the table and wound up a gold repeater with a hand that trembled almost too nervously to admit of the operation, was, beyond contradiction, Warner Howard Warner Esqre. The third, who turned to the side-board and filled a goblet of crimson wine, which was drunk afterwards in solemn silence, as if to the memory of the dead, bore the indisputable lineaments of H. F. Enara. But who was the fourth – that gaunt man leaning both his elbows on the table and his wolfish cheeks upon his spread palms, rolling his wandering eyes with a disturbed ghastly glitter from one face of his associates to another, contracting his forehead with a scowl, and dissevering his lips with a furious grin? That, Townshend, was Lord Hartford!

I looked for another face, but in vain. The Duke of Zamorna was not there.

Three of the statesmen shook hands with me as I advanced to the table. Hartford never stirred. I took my seat. There was silence for a little while. It seemed evident to me that some strange kind of scene had taken place just before my entrance, and when I looked round there were tokens that the Duke *had* been there. There was his arm-chair at the head of the table, and his pencil-case lying on an open map.

'Is he returning?' I asked Lord Arundel in a whisper.

Arundel was going to answer, when a sudden interruption of the silence prevented him.

'Well,' broke forth Lord Hartford. 'Well, you've all seen his d—d injustice to-night. You've all beheld me insulted and repulsed and trampled on, and none of you had the manliness to take my part – not one!'

'My lord, your conduct is unprecedented,' said Mr Warner. 'No ministry could have taken the step you solicited His Majesty to command my government to take without tarnishing its honour. My word was pledged. Sir, was I to recede from that? And if His Majesty rejected your proposal in a pointed and bitter manner, what else had you to expect?'

'It is infernal injustice!' retorted Hartford. 'I, who am the representative of one of the oldest families in Angria and whose whole worldly interests were staked in the country before Zamorna drew breath, I solicit an appointment of trust abroad, and am rejected with harsh sarcasm, while a parvenu officer of Hussars[101] is elevated to the post over my head. By heaven and all that's holy, I'll make him grind his teeth in remorse for this last thrust. I'll tell him that [which] will burn to the quick every nerve in his whole proud d—d blasted carcase!'

'Did you hear that, gentlemen?' said Enara, with a grim smile. 'Mind you mark it, for such eloquence is scarce. It is not often to be heard out of a lunatic asylum.'

Hartford glared at him, snatched his card-case from his pocket, and threw a challenge[102] to him on the spot.

'I'd desire no better sport,' growled Enara, coolly taking up the card and thrusting it within his waistcoat. 'It's just the chance I've long been looking out for, my lord; and the charging pill[103] that I shall administer will purge of lust and lunacy at once.'

I could have kissed the old grim Tiger, his words came so pat to the purpose. These words were echoed by a low laugh of cold and bitter sound. It came just from behind my chair, and at the same moment I was sensible of a hand strongly grasping the chair-back. I had no need to look round: I knew who was there.

He began to speak in a voice whose tone reminded me of the night before the battle of Leyden.[104] On that night, he had given me some orders in person, and I had never heard it since.

'Henri, you will not exhibit[105] that dose which you have so ably prescribed. A duel with an insane person will by no means add to the number of your honourable exploits, and, as my Maker shall judge me, I believe that Lord Hartford is not in a sound frame of mind. At this moment his eye shews all the uncertain glare of derangement.'

Lord Hartford looked up at him. His nostril quivered with passion, but he suppressed it.

'Your Majesty is opening your second campaign against me,'

said he with forced calmness. 'And you have now given me the clue to your system of tactics for the season. I am to be studiously excluded from employment in public, and denounced in private as a raving madman.'

'If you had said "confined in private" you would have expressed my intentions more correctly,' replied his Grace.

Hartford muttered something under his breath, and then he rose and walked round the table to the Duke.

'I have a secret to communicate to your Majesty,' said he. 'I should like to ease my mind of it before our council breaks up for the night.'

'I do not wish to hear it,' returned Zamorna with haughty indifference. 'Madmen often have strange crotchets.'

Hartford pressed nearer. The Duke did not retire, but he erected his lofty head and threw into his countenance more scorn than a horse could stomach.

'But I must confess all to your Majesty,' said Hartford.

He stepped a little behind him, placed his lips to his ear, and muttered, in a fiendish kind of undertone, some sentences which took about two minutes in delivering.

I watched Zamorna intently, and so did the rest. Whether it was that he was conscious our eyes were fixed upon him and he was resolved not to let us see that the communication affected him, or that he really took it with indifference, I know not, but not a muscle of his face moved. His features remained fixed in the same cold, haughty smile to which they were moulded before. However, he lost all colour. When Hartford finished the whisper and stepped back from that close proximity, his monarch's cheek was rather livid than ruddy.

'I am flattered by your confidence, my lord,' he said, with precisely the same sneering accent he had used all along, 'and will take an early opportunity of rewarding it by some corresponding token of regard. I pity the aberration of reason and the taint of morals which puts imaginations of that sort into your head. But courage, my lord. With proper attention from keepers and mad-doctors, you may yet do well.'

'Good evening to your Grace,' replied Hartford, grimly smiling.

'Good evening, my lord,' said his sovereign, with a smile equally grim, 'You and I will meet again yet.'

'Aye, in hell!' retorted Hartford, as he turned on his heel and left the room.

I noticed that Enara heaved an unusually profound sigh when he was gone, and directly afterwards the worthy Tiger remembered that he had a piece of business to transact that night which could on no account be neglected. He was rising to go and look after it when His Majesty placed his hand on his shoulder and so restrained him in his seat.

'No, Henri, that move shall not pass. I know what piece of business you allude to, but if you interfere in it, remember this: I shall consider it the unkindest cut[106] you ever gave me.'

'I am not accustomed to dispute your Majesty's commands,' said Enara, 'and so I shall hold my hand at your bidding. But allow me to say that I think you take a most mistaken view of the proper method to proceed in this matter.'

Mr Warner, who had been regarding the whole of these transactions with mute lips but not less vigilance of eye, now took up the word.

'I confess myself,' said he, 'unable to comprehend this affair in all its bearings. Scenes may have been acted behind the regular stage which, if known, would change the aspect of the business and amply justify many things which now seem of doubtful discretion. Yet judging according to the light which I have, I feel it this night to be my bounden duty to communicate without false play to my sovereign the opinion I have formed on this subject. Your Majesty knows I have always told you faithfully what to me seemed right and what far wrong in your dealings with your subjects; and I will follow that straight path now, though it may to me sometimes be a rugged one.

'My lord Duke, Lord Hartford spake truly this night when he said he sat here the representative of one of the oldest families in Angria; and being such, and also a man of sound political principle, whatever his private errors may have been, reason tells me he was entitled to consideration whenever a servant of the country was wanted to promote that country's deepest interests. Sir William Percy will allow me to say in his presence that I know not a braver or more honourable man than he, or one whose career in the service of Angria has been more free from the sin of selfish defection. But still, even he, I think, cannot resist the conviction that Hartford has higher claims to the confidence of his sovereign than could possibly have been possessed by a stranger to the country,[107] his subaltern in rank and by twenty years his junior in age.

'Your Majesty will recollect that I was not consulted about this appointment, or I should have stated these objections before. You applied to General Enara before, and on General Enara's shoulders be the responsibility of the advice he gave you.'

'I take it,' said Enara. 'I've borne worse weights than the sin of ousting a half-mad rake from office.'

'Well, Arundel, have you nothing to say?' asked the Duke, addressing his handsome chevalier, who sat silent opposite to him, displaying by far the finest head of the three councillors – but between ourselves, Townshend, I conceive, the least brains to furnish it.

He changed his position and, looking at His Majesty, answered,

'It seems to me that Mr Warner is disposed to assume a very dictatorial tone tonight. I wonder where he would limit his encroachments on the royal prerogative, if your Majesty is to be denied the privilege of excluding from your confidence a man who before now has abused that confidence so basely as Lord Hartford has done.'

Mr Warner was now getting irritated. He dismissed his calm manner and returned to his usual querulous tone.

'Your Majesty,' said he, 'is surrounded by flatterers – those filthy fungi that feed on the vices of royalty and eat into its heart. As far as I can understand the matter, Lord Hartford has entertained no thought of a nature to sully your Majesty's honour. He has only disobliged you where your irregular passions are concerned, and why, for such a venial offence as that, should a nobleman of the country be persecuted and neglected as he has been? I know very well by your Majesty's eye at this moment that your blood is boiling against me for my plain-speaking. I know your resolution is so fixed, of barring every door of prefer-ment and every avenue of court favour against that unfortunate nobleman, that you would rather put all to the hazard than admit him. Your Majesty is rash, revengeful.'

'Mr Warner!' said Lord Arundel in an undertone, expressing mingled surprise and indignation. 'Mr Warner, you had better pause. If you speak many more words in that strain, I shall feel it my duty to take measures I would rather abstain from.'

Mr Warner was now fully excited. He turned like a wild-cat on Lord A.

'Do you hector me, sir? Do you dictate what I shall say, and what I shall leave unsaid? I tell you, it is you and such as you who are the bane of monarchical government. You are the panderers to royal vice, the instigators to royal crime. A youthful king surrounded by men of your stamp and Enara's is like untried innocence exposed to the temptations of experienced infamy. You minister to his carnal desires; you inflame the lust of the flesh, the pride of the eye, and the pride of life;[108] you stifle every better and higher thought in him; you prejudice his heart and stop his ears against the solemn voice of whosoever would warn him of his danger. You tempt him down to hell along a path strewn with flowers.'[109]

'Amen!' exclaimed His Majesty who, during, the exordium had been alternately taking snuff and looking at a map. 'Amen, Warner! Is the sermon over? It went off with a twang. Now that was none of your sugared dainties – the cakes the Devil flings to poor deluded souls, with a view to persuade them they'll have such every day when they come to his place. It was a taste of the real bread of life, bitter as gall, sour as vinegar,[110] choky as chaff. Frederick and Henri, how do you like it?'

'It's what we're used to,' said Enara, quite coolly.

'But,' continued the Duke, 'don't you think the reverend gentleman was particularly strong in that last clause? The word "hell" comes in like the genuine thing. I've heard a fellow in the north whip it into his sermons with just such an emphasis.'

'My lord Duke, you may jest,' said Warner, 'but it is true, nevertheless. Sir, I can have no interested motives in what I have said. I am not partial to Lord Hartford – you know I am not. There was a time when Your Majesty made him your bosom companion, when his Lordship formed one of that very set against which I have just now been inveighing, and outdid them all in prostrate adulation of your Majesty's failings. His character, I think, is more nearly akin to Lord Arundel's and General Enara's than to mine; and when your Majesty was partial to him I used to warn you of his atrocities and shew you to what bourne they tended.'

'Yes!' retorted the Duke. 'When I thought well of Hartford, you traduced him, Warner. Now, when I hold him in utter detestation, and when you know I have formed resolutions against him too strong ever to be softened, you shift ground and call him an angel. Were I to do as you wish me and give him my hand again, he would be a devil tomorrow – and Enara, I've only to quarrel with you to produce the same effect. The moment we parted in wrath, Warner would discover sainted virtues in your character which he never dreamt of before. Oh Howard, but you're jealous, jealous!'

'Your Grace is privileged to insult me with impunity,' said Mr Warner, evidently touched at the quick by this insinuation.

'I don't insult you, Howard,' continued our czar, leaning over the table towards him. 'I know you wish me well and have a most magnanimous notion of doing your duty without reference to selfish considerations. Much, too, of what you say about these fellows is quite right. They're all raff, Howard, and but very little better than they should be. Moreover, it is not to tell the harm they've done me. Enara there has been my ruin. I was one of the best-intentioned young men that ever blew, before I made his acquaintance. You know what a spotless character I bore in the days of my marquisate, and now my reputation's so damaged it has hardly a leg left to stand on. However, one little puzzle has entered my head which I should like you to solve.

'I remember two or three years ago, when there was a harmless old aristocrat about, by the name of Northangerland, you entertained a somewhat different opinion of the persons here present. All the vials of your wrath[111] were then emptied on the innocent head of the elderly nobleman before alluded to. He was the seducer of my youth, the misleader of my morals, and, above all, the underminer of my royal popularity. These gentlemen were the true props of the throne, the real friends of the monarchy.

I can distinctly recollect growing very weary of the changes continually rung in my ears[112] on the honest worth and ill-rewarded fidelity of General Fernando di Enara and Frederick, Lord Arundel. How is this, Howard?'

'Your Majesty can best explain paradoxes of your own framing,' replied Warner.

'I shall explain it easily,' said the Duke. 'But to do so I should have to repeat that little word which annoyed you so before.'

'Then,' said the Premier, 'all my labours in your Majesty's cause turn on the point of jealousy, do they? And from that motive I am wasting life and health, sacrificing life and happiness in the service of a sovereign who rewards me by taunts?'

Warner was looking down. His head, which, judging from the heavy aspect of his eyes, seemed to ache, rested on his hand. He did not see the look which was turned on him by Zamorna, and the proud magnate would not express his feelings in words.

There was a silence of some time, and then his Grace, turning to me, said in a changed and cheerful tone,

'Well, Sir William, you will leave us to-morrow, if all be well. Now, my lad, do you think you'll have heart and nerve to go through with this ticklish business? Those must be quick away, Percy, who would work in secret and escape the dangers of detection.'

'I have considered that, my lord Duke,' returned I, 'and I don't see the sense of being terrified at risks which will be hazarded.'

He smiled quietly.

'I know you've some determination, Percy, or I should not have selected you to be the concealed agent of these transactions. You have, I believe, all instruments and documents needful in your commission.'

'All but one paper, Sire, which I was instructed to ask for here.'

'I know,' said he; and, taking out his pocket-book, he opened the silver clasp and handed to me a letter on which, when I cast my eyes, [I saw] an autograph direction including a name which somehow made my hand tremble. 'That will speed you on your way,' said he. 'You will halt one night at the place where you deliver that letter, and receive a few instructions which cannot be given you so satisfactorily elsewhere.'

I bowed. The letter, I will just tell you, was directed to 'Miss Laury, Lodge of Rivaulx, Hawkscliffe'.

Zamorna now rose from his arm-chair. It was a signal that the council was dissolved. At the same moment, a clock struck eleven, and the three statesmen rose also, and so did I. They bowed to the Duke, and wished him good evening. He, standing on the hearth, returned the greeting of each. Arundel and Enara left the room together. Warner was last, and I saw his eyes meet those of his master as he turned at the door. The Duke smiled and turned away.

You will ask me, Townshend, why I lingered when these great men departed. It was to make a request which I did not choose them to hear. When they were gone and the door was closed, I walked up to my mighty brother-in-law and said boldly,

'Sire, may I see my sister?'

He said something about its being late, but I did not withdraw the petition. Then he told me to follow him, and I did so. He took me through a great many winding ways, the mazes of which he seems very well acquainted with, though it was now pitch dark. He stopped at a little curtained door and went in, saying I was to wait without a moment.

I stood in the dark, listening to the low sound of his voice in the room, and the scarce audible answers of another person. I heard him call me, and I entered. My sister's apartment was what you might expect such a man to lodge his queen in.

She and Zamorna were standing together by the fire. I have always determined in my intercourse with her to demean myself towards [her] as an elder brother may without degradation. I feel towards her as the only thing in the world between whom and myself close blood-relationship has brought natural affection.

I went towards her.

'I thought, sister, I should like to bid you good-bye,' I said.

'You go away to-morrow, I believe?' she returned, in a low, hurried kind of voice.

'Yes.'

'Is there anything I can say or do for you before your departure?' she asked.

'No.'

'You do not know when you are likely to return?'

'No.'

'If you have time, it would interest me to hear from you during your absence.'

'I do not think I shall have any time for writing private letters.'

'Good-bye, William.'

She held out her hand, and I took it.

'Good-bye, Mary.'

'I wish you well,' she continued, turning her face away.

'God bless you.'

I pressed her hand again, bowed to my brother-in-law, who stood leaning his elbow on the mantle-piece and watching my sister, and so she and I parted.

Townshend, you prig, the postage for this packet will burn a hole in your pockets. Tomorrow, hurrah for Paris! Like a Cossack, I don't care a cracked penny for the whole world! I'm a made man. There'll be no old Talleyrand[113] to baffle me – and let meaner vermin set their houses in order.

Yours, the first statesman of the day,

    William Percy.

        C. BRONTE July 21st, 1838

HENRY HASTINGS

Introductory Note

In December 1838 Charlotte Brontë left her post as a teacher at Miss Wooler's school. She now had time to write a much longer and more ambitious fiction than any she had hitherto attempted. The result was *Henry Hastings*, the first part of which she finished on 24 February 1839.

Henry Hastings begins, like the previous tales, with Charles Townshend, here in self-mocking mode – advertising for a wife, meeting a disconcerting girl on a coach, quarrelling with his landlord about coals. Again, we have moved on from the events of the previous tale. Sir William Percy has returned from his diplomatic mission to Paris, and is sitting in the Verdopolitan parliament. Now much more an establishment figure, 'very much about the Angrian court', he is distancing himself from Charles Townshend: indeed, early in *Henry Hastings*, he is one of the 'nobs' who interrogates his disreputable former friend. In the course of that interrogation, we learn the reason for his mission to Paris, at this time full of Northangerland's supporters and Zamorna's enemies. He was sent in search of Henry Hastings, once the 'Poet of Angria' and also its historian, who has killed his superior officer and deserted to the other side. As the tale unfolds, it emerges that this 'daring, desperate miscreant' has returned to Verdopolis in disguise; Sir William is in hot pursuit. The girl on the coach was Elizabeth Hastings, his sister, who is employed as a kind of governess to Jane Moore.

Central to this tale are a brother and a sister; the former once full of promise, but now a disgraced drunkard, the latter an 'insignificant, unattractive young woman' with fine eyes and 'intense emotions', an outsider in the midst of aristocratic

Angrian society. It is hard not to see this as redolent of the situation in the Brontë family, where Charlotte was attempting to earn her living in uncongenial employment, and Branwell, the hope of the family, was possibly beginning to show signs of unsteadiness. Branwell himself seems to have identified closely with Hastings, who had since late 1834 been one of his favourite narrators (see n. 75), and whom he represents in his mss. of this period as descending into drunkenness. Indeed, there is perhaps a joking autobiographical reference in the account he gives of Hastings' return to Angria in two manuscripts written just prior to the first part of Charlotte's *Henry Hastings*. The first of these mss. is dated January 1839, shortly after Branwell had returned home from Bradford, where he had been seeking to establish himself as a portrait painter, perhaps in some kind of disgrace (Barker, p. 302). It is in the form of a letter from 'John King, Major in the 19th infantry' to 'the Right Hon Henri Fernando Earl of Enara, Secretary at War' telling of the return of the 'Abandoned Deserter HENERY HASTINGS!', leading a band of Frenchmen and 'Negroes from the interior' (*Angria and the Angrians V(d)*, in Neufeldt 3, pp. 249–51). The second, dated 4 February, tells of the arrival of 'Richard Wilson' in Verdopolis from the point of view of his landlady ('There was one thing about him clear enough he was a desperate drinker', p. 253), and of the attempt he makes on the Duke of Zamorna's life (*Angria and the Angrians V(d)*, in Neufeldt 3, pp. 251–9). This is the story that Charlotte Brontë picks up in *Henry Hastings*, finished later the same month.

[PART I]

A young man of captivating exterior, elegant address and most gentlemanlike deportment is desirous of getting his bread easy, and of living in the greatest possible enjoyment of comfort and splendour, at the least possible expense of labour and drudgery. To this end he begs to inform the public that it would suit him uncommon well to have a fortune left him, or to get a wife whose least merit should not be her pecuniary endowment.[1] The advertiser is not particular as to age, nor does he lay any stress on those fleeting charms of a merely personal nature which, according to the opinion of the best-informed medical men of all ages, a few days' sickness or the most trivial accident may suffice to remove. On the contrary, an imperfect symmetry of form – a limb laterally, horizontally or obliquely bent aside from the line of rigid rectitude, or even the absence of a feature, as an eye too few or a row of teeth minus – will be no material objection to this enlightened and sincere individual, provided only satisfactory testimonials be given of the possession of that one great and paramount virtue, that eminent and irresistible charm, C- A- S-H! Address CT, care of Mr Surena Ellrington, No. 12 Chapel Street, Verdopolis.

P.S. None need apply whose property – personal, landed and funded, amounts to less than 20,000£ sterling. The advertiser considers himself a cheap bargain at double this sum. He would have no objection to enter into an immediate negotiation with Miss Victoria Delph[2] of Brunswick Terrace or Miss Angelica Corbett of Melon Grove. These ladies or any others who may feel disposed to try their luck in this noble lottery are referred for character etc. to the most noble Viscount Macara Lofty, Sir

W. Percy, Bart, Mr Steaton Esqu., Rev. G. Bromley, Revd. W. Stephens, Revd M. Chambers, etc., etc.

Such was the advertisement that lately appeared in the columns of a metropolitan print,[3] being the last resource of an an unoffending and meritorious individual who, penniless and placeless, found himself driven upon the two horns of a hideous dilemma, and – all other attempts to raise the wind[4] by less desperate methods having failed – compelled either to write or to wed. For the last six months I have been living, as it were, on turtle-soup and *foie gras*. I have been rowing and revelling and rioting to my heart's content, but now, alas, my pockets are empty and my pleasures are gone. I must either write a book or marry a wife, to refill the one and to recall the other.

Which shall I do? Hymen with waving torch invites me – but no! I am beloved by too many to give up my liberty to one. Ever fascinating as a pheasant, I will still be free as an eagle. Wail not then, O dark-eyed daughters of the west! Lament not, ye ruddy virgins of the east! Sit not in sackcloth, soft maids of the sunny south, nor weep upon the hill-tops proud damsels of the north, nor yet send the voice of mourning from afar, O ye mermaids of the island realms! Charles Townshend will not marry. He is yet too young, too frisky, too untamed, to submit to the sober bonds of matrimony. Charles Townshend will still be the handsome bachelor, the cynosure of neighbouring eyes, the tempting apple of discord to the African fair.[5] Charles Townshend, therefore, gets pen, ink and paper, and sits down to write a book, though his charming noddle is about as empty of ideas as his pocket is of pence. '*Regardez donc; nous allons commencer.*'[6]

I have clean forgotten what day of the month it was, or even what month in the year, whether the last week in September or the first week in October, that I, comfortably seated in an Angrian stage-coach, found myself comfortably rolling up from Adrianopolis and on a western tack towards the mighty Megatherium,[7] the old capital of the country. However, it was autumn; the woods were turning brown. It was the season of partridge-shooting, for the popping of guns was continually to be heard over the landscape, and as we whirled past Meadowbank, the seat of John Kirkwall Esqr., M. P., I recollect catching a glimpse from the coach-window of three or four young gentlemen in green shooting-jackets followed by a yelling train of pointers and a brassy-browed gamekeeper. These sparks were just issuing from the park gate, and as one of them hailed our equipage with an impressive oath, another sportively directed his fowling piece toward a young girl on the outside, thereby causing her to ejaculate a scream of exemplary shrillness. A gentleman opposite to me observed:

'That is Mr Frank Kirkwall.' At the same time, he smiled significantly, as good as to add, 'a scoundrelly young blade'. 'And I believe,' he continued, 'the other with the gun is no other than Lieutenant James Warner, the youngest brother of our premier.'

'Indeed!' exclaimed a voice at my side, and at the same moment a person I had not before observed bolted[8] forward and almost rudely pushed past me to get a look from the window. The person was a lady, and therefore I could not well resent her want of ceremony. So I waited patiently till she chose to sit down again, and then I said, with a jocular smirk,

'You seem interested, ma'am, in the Lieutenant.'

'Why,' she answered, 'I don't often see celebrated men.'

'I am not sure that that young chap is particularly celebrated,' was my reply.

'Yes, but his brother, you know,' responded the lady with logical clearness of expression, 'and then I believe the Lieutenant himself is an officer of the illustrious 19th.'[9]

'Illustrious, ma'am! A parcel of blackguards!'[10] exclaimed the gentleman who had spoken before.

'Yes, they are,' said the lady, who seemed not strongly inclined to dispute any opinion that might be uttered by another. 'They are certainly very wild and reckless, according to all accounts. But then, after all, they have performed gallant exploits. Evesham would never have been won but for them.'

'Fit for nothing but storming towns,' answered the gentleman. 'And that's dirty work, after all – bloody work, ma'am.'

'Yes, it is,' again assented she. 'But if we have war there must be bloodshed; and then the 19ᵗʰ have other things to do besides that, and they have never failed – at least the newspapers say so.'

'They always prime so well before they explode. I've understood, ma'am, that that honourable regiment mostly drinks up to *trop*[11] in time of action.'

I expected the lady would turn enthusiastic and indignant at this, but she only smiled.

'Indeed, sir! Well, then, they do their duty drunk better than most men do sober.'

'I can tell you, madam, on the best authority, that at Westwood, half an hour before General Thornton put himself at their head to make the final charge, every officer and almost every private of the 19ᵗʰ were as drunk as they could sit in their saddles.'[12]

'Very shocking!' said the lady, still not at all roused. 'Yet that charge was most noble and successful. Was it not said that Lord Arundel thanked them on the field of battle for their gallantry?'

'Don't know,' said the gentleman coldly, 'and if he did, madam, his Lordship is very little better than they are.'

'No, certainly,' said she. 'I should think his courage to be much of the same order.'

'Very likely,' said the gentleman, whom by this time I more than suspected to be a millowner of Zamorna or Hartford Dale; and now, taking a newspaper from his pocket, he leant back in the coach and immersed himself in the perusal of a long speech which had been made by Edward Percy Esqu., M. P., at a dinner lately given him by his constituents. The lady leant back too and was silent.

Until the commencement of the little dialogue above recorded, I had not been sufficiently attracted by my fellow passenger to give her more than the slightest cursory glance imaginable, but I now scrutinized her a little more closely. I remembered, indeed, that early that morning, as, after travelling all night, our vehicle was traversing a wild tract of country in the Douro, its speed had suddenly been checked by a cry of 'Coach! Coach!', and on looking out I perceived that we neared a little inn, just where a branch-path winding down from among the loneliest hills formed a junction with the great high road, and by the grey light was just discernible a female figure in a shawl, bonnet and veil, waiting at the inn door, and a woman-servant standing guard over certain paraphernalia of boxes, packages, etc. The luggage was hoisted onto the top of the coach and the lady was helped inside, where, being but little and thin, she was easily stowed away between myself and a stout woman in a plurality of cloaks. I just saw her shake hands with her attendants. She said something which sounded like 'Good-bye, Mary', or 'Martha', or 'Hannah', and then, as the coach dashed off, she sat well back behind my shoulder and, comfortably hid in her veil and shawl, gave herself up to most unsocial and unfascinating taciturnity.

One can't feel interest in a person that will neither speak nor look. So after the lapse of near four mortal hours' silence, I had completely forgotten her existence, and should never have remembered it again if that sudden push of hers towards the window, in which she disarranged my hair with the contact of her shawl, had not reminded me of it. The few sentences she subsequently uttered prevented her from sinking again into immediate oblivion and, though no one could have deducted a character from them, yet they were sufficiently marked to make me feel a little curiosity as to what and who she might be. I had already made two or three attempts to get a view of her face, but in vain; her bonnet and veil effectually shaded it from observation. Besides, I thought she intentionally turned it from me, and though she had talked freely enough to the crusty, middle-aged manufacturer opposite, I had not yet been able to draw a syllable of conversation from her. By her voice I concluded she must be a young person, though her dress was of that general, simple nature that almost any age might have adopted it: a dark silk gown, a heavy chenille shawl, a straw bonnet plainly trimmed completed a costume unpretending but not unladylike.

Thinking, at last, that the best way to get a look at her was to begin to talk, I turned rather suddenly towards her for the purpose of commencing a conversation. Meantime, while I had been thinking of her, she, I found, had also been thinking of me, and as she sat shrinking behind me she had taken the opportunity of my seeming abstraction to scrutinize my physiognomy most closely. Consequently, when I made the unexpected movement of turning my head, I saw her veil thrown back and her eyes fixed full on me with a gaze of keen, sharp observation. I protest I felt almost flattered by the discovery. However, I soon recovered my wonted self-possession sufficiently to take revenge by an answering stare of, I flatter myself, at least equal intensity. The lady exhibited some command of countenance. She only coloured a little; and then, looking towards the window, remarked it was a beautiful country we were entering upon. It was, for we were now in the province of Zamorna, and the green and fertile plains of Stuart March[13] were unfolding on each side of the noble road. Had the lady been very old and very ugly I would have said no more to her. Had she been young and extremely handsome I would have commenced a series of *petits soins* and soft speeches. Young indeed she was, but not handsome. She had a fair, rather wan complexion, dark hair smoothly combed in two plain folds from her forehead, features capable of much and varied expression, and a quick, wandering eye of singular and by no means common-place significance.

'You are a native, madam, I presume, of Angria.'

'Yes,' said she.

'Fine, thriving nation, yours. No doubt you're very patriotic.'

'Oh, of course,' was her answer, and she smiled.

'Now I shouldn't wonder if you take a great deal of interest in politics,' continued I.

'People who live in retired places often do,' she returned.

'You are not from a very populous district then, ma'am?'

'No, a solitary hilly country on the borders of Northangerland.' And as she spoke, I remembered the place where she had been taken up, just at the entrance of a bye-path winding away amongst untrodden hills.

'You must find a pleasant change in visiting this busy, stirring region,' said I. 'Were you ever in Zamorna before?'

'Yes, it is a splendid province – the most populous and wealthy of all the seven.'[14]

'I daresay, now, you think it is worthy of giving a title to your gallant young monarch, eh, ma'am? You Angrian ladies are all very loyal, I know.'

'Yes,' she said. 'I suppose the women of Angria have that character, but I understand it is not peculiar to them. Most African ladies admire his Grace, don't they?'

'They make a great profession of doing so, ma'am, and of course you are not an exception.'

'Oh no!' she said, with extreme coolness. 'I never had the happiness of seeing him, however.'

'Perhaps that is the reason you speak so indifferently about him. I am quite astonished. All his fair subjects with whom I have conversed on the topic before speak in raptures.'

She smiled again.

'I make a point of never speaking in raptures, especially in a stage-coach.'

'Except about the gallant 19th,' I interposed significantly; then, with my most insinuating air: 'Perhaps some hero of that heroic corps is honoured with your especial interest?'

'All of them are, sir. I like them the better because they are so abused by the cold, whiggish Adrahians. I could even worship the Bloodhounds[15] for the same reason.'

'Humph!' said I, taking a pinch of snuff. 'I see how it is, madam. You don't scruple to admire in general terms any body of men, but you decline coming to individuals.'

'Just so,' said she, gaily. 'I'm not free to condescend on particulars.'[16]

'Do you travel far on this road, ma'am?'

'No, I get out at the Spinning Jenny in Zamorna – the inn where the coach stops.'

'Then you are going to visit some friend in that city?'

'I expect to be met there.'

This was an answer so indirect that it was as good as a rebuff. It was evident this young woman did not intend to make anybody the confidant either of her opinions or plans.

'She may keep her secrets to herself, then,' thought I, a little huffed at her reserve, and, folding my arms, I resumed my former silence and so did she hers.

It was about noon when we got into Zamorna. The bustle of a market day was throughout all the streets of the thriving commercial city. As the coach stopped at the Spinning Jenny, I saw my fellow-traveller give an anxious glance from the window as if in search of those she expected to meet her. I thought I would keep an eye upon her movements, for my curiosity was a little piqued concerning her.

The door being opened, I was just stepped out into the inn-yard, and was offering up my hand to assist her in alighting, when a man in livery pushed up and forestalled me in the office. Touching his hat to the lady, he inquired what luggage she had. She gave him her orders, and in five minutes after I saw her enter a handsome travelling carriage; and the trunks and portmanteaus being stowed away in the same conveyance. And a touch being given to the horses, the whole concern rolled lightly off, and in a twinkling had vanished like a dream.

'Surely she can't be anybody of consequence,' thought I. 'She has little of the bearing or mien of an aristocrat. That quiet aspect and plain, demure dress scarcely harmonize with so splendid an equipment.'

I always like to be in town at opening of the sessions, the commencement of the grand political season. When the mustering of forces begins, when carriages roll in daily, hourly from the country,[17] when town-houses fill, and manors, halls and castles are left to the dreariness of December rains, then it is that you meet country gentlemen walking the broad *pavés* of Verdopolis. Then do Angrian members swarm in the club-rooms of the capital, then do you hear the designations of eastern officials bandied from mouth to mouth like watch-words, and with the broad accent of that polished land the clan-names of their chiefs – Warner, Stuartville, Thornton, Arundel, etc. – are mouthed out with more emphasis than harmony. At every turn and every corner, in all the squares and streets and lanes within three miles of Parliament Street, you hear a Mr Howard calling to a Mr Kirkwall, and a Captain Fala shouting recognition to a Major Sydenham, and a Counsellor Hartford hailing a Sergeant Warner, while the Warrens, the

Westfields, the Stancliffes, the Binghams, the Moores, the Pighills, the Steatons, the Naylors and the Bugdens swarm like midges in the summer hayfields of their own Arundel. Then, too, the north sends down its St Clairs, its Denards, its Gordons and its Gilderoys, while, bearing up full sail from the south, the great men of war's men – Elphinston, Ilcomkill, Wilson, Patteson and Macaulay – cast anchor in neat, economical lodging-houses kept by canny Scotch landladies.

At this time, too, newspapers become interesting. Leading articles are piquant, parliamentary intelligence spicy. Prime ministers wax wild, ministerial supporters are troubled with cholera morbus,[18] while the opposition professes piety and patriotism. Pleasant, then, is it, after a good dinner at a friend's house, with just as much wine in a man as will float his spirits off the quick-sands of despondency into the open sea of bliss, to sally forth, not in a carriage and four, but rejoicingly six abreast (if the night is wet and wild, so much the better), thus to seek Parliament Street, to repair to the gallery and, seated there, to view the gladiators come forth upon the arena.

About midnight, when the war of words has waxed warm, what an exulting sight it is! The world shut out, candle-light, closed doors; a hell of hate and rage, an agony of attention and suspense within; around, the members of the House,[19] bench behind bench, with grim faces, young and old. They have forgotten to be handsome. Beauty, smiles and softness is the incense offered to pleasure. These are now sacrificing to ambition, and even such a fop as Lord Stuartville has dashed his curled locks into bristling confusion with one spasmodic movement of phrenzy, while the shade of a tall peer is standing opposite, looking at him like a devil and speaking of him words that make him less than man. In the other House, one man speaking, amid the silence of many, turns upon you a thin flushed face and an eye with the glitter of fever in its pupil. He stands in the centre of the floor by a table, and on the other side is another man, leaning over to him, asking him, in a steady, low tone, questions which he can hardly answer. Not for a moment does the hard-browed but pallid inquisitor spare his victim. He hears the stammer, the word uttered and then recalled. He turns to the house with a smile – the Devil's smile, for that is Macara Lofty, skinning alive a poor eel, a young member who has been making a maiden speech in favour of the Constitutionalists.[20] Just look, now, at that individual on the Angrian side of the house – a leader, for he sits on the front bench, a worn, delicate man, watching the combatants. He is smiling and curling his thin upper lip, not with hate at Macara, but with scorn at his baffled prey. He coldly admires that fiend's quick, firm hand in the operation, his subtlety, his unrelenting pursuit of the rash greenhorn. It is a trick in his own trade well executed, and it pleases him, though performed by an enemy. Bravo, Mr Warner! You are a saintly premier after all.

Yet what ninnies all these are! Upon my Christian d—n—n, I do think a man who is really interested in politics the greatest fool the sun looks on – unless, indeed, as a simple matter of gain. Ministers do right to hold hard on by their places, opposition members do right to try to oust and supplant them; but as to oratorical fame or party prejudices, all I can say is, I don't understand that sort of thing. The above concerning the agony of flayed eels, the attention of breathless lookers-on, the ferocity of infernal operators, I wrote merely as a specimen of a certain style.[21] My dear reader, when you are inclined to grow enthusiastic about such things, just recall my image, leaning over the gallery with my hat on, alternately squeezing and sucking a remarkably fine Madeira orange, and meantime cocking my eye at the honourable gent.[22] on his legs with an expression sufficiently indicative of the absorbing interest I take in his speechifications.

There is but one individual whom it refreshes me to look at – that lengthy-limbed young member[23] in the stiff black stock, half-reclined on the bench, with a white pocket-handkerchief judiciously arranged over his face, so as to leave you in doubt as to whether that ardour and attention may not be sufficiently expressed by his veiled features which the admirable nonchalance of his figure denies. That gentleman, as you may perceive, is on the Angrian side of the House, and you may derive edification from noticing the conscientious manner in which he acts with his party. Sir Marmaduke Howard is on his legs and

consequently astounding cheers are the order of the day. At
every thundering peal, this worthy individual, without rising,
lifts his fine eyes and utters a huzza like the dying fall of a jew's-
harp. Presently, when Mr Macombich rises to answer, he will
roar hot contempt like any sucking dove.[24] I respect that man.
When he speaks himself, which he does as seldom as he can
possibly help – though, being closely connected with the Angrian government, he is obliged now and then to answer questions and make statements – he saunters forward to the table,
says what he has to say in language that exhibits all the burning
glow of an icicle, all the figurative eloquence of a well-kept
ledger. His Grace the Duke of Wellington never was more
imaginative, diffusive and poetic in his most inspired moments.
He seems, now and then, to take a sort of lazy pleasure in rising
to answer such a man as Lindsay, especially when the pulse of
the House is beating quick after the outpouring of some torrents
of his rabid eloquence. Dry and cold are the answers he gives
to the indignant questioning of that foe. He bears his invective,
his satire, his scorn; turns a chilly eye of wonder on him; goes
on telling his own plain, quiet tale to the House; concludes with
a compliment to Lindsay on his calm, dispassionate demeanour;
deliberately sits down and takes snuff.

As I was coming out of the House rather late one night, and as
several of the members were leaving it at the same time, I got
mixed amongst them. Something light as a glove or handkerchief tapped my shoulder, and on turning I saw a figure somewhat taller than myself close at my shoulder. The light of a
street-lamp was brilliant enough to reveal the identity[25] at a
glance. No one could mistake the cloak with stand-up collar
closely drawn about the wasted person, the black silk kerchief
folded again and again round the throat, the hat with ample
brim pulled over the eyes, throwing the pale forehead and
strange eyes underneath into shade, implying the habitual half-
concealment of one always suspecting and always shrinking
from open notice.
    'A cold night, Townshend,' said my friend, as he and I ten-
derly immingled our gloved hands.

'Infernally so, my lord, but you have your carriage? You're not going to walk home?'

'Oh yes. It does not rain, I think. Come, lend me your arm. I'm almost finished with these late sittings of the House.'

The shivering lord leant upon me as we descended the steps and took our way up Parliament Street.

'How do you like the style in which our friend the Baronet comes out this sessions?' said he, meaning the gentleman above alluded to.

'Oh, very good, Viscount – a trifle too warm as usual. Pray, have you seen anything of him of late in a private way?'

'No, he has been very much about the Angrian court ever since his return from Paris. But you, Townshend, are in correspondence with him, of course?'

'Not I. Indeed, the Colonel is very fitful in his friendships. He has none of your constancy, my dear lord.'

'Ah! Townshend, you and I know each other's worth. Yet I thought I saw Percy move to you the other night, when you and he met in the lobby.'

'Just so; he did move, and passed on, though we were so close that I had an opportunity of nabbing the delicate cambric handkerchief which hung alluringly from his coat-pocket – the gift of some Parisian divinity, no doubt, for it had a coronet embroidered in black hair[26] on the corner, and the word "Agathe" underneath.'

'*Pathètique!* And really, Townshend, he did not speak to you?'

'Not a syllable, though it was the first time of our meeting for a quarter of a year.'

'A'nt you very low about such faithlessness?'

'*Au désespoir*,' said I, directing my forefinger to my heart. The viscount and I expressed our mutual grief, in a low sympathetic laugh.

'And what,' said Macara, 'what can it possibly be, dear Townshend, that has expelled your loved image from his breast?'

'Ah!' returned I. 'There are thoughts that breathe and words that burn.[27] Sir William has of late been in climes where softer feelings than those of friendship float from the pastille-perfumed bowers of the south.'

'You grow poetic, Townshend. It's your opinion, then, that our friend, frigid as he seems, is not altogether proof against temptation?'

'Did your Lordship think he was?'

'Why, I don't know. He's very *philosophique*.'

'Your Lordship, I perceive, judges from your own unsunned snow. You know yourself innocent, and you believe others to be the same.'

'Will you take a pinch of snuff, Townshend?'

'I'm obliged to you, my lord. Yet in this matter I believe you're somewhat too charitable. The Baronet's a remarkably sly hand. Depend on it, he's taken pleasure and business together during his late *diplomatique* excursion.'

'I've heard as much hinted before,' said Macara.

'By whom?'

'An individual not to be doubted in such things – our illustrious friend the Earl. I met him the other day at a dinner party. He was seated between Lady Stuartville and Georgina Greville and talking in as low a voice as you please, just like a turtle[28] cooing to his mates. I heard something about Sir William and a certain Marquise of Froncville – now I think on it, her name was Agathe. I heard the word "duel", too. Has the Colonel been fighting, do you think?'

'Very likely. However, here we are at your lodgings. Good-night. Give my love to Louisa when you see her.'

'I will. Good-night.'

'Stay a moment, Townshend!' – calling me back as I was turning from the door, where his Lordship stood with his hand on the bell-handle – 'You will come and take a quiet cup of tea with me to-morrow? I'll ask our friend to meet you if you like.'

'With pleasure. I'll be punctual at eight o'clock.'

His Lordship rung the bell and was admitted; I moved away.

Lord Macara's apartments are in a street of splendid lodging-houses, mostly let to M.P.s, towards the west end. The evening of the next day being very wet, and the wind besides being high,

I called a hackney coach, and at the appointed hour was set down under the imposing portico of his hotel. His valet let me in, and I was shewn through a well-lighted hall and up a handsome flight of stairs to a drawing-room of small size but tasteful arrangement, cheerfully shining in the light of a good fire and of four tall wax candles burning on the table. I perceived at once that Macara had been thoughtful enough to provide female superintendence. Her Ladyship was there, seated in a low chair by the hearth, and playing with the silken ears of a little spaniel. A lady, if there be but one in an apartment, always rivets the attention first, and I did not look for other visitors until I had satisfactorily scanned Louisa's easy[29] figure.

'Down, Pepin, down,' she was saying, as she tantalized the pigmy wretch with a bit of biscuit; then again, changing her tone, 'Poor thing, come,' and she laid her slim hand lightly on its head and soothed it till the crouching creature sprang into her lap. There it was caressed for a while, still with the same aristocratic hand whose touch seemed lighter than down, shaking her head meantime in affected rebuke, so as to produce a pretty waving motion in her long curls and cause them to stray shadily upon her cheeks and neck. This charming pantomime having been acted a due length of time, she thought fit to start and acknowledge my approach.

'Dear, Mr Townshend! How you do frighten one with stealing into the room! Pray, how long have you been standing at the door watching me and Pepin?'

'Perhaps five minutes, madam. It's rude, I know, but you must excuse me. The picture was such a pretty one.'

'Now,' said she, turning to a person in another part of the room whom I had not noticed before, 'we'll have no flattery to-night, will we, sir?'

'Not from me at least, ma'am,' answered a voice from a dark corner.

'You never flatter, I think,' she continued.

'I've not done lately,' was the reply. 'My tongue is out of practice.'

'Perhaps you disdain all soft nonsense,' said she.

'I'm a novice,' answered the unseen hastily. 'I don't understand it.'

'Come and learn, then,' interposed I. 'At Louisa Dance's feet, who would be a novice in love's worship long?'

'Curse it, I'm cold!' ejaculated the gentleman, and, rising hastily from the sofa where he had been lounging, he strode forward on to the hearth.

The gentleman, as he spread his hands over the fire, regarded me from top to toe with a rapid sharp glance, that implied in its sidelong scrutiny anything rather than an open comfortable state of mind. I pretended not to look at him, but yet from the corner of my eye I took a sufficiently scrutinizing survey of his person and demeanour. He was a man of a muscular and powerful frame, though not tall; of a worn and haggard aspect, though not old or even middle-aged. His hair had no gloss upon it, though it was jet-black and thick. Little care had been bestowed upon its arrangement; it crossed his forehead in disordered flakes, and yet his dress was good and fashionable. Judging by the man's face, he must have been blessed with a devil's temper. I never saw such a mad, suspicious irritability as glinted in his little black eyes. His complexion, of a dark sallowness, aided the effect of a scowl which seemed habitual to his hard, beetling brow. Leaning on the mantle-piece, he looked at Louisa. What a contrast was there between him and her!

'I've not seen his Lordship, madam. Where is he?'

'Oh, he'll be down soon. But the Viscount's health is really so very indifferent now; during the last week he has never left his bed till it was time to go to the House.'

'Hum!' said the gentleman; then, after a pause of some minutes, during which he looked ferociously into the fire, he added, 'Dash it – I feel a want!' The Marchioness was now playing with her dog; and her attention being wholly taken up with its gambols, the dark stranger turned to me and, putting his thumb to his nose-end,[30] said with felicitous politeness: 'Do you?'

'Can't say,' was my response.

' 'Cause,' he continued, 'if your case is a similar one to my own, I know the whereabouts and we'll apply a remedy.'

I thanked him for his civility, but said, 'I was well enough, and for the present at least would dispense with medicine.'

'You don't take?' returned he. 'However, please yourself. Every man to his mind, as the man said, etc.; but I must corn, or it's no go.'[31]

He walked toward a door and opened it. There was a room within. I watched him walk up to the far end, where was a lamp hanging over a sideboard. Decanters and glasses stood there; he filled a glass and drank it; another – again – again – again – even to the mysterious number of seven times.[32] He returned, wiping his lips with a handkerchief. Just then the door opened, and a figure in slippers and dressing-gown came bending into the apartment.

'Glad to see you, my lord,' said the stranger, advancing very brusquely. 'I've come according to invitation, you see. I hope your Lordship's well?'

'Indifferent, Mr Wilson, indifferent. I've made an effort to rise on your account. Louisa, will you lend me your arm to a seat? I don't feel strong this evening.'

'Certainly, my dear Viscount,' said the Marchioness, and rising, she supported her friend to an easy chair set by the hearth. He leant back on the cushions and thanked her with a placid, patient smile. To look at him, a stranger might have thought him a saint. He was as white as a sheet. Every feature expressed extreme exhaustion, but his eyes glittered with temporary excitement.

'What have you been doing with yourself since last night?' asked I, with surprise.

'Oh, I took cold,' he answered. 'Cold always weakens me so. But I shall be better soon. Townshend, you and Mr Wilson don't know each other, I believe? Let me introduce you. Townshend, Mr Wilson – Wilson, Mr Townshend.'

Wilson bowed to me with an assured, impudent air, and then he sat down immediately in front of the fire, folded his arms on his broad chest, and favoured me with one or two of his pleasant, ingenuous glances.

'My lord,' he said, addressing Macara, 'I hadn't expected to meet company here when I came.'

'Oh, Mr Townshend is a friend,' returned Lord Macara. 'I hope you and he will soon be on the best terms.'

'Have you ever been in the army, sir?' asked Mr Wilson, turning to me.

It was evident the man was too mad or too muddy[33] to have any perception of my real identity, so I answered calmly, 'No, though I had a large circle of military friends.'

'Humph! I suppose amongst the Constitutional troops, old stiff-backs of the Fidena school. Your friends, I have no doubt, distinguished themselves in the retreat before Massena of 1833?'[34]

'I believe not,' returned I, lighting a cigar. 'It strikes me that most of them were at that time lying snug with Squire Warner, who, you will remember, hopped about with his ragamuffins, keeping wide of both armies and always hiding from danger in those confounded dirty marshes of theirs, up in the nice Angrian hills.'[35]

'I know, I know,' returned Mr Wilson. 'That's a nasty country, that Angria. I never was there but once, when I was commercial traveller to the house of Macandlish and Jamieson, and I left the situation on that very account, that they sent me and my gig through sich a hell.'

'Indeed!' said I, with some surprise. 'Then you're not a native of the country?'

'A native!' roared Mr Wilson, his little eyes fixing upon me with tiger-fury, and an inexpressible searching gleam of distrust. 'A native! What d'ye mean, sir? Blast the country! I, a native! that never slept but one night within its frontiers, which I remember by the same token, that it was at that grand hotel of theirs at Zamorna – Suchcliffe's, Ratcliffe's, Stancliffe's, what d'ye call it – where I was brutally bitten by bugs and had such a face in the morning that I was forced to borrow the chambermaid's shawl to fold about it up to the eyes. Now, sir, what do you say to that?'

'Oh, I beg a thousand pardons. I merely hazarded the supposition from the circumstance of your having a strong twang of the Angrian accent.'

'It's the Scotch accent!' exclaimed he. 'I'll stand to it.[36] It's the Scotch accent. I was born in Rosstown and brought up in Rosstown, behind the counter. I took a trifle from the till and was consequently expunged to Stumpsland – Frederick's Town. There I went into the house of Macandlish and Jamieson as I told you before, and I'll break any man's bones who shall dare –'

'Mr Wilson, take some coffee,' interposed the voice of Miss Dance, and that lady stood before him in a bending attitude, with the cup in her hand and the smile of persuasion on her lip, almost as lavish in her fascinations to the commercial traveller as she could have been to her high and aristocratic lover, the fastidious Earl of N—. Wilson looked at her; and, taking the cup she offered him, said,

'Were it poison, I'd drink it.'

'I hope it will act as a sedative,' said she, smiling gently.

'No, madam, as a fiery stimulant. This draught, given by you, makes me a soldier again.' He swallowed the coffee. 'Now,' he continued, flashing at her a glance of fierce sentiment, 'I've done what you bid me. I wish it were a harder task.'

'I can impose one you will think harder,' returned she. 'Restrain that haughty temper of yours. Be quiet for at least five minutes. See, I seal your lips.'

She sportively touched his mouth with her finger and, laughing, returned to her seat.

'There,' said Lord Macara. 'You cannot break a prohibition so delivered.'

Who can account for the strange association of ideas in the human mind? During the brief operation of the silent spell that Louisa Dance had thrown over her visitor, I looked round me, and the *tout ensemble* of what I saw recalled to me another picture – like this, but yet how different! Here was a room in the heart of a great town, closed, curtained and lighted up. By a table, with silver and china before her, sat a lady, an elegant form in thin, meritricious robes, with a face a little faded by time, a little wasted by dissipation, but still lovely in softening lamplight. The syren look in her rolling blue eyes, the loose dishevellement of her hair, the studied languor of every glance and movement told plainly enough her character – the unprincipled, the insincere, the heartless, the unchaste, but still the seductive. By the fireside, that image in a dressing-gown, that man with a face like clay and hands like cold, white, fleshless bone, all the spirit of health and youth evidently gone from him, and lassitude, suffering quickened with devilishness, left. Then the other, Wilson, calling himself a Scotch trader; evidently, from bearing, mien and aspect, some scoundrelly, broken officer, some skulking, debauched military miscreant, who dared not own his country, and had blotted out his family name with stains of infamy. This picture, as I gazed on it, suggested to my mind another – a parlour in an old hall, a summer evening shining over a glorious park, near the open window a table surrounded by a circle of lovely women, young and unfaded with vice, and one bold, handsome, hardy soldier, admitted amongst them by the passport of fame.[37] But the scene is no longer vivid. I have forgotten it; its healthy hues will not stand in the vitiated atmosphere of this other tableau.

And even on that I will dwell no more. It is enough to say that I saw Wilson put into Macara's carriage that night blind drunk. Where it took him to I do not know, for the night was so cold and tempestuous I could not be at the pains to follow him. The Viscount I left sitting in his easy-chair, very still, with a leering, vacant simper fixed on his lips. Miss Dance had driven home to Azalia Bower some hours before, after lavishing the softest attentions on the intoxicated Wilson. I thought I could discern that Macara had employed her to act the basilisk,[38] and lure by her dangerous charms that reckless ruffian into his power. During the conversation of the evening, when wine removed restraint, I heard hints of political machinations. Wilson spoke of his associates, his pals, and a short time before he fell under the table he drank, in a brimming bumper, d—mn—n to the Soldan and his satellites. He insisted that I should pledge him,[39] to which I made no objection. I cared nothing who the Soldan might be. I did not even know, though perhaps I might guess, but *n'importe*.

Surena and I had just had a quarrel concerning the quantity of coal to be consumed in the back-parlour grate. I had conquered, and was enjoying the results of my triumph in a charming good fire, which I effectually monopolized by sitting full in front with a foot on each hob. Surena had retreated after his defeat to the shop, whence his voice, softened by distance and the intervening panels of a double door, was heard at intervals, swearing away his precious soul to attest the fact that he was now selling his goods at a lower price than he bought them. Tea was over. Hannah Rowley had closed the shutter and drawn the curtain of our single window. I was the sole occupant of the parlour, and, as I sat in the elegant position above described and leant back in my chair, I saw in the fitful firelight my gigantic shadow wavering wide on the ceiling.

It chanced that I had made a capital good tea, much to the disquietude of my landlord, and all being sufficiently tranquil about me, and my stomach in a state of comfortable and not overloaded repletion, I felt inclined to reverie, if not to drowsiness. The influence of a soft opiate seemed diffused over my brain. Already my eyes were closed, and thick-coming fancies were condensing into gentle dreams. I was very far from Verdopolis. I was in the presence of something fair and poetic, a silken sleeve and a fair white hand were resting on my arm, and she and I were wandering in a moonlight lane.[40] She – aye, what was her name? What were her features? I was just about to hear the name pronounced, and the face was turning towards me, when something stirred. A tinkle – a clang – 'the fire-irons!' thought I; and the conviction darted into my mind that Surena had entered the room and, meanly seizing the advantage my somnolent state afforded him, had commenced the process of taking off the fire with the tongs.

'Hillo!' I shouted, starting up. 'Let the fire alone, will ye, or I'll shiver your skull with the poker!'

Somebody laughed, and as I opened my eyes and woke up I perceived that the flame was ascending the chimney more brilliantly than before, and that fresh fuel had been added within the last few minutes. A dusk form was bending over the hearth in the very act of replacing the poker against its support.

'Who are you?' I demanded.

'Look!' was the concise answer.

I did look, and not small was my astonishment to discern an individual attired in the dress and bearing all the insignia of a policeman. There was no mistaking the dark blue uniform faced with red, the white gloves, the staff and sword-stick.[41]

'Who sent you, and what do you want?' I again interrogated.

'Only your company for a short distance,' returned the man.

'My company! Where to?'

'No need to alarm yourself, Mr Townshend; it's only a trifle. The nobs want a word or two of you. Meantime, if you'll use your eyes, you'll see I'm a friend. If it were not for previous acquaintance I should not have made bold to come upon you so sudden-like.'

In fact the man's features did seem familiar to me when I examined them nearly, and at length I recognized an old pal whom, under the name of James Ingham, I have mentioned in some of my former works.[42]

'Sure, it's not you, Jemmy!' I exclaimed.

'But it is, sir, and I mean to use you genteel, so I've got a cab at the door ready waiting for you.'

'But what for, Jem? What have I done?'

'Don't know. Your honour was always a gentleman of spirit. However, we must go and here's my warrant.'

'Is it a case of murder?' I demanded. 'Or of bigamy? Or of arson, or of burglary, or what?'

'Don't know. Your honour will soon find out. Come.'

And come I did, for just then stepped in two other chaps in the same blue coats and white gloves and, placing me between them, I was walked out through our kitchen and the back-door, placed in a hackney-coach, and nolens volens driven off, the d—l knows where.

We had scarcely proceeded the length of three streets when one of the policemen put his head out of the window and ordered the jarvey to stop, 'as the gen'leman would get out here'. Accordingly, I alighted at the door of a good-sized house, which being presently opened admitted me to a passsage lighted with gas, where were sundry great-coats dangling from pins and sundry hats lying on a slab. A servant in a striped jacket was waiting there.

'You'll show this gentleman upstairs,' said my friend Ingham.

'Yes, sir. Follow me if you please.'

And I did follow him, up a staircase into a gallery. He opened one of a row of doors along the side, and I was ushered into a moderate-sized, neatly furnished library. At a round table in the middle of the room two gentlemen were sitting, one with a desk before him, the other leaning his head on his hand. The latter rose as I entered.

'How do you do, Mr Townshend? Be seated, will you? I am sorry to have given you this trouble, but we will explain matters presently. Jenkins, place Mr Townshend a chair.'

Jenkins, the individual behind the desk, briskly rose, placed a chair for me just opposite his superior, and resumed his own seat. The manner in which this trifling movement was executed at once informed me that he occupied the situation of clerk. The other person I conjectured to be a magistrate. He was a professional-looking middle-aged man with a cold shrewd eye, a pale face and dark hair turning grey. A gas-lamp burning just above the table clearly showed his features – too clearly, indeed, for every line, every muscle, every furrow was revealed in the chilly white light. And as I looked methought this was not the first time I had seen that hard, man-of-the-world physiognomy. I was sure such a face had met my gaze often in electioneering crowds, in public dinners and political meetings, yet I could not recall his name.

'Mr Townshend,' he began. 'A gentleman such as I know you to be will not require an apology for a mode of procedure which seems harsh, but which legal formalities require should be adopted. You will recognize me as a member of the Angrian magistracy, and I have summonsed you hither to give in-formation concerning certain important matters which now occupy the attention of that government of which I am an unworthy servant.'

'Really, sir,' I replied, effectually puzzled at this preamble, 'I feel very much at a loss to imagine in what way I can be of use to you. May I know on whose authority besides your own the warrant of my arrest was issued?'

'You shall presently be satisfied that I do not act without

authority,' replied the magistrate. 'Meantime, my clerk will administer to you the oath, and I will then proceed to take your testimony.'

A Bible being brought, I commenced the prescribed ceremony, and had nearly completed it when the inner door opened and a third person appeared upon the scene. An individual in a surtout entered the apartment. Unbuttoning his coat with a cool, self-possessed air, he advanced to the fire-place.

'Good evening, Mr Moore,' said he, bowing to the magistrate; and Mr Moore rose and returned his bow with a suppleness that shewed he considered the newcomer no small shakes.[43]

'Hope you're well, Mr Townshend,' continued the person in question, inclining his body again with the slight bend of a poplar in a calm; and then he threw the breast of his surtout open, inserted his thumbs in the armholes of his waistcoat, erected himself before the fire, and looked at me with the air of some almighty nabob to whom I had formerly been shoe-black.

'Go it, my boy,' thought I. 'I'm not the chap to play off these airs upon. I'll give you change for your notes.'[44]

So, having duly kissed the book etc., I resumed my seat opposite Mr Moore, took out my snuff-box and, while deliberately taking a pinch between my finger and thumb, I pretended to scrutinize the two-legged fire-screen with a sidelong glance of keen observation. Small need was there for my eye to linger long on the young face with thin but unmarked features, the light hair brushed into curl on the temples, the martial mustaches and whiskers, the sinewy but very slight figure invested with the carriage of a ramrod.[45] Curse him! Was he not as fully known to me as my own heart? And there he stood like an icicle! However, the *dramatis personae* being assembled, we'll now go on with the play.

'The witness is just about to commence his deposition, I presume,' began the young dragoon.

'He is,' returned Mr Moore. 'Will you question him, Sir William, or shall I?'

'I will begin, if you please,' was the answer and, wiping his mouth with a cambric handkerchief, he put the first interrogation.

'Your name is Townshend, I believe?'

'It is.'

'Have you no other name – or you sometimes use an alias?'

'I frequently use an alias.'

'What other names then are you known by?'

'Gardiner, Jones, Collier and Wellesley.'[46]

'On what grounds do you found your claim to that last name?'

'I don't know.'

'Perhaps you have relations[47] who bear it?'

'Perhaps I have.'

'Have you been living long in Verdopolis?'

'About twenty-one years.'

'What is your age?'

'One and twenty.'

'Remember, witness, you are upon your oath. I again ask you, what is your age?'

'Twenty-one.'

'Indeed!' and the examiner paused, as if in great doubt. In a minute, he recommenced.

'Are you a married man or a bachelor?'

'I don't know.'

'Will you be kind enough to explain that last answer?'

'I never was married that I know of, but I've often wished to be.'

'What business do you carry on?'

'A very thriving one.'

'What is it?'

'I'm a jarvey.'

'What species of conveyance do you drive – an omnibus or cab?'

'Neither.'

'What then?'

'A quill.'

'If I were to require a character of you, do you think you could procure respectable testimonials?'[48]

'No.'

'That's a strange admission. To what circumstances of your life do you ascribe the loss of so valuable a thing as reputation?'

'To the circumstances of my having been at one time connected with a rascal of the name of Clarke – William Clarke,[49] a private in the Angrian army.'

'Soh! Well now, to come to the point. Where were you last Thursday?'

'In Verdopolis.'

'Where were you on the evening of that day?'

'I'm cursed if I can recollect.'

'Perhaps, in that case, I may be able to refresh your memory. You know Clarges Street?'

'Yes.'

'Is it not chiefly occupied by lodging-houses?'

'Very likely.'

'Can you recall the names of any individuals to whom these lodgings are let?'

'Perhaps I might by to-morrow night at this time.'

'You were there last Thursday evening.'

'Was I?'

'Mr Moore, undertake the witness.'

The magistrate obeyed.

'Lord Macara Lofty occupies apartments in that street, Mr Townshend, and you were there as a guest of his Lordship's last Thursday evening. Now, you are required on your oath to say what visitors you met on that occasion.'

'Hum!' thought I. 'Here's some mystery!'

I paused. I rapidly ran over in my own mind the state of the business; I calculated whether I had any interest in concealing names and screening the noble Viscount; I weighed the affair and adjusted the balance as evenly as I could; and as, after due consideration, I could not discern that one atom of advantage would accrue to me by telling a lie, I resolved to speak the truth.

'I was at Clarges Street last Thursday,' said I, 'and I saw Lord Lofty and the honourable Miss Dance. I took tea with them.'

'You were alone, then, in their company?'

'No, there was a sort of lap-dog, a poodle or spaniel of the name of Pepin.'

Sir William interposed a word.

'You and the poodle, then, were invited to meet each other, I presume, Mr Townshend, and the noble Viscount had not troubled himself to ask a third person?'

'Yes, a very respectable bagman.'

'Of the name of Wilson,' added Mr Moore.

'Just so.'

'Will you describe the person of this gentleman? Was he tall?'

'He was, in comparison of the poodle.'

'Mr Townshend, this won't do,' said Mr Moore. 'I must demand proper answers to my questions. I request you again to give me a description of Mr Wilson.'

'I will, then,' said I, 'and it shall be done *con amore*. He was a middle-sized man with a deep open chest, a very dark skin, strong black hair and whiskers, a dissipated profligate look, a kind of branded[50] brow hanging over his eyes, with a scowl, a remarkably bass voice for a man under thirty – which I should judge him to be, though strong drink and bad courses had ploughed lines in his face which might better have suited three score. He called himself a Scotchman, but had none of the Scotch physiognomical characteristics.'

'Did he talk much?'

'No.'

'Had you any wine in the course of the evening?'

'Just a drop.'

'Did Mr Wilson profess teetotalism?'

'Hardly.'

'Was he quite sober when he left the house?'

'I daresay he would be by next day at noon.'

'Was he carried out or did he walk?'

'Something between the two. He walked to the top of the stairs, fell to the bottom, and was carried to Lord Macara's carriage.'

'Who went home with him?'

'No one except the coachman.'

'Did you see the carriage drive off?'

'Yes. For that matter, I saw two carriages; at the moment I was labouring under the complaint called second sight.'

'In what direction did it drive? Up Clarges Street or down?'

'On my oath I can't say. I was in a kind of mist, and, to speak truth, one vision of it seemed to go one way and the other another. I was a little carried in liquor myself.'

'Were the Viscount and Mr Wilson apparently on friendly terms?'

'Yes, but Wilson and Miss Dance were on still friendlier, especially after Wilson's tenth tumbler.'

'Did Miss Dance take glass for glass with Wilson?' asked Sir William gravely.

'I didn't observe that she mixed herself any gin and water, but she certainly allowed Lord Macara to help her from the decanter very freely.'

'Did their conversation at all turn on political subjects?'

'Wilson blasted out once or twice about that d—n—d Turk in the east,[51] but whenever he did so Miss Dance drew her chair nearer to him, and by touching his hand and looking into his face got him off onto some other subject.'

'Did you infer from any part of Mr Wilson's conversation that he had lately been abroad – in France, for instance, or any foreign country?'

'He talked much to Miss Dance about the beauty of French women, and recommended her to dress her hair in the Parisian style. He was beginning a story, to[o], with the words, "When I was last at the Palais Royal", but Lord Macara stopped him, and turned the conversation another way.'

'On your oath, Mr Townshend, have you seen or heard anything of Wilson since the night in question?'

'On my oath, I have not.'

'Well,' said Mr Moore, turning to the Baronet, 'I think we have now got from Mr Townshend all the information on the subject he is capable of communicating. There can be no doubt of Wilson's identity, and, for the rest, time and vigilance will be our best assistants.'

'Mr Townshend is at liberty to depart,' observed Sir William.

I got up; a nod of the most distant civility was interchanged between me and the Baronet, and I turned to the door. Mr Moore followed me. In the gallery he apologized again for the seemingly harsh measures which the law had obliged him to adopt, assured me he should consider my future acquaintance as an honour, and that he could not help being glad of an occasion which had brought him into contact with a man of so much literary eminence. Of course I bowed acknowledgement, and we parted on the best mutual terms possible.

Perhaps before closing this chapter I should say a word about Mr Moore. My readers will not need to be told where they have seen him before – not in Verdopolis, but in the streets of mercantile Zamorna, which he cannot walk without hearing on all sides the whispered sentence, 'There goes Hartford's main man.' An eminent barrister, a wealthy land-holder, he is still the tool of a most haughty task-master. Yet I had just found him acting in close coalition with his superior's bitterest enemy, hiring himself out to be the instrument of that government which had spurned the Baron[52] from amongst them. Truly I now began to wonder who this Wilson was, that could occasion the junction of two such hostile powers. They must be on the scent of blood, thought I, or that implacable Percy would not hunt in couples with Hartford, even by proxy.

Where the Olympian crept along, slow, deep and quiet, after escaping from the rushing mill-races of Zamorna, a thin ice was beginning to crisp upon its surface. A frost was setting in that evening, which already had hardened the road down Hartford Dale to such iron firmness that when any solitary carriage passed up at that late hour the sound of its wheels tinkled among the dusk woods as if they had rolled over metal. Ascending above the dimness of the valley, a full moon filled the cloudless and breathless winter twilight with a sort of peace the largest star could but have faintly typified. Yet here was no summer softness. It was cold, icy, a night of marble, and fast beneath its influence did bagmen urge their gigs, and rejoicingly did mail-coach guards wind their horns when the lights of

Zamorna flashed in the distance and the vision of a tankard of hot ale and rum flashed upon their inward eye.[53]

A man in a cloak came over the bridge of Zamorna and, turning down the dale, held a straight course along the causeway of that noble road. He walked on foot, with his cloak gathered about him, his head and chest erected, and his hat so set on his brow that the brim rested very near on the bridge of his nose. Hartford Woods, unfolding on each hand, shewed, in a fissure between their dark sweep of shade, the sky filled with that glorious rising moon – which moon looked intently upon the traveller with that melancholy aspect it has always worn since the flood. The man stinted[54] his stride a moment when, on his right hand, he passed the great gates of Hartford Hall and beheld far within, towering amid the stretch of grounds, the wide front and wings of that lordly seat. While you gaze, reader, on those long windows shining in moonlight, on those stately and turret-like chimneys and that gleaming roof, the traveller has hurried on. Where is he? Not on the road. Has he vanished? Follow me, and we shall see.

He crossed a stile in that hedge. The field beyond was steep, green and wide. He skirted it quickly, and then, with a faster stride than ever, he threaded the broad, far-stretching ings of the Olympian. Distant, now, from the main road, he pursued a lone track through the silence of lanes and fields. Not a creature crossed his path. Flocks and herds were folded.[55] The farms here are vast, and the farm-houses far asunder. This was Lord Hartford's land, let in long leases half a century ago.

Well, he was now four miles from Zamorna, and the bells of a church were heard far away, chiming nine at night. That was from Massinger, and he stopped till they had ceased ringing, perhaps to listen, perhaps to draw breath. At last, he came to a field with a very noble row of magnificent old trees down the sides, and close along their trunks a broad gravelled footpath, which their boughs overhung like arches. Following this road, he came soon to a house called Massinger Hall, an ancient, spacious dwelling, situated all alone in those wide fields, very solitary and impressive, with a sombre rookery frowning behind it. The pillars of the garden gate were crowned with stone balls, as also were the gables of the house, and in the garden, on a lawn, there was a stone pillar and a time-stained dial-plate.

Massinger Hall was as silent as the grave. All the front was black, except where the moonlight shone on the masses of ivy clustered around every casement. Yet it was not ruined; a calm, stately order pervaded the scene. It was only antique, lonely and grey.

The man in the cloak roamed backwards and forwards before the front of the Hall, pausing, sometimes, as if to listen and, when no sound was audible and no light streamed from the many closed and frost-wrought casements, wandering on again with the same measured stride. At length, from within the house, a sound was heard of the deep bark of some large dog, not near at hand, but in a remote room away at the back. Fearful, evidently, of discovery, the traveller started at the noise. In a moment he had turned the corner of the house and stood sheltered under the more retired gable. Here, at last, his eye met some sign of habitation. The gable had but one large window, almost like that of a church, long and low, opening upon the turf of the lawn, and from this window glowed a reflection of warm light upon all the garden-shrubs about it. Every one knows how distinctly the interior of a lamp-lit room can be seen at night when there is no shutter or blind to screen the window; and, as the stranger knelt on the ground behind a large laurel whose branches partly shot over the lattice, he could see into the very penetralia of the grim house as distinctly as if he had been actually within its walls.

About the window there hung the festoons and drapery of a heavy moreen curtain, deep crimson in colour. These, looped up, showed a long room, glittering on all sides with the reflection of firelight from the darkest panels of oak. The room was carpeted, and in the middle was a massive table having the raven-gloss of ebony. There were no candles, no lamps; nothing but a glowing hearth. This might have been a cheerful room when filled with company, but to-night it wore, like the rest of Massinger Hall, an air of proud gloom, almost too impressive to the imagination. A figure came towards the window, and then paced back again, and was almost lost in the shadow of the opposite end. Again it appeared, drawing near slowly; as slowly, it withdrew to the dusk of distance. To and fro it paced with the same measured step down the whole length of the large old parlour, and there was nothing else visible. A single person walking about there, in that remote mansion embosomed amid boundless fields.

This person was a woman – rather, a girl of about nineteen. She looked like one who lived alone, for her dress showed none of the studied arrangement and decorative taste by which women – young women especially – endeavour to please those with whom they associate. She looked also like one who lived too much alone, for the expression of her face, as she roamed to and fro, was fixed and dreamy. Whether at this moment her thoughts were sad or bright I cannot tell, but they were evidently very interesting, for she had forgot heaven above and earth beneath[56] and all things that are therein in the charm that they wrapped about her. No doubt it was to excite in her mind these fevered dreams that she had left the curtains of the great window undrawn, so that whenever she looked towards it, there was the moon gliding out into a broad space of blue sky from behind the still, tall spire of a poplar, and under her beams, spreading to the horizon, there were wide, solitary pastures, with the noblest timber of the province along their swells.

At last she's waking, and it's time, for a clock somewhere in the house struck ten five minutes ago. She shakes of[f] her trance with a short sigh, walks to the fire, stirs it, and then thinks she'll let down the window-curtains. Being not very tall, she stepped on to a chair for this purpose, but she quickly jumped down again, for as she was stretching her hand to loose the crimson rope, a man rose from behind the laurel branches and stood straight up with his foot on the very sill of the window. The young woman gave back, and looked towards the door. Considerable dismay and amazement were at first depicted in her face, but before she had time to run away the apparition had passed the thin barrier of the glass door and stood in her very presence.

Most considerately, he closed the lattice behind him and also let down the curtains, a feat his stature enabled him to perform much more conveniently than the lady could have done. Then he took off his hat and, while he ran his fingers through his thick hair, said in an ordinary masculine voice,

'Now, Elizabeth, I suppose you know me?'

But this greeting, easy as it was, seemed for a while to produce no answering token of recognition. The young woman looked again and again in dismayed astonishment. At last, some conviction seemed fastening on her mind. It excited strong feeling; she lost the very little colour which had tinged her complexion before, and at last she said in a peculiar voice – a voice flesh and blood human beings never use but when the strongest and strangest sensations are roused,

'Henry! Can it be you?'

Smiling as well as he could, in a kind of way that shewed he was not used to that sort of thing, the man in the cloak offered his hand. It was clasped in two that together were not as large as that one, and wrung and pressed with wild and agitated eagerness. The girl would not speak till she had cleared her voice, so as to be able to utter her words without any choking, hysterical demonstrations; and then she said her visitor was cold and drew him towards the fire.

'I shall do, Elizabeth, I shall do,' said the man, 'only you get a trifle calmer. Come, come, I don't know that I've exactly deserved much of a welcome.'

'No, but I *must* give it you when I can't help it,' she answered sharply. 'Sit down. I never thought you were alive. According to the newspapers, you were in France – why have you left it for a country where you can't be safe? Do you think the police have a glimpse of suspicion which route you have taken? How cold you are, Henry! It is two years tonight since I saw you. Sit down.'

There was a large antique arm-chair on each side of the hearth, and he threw himself into one with the abandonment of a weary man.

'I've not had two hours' sleep for the last three nights,' said he. 'How their d—d police have dogged me since they got fairly on the scent!'

'What, officers are in pursuit of you now!' exclaimed the girl, in a tone of dread.

'Yes, yes, but I think I've shewn them a trick in coming here. They'd think Angria would be the last cover the fox would take. Give me a draught of wine, Elizabeth, I'm almost done.'

She went out of the room hurriedly, looking round at his harassed, pallid face as she closed the door. In her absence, he dropped his head upon the arm of the chair, and gave expression to his sufferings in a single groan, the language of a strong man's distress. When her step was heard returning, he started up, cleared his countenance, and sat erect. She brought wine, which he took from her hand and swallowed eagerly.

'Now,' said he, 'all's right again. Come, you look sadly scared, Elizabeth; but with regard to you, I'm just the same Harry Hastings that I always was. I daresay by this time you've learnt to think of me as a kind of ogre.'

He looked at her with that kind of mistrust born of conscious degradation, but his suspicions were allayed by the expressive glance with which she answered him. It said more convincingly than words: 'Your faults and yourself are separate existences in my mind, Henry.'

Now, reader, how were these two connected? They were not lovers; they were not man and wife. They must have been – a marked resemblance in their features attested it – brother and sister. Neither were [sic] handsome. The man had wasted his vigour and his youth in vice; there was more to repel than charm in a dark, fiery eye sunk far under the brow and an aspect marked with the various lines of suffering, passion and profligacy. Yet there were the remnants of a strong young frame, a bold, martial bearing in proud, confident and ready action, which in better days had won him smiles from eyes he adored like a fanatic. But you remember, reader, what I said of Wilson, and I need not paint his portrait anew. For this was Wilson, just the same dark reprobate in the lonely oak-parlour of Massinger Hall as he had been in Lord Lofty's elegant drawing-room at Verdopolis.

His sister was almost as fair as he was dark, but she had little colour. Her features could lay no claim to regularity, though they might to expression; yet she had handsome brown eyes and a lady-like and elegant turn of figure. Had she dressed herself stylishly and curled her hair, no one would have called her plain. But in a brown silk frock, a simple collar and hair parted on her forehead in smooth braids, she was just an insignificant, unattractive young woman, wholly without the bloom, majesty or fullness of beauty. She looked like a person of quick perceptions and dexterous address; and when the first tumult of emotion consequent on the adventure of the night had subsided, she spoke to her brother with an assumed tone of cheerfulness, as if desirous to conceal from his vigilant jealousy those pangs of anguish which his changed appearance, his dreadful and death-struck prospects, must have forced into her heart. He had gone away a young soldier full of hope; and what career of life must that have been which had brought him back a Cain-like wanderer[57] with a price upon his blood?

'I am not as bad as you think me,' said Henry Hastings suddenly. 'I'm a man that has been atrociously wronged. I could tell you, Elizabeth, a black tale about Adams and that gutter-blood, that fiend of hell, Lord Hartford.[58] They envied me – but I suppose you're on their side, and so it's of no use talking.'

'You think I care more about Hartford and Adams than I do about you, then, do you, Harry? And I know so little of you as to suppose you would shoot a man dead without galling and infamous provocation?'

'Aye, but besides that, I'm a deserter, and no doubt at Pendleton everybody is very patriotic, and it's ultra-heterodox to hate an Angrian renegade one whit less than the Devil. My father, for instance, would he see me, d'ye think?'

'No.'

The answer was short and decisive; but Hastings would not have tolerated evasion. The truth was a bitter pill, but he swallowed it in silence.

'Well, I don't care!' he exclaimed after a pause. 'I'm a man yet, and a better man and a better man |sic| than most of those that hate me, too. And don't think I've been spending the last two years in puling and whining, either, Elizabeth. I've lived like a prince at Paris, a good life, and feasted so well on pleasure that a little pain comes in conveniently to prevent a surfeit. Then this pursuit will soon blow over. I'll keep close with you at Massinger till the hounds are baffled, and then I'll slip down to Doverham, take ship and emigrate to one of the islands. I'll make myself rich there, and when I've built a good house and got an estate full of slaves, I'll stand for a borough. Then I'll come back. After seven years absence they can't touch me. I'll speak in Parliament; I'll flatter the people; I'll set hell burning through the land. I'll impeach half the peerage for their brutal corruptions and tyrannies. If Northangerland be dead I'll apotheize[59] his memory. Let my bloody-handed foes remember that

> 'If we do but watch the hour,
> There never yet was human power
> That could evade, if unforgiven,
> The patient search and vigil long
> Of him who treasures up a wrong.'[60]

Instead of soothing the renegade's excited ferocity and reasoning against his malignant vindictiveness, Miss Hastings caught his spirit, and answered in a quick excited voice, 'You have been basely persecuted. You have been driven to desperation. I know it, and I always did know it. I said so on the day that Mr Warner came to Pendleton and told my father you were broken by a court-martial[61] for desertion. My father took out his will, and while Mr Warner looked on, drew a long line through your name and said he disowned you for ever. Our landlord said, "You have done right, sir", but I told him he had done wrong and unnaturally. My father was then scarcely himself, and he is always quite as passionate as his son. He knocked me down in Mr Warner's presence. I got up and said the words over again. Mr Warner said I was an undutiful daughter, and was adding by my obstinacy to my father's misery. I cared nothing for his reproof, and I left Pendleton a few weeks after. I've been earning my bread since by my own efforts.'

'So I heard,' returned Hastings, 'and that is the reason you are at Massinger, I suppose?'

'Yes. The house belongs to the Moores. Old Mr Moore died lately, and his son, the barrister, is going to reside here. I am keeping it for him while he and his daughter are in Verdopolis. Miss Moore pretends to have a great regard for me and says she can't live without me, because I flatter her vanity and don't rival her beauty, and I teach her to speak French and read Italian, which of course is a convenience.'

'Well, Elizabeth, can you keep me here in safety for a day or two?'

'I'll do my best. There are only two or three old servants in the house. But, Henry, you are sick with weariness. You must have something to eat and go to bed directly. I'll order a room to be prepared for you.'

While Elizabeth Hastings leaves the parlour to find her way through dark passages to the distant kitchen, we also will turn for a time from the contemplation of her and her brother. My candle is nearly burnt out, and I must close the chapter.

Sir William Percy's Diary

Lay long abed this morning – couldn't get up because I was engaged with one of those pleasant dreams that sometimes fill a night with the joy of a lifetime. I wonder what I'd give to realize for one half hour the events of that trance – my hand, I think, or else my two front teeth. Hardly, though, teeth are precious things. I shan't soon forget what Monsieur Adam said about false ones – '*les trois maisons dans la bouche*'.[62] Well, but the dream – I think I was a God, or something quite as irresistible, and I just had in my power what I'd lose a chance of promotion to-morrow to obtain.[63] That's saying a great deal. We sometimes see very beautiful eyes in dreams – those were transcendent; and the whole face, just the living woman as she is. If I were a fool I might hang myself, knowing, as I do, that this dream is a false lie from hell. But I made a good breakfast as soon as I got up, and consoled myself by looking at the Marquise's miniature in the lid of my snuff-box. Bah! what was the made-up artificial French face to *hers*! But Agathe has dark eyes, I think, and that's the reason I flattered her. It's mighty convenient to be in love with Frenchwomen – one's passion never interferes with one's comfort. I think I'll never marry, but spend my life in finding out resemblances to the single shape I glorify – and when I'm very love-sick I'll remember that my idol is altogether terrestrial, and so far from perfect that the other day a modest young lady blushed when, in turning over a volume of portraits, she chanced to come to hers, and perceived at the same moment that my eye had caught the name. heavens, but it told tales!

Just given audience to Ingham. My police inspector tells me that he has quite ascertained that Wilson has left his haunts about town. My lads had smoked every hole where he could hide with such strong fumes of brimstone that he's been forced to leave it – an important object gained. It's easier to chase the fox over an open champaign than in the broken ground and pits and holes of a rabbit warren like Verdopolis – aye, or Paris either. Drove to York Place to communicate the intelligence to Moore. The oily-tongued, smooth-faced toadie of a blackguard cut-throat was sly enough to see the advantage at once. He rubbed his hands and said, chuckling,

'We have him now, Sir William. Only a little patience, a little time, and we'll all be in at the death.'

Well, when Hastings is down there's a wild-boar chase to come on, and then a wolf-hunt, and after that a bull-baiting. Simpson and Montmorency and Macqueen[64] are every one marked. We'll keep on their track; their

> Long gallop shall never tire
> The hound's deep hate, and hunter's fire.[65]

Moreover I must not forget an afterpiece, to be performed under the special patronage of royalty – the tiger hunt, the great striped animal of Bengal turned loose and Colonel Adrian

Augustus O'Shaughnessy[66] at his heels. Lord! The gladiatorial
wild beast fights of the Romans were nothing to these!

But what tack has Hastings taken? My lads must disperse far
and wide. I've ordered some to Edwardston to watch the east
road, and some to Alnwick to guard the west, and some to
Freetown to sentinel the north. If he does escape me, he's a
devil and not a man. Yet he has skill in baffling pursuit. Again
and again, when the hounds were on his very haunches, he has
doubled and slipt. I wonder what charm the miserable victim
can find in life to make him stick to it so? In Paris I more than
once so hemmed him in and harassed him, so crushed him to
the wall, that he must have been at the verge of absolute starvation. The man would have cut his throat long since if he
had been left alone, but while others seek his life to take it
his obstinate nature will lead him to defend the worthless
possession to the last.

Today, while thinking about him, I recollected a little incident
which I may hereafter turn to account in discovering his lair.
Some months since, I chanced to go to the opera one night.
While I was sitting in my box, and thinking myself in my
full-dress uniform an uncommon killing sight, I observed a sort
of sensation commencing round me, and heard, amidst many
whispers and a rising hum of admiration, the words often
repeated, 'It is the beautiful Angrian!' Translate me, if I didn't
at first think they were alluding to myself! The words 'Spare
my blushes' were at my tongue's end, and I was beginning to
deliberate whether or not it would be necessary to acknowledge
so much polite attention by a grateful bow, when I perceived
that the heads and eyes of the ninnies were not turned towards
me, but in a clean oppositie direction – to a box where a tall
young woman was sitting in the middle of a crowd of most
respectable-looking masculine individuals, who one and all
wanted nothing but a tail to make the prettiest counterfeit
monkeys imaginable. The young woman shone in blond and
satin, with plumes enough on her head to waft an ostrich from
Arabia to Sagalecon. The liberal display of neck and arms
shewed plainly enough that she knew both were as white and
round and statuesque as if Phidias had got up from the dead to

chisel them out of the purest marble he could hew from the quarries of Paros, and the pearls circling them round indicated that she had taste enough to be aware how effective was the contrast between the dazzling, living flesh and the cold, glistening gem. She'd a nose like Alexander the Great's,[67] and large, blue, imperial eyes, bright with the sort of ecstasy that a woman flattered into conviction of her own divinity must feel glowing at her heart. Nature had given her a profusion of hair, and art had trained it into long silky ringlets bright as gold. She was a superb animal – there's not a doubt of it – and I hardly know a face or form in Africa that would not have looked dim by her side. And a dim, dusk foil she had, indeed, to her diamond lustre, a little shade just at her elbow, hustled backwards and forwards by the men-pagans that were crowding to the shrine of this idol.

While I was looking at her, Townshend came into my box.

'D'ye see how triumphant Jane Moore is looking to-night?' said he.

'Yes,' I answered. 'She's poisoning half the female peerage with envy. But who in heaven's name has she got at her side, Townshend? What can that little blighted mortal be? Somebody she's hired at so much a night to keep near her for the purpose of shewing her off?'

Townshend took a sight with his opera-glass.

'D'ye mean that pale, under-sized young woman, dressed as plain as a Quakeress in grey, with her hair done à la Victoria Delph?[68] Small credit to her taste for that same! I think a few curls would not have been amiss, to relieve her singular features a trifle. And yet, I don't know; there's something studied about her dress. Every thing suits: white scarf, plain silver ribbon in her hair –'

I interrupted.

'D'ye know who she is, Townshend? Is she some heiress that has sufficient attractions of purse to dispense with those of person?'

'Hardly, I think, for if you observe, she has not a single beau in her train. If she'd had brass, now, half that raff of young Angrian scamps that are pressing their attentions upon Miss

Moore would have turned their thoughts to the holder of the
money-bags. It strikes me now, as that girl looks towards us,
I've seen her face before. I have, I'm sure. It was in a stage-coach
on the Angrian road; I travelled with her some distance, and I
remember from what she said I thought her a sharp, shrewd
customer enough. Did you hear her name?'

'No.'

Here the conversation dropped, for I could take no particular
interest in a person of that sort.

Just a day or two after, I went to dine at Thornton's. It was
a blow-out for the Angrians on the occasion of their omnigatherum[69] at the commencement of the Verdopolitan season. I
was a trifle late, as is my way occasionally, and when I entered
the drawing-room they were already marshalling themselves
for dinner. Jane Moore was the first person I saw, and three
gentlemen were offering her their arms at once – the Earl of
Stuartville, Captain Frank Kirkwall and the omnipotent Lord
Arundel. Of course, the last carried her off. While I was watching their manoeuvres all the other ladies had found conductors,
and lo, I was last in the long train of plumes and robes and, to
my horror and consternation, nothing left for me to patronize
but the same little dusk apparition I had seen at the opera, the
plain, pinched protégée of Miss Moore's. 'Well,' thought I, 'she
may go by herself before I'll offer her my arm,' and, pretending
not to see her, I carelessly followed the rest and took my place,
with all the ease and coolness of my natural habits, at the very
bottom of the table. She came stealing after. There was a single
chair below mine, and into this, being the only seat vacant, she
was obliged to induct herself. However, I'd a pleasant, pretty
girl on the other side of me, an Augusta Londsdale, and one of
the stately Ladies Seymour sat opposite to me. So, having
formed the determination not to notice my left-hand neighbour
by word or look, I made myself very comfortable.

Your Angrians have always a deal of laughing and conversation over their meals, and the party were exceedingly merry.
Looking up the table, I saw a great many handsome women
and much glittering of jewellery and sparkling of bright eyes.
Invitations to take wine were also passing from lip to lip, and

bows were interchanged across the table with infinite gravity. Ladies were leaning their heads to hear the flatteries of the men at their sides, and for my part, I was cajoling Miss Augusta Lonsdale with the finest possible compliments on the bloom of her complexion and the softness of her smiles. When all this flow of enjoyment was at its height, I chanced to look round for the purpose of taking some vegetables a footman was handing, and my eye unfortunately fell on the little individual I had resolved not to see. She was eating nothing, listening to nothing; not a soul had addressed a word to her; and her face was turned towards a large painting of a battle between the windows, which in that room by lamp-light had a peculiar aspect of gloom and horror. I can't pretend to say what thoughts were in her mind, but something she beheld in the rolling clouds of smoke, in the tossed manes and wild eyes of charging horses, and in the bloody forms of men trampled beneath their hoofs, which had filled her eyes with tears. More likely, however, she felt herself solitary and neglected. There is no bitterness the human heart knows like that of being alone and despised, whilst around it hundred hundreds [sic] are loved and idolized. I think I should have spoken to her, but something suggested to me, 'Every body has their own burden to bear. Let her drink the chalice fate commends to her lips.'[70] Besides, there was something that suited my turn of mind in the idea of a neglected human being turning from the hollow world, glittering with such ungenial and selfish splendour before her, to the contemplation of that grim vision of war, and finding, in the clouds of battle-dust and smoke there melting into air, something that touched her spirit to the quick. I would not break the charm by trying to remove the sorrow, and when a tear trickled from her eyelash to her cheek and she hastily lifted her handkerchief to wipe it away, and then, roused to recollection, called into her face an indifferent expression, and turning from the picture, looked like a person without an idea alien from those she was with, I took good care to seem engaged in deep discourse with Augusta Lonsdale, that she might not suspect what scrutiny she had been the subject of a moment before.[71]

After dinner, when the ladies had retired to the drawing-

room, I was, as I always am, one of the first to follow them.
I hate sotting over the decanters; it's a vulgar, beastly habit.
The whole of that evening I watched the protégée very closely,
but she evinced no other habit that took my fancy. She got a
little more notice. Several ladies talked to her, and she entered
into conversation with a good deal of fluency and address. She
assented, and gave up her opinion, and listened with seeming
interest to whatever others had to say. She asked Miss Moore
to sing just when Miss Moore wanted to be asked; she ran over
the list of her finest songs where Jane's grand show-off voice is
most efficiently displayed; and when the lady had fairly commenced she retired from the piano and left room for her
admirers to crowd about her. In two hours, she had grown
quite a favourite with the female part of the company. The men
she never looked at, nor seemed once desirous of attracting
their attention.

Yet the creature, on a close examination, was by no means
ugly. Her eyes were very fine, and seemed as if they could
express anything. She'd a fair smooth skin, a hand as fine as a
fairy's, and her face and ancles were like those of a crack dancer
in an opera-ballet corps. But her features were masked with an
expression foreign to them. Her movements were restrained
and guarded. She wanted openness, originality, frankness.

Before the evening was over, I contrived to learn her name
and family. It was Elizabeth Hastings, the sister of that devil,
Henry. I have never seen her since; till to-day I had forgotten
her. But it struck me all at once that if I could find her out I
might, by proper management, get some useful intelligence
respecting her brother. I'll call on Miss Moore, and ask her a
few careless questions about her protégée, taking care to throw
in deprecating remarks and a general air of contempt and indifference. A careful gleaner finds ears of good grain where a fool
passes by and sees only stubble.

Feb 10th – Dedicated the whole of this morning to an easy
lounge in Miss Moore's boudoir. How much wisdom there is
in taking things quietly! Instead of ferreting like Warner in
dismal government offices, I carry on my machinations amidst
the velvet and down of a lady's chamber. Jane Moore certainly

knows how to fascinate. She is what the world calls exquisitely sweet tempered. A sweet temper in a beautiful face is a divine thing to gaze on, and she has a kind of simplicity about her which disclaims affectation. She does not know human nature; she does not penetrate into the minds of those about her; she does not fix her heart fervently on some point which it would be death to take it from; she has none of that strange refinement of the senses which makes some temperaments thrill with unde-fined emotion at changes or chances in the skies or the earth, a softness in the clouds, a trembling of moonlight in water, an old and vast tree, the tone of a passing wind at night, or any other little accident of nature which contains in it more botheration than sense. Well, and what of that? Genius and enthusiasm may go and be hanged. I did not care a d—n for all the genius and enthusiasm on earth when Jane rose from her seat by the fire, and stood up in her graceful height of stature with her hand held out to welcome me, and 'Good morning, Sir William,' those fresh lips said with such a frank smile. I liked my name better for being uttered by her voice. 'Sit down close to the fire. You must be very cold.' So I did sit down, and in two minutes she and I were engaged in the most friendly bit of chat imaginable.

Jane asked me if I was getting warm, and rang for some more coal in my special behoof.[72] Then she inquired when I thought of going down into Angria, for she hoped whenever I chanced to be about Zamorna I would be sure to pay them a visit, provided they were at home.

'You've never been to our new house,' said she. 'You know we've left Kirkham Lodge since my grandfather died.'

'Indeed,' said I. 'But you live in the neighbourhood still, I suppose?'

'Oh yes, it's the family place near Massinger, an old, queer sort of house, but Papa intends to pull it down and build a proper seat. I'm rather sorry, because the people at Zamorna will be sure to say it is pride.'

'Oh, you shouldn't mind envy,' I returned; and then, by way of changing the conversation, I made a remark on the beauty of an ornamental vase on the mantle-piece, the sides of which were exquisitely painted with a landscape of Grecian ruins, olives and a dim mountain background.

'Is it not beautiful!' she said, taking it down. 'And it was done by the sister of poor Captain Hastings. By the bye, Colonel, it is very cruel of you to hunt young Hastings as they say you do. He was such a clever, fine, high-spirited fellow.'

'Aye, he shewed his spirit in that bloody murder of Adams,' I returned.

'Adams was not half as nice a man as he,' returned Jane. 'He was very arrogant. I daresay he insulted poor Hastings shamefully. Adams was just like Lord Hartford. I once met him at Hartford Hall when Papa and I dined there, and I told Papa when I came home I thought he was a very proud, disagreeable man.'

'Then you think his subaltern did right to shoot him through the brain?'

'No, not right; but it is a pity Hastings should die for it. I wish you knew his sister, Colonel. You would be sorry for her.'

'His sister? Who is she? Not that very plain girl I saw with you one night at the opera?'

'You wouldn't call her plain if you knew her, Colonel,' said Jane, with the most amiable earnestness of manner. 'She is so good and so clever. She knows everything, very nearly, and she's quite different to other people, I can't tell how.'

'Well,' said I, 'she's not a person, my dear Miss Moore, to attract my attention much. Is she really a friend of yours?'

'I won't tell you, Colonel, because you speak so sneeringly of her.'

I laughed.

'And so I suppose this paragon bothers you a great deal about her murdering brother – tells you tales of his heroism and genius and so forth?'

'No,' said Jane. 'There's one very odd thing that I've often wondered at – she never mentions him. And somehow I never dare begin to talk on the subject, for she has her peculiarities, and if she happened to take offence she'd leave me directly.'

'Leave you! What, does she live with you?'

'She's my governess, in a sense,' said Miss Moore. 'I learn French and Italian of her. She went to school at Paris, and she speaks French very well.'

'Where do the Hastings come from?' I inquired.

'From Pendleton, up in Angria; quite a rough, wild country, very different to Zamorna. There's no good society there at all, and the land is very little cleared. I once rode over to the neighbourhood on horse-back when I was on a visit to Sir Markham Howard's, and I was quite astonished at the moors and mountains. You've no idea – hardly any green fields, and no trees, and such stony bad roads. I called at old Mr Hastings' house. They don't live like us there. He's considered a gentleman, and his family is one of the oldest in that part of the country; and he was sitting in his kitchen – what they call the house. It was wonderfully clean, the floor scoured as fair, nearly, as this marble, and a great fire in the chimney such as we have in our halls. Still, it looked strange, and Mr Hastings was roughly dressed and had his hat on. He spoke quite with an Angrian accent, far broader than General Thornton's, but I liked him very much. He was so hospitable. He called me a bonny lass, and said I was as welcome to Colne Moss Tarn as the day.'

'Was Captain Hastings at home then?' I inquired.

'No. It was soon after he had entered the army, and when everybody was talking in his praise, and his songs were sung at public dinners and meetings.[73] But Elizabeth Hastings was at home, and she did look such an elegant, lady-like being in that homely place. But though she's quite fastidious in her refinement, I really believe she likes those dreary moors and that old manor house far better than Zamorna or even Verdopolis. Isn't it odd?'

'Very,' said I.

Jane continued,

'I often wonder what it was that made her leave Pendleton and go out into the world as she has done. Papa thinks it is for something her father has said or done against Henry, for old Mr Hastings is an exceedingly obstinate, passionate man. And indeed, all the family are passionate. Elizabeth has never been home for two years, and now she's living by herself at our place, Massinger Hall. Such a lonely situation and such gloomy old rooms – I wonder she can bear it.'

This last sentence of Miss Moore's comprised the information I wished to obtain, so it was not necessary I should prolong my visit much further. After a few minutes further chat, I took a final gaze on her kind, handsome face, shook hands, made my parting bow and exit. Then, when I got home, I found Ingham waiting for me with an important piece of intelligence. He had succeeded in ascertaining that the dog Wilson had certainly gone in an eastern direction. Angria is the word, then. I'll set off tomorrow, and as to this Massinger Hall, I mean to see the interior of it before two more suns set.

The stillest time[74] of a winter's day is often the afternoon, especially when the desolation of snow and tempest without seem to give additional value to the comfort of a warm hearth and sheltering roof within. Near the close of a wild day, just before twilight's shadows began to fold over the world, Captain Hastings and his sister were sitting by the hearth of the oak-parlour at Massinger Hall. Hastings watched the dreary snow-storm careering past that large Gothic casement, and after a long silence he said, 'There will be deep drifts on Boulshill.' The man was in a gloomy mood and so was his sister, for neither of them was the brightest, mildest, or gentlest of human beings, and one had the horror of a violent death always before him, and the other had the consciousness that a murderer, an outlaw, a deserter and a traitor were all united in the person of her only brother.

'And you think no intercession on your behalf would be listened to at court?' said Elizabeth Hastings, recurring to a conversation they [had] been engaged in some minutes previously.

'I think they are all unhanged villains at court,' replied Henry in a deep rough voice.

Before proceeding with my narration, I would pause a minute on the character of Captain Hastings.[75] The 19th regiment, of which the renegade had once been an officer, never lost from its bold, bad ranks a man so well calculated to sustain the peculiar species of celebrity which that corps have so widely earned. He was, at the outset of his career, just what a candidate for distinction there ought to have been. Before vice fixed her canker in him, he was a strong, active, athletic man, with all the health of his native hills glowing in his dark cheeks, with a daring ferocity of courage always awake in his eye, with an arrogance of demeanour that bore down weaker minds, and which, added to an intellect strong in the wings as an eagle, drew round him wherever he went a train of besotted followers. But the man was mutinous and selfish and accursedly malignant. His mind was of that peculiarly agreeable conformation, that if any one conferred a benefit upon him, he instantly jumped to the conclusion that they expected some act of mean submission in return; and the consequence was, he always bit the hand that caressed him. Then his former patrons looked coldly at him, shrugged their shoulders, and drew off in disgust, while Hastings followed their retreat with a howl of hate and a shout of defiance. Thus he ruined his public prospects, for the bashaws whom he insulted – the Richtons and Hartfords and Arundels – were already in possession of the high places, and they stood on the lofty steps of preferment, and with pride and tyranny more demoniac even than his own, shook their lordly fists at the baffled lion below, and swore, till the bottom of hell was moved by their oaths, that they'd go bodily to Beelzebub[76] before Hastings should rise an inch.

No doubt these aristocratic vows will be fulfilled all in good time. But meanwhile the Captain, like a wise man, thought he'd be beforehand with them. Ambition would not carry him fast enough to Pandemonium, so he harnessed the flying steeds of pleasure to aid it. His passions were naturally strong, and his imagination was warm to fever. The two together made wild work, especially when drunken delirium lashed them up to a gallop that the steeds of the Apocalypse thundering to Armageddon[77] would have emulated in vain. He was talked of everywhere for his excesses. People heard of them with dismay; the very heroes of the 19th held up their saintly hands and eyes at some of his exploits, and exclaimed, 'Dang it! that beats everything!'

One day during the campaign of the Cirhala, Hastings was on duty somewhere when a man in an officer's cloak rode by on horseback. He reined up and said,

'Hastings, is that you?'

'Yes,' said the Captain, not looking up from the butt end of his rifle, on which he was leaning, for he knew the voice, and the figure too, and it galled him that anything should come near him whose approach it would be necessary to recognize by an act of homage. However, the horseman was alone; so, as there were no witnesses of the humiliation, Hastings at last condescended to lift his military cap from his brow.

'You're going to the dogs, I understand, Hastings,' continued the other. 'What the D—l do you think your constitution's made of, man?'

'Devilment, if I may judge from what I feel,' answered the suffering profligate with the air of a rated bull-dog.

'D'ye mean to stop?' continued the interrogator.

'I've no present intention of that sort, my lord Duke.'

'Well, perhaps you're in the right,' continued the horseman coolly, managing his restless charger, which fretted impatiently beneath the restraint of the rein. 'Perhaps you're in the right, lad. It would be hardly worth your while to stop *now*. You're a lost, worn-out, broken-up scoundrel.'

The Captain bowed.

'Thank you, my lord. That's God's truth, however.'

'I once had a pleasure in looking at you,' added his adviser. 'I thought you a fine, promising fellow that was fit for anything. You're now just a poor d—l, nothing more.'

'And that's God's truth too,' was the answer.

The horseman stooped a moment from his altitude, laid his hand on Hastings' shoulder, and with a remarkably solemn air ejaculated,

'D—n you, sir!'

The horse was then touched with the spur, and it sprang off as if St Nicholas[78] had ridden it.

It was evening when this interview took place, and the next morning Hastings shot Colonel Adams. I will now return to Sir William Percy's diary.[79]

Feb 18th Stancliffe's is a real nice comfortable inn. I always feel as content as a king when I'm seated in that upper room of theirs that looks out on the court-house. I'd a wretchedly cold journey from Verdopolis down to Zamorna. Very wet, dreary day. Got in just about noon, and felt very philanthropic and benevolent when I was shewn into the aforesaid upper room with a good fire and as pretty a little luncheon as eye could wish to see set out on the table. Having appeased the sacred rage[80] of hunger, I began to consider whether I should order fresh horses to my barouche and drive forward to Massinger, but a single glance towards the window settled that matter. Such driving pelting rain, such a bitter, disconsolate wind, such sunless gloom in the sky, and streets brown and shining wet, clattering with pattens and canopied by umbrellas.

'No, it's no go,' I said to myself. 'I'll give anybody leave to cut off my ears that shall catch me romancing in search of old halls today.'

So I just laid me down easy on a sofa that stood convenient to the fireside, and with the aid of the last number of *Rookwood's Northern Magazine*[81] and a glass of pleasant Madeira placed on a little stand within the reach of my arm, I proposed spending an afternoon at once rational and agreeable. Well, for two hours all went uncommon well. The fire burnt calm and bright, the room was still, the elements without gibbered more infernal moans than ever, and I, hanging over the pages of a deliciously besotted tale entitled 'Leasehold Beck', was just subsiding into a heavenly slumber, when knock, knock, knock; some fiend of Tartarus[82] tapped at the door. I know how to punish intruders. I pretended not to hear. Tap, tap, tap. No answer. Rap, rap, rap. No go. Bang, bang, bang.

'Come in,' said I, with the most gentlemanly languor of tone imaginable. A ghoul[83] in the likeness of a waiter appeared at the invocation.

'A note for you, sir,' said he, poking a silver salver into my face.

'A note! I hope it's a billet-doux,' thought I, taking up the missive and lingering over the seal, as if breaking it would dissolve a charm.

'I believe it's from Hartford Hall,' continued the ghoul. 'A tiger[84] in their livery brought it.'

'A tiger!' I repeated. 'Aye, it's all the work of magic. Pray, is the wild beast waiting for an answer?'

'Wild beast, sir! It's a tiger – a boy. No, sir, he's gone.'

'Very well. Do me the favour, then, to follow his example.'

Thus rebuked, the ghoul vanished. Having opened the note, I found its contents to run as follows.

Lord Hartford, having learnt that Sir William Percy is at Stancliffe's Hotel, requests the favour of his immediate attendance at Hartford Hall, as Lord Hartford has important intelligence to communicate. He hopes Sir William will not delay complying with the solicitation contained in this note.

P. S. Lord Hartford is momently expecting the arrival of Ingham with the detachment of police stationed by Sir William's orders at Edwardston.

Having achieved the perusal of this despatch I found myself giving utterance to a whistle, and at the same instant the spirit moved me to ring the bell and order a horse. In about a quarter of an hour after I had been dreaming on a couch under the dozy influence of a stupid tale, I found myself pricked up[85] in a saddle, dashing over the bridge of Zamorna like a laundrymaid heading a charge of cavalry. When I got to Hartford Hall, I found a carriage drawn up at the entrance, and four of my own police ready mounted in the disguise of postillions. One of them was Ingham. He doffed his cap.

'Scent's as strong as stink, sir,' says he. Encouraged by this agreeable hint, I alighted, and hastened into the house to obtain more precise information. Passing through the hall, I perceived the door of the dining-room was open, so I walked in. The Great Creole[86] had just concluded his dinner and was in the act of helping himself to a glass of wine when I entered. His gloves and his hat lay on a side-table, and a servant stood with his cloak over his arm, waiting to assist him on with it.

'Well, Percy,' he began with his growling bass voice, as soon as ever his eye caught me. 'I hope the rascal is about to be disposed of at last. Fielding, is my cloak ready?'

'Yes, my lord.'

'Will you take wine, Sir William? Fielding, the carriage is at the door, I suppose?'

'Yes, my lord.'

'You have nothing to detain you, I presume, Sir William? Time is precious. Fielding, have the police had the whisky I ordered?'

'Yes, my lord.'

'I got upon the train[87] only this morning, Sir William. I laid my plans instantly. Fielding, did you load my pistols?'

'Yes, my lord.'

'A desperate scoundrel like that ought to be guarded against. By G—d, if he resists, if he proves troublesome, a small thing will make me blow his brains out. Fielding, my cloak. Help me on with it.'

'Yes, my lord.'

'By G—d, I wish he may only give me sufficient pretext. I'll provide for him handsomely. Ha! ha! I'm more than half in old Judge Jeffrey's[88] mind. Provided he'll save me the trouble of a trial, I'll put him out of pain a little quicker. Sir William, you're ready?'

'Yes, my lord.'

So the Baron swallowed another bumper of his claret, and then drew on his gloves and pulled his hat over his broad black eye-brows so as half to shade the orbs flickering underneath, with an unaccustomed smile, kindled partly by wine and partly by the instinct of bloodhound exultation. Out he strode into the hall, and I followed. I wonder if that man knows how intensely I hate him. Sometimes, I think he has a dim conscious-ness that some creeping thrills of abhorrence steal along my veins whenever he and I look into each other's eyes. At other times, I imagine he lives in stolid ignorance of the fact. I promise myself the pleasure of enlightening his mind on the subject sometime when a fair opportunity offers. Till then, I'll conceal.

Before getting into the carriage, I just stepped up to my two innocents and inquired how they were off for soap (alias fire-arms), for I knew the stag would gore when brought to bay. The dear babes shewed me each a couple of chickens[89] nestling in his bosom. I was satisfied, and took my seat calmly by the side of my noble friend. How my heart warmed towards him in the close proximity of our relative positions, especially when I looked at his viznomy, and saw him dissevering his lips with a devilish grin and setting his clenched teeth against the wild sheets of rain that, as we whirled down his park, came driving in our faces.

Evening was now setting in, and all the woods of the dale were bending under the gloom of heavy clouds and rushing to the impetus of a tremendous wind. As we swept out at the iron gates, which swung back at our approach with a heavy clang, lights glanced from the porter's lodge; they were gone in a moment, and on we thundered through rain and tempest and mist, Hartford cursing his coachman every five minutes and ordering him to make the horses get over the ground faster. I shall not soon forget that ride. My sensations were those of strange, blood-thirsty excitement; and woods and hills rolled by in dusky twilight, spangled with lights from the scattered houses of the valley, while rain drove slanting wildly over every thing, and the swollen and roaring Olympian seemed running a mad race with ourselves. Hartford, between his oaths, at last contrived to give me some sort of explanation of the errand we were going upon. His gamekeeper, he said, had been that morning down at Massinger, and while he was setting some springes in a wood near the old place called Massinger Hall, he had seen a fellow come out of the garden gate whose appearance exactly answered to the hand-bill description of Henry Hastings, Gent.

'And,' says Hartford, 'I know a sister of the man's is residing there as a housekeeper or housemaid or something of that sort, and this, in conjunction with the track Ingham has succeeded in tracing out, justifies me in supposing that we have unkennelled the right fox at last. Drive on, Johnson! D—n the villain, he crawls like a tortoise!'

Though it was now getting very dark, I could perceive that we had for some time left the high road, and were following the course of a bye-path, whose windings led us down into some region of fields and solitude, where hardly the twinkle of a single window could be seen through the gloom. The first intimation we had of a near approach to the hall was the rushing of trees above us and the vision of vast, dusky trunks lining the road with a long colonnade of timber. Hartford now countermanded his former orders to Johnson and desired him to drive softly; a mandate easily obeyed, for the path was carpeted with a thick bed of withered leaves never cleared since last autumn, and over these the wheels passed with a dead, muffled sound, scarcely heard at all through the confusion of wind and rain and groaning branches.

The carriage suddenly stopped, and when I looked up there was the dim outline of a gate with balls upon the pillars, and beyond, rising above trees, I saw a stack of chimneys and a gable-end.

'Here we are!' said Hartford, and he jumped out, as eager and impatient for his prey as the most unreclaimed tiger of the jungle.

'Have you got the manacles?' I asked quietly, bending over to Ingham.

'Yes, sir, and a strait-waistcoat.'

'Come, Sir William, you lose time,' growled bloodhound.

'I'll not be hurried by you,' was my internal resolution, while I stood up in the carriage and buttoned my surtout comfortably over my chest, and then I felt if my handkerchief was in my pocket, chance[90] I should find it necessary to shed any tears on the occasion of the poor d—l's capture. I also ascertained that a vinaigrette I usually carry about me was safe in its place, for I considerately thought of Miss Hastings, and imagined it was not impossible that she might faint in the course of the scene about to go off, especially if there was any pluffing of gunpowder. My waistcoat was then to pull down, and a shawl I had about my neck was to adjust more conveniently. Lastly,

I felt I could not live without priming with a pinch of snuff. During the settlement of all these small but essential preliminaries, my noble friend stood on the wet grass before the gate, fuming, cursing and ejaculating in a most exemplary way. First it began,

'Sir William, surely you're ready! What the d—l can you be about? Johnson, Ingham, Jones, can't you assist Sir William? The whole affair will be spoiled by this accursed dawdling – precious time passing away and nothing done. G—d d—n! Blast such folly! Cursed conceited humbug! Infernal petticoat perverseness![91] Fetid foppery! Are you ready, I say, sir?'

This interrogation was put in the harshest mode of savage, arbitrary insolence.

'I shall be, by and bye,' said I, and having now perfectly arranged myself, I proceeded to alight from the carriage with the care and deliberation of a lady fearful of soiling her silk gown by contact with the wheels.

'Your Lordship looks somewhat hurried,' I remarked, in an indifferent sort of way. 'Take your time – no fear,' and, in a consolatory whisper, 'Perhaps the fellow may not have fire-arms.'

I heard something about a d—d impertinent puppy! and his Lordship turned his ferocity on our assistants.

'What are you all standing gaping there for? To your stations, every one. Johnson, you idiot, take the carriage to the back way and have it ready. Do you hear, sir?'

And now serious work commenced. There were four policemen. One of them was to be stationed behind, one in front of the house, to bar all egress. The two others were destined for the business of the interior. I now led my men to their posts. All the garden paths were dark and wet. The house was silent, all the windows closed, and not a beam of light streaming from their panes. It seemed an old pile, and had something of haunted and romantic gloom about it.

My lads having received their orders and commenced their sentinel march in the yard and on the lawn, I stole round to join Lord Hartford. He was waiting for me on the front door steps. I could just discern his dusk-cloaked figure standing there like a goblin.

'Is all right?' said he.

'All is right,' I answered.

He turned to the door, lifted the knocker, and to the sound of his summons a long, desolate echo answered from within. In the interval that followed, how utterly I forgot that drenching rain. Wild wind and utter darkness enveloped me round.

A door opened, and a very light but very rapid step was heard to run quickly up the passage; then another step, and a hollow, treading sound as of some one ascending oaken stairs; then a pause, a silence of some minutes. Hartford began again with his growling solo of oaths.

'Hustling the lumber into concealment, I suppose,' said he. He gave another, louder rap, and in two minutes more the withdrawing of a bolt and the rattling of a chain was heard. The heavy front door turned grating on its hinges, and a woman-servant stood before us with a light. The look with which she scanned us said plainly enough, 'Who can there be making such a noise at this time of night?'

'Is Miss Hastings at home?' I asked.

'Yes, sir.'

'Can we see her?'

'Walk forward, sir.' And still with a perplexed air, the woman led the way through a long passage and, opening a door in the side, asked us to step in. She left her light on the table of the room into which she shewed us, and closing the door, went away. It was an apartment with the chill of a vault on its atmosphere, furnished in drawing-room style, but without fire in its bright steel grate, without light in its icy chandelier, whose drops streamed from the ceiling like a cold crystal stalactite. The mirror between the windows looked as if it had never reflected a human face for ages; the couch, the chairs, the grand piano, all stood like fixtures never to be moved. Over the piano was a large picture, the only one in the room. I could see by the dim candle on the table that it was a portrait, painted by some eminent hand, for the contours were flesh-like and brilliant. It was a girl of about twelve years old, with the lips and the eyes and the soft, shadowy hair that flattering villain Lawrence bestows on all his portraits. The image smiling all by itself in this frozen, dreary room reminded me of that legendary lady who pricked her finger, and having fallen into a trance, was enshrined in a splendid chamber where she sat twenty years, in all the stillness of death and all the beauty of life.[92]

I was still looking at this picture, and had just discovered in the features an indubitable likeness to Jane Moore, when the turning of the door-handle caused me also to turn, and having so done I saw a young female enter the room, curtsey to myself and Lord Hartford, and then stand with her fingers nervously twined in a watch-chain round her neck and her eyes fixed on us with a look of searching yet apprehensive inquiry.

'We shall want a few minutes' conversation with you, Miss Hastings,' said Hartford, shutting the door and handing a chair, while the stern arrogance of the dissipated old rake instantly softened to gentle condescension at the sight of a petticoat.

'I believe I am speaking to Lord Hartford,' said she, summoning a kind of high-bred, composed tact into her manner, though the leaf-like trembling of her thin, white hands let me into a secret as to the reality of that composure.

'Yes, madam, and I wish to treat you as considerately as I can. Now come, be under no alarm, and sit down.'

Now for my vinaigrette, thought I, for already the nervous being had lost her feint of calmness, and was beginning to look sick. She took the chair Hartford brought her.

'I am only surprised at your Lordship's visit. I am not alarmed. There is nothing to alarm me,' and a respectful air of reserve was assumed.

'I can trust to your sense,' said his Lordship politely. 'You will receive the communication I have to make with proper fortitude, I am sure. It grieves me that you happen to be the sister of a man proscribed by the law. But justice must have its course, madam, and it is now my painful duty to tell you that I am here tonight for the purpose of arresting Captain Henry Hastings on a charge of murder, desertion and treason.'

'Will she swoon now?' thought I. But humph! No! Up she got, like a doe starting erect at the sound of horns.

'But Henry Hastings is not here,' said she, and she stood

within a pace or two of Hartford, looking up into his face as if
she were going to challenge him. His Lordship, still drawing it
mild,[93] shook his head.

'It won't do, Miss Hastings. It won't do,' said he. 'Very
natural that you should wish to screen your brother, but my
information is decisive. My plans are laid. There are four
policemen about the house; your doors are guarded. So now
compose yourself. Stay here with Sir William Percy. I am going
to execute my warrant, and in two minutes the thing will
be done.'

Sparks of fire danced in Miss Hastings' eyes. There was very
little resemblance between what now stood before me and
the submissive, dexterous, retiring individual I had seen at
Verdopolis.

'Does your Lordship intend to search the house?' said she.

'Yes, madam; every cranny of it from the hall to a rat-hole.'

'And every cranny of it from the hall to a rat-hole is free for
your Lordship's inspection,' she rejoined.

Hartford moved towards the door.

'I shall certainly attend your Lordship,' she pursued; and
turning sharply to the table, she took up the candle and walked
after him, thus leaving me very unceremoniously in the dark.
I heard Hart[ford] stop in the passage.

'Miss Hastings, you must not follow me.'

There was a pause.

'I must lead you back to the drawing-room.'

'No, my lord.'

'I must.'

'Don't,' in an intreating tone. 'I'll shew you every room.'

But Hartford insisted; she was obliged to retreat. Still, she
did not yield. She only backed as the Baron advanced, a little
overawed by his towering stature and threatening look. She
made a stand at the drawing-room door.

'Will you compel me to use coercive measures?' said his
Lordship. He laid a hand on her shoulder. One touch was
enough. She shrunk away from it into the room. Hartford shut
the door and she was left standing, her eyes fixed on the vacant
panels. Mechanically she replaced the candle on the table, and

then she wrung her hands and turned a distressed, wild glance on me.

It was now my turn to address her, and my knowledge of her character shewed me in what way to proceed. Here, I saw, was little strength of mind, though there was a semblance of courage, the result merely of very overwrought and ardent feeling. Here was a being made up of intense emotions, in her ordinary course of life always smothered under diffidence and prudence and a skilful address. But now, when her affections were about to suffer almost a death-stab, when incidents of strange excitement were transpiring around her, on the point of bursting forth like lava, still she struggled to keep wrapt about her the veil of reserve and propriety.

She sat down at a distance from me, and turned her face from the light to evade the look with which I followed all her movements. I walked towards her chair.

'Miss Hastings, you look very much agitated. If it would be a relief to you, you shall accompany the officers in their search. I have authority to give you permission. I am sorry for you, my poor girl, very.'

Her head turned more and more away from me as I spoke. She rested her eyes and forehead on her hand, and when I uttered the last words, there was a short irrepressible sob. Every nerve in her frame quivered, and she gave way to the bitter weeping of despair. She got it over as soon as she could, and then she turned and thanked me for my compassion, in a way and with a tone that shewed all caution and disguise were gone and that impulse and imagination were now in full and unguarded play.

'I may go?' she said.

I gave her leave, and as quick as thought she was gone.

'But I must follow,' thought I, and it required my fastest stride to overtake her. The lower rooms had been already examined; we heard the policemen's tramp in the lobby overhead. She was speeding up the old staircase as if her feet had been winged. Hartford confronted her at the top of the stairs. He frowned prohibition and stretched out his arm to impede passage, but she darted under the bar, sprang before Ingham, who

was just in the act of opening a chamber door, dashed in before
him, exclaiming, 'Henry, the window!' and clapping the door
to, tried with all her strength to hold it, to bolt it, till the
murderer should have time to escape.

'The vixen!' thought I. 'The witch! That's the consequence
of minding female tears.'

I sprang to Ingham's assistance. In her agony she had had
strength to hold it against him for a fraction of time. I put my
foot and hand to the door. The inefficient arm within failed,
she was flung to the ground by the force of the rebound, and I
and my myrmidons rushed in. The room was dark, but there
by the window was the black outline of a man, madly tearing
at the stanchions and bars by which the old lattice was secured.
It was a nightmare.

'Seize him!' thundered Hartford. 'Men, your pistols! Shoot
him dead if he resists!'

There was a flash through the dark chamber – a crack –
somebody's pistol had exploded. Another, louder crash – the
whole frame-work of the lattice was dashed in, bars, glass
and all. The cold, howling storm swept through the hollow.
Hastings was gone. I gave a glance to see if I could follow; but
there was an unfathomed depth of darkness down below, and
I thought of legs jammed into the body like a telescope.[94]

'To the outside!' I shouted.

I cleared the stairs at two bounds and made for the front
door and, followed by I know not what hurly-burly of tramping
feet, rushed onto the front. The contest was already begun.
There was a grass-plat in front of the house, and in the middle
of it I saw a huddled struggle of two figures in deadly gripe,
Hastings and the sentinel that had been stationed outside. God
bless me! There sprung a flash of fire between them, and the
ringing crack of a pistol split the air again. The mass of wrestling
mortality dissolved. The arms of one were loosened from the
body of the other, and a heavy weight fell on the grass. Off
sprung the survivor, bounding like a panther. But he was surrounded, he was hemmed in; the three remaining policemen cut
across the lawn, intercepted his flight. He was too stunned to
struggle more, and while two held him down on his knees, the

third fixed his hands in a pair of bracelets more easily put on than taken off.

Just as this ceremony was completed, the moon, for the first time that night, came rolling out of a cloud. She was in her wane, but the decayed orb gave light enough to shew me the features I longed to see. He was in the act of rising up; his head was bare, his face lifted a little. A gleam, cold, wan and wild, revealed the aspect, the expression of the man I had followed for eighteen months and hunted down in blood at last – of that daring, desperate miscreant, Henry Hastings the Angrian!

C Townshend Feby 24th 1839

[PART II]

My last volume, I believe, terminated at the ringing of the Duchess's bell; which bell, acting like a charm on the dramatis personae of the narrative, all at once sealed their lips and sent the curtain rolling down 'like midnight loosed at noon'[95] over her Grace's ante-room. This, no doubt, was a providential interference; for, if my readers recollect, an angry parle was then in progress which, from the pitch at which it had arrived, seemed likely to terminate in nothing less than a duello between the Premier of Angria and one of his lease-holders' daughters. W. H. Warner Esqre. had just ordered Miss Hastings to stop, and Miss Hastings was just asking herself what right any living creature had to give her any orders whatever, and in dim perspective was making up her mind to leave Verdopolis instanter, committing herself and her fortunes to the first Angrian coach which should be ready to start, to return to Zamorna and there doggedly to wait whatever luck should befall her martyr brother, then to sit down with a consolatory and lasting hate at her heart towards all and sundry, the judge, jury, king, court and country, who had tried, condemned and suffered the execution of that notorious and ineffable saint; such, I say, was the tenor of Miss Hastings' embryo resolves, when that bell from within rung its short call, when the inner door opened and, in spite of herself, the young woman found that she was compelled to finish the adventure she had commenced.

How quietly and deferentially, with what a studied look of awe, she would, under other circumstances, have crossed that hallowed threshold! She would have considered only how best to prove her deep, innate sense of her own inferiority and of the transcendent supremacy of the royal lady she was about to petition. She would have called up all her tact, all her instinctive knowledge of human nature, especially of the human nature of beautiful and titled women. She would have laid by her scorn, shut up out of sight the trifling property of pride which, after all, gave the little woman the power of valuing to their full extent her own acute perceptions and mental gifts. She would have said, 'Here I am, dust and ashes, and I presume to speak to a Queen.' But the hazing Mr Warner had very properly administered was still burning at her heart. It had raised her dander, and had quickened in her mind diverse calculations as to the relative value of patrician and plebeian flesh and blood. Now, those calculations it had ever been her wont occasionally to indulge in by her own fireside, but she had never before attempted to solve the problem under the roofs of royalty or even of aristocracy. The effort, consequently, threw her into some agitation, and when she stepped into the imperial breakfast-room the tears were so hot and blinding in her eyes she could scarcely discern into what a region of delicate splendour her foot had intruded.

She saw, however, a table before her, and at the table there was a lady seated. When she had cleared the troublesome mist from her vision, she perceived that the lady was engaged with some loose sheets that looked like music and, as she turned them over, conversing with a person who stood behind her chair. That person was Sir William Percy and, when Miss Hastings entered, as his royal sister did not appear to notice her approach, he observed coolly,

'The young woman is waiting. Will your Grace speak to her?'

Her Grace raised her head; not quickly, as your low persons do when they are told an individual is expecting their attention, but with a calm deliberate movement, as if it was a thing of course that somebody should be waiting the honour of her notice. Her Grace's eyes were very large and very full. She turned them on Miss Hastings, let them linger a moment over her figure, and then withdrew them again.

'A sister of Captain Hastings, you say?' she remarked, addressing her brother.

'Yes,' was the answer.

Her Grace turned the leaves of a fresh sheet of music, put it quietly from her, and once more regarded the petitioner. Now, her Royal Highness's glance was not penetrating – that is, the brown eye had not that quick, arrowy flicker which darts to the heart in a minute – but it seemed to dwell quietly and searchingly. It had the effect of sinking through the countenance to the mind. It was grave, and the darkness of the eye-lashes, the languour of the lids, made it seem pensive. However, Miss Hastings stood that gaze, and her temper was so refractory at the time she could almost have curled her lip in token of defying it. Yet, as she stood opposite the fair princess, she felt by degrees the effect of that beautiful eye, changing her mood, awakening a new feeling, and her heart confessed, as it had a thousand times done before, the dazzling omnipotence of beauty, the degradation of personal insignificance.

'Come forward,' said the Duchess.

Miss Hastings barely moved a step. Still she would hardly endure the tone of dictation.

'Explain to me what you wish in your present circumstances, and I will consider if I can serve you.'

'I presume,' returned Miss Hastings, looking down and speaking in a low, quick voice, not at all supplicatory, 'I presume your Royal Highness is aware of the situation of Captain Hastings. My present circumstances are to be inferred from that situation.'

And so she abruptly stopped.

'I do not quite comprehend you,' returned the Duchess. 'I understand you came as a petitioner.'

'I do,' was the answer. 'But perhaps I have done wrong. Perhaps your Royal Highness would rather not be troubled with my request. I know what seems of importance to private individuals is often trivial to the great.'

'I assure you, I regard your brother's case with no unconcerned eye. Perhaps I may have already done all that I can to obtain a remission of his sentence.'

'In that case, I thank your Grace. But if your Grace has done what you can, it follows that your Grace can do no more, so it would be presumption in me to trouble your Grace further.'

The Duchess seemed rather puzzled. She looked at the little stubborn sight before her with a perplexed air, and then she turned an inquiring glance to Sir William, as good as to say, 'What does she mean?'

Sir William was stuffing a pocket handkerchief into his mouth, by way of stifling an incipient laugh. He stooped to his sister's ear, and said in a whisper,

'She has an odd temper. Something has occurred to ruffle it. Your Grace will excuse it.'

But the Duchess hardly looked as if she would. At any rate she did not condescend to continue the conversation till Miss Hastings should choose to explain. That individual, in the meantime, liable always to quick and strong revulsions of feeling, began to recollect that she was not going the right way to work if she intended to make an impression in favour of her brother.

'What a fool I am,' she thought to herself, 'to have spent the best part of my life in learning how to propitiate the vices and vanity of these aristocrats, and now, when my skill might do me some good, I am on the point of throwing it away for the sake of a pique of offended pride. Come, let me act like myself, or that beautiful woman will order her lackey to show me to the door directly.'

So she came a little nearer to the chair where the Queen of Angria was seated; and, looking up, she said with the emphatic earnestness of tone and manner peculiar to her, 'Do hear the few words I have to say.'

'I said before I would hear them,' was the haughty reply, a reply intended to show Miss Hastings that great people are not to be wantonly trifled with.

'Then,' continued the petitioner, 'I have nothing to urge in extenuation of my brother. His crimes have been proved against him. I have only to ask your Grace to remember what he was before he fell, how warm his heart was towards Angria, how bold his actions were in her cause. It is not necessary that

I should tell your Royal Highness of the energy that marks Captain Hastings' mind, of the powerful and vigorous talent that distinguished him above most of his contemporaries. The country rung with his name once,[96] and that is proof sufficient.'

'I know he was a brave and able man,' interposed the Duchess. 'But that did not prevent him from being a very dangerous man.'

'Am I permitted to reply to your Royal Highness?' asked Miss Hastings. The Duchess signified her permission by a slight indication of the head.

'Then,' said Miss Hastings, 'I will suggest to your Grace that his courage and his talents are the best guarantee against dishonourable meanness, against treachery, and if my brother's sovereign will condescend to pardon him, he will by that glorious action win back a most efficient subject to his standard.'

'An efficient subject!' repeated the Duchess. 'A man free from treachery! You are aware, young woman, that the King's life has been endangered by the treasonable attempt of the very man whose cause you are pleading. You know that Captain Hastings went near to become a regicide.'

'But the attempt failed,' pleaded she. 'And it was in distraction and despair that Hastings hazarded it.'

'Enough!' said the Duchess. 'I have heard you now, and I think you can say nothing more to me which can throw fresh light on the subject. I will give you my answer. Captain Hastings' fate will be regarded by me with regret, but I consider it inevitable. You seem shocked. I know it is natural you should feel, but I cannot see the use of buoying up your expectations with false hopes. To speak candidly, I have already used all the influence I possess in Hastings' behalf. Reasons were given me why my request should meet with a denial – reasons I could not answer, and therefore I was silent. If I recur to the subject again, it will be with reluctance, because I know that the word passed will not be revoked. However, I promise to try. You need not thank me. You may go.' And she turned her head quite away from Miss Hastings. The hauteur of her exquisite features expressed that if more was said she did not mean to listen to it.

Her humble subject looked at her a moment. It was difficult to say what language was spoken by her dark glowing eyes. Indignation, disappointment and shame seemed to be the prevailing feelings. She felt that somehow she did not take with[97] the Duchess of Zamorna, that she had hit on a wrong tack, had made a false impression at first, that she had injured her brother's cause, rather than benefited it. Above all, she felt that she had failed thus signally before the eyes and in the presence of Sir William Percy. She left the room quite heart-sick.

'Do you know much of that young woman?' asked the Duchess, turning to her brother.

'I've seen her a few times,' was Sir William's reply.

'Well, but do you know her? Are you acquainted with her character?'

'Not much. She's a warm-hearted girl,' returned the Baronet, and he smiled with an expression meant to be very inexplicable and mysterious.

'Where has she lived, and what are her connections?'

'Till lately, she was a sort of governess in the barrister Moore's family.'

'What, the father of Miss Moore? Jane, Julia, or – what is her name?'

'Just so, the beautiful Angrian, your Grace means.'

'Aye, well, this Miss Hastings is not very pleasing. I don't like her.'

'Why, please your Grace?'

'She's odd, abrupt. I would rather not grant another audience. You'll remember that.'

'Very well. By the bye, I'm tired of standing. Will it be lèse-majesté to sit down in your Grace's presence?'

'No, sir. Draw a chair to the table.'

Sir William left his station behind the royal sofa and took a seat near his sister's. They looked a rather remarkable pair, and seemed too on rather remarkable terms. Their conversation was short and terse; their looks at each other were quick, not very sentimental, but still such as indicated a sort of mutual understanding. The Duchess did not forget her rank. She addressed her relative with a regal freedom and brusquerie.

'What have you been about lately?' she asked, regarding him with a half-frown, half-smile, the random scamp who now rested his elbow on her sofa-arm.

'Could not justly tell you, madam. Been breathing myself[98] a trifle after the hard race I ran lately.'

'But where have you been? I assure you I've heard nothing but complaints of your absence from town. The Premier has more than once expressed himself very warmly on the subject.'

'Retirement is necessary now and then, your Grace knows, to give a man an opportunity for thought. The hurry and bustle of this wicked world is enough to drive him distracted.'

'Retirement, William! Stuff! Retirement gets you into mischief. I know it does. I wish you'd keep in action.'

'What, is your Grace going to trouble yourself about my morals?'

'Don't sneer, William. Your morals are your own concern, not mine. But tell me what you've been doing.'

'Nothing, Mary. As I'm a Christian, I tell you I've been in no mischief whatever. What makes you suspect me so?'

'Well, keep your confession to yourself then. And now, inform me what you're going to do. Can I further any of your intentions?'

'No, thank ye. My work is set for the present. I'm after Montmorency and Simpson.'

'Have you any idea where they are, William?'

'Scarcely, but I think they've left Paris.'

'I imagined so, from what I heard last night.'

'What did you hear?'

'Why, the Duke and my father were talking about them, and my father said he thought they were nearer home than France.'[99]

'Was that all?' asked Sir William, looking at his sister keenly.

'Yes. I heard nothing more. They stopped talking when I came into the room.'

Do you suppose,' asked the Baronet, 'that our respected and illustrious parent has any connection with his old friends now?'

'Not the least, I should think. He seldom alludes to politics. O William, I do wish he would keep out of them!'

'O Mary, I don't care the smallest pearl in that broach of yours whether he does or not. But it's very blackguardly of him to give his quondam associates the slip in that way.'

'Come, I'll have none of Edward's slang,' rejoined the Drover's daughter.[100]

'I'd say the same to his face,' answered that Drover's son. 'I've often thought, Mary, that a more peculiarly strange, insane scoundrel than the man who begot me never existed. As to Edward's coarse abuse, it's all fudge; and I've no irresistible natural impulse to hate our noble sire.'

'Then be silent, sir!' broke in Queen Mary.

'Nay, I've a right to speak,' was the answer. 'The man's a monomaniac, I'll swear to it. God bless me! I'd never marry if I thought I should inherit the wild delusion of believing that all the male children who might be born to me were devils.'

'He never said or believed that you and Edward were devils. He'd have been near the truth if he had.'

'No, the gentleman daren't say such a thing. It's too horrible a supposition to be expressed in words. In his hypochondria dread he must darkly have concluded that he himself was not altogether human, but a something with a cross of the fiend[101] in it. That's just the lunatic's idea; and he thinks his sons take after their demon father, and his daughter is the pure offspring of her pleasant human mother. Pray, Mary, have you any such notions about your children? There would be some sense in it if you had, for no doubt their father is a demon.'

'William, what a strange, scoffing sneerer you are. I've been angry with you once or twice ere now for talk of this kind, but it's of no use. I'll dismiss you, sir, and have as little to do with you as I have with Edward.'

'Do, madam. Deny me an audience once when I ask for it, and I'll just take revenge by rushing head-foremost into a little scrape I've been contemplating for the last two years. A single insult either from you, or the Great Cham, Chi Thaung-Gu, will make me come out onto the stage of publicity and turn out my fool[102] like a good 'un.'

'Do as you will. I'll not be threatened,' answered the Duchess 'Your dark hints are all nonsense. You've a bad temper, William.'

'So have you, Mary; and if you'd been married to a decent man like Sir Robert Pelham,[103] instead of the individual who now blesses you with his faithful love, you'd have shewn it ere now.'

'Happily, I was *not* married to Sir Robert Pelham. Let him thank his stars for it,' answered the Duchess.

'He does, I have no doubt,' was the quiet rejoinder.

'William, you're exceedingly disagreeable this morning,' continued her Grace.

'And you were most encouraging, kind and agreeable to that poor wretch who came to ask a favour of you half an hour since.'

'Oh, I vexed you, did I? How you smoothed over your anger, till it could explode with the best effect!'

'That's a quality natural to our family, a peculiarity derived from our satanic parentage.'

'William, your character is an odd one. I confess myself sometimes puzzled with it. Sometimes, you will come and sit in my apartment for an hour, stupidly silent, but with a placid smile of satisfaction on your quizzical face, as if you were the gentlest, most contented creature in the world. If the children are here, you'll play with them, and seem rather fond of them than otherwise. Then again, you'll walk in when I don't want you, looking as sour, as cynical, as – nay, I know no figure of speech that will express an adequate comparison. You sit down, and begin a series of taunts and innuendoes whose bitterness would lead me to conclude that you hated and envied me worse than Edward does. How am I to account for this inconsistency? Does it arise from the mere love of wantonly exercising the sort of influence which your relationship gives you? Do you think I am in danger of being too happy, if I am not occasionally reminded of my mortal state by the intrusion of a haughty, capricious brother, who tries to convert himself into a sort of phantasm to haunt me always with secret, gnawing uneasiness?'

'Why, bless my life! What have I done, what have I said, to

call forth all this tirade?' said Sir William. 'Secret, gnawing
uneasiness!' he repeated sarcastically. 'No, no, Mary, the Great
Cham spares me the trouble of all that sort of thing. You know
his last foible, I suppose?'

'No, but you may tell it me. I'll believe it or not as I please.'

'Oh, of course. You're too good a wife to believe it, but
the town believes it, notwithstanding. He went to a soirée at
Clarence House two nights ago, did he not?'

'Yes. What of that?'

'Nothing. Only that the lady you mentioned a while since –
the beautiful Angrian – was there too.'

'Go on, William, say your worst.'

'Nay, I've nothing more to say – except that the King and
Miss Jane were closeted together for nearly an hour in that little
cabinet opening to the drawing-room. You may remember it.'

'Alone?' asked the Duchess.

'Aye, alone – but don't look so exceedingly concerned. Perhaps there was no harm done after all.'

'Who told you of it?'

'I saw it. I was at the soirée, and I used my eyes. I saw Richton
take Miss Moore into the cabinet; I heard him tell her that the
Duke was there; I noticed how long she stayed, and I observed
her come out.'

The Duchess looked at her brother narrowly. His face was
pale, and had something very envenomed in its expression.

'What are you telling me this for, William?' said she.

'For a very good reason, madam, and I'll confess my motive
candidly. I rather liked that Miss Moore. I thought her a handsome, good-natured girl; and as I mean to marry before long, I
had some faint intention of asking her to be Lady Percy. But
when I saw that delectable transaction – saw her allow Richton
to lead her behind the curtain of a recess, heard a mock struggle
that ensued between them, was aware afterwards of her admittance into the cabinet, and witnessed the heated face and
flurried manner with which she left it – I felt such a scunner
of disgust, I could have insulted her before the whole party.
However, I determined to punish her in a safer and more effec-
tual way. I thought I'd communicate the business quietly to my

royal sister, and she might act as she pleased. My advice is – nay, what are you going to do? Stop a moment! Humph, she's off! Well, I was in a very bad temper this morning, but I feel much easier in my mind now. Mary took fire in the right style. How will she act? Is she gone to attack him instanter? I don't care whether she does or not. Am I going to cut my throat for disappointed love? No, nor even drop a tear. I find I did not love her, the buxom, hearty, heartless, laughing, brainless jilt. What in the world do I care for her with her snivelling simplicity? But I've had my revenge. I'm quite comfortable. Now, let's drop heroics and go home and take our luncheon. I'll call on Townshend today, I think, and we'll flay the world alive.'[104]

CHAPTER I

'Will ye tell Major King[105] I want to speak to him?' said Lord Hartford, opening his dressing-room door and addressing a housemaid who was dusting the gilded picture frames in the gallery.

'Yes, my lord.'

And with her brush in her hand the smart housemaid bustled down the great wide staircase as far as the last landing. There she stopped.

'Wood!' she called to a man-servant crossing the hall with a tray in his hand on which were some silver egg-cups and some toast. 'Wood, are the gentlemen at breakfast?'

'Yes, but they'll have done soon. What for, Susan?'

'You're to tell Major King that my lord wants him, and be sharp.' The housemaid ran up the staircase to return to her work, and the footman passed on to the breakfast-room.

Major King, Captain Berkley and Lieutenant Jones, being visitors at Hartford Hall, had come down a little after ten o'clock, and were now sitting in a handsome apartment engaged in the discussion of a capital good breakfast.

'How d'ye feel this morning, Berkley, my cock?' said Major King. 'Is that a chicken's wing you're picking? Your appetite seems only delicate to-day.'

'As good as yours, I've a notion. I've not seen you take anything but a mouthful of dry toast, and there's Jones is lingering over his coffee as fondly as if it were poison.'

'I wonder what breakfasts were made for?' grumbled Jones.

'You can't see the use of them, can you?' inquired Major King. 'Especially when your head and stomach are in the condition they are just now. Conscientiously, Jones, how many bottles do you think you decanted last night?'

'I forgot to count after the fourth,' answered Jones.

'And where did you sleep, my buck?'

'I don't know. I found myself amongst a lot of flowers when I awoke.'

'A lot of flowers, yes. When you framed[106] to steer out of the dining-room, instead of making for the door like a Christian, you took a grand tack to one side and went crash through the glass of the conservatory. Hartford swore he would make you pay for damages.'

'If you please, sir, you're wanted,' said the footman, addressing Major King.

'Who wants me, Wood?'

'My lord. He's in his dressing-room.'

'Oh,' said the Major, rising from the table with a wink, 'I suppose he's done – can't come down this morning. I'll recommend bleeding, and if the doctor'll prick him in the jugular, there's a chance for me. Take away the breakfast, Wood. Captain Berkley and Mr Jones are Roman Catholics, and they mean to fast to-day. Bring the liqueur-case, Wood, and a bottle or two of soda-water, and fetch Mr Jones a box of cigars and a novel from the library, or something light to amuse him.'

'D—n you, King. I wish you'd order for yourself,' said Mr Jones.

Major King laughed as he looked askance at the Lieutenant's sackless face, and while laughing he left the room.

The excellent Major went up the staircase and came with swinging stride along the gallery, looking as little like a rakish raff as any officer of the 19ᵗʰ could be expected to do on the morning succeeding a deep debauch. Susan, the housemaid mentioned before, was still at her work, still whisking her light

brush and duster over the burnished frames of all the dark
Salvators and Carracis and Corregios[107] which frowned along
that lengthened wall. Major King seemed to have something
particular to say to her. He stooped, and was for commencing
a conversation, which he would fain have preluded with a
salute, but Susan slipped away and took refuge in a neighbouring apartment, of which she bolted the door.

On, then, marched Major King, and at last made a halt before
a door at the far end of the gallery. He knocked.

'Come in, d—n you,' growled a voice as of one either in the
gout or the colic.

Major King sucked in his cheeks and obeyed orders.

Lord Hartford's dressing-room was somewhat dark, the
blinds being down and the curtains half drawn. However, a
freer admittance of light was scarcely to be desired, seeing that
both the room and its occupant were in what may be called 'a
mess'. The toilet was scattered over with shaving materials,
with broaches and rings, a loose miniature shut up in a case
and a magnificent gold repeater. A great cheval mirror[108] was
standing in the middle of the room, with an arm-chair placed
before it and a damask dressing-gown like a mussulman's robe
thrown untidily over the back thereof. The rich carpet was
ruffled up, and a footstool lay by the door, as if it had been
hurled missive-wise in some access of patrician furor. Full in
front of the fire there was a chair, and seated therein was a man
of savage, hirsute aspect, unwashed, uncombed, unshaven, with
hands plunged to an unknown depth in his pocket and long
legs widely sundered so that one morocco-slippered foot rested
upon one hob and the other on the corresponding pedestal
opposite. He was a charming figure, especially as his eyes were
fixed steadfastly on the back of the chimney with a smothered
choler of expression rather to be imagined than described.

'Well, what's the bulletin for today, Colonel?' inquired Major
King, swaggering up to his superior.

'Will ye shut the door,' said Hartford, with as little amenity
of tone as is expressed in the growl of a sick tiger.

King walked back and kicked the door to with his foot.

'Will ye read them documents?' continued the first gentleman in Angria, at the same time reluctantly drawing one hand from the pocket of his inexcusables[109] and directing his thumb towards a brace of letters which, with their envelopes, lay open on the table. The major obeyed orders.

'Will ye read up?' pursued the ornament of the peerage.

King cleared his throat, flourished the letters and, in the tone of a sentinel singing out the watch-word, began as follows:

'Victoria Square – Verdopolis – March –

'To Lord Hartford,
'Colonel of the 19th regiment of infantry,
'Judge of the Court-Martial at Zamorna.
'My lord,
    'I have received His Majesty's commands to lay before you the following decision, sanctioned by His Majesty in council, concerning the prisoner Hastings, now in your Lordship's custody in the county jail of Zamorna. It is desired that your Lordship shall proceed forthwith to lay before him the following articles, on agreeing to which the prisoner is to be set at liberty with the reservations hereafter stated.

    'Firstly, he is to make a full confession as to how far he was connected with the other individuals included with himself in the sentence of outlawry.

    'Secondly, he is to state all he knows of the plans and intentions of those individuals.

    'Thirdly, he is to give information where he last saw Hector Mirabeau Montmorency, George Frederick Caversham and Quashia Quamina Kashna; also, where he now supposes them to be; also, how far they were concerned with the late massacre in the east and the disembarkation of French arms at Wilson's creek; also, whether these persons are connected with any foreign political incendiaries, with Barras, Dupin and Bernadotte;[110] also – and this your Lordship will consider an important question – whether the courts of the southern states have maintained any secret correspondence with the Angrian renegades, whether they have given them any encouragement directly or indirectly.

    'Should Hastings consent to give such answers to these questions as His Majesty and the government shall deem satisfactory, his sentence of death will be commuted to degradation from his rank as an officer in the Angrian army, expulsion from the 19th regiment, and compulsory service as a private soldier in the troops commanded by Colonel Nicholas Belcastro.[111]

'Should Hastings decline answering all or any of these questions after being allowed half an hour for deliberation, your Lordship will cause his sentence to be executed without reserve. His Majesty particularly requests that your Lordship will not delay complying with his commands on these points, as he thinks it is high time the affair were brought to a conclusion, in order that your Lordship may be relieved from the anxiety of having the whole responsibility of this matter. The Government have given orders that Sir Wm. Percy shall be in attendance at the next sitting of your Lordship's court.

'I have the honour to remain

'Your Lordship's obedient humble servant,

'H. F. Etrei,[112] Secretary at War, Verdopolis, March 18th— 39.'

Major King, having finished the perusal of this despatch, was about to make his comment on it – he had already begun 'G—d d—n—n' – when he was stopped by the stormy uprising of the man in the morocco slippers with the black unshaven beard and the grizzled uncombed head.

'There,' roared Hartford, striding down the length of his dressing-room, 'there, that's what you may call black bile, that's something to stink in a man's nostrils till the day of his eternal death, that's a court-insult![113] They'll pardon the hound, they'll give him a fair chance – the fellow that should have been shot when caught, as you'd shoot a dirty girning wolf – and all to spite me! And they'll set their snivelling government agent, their hired spy, their toadie, their loathsome lickspittle, to watch my actions! To relieve me from anxiety, forsooth! To hector and bully the court martial of the 19th! And I'm to have Sir Wm Percy stuck at my elbow, and I'm to have every look and movement watched by him, and every word reported by his befouled hireling pen! Curse me – curse the globe!'

This last anathema was uttered with a perfect yell, for just then the irate nobleman, happening in his furious promenade to come in contact with the great cheval glass set in the middle of the floor, kicked his foot through it, thereby shivering to atoms the noble reflect it was affording of his own tall, dark, muscular shape and of his swarthy, strong-featured and most choleric physiognomy. Having performed this exploit, his Lordship began calling upon several fiends by their names. As nobody seemed to answer – unless, indeed, Major King might be considered as the representative of the infernal muster-roll – the noble lord at last cooled down so far as to resume his seat before the fire, and having verbally consigned the King and court of Angria to the custody of the infernal agents he had invoked, he fetched a deep sigh, and through mere exhaustion was silent.

Now, it so happened that the Major King did not at all sympathize in this explosion of his noble Colonel's furor. It seemed to him that no better or more exquisite revenge could be devised than that Hastings should be cashiered from his sublime post as Captain in the 19th, and forced, on the most degrading conditions, to enter the ranks of the Bloodhounds and put his neck under the grinding yoke of Colonel Nicholas Belcastro. 'It's the best card that has turned up for many a day,' thought he. 'We can make the rascals wince again with telling them how they're forced to take our dirtiest leavings. To be sure, they may give us tit for tat by replying that what is good enough for an officer in the 19th will only do for a private in the Bloodhounds. Bah! That's bad, but if any of them dare any such a thing there's always one remedy – pistols and six paces.'

The Major was amusing himself with these pleasing reflections when Hartford interrupted him by a request that he would read the other letter. It was short:

'General Sir Wilson Thornton is desired by His Majesty to intimate to Lord Hartford that, as there is some prospect of the army being called into active service erelong, it will be necessary that all the regiments should be efficiently officered. General Sir Wilson therefore has received directions to inquire whether Lord Hartford considers himself in a condition to take the field along with his troops in case the 19th should be called out, or whether the state of his health and spirits will not render such a mode of procedure unadvisable. In case Lord Hartford should be of the latter opinion, it will be considered necessary to appoint a substitute for his Lordship, even though, by so doing, His Majesty should have to request the permanent loss of Lord Hartford's valuable services. An immediate answer is requested.

'(signed) W. Thornton.'

'There's for you,' said Lord Hartford, and for the space of ten minutes he said no more. But at the expiration of that period of silence he in a faint voice bade Major King take a pen and a sheet of paper and write what he should dictate.

'Begin,' said he, '"Hartford Hall, Hartford Dale, Zamorna." I'll remind them I've a house to shelter in at any rate. Have ye written that?'

'Yes.'

'Now put "March the 18th 1839". I'll shew them I've sense enough to know what day of the month it is and what year of the century. Ye've written that?'

'Yes.'

'Now then, hearken, and jot away as fast as ye can. "Sir" – mind, I'm addressing farmer Thornton –

'Sir, Allow me through your medium to thank His Majesty with all the warmth and sincerity His Majesty's unprecedented kindness deserves, for the touching and philanthropic interest His Majesty has condescended to take in my welfare. It affords me matter of self-gratulation that through the blessing and protection of an omnipotent Providence I am enabled to return a most satisfactory answer to His Majesty's benignant inquiry. His Majesty's kind and generous heart will be rejoiced to hear that I never in all my life have been favoured with a state of more perfect, sound and uninterrupted health than what I at present enjoy, that my spirits are consequently light, free, and even at times exuberant, that so far from shrinking from active service with my regiment, I feel pleasure amounting to exultation at the thought of setting my foot in the stirrup again. His Majesty may rest assured that whenever His Majesty shall be pleased to summon the 19th to the field, not an officer or a soldier in that well-tried regiment will respond more cheerfully to the call than I shall do. I am ready for anything, the post of honour and the post of danger. I have been faithful to my country so far, and I mean to die with that quality untarnished. Report my allegiance to His Majesty and my heartfelt gratitude for all the honourable, justifiable attentions I have lately received.

    'I am,

        'Yours &c.

        'Edward Hartford.

'Now then, you'll ring the bell and send that letter off directly, King, and then you'll take horse and ride to Zamorna to order and prepare matters for the sitting of the court-martial to-morrow. As for me, I'm going to bed, and I shall keep it for the rest of the day, as I'm exceedingly sick. G—d d—n!'

And with these words Lord Hartford passed from his dressing-room to his chamber. When he was gone, Major King nearly suffered strangulation in a silent fit of laughter.

CHAPTER II

The city of Zamorna is a very pleasant place in fine sunny weather. The public buildings are all new, of very handsome architecture, and constructed of white gleaming stone. The principal streets are broad; the shops look busy and affluent; the ladies walking on the pavements are richly dressed, like the wives and daughters of wealthy merchants, and at the same time they have a stylish air about them, for the province of Zamorna is highly aristocratic. There is almost always an air of excitement over this town. Its population presents the appearance of an ant-hill, one moving mass of animation. The grand focus of bustle is Thornton Street, with Stancliffe's Hotel on one side of the way and the court-house on the other.

It was March, the 19th day of the month, and Tuesday by the week.[114] The day was fine, the sky bright blue with a hot sun,

and far on the horizon those silver-piled towering clouds that
foretell the rapid showers of spring. There had been rain an
hour ago, but the fresh breeze had dried it up, and only here
and there a glittering pool of wet remained on the bleached
street pavement. One could tell that in the country the grass
was growing green, that the trees were knotty with buds and
the gardens golden with crocuses. Zamorna, however, and the
citizens of Zamorna, thought little of these rural delights. Tuesday was market-day. The piece-hall and the commercial buildings were as throng as they could stand. The Stuartville Arms,
the Wool-Pack and the Rising Sun were all astir with the preparations for their separate market dinners, and the waiters were
almost run off their feet with answering the countless calls for
bottoms of brandy, glasses of gin and water, and bottles of
north-country ale.

Serene in the majesty of aristocracy, Stancliffe's Hotel stood
aloof from this commercial stir. Bustle there was, however, even
there, and that of no ordinary kind. To be sure, the gentlemen
passing in and out of its great door had a different air and
different *ton* to the red-whiskered travellers, the swearing,
brandy-drinking manufacturers crowding the inferior inns. Servants in military and aristocratic liveries, too, were to be seen
lounging in the passages and, had you gone into the stable-
yards, you would have found a dozen grooms busily engaged
in brushing down and corning some pairs of splendid carriage
horses, as well as three or four very grand-looking chargers –
proud, pawing beasts, who looked conscious of the glories of
Westwood and the bloodier triumphs of Leyden.[115]

No doubt there is some affair of importance transacting at
the court-house opposite, for the doors are besieged with a
gentlemanly crowd of black and green and brown, velvet-
collared frock-coats and black and drab[116] beaver hats; and,
moreover, every now and then the doors open and an individual
comes out, runs hastily down the steps, across the way to
Stancliffe's, there calls impatiently for wine and, having swallowed what is brought him, runs with equal haste back again, a
lane being simultaneously opened for him by the crowd through
which he passes with absorbed, important gravity, looking

neither to the left hand nor the right.[117] The door is jealously closed as he enters, allowing you but one glimpse of a man with a constable's staff standing inside.

On the morning in question, I was myself one of the crowd about the court-house doors, and I believe I stood four mortal hours at the bottom of a flight of broad steps, looking up at the solid and lofty columns supporting the portico above. Ever since nine o'clock the court-martial had been assembled within, and it was known throughout all Zamorna that Henry Hastings the renegade was at this moment undergoing a rigid examination, on the result of which hung the issues of life and death. Yes, just now the stern Hartford occupied his seat of judge; the crafty Percy sat by, watching every transaction, ferreting out every mystery, urging relentlessly the question that would fain be eluded, insinuating his sly acumen like the veriest Belial that ever clothed himself in flesh. All round are ranged the martial jury, whose character shall be their names alone – King, Kirkwall, Jones, Dickens, Berkley, Paget, etc etceterorum[118] – while the few gentlemen privileged to be spectators sit on benches near. And then, the prisoner Hastings, imagine him. At this instant, the mental torture is proceeding; a broad gleam of sunshine rests on the outside walls of this court-house; the pillared front and noble roof rise against an unclouded sky. But if Judas[119] Hastings is selling his soul to about a score of devils sitting upon him in judgment, what thought has he to spare for the cheerful daylight?

The town clock and the minster clock struck twelve.

'Bless my life, do they never mean to have done to-day?' said a chap standing near, and when I turned I recognized the peculiar phiz of the Sydenhams. It was John Sydenham, the eldest son of Wm. Sydenham Esqre. of Southwood.

'How d'ye do, Mr John?'

'Haven't the pleasure of knowing you, sir,' replied he with true Angrian politeness.

'My name's Townshend. You may remember meeting me in Sir Frederick Fala's box in the theatre at Verdopolis.'

'Oh, so I believe I do. Charles Townshend, really, beg your pardon! We went to a chop-house after the play, and had a night of it. I remember perfectly. Hope you're well, Mr Townshend.'

'Quite well, thank ye. Rather tired of standing, though. You've not heard anything of what's going on inside there, I suppose, Mr John?'

'Not a shiver. They're laying bets at Stancliffe's about the result. Some say Hastings'll sign terms, and some say he'll stand pepper.'[120]

'What's your own opinion?'

'Oh, I judge of others according to myself. Not a doubt he'll tip King's evidence.[121] I'd do it if I were him.'

'Why, the man that's turned his coat once will turn it again, I suppose.'

'Yes, yes. It's only the first time that's awkward. You get used to it after that.'

'They say they've nearly wound up,' said a third person, joining us.

'Indeed, Midgley. Who told you?'

'Paget. He's just been out, and they're reporting it in Stancliffe's that the prisoner has turned stupid.[122] Everybody there says he won't peach.'

'Why, some of the articles come it very strong,[123] I suppose.'

'Very. They hold him tight.'

'And the execution's to take place directly, if he declines conditions?'

'Yes, this afternoon. He's to be shot on Edwardston Common. Orders have been sent to the barracks that the soldiers are to be in readiness by three o'clock, they say.'

'Then that's a sure sign he's stupid.'

'I should think so. They'd press him very hard, no doubt, and serve him right.'

'Paget said the judge was swaggering bloodily.'

'What about?'

'Some interference of the government agents.'

'What, Sir Wm. Percy?'

'Yes.'

'Does Percy want to save the prisoner?'

'Nay, God knows. Paget said he pushed all ways and seemed to have eyes both before and behind.'[124]

'I say, what are they doing at that end of the crowd?'
'Don't know. They seem to be making a kind of sign.'
'D'ye think the court's rising?'
'Shouldn't wonder. They've sat four hours, I believe.'
'There's Mackay coming on to the steps.'
'Yes, and they're drawing up the blinds.'
'Now for't then; let's push to get a bit nearer the steps.'

With these words, Messrs Sydenham, Midgley and Townshend made a bold plunge into the throng and, by dint of
elbowing, pushing and kicking, succeeded in obtaining an
advantageous position very near the court-house door.

That door being now opened, the occupants of the magistrates' room began to issue from the interior. First came Mr
Edward Percy, in the act of blowing his nose and then thrusting
his silk handkerchief into his coat-pocket. He descended the
steps at two strides and went straight across the way to Stancliffe's. No intelligence was to be had from him. So far from
speaking to any one in his passage, he did not so much as
vouchsafe a look either to right hand or the left. Next came
some officers, four abreast, with spurs on their heels jingling as
they trod the stone pavement; then a professional-looking man
with a grey head and a pallid thoughtful face. That was Mr
Moore; he raised his hat to me as he passed. These all disappeared into Stancliffe's. Now a policeman or two turned out
onto the broad summit of the steps and stood erect by the
pillars. Mackay came down into the crowd and began to clear
a way with his official staff. A hackney-coach came wheeling
out of the hotel yard, and drew up just before the door.

Just then, Midgley said in a low voice, 'There's Hastings';
and when I looked up, there was a man emerging from the
shade of the portico, dressed in black, with his single-breasted
coat buttoned close over his broad chest, and his hat drawn
down on his brow. I can hardly say that I saw his face, and yet
one glimpse I caught, as he raised his head for a moment and
threw a hurried glance over the crowd. The expression of that
glance was one to be soon caught and long retained. It denoted
the jealous suspicion of a bad man who expects others to hate,
and the iron hardihood of a vindictive man who resolves to

hate others in return. His teeth were set, his countenance was one dark scowl. He seemed like one whose mind was troubling him with the gall of self-abhorrence. A policeman got into the hackney coach; then Hastings entered it, and a second policeman followed him. The vehicle drove away. Not a sound followed its departure, neither cheer nor hoot.

'He's Judas, I'll lay my life on it,' said I, turning to John Sydenham. John nodded assent.

'Sir William Percy's coming out,' said a voice near me, and in the door-way appeared the thin Hussar in his blue and white dress, settling his hat on his brow and looking straight before him at no object in particular, with that keen, quiet, unsmiling aspect he always wears when he's really busy about something important and has no time for his usual sneers of supercili-ousness or airs of nonchalance. He passed by us in his easy, leisurely way. I had a full view of his face, for he always carries his head very erect. His forehead, the only regularly handsome part of his phiz, had a trace of shade on its smoothness not often seen there. I believe just then he was burning with venom against somebody – perhaps his brother or Lord Hartford – yet how calm he looked! I lost sight of him in the all-absorbing abyss of Stancliffe's passage.

'Make way for Lord Hartford's carriage,' cried a voice from the yard; and out thundering upon us came a dashing barouche with four fiery greys. Last but not least, the judge appeared when his vehicle was announced. A grand judge he looked, in an officer's cloak, with boots and a travelling cap. This last article of dress suited his strongly marked face, swarthy skin and bushy black whiskers amazingly. It gave him very much the air of a gigantic ourang-outang; I'm sure he might have passed for that sort of gentleman in any menagerie in the king-dom. Arm in arm with his Lordship appeared a fine personage in a mackintosh and light drab caster. Of course, nobody was at a loss to recognize the ubiquitous Earl of Richton, who, no doubt grudging to lose so charming an amusement as was to be afforded by the spectacle of Hastings' final degradation, had come down for the day and, too proud to accept even the princely accommodations of Stancliffe's, was now about to accompany his noble friend to the Hall. The two entered the carriage, one looking as black as midnight, the other all smiles and suavity. In five minutes, they had swept up Thornton Street and were far on the Hartford road.

Two hours had elapsed before the result of the day's proceedings was known all over Zamorna. Hastings had accepted conditions; had delivered a mass of evidence against his quondam friends, whose purport, as yet a secret, would erelong be indicated by the future proceedings of government; had yielded up his captain's commission; had taken the striped jacket and scarlet belt of a private in Belcastro's Bloodhounds; and, in recompense, had received the boon of life – life without honour, without freedom, without the remnant of a character. So opens the new career of Henry Hastings, the young hero, the soldier poet of Angria! 'How are the mighty fallen!'[125]

CHAPTER III

Sir William Percy, like his father, is very tenacious of a favourite idea, any little pet whim of his fancy, and the less likely it is to be productive of good, either to the individual who conceives it or to others, the more carefully it is treasured and the more intently it is pursued. Northangerland has all his life been a child chasing the rainbow,[126] and into what wild abysses has the pursuit often plunged him! How often has it seduced him from his serious aims, called him back when ambition was leading him to her loftiest summit, when the brow was nearly gained and the kingdoms of the world and the glory of them[127] were lying in prospect below! How often at this crisis has Alexander Percy turned, because the illusion of beauty dawned on his imagination and, down the steep that cost him days and nights of toil to climb, sprung like a maniac to clasp the dream in his arms! When it mocked him and melted into mist, he never awoke to reason. Still he saw those soft hues crossing the clouds before him, and still he followed, though the clouds and their arch faded into nothingness.

Sir William, being of a cooler and less imaginative temperament than his father, has never yielded to delirium like this. Compared to Northangerland, he is a man of marble – but still, marble under a strange spell, capable of warming to life like the sculpture of Pygmalion.[128] He is a being of changeful moods. Now, the loveliest face will call from him nothing but a sneer on female vanity; and again, an expression flitting over ordinary features, a transient ray in an eye neither large nor brilliant, will fix his attention and throw him into romantic musing, merely because it chanced to harmonize with some preconceived whim of his own capricious mind. Yet having once caught an idea of this kind, hav[ing] once received the seeds of this sort of partiality – inclination, fondness, call it what you will – his heart offered a tenacious soil, likely to hold fast, to nurture long, to cultivate secretly but surely the unfolding germ of what might in time grow to a rooted passion.

Sir William, busied with the debates of cabinet councils, in posting to and fro on political errands, holding the portfolio of a trusted and heavily responsible government attaché, consequently living in an atmosphere of turmoil, still kept in view that little private matter of his own, that freak of taste, that small soothing amusement – his fancy for Miss Hastings. She had dropped out of his sight, he hardly knew where. After that audience with his royal sister, he had never troubled himself to inquire after her. The last view he had of her face was as it looked, flushed with painful feeling, when she retired from the presence-chamber. The warm-hearted young man chuckled with internal pleasure at the recollection of the cold, indifferent mien he had assumed as he stood behind the royal chair. He knew at the time she would apply to him no more, that she would, henceforth, shun his very shadow, fearful lest her remotest approach should be deemed an unwelcome intrusion. He knew she would leave Verdopolis that very hour if possible, and he allowed her to do so without a parting word from him. Still, Miss Hastings lingered in his recollection; still, he smiled at the thought of her ardour; still, it pleased him to picture again the quick glances of her eye when he spoke to her – glances in which he could read so plainly what she imagined buried out of sight in her inmost heart. Still, whenever he saw

a light form, a small foot, an intelligent, thin face, it brought a
vague feeling of something agreeable, something he liked to
dwell on. Miss Hastings, therefore, was not by any means to
be given up. No, he would see her again sometime. Events
might slip on; one thing he was certain of – he need be under
no fear of the impression passing away. No,

> His form would fill her eye by night
> His voice her ear by day
> The touch that pressed her fingers slight
> Would never pass away.

So when he came again to Zamorna, having ascertained that
she was still there, he began to employ his little odds and ends
of leisure time in quiet speculations as to how, when and where
he should reopen a communication with her. It would not do
at all to conduct the thing in an abrupt, straightforward way.
He must not seem to seek her; he must come upon her sometime
as if by accident. Then, too, this business of her brother's must
be allowed to get out of her head. He would wait a few days,
till the excitement of his trial had subsided, and the renegade
was fairly removed from Zamorna and on his march to the
quarters and companions assigned him beyond the limits of
civilization. Miss Hastings would then be very fairly alone in
the world, quite disembarrassed from friends and relations, not
perplexed with a multitude of calls on her affection. In such a
state of things, an easy chance meeting with a friend would, Sir
William calculated, be no unimpressive event. He'd keep his
eye, then, on her movements and, with care, he did not doubt,
he should be able to mould events so as exactly to suit his
purpose.

Well, a week or two passed on. Hastings' trial, like all nine
days' wonders, had sunk into oblivion. Hastings himself was
gone to the D—l, or to Belcastro, which is the same thing. He
had actually marched bodily out of Zamorna, in the white
trousers, the red sash, the gingham jacket of a thorough-going
Bloodhound, as one of a detachment of that illustrious regiment
under the command of Captain Dampier. To the sound of

fife, drum and bugle, the lost desperado had departed, leaving
behind him the recollection of what he had been, a man; the
reality of what he was, a monster.

It was very odd, but his sister did not think a pin the worse
of him for all his dishonour. It is private meanness, not public
infamy, that degrade[s] a man in the opinion of his relatives.
Miss Hastings heard him cursed by every mouth, saw him
denounced in every newspaper; still, he was the same brother
to her he had always been; still, she beheld his actions through
a medium[129] peculiar to herself. She saw him go away with a
triumphant hope (of which she had the full benefit, for no one
else shared it) that his future actions would nobly blot out
the calumnies of his enemies. Yet, after all, she knew he was an
unredeemed villain. Human nature is full of inconsistencies.
Natural affection is a thing never rooted out where it has once
really existed.

These passages of excitement being over, Miss Hastings, very
well satisfied that her brother had walked out of jail with the
breath of life in his body, and having the aforesaid satisfactory
impression on her mind that he was the finest man on the top
of this world, began to look about her and consider how she
was to make off life. Most persons would have thought themselves in a very handsome fix, majestically alone in the midst of
trading Zamorna. However, she set to work with the activity
of an emmet,[130] summoned her address and lady-manners to
her aid, called on the wealthy manufacturers of the city and the
aristocracy of the seats round, pleased them with her tact, her
quickness, with the specimens of her accomplishments,[131] and
in a fortnight's time had raised a class of pupils sufficient not
only to secure her from want, but to supply her with the means
of comfort and elegance. She was now settled,[132] to her mind.
She was dependent on nobody, responsible to nobody. She
spent her mornings in her drawing-room, surrounded by her
class; not wearily toiling to impart the dry rudiments of knowledge to yawning, obstinate children – a thing she hated, and
for which her sharp, irritable temper rendered her wholly unfit
– but instructing those who had already mastered the elements
of education; reading, commenting, explaining, leaving it to

them to listen; if they failed, comfortably conscious that the blame would rest on her pupils, not herself. The little dignified governess soon gained considerable influence over her scholars – daughters, many of them, of the wealthiest families in the city. She had always the art of awing young ladies' minds with an idea of her superior talent, and then of winning their confidence by her kind, sympathizing affability. She quickly gained a large circle of friends, had constant invitations to the most stylish houses of Zamorna, acquired a most impeccable character for ability, accomplishment, obliging disposition, and most correct and elegant manners. Of course, her class enlarged, and she was as prosperous as any little woman of five feet high and not twenty years old need wish to be. She looked well, she dressed well – plainer, if possible, than ever, but still with such fastidious care and taste; she moved about as brisk as a bee. Of course, then, she was happy.

No. Advantages are equally portioned out in this world. She'd plenty of money, scores of friends, good health, people making much of her everywhere, but still the exclusive, proud being thought she had not met with a single individual equal to herself in mind, and therefore not one whom she could love. Besides, it was respect, not affection, that her pompous friends felt for her, and she was one who scorned respect. She never wished to attract it for a moment, and still, somehow, it always came to her. She was always burning for warmer, closer attachment. She couldn't live without it. But the feeling never woke, and never was reciprocated. Oh, for Henry, for Pendleton, for one glimpse of the Warner Hills!

Sometimes when she was alone in the evenings, walking through her handsome drawing-room by twilight, she would think of home, and long for home, till she cried passionately at the conviction that she should see it no more. So wild was her longing that when she looked out on the dusky sky, between the curtains of her bay-window, fancy seemed to trace on the horizon the blue outline of the moors, just as seen from the parlour at Colne-moss. The evening star hung above the brow of Boulshill, the farm fields stretched away between. And when reality returned – houses, lamps and streets – she was phrenzied.

Again, a noise in the house seemed to her like the sound made by her father's chair when he drew it nearer to the kitchen hearth; something would recall the whine or the bark of Hector and Juno, Henry's pointers. Again, the step of Henry himself would seem to tread in the passage, and she would distinctly hear his gun deposited in the house corner. All was a dream. Henry was changed, she was changed; those times were departed for ever. She had been her brother's and her father's favourite; she had lost one and forsaken the other. At these moments, her heart would yearn towards the old lonely man in Angria till it almost broke. But pride is a thing not easily subdued. She would not return to him.

Very often, too, as the twilight deepened and the fire, settling to clear red, diffused a calmer glow over the papered walls, her thoughts took another turn. The enthusiast dreamed about Sir William Percy. She expected to hear no more of him; she blushed when she recollected how, for a moment, she had once dared to conceive the presumptuous idea that he cared for her; but still she lingered over his remembered voice and look and language with an intensity of romantic feeling that very few people in this world can form the remotest conception of. All he had said was treasured in her mind. She could distinctly tell over every word; she could picture vividly as life, his face, his quick hawk's eye, his habitual attitudes. It was an era in her existence to see his name or an anecdote respecting him mentioned in the newspapers. She would preserve such paragraphs to read over and over again when she was alone. There was one which mentioned that he was numbered amongst the list of officers destined for the expected campaign in the east; and thereupon her excitable imagination kindled with anticipation of his perils and glories and wanderings. She realized him in a hundred situations – on the verge of battle, in the long weary march, in the halt by wild river banks. She seemed to watch his slumber under the desert moon, with large-leaved jungle plants spreading their rank shade above him. Doubtless, she thought, the young Hussar would then dream of some one that he loved; some beautiful face would seem to bend over his pillow such as had charmed him in the saloons of the capital.

> And with that thought came an impulse
>   Which broke the dreamy spell,
> For no longer on the picture
>   Could her eye endure to dwell.
> She vowed to leave her visions
>   And seek life's arousing stir,
> For she knew Sir William's slumber
>   Would not bring a thought of her.
>
> How fruitless, then, to ponder
>   O'er such dreams as chained her now,
> Her heart should cease to wander
>   And her tears no more should flow.
> The trance was over – over,
>   The spell was scattered far,
> Yet how blest were she whose lover
>   Would be Angria's young Hussar!
>
> Earth knew no hope more glorious,
>   heaven gave no nobler boon
> Than to welcome him victorious
>   To a heart he claimed his own.
> How sweet to tell each feeling
>   The kindled soul might prove!
> How sad to die concealing
>   The anguish born of love!

Such were Miss Hastings' musings, such were almost the words that arranged themselves like a song in her mind; words, however, neither spoken nor sung. She dared not so far confess her phrenzy to herself. Only once she paused in her walk through the drawing-room by her open piano, laid her fingers on the keys and, wakening a note or two of a plaintive melody, murmured the last lines of the last stanza,

> How sad to die concealing
>   The anguish born of love!

And instantly snatching her hand away, and closing the instrument with a clash, she made some emphatic remark about
unmitigated folly, then lighted her bed-candle and, it being now
eleven at night, hastened upstairs to her chamber as fast as if a
nightmare[133] had been behind her.

CHAP[TER] IV

One mild, still afternoon, Miss Hastings had gone out to walk.
She was already removed from the stir of Zamorna and slowly
pacing along the causeway of Girnington Road. The high wall
and trees enclosing a gentleman's place ran along the road side;
the distant track stretched out into a quiet and open country.
Now and then, a carriage or a horseman rolled or galloped
past, but the general characteristic of the scene and day was
tranquillity. Miss Hastings, folded in her shawl and with her
veil down, moved leisurely on, in as comfortable a frame of
mind as she could desire, inclined to silence and with no one
to disturb her by talking, disposed for reverie and at liberty to
indulge her dreams unbroken. The carriages that passed at
intervals kept her in a state of vague expectation. She always
raised her eyes when they drew near, as if with the undefined
hope of seeing somebody, she hardly knew whom – a face from
distant Pendleton, perhaps.

Following a course she had often taken before, she soon
turned into a bye-lane with a worn white causeway running
under a green hedge and, on either hand, fields. The stillness
now grew more perfect. As she wandered on, the mail-road
disappeared behind her; the sense of perfect solitude deepened.
That calm afternoon sun seemed to smile with a softer lustre,
and away in a distant field a bird was heard singing with a fitful
note, now clear and cheerful, now dropping to pensive silence.
She came to an old gate. The posts were of stone, and moulder-
ing and grey; the wooden paling was broken; clusters of springing leaves grew beside it. It was just a fit subject for an artist's
sketch.[134] This gate opened into a large and secluded meadow,
or rather, into a succession of meadows, for the track worn in

the grass led on, through stiles and gates, from pasture to pasture, to an unknown extent. Here Miss Hastings had been accustomed to ramble for many an hour, indulging her morbid propensity for castle-building, as happy as she was capable of being, except when now and then scared by hearing the remote and angry low of a great Girnington bull which haunted these parts.

On reaching the gate, she instinctively stopped to open it. It was open, and she passed through. She stopped with a start. By the gate-post lay a gentlemanly-looking hat and a pair of gloves, with a spaniel coiled up beside them as if keeping guard. The creature sprung forward at the approach of a stranger and gave a short bark, not very furious. Its instinct seemed to tell it that the intruder was not of a dangerous order. A very low whistle sounded from some quarter quite close at hand, yet no human being was visible from whom it could proceed. The spaniel obeyed the signal, whined, and lay down again. Miss Hastings passed on.

She had hardly set her foot in the field when she heard the emphatic ejaculation, 'Bless my stars!' distinctly pronounced, immediately behind her. Of course she turned. There was a hedge of hazels on her right hand, under which all sorts of leaves and foliage grew green and soft. Stretched full length on this bed of verdure, and with the declining sun resting upon him, she saw a masculine figure, without a hat, and with an open book in his hand which, it is to be supposed, he had been perusing – though his eyes were now raised from the literary page and fixed on Miss Hastings. It being broad day-light, and the individual being denuded as to the head, features, forehead, hair, whiskers, blue eyes, etc., etc., were all distinctly visible. Of course my readers know him: Sir William Percy and no mistake. Though what he could possibly be doing here, ruralizing in a remote nook of the Girnington summerings, I candidly confess myself not sufficiently sagacious to divine.

Miss Hastings, being, as my readers are aware, possessed with certain romantic notions about him, got something of a start at this unexpected meeting. For about five minutes she'd little to say, and indeed was amply occupied in collecting her wits and contriving an apology for what she shuddered to think Sir William would consider an unwelcome intrusion. Meantime, the Baronet gathered himself up, took his hat, and came towards her, with a look and smile that implied anything rather than annoyance at her presence.

'Well, you've not a single word to say to me. How shocked you look, and as pale as a sheet. I hope I've not frightened you.'

'No, no,' with agitation in the tone, 'but it was an unusual thing to meet anybody in those fields, and she feared she had perhaps disturbed Sir William. She was sorry. She ought to have taken the spaniel's hint and retreated in time.'

'Retreated? What from? Were you afraid of Carlo? I thought he saluted you very gently. Upon my word, I believe the beast had sense enough to know that the new-comer was not one his master would be displeased to see. Had it been a great male scarecrow in jacket and continuations he'd have flown at his throat.'

The tone of Sir William's voice brought back again, like a charm, the feeling of confidence Miss Hastings had experienced before in conversing with him. It brought back, too, a throbbing of the heart and pulse and a kindling of the veins which soon flushed her pale face with sufficient colour. But never mind that; let us go on with the conversation.

'I was not afraid of Carlo,' said Miss Hastings.

'What, then, were you afraid of? Surely not me?'

She looked up at him. Her natural voice and manner, so long disused, returned to her.

'Yes,' she said quickly. 'You, and nothing else. It is so long since I had seen you, I thought you would have forgotten me and would think I had no business to cross your way again. I expected you would be very cold and proud.'

'Nay, I'll be as warm as you please. And as to pride, I calculate you are not exactly the sort of person to excite that feeling in my mind.'

'I suppose, then, I should have said contempt. You are proud, no doubt, to your equals or superiors. However, you have spoken to me very civilly, for which I am obliged, as it makes me unhappy to be scorned.'

'May I ask if you're quite by yourself here?' inquired Sir William. 'Or have you companions near at hand?'

'I'm alone. I always walk alone.'

'Humph! And I'm alone likewise. And as it's highly improper that a young woman such as you should be wandering by herself in such a lot of solitary fields, I shall take the liberty of offering my protection whilst you finish your walk and then seeing you safe home.'

Miss Hastings made excuses. 'She could not think of giving Sir William so much trouble. She was accustomed to manage for herself. There was nothing in the world to be apprehended, etc.'

The Baronet answered by drawing her arm through his.

'I shall act authoritatively,' said he. 'I know what's for the best.'

Seeing she could not so escape, she pleaded the lateness of the hour. 'It would be best to turn back immediately.'

'No.' Sir William 'had a mind to take her half a mile further. She would be able to get back to Zamorna before dark and, as he was with her, she needn't fear.'

On they went then, Miss Hastings hurriedly considering whether she was doing any thing really wrong, and deciding that she was not, and that it would be sin and shame to throw away the moment of bliss chance had offered her. Besides, she had nobody in the world to find fault with her, nobody to whom she was responsible, neither father nor brother. She was her own mistress, and she was sure it would be cant and prudery to apprehend harm.

Having thus set aside scruples and wholly yielded herself to the wild delight fluttering at her heart, she bounded on with so light and quick a step Sir William was put to his mettle to keep pace with her.

'Softly, softly,' said he at last. 'I like to take my time in a ramble like this. One can't walk fast and talk comfortably at the same time.'

'The afternoon is so exceedingly pleasant,' returned Miss Hastings, 'and the grass is so soft and green in these fields, my spirits feel cheerier than usual. But however, to please you I'll draw in.'[135]

'Now,' continued the Baronet, 'will you tell me what you're doing in Zamorna, and how you're getting on?'

'I'm teaching, and I have two classes of twelve pupils each. My terms are high – first-rate – so I'm in no danger of want.'

'But have you money enough? Are you comfortable?'

'Yes, I'm as rich as a Jew. I mean to begin to save for the first time in my life, and when I've got two thousand pounds I'll give up work and live like a fine lady.'

'You're an excellent little manager for yourself. I thought now, if I left you a month or two unlooked after, just plodding on as you could, you'd get into strait or difficulty and be glad of a friend's hand to help you out. But somehow you contrive provokingly well.'

'Yes, I don't want to be under obligations.'

'Come, let me have no proud speeches of that sort. Remember, Fortune is ever changing, and the best of us are not exempt from reverses. I may have to triumph over you yet.'

'But if I wanted a sixpence, you would be the last person I should ask for it,' said Miss Hastings, looking up at him with an arch expression very natural to her eyes, but which seldom indeed was allowed to shine there.

'Should I, young lady? Take care; make no rash resolutions. If you were compelled to ask, you would be glad to go to the person who would give most willingly, and you would not find many hands so open as mine would be. I tell you plainly, it would give me pleasure to humble you. I have not yet forgotten your refusal to accept that silly little cross.'[136]

'Nay,' said Miss Hastings, 'I knew so little of you at that time, I felt it would be quite a shame to take presents from you.'

'But you know me better now, and I have the cross here. Will you take it?'

He produced the green box from his waistcoat pocket, took out the jewel, and offered it.

'I won't,' was the answer.

'Humph!' said Sir William. 'I'll be revenged sometime. Such nonsense!' He looked angry, an unusual thing with him.

'I don't mean to offend you,' pleaded Miss Hastings, 'but it would hurt me to accept anything of value from you. I would take a little book, or an autograph of your name, or a straw, or a pebble, but not a diamond.'

The attachment implied by these words was so very flattering, and at the same time expressed with such utterly unconscious simplicity, that Sir William could not suppress a smile. His forehead cleared.

'You know how to turn a compliment after all, Miss Hastings,' said he. 'I'm obliged to you. I was beginning to think myself a very unskilful general, for turn which way I would and try what tactics I chose, the fortress would never give me a moment's advantage; I could not win a single outwork. However, if there's a friend in the citadel, if the heart speaks for me, all's right.'

Miss Hastings felt her face grow rather uncomfortably hot. She was confused for a few minutes, and could not reply to Sir William's odd metaphorical speech. The Baronet squinted towards her one of his piercing side-glances and, perceiving she was a trifle startled, he whistled a stave to give her time to compose herself, affected to be engaged with his spaniel, and then, when another squint had assured him that the flush was subsiding on her cheek, he drew her arm a little closer, and recommenced the conversation on a fresh theme.

'Lonely, quiet meadows these,' said he. 'And all this country has something very sequestered about it. I know it well, every lane and gate and stile.'

'You've been here before, then?' returned Miss Hastings. 'I've often heard that you were a rambler.'

'I've been here by day and by night. I've seen these hedges bright as they are now in sunshine and throwing a dark shade by moonlight. If there were such things as fairies I should have met them often, for these are just their haunts – foxglove leaves and bells, moss like green velvet, mushrooms springing at the roots of oak-trees, thorns a hundred years old grown over with ivy, all precisely in the fairy-tale style.'

'And what did you do here?' inquired Miss Hastings. 'What made you wander alone, early and late? Was it because you liked to see twilight gathering in such lanes as these, and the moon rising over such a green swell of pasture as that, or because you were unhappy?'

'I'll answer you with another question,' returned Sir William. 'Why do *you* like to ramble by yourself ? It is because you can think, and so could I. It never was my habit to impart my thoughts much, especially those that gave me the most pleasure, so I wanted no companion. I used to dream, indeed, of some nameless being, whom I invested with the species of mind and face and figure that I imagined I could love; I used to wish for some existence with finer feelings and a warmer heart than what I saw round me. I had a kind of idea that I could be a very impassioned lover, if I met with a woman who was young and elegant and had a mind above the grade of an animal.'

'You must have met with many such,' said Miss Hastings, not shrinking from the conversation, for its confidential tone charmed her like a spell.

'I've met with many pretty women, with some clever ones. I've seen one or two that I thought myself in love with for a time, but a few days or at most weeks tired me of them. I grew *ennuyé* with their insipid charms, and turned again to my ideal bride. Once, indeed, I plunged over head and ears into a mad passion with a real object. But that's over.'

'Who was she?'

'One of the most beautiful and celebrated women of her day.[137] Unfortunately, she was appropriated. I could have died to win that woman's smile; to take her hand and touch her lips, I could have suffered torture; and to obtain her love, to earn the power of clasping her in my arms and telling her all I felt, to have my ardour returned, to hear in her musical earnest voice the expression of responsive attachment, I could, if the D—l had asked me, have sold my redemption and consented to take the stamp of the hoof[138] on both my hands.'

'Who was she?' again asked Miss Hastings.

'I could not utter her name without choking. But she is one you have often heard of, a woman possessed of a singular charm. I never knew a man of strong and susceptible feelings yet who came near her without being more or less influenced by her attractions. She's beautiful in form and face and expression, most divinely so. She's impassioned, too; her feelings are concentrated and strong; and this gives a tone to her looks, her manners, her whole aspect that no heart can resist. Sorrow has made her grave. The recollection of important and strange events in which she has been deeply concerned have fixed a character of solemnity on her brow. She looks as if she could never be frivolous, seldom gay. She has endured a great deal, and with the same motive to animate her, she would endure it all again.'

'Does she live in Angria?'

'Yes. Now ask me no more questions, for I'll not answer them. Come, give me your hand, and I'll help you over this stile. There, we're out of the fields now. Were you ever so far as this before?'

'Never,' said Miss Hastings, looking round. The objects she saw were not familiar to her. They had entered upon another road, rough, rutty and grown over. Not a house or a human being was to be seen, but immediately before them stood a church with a low tower and a little churchyard scattered over with a few head-stones and many turf mounds. About four miles off stretched a line of hills, darkly ridged with heath, now all empurpled with a lovely sunset. Miss Hastings' eye kindled as she caught them.

'What moors are those?' she asked quickly.

'Ingleside and the Scars,' replied Sir William.

'And what is that church?

'Scar Chapel.'

'It looks old. How long do you think it is since it was built?'

'It is one of the earliest date in Angria. What caps me is why the d—l any church at all was set down in a spot like this where there is no population.'

'Shall we go into the church-yard?'

'Yes, if you like; and you'd better rest there for a few minutes, for you look tired.'

In the centre of the enclosure stood an ancient yew, gnarled,

sable and huge. The only raised tomb in the place rested under
the shadow of this grim old sentinel. 'You can sit down there,'
said Sir William, pointing to the monument with his cane. Miss
Hastings approached, but before she took her seat on the slab,
something in its appearance caught her attention. It was of
marble, not stone; plain and unornamented, but gleaming
with dazzling whiteness from the surrounding turf. At first sight
it seemed to bear no inscription, but on looking nearer one
word was visible: 'RESURGAM'.[139] Nothing clsc; no namc,
date or age.

'What is this?' asked Miss Hastings. 'Who is buried here?'

'You may well ask,' returned Sir William, 'but who d'ye think
can answer you? I've stood by this grave many a time when
that church clock was striking twelve at midnight, sometimes
in rain and darkness, sometimes in clear, quivering starlight,
and looked at that single word, and pondered over the mystery
it seemed to involve, till I could have wished the dead corpse
underneath would rise and answer my unavailing questions.'

'And have you never learnt the history of this tomb?'

'Why, partly. You know I've a sort of knack of worming out
any trifling little secret that I get it into my [head] I should like
to discover, and it's not very likely that a slab like this should
be laid down in any church-yard, however lonely, without
somebody knowing something about it.'

'Tell me what you know, then,' said Miss Hastings, raising
her eyes to Sir William's with a look that told how magical was
the effect, how profound was the interest of all this sweet
confidential interchange of feeling. It was more bewitching even
than the open language of love. She had no need to blush and
tremble. She had only to listen when he spoke to feel that he
trusted her, that he deemed her worthy to be the depository of
those half-romantic thoughts he had never perhaps breathed
into human ear before. These sensations might all be delusive,
but they were sweet, and, for the time, Doubt and Apprehension
dared not intrude their warnings.

'Come, sit down,' said the Baronet, 'and you shall hear all I
can tell you. I see you like anything with the savour of romance
in it.'

'I do,' replied Miss Hastings. 'And so do you, Sir William, only you're rather ashamed to confess it.'

He smiled and went on.

'Well, the first clue I got to this business was by a rather remarkable chance. I had been shooting on Ingleside there one day last August, and towards afternoon, as it was very hot, I got tired, and so I thought I would take a stroll down to Scar Chapel and rest myself a while under this old yew, proposing to make and meditate and perhaps concoct a poem over the eccentric grave-stone with one word on it. By the bye, Elizabeth, it has just struck me what a capital economist the individual must have been who ordered the inscription. You know, stone-cutters always charge so much a letter. He could not have had much to pay. On my life, I'll mention that notion to my brother Edward next time I see him; it will suit him to a hair.[140] But excuse me, you don't like practical remarks of that sort. It interferes with the romance.

'To proceed. I was just opening the little gate yonder and, as it stuck against a stone, I had bestowed upon it an emphatic kick to make it fly back more sharply, when I saw to my horror that the church-yard was not empty. You can't conceive how aggravated I was. I had come here so often, and had always found it so utterly lonely, that I had begun to imagine somehow it was my own property, and that nobody ever came near it but myself . However, I now perceived that this idea was an egregi-ous mistake. A chap in a shooting-dress was standing by this very tomb, my own blank tablet of mystery, leaning with both his hands on a long fowling-piece, and about a yard off, on that mound of turf, two pointers were laid stretched out with their tongues lolling from their jaws, panting after a long day's run on the summer hills. I was on the point of levelling my rifle at the interesting group when prudence checked me by two considerations – firstly, that the fellow's head might be of too leaden a consistency to be susceptible of injury from a bullet, and secondly, that there were such things as coroner's inquests and verdicts of wilful murder. So I thought I'd stand and watch.

'The sportsman had his face turned from me, but he was a

tall, strapping specimen of mortality, with a contour of form
that, when I looked hard at him for five minutes on end, seemed
to me particularly familiar to my eye. He stood a long time,
still as a statue, till I began to think he must be the victim of
sentiment. This idea was confirmed by seeing him once or twice
take a handkerchief from his pocket and apply it to his eyes.
I had placed my thumb to the side of my nose, and was on the
point of calling out in a loud clear voice to know how he was
off for soap,[141] when he used his handkerchief for the last time,
thrust it hastily into his pocket and, calling "Dash" and "Bell",
came striding down towards the gate with his dogs at his heels.
My God, here was a kettle of fish![142] I knew his face as well as
I know yours; it was one I had seen under the rim of a crown.
In short, it was our governing lord, Adrian Augustus himself.'

'The Duke of Zamorna!' exclaimed Miss Hastings.

'Yes.'

'And did he see you?'

'See me? The D—l, no! I cut,[143] the moment I recognized his
Satanic Majesty, and ran – my stars, how I did run!'

'Well, and what had he to do with the gravestone? Why did
he cry?'

'Oh, because one of his women is buried under it, a woman
very much talked of five years ago, Rosamund Wellesley.[144] She
died at a house somewhere between here and Ingleside, where
she had lived for some months under a feigned name. From
what I have heard, I should think she gave nature a lift – helped
herself out of the world when she was quite tired of it.'

'Killed herself, do you mean? Why?'

'Because she was ashamed of having loved His Majesty not
wisely but too well.[145] I remember seeing her. She was very
beautiful; not unlike your friend Jane Moore in features, figure
and complexion; very tall and graceful, with light hair and fine
blue eyes. Very different to Miss Moore in mind, though; clever,
I daresay, and sensitive. The Duke undertook to be her guardian
and tutor. He executed his office in a manner peculiar to himself. Guarded her with a vengeance, and tutored her till she
could construe the Art of Love,[146] at any rate. She enjoyed the
benefit of his protection and instructions for about a year, and

then, somehow, she began to pine away. Awkward little reports
were spread. She got to hear them. Her relations insisted upon
it that she should leave her royal mentor. He swore she should
not; they persisted in claiming her. So His Majesty sequestered
her in one of his remote haunts out of their reach. Then he
dared them to come into the heart of his kingdom and fetch
her out. She did not give them the chance. Shame and horror,
I suppose, had worked her feelings into delirium and she died
very suddenly – whether fairly[147] or not, heaven knows. Here
she was interred, and this is the stone her lover laid over her.
Now, Elizabeth, what do you say to such a business as that?'

'It seems the Duke of Zamorna never forsook her, and that he
remembered her after she was dead,' remarked Miss Hastings.

'Oh! and that's sufficient consolation, as the Duke of
Zamorna is a very fine, grand God incarnate, I suppose! G—d
d—n!'

'The Duke of Zamorna is a sort of scoundrel, from all that
ever I heard of him. But then, most men of rank are, from what
I can understand.'

'Were you ever blessed with a sight of His Majesty?' inquired
Sir William.

'Never.'

'But you've seen his portraits, which are, one and all, very
like. Do you admire them?'

'He's handsome, no doubt.'

'Oh, of course; killingly, infernally handsome. Such eyes and
nose, such curls and whiskers – and then his stature! Magnificent! And his chest, two feet across! I never knew a woman yet
who did not calculate the value of a man by the proportion of
his inches.'

Miss Hastings said nothing. She only looked down and
smiled.

'I'm exceedingly nettled and dissatisfied,' remarked Sir
William.

'Why?' inquired Miss Hastings, still smiling.

Sir William, in his turn, gave no answer. He only whistled a
stave or two. After a moment's silence, he looked all round him
with a keen, careful eye. He then turned to his companion.

'Do you see,' said he, 'that the sun is set, and that it is getting dark?'

'Indeed it is,' replied Miss Hastings, and she started instantly to her feet. 'We must go home, Sir William – I had forgotten – how could I let time slip so?'

'Hush,' said the young Baronet, 'and sit down again for a few minutes. I will say what I have to say.'

Miss Hastings obeyed him.

'Do you see,' he continued, 'that everything is still round us, that the twilight is deepening, that there is no light but what that rising half-moon gives?'

'Yes.'

'Do you know that there is not a house within two miles, and that you are four miles from Zamorna?'

'Yes.'

'You are aware, then, that in this shade and solitude you and I are alone?'

'I am.'

'Would you have trusted yourself in such a situation with any one you did not care for?'

'No.'

'You care for me, then?'

'I do.'

'How much?'

There was a pause – a long pause. Sir William did not urge the question impatiently. He only sat keenly and quietly watching Miss Hastings and waiting for an answer. At last she said in a low voice,

'Tell me first, Sir William Percy, how much you care for me.'

'More than at this moment I do for any other woman in the world.'

'Then,' was the heart-felt rejoinder, 'I adore you – and that's a confession death should not make me cancel.'

'Now, Elizabeth,' continued Sir William, 'listen to the last question I have to put, and don't be afraid of me. I'll act like a gentleman whatever your answer may be. You said just now that all men of rank were scoundrels. I'm a man of rank. Will you be my mistress?'

'No.'

'You said you adored me.'

'I do, intensely. But I'll never be your mistress. I could not, without incurring the miseries of self-hatred.'

'That is to say,' replied the Baronet, 'you are afraid of the scorn of the world.'

'I am. The scorn of the world is a horrible thing, and more especially, I should dread to lose the good opinion of three persons, of my father, of Henry and of Mr Warner. I would rather die than be despised by them. I feel a secret triumph now, in the consciousness that, though I have been left entirely to my own guidance, I have never committed an action, or hazarded a word, that would bring my character for a moment under the breath of suspicion. My father and Mr Warner call me obstinate and resentful, but they are both proud of the address I have shewn in making my way through life, and keeping always in the strictest limits of rectitude. Henry, though a wild wanderer himself, would blow his brains out if he heard of his sister adding to the pile of disgrace he has heaped so thickly on the name of Hastings.'

'You would risk nothing for me, then?' returned Sir William. 'You would find no compensation for the loss of world's favour in my perfect love and trusting confidence? It is no pleasure to you to talk to me, to sit by my side as you do now, to allow your hand to rest in mine?'

The tears came into Miss Hastings' eyes.

'I dare not answer you,' she said, 'because I know I should say something frantic. I could no more help loving you than that moon can help shining. If I might live with you as your servant I should be happy. But as your mistress! It is quite impossible.'

'Elizabeth,' said Sir William, looking at her and placing his hand on her shoulder, 'Elizabeth, your eyes betray you. They speak the language of a very ardent, very imaginative temperament. They confess not only that you love me, but that you cannot live without me. Yield to your nature, and let me claim you this moment as my own.'

Miss Hastings was silent, but she was not going to yield. Only the hard conflict of passionate love with feelings that shrunk, horror-struck, from the remotest shadow of infamy compelled her, for a moment, to silent agony.

Sir William thought his point was nearly gained.

'One word,' said he, 'will be sufficient, one smile or whisper. You tremble. Rest in my shoulder [sic]. Turn your face to the moonlight, and give me a single look.'

That moonlight shewed her eyes swimming in tears. The Baronet, mistaking these tears for the signs of resolution fast dissolving, attempted to kiss them away. She slipt from his hold like an apparition.

'If I stay another moment, God knows what I shall say or do,' said she. 'Good-bye, Sir William. I implore you not to follow me. The night is light; I am afraid of nothing but myself. I shall be in Zamorna in an hour. Good-bye, I suppose, for ever!'

'Elizabeth!' exclaimed Sir William.

She lingered for a moment; she could not go. A cloud just then crossed the moon. In two minutes it had passed away.

Sir William looked towards the place where Miss Hastings had been standing. She was gone. The church-yard gate swung to. He muttered a furious curse, but did not stir to follow. There he remained, where she had left him, for hours, as fixed as the old yew whose black arms brooded over his head. He must have passed a quiet night – church and graves and tree all mute as death, Lady Rosamund's tomb alone proclaiming in the moonlight 'I shall rise!'

CHAPTER V

You must now, reader, step into this library, where you shall see a big man sitting at a table with a long swan-quill pen in his hand and an ink-stand before him. Behind the big man's chair stands a little man, holding a green bag from which he hands papers for the big man to sign. The scene is a silent one.

When you have looked awhile you begin to imagine that both performers are dummies. It reminds you of the mute allegories shown by the Interpreter to Christian,[148] or of the old Dutch groups of ghosts who play dice and nine-pins a hundred years after they are dead.[149] At last the profound taciturnity of the scene is relieved by an audible sigh heaved from the deep chest of the big man.

'I think,' he says, 'there's no bottom to that d—d bag.'

'Patience,' replies the little man. 'Some persons are soon tired, I think. Where is the labour of affixing a signature?'

'Another pen,' demands the big man, throwing away his swan-quill.

'There is a loss of time in changing the pen often,' replies the little man. 'Cannot your Grace make that do?'

'Look at it,' was the answer. The quill was split up in some emphatic dash or down stroke.

'Strange mismanagement,' says the little man, handing, however, another pen.

The pantomime again proceeded. In a while its monotony was broken by a gentle knock at the library door.

'Come in,' said the big man.

'Absurd interruption of business,' muttered the little man.

The door opened. The person entering closed it again, and crossed the soft carpet without much sound. A lady approached the table, of tall and dignified appearance. She wore a hat with black feathers and a veil thrown back.

'How d'ye do?' said she, placing her hand on the table.

'How d'ye do?' responded the signer of documents, and that was all the interchange of words that took place. Him of the green bag bowed, with an air of mixed respect and annoyance; and the lady said something that sounded like a 'good morning'. She stood a moment by the table, looking half abstractedly at what was transacting there. She then moved away to the hearth, and stood for about five minutes turning over the coins and shells laid on the mantle-piece and surveying the features of three bronze busts that stood there as ornaments. Finally, she loosened the strings of her hat, removed a fur boa from her neck, and having thrown that and her shawl on a sofa that stood near the fire, she seated herself there also and remained perfectly still.

'All things must have an end',[150] and so, at long last, the green bag and its contents were exhausted. 'I have given your Grace the last paper,' said Mr Warner, when his master, now broken into the service, looked round with the patience of despair, expecting another document and yet another.

'God be thanked for all his mercies,' replied the King solemnly. Mr Warner, who was in a ruinous temper, did not vouchsafe a reply. He merely locked his bag with particular emphasis, drew on his gloves and, bowing stiffly, said,

'I wish your Majesty a very good morning.' Another silent bow to the lady followed, and then the Premier of Angria formally backed out of his master's presence.

The Duke of Zamorna now crossed his legs, leant his arm on the back of his chair, and turned half round to his stately visitor.

'The little man's cursedly peevish today,' said he, smiling. The lady uttered a scarcely articulate monosyllable of assent, and continued to sit gravely gazing at the window opposite. The Duke reached out his arm, and drew from under a pile of books and papers an immense folio.

'You've seen these new maps, I suppose?' said he, opening the vast boards. 'They're the pride of my life, so beautifully accurate.'

The lady got up, stood behind him, and stooped over his shoulder as he turned the leaves.

'The first military chartists[151] in Angria have been employed to get up these,' he continued.

'I daresay they're good,' replied the lady.

'Good! they're exquisite!' exclaimed the monarch. 'And the engraving is first rate, too. Look there, and there – how distinct.'

He traced his ringed fore-finger along certain ridges of mountains and courses of rivers and markings of sand-hills and boundaries of trackless wildernesses.

'Very clear,' said the lady.

'And correct, that's the point,' added her companion. 'No guessing here, no romancing. One can depend on such stuff as this. My word, if the fellows had given rope to their imaginations, here Etrei would soon have twisted it into a halter for their own necks. But bring a chair, Zenobia, and I'll shew you the whole thing, and all my pencil-marks.'

Zenobia brought a chair. She leant her arm on the table, and inclined her head to look and listen while the maps were shewn and their bearings explained.

'Take your hat off first,' began His Majesty. 'The feathers throw a shade on the paper so that you cannot see.'

She complied in silence, removed her hat, and let it drop onto the floor beside her. The process of demonstration and elucidation then began. In other words, His Majesty proceeded to make a famous bore of himself. He was listened to with exemplary patience, a patience the more remarkable as the royal lecturer, like all very formidable bores, exacted the most rigid attention from his hearer; and every now and then, to convince himself that she comprehended what he said, required prompt answers to very botheracious questions. One of his interrogations not being readily replied to, he got vexed.

'Now, Zenobia, I wish you would attend more closely. Why, I explained all that only five minutes ago.'

'Well, just repeat it once more.'

So in a deliberate, doctrinal tone, His Majesty proceeded to lay down the law again. In about a quarter of an hour, another bungle occurred. Zenobia requested some explanation which seemed to produce the effect of an electrical shock on her royal instructor. He dropped his pencil, raised his eyes to the ceiling in rapt astonishment and, turning his chair completely round from the table to the fire, gave the important information that 'since she did not understand *that*, the game was up'. In a while he seized the poker, and having made an emphatic assault on the already blazing coals, he read[152] on thus:

'What the D—l you're thinking about this morning, I can't tell. I never knew you so stupid before – never. When I've spent the last hour in explaining to you the finest system of tactics that ever a d—d infernal sand-hill and jungle warfare was conducted on, and proved to a moral certainty that if I can only have my own way not a black piccaninny will be left to cheep between this and Tunis,[153] all at once you pose me with a question that shews you no more heard or understood a word of my argument than the babe unborn.'

'Well, Zamorna,' said the Countess, 'you know that sort of abstruse reasoning is not my forte. You always said I never could deduce an inference.'[154]

'Yes, I know that. Mathematics and logic are chaos and confusion in your estimation, I'm perfectly aware. But this caps the globe,[155] as they say in Angria. I tell you, Zenobia, if I'd spent as much time over my Frederick, in teaching him the facts of the case, and he'd cut me short with such a speech as that, by the Lord, I'd have whipped him.'

'Well, I'll do better another time,' continued the Countess. 'But the truth is, Zamorna, my thoughts were running on something else all the time you were speaking. I'm downright unhappy.'

'Oh, that's another thing!' returned the Duke. 'You should have told me so at once. But what's the matter?'

'Percy vexes me so. I shall have to leave him.'

'What, his vagaries are not over, are they?'

'No indeed, worse than ever. I feel persuaded he will not settle till he has done something very wild and *outré*.'

'Come, you're looking on the dark side, Zenobia. Cheer up! Has he done anything very extraordinary lately?'

'He seems so strange and fitful,' returned the Countess. 'Every evening, he goes into the red saloon and plays on the organ there for hours together. If I happen to be there, not a single word does he speak. He seems altogether absorbed in the music. He looks up in that inspired kind of way he has when he feels excited, then he takes his fingers from the keys and sits silent with his head on his hand. If I ask him a question, he says "I don't know" or "I can't tell". Nothing can draw him into conversation. At last he'll get up and ring for his hat and set off God knows where. I understand he often goes to Lady Georgiana Greville's[156] or Lady St James'– sometimes even to that little insignificant wretch's, Miss Delph's. But I *will* not bear it, and I solemnly declare to you, Zamorna, that if he does not change soon I'll leave him and go away to the west.'

'No, Zenobia,' returned his Grace. 'Take my advice and

make no public move of that sort, nothing to cause éclat; it will only hurry on some frantic catastrophe. Besides, you know you'll come back to him as soon as ever he chooses to coax you. Refuse to see him if you like, confine yourself entirely to your own suite of rooms and give him to understand that your apartments are forbidden ground, then shut your eyes and let him go to the D—l his own way. He'll sit down quietly enough in a while.'

'What!' exclaimed the Countess. 'Then I'm to let him follow a score of mistresses, waste all his love on Greville and Lalande – who, by the by, like a dirty French demi-rep as she is, has actually come over from Paris and taken up her quarters at Dèmars Hotel, that she may make hay while the sun shines[157] – I'm to endure all this tamely, am I? No, Augustus, that's a trifle too much to require of me; you know I could not do it.'

'Then box his ears, Zenobia – he deserves it – and invite all his ladies to a good dinner, feed them well, give them a few glasses of wine, and then flog them all round. I shouldn't hesitate to back you against any ten of them. One down, and another come on –'[158]

'It would do me good,' replied the Countess, half-crying, half-smiling. 'I should like to chastise some of them, especially that Delph and that Lalande. I say again, Augustus, it's too bad, when I love him so well for himself alone, that he should refuse to give me so much as a word or look, and lavish all his affection on these nasty, mercenary wretches.'

'Yes, men are cursed animals,' replied Zamorna. 'That's a fact and it won't deny. And your Alexander is a charming specimen of the worst of a bad set. But Zenobia, you may exaggerate a little. You may be misinformed. There's such a thing, you know, as ladies being jealous without a reason. I happen just now to be acquainted with a case in point, and as you and I are on the subject of matrimonial grievances, I'll tell you what it is, in order that we may condole with each other.'

'Oh, Zamorna,' interrupted the Countess, 'you're going to turn the whole affair into ridicule in your usual way.'

'No, indeed. I was merely about to tell you that I've quite a weight on my mind at present, on account of the freezing distance at which her Grace the Duchess has thought proper to keep me lately, and the unaccountable coolness and frigidity which has marked her whole manner towards me for this fortnight last past. I've thought every day that I'd request an explanation, but somehow I felt a sort of impulse to let matters take their own course and look as if I was not greatly concerned about the business. When I do so, she makes a point of crying – yes, actually shedding tears and looking considerably heartbroken, and I declare before heaven I can't guess what it's all about.'

The Countess shook her head.

'You're a Nathaniel without guile,[159] all the world knows that,' said she. 'But I see you'll not consider my distresses in a serious light, and yet I'm such a fool I can't help complaining to you.'

'Well,' returned his Grace, 'I complain to you and you won't pity me, and so we're even. Come, Zenobia, dismiss sad thoughts from your mind. It's precisely three o'clock by my repeater. I've had a very hard morning's work, and am just in tune for an hour or two's relaxation. Go and put on your riding habit and beaver. I'll order a pair of my hunters to be saddled, and we'll have a gallop on the Alnwick road in the old style, neck and neck.'

The Countess rose, wiping her eyes and smiling in spite of herself.

'Mercurial as ever,' said she. 'Care does not cling to you, Augustus.'

'Nor to you either,' was the answer. 'In half an hour, as soon as you've inhaled a draught of fresh air and got fairly into the country, you'll be as fresh as a lark and thinking only how to beat me in the hard trot and sharp canter. But the chances are not as equal as they used to be, Zenobia. Though you are magnificently round, my height and bone will outweigh you now.'

'Well,' said the Countess, 'I suppose I must humour you. I shall not be long in preparing. Do you mean to ride till dinner time?'

'Yes. We shall only have two hours and a half, so make haste.

It's a glorious day, bright and breezy. Hey, what's that passing
the window? Zenobia, just come and look.'

Zenobia approached the casement where his Grace was
standing. Two elfish figures rode by, mounted on diminutive
and shaggy ponies and followed by a tall and stately footman in splendid scarlet livery, mounted on a glossy black steed.
The first cavaliers were little fellows in blue dresses[160] with
tassled caps. They sat in their saddles as erect as arrows, and
looked about them with an air of shy, proud consequence, truly
aristocratic.

'Not bad riders, are they?' said the Duke, gazing after them
with a grin of complacency that displayed all his white teeth.

'They manage their chargers wonderfully well,' replied the
Countess. 'And the ponies look spirited too. You must have
begun to teach them in good time.'

'Only half a year ago. The lads took to their saddles well.
Look at Frederick! D—n the little toad! He's laying it into his
nag most viciously.'

At this moment one of the shelties turned somewhat restive,
and the slim rider, a pale, light-haired boy of between four and
five, lifted his switch and, setting his teeth, laid on about the
pony's head like a savage. The creature kicked and reared,
and if the footman had not interfered a drawn battle might
have ensued. With his aid, the matter was at last settled. Both
the little chaps then started into a canter, and sweeping across
Victoria Square entered Fidena Park.

'There go the hopes of Angria,' said Zamorna, laughing.
'That was a touch of the grandfather.[161] He looked very like
him at the moment. He deserves licking.'

CHAP[TER] VI

Evening being come on, the time for closing curtains and rous-
ing fires, I will introduce my readers to a domestic scene in
Wellesley House, all very innocent and homely. The daylight,
perhaps, is not quite drawn in, for winter, you must remember,
is past, and the sunset of a fine day leaves a long glimmer behind

it. However, it is dusk enough to bring out the full glow of a good fire, and in this drawing[-room], which I wish you now to imagine, there is more of red reflection from the hearth than of pale gleam from the windows.

Don't suppose you are about to witness a scene of unalloyed peace. On the contrary, the room is full of talk and noise. Or rather, there are two divisions in the place: calm reigns on one side, chaos on the other. By some tacit regulation, nothing tumultuous dare approach the region of the rug and mantle-piece. A sofa covered with crimson occupies one side of the hearth. The further end of this sofa comes against a window, through which the shrubs of a garden are seen dimly clustered in twilight, and above them ascends a half-moon, softening a sky of clear, cold azure. This moon directs a very pale beam on to the brow of a gentleman who sits on the sofa and gazes serenely at vacancy, without proffering a word to man or beast.

Now, a person of slim, genteel stature and mellow years, with a bald, smooth, lofty brow glistening in moonlight and bust-like features ditto, must needs look very poetical, especi-ally when he is dressed in an angelical blue swallow-tail coat, a pallid primrose vest, and pantaloons which are a sight to see, not speak of. Nor was there wanting, to give full effect to this aërial picture, the force of contrast. Behold, at the feet of this celestial form, this heavenly thought embodied in marble, sat or crept or rolled a human infant, yea, an absolute child, small and plump, with a white frock and round face, features as yet invisible, and a pair of saucer eyes a shade darker than jet in their hue. This child seemed to hold the territory of the rug with undivided sway, and it crept from end to end of its dominions with an unwearied and ceaseless vigilance of surveil-lance not easily accounted for on any known principal of government. Now and then it laid ten minute fingers on the rim of the burnished brass fender which formed the boundary to one side of its realm, and seemed inclined to overpass this formidable barrier and make an incursion into the fiery district beyond. Whenever these signs of a rising spirit of discovery occurred, the tall pensive gentleman would bend down, and with a gentle hand remove the adventurer to its own limits, just as one would put back a white mouse convicted of attempting to escape beyond its cage. These transactions took place in silence. Neither god-like man nor impish child seemed gifted with the faculty of speech.

Individuals of a different calibre peopled the other end of the room. There, three boys were making a famous clatter. Chairs and foot-stools were hauled about with small regard to decorum, and a yelp of voices was kept up much like what you might expect to hear in a kennel of pointer puppies. Two of the lads were pale, slight fellows with curling light hair. The other was a rounder, rosier animal, with a dimple in his cheek and with hair a shade darker, more thickly curled. Large brown eyes seemed a family peculiarity common to them all. The uproar they were keeping up seemed partly controlled, partly excited by a powerful-built gentleman who sat on a music-stool in the midst of them. At the identical moment we speak of, he had them in a half-circle before him, and appeared to be asking them some questions.

'Frederick, did you and Edward say your lessons this morning before you rode out?'

'Yes, Papa.'

'All of them?'

A pause.

'I did, but he didn't!' exclaimed Edward.

'And why didn't he, sir?'

'Because he wouldn't.'

'Wouldn't? What's the meaning of that, Frederick? I said you were not to come down in the evening next time you missed your lessons.'

'I did all but spelling,' said the accused.

'And why didn't you do spelling, too?'

''Cause Dr Cook wanted me to say G— and I wanted to say J—.'

'A pretty reason, sir. Truly, I hope Dr Cook will lick you soundly next time you take that whim. Do you know, sir, what Solomon says on the subject of flogging?'

Silence was the expressive answer to this question.

'Spare the rod and spoil the child,'[162] pursued the paternal monitor. 'And moreover, Frederick, my lad, let me tell you that the very next time I see that switch of yours laid on in the way it was this morning, I'll take the pony from you, and you shall ride no more for a month to come.'

'It wouldn't go right,' said Frederick, 'and Edward did just the same, only worse, when we got into the park.'

'Very well, gentlemen, I'll speak to your groom, and you shall walk out with Miss Clifton tomorrow, like little girls. Now, Arthur, what are you looking so eager about?'

'I want to ask you something, Papa.' The rosy wretch, setting a stool, proceeded rumbustiously to climb on to his father's knee. Having seated himself *en cavalier*, he began:

'I've said all my lessons today.'

'Well, that's a fine lad. What then?'

'May I have a pony?'

'He neither read yesterday nor the day before,' interposed Edward, who, with his brother, had been struck with chill dismay on hearing the sentence pronounced that they were to walk out with Miss Clifton like little girls.

'And he cried and screamed all the time we were out this morning, because he mightn't ride too,' added Frederick.

The Duke shook his head at hearing this.

'Bad account, Arthur.'

Arthur knew how to manage. Instead of crying, he eyed his father with a twinkling, merry glance out of the corner of his roguish dark eye, and repeated,

'Let me have a pony. Mamma says I ought.'

'Mamma spoils thee, my lad,' said Zamorna, 'because thou happenest to have a cheek like an apple and a vile dimple mark upon it, with sundry tricks of smiles and glances that, judging by my own experience, are never likely to win thee a share in saving grace.'

'A pony, a pony,' persisted the petitioner.

'Well, well, be a good boy for three days, and then we'll see about it.'

'I suppose Maria is to have a pony next,' muttered Frederick, regarding the diminutive thing on the rug with a look of lordly scorn, and then turning a displeased eye on Arthur. Happily, his father did not hear this remark, or it would probably have been rewarded by a manual application onto the auricular organs. Edward, retreating a little behind his father, expressed his feelings on the subject in the more delicate language of signs. Applying his thumb to his nose, he took a sight,[163] thereby meaning to intimate, 'Never mind, Fred. Let Arthur have his pony. He'll never sit in the saddle, and what fun the tumbling will be.'

Frederick, being a trifle in the sullens,[164] strayed away to the quiet region of the fire-place, and stood looking into the embers for some time. His noble grandsire, opposite to whom he had planted himself, noticed his proximity only by an uncertain glitter of the eye, with which he surveyed him at intervals. At last Northangerland made a movement as if he were going to speak, though reluctantly.

'Where's your mother?' he said abruptly, at the same moment directing a singular squint at the young heir of Angria and withdrawing his gaze instantly. The pale, sharp lad looked up.

'What did ye say, sir?' he asked, with the quick utterance that seemed natural to him.

'I asked you where your mother was,' replied the earl somewhat sternly.

'Mamma's in her room, sir.'

'And why doesn't she come down?'

'I don't know, sir.'

'Go and ask your father, then.'

'Ask him what, sir?'

'Blockhead!' said Northangerland, scowling. 'Ask your father why your mother is not here.'

'Very well, sir.'

Frederick whipped off.

'Please, Papa, my grandfather wants to know why Mamma is not come down.'

'Tell your grandfather,' replied his Grace, 'that I have been asking myself the same question, and that I had just screwed my courage up to the exploit of ascertaining the reason *in propria persona*.'

'In what, Papa?'

'In my own august person, Frederick.'

The ambassador returned.

'Papa's screwed up his courage to go and ask in his own august person.'

Northangerland curled his upper lip.

'I've done with you, sir,' he said, nodding to Frederick. But the imp, like a true Angrian, would not take a hint. He continued to stand by the fender, and shew to his annoyed progenitor the small correct features and pale auburn curls of the house of Percy gleaming in firelight. Zamorna drew near, a tower of strength.

'Frederick,' said he, 'go to the other side of the room.'

'What for, Papa? Maria's always let to be on the rug, and we never are.'

'To the right-about instantly,' said the Duke. 'No words from you, my lad. Do as you're bid.' And placing a hand on the slim malcontent's shoulder, he impelled him some yards on his way.

'If you return here while I am out of the room, I shall send you to bed directly,' said his Grace, and with these words, he opened a side door and departed.

The Duchess of Zamorna was sitting in a room as beautiful as jeweller's work, but without a fire, and therefore chilly and ungenial in spite of its splendour. One taper was shining on the toilet, and by the light it shed her Grace, seated in an arm-chair, seemed reading. At least, she had an open book in her hand and her eyes were fixed on the page, though the fair, slight finger resting between the leaves was not often raised to turn them over. Her dress was all elegant and queenly, and her hair, divided from her forehead in a silken braid, separated into wavy curls on the temples and relieved her rounded cheek and delicate features with its soft shade. She looked somewhat proud and somewhat sad, but most perfectly, most picturesquely lovely. What could be imagined fairer? De Lisle's pencil could not add a charm, and Chantry's chisel[165] could not remove a defect.

A rather smart rap at the door roused her. She lifted her cheek from the hand of ivory on which it rested, and seemed to consider a moment before she replied. It was not like the tap of her attendants; their summons was usually more gentle and subdued. And the one other person who had a right to enter this room always claimed his full privilege by appearing unannounced. While she doubted, the rap was repeated, with a still smarter, more prolonged application of the knuckles.

'Come in,' she said, with a stately composure of tone and mien which seemed to rebuke the impetuosity of the summons.

The door unclosed. 'I hope I've done right,' said the Duke of Zamorna, stepping forward and shutting himself in. 'I'd be sorry to be too bold, and hurt anybody's notions of delicacy, even if they were a little fastidious, or so.'

'Your Grace wishes to speak with me, perhaps,' returned the Duchess, laying down her book and looking up, with an aspect of serene attention.

'Yes, merely to speak; I pledge my word, nothing more. In surety whereof, I'll take a chair here just by the door, which will leave at least four yards between your ladyship and me.'

Accordingly, he placed a chair with its back against the door, and there seated himself. The Duchess looked down, and something stole into her eye which made it glisten with a more humid shine than heretofore.

'Your Grace will be cold there, I think,' said she, and a half smile lit the incipient tear.

'Cold? Aye, it seems to be a hard frost tonight, I think, Mary. Pray, if I might presume to put the question, will you be kind enough to tell me why you prefer sitting here reading a homily or a sermon by yourself, instead of coming down into your drawing-room and looking after the children? Frederick has been bothering his grandfather again, and little Maria has kept him engaged all the evening.'

'I'll come down if you wish me,' replied the Duchess. 'But my head ached a little after dinner, and I thought, perhaps, if I sat in the room and looked out of spirits, you would think me sullen.'

'Why, you've been looking out of spirits for the last fortnight, and therefore I should most likely never have noticed what I am now grown so much accustomed to. But if you'll favour me with the reason of it all, I'll consider myself obliged to you.'

Her Grace sat silent. She reopened her book and turned over the leaves.

'Are you going to read me a sermon?' asked His Majesty. The Duchess turned her head aside, and wiped away the single tear now stealing down her cheek.

'I can't talk to you at that distance,' said she.

'Well,' returned Zamorna, 'I would wish always to observe the strictest propriety, but if you'll give me an invitation, perhaps I may venture a yard or two nearer.'

'Come,' said the Duchess, still engaged with her hand-kerchief.

His Grace approached. 'You'll perhaps faint if I stir another step,' said he, pausing half-way between the door and the toilet. The Duchess held out her hand, though still her head was turned away. Thus encouraged, his diffident Grace drew nearer by degrees, and at last cast anchor with his chair alongside of his royal consort. He possessed himself, too, of the hand which had not been withdrawn, and then, with his peculiar smile, sat waiting for the sequel.

'You haven't been to Flower House lately, have you?' asked the Duchess.

'Not very, but what of that? Do you suspect a growing friendship between me and the Countess?'

'No, no; but, Adrian –'

A pause.

'Well, Mary?'

'You were at Flower House a few weeks ago?'

'I believe I was,' said his Grace, and he blushed to the eyes.

'And you forgot me, Adrian. You saw someone you liked better.'

'Who told you that snivelling lie?' returned his Grace. 'Did Richton?'

'No.'

'Warner?'

'No.'

'The Countess, or some other busybody in petticoats?'

'No.'

'Who, then?'

320 TALES OF ANGRIA

'I dare not tell you who, Adrian, but a person I was forced to believe.'

'Well, what more? What goddess was it that I liked better than you?'

'It was a lady I have heard you praise myself. You called her the most beautiful woman in Angria. Miss Moore.'

His Grace laughed aloud.

'And that's all, Mary, is it?' said he. 'That's what you've been pining over for two mortal weeks! And I like Miss Moore better than you, do I? I've a strange taste! Miss Moore?' he continued, as if endeavouring to recall the lady's identity. 'Miss Moore? Aye, I recollect – a tall girl, with light hair and a somewhat high colour. I believe I did once say that she was a fine specimen of the Angrian female. And on second thoughts, I remember now that the last time I was at Flower House, Richton brought her into the room where I was taking off my coat, and she bothered me a little with some kind of request about Henry Hastings – all in a very modest way, though; she was not intrusive. I told her I was sorry I could not oblige her, and gave her a little serious advice about not being too ready to take up the causes of scoundrelly young red-coats, as it might subject her to unpleasant imputations. She blushed with due propriety and there the matter ended. Now, Mary, there's the naked truth.'

'Is it all the truth, Adrian?'

'All, upon my Christian d—n—tion.'

The Duchess looked willing and yet afraid to believe.

'I wish I could feel convinced,' said she. 'A heavy weight would be removed from my mind.'

'Dismiss it instantly,' said his Grace. 'It's all imaginary, a mere nervous affection. You inherit your father's turn for hypochondria, Mary.'

'But,' pursued her Grace, 'I am sure, Adrian, you have been very cold to me for some days past. I have hardly had an opportunity of exchanging a word with you.'

Again Zamorna laughed.

'Well, the inconsistency of woman!' exclaimed he. 'Reproaching me with the effects of her own caprice! Have you not been shrinking from me like a sensitive plant, answering my questions in monosyllables, crying when I spoke to you kindly, and contriving to slip away whenever by any chance you happened to be left alone with me?'

'You exaggerate,' said the Duchess.

'Not in the least. And pray, what was I to make of all this? Of course, I imagined you had taken some kind of odd whim into your head, perhaps begun to entertain scruples regarding the lawfulness of matrimony, and in fact, every day I expected a formal application for a dissolution of the conjugal tie, and an intimation that it was your purpose to seek some sacred retreat where the follies of carnal affection might beset you no more.'

'Adrian!' said the Duchess, smiling at his taunts while she deprecated their severity. 'You know such ideas never crossed your mind. While you talk in that way, your eyes are full of triumph. Yes, Adrian, from the very first moment you saw me, six years ago, you perceived your own power. You perceive it now. It's of no use resisting; I'll believe all you tell me. I've acted foolishly. Forgive me, and don't retaliate.'

'Then you drop the idea of a convent, do you, Mary? You think there will be time enough to turn devout some thirty years hence, when that pretty face is not quite so fair and smooth and those eyes are not altogether so subduing, and, moreover, when your husband's head has grown a little grizzled, and his brow has a furrow or two across, deep enough to give him the air of a stern old fire-eater, as he will be? Then, you'll refuse him a kiss, but now –'

Two or three kisses were offered and received, and warmly returned. Duke and Duchess then rose. The candle remained burning on the toilet, the two chairs stood vacant before it, the splendid little room reflected around its fairy beauty, but the living figures of the scene were gone. Solitude and silence lingered behind them. The candle burnt soon to its socket. The flame flickered, waned, streamed up in a long tongue of light, sank again, trembled a moment, and finally vanished in total darkness. Then a piano was heard playing in the drawing-room below, and, when the first note had stilled the clamour of children, a voice sung:

'Life, believe, is not a scene
        So dark as sages say.
Oft, a little morning rain
        Will bring a pleasant day.
Sometimes there are clouds of gloom,
        But these are transient all,
If the shower will make the roses bloom,
        O why lament its fall?
                Merrily, rapidly,
        Our sunny hours flit by,
                Then gratefully, cheerily,
        Enjoy them as they fly.

'What though Death at times steps in,
        And calls our best away?
What though sorrow seems to win
        O'er Hope a heavy sway?
Yet Hope again elastic springs
        Unconquered, though she fell.
Still buoyant are her golden wings,
        Still strong to bear us well.
                Then manfully, fearlessly
        The day of trial bear,
                For gloriously, victoriously,
        Can Courage quell Despair!'

            Charles Townshend, March 26th 1839

CAROLINE VERNON

Introductory Note

From May to July 1839, Charlotte Brontë went for the first and only time to work as a governess with a private family, the Sidgwicks, first at Stonegappe near Skipton and then at Swarcliffe, a summer residence near Harrogate in Yorkshire taken by relatives of the family which employed her – 'a beautiful place in a beautiful country – rich and agricultural' (*CBL I*, p. 193). *Caroline Vernon* seems to have been begun after her return, in early July. The ms., which is in two distinct parts, is undated. The second part was probably begun, as its opening paragraph suggests, some four months later, after Brontë had returned from her first independent holiday, with her friend Ellen Nussey, at Easton near Bridlington.

Here, as in *Henry Hastings*, Charles Townshend is living in Verdopolis and leading the insouciant life of a young 'blade'. He is still a cash-strapped hack writer, and still a sardonic observer of romantic sentimentality. Zenobia, still stout, is still at odds with her husband, the ageing but still straying Earl of Northangerland. The Angrians are still demonstrating against Northangerland. Mary Percy is still anxious to keep her husband's affections. Northangerland and Zamorna are still sparring, and still indissolubly bound. But time – as the latter is sharply reminded when he learns the age of his daughter – has moved on. Louisa Vernon is now a superannuated courtesan, living in country retirement with her daughter, Caroline, teenage ward of Zamorna, and half-sister of his wife.

Caroline Vernon opens with a series of scenes in which, before we meet her, Caroline figures largely in others' thoughts and schemes. The drunken, exiled Quashia writes almost unintelligibly to her father, demanding her hand in marriage. Zenobia becomes 'very red and choleric' at the mere mention of her name. Zamorna has his 'notions as to how [she] ought to be managed'. Northangerland decides 'to introduce her to the world'. But Caroline, when she appears, also has her own ideas. This hoydenish, daydreaming, not-entirely-innocent heroine, who is to learn a thing or two in Paris and to stage her own 'voluntary elopement, without a companion, alone, entirely of her own free will', is 'not quite so simple and communicative as she seem[s].'

PART 1

When I concluded my last book, I made a solemn resolve that I would write no more till I had somewhat to write about, and at the time I had a sort of notion that perhaps many years might elapse before aught should transpire novel and smart enough to induce me to resume my relinquished pen. But lo you! scarce three moons have waxed and waned ere 'the creature's at his dirty work again'.[1]

And yet it is no novelty, no fresh and startling position of affairs, that has dipped my quill in ink and spread the blank sheet before me. I have but been looking forth as usual over the face of society; I have but been eating my commons in Chapel Street, dressing and dining out daily, reading newspapers, attending the theatres nightly, taking my place about once a week in the fire-flaught Angrian Mail, rushing as far as Zamorna, sometimes continuing my career till I saw the smoke of Adrianapolis, snatching a look at the staring shops and raw new palaces of that great baby capital, then, like a water-god, taking to the Calabar – not, however, robing myself in flags and crowning myself with sedge, but with a ticket in my fist getting on board a steamer, and away, all fizz and foam, down past Mouthton and coasting it along by Doverham back to Verdopolis again. When subdued by a fit of pathos and senti-mentalities, I've packed a hamper with sandwiches and gone to Alnwick or somewhere there awa' – but I'll try that no more, for last time I did it, chancing to sit down under a willow[2] in the grounds to eat a cold fowl and drink a bottle of ginger-beer, I made use of the pedestal of a statue for my table, whereat a keeper thought fit to express himself eminently scandalized, and in an insolent manner to give notice that such liberties were not permitted at the castle, that strangers were excluded from this part of the grounds, that the statue was considered a valuable piece of sculpture, being the likeness of some male or female of the house of Wharton who had died twenty years ago,[3] with a lot of rhodomontade all tending to shew that I had committed sacrilege or something like it by merely placing a mustard-glass and pepper-box with a dinner-bun and knife and fork at the base of a stupid stone idol representing somebody in their chemise fatuitously gazing at their own naked toes.

Howsumdever, even in this course of life I've seen and heard a summat that, like the notes of a tourist,[4] may sell when committed to paper. Lord, a book-wright need never be at a loss! One cannot expect earthquakes and insurrections every day. There's not always

> An Angrian campaign going on in the rain,
> Nor a gentleman squire lighting his fire
> Up on the moors with his blackguards and boors,
> Nor a duke and a lord drawing the sword,
> Hectoring and lying, the whole world defying,
> > Then sitting down crying.

There's not always

> A shopkeeper militant coming out iligant,
> With King Boy and King Jack both genteelly in black,
> Forming Holy Alliance and breathing defiance,
> Nor a prince finding brandy every day coming handy,
> While he's conquering of lands with his bold nigger bands,
> > Like a man of his hands.

There's not always

> A death and a marriage, a hearse and a carriage,
> A bigamy cause, a king versus laws,
> Nor a short transportation for the good of the nation,
> Nor a speedy returning, mid national mourning,

> While him and his father refuse to foregather,
>   'Cause the Earl hadn't rather.[5]

Reader, these things don't happen every day. It's well they don't, for a constant recurrence of such stimulus would soon wear out the public stomach and bring on indigestion.

But surely one can find something to talk about, though miracles are no longer wrought in the world. Battle-fields, it is true, are now growing corn. According to a paragraph in a westland newspaper which I had a while since in my hand, 'Barley and oats are looking well in the neighbourhood of Leyden, and all the hay is carried from the fields about Evesham.[6] Nay, they tell us the navigation of the Cirhala is about to be improved by a canal which will greatly facilitate the conveyance of goods up the country, and that subscriptions are on foot for erecting a new and commodious piece-hall in the borough of Westwood.' What then? Is all interest to stagnate, because blood has ceased to flow? Has life no variety now? Is all crime the child of war? Does Love fold his wings when Victory lowers her pennons?[7] Surely not! It is true a tone of respectability has settled over society, a business-like calm. Many that were wild in their youth have grown rational and sober. I really trust morals, even court morals, have improved. We hear of no outbreaks now. Some small irregularities, indeed, of a certain very elevated nobleman are occasionally rumoured in the public ear; but habit with him has become second nature, and the exquisite susceptibility of his feelings is too well known to need comment. And elsewhere there is certainly a change, a reformation.[8] Let us now who have so long gazed on glaring guilt solace ourselves with a chastened view of mellowed morality.

CHAPTER I

On the morning of the 1st of July a remarkable event happened at Ellrington House. The Earl and Countess were both eating their breakfast – at least the Countess was, the Earl was only looking at his – when all at once the Earl, without previous warning or apparent cause, laughed!

Now, the scene of this singular occurrence was the Countess's own dressing-room. Her Ladyship had that morning coaxed his Lordship to rise early, with the intention that, as it was a very fine summer day, they should take a drive out to Alnwick for the benefit of his Lordship's health and spirits. For about a fortnight or three weeks past, his Lordship had ceased certain eccentric deviations from his lawful path. The saloons – I should rather say, the boudoirs – of certain noble mansions had vainly waited to reverberate the gentle echo of his voice and step. Mesdames Greville, Lalande and St James had been mourning like nightingales on their perches, or like forsaken turtle-doves cooing soft reproaches to their faithless mate.[9] He came not, and bootless was the despatch of unnumbered tender billets charged at once with sighs and perfumes and bedewed with tears and rose-water. More than one such delicate messenger had been seen shrivelling 'like a parched scroll' in the grate of his Lordship's apartment, and answer there was none. Sick of music, surfeited with sentiment, the great ex-president[10] had come home to his unmusical, plain-spoken Countess. The roll of languishing eyes gave him the exies, so he sought relief in the quick, piercing glances that bespoke more hastiness than artifice of temper.

Her Ladyship was very cross-grained and intractable at first. She would not come to at all for about a week. But after the Earl had exhibited a proper modicum of hopeless melancholy and lain on the sofa for two or three days in half-real, half-feigned illness, she began first to look at him, then to pity him, then to speak to him, and last of all to make much of him and caress him. This re-awakened interest was at its height about the time when my chapter opens. On the very morning in question, she had been quite disquieted to see how little appetite her noble helpmate evinced for his breakfast, and when, after an unbroken silence of about half an hour, he all at once, while looking down at his untasted cup, dissipated that silence by a laugh – an unexpected, brief, speechless, but still indisputable laugh – Zenobia was half alarmed.

'What is it, Alexander?' said she. 'What do you see?'

'You, and that's enough in all conscience,' answered the Earl, turning upon her an eye that had more of sarcasm than mirth in it, and more of languor than either.

'Me! Are you laughing at me, then?'

'Who, I? No.' And he relapsed again into silence, a silence so pensive and dejected that the worthy Countess began to doubt her ears, and to think she had only fancied the laugh which still rang in them.

Breakfast being concluded, she rose from table and, advancing to the window, drew up the blind which had hitherto screened the sunshine. She opened the sash top, and a free admission of morning light and air cheered the apartment. It was a fine day, too, bright and summer-like for a city. Every heart and every eye under the influence of such a day longs for the country.

'Let the carriage be got ready quickly,' said the Countess, turning to a servant who was clearing the breakfast-table and, as the servant closed the door, she sat down at her glass to complete the arrangement of her dress, for as yet she was only in deshabille. She had plaited and folded her hair, and thought with some pride that its sable profusion became her handsome features as well now as it had done ten years ago. She had adjusted her satin apparel to a shape that, though it might not befit a sylph, did well enough for a fine, tall woman who had the weight of as much pride and choler to support as would overwhelm any two ordinary mortals. She had put on her watch, and was embellishing her white, round hands with sundry rings, when the profound hush which had till now attended her operations was interrupted by a repetition of that low, involuntary laugh.

'My lord!' exclaimed the Countess, turning quickly round. She would have started, if her nerves would have permitted such a proof of sensitiveness.

'My lady!' was the dry answer.

'Why do you laugh?' said she.

'Don't know.'

'Well, but what are you laughing at?'

'Can't tell.'

'Are you ill? Is it hysterical?'[11]

'I'm never in rude health that I know of, Zenobia; but as to hysterics, ask Miss Delph.'[12]

With a gesture of scorn, the Countess turned again to her glass. Wrath is seldom prudent, and as her Ladyship's was vented upon her hair, on which she had so recently lavished such care and taste, combs and fillets flew, and the becoming braids which had wreathed her temples and brow quickly floated in a confused cloud of darkness over her shoulders. Again the Earl laughed, but now it was evidently at her. He approached her toilette, and leaning on the back of the armchair she filled (emphatically I say filled, for indeed, there was no room for anybody else), he began to talk.

'Softly, Zenobia. I thought you had done your hair. It was well enough, rather a little sombre or so, not quite enough in the floating, airy tendril style. But then, that requires a lightish figure, and yours – ahem!'

Here, the glass was shifted with a hasty movement, the brush thrown down and the comb snatched up with emphatic promptitude. The Earl continued with gentleness.

'The Furies,[13] I believe, had hair of live snakes,' said he. 'What a singular taste! How was it, eh, Zenobia? Eh?'

'How was it, my lord? What do you mean? I have not the honour of understanding your Lordship.'

'Don't know exactly what I meant. It was some dim notion of analogy haunting my mind that made me put the question. I've so many embryo ideas nowadays, Zenobia, that are crushed, blighted by the stormy climate I live in. Gentler nurture, a little soft sunshine and quiet showers might encourage the infant buds to expand, and in the tender shining after rain I might now and then say a good thing, make a hit,[14] but as it is, I daren't speak, lest I should be snapped up and snarled at out of all reason. It makes me quite low.'

The Countess, as she brushed her tresses, whisked a thick, dark mass over her face, to conceal the smile she could not repress.

'You're hardly used,' said she.

'But, Zenobia,' pursued the Earl, 'I've something to tell, something to shew you.'

'Indeed, my lord?'

'Aye. We all love them that love us, Zenobia.'

'Do we?' was the succint answer.

'And,' pursued his Lordship with pathos, 'when we've neglected an attached friend, you know, turned a cold shoulder to him, kicked him, perhaps, by mistake, how touching it is to find that, after long years of separation and misunderstanding, he still remembers us, and is still willing to borrow that half-crown he has asked for seventy and seven times and has seventy and seven times[15] been refused. Zenobia, they brought this letter last night.'

'Who, my lord?'

'The people. James, I think. I don't often get a letter, you know. Mr Steaton manages these things.'

'And I suppose your letter is from Zamorna?'

'Oh, no. Mr Steaton generally relieves me of the trouble of correspondence in that quarter. Besides, I think his documents are more frequently addressed to you than me. I object, you know, to his style. It is unpleasant; smells so very strong of oat-cake and grouse.'

'Alexander!' expostulated Zenobia.

'And then,' continued the Earl, 'you forget that he is in the country at present, and therefore too fully occupied in devising a new compost for Thornton's beans, farming Warner's turnips and curing the rot in Sir Markham Howard's sheep, to think of writing letters. Besides, his own hay about Hawkscliffe is not all carried; and depend on it, he's making the most of this fine morning, out in his shirt sleeves, with straw hat on his head, swearing at the hay-tenters,[16] now and then giving a hand to help to load the waggons, and at noon and drinking-time sitting down on a cock to eat his bread and cheese and drink his pot of ale like a king and a clod-hopper. Can't you fancy him, Zen, all in a muck of sweat, for it's hard work and hot weather, arrayed in his shirt and white tights and nothing else, and then, you know, "at the close of the day when the hamlet is still"[17] going with his dear brother in arms, Lord Arundel, to

take a prudent dip and swim in the beck, and coming out
with a bad inflammation occasioned by a sudden check of the
perspiration, and going home to be blistered and bled *ad libitum*, and then with interesting wilfulness insisting on t'other
tankard and a frcsh go of bathing when he's in a raging fever
and, being very properly yielded to, allowed to have his way,
and so waxing delirious, cutting his throat and walking off
stage with a flourish of trumpets worthy of the most mighty
and magnanimous monarch that ever understood dog-diseases
or practised the noble science of farrier?'

'Who is that letter from, please, my lord?'

'Ah, the letter! You shall read it, and the signature will tell
you who it is from.'

His Lordship took out his pocket-book and handed therefrom a singularly folded epistle, directed in a large black autograph whose terrible down-strokes, cross-dashes and circular
flourishes seemed to defy all hands, mercantile, genteel and
juvenile, that ever existed. The Countess read as follows:

Boulogne, June 29th 1839

Daddy Long-legs,

Sober[18] I am, and sober I have been, and by the bleached bones
of my fathers, sober I mean to be to the end of the chapter. Aye,
by the bones of my fathers, and by their souls, their burning
souls, which in the likeness of game-cocks, cropped and spurred,
are even now sitting on my right hand and on my left,[19] and
crowing aloud for vengeance!

The night was dark when I saw them; it lightened and there
was thunder. Who bowed from the cloud as it rolled? Who spake
a word in mine ear? Didst not thou, O dark but comely one, Sai
Too-Too, and thou, the brother of my mother's grand-mother,
Sambo Mungo Anamaboo?[20]

I'll tell ye what, ye're a cozening old rascal. Ye never made me
a promise in your life but you broke it. Deny that, deny it, I say,
will ye? Give me the lie, beard me, spit in my face, tweak my
nose! Come on, I'm your man, up with your daddles! Who's
afraid? 'What's the fun?'[21]

The marrow of the affair, the root of the matter, is this: a more scoundrelly set of men than some that I could mention were never beheld, nor a more horrifying series of transactions than some that I have in my eye. Why, the earth reels, the heavens stagger, the seas totter to their downfall, and old Ocean himself trembles[22] in his highest hills and shudders horror-struck through all his woods.

To come to the point at once. May I forget myself and be counted as a child of perdition if the present generation be not very little better than the last. Why, I remember when there was a Bible in every house, and as much brandy sold for a cab of dove's dung[23] as you could buy now for half a sovereign. The fact is, and I am certain of it, religion's not popular – real, genuine religion I mean. I've seen more Christianity in the desert than it would be worth any man's while to take account of.

Daddy, where are you? There seems to be a kind of a darkness, a sort of a mist in the hoyle, a round-about whirligig circumferential cloudiness. Prop the leg of this here table, will ye, daddy? It's sinking with me through the floor. Snuff out the candlestick – there, we've a better light now, we write steadier. Hark ye, then, the play's nearly played out.[24]

Bloody old robber, you walk in silks and velvets, and live in a diamond house with golden windows, while I have foxes and holes and the birds of the air have neither. You toil and spin, while I am Solomon in all his glory arrayed like one of these. But I warn you, Scaramouch,[25] you'd better provide for me, for my wife must share my poverty, and then what will you say? I've made up my mind to marry. I tell you it's a done thing, and the Queen of Heaven herself should not prevail on me to alter it.

Beautiful and benign being, thou pinest in captivity! Loved lady of my heart, thou weepest in the prison-house! But heaven opens, and thy bridegroom waits.[26] She shall be mine!

Won't you give your consent, old scum? You promised me another, but she 'like a lily drooping bowed her head and died' – at least as good as died, for was not that a living death that consigned her to the arms of a numb-scull?[27]

A better lot is thine, fair maid,[28]
   A happier lot is thine,
And who would weep in dungeon shade
   Whom fate has marked for mine?
   Come, do not pine,
But fly to arms that open to receive
   Thy youthful form divine.
Clasped to this heart of fire thoul't never grieve,
   No, thou shalt shine
Happy as houris fair that braid their hair
   Glorious in Eden's bowers
   Where noxious flowers
With fragrant reptiles twine.
But thou, my blooming gem, wilt far out-flourish them,
   My radiant Caroline!

Now, daddy, what d'ye say to that? Shew her them lines and see
if they won't plead my cause for me.

She's young, you say. The more need she has of a father, and
won't I be both father and husband to her in one? T'other was
not much older when you gave me the refusal of her fair, snow-
white hand. True, I rejected her,[29] but what then? I'd my eye on
the younger, softer bud. Caroline's a more alluring name than
Mary, more odoriferously and contumaciously musical. Then,
she loves me. So did the other, you'll say; desperately, divinely.
I know it, old cock, I know it. I have it under her hand, sealed
and signed in legal form. But this sweet blossom, this little,
fluttering, fickle, felicitous fairy, this dear, delicious, delirious
morsel, comes into my dreams and announces her intention of
marrying me straight away off-hand, whether I will or no.

I'll be moderate on the subject of settlements. A handsome
house, ten thousand a year, the custody of your will, and the
making of it all over again according to my own directions, that's
what I want and what I'll have. Answer by return of post, and
enclose a letter from my lovely one, also a bank-note or two. In
the shadows of approaching sunrise and the profound roar of
the storm when it subsides to silence, in Love's intoxication,
Hope's fury and Despair's wild madness, in Beauty's blaze, in

Eden's bliss, in hell's troubled and terrific turbulence, in Death's
deep and dangerous delirium,
    I am, and was not, a squire of high degree,
        Q in the corner.[30]

'You know the fine Roman hand,[31] I presume?' said the
Earl, when his Countess had finished reading this surprising
lucubration.

'Yes, Quashia, of course. But who does he mean? What is he
driving at?'

'He wants to marry a little girl of ten or eleven years old,'
returned Northangerland.

'What, Miss Vernon?' said her ladyship, uttering the name
between her teeth.

'Aye.'

'And is Miss Vernon no more than ten or eleven?'

'No, I think not.'

A servant just then entered to announce the carriage. The
Countess went on dressing herself very fast and looking very
red and choleric. While she finished her toilette, Northangerland stood by the window, thinking. His thoughts were wound
up by a word that seemed to burst involuntary from his lips. It
was 'D—n—t—n!' He then asked his wife where she was going.
She said, to Alnwick.

'No,' he replied. 'I'll go to Angria. Bid them turn the horses'
heads east.'

Mr Jas Shaver brought his hat and gloves, and he went down
into the hall, and so vanished.

CHAPTER II

Zamorna was literally standing in a hay-field, just below the
house at Hawkscliffe, talking to a respectable man in black. It
was a hot afternoon, and he wore a broad-brimmed hat of
straw, and though not exactly in his shirt sleeves, yet a plaid
jacket and trousers testified but a remote approximation to full
dress.

It was a large field, and at the further end about a score of hay-makers, male and female, were busily engaged at their work. Zamorna, leaning against the trunk of a fine tree, with a dog laid on the hay at his feet, was watching them. Especially, his eyes followed one or two smart, active girls, who were amongst the number of the tenters. At the same time, he talked to his companion, and thus their conversation ran.

'I reckon, now,' said the respectable man in black, 'if your Grace gets this hay well in, it'll be a varry fair crop.'

'Yes, it's good land,' returned the monarch, 'very good grazing land.'

'I sud thin[k] grain would hardly answer so well. Have ye tryed it wi' ony mak o'corn seed?'

'There's a croft on the other side of the beck where the soil is just like this. I sowed it with red wheat last spring, and it's bearing beautifully now.'

'Humph – wha, ye see, ye cannot err mich, for where trees grow as they do here there's hardly any mak o' grain but what'll prosper. I find t' truth o' that at Girnington. Now, up i't' north, about Mr Warner's place, it's clear different.'

'Yes, Warner has a great deal of bother with tillage and manure. That bog-soil is so cold and moist, it rots the seed instead of cherishing it. Well, my lass, are you tired?' going forward, and speaking to a tight girl with cheeks like a rose who, with her rake, had approached nearer to the royal station.

'Nay, sir,' was the answer, while the young rustic's vanity, gratified by the notice of a fine gentleman with whiskers and mustaches, sent a deeper colour than ever to her brown, healthy complexion.

'But it's hot, don't you think so?' continued his Grace.

'Nay, not so varry.'

'Have ye been working all day among the hay?'

'Nay, nobbut sin' nooin.'

'It's Hawkscliffe Fair tomorrow, is not it, my lass?'

'Yes, sir, they call't so.'

'And you'll go there, no doubt?'

'I happen sall,' giggling, and working with her rake very busily to conceal her embarrassment.

'Well, there's something to buy a fairing with.'

There was a shew of reluctance to accept the present which was tendered. But his Grace said 'Pshaw!' and pressed it more urgently, so the damsel suffered her fingers to close upon it, and, as she put it in her pocket, dropped two or three short, quick curtseys in acknowledgement.

'You'd give me a kiss, I daresay, if that gentleman was not by,' said Zamorna, pointing to his friend, who regarded the scene with an expression that shewed he thought it excellent fun. The lass looked up at both the gentlemen, coloured again very deeply and, laughing, began to withdraw in silence. Zamorna let her go.

'There's a deal of vanity there,' said he, as he returned to the oak tree.

'Aye, and coquetry too.'

'Look, the witch is actually turning back, and surveying me with the corner of her eye.'

'I doubt she's a jilt,' replied Thornton.

His Grace pushed out his under-lip, smiled, and said something about 'palace and cottage' and 'very little difference'.

'But she's a bonny lass,' pursued the Laird of Girnington.

'Tight and trim and fresh and healthy,' was the reply.

'There's mony a lady would be glad to exchange shapes with her,' remarked Sir Wilson again.

'Varry like,' said his Grace, leaning lazily against the bank, and looking down with a bantering smile at Thornton as he imitated his tone.

'Does your Grace know the lass's name?' asked the General, not noticing his master's aspect. A pause, closed by a laugh, was the answer. Thornton turned to him in surprise.

'What the D—l!' said he hastily, when he saw the sarcasm expressed by eye and lip. 'Does your Grace mean to insinuate – ?'

'Nay, Thornton, be cool. I'm only thinking what a soft heart you have.'

'Nonsense, nonsense,' returned Sir Wilson. 'But your Grace is like to have your own cracks. As if I had spokken to t' lass – when it was all your Majesty, 'at cannot let ought be under thirty.'

'Cannot I? That's a lie. Here I stand, and I care as much for that foolish little jilt, or any other you can mention – high or low – as Bell here at my feet does. Bell's worth them all. Hey, old girl, there's some truth in thy carcase! There, there. Down now, that's enough.'

'I know yer Grace is steadier nor you used to be, and that's raight enough, but you *have* been wild.'

'Never!' was the unblushing rejoinder.

'But I know better.'

'Never, by G—d, never!' repeated his Grace.

'Oh whah!' said Thornton, coolly. 'Your Majesty's a right to lie abaat yese'ln. It's naught to me 'at I know on.'[32]

Could it possibly have been Quashia's mad letter which induced Lord Northangerland to set off then and there to Hawkscliffe at the far end of Angria, a house and a country[33] where he had not shewn his nose for years? His Lordship's movements are often very inexplicable, but this, as Mr Jas Shaver expressed it (when he received sudden orders to pack up the Earl's dressing-case and wardrobe) was the beat'em of all. The Countess offered to go with her lord, but he made answer that she 'had better not'. So he put himself into the carriage solus, and solus he continued through the whole of the journey. Neither did he speak word to man or beast, except to desire them 'to get on'.

And get on they did, for they stopped neither day nor night, till half the breadth of Angria was traversed and the Moray Hills began to undulate on the horizon. He did not travel incognito, and of course he was known at every inn and ale-house, where the horses got a pailful of meal and water and the postillions a bottle of Madeira. Trivial preparations were commenced in Zamorna for a riot and a stoning. But before Mr Edward Percy could loose his mill and furnish his people with brick-bats, the object of filial attention was a mile out of town, and cleaving the woods of Hartford in a whirlwind of summer dust. His progress was similarly hailed at the other towns and villages that intercepted his route. At Islington, a dead cat, nimble as when alive, leapt up at the carriage window and broke it. At Grantley, the hissing and yelling rivalled the music of a legion of cats, and at Rivaulx, the oblations of mud offered to his divinity were so profuse as to spread over the chariot panels a complete additional coating of varnish. Whether the Earl derived pleasure or vexation from these little testimonials of national regard, it would be hard to say, inasmuch as the complexion of his countenance varied no more than the hue of his coat, and his brow and features looked, evermore, to the full as placid as the glass-face of a repeater which he held in his hand and continually gazed at.

One thinks there is something pleasant in slowly approaching solitude towards the close of a bustling journey. Driving over the burning pavements, through the smoke and filth of manufacturing towns in the height of summer, must form, one would fancy, no unimpressive preparation for the entrance on a fine, green country of woods, where everything seems remote, fresh and lonely. Yet for all Jas Shaver Esqre could see in Lord Northangerland, and for all Lord Northangerland could remark in Jas Shaver, neither of these illustrious persons found any remarkable difference when a July afternoon saw their carriage entering the vast and silent domain of Hawkscliffe, town and tumult being left far behind, and only a rustling of trees and a trickling of becks being audible. Where the habitation of man is fixed, there are always signs of its proximity. The perfect freshness of nature disappears; her luxuriousness is cleared away. And so, erelong, Hawkscliffe began to break into glades, the path grew rolled and smooth, and more frequent prospects of distant hills burst through the widening glimpses of foliage.

Out at last they rolled upon a broad and noble road, as well beaten, as white and as spacious as the far-distant highway from Zamorna to Adrianapolis. That track, however, seems endless; but this, at the close of about a hundred yards was crossed by the arch of an architectural gateway. The turret on each side served for a lodge, and the heavy iron gates were speedily flung back by the keeper. As the carriage paused for a moment, ere it shot through, the yelping of a kennel of hounds was heard somewhere near, and a large Newfoundlander laid under the lodge-porch rose up and gave a deep-mouthed bark of welcome. Beyond these gates, there was no more forest, only detached clumps of trees and vast solitary specimens varying the expanse of a large and wild park, which ascended and half clothed with light verdure the long aclivity[34] of one of the Sydenhams. The remoter hills of the same range rolled away, clad in dusky woodland, till distance softened them and the summer sky embued them with intense violet. Near the centre of the park stood Hawkscliffe House, a handsome pile, but by no means so large nor so grand as the extent of the grounds seemed to warrant. It could aspire to the title neither of palace nor castle; it was merely a solitary hall, stately from its loneliness, and pleasant from the sunny and serene effect of the green region which expanded round it. Deer, a herd of magnificent cattle, and a troop of young unbroken horses shared the domain between them.

As the carriage stopped at the front door, Northangerland put up[35] his repeater, whose hand was pointing to six o'clock p.m. and, the steps being let down and door opened, he alighted and quietly walked into the house. He had got half through the hall before he asked a question of any servant, but the butler, advancing with a bow, inquired to what apartment he should conduct him. North[angerland] stopped, as if at fault.

'Perhaps I am wrong,' said he. 'This is not Hawkscliffe.' And he looked dubiously round on the plain, unadorned walls and oak-painted doors about him, so unlike the regal splendours of Victoria Square. A noble branch of stag's antlers seemed to strike him with peculiar horror. He recoiled instantly and, muttering something indistinct about 'Angrian squire's den – a strange mistake', he was commencing a precipitate retreat to his carriage when James Shaver interposed.

'Your Lordship is in the right,' said he, whispering low. 'This is the royal residence' (with a sneer). 'But country plainness – no style kept up. Fear I sha'n't be able to muster proper accommodations for your Lordship.'

'James,' said the Earl after a pause, 'will you ask those people where the Duke of Zamorna is?'

James obeyed.

'Gone out,' was the reply. 'His Grace is generally out all day.'

'And where was the Duchess?'

'Gone out too, but most likely would be back presently.'

'Shew me into a room,' said the Earl, and his Lordship was ushered into a library where, without looking round him, he sat down, his back to the window and his face to an enormous map, unrolled and covering half the opposite wall. There was nothing else in the room except books, a few chairs, a desk, and a table loaded with pamphlets and papers; no busts, or pictures, or any of the other elegant extras[36] commonly seen in a nobleman's library. A large quarto lay on the floor at Northangerland's feet. He kicked it open with a slight movement of his toe. It was full of gay feathers, coloured wools and brilliant flies for fishing. Another and apparently still slighter movement sufficed to discharge the volume to the other end of the room. It fell by a row of thick volumes standing side by side in the lowest shelf of books; the words *Agricultural Magazine* glittered in gilt letters on the back of each.

When Northangerland was quite tired of sitting, he got up and restlessly paced through the apartment, pausing at a side-table where a small book was lying open. He began mechanically to finger the leaves. It was the planter's *vade mecum*.[37] Northangerland withdrew his fingers as if they had been burnt. On the same table lay two packets neatly tied up and labelled 'Sample of red wheat from General Thornton', 'Sample of Oats from Howard'. The Earl was still gazing at these packets, riveted by them, apparently, as if they had been the two eyes of a basilisk, when a shade crossed the window outside. Soon after, somebody was heard entering by the front door. A word or two passed in the hall, and then a step quietly approached the library.

It was the Duchess who came. She went to her father, and he had to stoop to give the kiss for which she looked up in silent eagerness.

'I thought it was a farm-house,' said he, when he had held her a moment and surveyed her face. 'But I suppose, Mary, you don't milk cows?'

'How long have you been here?' returned his daughter, evading his sarcasm with a smile. 'They should have fetched me in before. I was only walking down the avenue.'

'Down the yard, I thought you would say,' continued the Earl. 'Surely, Mary, you term that a croft?' (pointing to the park). 'And this bigging, we are in no doubt, is called the grange. Have you a room to yourself? Or [do] you sit in the house,[38] and eat your porridge with the plough-men and dairy-maids?'

The Duchess still smiled, and she slipped the obnoxious packets into a drawer. 'Is there a small inn in the place?' went on her father. 'Because if there is, I'll put up there. You know I can't eat bacon and eggs, and though your kitchen may be very comfortable, it will smell, perhaps, of the stable – which, you know, comes close up to the door for convenience sake, because when the big farmer comes home from the market a trifle sprung or so, it's more convenient to dismount him rather nigh the house, as he's a good weight to carry in.'

'Don't, Father,' said the Duchess, as, half-vexed, she held her head down, looking at her father's hand, which she retained in hers, and pulling the ring from his little finger.

'What then, is he a better horse-jockey or cow-jobber?' inquired the inexorable Northangerland. 'Does he kill his own meat? Or he buys it? Does he feed pigs, Mary?'

The Duchess pouted.

'I should like to see him riding home a-horseback, after driving a hard bargain down at Grantley there about a calf which he is to bring home in a rope.[39] The excellent fellow, of course, will be very drunk, extremely so, for the bargain has been on and off at least ten times, and it took at least sixteen tumblers of whisky and water to consolidate it in the end. Then the calf will be amazingly contrary, as bad to get on as himself; and what with tumbling from his saddle, rolling in the mud, fighting with his bargain etc., he will, I should imagine, cut much such a figure as I have seen that fool Arthur O'Connor do under similar circumstances.'

'Hush, Father!' said the Duchess earnestly. 'Don't talk so! I hear him in the passage; now pray –'

She had not time to complete her entreaty, when the door was promptly opened and his Grace walked in. Some dogs walked in, too. The whole party, equally heedless of who might or might not be in the room, advanced to a cabinet with some drawers in it; and while the Duke sought in one of the drawers for a coil of gut that he wanted for his line, the dogs pushed their noses in his face as he stooped down, or smelt at his pannier which he had laid on the carpet.

'Be quiet, Juno,' said Zamorna, putting a large pointer from him, whose caresses interrupted him in his sedulous search; then, calling to somebody in the passage, 'William, tell Homes I can't find the tackle; it must be at his lodge. But I shall not want it tonight, so he may send it up first thing to-morrow morning.'

'Very well, my lord,' answered a gruff voice without. Zamorna shut up the drawers.

'Oh, stop!' said he, speaking suddenly to himself. 'I had almost forgotten.' He walked quickly out of the room. 'William!' (standing on the front-door steps and calling down the park).

'Yes, please your Grace.'

'You may give my compliments to Homes, and say that the river has been poached on. I was fishing there to-day, and I only got three trout. Tell him he's a d—d idle dog, and keeps no right look-out at all when I'm away. But things must be managed differently. I'll have law and order observed here, or else I'll try for it.'[40]

He came back, crossing the passage with firm, even stride. He entered the library again, rather more deliberately. He had now time to notice that it was occupied by other persons besides himself and his dogs. His wife caught his eye first.

'Well, Mary, have you been walking?'

'Yes.'

'Rather late, isn't it? You should mind not to be out after sunset.'

'It was very warm.'

'Yes, fine weather.' And he pulled off his gloves and began to take his long fishing rod to pieces.

As he was busily intent on disengaging the hook from the line, Northangerland advanced a little step from the sort of recess where he had been standing. Zamorna, attracted by the movement, turned. He looked keenly, pausing from his employment. He was obviously astonished for a moment at this unexpected apparition of his father-in-law. Only for a moment. There was no salutation on either side. Zamorna stared; North-angerland gazed coolly. Zamorna turned his back, went on disjointing his rod, hung up that and his pannier, took off a broad-brimmed straw hat which had hitherto diademed his head, and then, at last, as he sat down in an arm-chair by the table, found time to ask, 'When the Earl had arrived?'

'I didn't look at the clock,' was the answer; and, 'Yet 'faith, I remember, I did. It was about six this evening.'

'Hmm. Have ye had any dinner? We dine early; seldom later than three.'[41]

'James gave me a biscuit in the carriage. 'Tis as well he did so, for, as I've been remarking to Mrs Wellesley, I can't take porridge and fried bacon.'

'No, nor omlets and patés[42] either, for that matter,' muttered the Duke in an under-tone. 'Nor hardly a mouthful of any Christian edible under the sun.' Then he continued aloud, 'Pray, have ye been ordered to take a journey here for your health?'

'What, to a fish-monger's and farrier's? No, stale herring gives me the nausea. I'm come on business. But may that basket of stinking sprat be sent away?' (pointing to the pannier, and holding a perfumed cambric handkerchief to his nose).

'It's fresh trout,' answered his son, calmly. 'But you're a valetudinarian, and must be excused for having sickly anti-pathies. Come, I'll humour you for once.' He rung the bell, and the nuisance was quickly removed. 'How did ye get along through the country?' continued the Duke, taking up a news-paper and unfolding it. 'Were you much fêted and flattered? Or they forgot to ring the bells and call out the bands in your honour?'

'I don't remember,' responded Northangerland.

'Don't you? Humph! But perhaps your postillions and horses will. I have some dim notion that the kennel rubbish of Edwardston and Zamorna and Islington and some of those places has been made uncommon useful not long since.'

The Duchess here approached his Grace's chair and, leaning over the back as if to look at the newspaper which he was still reading or feigning to read, she whispered, 'Don't try to vex him to-night, Adrian. I am sure he's tired with his journey.'

The Duke merely seated her beside him and, resting his hand on her shoulder, went on talking.

'Where d'ye think you're most popular now, sir?' said he.

'With a small handful of coloured men under the command of Mr Kashua,'[43] returned Northangerland.

'Long may your popularity be confined to that limited and devoted band,' rejoined his dutiful son.

'What for, Arthur?' inquired the Earl, in a gentle insinuating tone.

'Because you'll never more be fit for the confidence of decent Christians.'

'Was I once?'

'Not that I can remember.'

'No, only for such debauched dogs as Douro the dandy,'[44] returned Northangerland.

'Could you get up a meeting now anywhere in Angria, or form a Society for the Diffusion of Genuine Vitality?'[45]

'I could, if my dear young friend, Arthur Wellesley, would stick the bills as he used to do.'

'Arthur Wellesley, instead of sticking the bills now, would stick[46] the whole concern – aye, to the D—l.'

'As he does everything else he meddles with,' said Northangerland, closing the verbal sparring match with a gentle nicher.

His son's reply was prevented by the Duchess, who sat between the combatants, trembling with anxiety, lest this skirmish of words should overstep the brink of mere sarcasm and plunge into invective.

'Well,' said the Duke, in answer to her silent entreaty for forbearance. 'He shall have it his own way this time, in consideration that he's done up with riding a few miles in an easy carriage like a bed. But I'll balance the reckoning to-morrow.'

'Good-night, Mary,' said the Earl, rising abruptly. She followed her father from the room, and the Duke, being left by himself, rang for candles, and sat down to write a lot of letters.

CHAPTER III

Well, reader, you have not yet heard what business it was
that brought Northangerland all that long way from Ellrington
House to Hawkscliffe Hall. But you shall, if you'll suppose it
to be morning, and step with the Earl out of this little parlour
where the Duchess is at work, sitting by a window surrounded
with roses.

As soon as ever Zamorna had had his breakfast, he had
set off and the Earl was now following him. Fortunately, he
met him on the steps at the front door, leaning against the pillar
and enjoying the morning sunshine and the prospect of his
wild park, but half-reclaimed from the forest, for one tranquil
moment, before starting on a day-long campaign in the fields.

'Where are you going, Arthur?' asked the Earl.

'To that wood beyond the river.'

'What to do there?'

'To see some young trees transplanted.'

'Will there be an earthquake if you defer that important
matter until I have spoken a word with you on a trivial business
of my own?'

'Perhaps not. What have you to say?'

Northangerland did not immediately answer. He paused,
either from reluctance to commence, or from a wish to ascertain
that all was quiet and safe around and that no intruder was
nigh. The Hall behind was empty. The grounds in front
were still dewy and solitary. He and his son-in-law stood by
themselves. There was no listener.

'Well, why don't you begin?' repeated Zamorna, who was
whistling carelessly and evincing no inclination to attach special
importance to the coming communication.

When our own minds are intensely occupied with a subject,
we are apt to imagine that those near us are able to pry
into our thoughts. The side-glance with which Northangerland
viewed his son was strange, dubious and distorted. At last he
said, in a remarkable tone,

'I wish to know how my daughter Caroline is.'

'She was very well when I saw her last,' replied the Duke of Zamorna, not moving a muscle, but looking straight before him at the waving and peaked hills which marked the unclouded horizon.

There was another pause. Zamorna began his whistle again. It was more studiedly careless than before, for whereas it had just flowed occasionally into a pensive strain, it now only mimicked rattling and reckless airs broken into fragments.

'My daughter must be grown,' continued Northangerland.

'Yes, healthy children always grow.'

'Do you know anything about the progress of her studies? Is she well educated?'

'I took care that she should be provided with good masters, and from their report I should imagine she has made very considerable proficiency for her age.'

'Does she evince any talent? Musical talent she ought to inherit.'[47]

'I like her voice,' answered Zamorna, 'and she plays well enough, too, for a child.'

Northangerland took out a pocket-book. He seemed to calculate in silence for a moment, and writing down the result with a silver pencil-case,[48] he returned the book to his pocket, quietly remarking,

'Caroline is fifteen years old.'

'Aye, her birthday was the first or second of this month, was it not?' returned Zamorna. 'She told me her age the other day. I was surprised; I thought she had hardly been more than twelve or thirteen.'

'She looks childish, then, does she?'

'Why, no; she is well-grown and tall. But time in some cases cheats us. It seems only yesterday when she was quite a little girl.'

'Time has cheated me,' said the Earl. There was another pause. Zamorna descended the steps.

'Well, good-morning,' said he. 'I'll leave you for the present.' He was moving off, but the Earl followed him.

'Where is my daughter?' asked he. 'I wish to see her.'

'Oh, by all means. We can ride over this afternoon. The house is not above three miles off.'

'She must have a separate establishment instantly,' pursued the Earl.

'She has,' said Zamorna. 'That is, in conjunction with her mother.'

'I shall either have Selden House or Eden Hall fitted up for her,' continued his Lordship, without heeding this remark. He and his son-in-law were now pacing slowly through the grounds side by side. Zamorna fell a little into the rear. His straw hat was drawn over his eyes, and it was not easy to tell with what kind of a glance he regarded his father-in-law.

'Who is to go with her and take care of her?' he asked after a few minutes' silence. 'Do you mean to retire into the north or south yourself, and take up your abode at Eden Hall or Selden House?'

'Perhaps I may.'

'Indeed, and will Zenobia adopt her, and allow the girl to live under the same roof without the penalty of a daily chastisement?'

'Don't know. If they can't agree, Caroline must marry. But I think you once told me she was not pretty?'

'Did I? Well, tastes differ, but the girl is a mere child. She may improve. In the meantime, to talk of marrying her is rather good; I admire the idea. If she were my daughter, sir, she should not marry these ten years. But the whole scheme sounds excessively raw, just like one of your fantastic, expensive whims. About establishments etc. – you know nothing of management, nor of the value of money; you never did.'

'She must be established; she must have her own servants and carriage and allowance,' repeated the Earl.

'Fudge!' said the Duke, impatiently.

'I have spoken to Steaton, and matters are in train,' continued his father-in-law, in a deliberate tone.

'Unbusinesslike, senseless ostentation!' was the reply. 'Have you calculated the expense, sir?'

'No, I've only calculated the fitness of things.'[49]

'Pshaw!'

Both gentlemen pursued their path in silence. Northanger-land's face looked serene, but extremely obstinate. Zamorna could compose his features, but not his eye; it was restless and glittering.

'Well,' he said after the lapse of some minutes, 'do as you like. Caroline is your daughter, not mine. But you go to work strangely. That is, according to my notions as to how a young, susceptible girl ought to be managed.'

'I thought you said she was a mere child.'

'I said, or I meant to say, I considered her as such. She may think herself almost a woman. But take your own way, give her this separate establishment, give her money and servants and equipages, and see what will be the upshot.'

Northangerland spoke not. His son-in-law continued,

'It would be only like you, like your unaccountable, frantic folly, to surround her with French society,[50] or Italian if you could get it. If the circle in which you lavished your own early youth were now in existence, I ver[il]y believe you'd allow Caroline to move as a queen in its centre.'

'Could my little daughter be the queen of such a circle?' asked Northangerland. 'You said she was no beauty, and you speak as if her talents were only ordinary.'

'There!' replied his son. 'That question confirms what I say. Sir,' he continued, stopping, and looking full at Northanger-land and speaking with marked emphasis, 'if your fear is that Caroline will not have beauty sufficient to attract licentiousness, and imagination warm enough to understand approaches, to meet them and kindle at them, and a mind and passions strong enough to carry her a long way in the career of dissipation if she once enters it, set yourself at rest, for she is, or will be, fit for all this and much more.'

'You may as well drop that assumed tone,' said Northanger-land, squinting direfully at his comrade. 'You must be aware that I know your royal Grace, and cannot for a moment be deluded into the supposition that you are a saint, or even a repentant sinner.'

'I'm not affecting either saintship or repentance,' replied the

Duke, 'and I'm well aware that you know me. But I happen to have taken some pains with the education of Miss Vernon. She has grown up an interesting, clever girl, and I should be sorry to hear of her turning out no better than she should be, to find that I have been rearing and training a mistress for some blackguard Frenchman. And this, or something worse, would certainly be the result of your plans. I have studied her character; it is one that ought not to be exposed to dazzling temptation. She is at once careless and imaginative; her feelings are mixed with her passions; both are warm, and she never reflects. Guidance like yours is not what such a girl ought to have. She could ask you for nothing which you would not grant. Indulgence would foster all her defects. When she found that winning smiles and gentle words passed current for[51] reason and judgment, she would speedily purchase her whole will with that cheap coin, and that will would be as wild as the wildest bird, as fantastic and perverse as if the caprice and perverseness of her whole sex were concentrated in her single little head and heart.'

'Caroline has lived in a very retired way hitherto, has she not?' asked Northangerland, not at all heeding the Duke's sermonizing.

'Not at all too retired for her age,' was the reply. 'A girl with lively spirits and good health needs no company, until it is time for her to be married.'

'But my daughter will be a little rustic,' said the Earl, 'a milkmaid. She will want manners when I wish to introduce her to the world.'

'Introduce her to the world!' repeated Zamorna, impatiently. 'What confounded folly! And I know in your own mind you are attaching as much importance to the idea of bringing out this half-grown schoolgirl – providing her with an establishment and all that sort of humbug – as if it were an important political manoeuvre, on the issue of which the existence of half a nation depended.'

'Oh!' replied the Earl, with a kind of dry, brief laugh. 'I assure you, you quite underrate my ideas on the subject. As to your political manoeuvres, I care nothing at all about them.

But if my Caroline should turn out a fine woman, handsome and clever, she will give me pleasure. I shall once more have a motive for assembling a circle about me, to see her mistress and directress of it.'

An impatient 'Pshaw!' was Zamorna's sole answer to this.

'I expect she will have a taste for splendour,' continued the Earl, 'and she must have the means to gratify it.'

'Pray, what income do you intend to allow her?' asked his son.

'Ten thousand per annum to begin with!'

Zamorna whistled, and put his hands in his pockets. After a pause he said,

'I shall not reason with you, for on this subject you're just a natural-born fool, incapable of understanding reason. I'll just let you go on your own way, without raising a hand either to aid or oppose you. You shall take your little girl just as she is, strip her of her frock and sash and put on a gown and jewels, take away her child's playthings and give her a carriage and an establishment, place her in the midst of one of your unexceptionable Ellrington House and Eden Hall coteries, and see what will be the upshot. God d—n! I can hardly be calm about it! Well enough do I know what she is now – a pretty, intelligent, innocent girl; and well enough can I guess what she will be some few years hence – a beautiful, dissipated, dissolute woman, one of your syrens, your Donna Julias, your Signora Cecilias.[52] Faugh! Good-morning, sir. We dine at three. After dinner we'll take a ride over to see Miss Vernon.'

His Grace jumped over a field wall and, as he walked away very fast, he was soon out of sight.

CHAPTER IV

Punctually at three o'clock, dinner was served in a large antique dining-room at Hawkscliffe, whose walls, rich in carved oak and old pictures, received a warm but dim glow from the bow-window screened with amber curtains. While one footman removed the silver covers from two dishes, another opened the folding door to admit a tall middle-aged gentleman with a very sweet young lady resting on his arm and another gentleman walking after. They seated themselves, and when they were seated there was as much an air of state about the table as if it had been surrounded by a large party instead of this select trio. The gentlemen, as it happened, were both very tall; they were both, too, dressed in black, for the young man had put off the plaid jacket and checked trousers which it was his pleasure to sport in the morning, and had substituted in their stead the costume of a well-dressed clergyman. As for the young lady, a very fair neck and arms, well displayed by a silk dress made low and with short sleeves, were sufficient of themselves to throw an air of style and elegance over the party. Besides that, her hair was beautiful and profusely curled, and her mien and features were exceedingly aristocratic and exclusive.[53]

Very little talk passed during dinner. The younger gentleman ate uncommon well; the elderly one trifled a considerable time with a certain mess in a small silver tureen, which he did not eat. The young lady drank wine with her husband when he asked her, and made no bones of some three or four glasses of champagne. The Duke of Zamorna looked as grave as a judge. There was an air about him, not of unhappiness, but as if the cares of a very large family rested on his shoulders. The Duchess was quiet; she kept glancing at her help-mate from under her eye-lids. When the cloth was taken away, and the servants had left the room, she asked him if he was well – a superfluous question, one would think, to look at his delicate Grace's damask complexion and athletic form and to listen to his sounding, steady voice. Had he been in a good humour, he would have answered her question by some laughing banter about her over-anxiety. As it was, he simply said he was well. She then inquired if he wished the children to come down. He said, 'No; he should hardly have time to attend to them that afternoon. He was going out directly.'

'Going out! What for? There was nothing to call him out.'

'Yes, he had a little business to transact.'

The Duchess was nettled, but she swallowed her vexation and looked calm upon it.

'Very well,' said she. 'Your Grace will be back to tea, I presume?'

'Can't promise, indeed, Mary.'

'Then I had better not expect you till I see you.'

'Just so. I'll return as soon as I can.'

'Very well,' said she, assuming as complacent an air as she possibly could, for her tact told her this was not a time for the display of wife-like petulance and irritation. What would amuse his Grace in one mood she knew would annoy him in another. So she sat a few minutes longer, made one or two cheerful remarks on the weather and the growth of some young trees his Grace had lately planted near the window, and then quietly left the table. She was rewarded for this attention to the Duke's humours by his rising to open the door for her. He picked up her handkerchief, too, which she had dropped, and as he returned it to her he favoured her with a peculiar look and smile, which as good as said he thought she was looking very handsome that afternoon. Mrs Wellesley considered that glance sufficient compensation for a momentary chagrin. Therefore, she went into her drawing-room and, sitting down to the piano, soothed away the remains of irritation with sundry soft songs and solemn psalm tunes which, better than gayer music, suited her own fine, melancholy voice.

She did not know where Northangerland and Zamorna were going, nor who it was that occupied their minds, or she would not have sung at all. Most probably, could she have divined the keen interest which each took in little Caroline Vernon, she would have sat down and cried. It is well for us that we cannot read the hearts of our nearest friends. It is an old saying, 'where ignorance is bliss 'tis folly to be wise',[54] and if it makes us happy to believe that those we love unreservedly give us, in return, affections unshared by another, why should the veil be withdrawn and a triumphant rival be revealed to us? The Duchess of Zamorna knew that such a person as Miss Vernon existed, but she had never seen her. She imagined that Northangerland thought and cared little about her, and as to Zamorna, the two ideas of Caroline and the Duke never entered her head at the same time.

While Mrs Wellesley sung to herself 'Has sorrow thy young days shaded?',[55] and while the sound of her piano came through closed doors with faint sweet effect, Mr Wellesley Junr and Mr Percy Senior sat staring opposite to each other like two bulls. They didn't seem to have a word to say, not a single word; but Mr Wellesley manifested a disposition to take a good deal of wine, much more than was customary with him, and Mr Percy seemed to be mixing and swallowing a number of little tumblers of brandy and water. At last, Mr Wellesley asked Mr Percy 'whether he meant to stir his stumps that afternoon or not?' Mr Percy said he felt very well where he was, but however, as the thing must be done some day, he thought they had better shog. Mr Wellesley intimated that it was not his intention to make any further objection, and that therefore Mr Percy should have his way, but he further insinuated that that way was the direct road to hell, and that he wished with all his heart Mr Percy had already reached the end of his journey. Only it was a pity a poor, foolish little thing like Caroline Vernon should be forced to trot off along with him.

'You, I suppose,' said Mr Percy drily, 'would have taken her to heaven. Now, I've an odd sort of a crotchety notion that the girl will be safer in hell with me than in heaven with thee, friend Arthur.'

'You consider my plan of education defective, I suppose,' said his Grace with the air of a schoolmaster.

'Rather,' was the reply.

'You're drinking too much brandy and water,' pursued the royal mentor.

'And you have had quite enough champagne,' responded his friend.

'Then we'd better both be moving,' suggested the Duke, and he rose, rung the bell and ordered horses. Neither of them were quite steady when they mounted their saddles and, unattended by servants, started from the front door at a mad gallop as if they were chasing wild-fire.[56]

People are not always in the same mood of mind, and thus, though Northangerland and Zamorna had been on the point of quarrelling in the morning, they were wondrous friends this afternoon, quite jovial. The little disagreement between them as to the mode of conducting Miss Caroline's further education was allowed to rest. Indeed, Miss Caroline herself seemed quite forgotten. Her name was never mentioned as they rode on through sombre Hawkscliffe, talking fast and high and sometimes laughing loud. I don't mean to say that Northangerland laughed loud, but Zamorna did very frequently. For a little while, it was Ellrington and Douro resuscitated.[57] Whether champagne and brandy had any hand in bringing about this change, I can't pretend to decide. However, neither of them were ree; they were only gay. Their wits were all about them, but they were sparkling.

We little know what fortune the next breath of wind may blow us, what strange visitor the next moment may bring to our door. So Lady Louisa Vernon may be thinking just now, as she sits by her fireside in this very secluded house, whose casements are darkened by the boughs of large trees. It is near seven o'clock, and the cloudy evening is closing in somewhat comfortless and chill, more like October than July. Her Ladyship consequently has the vapours.[58] In fact, she has had them all day. She imagines herself very ill, though what her ailments are she can't distinctly say, so she sits upstairs in her dressing-room, with her head reclined on a pillow and some drops and a smelling-bottle close at hand. Did she but know what step was now near her door, even at her threshold, she would hasten to change her dress and comb her hair, for in that untidy deshabille, with that pouting look and those dishevilled tresses, her Ladyship looks haggard.

'I must go to bed, Elise. I can't bear to sit up any longer,' says she to her French maid, who is sewing in a window recess near.

'But your Ladyship will have your gown tried on first?' answered the girl. 'It is nearly finished.'

'Oh no! Nonsense! What is the use of making gowns for me? Who will see me wear them? My God! Such barbarous usage I receive [from] that man who has no heart!'

'Ah, Madame!' interposed Elise. 'He has a heart, don't doubt it. *Attendez un peu*, Monsieur loves you *jusqu'à folie*.'[59]

'Do you think so, Elise?'

'I do. He looks at you so fondly.'

'He never looks at me at all. I look at him.'

'But when your back is turned, Madame, then he measures you with his eyes.'

'Aye, scornfully.'

'*Non, avec tendresse, avec ivresse*.'[60]

'Then why does not he speak? I'm sure I've told him often enough that I am very fond of him, that I adore him, though he is so cold and proud and tyrannical and cruel!'

'*C'est trop modeste*,'[61] replied Elise, very sagely. Apparently, this remark struck her Ladyship in a ludicrous point of view. She burst into a laugh.

'I can't quite swallow that, either,' said she. 'You are almost an idiot, Elise. I daresay you think he loves you too. *Ecoutez la fille! C'est un homme dur. Quant'à l'amour, il ne sait guère qu'est-ce que c'est. Il regarde les femmes comme des esclaves. Il s'amuse de leur beauté pour un instant, et alors il les abandonne. Il faut haïr un tel homme et l'éviter, et moi, je le haïs beaucoup. Oui, je le déteste. Hèla! combien il est different de mon Alexandre! Elise, souvenez vous de mon Alexandre, du beau Northangerland!*'[62]

'*C'etait fort gentil*,'[63] responded Elise.

'*Gentil!*' ejaculated her ladyship. '*Elise, c'etait un ange! Il me semble que je le vois dans ce chambre même, avec ses yeux bleus, sa physiognomy qui exprimait tant de douceur, et son front de marbre environné des cheveux chataignes*.'[64]

'*Mais le Duc a des cheveux chataignes aussi*,'[65] interposed Elise.

'*Pas comme ceux de mon pre[cie]ux Percy*,'[66] sighed her faithful Ladyship. And she continued in her own tongue, 'Percy had so much soul, such a fine taste. *Il sut apprécier mes talen[t]s*.[67] He gave me trinkets. His first present was a broach like a heart set with diamonds; in return he asked for a lock of his lovely Allan's hair. My name was Allan then, Elise. I sent him such a long, streaming tress. He knew how to receive the gift like a gentleman; he had it plaited into a watch-guard. And the next night I acted at the Fidena Theatre. When I came on to the stage, there he was in a box just opposite, with the black braid across his breast. Ah, Elise, talk of handsome men! He was irresistible in those days – stronger and stouter than he is now. Such a chest he shewed! And he used to wear a green Newmarket coat and a white beaver – well, anything became him. But you can't think, Elise, how all the gentlemen admired me when I was a girl, what crowds used to come to the theatre to see me act, and how they used to cheer me. But he never did, he only looked – ah, just as if he worshipped me. And when I used to clasp my hands, and raise my eyes just so, and shake back my hair in this way, which I often did in singing solemn things, he seemed as if he could hardly hold from coming on to the stage and falling at my feet, and I enjoyed that.

'The other actresses did envy me so. There was a woman called Morton, whom I always hated so much. I could have run a spit through her or stuck her full of needles any day, and she and I once quarrelled about him. It was in the green room; she was dressing for a character. She took one of her slippers and flung it at me; I got all my fingers into her hair, and I twisted them round and round and pulled and dragged till she was almost in fits with pain. I never heard anybody scream so. The manager tried to get me off, but he couldn't, nor could anybody else. At last he said, "Call Mr Percy. He's in the saloon." Alexander came, but he had had a good deal of wine, and Price, the manager, could not rightly make him comprehend what he wanted him for. He was in a swearing passionate humour, and he threatened to shoot Price for attempting to humbug him, as he said. He took out his pistols and cocked them. The green room was crowded with actors and actresses and dressers. Every body was so terrified, they appealed to me to go and pacify him. I was so proud to shew my influence before them all. I knew that, drunk as he was, I could turn him round my little finger, so at last I left Morton, with her head almost bald and her hair torn off by handfuls, and went to the Drover. I believe he would really have shot Price if I hadn't stopped him, but I soon changed his mood. You can't think, Elise, what power

I had over him. I told him I was frightened of his pistols, and
began to cry. He laughed at me first, and when I cried more,
he put them away. Lord George,[68] poor man, was standing
by, watching. I did used to like to coquette between Vernon
and Percy. Ah, what fun I had in those days! But it's all gone
by now – nothing but this dismal house, and that garden
with its high wall like a convent, and these great dark trees,
always groaning and rustling. Whatever have I done, to be
punished so?'

Her Ladyship began to sob.

'Monseigneur will change all this,' suggested Elise.

'No, no, that's worst of all,' returned her Ladyship. 'He does
not know how to change – such an impenetrable, iron man, so
austere and sarcastic. I can't tell how it is I always feel glad
when he comes. I always wish for the day to come round when
he will visit us again, and every time I hope he'll be kinder, and
less stately and laconic and abrupt, and yet, when he does come,
I'm so tormented with mortification and disappointment. It's
all nonsense looking into his handsome face; his eyes won't
kindle any more than if they were of glass. It's quite in vain
that I go and stand by him and speak low. He won't bend to
listen to me, though I'm so much less than him.[69] Sometimes,
when he bids me good-bye, I press his hand tenderly; sometimes
I'm very cold and distant. It makes no difference; he does not
seem to notice the change. Sometimes I try to provoke him, for
if he would only be exceedingly savage, I might fall into great
terror and faint, and then perhaps he would pity me afterwards.
But he won't be provoked. He smiles as if he were amused at
my anger and that smile of his is so – I don't know what,
vexing, maddening! It makes him look so handsome, and yet it
tears one's heart with passion. I could draw my nails down his
face, till I had scraped it bare of flesh; I could give him some
arsenic in a glass of wine. Oh, I wish something would happen,
that I could get a better hold of him! I wish he would fall
desperately sick in this house, or shoot himself by accident, so
that he would be obliged to stay here and let me nurse him. It
would take down his pride if he were so weak that he could do
nothing for himself, and then, if I did everything for him, he

would be thankful. Perhaps he would begin to take a pleasure in having me with him, and I could sing his kind of songs and seem to be very gentle. He'd love me, I'm sure he would. If he didn't, and if he refused to let me wait on him, I'd come at night to his room and choke him while he was asleep – smother him with the pillow, as Mr Ambler used to smother me when he had the part of Othello and I had that of Desdemona. I wonder if I dare do such a thing?'

Her Ladyship paused for a minute, as if to meditate on the moral problem she had thus proposed for her own solution. Ere long she proceeded:

'I should like to know, now, how he behaves towards people that he does love, if indeed he ever loved anybody. His wife, now, does he always keep her at a distance? And they say he has a mistress or two. I've heard all sorts of queer stories about him. It's very odd; perhaps he likes only blondes. But no, Miss Gordon[70] was as dark as me, and eight years ago what a talk there was in the north about him and her. He was a mere schoolboy then, to be sure. I remember hearing Vernon and O'Connor bantering Mr Gordon about it, and they joked him for being cut out by a beardless lad. Gordon did not like the joke. He was an ill-tempered man, that. Elise, you're making my gown too long; you know I always like rather short skirts. Morton used to wear long ones because, as I often told her, she'd ugly, thick ancles. My ancles, now, were a straw-breadth less in circumference than Julia Corelli's, who was the first *figurante* at the Verdopolitan Opera. How vexed Corelli was that night that we measured, and my ancles were found to be slimmer than hers! Then neither she nor any of the other dancers could put on my shoes; and – it's a fact, Elise – a colonel in the army stole a little black satin slipper of mine, and wore it a whole week in his cap as a trophy. Poor man, Percy challenged him. They had such a dreadful duel across a table. He was shot dead. They called him Markham, Sydenham Markham; he was an Angrian.'

'Madame, *c'est finie*,'[71] said Elise, holding up the gown which she had just completed.

'Oh well, put it away. I can't try it on; I don't feel equal to the fatigue. My head's so bad, and I've such a faintness and such a fidgetty restlessness. What's that noise?'

A distant sound of music in a room below was heard, a piano very well touched.[72]

'Dear, dear! There's Caroline strumming over that vile instrument again! I really *cannot* bear it, and so it doesn't signify. That girl quite distracts me with the racket she keeps up.'

Here, her Ladyship rose very nimbly, and going to the top of the stairs, which was just outside her room, called out with much power of lungs,

'Caroline! Caroline!'

No answer, except a brilliant bravura run down the keys of the piano.

'Caroline!' was reiterated. 'Give up playing this instant! You know how ill I have been all day, and yet you will act in this way.'

A remarkably merry jig responded to her Ladyship's objurgations, and a voice was heard far off, saying,

'It will do you good, Mamma!'

'You are very insolent,' cried the fair invalid, leaning over the bannisters. 'Your impertinence is beyond bearing. You will suffer for it one day. You little forward piece, do as I bid you!'

'So I will directly,' replied the voice. 'I have only to play "Jim Crow"[73] and then – ', and 'Jim Crow' was played, with due spirit and sprightliness. Her Ladyship cried once again, with a volume of voice that filled the whole house,

'D'ye know I'm your mother, madam? You seem to think you are grown out of my control. You have given yourself fine impudent airs of late. It's high time your behaviour was looked to, I think. Do ye hear me?'

While 'Jim Crow' was yet jigging his round, while Lady Vernon, bent above the bannisters, was still shaking the little passage with her voice, the wire of the door-bell vibrated. There was a loud ring, and thereafter a pealing aristocratic knock. 'Jim Crow' and Lady Louisa were silenced simultaneously. Her Ladyship effected a precipitate retreat to her dressing-room. It seemed also as if Miss Caroline were making herself scarce, for there was a slight rustle and run heard below, as of some one retiring to hidden regions.

I need not say who stood without. Of course, it was Messrs Percy and Wellesley. In due time the door was opened to them by a manservant, and they walked straight on to the drawing-room. There was no one to receive them in that apartment, but it was evident somebody had lately been there. An open piano and a sheet of music with a grinning, capering nigger litho-graphed on the title-page,[74] a capital good fire, an easy chair drawn close to it, all gave direct evidence to that effect.

His Grace the Duke of Zamorna looked warily round. Nothing alive met his eye. He drew off his gloves and, as he folded them one in the other, he walked to the hearth. Mr Percy was already bent over a little work-table near the easy chair. Pushed out of sight, under a drapery of half-finished embroidery, there was a book. Percy drew it out; it was a novel, and by no means a religious one, either. While Northangerland was turning over the leaves, Zamorna rung the bell.

'Where is Lady Vernon?' he asked of the servant who answered it.

'Her Ladyship will be downstairs directly. I have told her your Grace is here.'

'And where is Miss Caroline?' The servant hesitated.

'She's in the passage,' he said, half smiling and looking behind him. 'She's rather bashful, I think, because there's company with your Grace.'

'Tell Miss Vernon I wish to see her, will you, Cooper?' replied the Duke. The footman withdrew. Presently the door re-opened, very slowly. Northangerland started, and walked quickly to the window, where he stood gazing intently into the garden. Meantime, he heard Zamorna say 'How do you do?' in his deep low voice, most thrilling when it is most subdued. Somebody answered 'Very well, thank ye', in an accent indicat-ing girlish *mauvaise honte*[75] mixed with pleasure. There was then a pause. Northangerland turned round.

It was getting dusk, but daylight enough remained to shew him distinctly what sort of a person it was that had entered the room and was now standing by the fire-place, looking as if she did not exactly know whether to sit down or to remain on her feet. He saw a girl of fifteen, exceedingly well-grown and well-made of her age,[76] not thin or delicate, but, on the contrary, very healthy and very plump. Her face was smiling. She had fine dark eyelashes and very handsome eyes. Her hair was almost black; it curled as nature let it, though it was now long and thick enough to be trained according to the established rules of art. This young lady's dress by no means accorded with her years and stature. The short-sleeved frock, worked trousers,[77] and streaming sash would better have suited the age of nine or ten than that of fifteen. I have intimated that she was somewhat bashful, and so she was, for she would neither look Zamorna nor Northangerland in the face; the fire and the rug were the objects of her fixed contemplation. Yet it was evident that it was only the bashfulness of a raw schoolgirl unused to society. The dimpled cheek and arch, animated eye indicated a constitutional vivacity which a very little encouragement would soon foster into sprightly play enough; perhaps it was a thing rather to be repressed than fostered.

'Won't you sit down?' said Zamorna, placing a seat near her. She sat down. 'Is your mamma very well?' he continued.

'I don't know. She's never been down to-day, and so I haven't seen her.'

'Indeed! You should have gone up-stairs and asked her how she did.'

'I did ask Elise, and she said Madame had the megrims.'[78]

Zamorna smiled, and Northangerland smiled too.

'What have you been doing, then, all day?' continued the Duke.

'Why, I've been drawing and sewing. I couldn't practise, because Ma said it made her head ache.'

'What is "Jim Crow" doing on the piano then?' asked Zamorna.

Miss Vernon giggled. 'I only just jigged him over once,' she replied. 'And Ma did fly![79] She never likes "Jim Crow".'

Her guardian shook his head. 'And have you never walked out this fine day?' he continued.

'I was riding on my pony most of the morning.'

'Oh, you were! Then how did the French and Italian lessons get on, in that case?'

'I forgot them,' said Miss Caroline.

'Well,' pursued the Duke, 'look at this gentleman, now, and tell me if you know him.'

She raised her eyes from the carpet, and turned them furtively on Percy. Frolic and shyness was the mixed expression of her face as she did so.

'No,' was her first answer.

'Look again,' said the Duke, and he stirred the fire to elicit a brighter glow over the now darkening apartment.

'I do!' exclaimed Caroline, as the flame flashed over North-angerland's pallid features and marble brow. 'It's Papa!' she said, rising, and without agitation or violent excitement she stepped across the rug towards him. He kissed her. The first minute, she only held his hand; and then she put her arms round his neck, and would not leave him for a little while, though he seemed oppressed and would have gently put her away.

'You remember something of me, then?' said the Earl at last, loosening her arms.

'Yes, Papa, I do.' She did not immediately sit down, but walked two or three times across the room, her colour heightened and her respiration hurried.

'Would you like to see Lady Vernon tonight?' asked Zamorna of his father-in-law.

'No, not to-night. I'd prefer being excused.'

But who was to prevent it? Rustle and sweep, a silk gown traversed the passage. In she came.

'Percy! Percy! Percy!' was her thrice repeated exclamation. 'My own Percy, take me again! Oh, you shall hear all, you shall! But I'm safe now, you'll take care of me. I've been true to you, however.'

'God bless me, I shall be choked!' ejaculated the Earl, as the little woman vehemently kissed and embraced him. 'I never can stand this,' he continued. 'Louisa, just be quiet, will ye?'

'But you don't know what I've suffered,' cried her Ladyship, 'nor what I've had to contend against! He has used me so ill, and all because I couldn't forget you.'

'What, the Duke there?' asked Percy.

'Yes, yes. Save me from him! Take me away with you! I cannot exist if I remain in his power any longer.'

'Ma, what a fool you are,' interposed Caroline very angrily.

'Does he make love to you?' said the Earl.

'He persecutes me; he acts in a shameful, unmanly, brutal manner.'

'You've lost your senses, Ma,' said Miss Vernon.

'Percy, you love me, I'm sure you do,' continued her Ladyship. 'Oh, protect me! I'll tell you more when we've got away from this dreadful place.'

'She'll tell you lies,' exclaimed Caroline in burning indignation. 'She's just got up a scene, Papa, to make you think she's treated cruelly, and nobody ever says a word against her.'

'My own child is prejudiced and made to scorn me,' sobbed the little actress. 'Every source of happiness I have in the world is poisoned, and all from his revenge, because –'

'Have done, Mamma,' said Caroline promptly. 'If you are not quiet, I shall take you up-stairs.'

'You hear how she talks,' cried her Ladyship, 'my own daughter, my darling Caroline – ruined, miserably ruined!'

'Papa, Mamma's not fit to be out of her room, is she?' again interrupted Miss Vernon. 'Let me take her in my arms and carry her upstairs. I can do it easily.'

'I'll tell you all!' almost screamed her Ladyship. 'I'll lay bare the whole vile scheme! Your father shall know you, Miss, what you are, and what *he* is. I never mentioned the subject before, but I've noticed, and I've laid it all up, and nobody shall hinder me from proclaiming your baseness aloud.'

'Good heavens, this won't do,' said Caroline, blushing as red as fire. 'Be silent, Mother! I hardly know what you mean, but you seem to be possessed. Not another word, now. Go to bed, do. Come, I'll help you to your room.'

'Don't fawn, don't coax,' cried the infuriated little woman. 'It's too late. I've made up my mind. Percy, your daughter is a bold, impudent minx. Young as she is, she's a –'

She could not finish the sentence. Caroline fairly capsized her mother, took her in her arms, and carried her out of the room. She was heard in the passage, calling Elise and firmly ordering her to undress her lady and put her to bed. She locked the door of her bed-room, and then she came downstairs with the key in her hand. She did not seem to be aware that she had done anything at all extraordinary, but she looked very much distressed and excited.

'Papa, don't believe Mamma,' were her first words as she returned to the drawing-room. 'She talks such mad stuff when she's in a passion, and sometimes she seems as if she hated me. I can't tell why. I'm never insolent to her. I only make fun sometimes.'

Miss Vernon lost command over herself and burst into tears. His Grace of Zamorna, who had been all this time a perfectly silent spectator of the whole strange scene, rose and left the room. Miss Vernon sobbed more bitterly when he was gone.

'Come here, Caroline,' said Northangerland. He placed his daughter on a seat close to his side, and patted her curled hair soothingly. She gave up crying very soon and said, smiling, she didn't care a fig about it now, only Mamma was so queer and vexatious.

'Never mind her, Caroline,' said the Earl. 'Always come to me when she's cross. I can't do with your spirit being broken by such termagant whims. You shall leave her and come and live with me.'

'I wonder what in the world Mamma would do quite by herself,' said Caroline. 'She would fret away to nothing. But to speak truth, Papa, I really don't mind her scolding. I'm so used to it, it does not break my spirit at all. Only she set off on a new tack just now. I didn't expect it; she never talked in that way before.'

'What did she mean, Caroline?'

'I can't tell. I've almost forgot what she did say now, Papa, but it put me into a regular passion.'

'It was something about the Duke of Zamorna,' said Northangerland, quietly. Caroline's excitement returned.

'She's lost her senses,' she said. 'Such wild, mad trash!'

'What mad trash?' asked Percy. 'I heard nothing but half sentences, which amazed me, I confess, but certainly didn't inform me.'

'Nor me, either,' replied Miss Vernon. 'Only I had an idea that she was going to tell some tremendous lie.'

'Of what nature?'

'I can't tell, Papa. I know nothing about it. Ma vexed me.'

There was a little pause, then Northangerland said,

'Your mother used to be fond of you, Caroline, when you were a little child. What is the reason of this change? Do you provoke her unnecessarily?'

'I never provoke her but when she provokes me worse. She's like as if she was angry with me for growing tall, and when I want to be dressed more like a woman, and to have scarfs and veils and such things, it does vex her so. Then, when she's raving and calling me vain and conceited and a hussey, I can't help sometimes letting her hear a bit of the real truth.'

'And what do you call the real truth?'

'Why, I tell her that she's jealous of me, because people will think she is old if she has such a woman as I am for her daughter.'

'Who tells you you are a woman, Caroline?'

'Elise Touquet. She says I'm quite old enough to have a gown, and a watch, and a desk, and a maid to wait on me. I wish I might. I'm quite tired of wearing frocks[80] and sashes, and indeed, Papa, they're only fit for little girls. Lord Enara's children came here once, and the eldest, Senora Maria as they call her, was quite fashionable compared to me, and she's only fourteen, more than a year younger than I am. When the Duke of Zamorna gave me a pony, Mamma would hardly let me have a riding habit. She said a skirt was quite sufficient for a child. But his Grace said I should have one, and a beaver too, and I got them. Oh, how Ma did go on! She said the Duke of Zamorna was sending me to ruin as fast as I could go, and whenever I put them on to ride out she plays up beautifully. You shall see me wear them to-morrow, Pa, if I may ride somewhere with you. Do let me!'

Northangerland smiled.

'Are you very fond of Hawkscliffe?' he asked, after a brief interval of silence.

'Yes, I like it well enough. Only I want to travel somewhere. I should like when winter comes to go to Adrianopolis; and if I were a rich lady, I'd have parties and go to the theatre and opera every night, as Lady Castlereagh does. Do you know Lady Castlereagh, Papa?'

'I've seen her.'

'And have you seen Lady Thornton too?'

'Yes.'

'Well, they're both very fine fashionable ladies, aren't they?'

'Yes.'

'And very handsome, too. Do you think them handsome?'

'Yes.'

'Which is the best looking, and what are they like? I often ask the Duke of Zamorna what they're like, but he'll tell me nothing, except that Lady Castlereagh is very pale and that Lady Thornton is extremely stout. But Elise Touquet, who was Lady Castlereagh's dress-maker once, says they're beautiful. Do you think them so?'

'Lady Thornton is very well,' replied Northangerland.

'Well, but has she dark eyes and a Grecian nose?'

'I forget,' answered the Earl.

'I should like to be exceedingly beautiful,' pursued Caroline. 'And to be very tall, a great deal taller than I am. And slender – I think I'm a great deal too fat. And fair – my neck is so brown, Ma says I'm quite a negro. And I should like to be dashing and to be very much admired. Who is the best-looking woman in Verdopolis, Papa?'

Northangerland was considerably nonplussed.

'There are so many, it's difficult to say,' he answered. 'Your head runs very much on these things, Caroline.'

'Yes, when I walk out in the wood by myself, I build castles in the air, and I fancy how beautiful and rich I should like to be, and what sort of adventures I should like to happen to me – for you know, Papa, I don't want a smooth common-place life, but something strange and unusual.'

'Do you talk in this way to the Duke of Zamorna?' asked Mr Percy.

'In what way, Papa?'

'Do you tell him what kind of adventures you should like to encounter, and what sort of nose and eyes you should choose to have?'

'Not exactly. I sometimes say I'm sorry I'm not handsome, and that I wish a fairy would bring me a ring, or a magician would appear and give me a talisman like Aladdin's lamp,[81] that I could get everything I want.'

'And pray what does his Grace say?'

'He says time and patience will do much, that plain girls with manners and sense often make passable women, and that he thinks reading Lord Byron has half turned my head.'[82]

'You do read Lord Byron, then?'

'Yes, indeed I do; and Lord Byron and Bonaparte and the Duke of Wellington and Lord Edward Fitzgerald are the four best men that ever lived.'

'Lord Edward Fitzgerald? Who the d—il is he?' asked the Earl in momentary astonishment.

'A young nobleman that Moore[83] wrote a life about,' was the reply. 'A regular grand republican. He would have rebelled against a thousand tyrants if they'd dared to trample on him. He went to America because he wouldn't be hectored over in England, and he travelled in the American forests, and at night he used to sleep on the ground like Miss Martineau.'[84]

'Like Miss Martineau!' exclaimed the Earl, again astounded out of his propriety.

'Yes, Papa, a lady who must have been the cleverest woman that ever lived. She travelled like a man, to find out the best way of governing a country. She thought a republic far the best, and so do I. I wish I had been born an Athenian. I would have married Alcibiades, or else Alexander the Great.[85] Oh, I do like Alexander the Great!'

'But Alexander the Great was not an Athenian, neither was he a republican,' interposed the Earl in a resigned, deliberate tone.

'No, Papa, he was a Macedonian, I know, and a king too.

But he was a right kind of king – martial, and not luxurious and indolent. He had such power over all his army! They never dared mutiny against him, though he made them suffer such hardships. And he was such an heroic man! Haephestion[86] was nearly as nice as he was, though; I always think he was such a tall, slender, elegant man. Alexander was little – what a pity!'

'What other favourites have you?' asked Mr Percy. The answer was not quite what he expected. Miss Caroline, who probably had not often an opportunity of talking so unreservedly, seemed to warm with her subject. In reply to her excellent father's question, the pent-up enthusiasm of her heart came out in full tide. The reader will pardon any little inconsistencies he may observe in the young lady's declaration.

'O Papa, I like a great many people, but soldiers most of all! I do adore soldiers! I like Lord Arundel, Papa, and Lord Castlereagh, and General Thornton, and General Henri Fernando di Enara, and I like all gallant rebels. I like the Angrians because they rebelled, in a way, against the Verdopolitans. Mr Warner is an insurgent, and so I like him. As to Lord Arundel, he's the finest man that can be. I saw a picture of him once on horseback. He was reining in his charger and turning round with his hand stretched out, speaking to his regiment as he did before he charged at Leyden. He was so handsome.'

'He is silly,'[87] whispered Northangerland, very faintly.

'What, Pa?'

'He is silly, my dear. A big man, but nearly idiotic; calfish, quite heavy and poor-spirited. Don't mention him.'

Caroline looked as blank as the wall. She was silent for a time.

'Bah!' said she at last. 'That's disagreeable.' And she curled her lip as if nauseating the recollection of him. Arundel was clearly done for in her opinion.

'You are a soldier, aren't you, Papa?' she said, erelong.

'No, not at all.'

'But you are a rebel and a republican,' continued Miss Vernon. 'I know that, for I've read it over and over again.'

'Those facts won't deny,' said Northangerland.

She clapped her hands, and her eyes sparkled with delight.

'And you're a pirate and a democrat too,' said she. 'You scorn worn-out constitutions and old rotten monarchies, and you're a terror to those ancient doddered kings up at Verdopolis. That crazy, ill-tempered old fellow, Alexander, dreads you, I know. He swears in broad Scotch whenever your name is mentioned. Do get up an insurrection, Papa, and send all those doting constitutionalists to Jericho.'[88]

'Rather good for a young lady that has been educated under royal auspices,' remarked Northangerland. 'I suppose these ideas on politics have been carefully instilled into you by his Grace of Zamorna, eh, Caroline?'

'No, I've taken them all up myself. They're just my unbiased principles.'

'Good!' again said the Earl, and he could not help laughing quietly, while he added in an undertone, 'I suppose it's hereditary, then. Rebellion runs in the blood.'

By this time, the reader will have acquired a slight idea of the state of Miss Caroline Vernon's mental development, and will have perceived that it was as yet only in the chrysalis form; that in fact she was not altogether so sage, steady and consistent as her best friends might have wished. In plain terms, Mademoiselle was evidently raw, flighty and romantic. Only there was a something about her, a flashing of her eye, an earnestness, almost an impetuosity, of manner, which I cannot convey in words, and which yet, if seen, must have irresistibly impressed the spectator that she had something of an original and peculiar character under all her rubbish of sentiment and inconsequence. It conveyed the idea that though she told a great deal, rattled on, let out, concealed neither feeling nor opinion, neither predilection nor antipathy, it was still just possible that something might remain behind, which she did not choose to tell nor even to hint at. I don't mean to say that she'd any love-secret, or hate-secret either, but she'd sensations somewhere that were stronger than fancy or romance. She shewed it when she stepped across the rug to give her father a kiss and could not leave him for a minute; she shewed it when she blushed at what her mother said and, in desperation lest she should let out more, whisked her out of the room in a whirlwind.

All the rattle about Alexander and Alcibiades and Lord Arundel and Lord Edward Fitzgerald was, of course, humbug and the rawest hash of ideas imaginable, yet she could talk better sense if she liked, and often did do so when she was persuading her mother to reason. Miss Caroline had a fund of vanity about her, but it was not yet excited. She really did not know that she was good-looking, but rather, on the contrary, considered herself unfortunately plain. Sometimes, indeed, she ventured to think that she had a nice foot and ancle and a very little hand. But then, alas, her form was not half slight and sylph-like enough for beauty – according to her notions of beauty, which of course, like those of all school-girls, approached the farthest extreme of the thread-paper and may-pole style.[89] In fact, she was made like a model. She could not but be graceful in her movements, she was so perfect in her proportions. As to her splendid eyes, dark enough and large enough to set twenty poets raving about them, her sparkling, even teeth and her profuse tresses, glossy, curling and waving, she never counted these as beauties; they were nothing. She had neither rosy cheeks, nor a straight Grecian nose, nor an alabaster neck, and so she sorrowfully thought to herself she could never be considered as a pretty girl. Besides, no one ever praised her, ever hinted that she possessed a charm. Her mother was always throwing out strong insinuations to the contrary, and as to her royal guardian, he either smiled in silence when she appealed to him, or uttered some brief and grave admonition to think less of physical and more of moral attraction.

It was after eleven when Caroline bade her papa good-night. His Grace the Duke did not make his appearance again that evening in the drawing-room. Miss Vernon wondered often what he was doing so long up-stairs, but he did not come. The fact is, he was not up-stairs, but comfortably enough seated in the dining-room, quite alone, with his hands in his pockets, a brace of candles on the table by him, unsnuffed[90] and consequently burning rather dismally dim. It would seem he was listening with considerable attention to the various little movements in the house, for, the moment the drawing-room door opened, he rose, and when Caroline's 'Good-night, Papa' had been softly spoken, and her step had crossed the passage and tripped up the staircase, Mr Wellesley emerged from his retreat. He went straight to the apartment Miss Vernon had just left.

'Well,' said he, appearing suddenly before the eyes of his father-in-law. 'Have ye told her?'

'Not exactly,' returned the Earl. 'But I will do, to-morrow.'

'You mean it still, then?' continued his Grace, with a look indicating thunder.

'Of course I do.'

'You're a d—d noodle,' was the mild reply, and therewith the door banged to and the Majesty of Angria vanished.

CHAP[TER] V

To-morrow came. The young lover of rebels and regicides awoke as happy as could be. Her father, whom she had so long dreamed about, was at last come. One of her dearest wishes had been realized, and why might not others, in due course of time? While Elise Touquet dressed her hair, she sat pondering over a reverie of romance, something so delicious, yet so undefined – I will not say that it was all love, yet neither will I affirm that love was entirely excluded therefrom. Something there was of a hero, yet nameless and formless, a mystic being, a dread shadow, that crowded upon Miss Vernon's soul, haunted her day and night when she had nothing useful to occupy her head or her hands. I almost think she gave him the name of Ferdinand Alonzo Fitz-Adolphus, but I don't know. The fact was, he frequently changed his designation, being sometimes no more than simple Charles Seymour or Edward Clifford and at other times soaring to the title of Harold Aurelius Rinaldo Duke of Montmorency di Valdacella, a very fine man no doubt – though whether he was to have golden or raven hair, or straight or aquiline proboscis, she had not quite decided. However, he was to drive all before him in the way of fighting, to conquer the world and build himself a city like Babylon, only it was to be in the Moorish style, and there was to be a palace called the Alhambra, where Mr Harold Aurelius was to live, taking upon himself the title of Caliph,[91] and she, Miss C Vernon, the professor of republican principles, was to be his chief lady and to be called the Sultana Zara Esmerelda, with at least a hundred slaves to do her bidding. As for the gardens of roses and the halls of marble and the diamonds and the pearls and the rubies, it would be vanity to attempt a description of such heavenly sights. The reader must task his imagination and try if he can conceive them.

In the course of that day Miss Vernon got something better to think of than the crudities of her own over-stretched fancy. That day was an era in her life. She was no longer to be a child; she was to be acknowledged a woman. Farewell to captivity, where she had been reared like a bird! Her father was come to release her, and she was to go with him to be his daughter and his darling. The Earl's splendid houses, which she had never entered, were to be opened to her, and she was to be almost mistress there. She was to have servants and wealth, and whatever delighted her eye she was to ask for and receive. She was to enter life, to see society; to live all the winter in a great city, Verdopolis; to be dressed as gaily as the gayest ladies; to have jewels of her own; to vie even with those demi-goddesses, the Ladies Castlereagh and Thornton. It was too much. She could hardly realize it.

It may be supposed, from her enthusiastic character, that she received this intelligence with transport, that as Northangerland unfolded these coming glories to her view, she expressed her delight and astonishment and gratitude in terms of extacy. But the fact is, she sat by the table with her head on her hand, listening to it all with a very grave face. Pleased she was, of course, but she made no stir. It was rather too important a matter to clap her hands about; she took it soberly. When the Earl told her she must get all in readiness to set off early to-morrow she said, 'To-morrow, Papa!' and looked up with an excited glance.

'Yes, early in the morning.'

'Does Mamma know?'

'I shall tell her.'

'I hope she'll not take it to heart,' said Caroline. 'Let her go with us for about a week or so, Papa! It will be so dreary to leave her behind.'

'She's not under my control,' replied Percy.

'Well,' continued Miss Vernon, 'if she were not so excessively perverse and bad to manage as she is, I'm sure she might get leave to go. But she makes the Duke of Zamorna think she's out of her wits by her frantic ways of going on, and he says she's not fit to be let loose on society. Actually, Papa, one day when the Duke was dining with us she started up without speaking a word in the middle of dinner and flew at him with a knife. He could hardly get the knife from her, and afterwards he was obliged to tell Cooper to hold her hands. And another time, she brought him a glass of wine, and he just tasted it and threw the rest at the back of the fire. He looked full at her, and Mamma began to cry and scream as if somebody was killing her. She's always contriving to get laudanum and prussic acid and such trash. She says she'll murder either him or herself, and I'm afraid if she's left quite alone she'll really do some harm.'

'She'll not hurt herself,' replied the Earl. 'And as to Zamorna, I think he's able to mind his own affairs.'

'Well,' said Miss Vernon, 'I must go and tell Elise to pack up.' And she jumped up and danced away as if care laid but lightly on her.

I believe the date of these present transactions is July, but I've almost forgotten. If so, summer days were not gone by, nor summer evenings either, and it is with a summer evening that I have now to do. Miss Caroline Vernon, alias Percy, had finished her packing up, and she had finished her tea too. She was in the drawing-room alone, and she was sitting in the window-seat as quiet as a picture. I don't exactly know where the other inmates of the house were, but I believe Mr Percy was with Lady Louisa, and Lady Louisa was in her own room, as sick as you please. Whether, at this particular moment of time, she was playing the houri or the fiend, kissing or cuffing the Earl, her lover, I really can't tell. Neither, as far as I know, does it much signify. However, be that as it may, Caroline was by herself, and also she was very still and pensive. What else could she be, looking out on to the quiet walks of that garden and on to that lawn, where the moon is already beginning dimly to shine? A summer moon is yellow, and a summer evening sky is often more softly blue than pen can describe, especially when that same moon is but newly risen, and when its orb hangs low and large over a background of fading hills, and looks into your face from under the boughs of forest beeches. Miss Caroline is to leave Hawkscliffe to-morrow, so she is drinking in all its beauties to-night.

So you suppose, reader, but you're mistaken. If you observe her eyes, she's not gazing, she's watching. She's not contemplating the moon; she's following the motions of that person who, for the last half hour, has been leisurely pacing up and down that gravel walk at the bottom of the garden. It is her guardian, and she is considering whether she shall go and join him and have a bit of talk with him for the last time – that is, for the last time at Hawkscliffe; she's by no means contemplating anything like the solemnity of an eternal separation. This guardian of hers has a blue frock-coat on, white inexpugnables,[92] and a stiff black stock; consequently, he considerably resembles that angelic existence called a military man. You'll suppose Miss Vernon considers him handsome, because other people do. All the ladies in the world, you know, hold the Duke of Zamorna to be matchless, irresistible. But Miss Vernon doesn't think him handsome. In fact, the question of his charms has never yet been mooted in her mind. The idea as to whether he is a god of perfection or a demon of defects has not crossed her intellect once, neither has she once compared him with other men. He is himself, a kind of abstract isolated being, quite distinct from aught beside under the sun. He can't be handsome, because he has nothing at all in common with Messrs Ferdinand Alonzo Fitzadolphus, Harold Aurelius Rinaldo and company. His complexion is not like a lady's, nor has he cheeks tinged with transparent roses, nor glossy golden hair, nor blue eyes. The Duke's whiskers and mustaches are rather terrible than beautiful, and the Duke's high mien and upright port and carriage are more awful than fascinating, and yet Miss Caroline is only theoretically afraid of him. Practically, she is often familiar enough. To play with the lion's mane is one of her greatest pleasures. She would play with him now, but he looks grave, and is reading a book.

It seems, however, that Miss Vernon has at length conquered her timidity, for lo! as the twilight deepens and the garden is all dim and obscure, she, with her hat on, comes stealing quietly out of the house, and through the shrubs, the closed blossoms and dewy leaves, trips like a fairy to meet him. She thought she would surprise him, so she took a circuit and came behind. She touched his hand before he was aware. Cast iron, however, can't be startled, and so no more was he.

'Where did you come from?' said the guardian, gazing down from supreme altitude upon his ward, who passed her arm through his and hung upon him, according to her custom when they walked together.

'I saw you walking by yourself, and so I thought I'd come and keep you company,' she replied.

'Perhaps I don't want you,' said the Duke.

'Yes, you do. You're smiling, and you've put your book away as if you meant to talk to me instead of reading.'

'Well, are you ready to set off to-morrow?' he asked.

'Yes, all is packed.'

'And the head and the heart are in as complete a state of preparation as the trunk, I presume?' continued his Grace.

'My heart is wae,'[93] said Caroline. 'At last of all, I'm sorry to go – especially this evening. I was not half so sorry in the middle of the day while I was busy, but now –'

'You're tired, and therefore low-spirited. Well, you'll wake fresh in the morning, and see the matter in a different light. You must mind how you behave, Caroline, when you get out into the world. I shall ask after you sometimes.'

'Ask after me? You'll see me. I shall come to Victoria Square almost constantly when you're in Verdopolis.'

'You will not be in Verdopolis longer than a few days.'

'Where shall I be, then?'

'You will go either to Paris, or Fidena, or Rossland.' Caroline was silent. 'You will enter a new sphere,' continued her guardian, 'and a new circle of society, which will mostly consist of French people. Don't copy the manners of the ladies you see at

Paris or Fontainebleau.[94] They are most of them not quite what they should be. They have very free, obtrusive manners, and will often be talking to you about love, and endeavouring to make you their confidante. You should not listen to their notions on the subject, as they are all very vicious and immodest. As to the men, those you will see will be almost universally gross and polluted. Avoid them.'

Caroline spoke not.

'In a year or two, your father will begin to talk of marrying you,' continued her guardian, 'and I suppose you think it would be the finest thing in the world to be married. It is not at all impossible that your father may propose a Frenchman for your husband. If he does, decline the honour of such a connexion.'

Still Miss Vernon was mute.

'Remember always,' continued his Grace, 'that there is one nation under heaven filthier even than the French; that is, the Italians. The women of Italy should be excluded from your presence, and the men of Italy should be spurned with disgust even from your thoughts.'

Silence still. Caroline wondered why his Grace talked in that way. He had never been so stern and didactic before.[95] His allusions to matrimony etc., too, confounded her. It was not that the idea was one altogether foreign to the young lady's mind. She had most probably studied the subject now and then, in those glowing day-dreams before hinted at; nay, I would not undertake to say how far her speculations concerning it had extended, for she was a daring theorist. But as yet these thoughts had all been secret and untold. Her guardian was the last person to whom she would have revealed their existence, and now it was with a sense of shame that she heard his grave counsel on the subject. What he said, too, about the French ladies and the Italian men and women made her feel very queer. She could not for the world have answered him, and yet she wished to hear more. She was soon gratified.

'It is not at all improbable,' pursued his Grace, after a brief pause, during which he and Caroline had slowly paced the long terrace-walk at the bottom of the garden, which skirted a stately aisle of trees, 'it is not at all improbable that you may meet occasionally in society a lady of the name of Lalande and another of the name of St James,[96] and it is most likely that these ladies will shew you much attention, flatter you, ask you to sing or play, invite you to their houses, introduce you to their particular circles, and offer to accompany you to public places. You must decline it all.'

'Why?' asked Miss Vernon.

'Because,' replied the Duke, 'Madame Lalande and Lady St James are easy about their characters. Their ideas on the subject of morality are very free. They would get you into their boudoirs, as the ladies of Paris call the little rooms where they sit in a morning and read gross novels[97] and talk over their own secrets with their intimate friends. You would hear of many love-intrigues, and of a great deal of amorous manoeuvering. You would get accustomed to impudent conversation, and perhaps become involved in foolish adventures which would disgrace you.'

Zamorna still had all the talk to himself, for Miss Vernon seemed too busily engaged in contemplating the white pebbles on which the moon was shining that lay here and there on the path at her feet to take much share in the conversation. At last she said in rather a low voice,

'I never intended to make friends with any Frenchwomen. I always thought that when I was a woman I would visit chiefly with such people as Lady Thornton and Mrs Warner, and that lady who lives about two miles from here, Miss Laury. They are all very well-behaved, are they not?'

Before the Duke answered this question, he took out a red silk handkerchief and blew his nose. He then said,

'Mrs Warner is a remarkably decent woman. Lady Thornton is somewhat too gay and flashy; in other respects I know no harm in her.'

'And what is Miss Laury like?' asked Caroline.

'What is she like? She's rather tall, and pale.'

'But I mean, what is her character? Ought I to visit with her?'

'You will be saved the trouble of deciding on that point, as she will never come in your way. She always resides in the country.'

'I thought she was very fashionable,' continued Miss Vernon, 'for I remember, when I was in Adrianopolis, I often saw pictures in the shops of her, and I thought her very nice-looking.'

The Duke was silent in his turn.

'I wonder why she lives alone,' pursued Caroline, 'and I wonder she has no relations. Is she rich?'

'Not very.'

'Do you know her?'

'Yes.'

'Does Papa?'

'No.'

'Do you like her?'

'Sometimes.'

'Why don't you like her always?'

'I don't always think about her.'

'Do you ever go to see her?'

'Now and then.'

'Does she ever give parties?'

'No.'

'I believe she's rather mysterious and romantic,' continued Miss Vernon. 'She's a romantic look in her eyes. I should not wonder if she has had adventures.'

'I daresay she has,' remarked her guardian.

'I should like to have some adventures,' added the young lady. 'I don't want a dull, droning life.'

'You may be gratified,' replied the Duke. 'Be in no hurry. You are young enough yet; life is only just opening.'

'But I should like something very strange and uncommon, something that I don't at all expect.'

Zamorna whistled.

'I should like to be tried to see what I had in me,' continued his ward. 'Oh, if I were only rather better looking! Adventures never happen to plain, fat people.'

'No, not often.'

'I'm so sorry I'm not as pretty as your wife, the Duchess. If she had been like me, she would never have been married to you.'

'Indeed, how do you know that?'

'Because I'm sure you would not have asked her. But she's so nice and fair, and I'm all dark – like a mulatto, Mamma says.'

'Dark yet comely,' muttered the Duke involuntarily, for he looked down at his ward and she looked up at him, and the moonlight disclosed a clear forehead, pencilled with soft, dusk curls, dark and touching eyes, and a round, youthful cheek, smooth in texture and fine in tint as that of some portrait hung in an Italian palace, where you see the raven eyelash and southern eye relieving a complexion of pure, colourless olive, and the rosy lips smiling brighter and warmer for the absence of bloom elsewhere.

Zamorna did not tell Miss Vernon what he thought, at least not in words. But when she would have ceased to look up at him and returned to the contemplation of the scattered pebbles, he retained her face in that raised attitude by the touch of his finger under her little oval chin. His Grace of Angria is an artist. It is probable that that sweet face, touched with soft lunar light, struck him as a fine artistical study.

No doubt it is terrible to be looked fixedly at by a tall, powerful man, who knits his brows, and whose dark hair and whiskers and mustaches combine to shadow the eyes of a hawk and the features of a Roman statue. When such a man puts on an expression that you can't understand, stops suddenly as you are walking with him alone in a dim garden, removes your hand from his arm, and places his hand on your shoulder, you are justified in feeling nervous and uneasy.

'I suppose I've been talking nonsense,' said Miss Vernon, colouring, and half frightened.

'In what way?'

'I've said something about my sister Mary that I shouldn't have said.'

'How?'

'I can't tell. But you don't like her to be spoken of, perhaps. I remember you once said that she and I ought to have nothing to do with each other, and you would never take me to see her.'

'Little simpleton!' remarked Zamorna.

'No,' said Caroline, deprecating the scornful name with a

look and smile; and shewed her transient alarm was evaporating. 'No, don't call me so.'

'Pretty little simpleton. Will that do?' said her guardian.

'No, I'm not pretty.'

Zamorna made no reply – whereat, to confess the truth Miss Vernon was slightly disappointed, for of late she had begun to entertain some latent, embryo idea that his Grace did think her not quite ugly. What grounds she had for supposing so it would not be easy to say. It was an instinctive feeling, and one that gave her little, vain, female heart too much pleasure not to be encouraged and fostered as a secret prize. Will the reader be exceedingly shocked if I venture to conjecture that all the foregoing lamentations about her plainness were uttered with some half-defined intent of drawing forth a little word or two of cheering praise? Oh, human nature! human nature! And oh, inexperience! In what an obscure, dim, unconscious dream Miss Vernon was enveloped! How little she knew of herself!

However, time is advancing and the hours – those 'wild-eyed charioteers', as Shelley calls them – are driving on. She will gather knowledge by degrees. She is one of the gleaners of grapes in that vineyard where all man- and woman-kind have been plucking fruit since the world began, the vineyard of experience. At present, though, she rather seems to be a kind of Ruth in a corn-field. Nor does there want a Boaz to complete the picture, who also is well disposed to scatter handfuls[98] for the damsel's special benefit. In other words, she has a mentor who, not satisfied with instilling into her mind the precepts of wisdom by words, will, if not prevented by others, do his best to enforce his verbal admonitions by practical illustrations that will dissipate the mists on her vision at once and shew her, in light both broad and burning,[99] the mysteries of humanity now hidden, its passions and sins and sufferings, all its passages of strange error and all its after-scenes of agonized atonement. A skilful preceptor is that same; one accustomed to tuition. Caroline has grown up under his care a fine and accomplished girl, unspoilt by flattery, unused to compliment, unhackneyed in trite fashionable conventionalities, fresh, naïve and romantic, really romantic, throwing her heart and soul into her dreams, longing only for an opportunity to do what she feels she could do, to die for somebody she loves – that is, not actually to become a subject for the undertaker, but to give up heart, soul, sensations to one adored hero, to lose independent existence in the perfect adoption of her lover's being. This is all very fine, isn't it, reader? Almost as good as the notion of Mr Rinaldo Aurelius! Caroline has yet to discover that she is as clay in the hands of the potter, that the process of moulding is even now advancing, and that erelong she will be turned off the wheel a perfect polished vessel of grace.[100]

Mr Percy Senr had been a good while up-stairs, and Lady Louisa had talked him nearly deaf, so at last he thought he would go down into the drawing-room by way of change and ask his daughter to give him a tune on the piano. That same drawing-room was a nice little place with a clean bright fire, no candles, and the furniture shining in a quiet glow. But however, as there was nobody there, Mr Percy regarded the vacant sofa, the empty easy chair, and the mute instrument with an air of gentle discontent. He would never have thought of ringing and asking after the missing indvidual; but however, as a footman happened to come in with four wax candles, he did just inquire where Miss Vernon was. The footman said,

'He really didn't know, but he thought she was most likely gone to bed, as he had heard her saying to Mademoiselle Touquet that she was tired of packing.'

Mr Percy stood a little while in the room. Erelong he strayed into the passage, laid his hand on a hat, and wandered placidly into the garden. Mr Percy was very poetical in his youth.[101] Consequently, he must have been very much smitten with the stillness of the summer night, the fine, dark, unclouded blue of the sky, and the glitter of the pin-point stars that swarmed over it like mites. All this must have softened his spirit; not to mention anything of a full moon, which was up a good way in the element just opposite, and gazed down on him as he stood on the front door steps just as if she mistook him for Endymion.[102]

Mr Percy, however, would have nothing to say to her. He

pulled the brim of his hat a trifle lower down on his forehead, and held the noiseless tenor of his way[103] amongst the shades and flowers of the garden. He was just entering the terrace-walk when he heard somebody speak. The voice came from a dim nook where the trees were woven into a bower and a seat was placed at their roots.

'Come, it is time for you to go in,' were the words. 'I must bid you good-bye.'

'But won't you go in, too?' said another voice, pitched in rather a different key to that of the first speaker.

'No, I must go home.'

'But you'll come again in the morning before we set off?'

'No.'

'Won't you?'

'I cannot.'

There was silence. A little repressed sound was heard, like a sob.

'What is the matter, Caroline? Are you crying?'

'Oh, I am so sorry to leave you! I knew, when Papa told me I was to go, I should be grieved to bid you good-bye. I've been thinking about it all day. I can't help crying.'

The sound of weeping filled up another pause.

'I love you so much,' said the mourner. 'You don't know what I think about you, or how much I've always wanted to please you, or how I've cried by myself whenever you've seemed angry with me, or what I'd give to be your little Caroline and to go with you through the world. I almost wish I'd never grown a woman, for when I was a little girl you cared for me far more than you do now. You're always grave now.'

'Hush, and come here to me,' was the reply, breathed in a deep, tender tone. 'There, sit down as you did when you *were* a little girl. Why do you draw back?'

'I don't know. I didn't mean to draw back.'

'But you always do, Caroline, now, when I come near you, and you turn away your face from me if I kiss you – which I seldom do, because you are too old to be kissed and fondled like a child.'

Another pause succeeded, during which it seemed that Miss

Vernon had had to struggle with some impulses of shame. For her guardian said, when he resumed the conversation,

'Nay, now, there is no need to distress yourself and blush so deeply; and I shall not let you leave me at present. So sit still.'

'You are so stern,' murmured Caroline. Her stifled sobs were heard again.

'Stern, am I? I could be less so, Caroline, if circumstances were somewhat different. I would leave you little to complain of on that score.'

'What would you do?' asked Miss Vernon.

'God knows.'

Caroline cried again, for unintelligible language is very alarming.

'You must go in, child,' said Zamorna. 'There will be a stir if you stay here much longer. Come, a last kiss.'

'Oh, my lord!' exclaimed Miss Vernon, and she stopped short, as if she had uttered that cry to detain him and could say no more. Her grief was convulsive.

'What, Caroline?' said Zamorna, stooping his ear to her lips.

'Don't leave me so! My heart feels as if it would break.'

'Why?'

'Oh, I don't know.'

Long was the paroxysm of Caroline's sore distress. She could not speak. She could only tremble and sob wildly. Her mother's excitable temperament was roused within her. Zamorna held her fast in his arms, and sometimes he pressed her more closely, but for a while he was as silent as she was.

'My little darling,' he said, softening his austere tone at last, 'take comfort. You will see or hear from me again soon. I rather think neither mountains nor woods nor seas will form an impassable barrier between you and me; no, nor human vigilance, either. The step of separation was delayed till too late. They should have parted us a year or two ago, Caroline, if they had meant the parting to be a lasting one. Now leave me. Go in.'

With one final kiss, he dismissed her from his arms. She went. The shrubs soon hid her. The opening and closing of the front door announced that she had gained the house.

Mr Wellesley was left by himself on the terrace-walk. He took a cigar out of his pocket, lighted it by the aid of a Lucifer-match, popped it into his mouth and, having reared himself up against the trunk of a large beech, looked as comfortable and settled as possible. At this juncture, he was surprised by hearing a voice at his elbow gently inquiring whether his mother knew he was out?[104] He had barely to turn his head to get a view of the speaker, who stood close to his side, a tall man with a pale aspect and a particular expression in his eyes, which shewed a good deal of their whites and were turned laterally on to Mr Wellesley.

PART 2

CHAP[TER] I

We were talking of a young lady of the name of Miss Caroline Vernon, who by herself and her more partial friends was considered to have pretty nigh finished her education, who consequently was leaving retirement and on the point of taking her station somewhere in some circle of some order of highly fashionable society. It was in July when affairs reached this climax. It is now November, nearly December,[105] and consequently a period of about four months has lapsed in the interim. We are not to suppose that matters have all this while remained *in statu quo*, that Miss Caroline has been standing for upwards of a quarter of a year with her foot on the carriage-step, her hand on the lackey's arm, her eyes pathetically and sentimentally fixed on the windows and chimneys of the convent-like place she is about to leave for good, all in a cataleptic condition of romantic immutability. No, be assured, the young person sighed over Hawkscliffe but once, wept two tears on parting with a groom and a pony she had been on friendly terms with, wondered thrice what her dear mamma would do without anybody to scold, for four minutes had a childish feeling of pity that she should be left behind, sat a quarter of an hour after the start in a fit of speechless thought she did not account for, and all the rest of the way was as merry as a grig.[106]

One or two instances did, indeed, occur on their route through Angria which puzzled her a little. In the first place, she wondered to hear her noble father give orders, whenever they approached a town, that the carriage should be taken through

all sorts of odd, narrow bye-ways, so as to avoid the streets;
and when she asked the reason of this, he told her with a queer
sort of smile that the people of Angria were so fond of him
he was afraid that a recognition of the arms on his carriage
might be attended with even a troublesome demonstration of
their affection. When, towards evening, they entered the city of
Zamorna, which they were necessitated to pass through because
it lay directly in their way, Miss Caroline was surprised to hear
all sorts of groans and yells uttered by grimy-looking persons
in paper caps, who seemed to gather about the lamp-posts[107]
and by the shop windows as they passed along. She was almost
confounded when, as the carriage stopped a moment at a large
hotel, an odd kind of howl broke from a crowd of persons who
had quickly collected by the door, and at the same instant the
window of plate-glass on her right hand shivered with a crash
and an ordinary-sized brick-bat leapt through it and settled
on her lap, spoiling a pretty silk frock which she had on, and
breaking a locket which was a keepsake and which she very
much valued.

It will now be a natural question in the reader's mind, what
has Miss Vernon been about during the last four months? Has
she seen the world? Has she had any adventures? Is she just the
same as she was? Is there any change where has she been?
Where is she now? How does the globe stand in relation to her,
and she in relation to the globe? During the last four months,
reader, Miss Vernon has been at Paris.[108] Her father had a
crotchety, undefined notion that it was necessary she should
go there to acquire a perfect finish. And in fact, he was right in
that notion, for Paris was the only place to give her what he
wished her to have – the *ton*, the air, the elegance of those who
were highest on the summit of fashion. She changed fast in the
atmosphere of Paris. She saw quickly into many things that
were dark to her before. She learnt life, and unlearnt much
fiction. The illusions of retirement were laid aside with a smile,
and she wondered at her own rawness when she discovered
the difference between the world's reality and her childhood's
romance. She had a way of thinking to herself, and of comparing what she saw with what she had imagined. By dint of

shrewd observation, she made discoveries concerning men and
things which sometimes astounded her. She got hold of books
which helped her in the pursuit of knowledge. She lost her
simplicity by this means, and she grew knowing and, in a sense,
reflective. However, she had talent enough to draw from her
theories a safe practice, and there was something in her mind or
heart or imagination which, after all, filled her with wholesome
contempt for the goings on of the bright refined world around
her. People who have been brought up in retirement don't soon
get hackneyed to society. They often retain a notion that they
are better than those about, that they are not of their sort, and
that it would be a letting down to them to give the slightest
glimpse of their real natures and genuine feelings to the chance
associates of a ball-room.

   Of course, Miss Caroline did not forget that there was such
a thing in the world as love. She heard a great deal of talk about
that article amongst the gallant monsieurs and no less gallant
madames around her. Neither did she omit to notice whether
she had the power of inspiring that superfine passion. Caroline
soon learnt that she was a very attractive being, and that she
had that power in a very high degree. She was told that her eyes
were beautiful, that her voice was sweet, that her complexion
was clear and fine, that her form was a model; she was told all
this without mystery, without reserve. The assurance flattered
her highly and made her face burn with pleasure, and when, by
degrees, she ascertained that few even of the prettiest women
in Paris were her equals, she began to feel a certain consciousness of power, a certain security of pleasing more delicious and
satisfactory than words can describe.

   The circumstance of her high parentage gave her éclat. Northangerland is a kind of king in Paris, and his youthful daughter
received from her father's followers the homage of a princess.
In the French fashion, they hailed her as a rising and guiding star
of their faction. The Dupins, the Barrases and the Bernadottes[109]
called her a new planet in the republican heaven. They knew
what an ornament to their dark revolutionary coteries a lady
so young and intelligent must be, and it will be no matter of

wonder to the reader when I say that Miss Vernon received their homage, imbibed their sentiments, and gave heart and soul to the politics of the faction that called her father its leader.

Her career at Paris soon assumed the aspect of a triumph.[110] After she had made one or two eloquent and enthusiastic declarations of her adoration for republics and her scorn of monarchies, she began to be claimed by the *jeunes gens* of Paris as their queen and goddess. She had not yet experience enough to know what sort of a circle she had gathered round her, though she guessed that some of those sons of young France who thronged about her sofa in the saloon and crowded her box at the theatre were little better than regular *mauvais sujets*. Very different, indeed, were these from the polite, grimacing men-monkeys[111] of the old regime. There was a touch of the unvarnished blackguard about most of them, infinitely more gross and unequivocal than is to be met with in any other capital of civilized Europe. Miss Vernon, who was tolerably independent in her movements, because her father restrained her very little and seemed to trust with a kind of blind confidence to I know not what conservative principle in his daughter's mind, Miss Vernon, I say, often at concerts and nightly soirées met and mingled with troops of these men. She also met with a single individual who was as bad as the worst of the *jeunes gens*. He was not a Frenchman, however, but a countryman of her father's, and a friend of his first youth. I allude to Hector Montmorency Esqre.[112]

She had seen Mr Montmorency first at an evening party at Sir John Denard's hotel, in a grand reunion of the Northangerland faction. As usual, her seat was surrounded by the youngest and handsomest men in the room, and as usual, she was engaged in passionate and declamatory conversation on the desperate politics of her party, and whenever she turned her head, she noticed a man of middle age, of strong form, and peculiar, sinister, sardonic aspect, standing with his arms folded, gazing hard at her. She heard him ask Sir John Denard, in the French language, 'who the De—l *cette jolie petite fille à cheveux noirs*[113] could possibly be?' She did not hear Sir John's reply;

it was whispered; but directly afterwards, she was aware of some one leaning over her chair-back. She looked up. Mr Montmorency's face was bending over her.

'My young lady,' said he. 'I have been looking at you for a good while, and I wondered what on earth it could possibly be in your face that reminded me so of old times. I see how it is now, as I've learnt your name. You're Northangerland's and Louisa's child, I understand. Hum, you're like to do them credit! I admire this; it's a bit in Augusta's way. I daresay your father'll admire it too. You're in a good line; nice young men you have about you. Could you find in your heart to leave them a minute, and take my arm for a little promenade down the room?'

Mr Montmorency offered his arm with the manner and look of a gentleman of the west.[114] It was accepted, for, strange to say, Miss Vernon rather liked him. There was an off-hand gallantry in his mien which took her fancy at once. When the honourable Hector had got her to himself, he began to talk to her in a half-free, half-confidential strain. He bantered her on her numerous train of admirers, he said one or two warm words about her beauty, he tried to sound the depth of her moral principles and, when his experienced eye and ear soon discovered that she was no Frenchwoman and no callous and hackneyed and well-skilled flirt, that his hints did not take and his innuendos were not understood, he changed the conversation and began to inquire about her education – where she had been reared and how she had got along in the world.

Miss Vernon was as communicative as possible. She chattered away with great glee about her mother and her masters, about Angria and Hawkscliffe, but she made no reference to her guardian. Mr Montmorency inquired whether she was at all acquainted with the Duke of Zamorna. She said she was, a little. Mr Montmorency then said he supposed the Duke wrote to her sometimes. She said, 'No, never.' Mr Montmorency said he wondered at that, and meantime he looked into Miss Vernon's face as narrowly as if her features had been the Lord's Prayer written within the compass of a sixpence.[115] There was nothing particular to be seen, except a smooth, brunette complexion and dark eyes looking at the carpet. Mr Montmorency remarked in a random, careless way, 'that the Duke was a sad hand in some things.' Miss Vernon asked,

'In what?'

'About women,' replied Montmorency, bluntly and coarsely. After a momentary pause, she said, 'Indeed!', and that was all she did say. But she felt such a sensation of astonishment, such an electrical, stunning surprise that she hardly knew for a minute where [she] was. It was the oddest, the most novel thing in the world for her to hear her guardian's character freely canvassed. To hear such an opinion expressed concerning him as that Mr Montmorency had so nonchalantly uttered was strange to a degree. It gave a shock to her ordinary way of thinking. It revolutionized her ideas. She walked on through the room, but she forgot for a moment who was round her or what she was doing.

'Did you never hear that before?' asked Mr Montmorency, after a considerable interval, which he had spent in humming a tune which a lady was singing to a harp.

'No.'

'Did you never guess it? Has not his Grace a rakish, impudent air with him?'

'No, quite different.'

'What, he sports the Simon Pure,[116]does he?'

'He's generally rather grave and strict.'

'Did you like him?'

'No – yes – no – not much –'

'That's queer. Several young ladies have liked him a good deal too well. I daresay you've seen Miss Laury, now, as you lived at Hawkscliffe?'

'Yes.'

'She's his mistress.'

'Indeed!' repeated Miss Vernon, after the same interregnum of appalled surprise.

'The Duchess has not particularly easy times of it,' continued Montmorency. 'She's your half-sister, you know.'

'Yes.'

'But she knew what she had to expect before she married

him, for when he was Marquis of Douro he was the most consumed blackguard in Verdopolis.'

Miss Caroline in silence heard, and in spite of the dismay she felt, wished to hear more. There is a wild interest in thus suddenly seeing the light rush in on the character of one well known to our eyes but, as we discover, utterly unknown to our minds. The young lady's feelings were not exactly painful. They were strange, new and startling. She was getting to the bottom of an unsounded sea, and lighting on rocks she had not guessed at. Mr Montmorency said no more in that conversation, and he left Miss Vernon to muse over what he had communicated.

What his exact aim was in thus speaking of the Duke of Zamorna it would be difficult to say. He added no violent abuse of him, nor did he attempt to debase his character as he might easily have done. He left the subject there. Whether his words lingered in the mind of the listener, I can hardly say. I believe they did, for though she never broached the matter to any one else, or again applied to him for farther information, yet she looked into magazines and into newspapers, she read every passage and every scrap she could find that referred to Zamorna and Douro, she weighed and balanced and thought over every thing, and in a little while, though removed five hundred miles from the individual whose character she studied, she had learnt all that other people know of him and saw him in his real light, no longer as a philosopher and apostle, but as – I need not tell my readers what they know, or at least can guess. Thus did Zamorna cease to be an abstract principle in her mind; thus did she discover that he was a man, vicious like other men – perhaps I should say more than other men – with passions that some-times controlled him, with propensities that were often stronger than his reason, with feelings that could be reached by beauty, with a corruption that could be roused by opposition. She thought of him no longer as 'the stoic of the woods, the man without a tear',[117] but as – don't let us bother ourselves with considering as what.

When Miss Vernon had been about a quarter of a year in Paris, she seemed to grow tired of the society there. She begged her father to let her go home, as she called it, meaning to

Verdopolis. Strange to say, the Earl appeared disquieted at this request. At first, he would not listen to it. She refused to attend the soirées and frequent the opera; she said she had had enough of the French people; she spent the evenings with her father, and played and sung to him. Northangerland grew very fond of her and, as she continued her entreaties to be allowed to go home, often soliciting him with tears in her eyes, he slowly gave way, and at length yielded a hard-wrung and tardy assent. But though his reluctance was overruled, it was evidently not removed. He would not hear her talk of Verdopolis; he evidently hated the thoughts of her return thither; he seemed disturbed when she secluded herself from society and declined invitations. All this, to an ordinary observer, would seem to partake of a tincture of insanity, for well did his Lordship know the character of those circles in which his daughter moved, the corrupt morality, the cold, systematic dissoluteness universal there. Yet he never hinted a word of advice or warning to her. He let her go seemingly unwatched and unguarded. He shewed no anxiety about her till the moment when she wished to withdraw from the vitiated atmosphere, and then he demurred and frowned, as though she had asked to enter into some scene of temptation instead of to retire from it. In spite of this seeming paradox, however, the probability is that Northangerland knew what he was about. He was well acquainted with the materials he had to work upon and, as he said himself, he deemed that Caroline was safer as the prima donna of a Parisian saloon than as the recluse of a remote lodge in Angria.

But Northangerland is not proof to a soft, imploring voice and a mournful look. Miss Vernon loathed Paris and pined after Verdopolis, and she got her way. One evening, as she kissed her father good-night, he said she might give what orders she pleased on the subject of departure. A very few days after, a packet freighted with the Earl and his household were steaming across the channel.

CHAP[TER] II

Northangerland was puzzled and uncomfortable when he got his daughter to Verdopolis. He evidently did not like her to remain there. He never looked settled or easy. There was no present impediment to her residing at Ellrington House, because the Countess happened to be then staying in Angria, but when Zenobia came home, Caroline must quit. Other considerations also disturbed the calm of the Earl's soul; by him untold, by his daughter unsuspected.

Mr Percy has his own peculiar way of expressing his dissatisfaction. Rarely does a word drop from his lips which bears the tone of expostulation, of reproof, or even command. He does it all by looks and movements, which the initiated only can understand. Miss Vernon discerned a difference in him, but could not dive to the origin thereof. When she came to him with her bonnet on, dressed to go out and looking, as her mirror had told her, very pretty and elegant, he did not express even his usual modicum of quiet pleasure. He would insinuate that the day was wet or cold or windy, or in some way unfit for an excursion. When she came to his drawing-room after tea and said she had nowhere to go, and was come to spend the evening with him, he gave her no welcome, hardly smiled, only sat passive. Now, his daughter Mary would have keenly felt such coldness, and would have met it with silent pride and a bitter regret, but Caroline had no such acute sensitiveness, no such subtle perception. Instead of taking the matter home to herself, and ascribing this change to something she had done or left undone, she attributed it to her father's being ill, or in low spirits, or annoyed with business. She could not at all conceive that he was angry with her, and accordingly, in her caressing way, she would put her arms round his neck and kiss him. And though the Earl received the kiss more like a piece of sculpture than anything living, Caroline, instead of retiring in silence, would begin some prattle to amuse him and, when that failed of its effect, she would try music, and when he asked her to give up playing, she would laugh and tell him he was as capricious as

Mamma, and when nothing at all would do, she would take a book, sit down at his feet and read to herself. She was so engaged one evening when Mr Percy said after a long, long lapse of silence,

'Are you not tired of Verdopolis, Caroline?'

'No' was the answer.

'I think you had better leave it,' continued the Earl.

'Leave it, Papa, when winter is just coming on!'

'Yes.'

'I have not been here three weeks,' said Miss Vernon.

'You will be as well in the country,' replied her father.

'Parliament is going to meet and the season is beginning,' pursued she.

'Are you turned a monarchist?' asked the Earl. 'Are you going to attend the debates, and take interest in the divisions?'

'No, but town will be full.'

'I thought you had had enough of fashion and gaiety at Paris?'

'Yes, but I want to see Verdopolitan gaiety.'

'Eden Cottage is ready,' remarked Northangerland.

'Eden Cottage, Papa?'

'Yes, a place near Fidena.'

'Do you wish to send me there, Papa?'

'Yes.'

'How soon?'

'To-morrow or the day after if you like.'

Miss Vernon's face assumed an expression which it would be scarcely correct to describe by softer epithets than dour and drumly. She said, with an emphatic slow enunciation,

'I should *not* like to go to Eden Cottage.'

Northangerland made no remark.

'I hate the north extremely,' she pursued, 'and have no partiality to the south.'

'Selden House is ready too,' said Mr Percy.

'Selden House is more disagreeable to me still,' replied his daughter.

'You had better reconcile yourself either to Fidena or Rossland,' suggested Mr Percy quickly.

'I feel an invincible repugnance to both,' was her reply, uttered with a self-sustained haughtiness of tone almost ludicrous from such lips.

Northangerland is long-suffering. 'You shall choose your own retreat,' said he. 'But as it is arranged that you cannot long remain in Verdopolis, it will be well to decide soon.'

'I would rather remain at Ellrington House,' responded Mademoiselle Vernon.

'I think I intimated that would not be convenient,' answered her father.

'I would remain another month,' said she.

'Caroline!' said a warning voice. Percy's light eye flickered.

'Papa, you are not kind.'

No reply followed. 'Will I be banished to Fidena?' muttered the rebellious girl to herself.

Mr Percy's visual organs began to play at cross-purposes. He did not like to be withstood in this way.

'You may as well kill me, as send me to live by myself at the end of the world where I know nobody except Denard, an old grey badger.'[118]

'It is optional whether you go to Fidena,' returned Percy. 'I said you might choose your station.'

'Then I'll go and live at Paquena in Angria. You have a house there, Papa.'

'Out of the question,' said the Earl.

'I'll go back to Hawkscliffe, then.'

'Oh no, you can't have the choice of that. You are not wanted there.'

'I'll live in Adrianopolis, then, at Northangerland House.'

'No.'

'You said I might have my choice, Papa, and you contradict me in everything.'

'Eden Cottage is the place,' murmured Percy.

'Do – do let me stay in Verdopolis!' exclaimed Miss Vernon, after a pause of swelling vexation. 'Papa, do! Be kind, and forgive me if I'm cross.' Starting up, she fell to the argument of kisses, and she also cried abundantly. None but Louisa Vernon, or Louisa Vernon's daughter, would have thought of kissing Northangerland in his present mood.

'Just tell me why you won't let me stay, Papa,' she continued. 'What have I done to offend you? I only ask for another month, or another fortnight, just to see some of my friends when they come to Verdopolis.'

'What friends, Caroline?'

'I mean, some of the people I know.'

'What people do you know?'

'Well, only two or three, and I saw in the newspaper this morning that they were expected to arrive in town very soon.'

'Who, Caroline?'

'Well, some of the Angrians. Mr Warner and General Enara and Lord Castlereagh. I've seen them many a time, you know, Papa, and it would be only civil to stop and call on them.'

'Won't do, Caroline,' returned the Earl.

'Why won't it do, Papa? It's only natural to wish to be civil, is[n't] it?'

'You don't wish to be civil, and we'd better say no more about it. I prefer your going to Fidena the day after to-morrow at the farthest.'

Caroline sat mute for a moment, then she said,

'So, I am *not* to stay in Verdopolis, and I *am* to go to Eden Cottage.'

'Thou hast said it,' was the reply.

'Very well,' she rejoined quickly. She sat looking at the fire for another minute; then she got up, lit her candle, said good-night, and walked upstairs to bed. As she was leaving the room, she accidentally hit her forehead a good knock against the side of the door. A considerable organ[119] rose in an instant. She said nothing, but walked on. When she got to her own room, the candle fell from its socket and was extinguished. She neither picked it up nor rang for another. She undressed in the dark, and went to bed ditto. As she lay alone, with night round her, she began to weep. Sobs were audible a long time from her pillow, sobs not of grief, but of baffled will and smothered passion. She could hardly abide to be thus thwarted, to be thus

forced from Verdopolis, when she would have given her ears
to be allowed to stay.

The reader will ask why she had set her heart so fixedly on
this point. I'll tell him plainly, and make no mystery of it. The
fact was, she wanted to see her guardian. For weeks, almost
months, she had felt an invincible inclination to behold him
again by the new lights Mr Montmorency had given her as to
his character. There had also been much secret enjoyment in
her mind from the idea of shewing herself to him, improved as
she knew she was by her late sojourn in Paris. She had been
longing for the time of his arrival in town to come, and that
very morning she had seen it announced in the newspaper
that orders had been given to prepare Wellesley House for the
immediate reception of his Grace the Duke of Zamorna and
suite, and that the noble Duke was expected in Verdopolis
before the end of the week. After reading this, Miss Caroline
had spent the whole morning in walking in the garden behind
Ellrington House, reverieing on the interesting future she imagined to be in store for her, picturing the particulars of her first
interview with Mr Wellesley, fancying what he would say,
whether he would look as if he thought her pretty, whether he
would ask her to come and see him at Wellesley House, if she
should be introduced to the Duchess, how the Duchess would
treat her, what she would be like, how she would be dressed,
etcetera etceterorum. All this was now put a stop to, cut off,
crushed in the bud, and Miss Caroline was thereupon in a
horrid bad temper, choked, almost, with obstinacy and rage
and mortification. It seemed to her imposssible that she could
endure the disappointment. To be torn away from a scene
where there was so much of pleasure, and exiled into comparative dark, blank solitude was frightful. How could she live?
After long musing in midnight silence, she said half-aloud, 'I'll
find some way to alter matters,' and then she turned on her
pillow and went to sleep.

Two or three days elapsed. Miss Vernon, it seemed, had not
succeeded in finding a way to alter matters, for on the second
day she was obliged to leave Ellrington House, and she took
her departure in tearless taciturnity, bidding no one good-bye

except her father, and with him she just shook hands and offered him no kiss. The Earl did not half like her look and manner. Not that he was afraid of anything tragic, but she seemed neither fretful nor desponding. She had the air of one who had laid a plan, and hoped to compass her ends, yet she scrupled not to evince continued and haughty displeasure towards his Lordship, and her anger was expressed with all her mother's temerity and acrimony; with something, too, of her mother's whimsicality, but with none of her fickleness. She seemed quite unconscious of any absurdity in her indignation, though it produced much the same effect as if a squirrel had thought proper to treat a Newfoundland dog with lofty hauteur. Northangerland smiled when her back was turned. Still, he perceived that there was character in all this, and he felt far from comfortable. However, he had written to Sir John Denard desiring him to watch her during her stay at Eden Cottage and he knew Sir John dared not be a careless sentinel.

The very morning after Miss Vernon's departure, Zenobia, Countess of Northangerland, arrived at Ellrington House, and in the course of the same day a cortège of six carriages conveyed the Duke and Duchess of Zamorna, their children and household to the residence in Victoria Square. Mr Percy had made the coast clear only just in time.

CHAP[TER] III

One day, when the Duke of Zamorna was dressing to go and dine in state at Waterloo Palace with some much more respectable company than he was accustomed to associate with, his young man, Mr Rosier, said, as he helped him on with his Sunday coat,

'Has your Grace ever noticed that letter on the mantle-piece?'

'What letter? No. Where did it come from?'

'It's one that I found on your Grace's library table the day we arrived in town – that's nearly a week ago – and as it seemed to be from a lady, I brought it up here, intending to mention it to your Grace; and somehow it slipped down between the toilet and the wall, and I forgot it till this morning, when I found it again.'

'You're a blockhead. Give me the letter.'

It was handed to him. He turned it over, and examined the superscription and seal. It was a prettily folded, satin paper production, nicely addressed, and sealed with the impression of a cameo. His Grace cracked the pretty classic head, unfolded the document, and read.

My Lord Duke,

I am obliged to write to you, because I have no other way of letting you know how uncomfortable everything is. I don't know whether you will expect to find me in Verdopolis, or whether you've ever thought about it, but I'm not there. At least, I shall not be there to-morrow, for Papa has settled that I am to go to Eden Cottage near Fidena, and live there all my life, I suppose. I call this very unreasonable, because I have no fondness for the place and no wish ever to see it, and I know none of the people there, except an old plain person called Denard, whom I exceedingly dislike. I have tried all ways to change Papa's mind, but he has refused me so often that I think it would shew a want of proper spirit to beg any longer. I intend, therefore, not to submit, but to do what I can't help doing, though I shall let Papa see that I consider him very unkind, and that I should be very sorry to treat him in such a way. He was quite different at Paris, and seemed as if he had too much sense to contradict people and force them to do things they have a particular objection to.

Will your Grace be so kind as to call on Papa, and recommend him to think better of it, and let me come back to Verdopolis? It would perhaps be as well to say that very likely I shall do something desperate if I am kept long at Eden Cottage. I know I cannot bear it, for my whole heart is in Verdopolis. I had formed so many plans, which are now all broken up. I wanted to see your Grace. I left France because I was tired of being in a country where I was sure you would not come, and I disliked the thought of the sea being between your Grace and myself. I did not tell

Papa that this was the reason I wished to remain in Verdopolis, because I was afraid he would think me silly, as he does not know the regard I have for your Grace.

I am in a hurry to finish this letter, as I wish to send it to Wellesley House without Papa knowing, and then you will find it there when you come. Your Grace will excuse faults, because I have never been much accustomed to writing letters, though I am nearly sixteen years old. I know I have written in much too childish a way. However, I cannot help it, and if your Grace will believe me, I talk and behave much more like a woman than I did before I went to Paris, and I can say what I wish to say much better in speaking than I can in a letter. This letter, for instance, is all contrary to what I had intended. I had not meant to tell your Grace that I cared at all about you. I had intended to write in a reserved, dignified way, that you might think I was changed – which I am, I assure you, for I have by no means the same opinion of you that I once had, and, now that I recollect myself, it was not from pure friendship that I wished to see you, but chiefly from the desire I had to prove that I had ceased to respect your Grace so much as formerly. You must have a great deal of cover in your character, which is not a good sign.

    I am, my Lord Duke,

      Your obedient servant,

        Caroline Vernon.

P.S. I hope you will be so kind as to write to me. I shall count the hours and minutes till I get an answer. If you write directly, it will reach me the day after tomorrow. Do write! My heart aches; I am so sorry and so grieved. I had thought so much about meeting you. But perhaps you don't care much about me, and have forgotten how I cried the evening before I left Hawkscliffe. Not that this signifies, or is of the least consequence; I hope I can be comfortable whoever forgets me. And of course, you have a great many calls on your thoughts, being a sort of king – which is a great pity; I hate kings. It would conduce to your glory if you would turn Angria into a Commonwealth, and make yourself Protector. Republican principles are very popular in France. *You*

are not popular there; I heard you very much spoken against.
I never defended you; I don't know why. I seemed as if I disliked
to let people know I was acquainted with you.

Believe me,

Yours respectfully,

C V.

Zamorna, having completed the perusal of this profound and
original document, smiled, thought a minute, smiled again,
popped the epistle into the little drawer of a cabinet which
he locked, pulled down his brief black silk waistcoat, adjusted
his stock, settled himself in his dress-coat, ran his fingers three
times through his hair, took his hat and new light lavender
kid gloves, turned a moment to a mirror, backed, erected his
head, took a survey of his whole longitude from top to toe,
walked downstairs, entered a carriage that was waiting for him,
sat back with folded arms, and was whirled away to Waterloo
Palace. He dined very heartily with a select gentleman party,
consisting of his Grace the Duke of Wellington, his Grace the
Duke of Fidena, the Right Honourable the Earl of Richton, the
Right Honourable Lord St Clair, General Granville and Sir R
Weaver Pelham. During the repast he was too fully occupied in
eating to have time to commit himself much by any marked
indecorum of behaviour, and even when the cloth was withdraw[n] and the wine placed on the table, he comported himself
pretty well for some time, seeming thoughtful and quiet. After
a while, he began to sip his glass of champagne and crack his
walnuts with an air of easy impudence much more consistent
with his usual habits. Erelong, he was heard to laugh to himself
at some steady constitutional conversation going on between
General Grenville and Lord St Clair. He likewise leant back in
his chair, stretched his limbs far under the table, and yawned.
His noble father remarked to him aside that if he were sleepy
he knew the way up-stairs to bed, and that most of the guests
there present would consider his room fully an equivalent for
his company. He sat still, however, and before the party were
summoned to coffee in the drawing-room he had proceeded to
the indecent length of winking at Lord Richton across the table.

When the move was made from the dining-room, instead of following the rest up-stairs, he walked down into the hall, took his hat, opened the door, whistling, to see if it was a fine night, having ascertained that it was, turned out into the street without carriage or servant, and walked home with his hands in his breeches pockets, grasping fast hold of a bob and two joeys.[120]

He got home in good time, about eleven o'clock, as sober as a water-cask, let himself in by the garden-door at the back of Wellesley House, and was ascending the private staircase in a most sneaking manner, as if he was afraid of somebody hearing him and wanted to slink to his own den unobserved, when hark! a door opened in the little hall behind him. It was her Grace the Duchess of Zamorna's drawing-room door. Mr Wellesley had in vain entered from the garden like a thief, and trodden across the hall like a large tom-cat, and stepped on his toes like a magnified[121] dancing-master as he ascended the softly carpeted stairs. Some persons' ears are not to be deceived, and in a quiet hour of the night, when people are sitting alone, they can hear the dropping of a pin within doors or the stirring of a leaf without.

'Adrian!' said one below, and Mr Wellesley was obliged to stop midway up the stairs.

'Well, Mary?' he replied, without turning round or commencing a descent.

'Where are you going?'

'Up-stairs, I rather think. Don't I seem to be on that tack?'

'Why did you make so little noise in coming in?'

'Do you wish me to thunder at the door like a battering-ram, or come in like a troop of horse?'

'Now that's nonsense, Adrian. I suppose the fact is, you're not well. Now just come down and let me look at you.'

'Heaven preserve us! There's no use in resisting. Here I am.'

He descended, and followed the Duchess from the hall to the room to which she retreated.

'Am I all here, do you think?' he continued, presenting himself before her. 'Quite as large as life?'

'Yes, Adrian, but –'

'But what? I presume there's a leg or an arm wanting, or my

nose is gone, or my teeth have taken out a furlough,[122] or the hair of my head has changed colour, eh? Examine well, and see that your worser half is no worse than it was.'

'There's quite enough of you, such as you are,' said she. 'But what's the matter with you? Are you sure you've been to Waterloo Palace?'

'Where do you think I have been? Just let us hear. Keeping some assignation, I suppose? If I had, I would not have come home so soon; you may be pretty certain of that.'

'Then you have been only to Waterloo Palace?'

'I rather think so. I don't remember calling anywhere else.'

'And who was there? And why did you come home by yourself, without the carriage? Did the rest leave when you did?'

'I've got a head-ache, Mary.' This was a lie, told to awaken sympathy and elude further cross-examination.

'Have you, Adrian? Where?'

'I think I said I had a *head*-ache. Of course it would not be in my great toe.'

'And was that the reason you came away so soon?'

'Not exactly. I remembered I had a love-letter to write.'

This was pretty near the truth. The Duchess, however, believed the lie, and disregarded the truth. The matter was so artfully managed that jest was given for earnest and earnest for jest.[123]

'Does your head ache very much?' continued the Duchess.

'Deucedly.'

'Rest it on this cushion.'

'Hadn't I better go to bed, Mary?'

'Yes; and perhaps if I were to send for Sir Richard Warner – ? You may have taken cold.'

'Oh no, not to-night. We'll see to-morrow morning.'

'Your eyes don't look heavy, Adrian.'

'But they feel so, just like bullets.'

'What kind of a pain is it?'

'A shocking bad one.'

'Adrian, you are laughing. I saw you turn away your head and smile.'

His Grace smiled without turning away his head. That smile

confessed that his head-ache was a sham. The Duchess caught its meaning quickly. She caught also an expression in his face which indicated that he had changed his mood since he came in, and that he was not so anxious to get away from her as he had been. She had been standing before him, and she now took his hand. Mary looked prettier than any of her rivals ever did. She had finer features, a fairer skin, more eloquent eyes. No hand more soft and delicate had ever closed on the Duke's than that which was detaining him now. He forgot her superiority often, and preferred charms which were dim to hers. Still she retained the power of wakening him at intervals to a new consciousness of her price, and his Grace would every now and then discover with surprise that he had a treasure always in his arms that he loved better, a great deal, than the far-sought gems he dived amongst rocks so often to bring up.

'Come, all's right,' said his Grace, sitting down, and he mentally added, 'I shall have no time to write a letter to-night. It's perhaps as well let alone.' Dismissing Caroline Vernon with this thought, he allowed himself to be pleased by her elder and fairer sister, Mary.

The Duchess appeared to make no great bustle or exertion in effecting this. Nor did she use the least art, or *agacerie*, as the French call it, which indeed, she full well knew, with the subject she had to manage, would have instantly defeated its own end. She simply took a seat near the arm-chair into which his Grace had thrown himself, inclined herself a little towards him, and in a low, agreeable voice began to talk on miscellaneous subjects of a household and family nature. She had something to say about her children, and some advice to ask. She had also quietly to inquire into his Grace's opinions on one or two political points, and to communicate her own notions respecting divers matters under discussion – notions she never thought of imparting to any living ear except that of her honourable spouse, for in everything like gossip and chit-chat the Duchess of Zamorna is ordinarily the most reserved person imaginable.

To all this the Duke hearkened almost in silence, resting his elbow on the chair and his head on his hand, looking sometimes at the fire and sometimes at his wife. He seemed to take her talk as though it were a kind of pleasant air on a flute, and when she expressed herself with a certain grave, naïve simplicity which is a peculiar characteristic of her familiar conversation, which she seldom uses but can command at will, he did not smile, but gave her a glance which somehow said that those little original touches were his delight. The fact was, she could, if she liked, have spoken with much more depth and sense. She could have rounded her periods like a blue,[124] if she had had a mind, and discussed topics worthy of a member of parliament. But this suited better. Art was at the bottom of the thing, after all. It answered. His Grace set some store on her as she sat telling him every thing that came into her mind in a way which proved that he was the only person in whom she reposed this confidence, now and then, but very seldom, raising her eyes to his. And then her warm heart mastered her prudence, and a glow of extreme ardour confessed that he was so dear to her that she could not long feign indifference or even tranquillity while thus alone with him, close at his side.

Mr Wellesley could not help loving his Mary at such a moment, and telling her so, too, and, I daresay, asseverating with deep oaths that he had never loved any other lady half so well, nor ever seen a face that pleased his eye so much, or heard a voice that filled his ear with such sweetness. That night, she certainly recalled a wanderer. How long it will be before the wish to stray returns again is another thing. Probably, circumstances will decide this question. We shall see, if we wait patiently.

CHAP[TER] IV

Louisa Vernon, sixteen years ago, gave the name of Eden to her romantic cottage at Fidena; not, one would suppose, from any resemblance the place bears to the palmy shades of an Asiatic paradise, but rather because she there spent her happiest days in the society of her lover, Mr Percy, the Drover, and because that was the scene where she moved as a queen in the midst of a certain set, and enjoyed that homage and adulation whose recollection she to this day dwells on with fondness, and whose absence she pines over with regret.

It was not with her mother's feelings that Caroline Vernon viewed the place, when she arrived there late on a wet and windy November night, too dark to shew her the amphitheatre of highlands towards which her cottage looked, for the mountains had that evening muffled their brows in clouds, instead of crowning them 'with the wandering star'. Caroline, as may be supposed, cherished other feelings towards the place than her mother would have done; other than she herself might very probably have entertained had the circumstances attending her arrival there been somewhat different. Had the young lady, for instance, made it her resting-place in the course of a bridal tour, had she come to spend her honeymoon amid that amphitheatre of highlands towards which the cottage looked, she might have deigned to associate some high or soft sensations with the sight of those dim mountains – only the portals, as it were, to a far wilder region beyond, especially when, in an evening, 'they crowned their blue brows with the wandering star'.[125] But Miss Caroline had arrived on no bridal tour. She had brought no inexpressibly heroic-looking personage as her *camarade de voyage* and also her *camarade de vie*. She came a lonely exile, a persecuted and banished being, according to her own notions; and this was her Siberia, and not her Eden.[126]

Prejudiced thus, she would not for a moment relax in her detestation of the villa and the neighbourhood. Her heaven for that season, she had decided, was to be Verdopolis. There were her hopes of pleasure, there were all the human beings on earth in whom she felt any interest, there were those she wished to live for, to dress for, to smile for. When she put on a becoming frock here, what was the good of it? Were those great staring mountains any judge of dress? When she looked pretty, who praised her? When she came down of an evening to her sitting-room, what was there to laugh with her, to be merry with her? Nothing but arm-chairs and ottomans and a cottage-piano. No hope, here, of happy arrivals, of pleasant rencontres.

Then she thought, if she were but at that moment passing

through the folding door of a saloon at Ellrington House, perhaps just opposite to her, by the marble fire-place, there would be somebody standing that she should like to see, perhaps nobody else in the room. She had imagined such an interview. She had fancied a certain delightful excitement and surprise connected with the event. The gentleman would not know her at first; she would be so changed from what she was five months ago. She was not dressed like a child now, nor had she the air and tournure of a child. She would advance with much state; he would, perhaps, move to her slightly. She would give him a glance, just to be quite certain who it was. It would of course be him and no mistake; and he would have on a blue frock-coat and white irreproachables,[127] and would be very much bewhiskered and becurled as he used to be. Also, his nose would be in no wise diminished or impaired; it would exhibit the same aspect of a tower looking towards Lebanon[128] that it had always done. After a silent inspection of two or three minutes, he would begin to see daylight. And then came the recognition. There was a curious uncertainty about this scene in Miss Caroline's imagination. She did not know exactly what his Grace would do or how he would look. Perhaps he would only say, 'What, Miss Vernon, is it you?' and then shake hands. That, the young lady thought, would be sufficient if there was anybody else there; but if not – if she found his Grace in the saloon alone – such a cool acknowledgement of acquaintance-ship would never do. He must call her his little Caroline, and must bestow at least one kiss. Of course there was no harm in such a thing. Wasn't she his ward? And then there came the outline of an idea of standing on the rug talking to him, looking up sometimes to answer his questions about Paris, and being sensible how little she was near him. She hoped nobody would come into the room, for she remembered very well how much more freely her guardian used to talk to her when she took a walk with him alone than when there were other persons by.

So far Caroline would get in her reverie, and then something would occur to rouse her – perhaps the tinkling fall of a cinder from the grate. To speak emphatically, it was then dickey with all these dreams. She awoke, and found herself at Fidena, and knew that Verdopolis and Ellrington House were just three hundred miles off, and that she might wear her heart with wishes, but could neither return to them nor attain the hope of pleasure they held forth. At this crisis, Miss Vernon would sit down and cry; and when a cambric handkerchief had been thoroughly wet, she would cheer up again at the remembrance of the letter she had left at Wellesley House, and commence another reverie on the effects that profound lucubration was likely to produce. Though day after day elapsed and no answer was returned, and no messenger came riding in breathless haste, bearing a recall from banishment, she still refused to relinquish this last consolation. She could not believe that the Duke of Zamorna would forget her so utterly as to neglect all notice of her request. But three weeks elapsed, and it was scarcely possible to hope any longer. Her father had not written, for he was displeased with her. Her guardian had not written, for her sister's charms had succeeded in administering a soft opiate to his memory, which for the time lulled to sleep all recollection of every other female face and deadened every faithless wish to roam.

Then did Miss Caroline begin to perceive that she was despised and cast off, even as she herself hid away a dress that she was tired of, or a scarf that had become frayed and faded. In deep meditation, in the watches of the night, she discerned, at first by glimpses, and at last, clearly, that she was not of that importance to the Earl of Northangerland and the Duke of Zamorna which she had vainly supposed herself to be.

'I really think,' she said to herself doubtfully, 'that because I am not Papa's proper daughter, but only his natural daughter, and Mamma was never married to him, he does not care much about me. I suppose he is proud of Mary Henrietta, because she married so highly and is considered so beautiful and elegant. And the Duke of Zamorna just considers me as a child, whom he once took a little trouble with, in providing her with masters, and getting her taught to play a tune on the piano and to draw in French chalk and to speak with a correct Parisian accent and to read some hard, dry, stupid, intricate Italian poetry. And now that I'm off his hands, he makes no more account of me than of one of those ricketty little Flowers[129] whom he sometimes used to take on his knee a few minutes to please Lord Richton. Now, this will never do! I can't bear to be considered in this light. But how do I wish him to regard me? What terms should I like to be on with him? Really, I hardly know. Let me see. I suppose there's no harm in thinking about it at night to oneself, when one can't sleep, but is forced to lie awake in bed, looking into the dark and listening to the clock strike hour after hour.'

And having thus satisfied herself with the reflection that silence could have no listener and solitude no watcher, she turned her cheek to her pillow and, shrouding her eyes even from the dim outline of a large window which alone relieved the midnight gloom of her chamber, she would proceed thus with her thoughts:

'I do believe I like the Duke of Zamorna very much. I can't exactly tell why. He is not a good man, it seems, from what Mr Montmorency said, and he is not a particularly kind or cheerful man. When I think of it, there were scores of gentlemen at Paris who were a hundred times more merry and witty and complimentary than ever he was. Young Vaudeville and Troupeau said more civil things to me in half an hour than ever he did in all his life. But still, I like him so much, even when he is behaving in this shameful way. I think of him constantly; I thought of him all the time I was in France. I can't help it. I wonder whether – '

She paused in her mental soliloquy, raised her head and look[ed] forth into her chamber. All was dark and quiet. She turned again to her pillow. The question which she had thrust away returned, urging itself on her mind: 'I wonder whether I love him?'

'Oh, I do!' cried Caroline, starting up in fitful excitement. 'I do, and my heart will break.' 'I'm very wicked,' she thought, shrinking again under the clothes. 'Not so very,' suggested a consolatory reflection. 'I only love him in this way: I should like always to be with him and always to be doing something that would please him. I wish he had no wife, not because I want to be married to him, for that is absurd, but because if he were a bachelor he would have fewer to think about and then there would be more room for me. Mr Montmorency seemed to talk as if my sister Mary was to be pitied. Stuff! I can't imagine that. He must have loved her exceedingly when they were first married, at any rate, and even now she lives with him, and sees him, and talks to him. I should like a taste of her unhappiness, if she would be Caroline Vernon for a month and let me be Duchess of Zamorna.

'If there was such a thing as magic, and if his Grace could tell how much I care for him and could know how I am lying awake just now and wishing to see him, I wonder what he would think? Perhaps he would laugh at me, and say I was a fool. Oh, why didn't he answer my letter? What makes Papa so cruel? How dark it is! I wish it was morning. The clock is striking only one. I can't go to sleep; I'm so hot and so restless. I could bear now to see a spirit come to my bedside and ask me what I wanted. Wicked or not wicked, I would tell all, and beg it to give me the power to make the Duke of Zamorna like me better than ever he liked anybody in the world before, and I would ask it to unmarry him and change the Duchess into Miss Percy again, and he should forget her, and she should not be so pretty as she is, and I believe – yes, in spite of fate – he should love me and be married to me. Now then, I'm going mad. But there's the end of it.'

Such was Miss Vernon' midnight soliloquy, and such was the promising frame of mind into which she had worked herself by the time she had been a month at Fidena. Neglect did not subdue her spirit; it did not weaken her passions. It stung the first into such desperate action that she began to scorn prudence, and would have dared anything – reproach, disgrace, disaster – to gain what she longed for; and it worked the latter into such a ferment that she could rest neither day nor night. She could not eat, she could not sleep. She grew thin. She began to contemplate all sorts of strange, wild schemes. She would assume a disguise; she would make her way back to Verdopolis; she would go to Wellesley House and stand at the door and watch for the Duke of Zamorna to come out. She would go to him hungry, cold and weary, and ask for something. Perhaps he would discover who she was, and then, surely, he would at least pity her.[130] It would not be like him to turn coldly away from his little Caroline, whom he had kissed so kindly when they had last parted on that melancholy night at Hawkscliffe.

Having once got a notion like this into her head, Miss Vernon was sufficiently romantic, wilful and infatuated to have attempted to put it into execution. In fact she had resolved to do so. She had gone so far as to bribe her maid by a present of her watch – a splendid trinket set with diamonds – to procure her a suit of boy's clothes from a tailor's at Fidena. That watch might have been worth two hundred guineas; the value of the clothes was at the utmost six pounds. This was just a slight hereditary touch of lavish folly. With the attire thus dearly purchased she had determined to array herself on a certain day, slip out of the house unobserved, walk to Fidena four miles, take the coach there, and so make an easy transit to Verdopolis.

Such was the stage of mellow maturity at which her wise projects had arrived when, about ten o'clock one morning, a servant came into her breakfast-room and laid down on the table beside her coffee-cup a letter; the first, the only one she had received since her arrival at Eden Cottage. She took it up; she looked at the seal, the direction, the post-mark. The seal was only a wafer-stamp,[131] the direction, a scarcely legible scrawl, the post-mark, Freetown. Here was mystery. Miss Caroline was at fault. She could not divine who the letter came from. She looked at it long; she could not bear to break the seal. While there was doubt, there was hope. Certainty might crush that hope so rudely. At last, she summoned courage, broke it, opened the missive, and read:

> Woodhouse Cliff
> Freetown
> Nov[br] 29th

My dear little Caroline,

Miss Vernon read so far, and she let the letter fall on her knee and her head drop forward on to the table, and fairly burst into a flood of tears. This was odd, but romantic young ladies are said to be often unaccountable. Hastily wiping away the tears from her eyes, she snatched the letter up again, looked at it, cried once more, smiled in the midst of her weeping, rose, walked fast about the room, stopped by the window and, while the letter trembled in the hand that held it, read with dim eyes that still flowed over the singular epistle that follows.[132]

My dear little Caroline

Business has called me for a few days to Woodhouse Cliff, a place of Mr Warner's in the neighbourhood of Freetown. Freetown is a hundred miles nearer to Fidena than Verdopolis, and the circumstance of closer proximity has reminded me of a certain letter left some weeks ago on the library table at Wellesley House. I have not that letter now at hand, for as I recollect, I locked it up in the drawer of a cabinet in my dressing-room, intending to answer it speedily, but the tide changed, and all remembrance of the letter was swept away as it receded. Now, however, that same fickle tide is flowing back again and bringing the lost scroll with it.

No great injury has been done by this neglect on my part, because I could not fulfil the end for which your letter was written. You wished me to act as intercessor with your father, and persuade him, if possible, to change his mind as to your place of residence, for it seems Eden Cottage is not to your taste. On this point, I have no influence with him. Your father and I never converse about you, Caroline; it would not do at all. It was very well to consult him now and then about your lessons and your masters when you were a little girl. We did not disagree much on those subjects. But since you have begun to think yourself a woman, he and I have started on a different tack in our notions concerning you.

You know your father's plan. You must have had sufficient experience of it lately at Paris and now at Fidena. You don't know much about mine; and, in fact, it is as yet in a very un-finished state, scarcely fully comprehended even by its originator. I rather think, however, your own mind has anticipated some-thing of its outline. There were moments now and then at Hawks-cliffe when I could perceive that my ward would have been a constituent of her guardian's, in case the two schemes had been put to the decision of a vote, and her late letter bears evidence that the preference has not quite faded away. I must not omit to notice a saucy line or two concerning my character, indicating that you have either been hearing or reading some foolish nonsense on that head. Caroline, find no fault with it, until experience gives you reason so to do. Foolish little girl! What have you to complain of? Not much, I think.

And you wish to see your guardian again, do you? You would like another walk with him in the garden at Hawkscliffe? You wish to know if I have forgotten you? Partly. I remember something of a rather round face, with a dimpled, childish little chin, and something of a head very much embarrassed by its unreasonable quantity of black curls, seldom arranged in anything like Christian order. But that is all; the picture grows very dim. I suppose when I see you again there will be a change. You tell me you are grown more of a woman. Very likely. I wish you good-bye. If you are still unhappy at Eden Cottage, write and tell me so.

Yours etc.,

Zamorna

People in a state of great excitement sometimes take sudden resolves, and execute them successfully on the spur of the moment, which in their calmer and more sane moments they would neither have the phrenzy to conceive nor the courage and promptitude to put in practice – as somnambulists are said in sleep to cross broken bridges unhurt and to walk on the leads of houses in safety, where awake, the consciousness of all the horrors round them would occasion instant and inevitable destruction.[133] Miss Vernon, having read this letter, folded it up, and committed it to the bosom of her frock. She then, without standing more than half a minute to deliberate, left the room, walked quickly and quietly upstairs, took out a plain straw bonnnet and a large shawl, put them on, changed her thin satin slippers for a pair of walking shoes, unlocked a small drawer in her bureau, took therefrom a few sovereigns, slipped them into a little velvet bag, drew on her gloves, walked downstairs very lightly, very nimbly, crossed the hall, opened the front door, shut it quickly after her, passed up a plantation, out at a wicket gate, entered the high road, set her face towards Fidena with an intrepid, cheerful, unagitated air, kept the crown of the causeway, and in about an hour was at the door of the General Coach Office asking at what time a coach would start for Freetown. The answer was that there were conveyances in that direction almost every hour of the day, and that the Verdopolitan Mail was just going out. She took her place, paid her fare, entered the vehicle and, before any one at Eden Cottage was aware of her absence, was already a good stage on the road to Woodhouse Cliff.

Here was something more than the devil to pay![134] A voluntary elopement, without a companion, alone, entirely of her own free will, on the deliberation of a single moment! That letter had so crowded her brain with thoughts, with hopes, with recollections and anticipations, had so fired her heart with an unconquerable desire to reach and see the absent writer, that she could not have lived through another day of passive captivity. There was nothing for it but flight. The bird saw its cage open, beheld a free sky, remembered its own remote isle and grove and nest, heard in spirit a voice call it to come, felt its pinion nerved with impatient energy, launched into air, and was gone. Miss Vernon did not reflect, did not repent, did not fear. Through the whole day and night the journey lasted, she had no moment of misgiving. Some would have trembled from the novelty of their situation, some would have quailed under the reproaches of prudence, some would have sickened at the dread of a cold or displeased reception at their journey's end. None of these feelings daunted Caroline a whit. She had only one thought, one wish, one aim, one object – to leave Fidena, to reach Freetown. That done, hell was escaped and heaven attained. She could not see the blind folly of her undertaking. She had no sense of the erroneous nature of the step. Her will urged it; her will was her predominant quality and must be obeyed.

CHAP[TER] V

Mrs Warner, a quiet, nice little woman, as everybody knows, had just retired from the dinner-table to her own drawing-room, about six o'clock one winter's evening. It was nearly dark, very still. The first snow had begun to fall that afternoon, and the quiet walks about Woodhouse Cliff were seen from the long, low windows all white and wildered. Mrs Warner was without a companion. She had left her husband and her husband's prodigious guest in the dining-room, seated each with a glass before him and decanters and fruit on the table. She walked to the window, looked out a minute, saw that all was cold and cheerless, then came to the fireside, her silk dress rustling as she moved over the soft carpet, sank into a *bergère* (as the French call it), and sat alone and calm, her ear-rings only glittering and trembling, her even brow relieved with smooth, braided hair, the very seat of serene good temper.

Mrs Warner did not ring for candles. She expected her footman would bring them soon, and it was her custom to let him choose his own time for doing his work. An easier mistress never existed than she is. A tap was heard at the door.

'Come in,' said the lady, turning round. She thought the candles were come. She was mistaken.

Hartley, her footman, indeed appeared, with his silk stockings and his shoulder knots, but he bore no shining emblems[135] of the seven churches which are in Asia. The least thing out of the ordinary routine is a subject of gentle wonderment to Mrs Warner, so she said, 'What is the matter, Hartley?'

'Nothing, madam, only a post-chaise has just driven up to the door.'

'Well, what for?'

'Some one has arrived, madam.'

'Who is it, Hartley?'

'Indeed, madam, I don't know.'

'Have you shewn them into the dining-room?'

'No.'

'Where, then?'

'The young person is in the hall, madam.'

'Is it some one wanting Mr Warner, do you think?'

'No, madam, it is a young lady, who asked if the Duke of Zamorna were here.'

Mrs Warner opened her blue eyes a trifle wider.

'Indeed, Hartley! What must we do?'

'Why, I thought you had better see her first, madam. You might recognize her. I should think, from her air, she is a person of rank.'

'Well, but, Hartley, I have no business with it. His Grace might be displeased. It may be the Duchess, or some of those other ladies.'

What Mrs Warner meant by the term 'other ladies', I leave it to herself to explain. However, she looked vastly puzzled and put about.

'What had we best do?' she inquired again, appealing to Hartley for advice.

'I really think, madam, I had better shew her up here. You can then speak to her yourself, and inform his Grace of her arrival afterwards.'

'Well, Hartley, do as you please. I hope it's not the Duchess, that's all. If she's angry about anything, it will be very awkward. But she would never come in a post-chaise, that's one comfort.'

Hartley retired. Mrs Warner remained, fidgetting from her arm-chair to her work-table, putting on her gold thimble, taking it off, drawing her foot-stool to her feet, pushing it away. In spite of the post-chaise, she still entertained a lurking dread that the new-comer might be her mistress, the Duchess; and the Duchess was, in Mrs Warner's idea, a very awful, haughty, formidable little personage. There was something in the high, melancholy look of the royal lady's eyes which, when Mrs Warner met it, always made her feel uncomfortable and inspired with a wish to be anywhere rather than in her presence. Not that they had ever quarrelled, nothing of the kind, and her Grace was usually rather conspicuously civil to the lady of one of the most powerful men in Angria.[136] Still, the feeling of restraint did exist, and nothing could remove it.

Steps were heard upon the staircase. Hartley threw open the

panelled folding door of the drawing-room, ushered in the visitor, and closed it; first, however, depositing four thick and tall tapers of wax upon the table. Mrs Warner rose from her arm-chair, her heart fluttering a little, and her nice face and modest countenance exhibiting a trivial discomposure. The first glance at the stranger almost confirmed her worst fears. She saw a figure bearing a singular resemblance to the Duchess of Zamorna in air, size and general outline. A bonnet shaded the face, and a large shawl partially concealed the shape.

'I suppose you are Mrs Warner,' said a subdued voice, and the stranger came slowly forward.

'I am,' said that lady, quite reassured by the rather bashful tone in which those few words were spoken, and then, as a hesitating silence followed, she continued in her kind way, 'Can I do anything for you? Will you sit down?'

The young person took the seat which was offered her. It was opposite Mrs Warner, and the brilliant wax lights shone full in her face. All remains of apprehension were instantly dissipated. Here was nothing of the delicate, fair and pensive aspect characteristic of Mary Henrietta. Instead of the light shading of pale brown hair, there was a profusion of dark tresses crowded under the bonnet, instead of the thoughtful, poetic hazel eye, gazing rather than glancing, there was a full, black orb charged with fire, fitful, quick and restless. For the rest, the face had little bloom, but was youthful and interesting.

'You will be surprised to see me here,' said the stranger, after a pause, 'but I am come to see the Duke of Zamorna.'

This was said quite frankly. Mrs Warner was again relieved. She hoped there was nothing wrong, as the young lady seemed so little embarrassed in her announcement.

'You are acquainted with his Grace, are you?' she inquired.

'Oh, yes,' was the answer. 'I have known him for a great many years. But you will wonder who I am, Mrs Warner. My name is Caroline Vernon. I came by the coach to Freetown this afternoon. I was travelling all night.'

'Miss Vernon!' exclaimed Mrs Warner. 'What, the Earl of Northangerland's daughter! Oh, I am sorry I did not know you! You are quite welcome here. You should have sent up your name. I am afraid Hartley was cold and distant to you.'

'No, not at all. Besides, that does not much signify. I have got here at last. I hope the Duke of Zamorna is not gone away.'

'No, he is in the dining-room.'

'May I go to him directly? Do let me, Mrs Warner!'

Mrs Warner, however, perceiving that she had nothing to fear from the hauteur of the stranger, and experiencing likewise an inclination to exercise a sort of motherly or elder-sisterly kindness and protection to so artless a girl, thought proper to check this extreme impatience.

'No,' said she. 'You shall go upstairs first, and arrange your dress. You look harassed with travelling all night.'

Caroline glanced at a mirror over the mantle-piece. She saw that her hair was dishevelled, her face pale, and her dress disarranged.

'You are right, Mrs Warner. I will do as you wish me. May I have the help of your maid for five minutes?'

A ready assent was given to this request. Mrs Warner herself shewed Miss Vernon to an apartment upstairs, and placed at her command every requisite for enabling her to reappear in somewhat more creditable style. She then returned to her drawing-room, sat down again in her arm-chair, put her little round foot upon the foot-stool and, with her finger on her lip, began to reflect more at leisure upon this new occurrence. Not very quick in apprehension, she now began to perceive for the first time that there was something very odd in such a very young girl as Miss Vernon coming alone, unattended, in a hired conveyance to a strange house, to ask after the Duke of Zamorna. What could be the reason of it? Had she run away, unknown to her present protectors? It looked very like it. But what would the Duke say when he knew? She wished Howard would come in; she would speak to him about it. But she didn't like to go into the dining-room and call him out. Besides, she did not think there was the least harm in the matter. Miss Vernon was quite open and free. She made no mystery about the business. The Duke had been her guardian; it was natural she should come to see him. Only the oddity was that she should

be without carriage or servants. She said she had come by the
coach. Northangerland's daughter by the coach! Mrs Warner's
thinking faculties were suspended in amazement.

The necessity of pursuing this puzzling train of reflections
was precluded by Miss Vernon coming down. She entered the
room as cheerfully and easily as if Mrs Warner had been her
old friend and she an invited guest at a house perfectly familiar.

'Am I neat now?' were her first words, as she walked up to
her hostess. Mrs Warner could only answer in the affirmative,
for indeed there was nothing of the traveller's negligence now
remaining in the grey silk dress, the smooth curled hair, the
delicate silk stockings and slippers. Besides, now that the shawl
and bonnet were removed, a certain fine turn of form was
visible, which gave a peculiarly distinguished air to the young
stranger. A neck and shoulders elegantly designed, and arms
round, white and taper, fine ancles and small feet imparted
something classic, picturesque and highly patrician to her whole
mien and aspect. In fact, Caroline looked extremely lady-like;
and it was well she had that quality, for her stature and the
proportions of her size were on too limited a scale to admit of
more superb and imposing charms.

She sat down.

'Now I do want to see the Duke,' said she, smiling at Mrs
Warner.

'He will be here presently,' was the answer. 'He never sits
very long at table after dinner.'

'Don't tell him who I am when he comes in,' continued
Caroline. 'Let us see if he will know me. I don't think he will.'

'Then he does not at all expect you?' asked the hostess.

'Oh no! It was quite a thought of my own coming here. I told
nobody. You must know, Mrs Warner, Papa objected to my
staying in Verdopolis this season, because, I suppose, he thought
I had had enough gaiety in Paris, where he and I spent the
autumn and part of the summer. Well, as soon as ever town
began to fill, he sent me up beyond Fidena to Eden Cottage.
You've heard of the place, I daresay – a dismal solitary house
at the very foot of the highlands. I have lived there about a
month, and you know how stormy and wet it has been all the

time. Well, I got utterly tired at last, for I was determined not to care anything about the misty hills, though they looked strange enough sometimes. Yesterday morning, I thought I'd make a bold push for a change. Directly after breakfast, I set off for Fidena, with only my bonnet and shawl on, as if I were going to walk in the grounds. When I got there, I took the coach, and here I am.'

Caroline laughed. Mrs Warner laughed too. The nonchalant, off-hand way in which this story had been told her completely removed any little traces of suspicion that might still have been lurking in her usually credulous mind.

The reader by this time will have discerned that Miss Vernon was not quite so simple and communicative as she seemed. She knew how to give her own colouring to a statement without telling any absolute lies. The very warm sentiments which she indulged towards her guardian were, she flattered herself, known to no living thing but the heart that conceived and contained them. As she sat on a sofa near the fire, leaning her head against the wall so that the shade of a projecting mantle-piece almost concealed her face, she did not tell Mrs Warner that while she talked so lightly to her, her ear was on the stretch[137] to catch an approaching foot-step, her heart fluttering at every sound, her whole mind in a state of fluttering and throbbing excitement, longing, dreading for the door to open, eagerly anticipating the expected advent, yet fearfully shrinking from it with a contradictory mixture of feelings.

The time approached. A faint sound of folding doors unclosing was heard below. The grand staircase ascending to the drawing-room was again trodden, and the sound of voices echoed through the lobby and hall.

'They are here,' said Mrs Warner.

'Now, don't tell who I am,' returned Miss Vernon, shrinking closer into her dim corner.

'I will introduce you as my niece, as Lucy Grenville,' was the reply, and the young matron seemed beginning to enter into the spirit of the young maid's espièglerie.

'Your Grace is perfectly mistaken,' said a gentleman, opening the drawing-room door and permitting a taller man to pass. 'It is singular that reason does not convince your Grace of the erroneous nature of your opinion. Those houses, my lord Duke, will last for fifty years to come, with the expenditure of a mere trifle on repairs.'

'With the expenditure of two hundred pounds on the erection [of] new walls and roofs, plaster, painting and wood-work, they will last a few years longer, I make no doubt,' was the reply.

'Your Grace speaks ignorantly,' rejoined Warner Howard Warner Esqre. 'I tell you, those houses have stood in their present state for the last twenty years. I recollect them perfectly when I was only twelve years old, and they looked neither better nor worse than they do now.'

'They could not well look worse,' returned the taller man, walking up to the hearth and pushing away an ottoman with his foot, to make room for himself to stand on the rug.

'Are you talking about the Cliff Cottages still?' asked Mrs Warner, looking up.

'Yes, mistress, they have been the sole subject of conversation since you left the room. Your master has increased his estimate of their value every five minutes, and now at last he describes the rotten, roofless hovels as capital, well-built mansion-houses, with convenient out-houses, to wit a pig-stye each, and large gardens, *id est* a pitch of dunghill two yards square, suitable for the residence of a genteel family. And he tells me, if I would only buy them, I should be sure to make a rental of twenty pounds per annum from each. That won't wash,[138] will it, mistress?'

'What won't wash, please your Grace? The rug?'

'No, Mr Ferguson's pocket-handkerchief.'

'I don't know. Who is Mr Ferguson,[139] and what kind of handkerchiefs does he wear?'

'Very showy ones, manufactured at Blarney Mills.[140] Your master always buys of him.'

'Now your Grace is jesting. Howard does nothing of the kind. His pocket-handkerchiefs are all of cambric.'

A half-smothered laugh, excited no doubt by Mrs Warner's simplicity, was heard from the obscure sofa-corner. The Duke of Zamorna, whose back had been to the mantle-piece and whose elbow had been supported by the projecting slab thereof, quickly turned. So did Mr Warner. Both gentlemen saw a figure seated and reclining back, the face half hid by the shade and half by a slim and snowy hand, raised as if to screen the eyes from the flickering and dazzling fire-light.

The first notion that struck His Majesty of Angria was the striking similarity of that grey silk dress, that pretty form and tiny slender foot to something that might be a hundred miles off at Wellesley House. In fact, a vivid though vague recollection of his own Duchess was suggested to his mind by what he saw. In the surprise and conviction of the moment, he thought himself privileged to advance a good step nearer, and was about to stoop down, to remove the screening hand and make himself certain of the unknown's identity, when the sudden and confused recoil, the half-uttered interjection of alarm with which his advances were received, compelled him to pause. At the same time, Mrs Warner said hurriedly,

'My niece, Lucy Grenville.'

Mr Warner looked at his wife with astonishment. He knew she was not speaking the truth. She looked at him imploringly. The Duke of Zamorna laughed.

'I had almost made an awkward mistake,' said he. 'Upon my word, I took Miss Lucy Grenville for some one I had a right to come within a yard of without being reproved for impertinence. If the young lady had sat still half a minute longer, I believe I should have inflicted a kiss. Now I look better, though, I don't know. There's a considerable difference, as much as between a dark dahlia and a lily.'

His Grace paused, stood with his head turned fixedly towards Miss Grenville, scrutinized her features with royal bluntness, threw a transfixing glance at Mrs Warner, abruptly veered round, turning his back on both in a movement of much more singularity than politeness, erelong dropped into a chair, and crossing one leg over the other, turned to Mr Warner and asked him if he saw daylight. Mr Warner did not answer, for he was busily engaged in perusing a newspaper. The Duke then inclined his head towards Mrs Warner and, leaning half across her work-table, inquired in a tone of anxious interest 'whether she thought *this* would wash?'

Mrs Warner was too much puzzled to make a reply. But the young lady laughed again, fitfully and almost hysterically, as if there was some internal struggle between tears and laughter. Again she was honoured with a sharp, hasty survey from the King of Angria, to which succeeded a considerable interval of silence, broken at length by His Majesty remarking that he should like some coffee. Hartley was summoned and His Majesty was gratified. He took about six cups, observing, when he had finished, that he had much better have taken as many eight-penn'orths of brandy and water, and that if he had thought of it before, he would have asked for it. Mrs Warner offered to ring the bell and order a case-bottle and a tumbler then, but the Duke answered that he thought, on the whole, he had better go to bed, as it was about half-past eight o'clock, a healthy, primitive hour, which he should like to stick to. He took his candle, nodded to Mr Warner, shook hands with Mrs Warner, and, without looking at the niece, said in a measured, slow manner, as he walked out of the room,

'Good-night, Miss Lucy Grenville.'

CHAPTER VI

How Miss Vernon passed the night which succeeded this interview, the reader may amuse himself by conjecturing. I cannot tell him. I can only say that when she went up-stairs, she placed her candle on a dressing-table, sat down at the foot of the bed where she was to sleep, and there remained, perfectly mute and perfectly motionless, till her light was burnt out. She did not soliloquize, so what her thoughts were it would be difficult to say. Sometimes she sighed, sometimes tears gathered in her eyes, hung a little while on her long eye-lashes, and then dropped to her lap, but there was no sobbing, no strong emotion of any kind. I should say, judging from her aspect, that her thoughts ran all on doubt, disappointment and suspense, but not on desperation or despair. After the candle had flickered a long time, it at last sank into darkness. Miss Vernon lifted up her head, which had been bent all the while, saw the vital spark lying on the table before her, rose and slowly undressed. She might have had a peculiar penchant for going to bed in the dark when anything happened to disturb her. If you recollect, reader, she did so before, the night her father had announced his resolution to send her to Eden Cottage.

The next morning, she woke late, for she had not fallen asleep before the dawn began to break. When she came down, she found that the Duke and Mr Warner were gone out to take a survey of the disputed Cliff Cottages – two superannuated old hovels, by the bye, fit habitations for neither man nor beast. They had taken with them a stone-mason and an architect, also a brace of guns, two brace of pointers and a game-keeper. The probability, therefore, was that they would not be back before night-fall. When Miss Vernon heard that, her heart was so bitter she could have laid her head on her hand and fairly cried like a child. If the Duke had recognized her – and she believed he had – what contemptuous negligence or cold displeasure his conduct evinced!

However, on second thoughts, she scorned to cry. She'd bear it all. At the worst, she could take the coach again, and return to that dungeon at Fidena. And what could Zamorna have to be displeased at? He did not know that she had wished her sister dead and herself his wife.[141] He did not know the restless, devouring feeling she had when she thought of him. Who could guess that she loved that powerful and austere Zamorna when, as she flattered herself, neither look nor word nor gesture had ever betrayed that frantic dream? Could he be aware of it, when she had not fully learnt it herself till she was parted from him by mountain, valley and wave? Impossible, and since he was so cold, so regardless, she would crush the feeling and never tell that it had existed. She did not want him to love her in return. No, no, that would be wicked. She only wanted him to be kind, to think well of her, to like to have her with him, nothing more. Unless, indeed, the Duchess of Zamorna were to happen to die, and then – but she would drop this foolery, master it entirely, pretend to be in excellent spirits, and if the Duke should really

TALES OF ANGRIA

find her out, affect to treat the whole transaction as a joke, a sort of eccentric adventure undertaken for the fun of the thing.

Miss Vernon kept her resolution. She drest her face in smiles, and spent the whole day merrily and sociably with Mrs Warner. Its hours passed slowly to her, and she still, in spite of herself, kept looking at the window, and listening to every movement in the hall. As evening and darkness drew on, she waxed restless and impatient. When it was time to dress, she arranged her hair and selected her ornaments with a care she could hardly account for herself.

Let us now suppose it to be eight o'clock. The absentees returned an hour since and are now in the drawing-room. But Caroline is not with them; she has not yet seen them. For some cause or other, she has preferred retiring to this large library in another wing of the house. She is sitting moping by the hearth like Cinderella; she has rung for no candles; the large fire alone gives a red lustre and quivering shadows upon the books, the ceiling, the carpet. Caroline is so still that a little mouse, mistaking her no doubt for an image,[142] is gliding unstartled over the rug and around her feet. On a sudden, the creature takes alarm, makes a dart, and vanishes under the brass fender. Has it heard a noise? There is nothing stirring. Yes, something moves somewhere in this wing, which was before so perfectly still.

While Miss Vernon listened, yet doubtful whether she had really heard or only fancied the remote sound of a step, the door of her retreat was actually opened, and a second person entered its precincts. The Duke of Zamorna came straying listlessly in, as if he had found his way there by chance. Miss Vernon looked up, recognized the tall figure and overbearing build, and felt that now, at last, the crisis was come. Her feelings were instantly wound to their highest pitch; but the first word brought them down to a more ordinary tone.

'Well, Miss Grenville, good evening.'

Caroline, quivering in every nerve, rose from her seat and answered,

'Good evening, my lord Duke.'

'Sit down,' said he, 'and allow me to take a chair near you.'

She sat down. She felt very queer when Zamorna drew a seat close to hers and coolly installed himself beside her. Mr Wellesley was attired in evening dress, with something more of brilliancy and show than has been usual with him of late. He wore a star on his left breast, and diamonds on his fingers. His complexion was coloured with exercise, and his hair curled round his forehead with a gloss and profusion highly characteristic of the most consummate coxcomb going.

'You and I,' continued His Sublimity, 'seemed disposed to form a separate party of ourselves to-night, I think, Miss Lucy. We have levanted from the drawing-room and taken up our quarters elsewhere. I hope, by the bye, my presence is no restraint. You do not feel shy and strange with me, do you?'

'I don't feel strange,' answered Miss Vernon, 'but rather shy just at the first. I presume – '

'Well, a better acquaintance will wear that off. In the meantime, if you have no objection, I will stir the fire, and then we shall see each other better.'

His Grace stooped, took the poker, woke up the red and glowing mass, and elicited a broad blaze, which flashed full on his companion's face and figure. He looked, first, with a smile, but gradually with a more earnest expression. He turned away and was silent. Caroline waited, anxious, trembling, with difficulty holding in the feelings which swelled her heart. Again the Duke looked at her, and drew a little nearer.

'He is not angry,' thought Miss Vernon. 'When will he speak and call me Caroline?'

She looked up at him. He smiled. She approached, still seeking in his eye for a welcome. Her hand was near his. He took it, pressed it a little.

'Are you angry?' asked Miss Vernon in a low, sweet voice. She looked beautiful, her eye bright and glowing, her cheek flushed, and her dark, wavy hair resting lightly upon it like a cloud. Expectant, impatient, she still approached the silent Duke, till her face almost touched his.

This passive stoicism on his part could not last long. It must bring a reaction. It did. Before she could catch the lightning change in face and eye, the rush of blood to the cheek, she found herself in his arms. He strained her to his heart a moment, kissed her forehead, and instantly released her.

'I thought I would not do that,' said Zamorna, rising and walking through the room. 'But what's the use of resolution? A man is not exactly a statue.' Three turns through the apartment restored him to his self-command. He came back to the hearth.

'Caroline! Caroline!' said he, shaking his head as he bent over her. 'How is this? What am I to say about it?'

'You really know me, do you?' answered Miss Vernon, evading her guardian's words.

'I think I do,' said he. 'But what brought you from Fidena? Have you run away?'

'Yes,' was the reply.

'And where are you running to?'

'Nowhere,' said Caroline. 'I have got as far as I wished to go. Didn't you tell me in your letter that if I was still unhappy at Fidena Cottage, I was to write and tell you so? I thought I had better come.'

'But I am not going to stay at Woodhouse Cliff, Caroline. I must leave to-morrow.'

'And will you leave me behind you?'

'God bless me!' ejaculated Mr Wellesley, hastily raising himself from his stooping attitude, and starting back as if a wasp had stung his lip. He stood a yard off, looking at Miss Vernon, with his whole face fixed by the same expression that had flashed over it before. 'Where must I take you, Caroline?' he asked.

'Anywhere.'

'But I am to return to Verdopolis, to Wellesley House. It would not do to take you there. You would hardly meet with a welcome.'

'The Duchess would not be glad to see me, I suppose,' said Miss Vernon.

'No, she would not,' answered the Duke, with a kind of brief laugh.

'And why should she not?' inquired the young lady. 'I am her sister. Papa is as much my father as he is hers. But I believe she would be jealous of anybody liking your Grace besides herself.'

'Aye, and of my Grace liking anybody, too, Caroline.'

This was a hint which Miss Vernon could not understand. These words, and the pointed emphasis with which they were uttered, broke down the guard of her simplicity and discomfited her self-possession. They told her that Zamorna had ceased to regard her as a child; they intimated that he looked upon her with different eyes to what he had done, and considered her attachment to him as liable to another interpretation than the mere fondness of a ward for her guardian. Her secret seemed to be discovered. She was struck with an agony of shame. Her face burned; her eyes fell; she dared look at Zamorna no more.

And now the genuine character of Arthur Augustus Adrian Wellesley began to work. In this crisis, Lord Douro stood true to his old name and nature. Zamorna did not deny, by one noble and moral act, the character he has earned by a hundred infamous ones. Hitherto we have seen him rather as restraining his passions than yielding to them; he has stood before us rather as a Mentor than a misleader; but he is going to lay down the last garment of light[143] and be himself entirely. In Miss Vernon's present mood, burning and trembling with confusion, remorse, apprehension, he might by a single word have persuaded her to go back to Eden Cottage. She did not yet know that he reciprocated her wild, frantic attachment. He might have buried that secret, have treated her with an austere gentleness he well knew how to assume, and crushed in time the poison flowers of a passion whose fruit, if it reached maturity, would be crime and anguish. Such a line of conduct might be trodden by the noble and faithful Fidena. It lies in his ordinary path of life. He seldom sacrifices another human being's life and fame on the altar of his own vices. But the selfish Zamorna cannot emulate such a deed. He has too little of the moral Greatheart[144] in his nature. It is his creed that all things bright and fair live for him; by him they are to be gathered and worn, as the flowers of his laurel crown. The green leaves are victory in battle; they never fade. The roses are conquests in love; they decay and drop off. Fresh ones blow round him, are plucked and woven with the withered

stems of their predecessors. Such a wreath he deems a glory
about his temples. He may in the end find it rather like the
snaky fillet which compressed Calchas's brows, steeped in blue
venom.[145]

The Duke reseated himself at Miss Vernon's side.

'Caroline,' said he, desiring by that word to recall her attention, which was wandering wide in the distressful paroxysm of
shame that overwhelmed her. He knew how to give a tone, an
accent, to that single sound which should produce ample effect.
It expressed a kind of pity. There was something protecting and
sheltering about it, as if he were calling her home.

She turned. The acute pang which tortured her heart and
tightened her breath dissolved into sorrow. A gush of tears
relieved her.

'Now then,' said Zamorna, when he had allowed her to weep
a while in silence, 'the shower is over. Smile at me again, my
little dove. What was the reason of that distress? Do you think
I don't care for you, Caroline?'

'You despise me. You know I am a fool.'

'Do I?' said he, quietly; then, after a pause, he went on. 'I
like to look at your dark eyes and pretty face.'

Miss Vernon started and deeply coloured. Never before had
Zamorna called her face pretty.

'Yes,' said he. 'It is exquisitely pretty, and those soft features
and dusky curls are beyond the imitation of a pencil. You blush
because I praise you. Did you never guess before that I took a
pleasure in watching you, in holding your little hand, and in
playing with your simplicity, which has sported many a time,
Caroline, on the brink of an abyss you never thought of?'

Miss Vernon sat speechless. She darkly saw, or rather felt,
the end to which all this tended, but all was fever and delirium
round her. The Duke spoke again, in a single blunt and almost
coarse sentence compressing what yet remained to be said.

'If I were a bearded Turk, Caroline, I would take you to my
harem.'[146]

His deep voice as he uttered this, his high featured face and
dark large eye, burning bright with a spark from the depths of
Gehenna, struck Caroline Vernon with a thrill of nameless

dread. Here he was, the man that Montmorency had described to her! All at once she knew him. Her guardian was gone; something terrible sat in his place. The fire in the grate was sunk down without a blaze, the silent, lonely library, so far away from the inhabited part of the house, was gathering a deeper shade in all its Gothic recesses.[147] She grew faint with dread. She dared not stir, from a vague fear of being arrested by the powerful arm flung over the back of her chair. At last, through the long and profound silence, a low whisper stole from her lips.

'May I go away?'

No answer. She attempted to rise. This movement produced the effect she had feared. The arm closed round her. Miss Vernon could not resist its strength; a piteous upward look was her only appeal. He, Satan's eldest son, smiled at this mute prayer.

'She trembles with terror,' said he, speaking to himself. 'Her face has turned pale as marble within the last minute or two. How did I alarm her? Caroline, do you know me? You look as if your mind wandered.'

'You are Zamorna,' replied Caroline. 'But let me go.'

'Not for a diadem, not for a Krooman's head, not for every inch of land the Joliba[148] waters.'

'Oh, what must I do?' exclaimed Miss Vernon.

'*Crede Zamorna!*'[149] was the answer. 'Trust me, Caroline, you shall never want a refuge. I said I could not take you to Wellesley House, but I can take you elsewhere. I have a little retreat, my fairy, somewhere near the heart of my own kingdom, Angria, sheltered by Ingleside and hidden in a wood. It is a plain old house outside, but it has rooms within as splendid as any saloon in Victoria Square. You shall live there. Nobody will ever reach it to disturb you. It lies on the verge of moors; there are only a few scattered cottages and a little church for many miles round. It is not known to be my property. I call it my treasure-house, and what I deposit there has always hitherto been safe, at least' (he added in a lower tone) 'from human vigilance and living force. There are some things which even I cannot defy. I thought so that summer afternoon when I came to Scar House and found a King and Conqueror had been before me,[150] to whom I was no rival but a trampled slave.'

The gloom of Zamorna's look, as he uttered these words, told a tale of what was passing in his heart. What vision had arisen before him, which suggested such a sentence at such a moment, it matters little to know. However dark it might have been, it did not linger long.[151] He smiled as Caroline looked at him with mixed wonder and fear. His face changed to an expression of tenderness more dangerous than the fiery excitement which had startled her before. He caressed her fondly, and lifted with his fingers the heavy curls which were lying on her neck. Caroline began to feel a new impression. She no longer wished to leave him; she clung to his side. Infatuation was stealing over her. The thought of separation and a return to Eden was dreadful. The man beside her was her guardian again, but he was also Mr Montmorency's Duke of Zamorna.[152] She feared; she loved. Passion tempted, conscience warned her; but, in a mind like Miss Vernon's, conscience was feeble opposed to passion.[153] Its whispers grew faint, and were at last silenced; and when Zamorna kissed her and said, in that voice of fatal sweetness which has instilled venom into many a heart, 'Will you go with me to-morrow, Caroline?', she looked up in his face with a kind of wild, devoted enthusiasm and answered, 'Yes.'

[gap in ms.]

The Duke of Zamorna left Woodhouse Cliff on Friday the 7th of Dec^br, next morning, and was precisely seven days in performing the distance between that place and Verdopolis. At least, seven days had elapsed between his departure from Mr Warner's and his arrival at Wellesley House. It was a cold day when he came, and that might possibly be the reason that he looked pale and stern as he got out of his carriage, mounted the kingly steps of his mansion, and entered under its roof. He was necessitated to meet his wife after so long a separation, and it was a sight to see their interview. He took little pains to look at her kindly. His manner was sour and impatient, and the Duchess, after the first look, solicited no fonder embrace.

She receded, even, from the frozen kiss he offered her, dropped his hand, and, after searching his face and reading the meaning of that pallid, harassed aspect, told him – not by words, but by a bitter smile – that he did not deceive her, and turned away with a quivering lip, with all the indignation, the burning pride, the heart-struck anguish stamped on her face that those beautiful features could express. She left him, and went to her room, which she did not leave for many a day afterwards.

The Duke of Zamorna seemed to have returned in a business mood. He had a smile for no one. When Lord Richton called to pay his respects, the Duke glanced at the card which he sent up, threw it on the table, and growled like a tiger, 'Not at home.' He received only his ministers; he discussed only matters of state. When their business was done he dismissed them. No hour of relaxation followed the hour of labour. He was as scowling at the end of the council as he was at the beginning.

Enara was with him one night and, in his blunt way, had just been telling him a piece of his mind, and intimating that he was sure all that blackening and sulking was not for nothing, and that he had as certainly been in some hideous mess as he now wore a head. The answer to this was a recommendation to Enara to go to hell. Henri was tasting a glass of spirits and water preparatory to making a reply, when a third person walked into the apartment and, advancing up to him, said,

'I'll thank you to leave the room, sir.'

The Colonel of Bloodhounds looked up fierce at this address but, having discerned from whom it proceeded, he merely replied,

'Very well, my lord; but, with your leave, I'll empty this tumbler of brandy and water first. Here's to the King's health and better temper.' He drained his glass, set it down, and marched away.

The newcomer, judging from his look, seemed likely to give the Duke of Zamorna his match in the matter of temper. One remarkable thing about his appearance was that, though in the presence of a crowned king, he wore a hat upon his head which he never lifted a hand to remove. The face under that hat was like a sheet, it was so white; and like a hanged malefactor's, it was so livid. He could not be said to frown, as his features were quiet, but his eye was petrifying. It had that in its light irid which passes shew.[154] This gentleman took his station facing the Duke of Zamorna and, when Lord Etrei had left the room, he said, in a voice such as people use when they arc coming instantly to the point and will not soften their demand a jot,

'Tell me what you have done with her!'

The Duke of Zamorna's conscience, a vessel of a thousand tons burthen, brought up a cargo of blood to his face. His nostrils opened. His head was as high, his chest as full, and his attitude standing by the table as bold as if from the ramparts of Gazemba he was watching Arundel's[155] horsemen scouring the wilderness.

'What do you mean?' he asked.

'Where is Caroline Vernon?' said the same voice of fury.

'I have not got her.'

'And you have never had her, I suppose? And you will dare to tell me that lie?'

'I have never had her.'

'She is not in your hands now?'

'She is not.'

'By G—d, I know differently, sir. I know you lie.'

'You know nothing about it.'

'Give her up, Zamorna.'

'I cannot give up what I have not got.'

'Say that again.'

'I do.'

'Repeat the lie.'

'I will.'

'Take that, miscreant.'

Lord Northangerland snatched something from his breast. It was a pistol. He did not draw the trigger, but he dashed the butt end viciously at his son-in-law's mouth. In an instant, his lips were crimson with gore. If his teeth had not been fastened into their sockets like soldered iron, he would have been forced to spit them out with the blood with which his mouth filled and ran over. He said nothing at all to this compliment, but only leant his head over the fire and spat into the ashes, and then wiped his mouth with a white handkerchief which in five minutes was one red stain. I suppose this moderation resulted from the deep conviction that the punishment he got was only a millionth part of what he deserved.

'Where is she?' resumed the excited Percy.

'I'll *never* tell you.'

'Will you keep her from me?'

'I'll do my best.'

'Will you dare to visit her?'

'As often as I can snatch a moment from the world to give to her.'

'You say that to my face?'

'I'd say it to the D—l's face.'[156]

A little pause intervened, in which Northangerland surveyed the Duke and the Duke went on wiping his bloody mouth.

'I came here to know where you have taken that girl,' resumed Percy. 'I mean to be satisfied. I mean to have her back. You shall not keep her. The last thing I had in the world is not to be yielded to you, you brutal, insatiable villain!'

'Am I worse than you, Percy?'

'Do you taunt me? You are worse. I never was a callous brute.'

'And who says I am a brute? Does Caroline? Does Mary?'

'How dare you join those names together? How dare you utter them in the same breath, as if both my daughters were your purchased slaves? You coarse voluptuary, filthier than that filthy Jordan!'

'I am glad it is you who give me this character, and not Miss Vernon, or her sister.'

'Arthur Wellesley, you had better not unite those two names again. If you do, neither of them shall ever see you more, except dead.'

'Will you shoot me?'

'I will.'

Another pause followed, which Percy again broke.

'In what part of Angria have you put Caroline Vernon? For I know you took her to Angria.'

'I placed her where she is safe and happy. I should say no

more if my hand were thrust into that fire. And you had better
leave the matter where it is, for you cannot undo what is done.'

Northangerland's wild blue eye dilated into wilder hatred
and fury.

He said, raising his hand and striking it on the table,

'I wish there was a hell for your sake! I wish –'

The sentence broke off, and was resumed, as if his agitation
shortened his breath too much to allow him to proceed far
without drawing it afresh. 'I wish you might now be withered
hand and foot and struck into a paralytic heap –' Again it
broke. 'What are you? You have pressed this hand and said
you cared for me. You have listened to all I had to tell you:
what I am, how I have lived, and what I have suffered. You
have assumed enthusiasm, blushed almost like a woman, and
even wearied me out with your boyish ardour.[157] I let you have
Mary, and you know what a curse you have been to her,
disquieting her life with your constant treacheries and your
alternations of frost and fire. I have let you go on with little
interference, though I have wished you dead, many a time,
when I have seen her pale harassed look, knowing how different
she was before she knew you and was subjected to all your
monstrous tyrannies and tantalizations,[158] your desertion that
broke her spirit, and your returns that kept her lingering on
with just the shadow of a hope to look to.'

'Gross exaggeration!' exclaimed Zamorna with vehemence.
'When did I ever tyrannize over Mary? Ask herself, ask her
at this moment, when she is as much exasperated against me
as ever she was in her life. Tell her to leave me. She will not
speak to me or look at me – but see what her answer would be
to that!'

'Will you be silent and hear me out?' returned Percy. 'I have
not finished the detail of your friendship. That Hebrew imposter
Nathan tells David, the man after God's own heart, a certain
parable of an ewe lamb and applies it to his own righteous
deeds. You have learnt the chapter by heart, I think, and fructified by it.[159] I gave you everything but Caroline. You knew my
feelings to her. You know how I reckoned on her as my last
and only comfort. And what have you done? She is destroyed;

she can never hold her head up again. She is nothing to me, but she shall not be left in your hands.'

'You cannot take her from me, and if you could, how would you prevent her return? She would either die or come back to me now. And remember, sir, if I had been a Percy instead of a Wellesley, I should not have carried her away, and given her a home to hide her from scorn and shelter her from insult. I should have left her forsaken at Fidena, to die there delirious in an inn, as Harriet O'Connor[160] did.'

'I have my last word to give you now,' said Percy. 'You shall be brought into the courts of law for this very deed. I care nothing for exposure. I will hire Hector Montmorency to be my counsel. I will furnish him with ample evidence of all the atrocities of your character, which, handled as he will delight to handle it, will make the flesh quiver on your bones with agony. I will hire half the press and fill the newspapers with libels on you and your court, which shall transform all your fools of followers into jealous enemies. I will not stick at a lie. Montmorency shall indite the paragraphs, in order that they many be pungent enough. He will not scruple involving a few dozens of court ladies in the ruin that is to be hurled on you. He shall be directed to spare none. Your cabinet shall be a herd of horned cattle.[161] The public mind shall be poisoned against you. A glorious triumph shall be given to your political enemies. Before you die, you shall curse the day that you robbed me of my daughter.'

So spoke Northangerland. His son answered with a smile,

'The ship is worthless that will not live through a storm.'

'Storm!' rejoined the Earl. 'This is no storm, but fire in the hold – a lighted candle hurled into your magazine! See if it will fall like a rain-drop!'

The Duke was still unquelled. He answered as he turned and walked slowly through the room,

'In nature there is no such thing as annihilation. Blow me up, and I shall live again.'[162]

'You need not talk this bombast to me,' said Percy. 'Keep it, to meet Montmorency with, when he makes you the target of *his* shafts; keep it, to answer Warner and Thornton and

Castlereagh, when their challenges come pouring on you like chain-shot.'

His Grace pursued his walk, and said in an undertone,

> 'Moored in the rifted rock,
> Proof to the tempest shock,
> Firmer he roots him the ruder it blow.'[163]

THE ROE HEAD JOURNAL
FRAGMENTS

Introductory Note

In July 1835, at the age of nineteen, Charlotte Brontë went as an assistant teacher to Miss Wooler's school for young ladies, at Roe Head, near Mirfield, about twenty miles from Haworth, at which she had been a pupil three years earlier. She was to teach at the school until 22 December 1838. The six fragments that follow were written during this period, in 1836 and 1837. They have become known as the Roe Head Journal, but they do not constitute a journal in the usual sense of the word. They are not entries in a single notebook, but a series of disconnected fragments, scribbled on spare scraps of paper in a miniscule uneven print. Although they are frankly expressive of passionate private feeling – the writer's irritation at the 'ongoings' that surround her, her frustration with the duties she is expected to perform, her longing, perhaps above all, for time and space in which to write – they are not simply confessional. For they also contain a series of sharply realized images of scenes and characters from the totally imaginary world of Angria.

Roe Head School was quite unlike the Clergy Daughters' School at Cowan Bridge, where the Brontë sisters had been sent as young children, and which Charlotte was to portray as Lowood Institution in *Jane Eyre*. It occupied an elegant, light and airy house, commanding open views of a prosperous, populous district. There were rarely more than eight or nine pupils, daughters of well-to-do families in the area, who learned geography, history, French, English grammar and lady-like 'accomplishments' – drawing, music, elocution, letter-writing. Such discipline as there was was kindly. Margaret Wooler, the headmistress, who was assisted in teaching by her sisters, was intelligent, well educated, and sensitive to her students' needs. 'Since I must enter a situation, "my lines have fallen in pleasant places",' Charlotte wrote to her friend Ellen Nussey; certainly, this employment was preferable to the 'one or two proposals of Private Governesship' which she had recently received.[1] She was not entirely without congenial companionship. Ellen and her other close school-friend Mary Taylor lived nearby and could visit and be visited. Her sister Emily accompanied her to the school, having been offered free schooling in part payment for Charlotte's services; when Emily returned, ill with homesickness, to Haworth in October 1835 she was replaced by the youngest Brontë sister, Anne. There was also the kindly Miss Wooler, with whom, after some disagreements, Charlotte forged an enduring friendship. Yet her time at the school was difficult.

Here, in her first employment, she confronted the limited opportunities open to women in early nineteenth-century England. The work seemed to her uncongenial and monotonous: 'nothing but teach, teach, teach, from morning till night'.[2] She missed her absent family. She missed the relative freedom of life at home in Haworth, where household duties left time for writing, music and drawing, and extensive walks on the moors. Above all, as these journal fragments reveal, she missed the imaginary world of Angria, which she and her brother Branwell had been constructing together for some time. The routine of Roe Head School, the lack of privacy there, gave her little opportunity to think of it. It was only secretly and in snatches that she could allow her imagination to dwell on its scenes and characters – more vivid and more compelling than those amongst which she lived. 'If you knew my thoughts; the dreams that absorb me; and the fiery imagination that at times eats me up and makes me feel Society as it is, wretchedly insipid, you would pity me and I dare say despise me,' she wrote, in half-confession, to her faithful friend Ellen Nussey; but she did not disclose the nature of those absorbing 'thoughts' and 'dreams'.[3]

Twenty miles away at Haworth, her collaborator Branwell was writing prolifically of Angria.[4] In a manuscript completed on 25 July 1835, just before Charlotte departed for Roe Head, he had described the 'stormy and ominous' scenes in the Verdo-politan parliament which were eventually to lead to war.[5] Throughout the following autumn – Charlotte's first term as a teacher – there was, he tells, 'incessant agitation' in Africa. When his sister came home for the Christmas holidays, he brought events to a climax, recording the expulsion of Angria from the Verdopolitan Union, the Angrians' desperate battles for survival, and the fall of 'youthful magnificent Adrianopolis'.[6] No Angrian manuscripts written by Charlotte during this Christmas period survive. Yet she too was still absorbed in that shared 'bright darling dream'. On the same day as Angria was expelled from the Verdopolitan Union, she wrote a long, impassioned poem celebrating its continuing power.[7] And the first of the journal fragments reprinted in this volume, written apparently shortly after her return to Roe Head, speaks in the language of biblical prophecy of the fall of Adrianopolis.

Throughout the two years that followed, the crisis in Angria unfolded, as Charlotte continued to labour at Roe Head. Zamorna and Northangerland at first combined against their enemies; then, largely owing to Northangerland's treacherous ambition, their alliance fell apart and Angria was devastated by civil war. This story (whose main events are set out in the Chronology of Angria in this volume) is recounted in detail in Branwell's manuscripts of this time. Charlotte, however, could contribute only during holidays at home. The letters she received from her brother offered tantalizing glimpses of a world in the shaping of which she could no longer play much part. Whereas he was writing extensive 'histories' that chron-icled the developing 'Angrian saga', she, stuck in the school-room, could not, she lamented, 'enter into a continued narrative'. Yet these fragments are not merely records of the young Charlotte Brontë's frustration. In their 'vivid realis-ations' of characters and vignettes from Angria they evince an imaginative process that seems very different from her brother's: a constant, creative tension between the development of 'continued narrative' and the rich particularity of sharply visualized 'scene'. In this they point suggestively forward, toward the distinctive method of her final Angrian tales.

NOTES

1. Brontë to Ellen Nussey, 2 July 1835, Margaret Smith, ed., *The Letters of Charlotte Brontë* (3 vols.; Oxford: Clarendon Press, 1995–2004), 1, p. 140.
2. Brontë to Ellen Nussey [early June, 1837], Smith, ed., *Letters*, 1, p. 171.
3. Brontë to Ellen Nussey 10 May 1836, Smith, ed., *Letters*, 1, p. 144.
4. Branwell seems to have been living in Haworth throughout 1836 and 1837, possibly trying to establish himself as a portrait painter; see Juliet Barker, *The Brontës* (London: Weidenfeld & Nicolson, 1994), pp. 226–34, 248.
5. *[Angria and the Angrians] I(e)*, Victor A. Neufeldt, ed., *The Works of Patrick Branwell Brontë*, 3 vols. (New York and London: Garland Publishing, 1999), 2, pp. 400–411.
6. *[Angria and the Angrians] I(e)*, pp. 464, 469.
7. 'We wove a web in childhood', Juliet Barker, ed., *Charlotte Brontë: Juvenilia 1829–1835* (Harmondsworth: Penguin, 1996), pp. 262–9.

[a] Well here I am at Roe Head,[1] it is seven o'clock at night the young ladies are all at their lessons the school-room is quiet the fire is low. a stormy day is at this moment passing off in a murmuring and bleak night. I now assume my own thoughts my mind relaxes from the stretch on which it has been for the last twelve hours & falls back onto the rest which no-body in this house knows of but myself. I now after a day's weary wandering return to the ark which for me floats alone on the face of this world's desolate & boundless deluge[2] it is strange. I cannot get used to the ongoings that surround me. I fulfil my duties strictly & well, I ~~not~~ so to speak if the illustration be not profane as God was not in the wind nor the fire nor the earth-quake so neither is my heart in the task, ~~that~~ the theme or the exercise. it is the still small voice[3] alone that comes to me at eventide, that which like a breeze with a voice in it over the deeply blue hills & out of the now leafless forests & from the cities on distant river banks it is ~~that now calling~~ of a far & bright continent.[4] It is that which takes my spirit & engrosses all my living feelings, all my energies which are not merely mechanical & like Haworth & home wakes sensations which lie dormant elsewhere. last night I did indeed ~~hav~~ lean upon the thunder-wakening wings of such a stormy blast as I have seldom heard blow & it whirled me away like heath in the wilderness[5] for five seconds of ecstasy – and as I sat by myself in the dining-room while all the rest were at tea the trance seemed to descend on a sudden & verily this foot trod the war-shaken

shores of the Calabar & these ~~light~~ eyes saw the defiled &
violated Adrianopolis shedding its lights on the river from lat-
tices whence the invader looked out & was not darkened:[6] I
went through a trodden garden whose groves were crushed
down I ascended a ~~colossal~~ great terrace, ~~whose marble~~ the
marble surface of which shone wet with rain where it was
not darkened by the crowds of dead leaves which were now
showered on & now swept off by the vast & broken boughs
which swung in the wind above them. I went to the wall of the
palace to the line of latticed arches which shimmered in light,
passing along quick as thought I glanced at what the internal
glare revealed through the crystal. there was a room lined with
mirrors & with lamps on tripods & very decorated [?] &
splendid couches & carpets & large half lucid vases white as
snow, thickly embossed with whiter mouldings & one large
picture in a frame of massive beauty representing a young man
[Zamorna] whose gorgeous & shining locks seemed as if they
would wave on the breath & whose eyes were half hid by the
hand carved in ivory that shaded them & supported the awful
looking coron[eted?] head: a solitary picture, too great to admit
of a companion – a likeness to be remembered full of ~~luxuriant~~
beauty not displayed for it seemed as if the form had been
copied so often in all imposing attitudes that at length the
painter satiated with its luxuriant perfection had resolved to
conceal half & make the imperial Giant bend & hide under his
cloud like tresses, the radiance he was grown tired of gazing
on. Often had I seen this room before and felt as I looked at it
the simple and exceeding magnificence of its single picure, its
five colossal cups of sculptured marble – its soft carpets of most
deep and brilliant hues, & its mirrors broad, lofty & liquidly
clear. I had seen it in the stillness of evening when the lamps so
quietly & steadily burnt in the tranquil air & when their rays
fell upon but one living figure: a young lady who generally at
that time appeared sitting on a low sofa, a book in her hand
her head bent ~~gently~~ over it as she read her light brown hair
~~falling~~ dropping in loose & unwaving curls her ~~dressing~~ falling
to the floor as she sat in sweeping folds of silk. All stirless about
her except her heart softly heaving under her dark satin bodice

& all silent except her regular and very gentle respiration. The haughty sadness of grandeur beamed out of her intent fixed hazel eye & though so young I always felt as if I dared not have spoken to her for my life. how lovely were the lines of her straight delicate features how exquisite was her small & rosy mouth but how very proud her white brow, spacious and wreathed with ringlets & her neck which though so slender had the superb curve of a queen's about the snowy throat! I knew why she chose to be alone at that hour & why she kept that shadow in the golden frame to gaze on her & why she turned sometimes to her mirrors & looked to see if her loveliness & her ~~dread~~adornments were quite perfect. However this night she was not visible – no – but neither was her bower void. the red ray of the fire flashed upon a table covered with wine flasks some drained and some brimming with the crimson juice. the cushions of a voluptuous ottoman[7] which had often supported her slight fine form were crushed by a dark bulk flung upon them in drunken prostration. Aye where she had lain ~~robed~~ imperially robed and decked with pearls, every waft of her garments as she moved diffusing perfume, her beauty slumbering & still glowing as dreams of him for whom she kept herself in such hallowed and shrine-like separation, wandered over her soul on her own silken couch, a swarth & sinewy moor intoxicated to ferocious insensibility had stretched his athletic limbs weary with wassail and stupefied with drunken sleep. I knew it to be Quashia himself and well could I guess why he had chosen the queen of Angria's sanctuary[8] for the scene of his soliatry revelling. While he was full before my eyes lying in his black dress on the disordered couch, his sable hair dishevelled on his forehead & tusk-like teeth glancing vindictively through his parted lips his brown complexion flushed with wine & his broad chest heaving wildly as the breath issued in snorts from his distended nostrils while I watched the fluttering of his white shirt ruffles starting through the more than half-unbuttoned waistcoat & beheld the expression of his Arabian countenance savagely exulting even in sleep[9] – Quamina triumphant Lord in the halls of Zamorna! in the bower of Zamorna's lady! while this apparition was before

me the dining-room door opened and Miss W[ooler] came in
with a plate of butter in her hand. "A very stormy night my
dear!" said she: "it is ma'am" said I

[b] Friday afternoon – Feb 4th 1836[10]
Now as I have a little bit of time there being no French lessons
this afternoon I should like to write something. I can't enter
into any continued narrative[11] – my mind is not settled enough
for that but if I could call up some slight & pleasant sketch, I
would amuse myself by jotting it down[12] let me consider the
other day I appeared to realize a ~~most~~ delicious hot day in the
most burning height of summer A gorgeous afternoon of idleness & enervation descending upon the hills of our Africa An
evening enfolding a sky of profoundly deep blue & fiery gold
about the earth. dear me! I keep heaping epithets together and
I cannot describe what I mean – I mean a day whose rise
progress & decline seem made of sunshine. As you are travelling
you see the wide road before you the fields on each side & the
hills far, far off all smiling, glowing in the same amber light
and you feel such an intense ~~light~~ heat, quite incapable of
chilling damp or even refreshing breeze a day when fruits visibly
ripen, when orchards appear suddenly to change from green to
gold. ~~it seemed to me~~ such a day I saw flaming over the distant
Sydenham hills in Hawkscliffe Forest. I saw its sublime sunset,
pouring beams of crimson through ~~as~~ the magnificent glades. It
seemed to me that the war was over,[13] that the trumpet had
ceased but a short time since and that its last tones had been
pitched on a triumphant key It seemed as if exciting events
tidings of battles of victories of treaties of meetings of mighty
powers had diffused an enthusiasm over the land that made its
pulses beat with feverish quickness After months of bloody toil
a time of festal rest was now bestowed on Angria; the Noblemen
the Generals & the Gentlemen were at their country seats
& the Duke young, but war-worn was at Hawkscliffe A still
influence stole out of the stupendous forest, whose calm was
now more awful than the sea-like rustling that swept through its
glades in time of storm. Groups of deer appeared & disappeared
silently amongst the prodigious stems & now & then a single

roe glided down the savannah park, drank of the Arno &
fleeted back again

Two gentlemen in earnest conversation[14] were walking in
St Mary's Grove & their deep commingling voice tones very
much subdued softly broke the silence of the evening. Secret
topics seemed to be employed implied in what they said, for
the import of their words was concealed from every chance
listener by the accents of a foreign tongue All the soft vowels
of Italian articulation[15] flowed from their lips as fluently as if
they had been natives of the European Eden. "Henrico"[16] was
the appellative by which the taller & younger of the two
addressed his companion & the other replied by the less familiar
title of Monsignore. that young Signior or Lord, often looked
up at the Norman towers of Hawkscliffe that which rose even
above the lofty elms of St Mary's grove the sun was shining on
their battlements kissing them with its last beam that rivalled
in hue the fire-dyed banner hanging motionless above them.
"Henrico" said he speaking still in musical Tuscan. "this is the
29th of June.[17] neither you nor I ever saw a fairer day to me it
will return no more What does it remind you of? all such sunsets
have associations." Henrico knitted his stern brow in thought
& at the same time fixed his very penetrating dar black eye on
the features of his noble comrade, which invested by habit &
nature with the aspect of command & pride were at this sweet
hour relaxing to the impassioned & fervid expression of
romance "What does it remind you of, my lord" said he briefly.
"Ah! many things Henrico! ever since I can remember the rays
of the setting sun have acted on my heart, as they did on
Memnon's wondrous statue.[18] the strings always vibrate, sometimes the tones swell in harmony sometimes in discord they
play a wild air just now – but sweet & ominously plaintive.
Henrico can you immagine what I feel when I look into the dim
& gloomy vistas of this my forest & at yonder turrets which
the might of my own hands has raised not the halls of my
ancestors like hoary Mornington. Calm diffuses over this wild
wide wood a power to stir & thrill the mind such as words can
never express. Do ye Look at the red west the sun is gone & it

is fading to Gas & into those mighty groves supernaturally still
& full of gathering darkness listen how the Arno moans!

[2]

[a] Friday August 11th – All this day I have been in a dream,
half-miserable & half ecstatic miserable because I could not
follow it out uninterrruptedly, ecstatic because it shewed almost
in the vivid light of reality the ongoings of the infernal world.[19]
I had been toiling for nearly an hour with Miss Lister, Miss
Marriott & Ellen Cook striving to teach them the distinction
between an article and a substantive.[20] The parsing lesson was
completed, a dead silence had succeeded it in the school-room
& I sat sinking from irritation & weariness into a kind of
lethargy. The thought came over me am I to spend all the best
part of my life in this wretched bondage, forcibly suppressing
my rage at the idleness the apathy and the hyperbolical & most
asinine stupidity of those fat-headed oafs and on compulsion
assuming an air of kindness, patience & assiduity? Must I from
day to day sit chained to this chair prisoned within these four
bare walls, while these glorious summer suns are burning in
heaven & the year is revolving in its richest glow & declaring
at the close of every summer day it the time I am losing will
never come again? Stung to the heart with this reflection I
started up & mechanically walked to the window. a sweet
August morning was smiling without The dew was not yet dried
off the field. the early shadows were stretching cool & dim
from the hay-stack & the roots of the grand old oaks & thorns
scattered along the sunk fence. All was still except the murmer
of the scrubs about me over their tasks. I flung up the sash. an
uncertain sound of inexpressible sweetness came on a dying
gale from the south, I looked in that direction Huddersfield &
the hills beyond it were all veiled in blue mist, the woods of
Hopton & Heaton Lodge[21] were clouding the waters edge &
the Calder silent but bright was shooting among them like a
silver arrow. I listened the sound sailed full & liquid down the
descent. it was the bells of Huddersfield Parish church. I shut

the window & went back to my seat. Then came on me rushing impetuously, all the mighty phantasm that we had conjured from nothing from nothing to a system strong as some religious creed. I felt as if I could have written gloriously – I longed to write. The spirit of all Verdopolis – of all the mountainous North of all the woodland West of all the river-watered East[22] came crowding into my mind. if I had had time to indulge it I felt that the vague sensations of that moment would have settled down into some narrative better at least than any thing I ever produced before. But just then a Dolt came up with a lesson. I thought I should have vomited.

[b] In the afternoon Miss E—L—was trigonometrically oecu-menical[23] about her French lessons she nearly killed me between the violence of the irritation her horrid wilfulness excited and the labour it took to subdue it to a moderate appearance of calmness. My fingers trembled as if I had had twenty four hours tooth-ache, & my spirits felt worn down to a degree of desperate despondency. Miss Wooler tried to make me talk at tea-time and was exceedingly kind to me but I could not have roused if she had offered me worlds. After tea we took a long dreary walk. I came back abymé to the last degree for Miss L— and Miss M—t[24] had been boring me with their vulgar famill iar [sic] trash all the time we were out if those Girls knew how I loathe their company they would not seek mine so much as they do The sun had set nearly a quarter of an hour before we returned and it was getting dusk – The Ladies went into the school-room to do their exercises & I crept up to the bed-room to be alone for the first time that day. Delicious was the sen-sation I experienced as I laid down on the spare-bed & resigned myself to the Luxury of twilight & solitude. The stream of Thought, checked all day came flowing free & calm along its channel. My ideas were too shattered to form any defined picture as they would have done in such circumstances at home, but detatched thoughts soothingly flitted round me & uncon-nected scenes occurred and then vanished producing an effect certainly strange but to me very pleasing.[25] the toil of the Day succeeded by this moment of divine leisure had acted on me

like opium & was coiling about me a disturbed but fascinating
spell such as I never felt before. What I imagined grew morbidly
vivid. I remember I quite seemed to see with my bodily eyes –
a lady[26] standing in the hall of a Gentleman's house as if waiting
for some one. it was Dusk & there was the dim outline of
antlers with a hat & a rough great-coat upon them it was dusk
she had a flat candle-stick in her hand & seemed coming from
the kitchen or some such place she was very handsome it is not
often we can form from pure idea faces so individually fine she
had black curls hanging rather low on her neck a very blooming
skin & dark anxious looking eyes I imagined it the sultry close
of a summer's day and she was dressed in muslin not at all
romantically a flimsy, printed fabric with large sleeves & a full
skirt. as she waited I most distinctly heard the front door open
& saw the soft moonlight disclosed upon a lawn outside, &
beyond the lawn at a distance I saw a town with lights twinkling
through the gloaming. Two or three gentlemen entered one of
whom I knew by intuition to be called Dr Charles Brandon
and another William Locksley Esqr[27] The Doctor was a tall
handsomely built man habited in cool ample looking white
trowsers and a large straw hat which being set one one side
shewed a great deal of dark hair & a sun-burnt but smooth &
oval cheek. Locksley & the other went into an inner room but
Brandon stayed a minute in the hall. There was a bason of
water on a slab & he went & washed his hands while the lady
held the light. "How has Ryder borne the operation she asked.
"Very cleverly he'll be well in three weeks was the reply – "But
Lucy[28] won't do for a nurse at the hospital – you must take her
for your head servant, to make my cambric fronts & handkerchiefs & to wash & iron your lace aprons. little silly thing she
fainted at the very sight of the instruments Whilst Brandon
spoke a dim concatenation of ideas describing a passage in
some individual's life a varied scene in which persons & events
features & incidents revolved in misty panorama[29] entered my
mind. The mention of the hospital, of Ryder, of Lucy each
called up a certain set of reminiscences or rather fancies it
would be endless to tell all that was at that moment suggested.
Lucy first appeared before me as sitting at the door [of] a lone

cottage on a kind of moorish waste sorrowful and sickly – a young woman with those mild regular features, that always interest us however poorly set off by the meanness of surrounding adjuncts – it was a calm afternoon her eyes were turned towards a road crossing the heath. A speck appeared on it far far away – Lucy smiled to herself as it dawned into view – & while she did so there was something about her melancholy brow, her straight nose & faded bloom, that reminded me of one who might for anything I at that instant knew be dead & buried under the newly plotted sod.[30] It was this likeness & the feeling of its existence that had called Dr Brandon so far from his daily circle & that made him now when he stood near his patient regard her meek face turned submissively & gratefully to him with tenderer kindness than he bestowed on employers of aristocratic rank and wealth Her eye said No more I have not time to work out the fiction vision. a thousand things were connected with it, a whole country, statesmen & Kings, a Revolution, thrones & princedoms subverted & reinstated meantime the tall man washing his bloody hands in a bason & the dark beauty standing by with a light remained pictured in my mind's eye with irksome and alarming distinctness I grew frightened at the vivid glow of the candle at the reality of the lady's erect & symmetrical figure[31] of her spirited & handsome face of her anxious eye watching Brandon's & seeking out its meaning diving for its real expression through the semblance of severity that habit & suffering had given to his stern aspect. I felt confounded & annoyed I scarcely knew by what. At last I became aware of a feeling like a heavy weight laid across me. I knew I was wide awake & that it was dark, & that moreover the ladies were now come into the room to get their curl-papers – they perceived me lying on the bed & I heard them talking about me. I wanted to speak, to rise – it was impossible. I felt that this was a frightful predicament – that it would not do, the weight pressed me as if some huge animal had flung itself across me[32] – a horrid apprehension quickened every pulse I had. I must get up I thought & I did so with a start. I have had enough of morbidly vivid realizations. every advantage has its corresponding disadvantage. tea's read[y] Miss Wooler is impatient.

[3]

October 14th 1836 I'm just going to write[33] because I cannot help it. Wiggins might indeed talk of scriblo-mania if he were to see me just now encompassed by the bulls (query calves of Bashan)[34] all wondering why I write with my eyes shut – staring, gaping, hang their astonishment. A C—k on one side of me E L—r on the other and Miss W—er[35] in the back-ground, Stupidity the atmosphere, school-books the employment, asses the society. what in all this is there to remind me of the divine, silent, unseen land of thought, dim now & indefinite as the dream of a dream, the shadow of a shade. There is a voice, there is an impulse that wakens up that dormant power which in its torpidity I sometimes think dead. That wind pouring in impetuous current through the air, sounding wildly unremittingly from hour, to hour, deepening its tone as the night advances, coming, not in gusts, but with a rapid gathering stormy swell, that wind I know is heard at this moment far away on the moors at Haworth. Branwell & Emily hear it and as it sweeps over our house down the church-yard & round the old church, they think perhaps of me & Anne – Nort Glorious! that blast was mighty it reminded me of Northangerland, there was something so merciless in the heavier rush, that made the very house groan as if it could scarce bear this acceleration of impetus. O it has wakened a feeling that I cannot satisfy – a thousand wishes rose at its call which must die with me for they will never be fulfilled. now I should be agonized if I had not the dream to repose on. its existences, its forms its scenes do fill a little of the craving vacancy Hohenlinden! Childe Harold! Flodden Field! the Burial of Moore![36] why cannot the blood rouse the heart the heart wake the head the head prompt the head [sic] to do things like these? Stuff! – Pho! I wonder if Branwell has really killed the Duchess[37] – Is she dead, is she buried is she alone in the cold earth on this dreary night with the ponderous gold coffin plate on her breast under the bleak pavement of a church in a vault closed up with lime mortar. Nobody near where she lies – she who was watched through

months of suffering – as she lay on her bed of state. now quite
forsaken because her eyes are closed, her lips sealed and her
limbs cold and rigid the stars as they are fitfully revealed
through severed clouds looking – in through the church-
windows on her monument. A set of wretched thoughts are
rising in my mind, I hope she's alive still partly because I can't
abide to think how hopelessly & cheerlessly she must have died.
and partly because her removal if it has taken place must have
been to North—d like the quenching of the last spark that
averted utter darkness. What are Zenobia's thoughts among
the stately solitudes of Ennerdale?[38] She's by herself now in a
large, lofty room that ~~twenty~~ thirty years ago used nightly to
look as bright & gay as it now looks lone & dreary. Her mother
was one of the beauties of the West, she's sleeping in the dust
of a past generation – and there is her portrait a fine woman at
her toillette – Vanity dictated that attitude, Paulina was noted
for her profuse raven tresses, and the artist has shewn her
combing them all out, the heavy locks uncurled & loose falling
over her white arms as she lifts them to arrange the dishevelled
masses. There for nine & twenty years has that lovely Spaniard
sat ~~dressing~~ looking down on the saloon that used to be her
drawing-room. Can she see her descendant a nobler edition of
her self – the Woman of a haughty & violent spirit – seated at
that table meditating how to save her pride & crush her feelings
– Zenobia is not easily warped by imagination. Yet she feels
unconsciously the power of –[39]

[4]

My Compliments to the weather. I wonder what it[40] would be
at. snow and sunshine: but however let me forget it I've sat
down for the purpose of calling up spirits from the vasty deep[41]
and holding half an hour's converse with them. Hush! there's
a knock at the gates of thought and Memory ushers in the
visitors. The visitors! There's only one a tall gentleman ~~of~~ with
a presence, in a blue surtout & jane[42] trowsers "how do do Sir?
I'm glad to see you, take a seat – very uncommon weather this

sir! how do you stand the changes?" The Gentleman instead of answering slowly divests his neck & chin of the folds of a large black silk handkerchief deposits the light cane he carried, in a corner ~~and~~ assume~~sing~~ a seat with deliberate state & bending his light-brown beetling eye-brows over his lighter blue menacing eyes looks fixedly at me – "Scarcely civil sir what's your name?" "John of the Highlands"[43] answers the Gentleman in a voice whose depth of base makes the furniture vibrate "John of the Highlands – you called me and I am come, now what's your business –" Your servant ~~Mr Sneachie~~ says Saunderson" says I "beg your pardon for not recognizing you at once – but really you've grown so exceedingly mild-looking and unsaturnine since I saw you last, and you do look so sweet-tempered hows Mrs Saunderson and how are the old people & the dear little hope of all the Saundersons – "Pretty well thank ye – I'll take a little snuff if ye have any – my box is empty –" So saying Mr Saunderson held out his empty gold mull which I speedily filled with black rappee[44] the conversation then proceeded – "What news is stirring in your parts?" I asked "Nothing special" was the answer "Only March has left the Angrians madder than ever" "What they're fighting still are they?" Fighting! aye! and every man amongst them has sworn by his hilts[45] that he'll continue fighting while he has two rags left stitched together upon his back." "In that case I should think peace would soon be restored" said I Mr Saunderson winked – "a very sensible remark said he "Mr Wellesley Senr. made me the fellow to it last time I saw him" – "The sinews of war not particularly strong in the East?"[46] I continued Mr S—n winked again, and asked for a pot of porter – I sent for the beverage to the Robin Hood across the way – & when it was brought Mr Saunderson after blowing off the froth – took a deep draught to the health of "the brave and shirtless!" I added in a low voice "to the vermined & victorious!" he heard me & remarked with a grave nod of approbation "very jocose" After soaking[47] a little while each in silence Mr Saunderson spoke again –[48]

Mr Saunderson did *not* speak again – he departed like the fantastic creation of a dream. I was called to hear a lesson &

when I returned to my desk again, I found the mood which had suggested that allegorical whim was irrevocably gone – A fortnight has elapsed since I wrote the above – this is my first half-hour's leisure since then and now once more on a dull Saturday afternoon, I sit down to try to summon round me the dim shadows, not of coming events, but of incidents long departed of feelings, of pleasures, whose exquisite relish I sometimes fear it will never be my lot again to taste – How few would believe that from sources purely imaginary such happiness could be derived. Pen cannot pourtray the deep interest of the scenes, of the continued trains of events, I have witnessed in that little room with the low narrow bed & bare whitewashed walls – twenty miles away – What a treasure is thought! What a privilege is reverie – I am thankful that I have the power of solacing myself with the dream of creations whose reality I shall never behold – May I never lose that power – may I never feel it growing weaker – If I should how little pleasure will life afford me – its lapses of shade are so wide so gloomy Its gleams of sunshine so limited & dim!⁴⁹

Remembrance yields up many a fragment of past twilight hours – spent in that little unfurnished room – There have I sat on the low bed-stead my eyes fixed on the window, through which appeared no other landscape than a monotonous stretch of moorland, a grey church tower, rising from the centre of a church-yard so filled with graves, that the rank – weed and coarse grass scarce had room to shoot up between the monuments. Over these hangs in the eye of memory a sky of such grey clouds as often veil the chill close of an October day & low on the horizon ~~appear~~ glances at intervals through the rack⁵⁰ the orb of a lurid & haloed moon. Such was the picture that threw its reflection upon my eye but communicated no impression to my heart – The mind knew but did not feel its existence – It was away It had launched on a distant voyage – haply it was nearing the shores of some far & unknown Island under whose cliffs no bark had ever before cast anchor In other words a long tale was perhaps then evolving itself in my mind, the history of an ancient & aristocratic family – The legendary

records of its origin, not preserved in writing – but delivered
from the lips of old retainers, floating in tradition up & down
the woods & vales of the Earldom, or Dukedom or Barony.
The [?feeling] of old oak avenues planted by the ancestors
of three hundred years ago, of halls neglected by the present
descendants of Galleries peopled with silent pictures, no longer
loved & valued for none now live who remember the substance
of those shadows – Then with a parting glance at the family –
church, with a thought reverting to the wide deep vault underneath its pavement, my dream shifted to some distant city, some
huge imperial metropolis – where the descendants of the last
nobleman the young lords and ladies, shine in gay circles of
patricians – Dazzled with the brilliancy of courts, haply with
the ambition of senates, Sons & Daughters have almost forgotten the groves where they were born & grew – as I saw them
stately & handsome, gliding through those saloons[51] where
many other well-known forms crossed my sight, where there
were faces looking up, eyes smiling & lips moving in audible
speech, that I knew better almost than my brother & sisters,
yet whose voices had never woke an echo in this world whose
eyes had never gazed upon the day-light, what glorious associations crowded upon me, what excitement heated my face &
made me clasp my hands in ecstasy – I too forgot the ancient
country seat I forgot the great woods with their lonely glades
peopled only by deer – I thought no more of the Gothic Chapel
under whose floor mouldered the bones of a hundred barons –
What then to me were the ballads of the Grand-mothers the
tales of the grey-headed old men of that remote village on the
Annesley Estate – I looked at Lady Amelia the eldest Daughter
standing by a wide lofty window descending by marble steps
on to a sunshiny lawn amidst a flush of rose-trees in bloom, a
lady of handsome features & full growth, just now she is exquisitely beautiful though that extreme brightness which excitement
& happiness are bestowing will soon pass away. I see the sweep
of her light summer dress – the fall & waving of her curled hair
on her neck, the unaccustomed glow of her complexion & shine
of her smiling eyes I see them now – she is looking round at
that ring of patricians, she is hearing her brother tell over the

names & titles of many that are become the darlings of fame, the monarchs of mind – She has been introduced to some, as they pass they speak to her. I hear them speak as well as she does, I see distinctly their figures – and though alone, I experience all the feelings of one admitted for the first time into a grand circle of classic beings – recognizing by tone, gesture and aspect hundreds whom I never saw before, but whom I have heard of and read of many a time, and is not this enjoyment? I am not accustomed to such magnificence as surrounds me, to the gleam of such large mirrors, to the beauty of marble figures, to such soft eastern foreign carpets, to such long wide rooms to lofty gilded ceilings. I know nothing of people of rank & distinction, yet there they are before me in throngs, in crowds, they come, they go, they speak, they beckon & that not like airy phantoms but as noblemen & ladies of flesh & blood. there is an aim in all – I know the house. I know the square it stands in, I passed through it this day I ascended the steps leading to the vestibule I saw the porter at the door, I went along hall & gallery till I reached this saloon. Is it not enjoyment to gaze around upon those changeful countenances; to mark the varied features of those high-born & celebrated guests, some gay & youthful some proud cold & middle-aged, a few bent & venerable here & there a head throwing the rest into shade, a bright perfect face, with eyes & bloom & divine expression whose realization thrills the heart to its core – There is one just now, crossing – a lady I will not write her name just now though I know it – no history is connected with her identity, she is not one of the transcendently fair & inaccessibly sacred beings – whose fates are interwoven with the highest of the high – beings I am not alluding to in this general picture, far from home I cannot write of them except in total solitude I scarce dare speak think of them. This nameless & casual visitant has crossed the drawing-room & is standing close by Lady Amelia, she is looking up & speaking to her – I wish I could trace the picture, so vivid, so obvious at this moment – She is a native of the East I never saw a more richer per specimen of an Angrian Lady with all the characteristics of her country-women in such perfection – She is rather tall, under-sized, plumply & well &

roundly formed, with plump neck & shoulders as white as drift
snow, profuse tresses in coulour almost red but fine as silk &
lying in soft curls upon her cheeks & round her forehead
the sweetness of the features thus shaded is inexpressible, the
beautiful little mouth, the oval chin & fine animated eyes, the
frank cheerful look, the clear skin with its pure healthy bloom
– The dress of light blue satin beautifully contrasting with her
hair & complexion – the pearls circling her round white wrist,
the movements of her figure not marked by the inceding grace
of the West, but unstudied prompt & natural, her laugh always
ready – the sound of her voice, her rapid rather abrupt, but
sweet & clear utterance, possessing a charm of its own, very
different from the rich, low subdued melody that flows from
the lips of Senegambia's daughters[52] – The quick glances of her
eye indicating a warm & excitable temperament the mingled
expression of good nature & pride, spirit & kind-heartedness
predominating in every feature all these are as clearly before
me as Ann's[53] quiet ~~face~~ image, sitting at her lessons on the
opposite side of the table –

Jane Moore,[54] that is her name has long been celebrated as a
beauty all over the province of Arundel, amongst whose green
swells of pasture, her father's handsome new mansion, lies with
all its pleasant grounds & young plantations, on this warm
spring – day opening their delicate foliage as rapidly as the
forests of Kentucky[55] – ~~John Mc~~ George ~~Armstrong~~ Moore
Esqr is a rising man, one of those whose fortunes were made
on the night Angria was declared a kingdom he is a mercantile
man moreover & has a huge warehouse down at Doverham,
& a vessel or two lying in the Docks, built by himself &
christened the lady Jane after his fair daughter – She is no petted
only child, Moore like a true Angrian has given to the State
some half dozen of stout youths and an equal number of ~~fair
maid~~ well grown girls, most of whom, now grave professional
men & dignified young matrons, are married into the first
families of the province & each established in a hall of their own
amongst the prairies.[56] But Jane is the youngest, the prettiest, the
rose of the whole bouquet, she has been the most highly educated, & by nature she was one of those whose minds manners

appearance must tend to elevate them wherever they go Jane
has ambition enough about her to scorn any offer that does not
comprise a coronet and it must be an Angrian Coronet too and
there must be wealth & Estates & a noble mansion & servants
& carriages & all the other means & appliances a dashing
beauty ~~may~~ be supposed to require to set her off. I am afraid
Jane Moore ~~with~~ notwithstanding her natural quickness & high
education has none of the deep refined romance of the west –
I am afraid she scarcely knows what it means, she is as matter
of fact as any manufacturer of Edwardston, & likes as well to
receive her penny's-worth for her penny – With undisguised
frankness she acknowledges that this world would be nothing
without a flash & glitter[57] now & then, if Jane does any thing
well she eminently likes to be told so – She delights in society –
not for worlds would she live alone, she has no idea even of
playing a tune, or singing a melancholy stanza to herself by
twilight ~~Now & then~~ Once or twice she has by some chance
found herself alone in the evening about dusk in some the large
parlour at Kirkham Wood & she has gone to the window &
looked out at the garden clustered over with dewy buds, & at
the lawn carpeted with mossy ~~grass~~ verdure & at the carriage
walk ~~sweeping~~ winding down to the gate & beyond that at the
wide & sweeping swell of grazing country all green, all opening
with a smile to the moon light beaming from the sky upon it –
And as Jane looked some unaccustomed feeling did seem to
swell in her heart, but if you had asked her why her eyes
glistened so, she would not have answered "the moonlight is
so lovely" but "Angria is such a glorious land!" Then as Miss
Moore turned from the window & looked round on the
deserted room with the restless firelight flickering over its walls
& making the pictures seem to stir in their frames as she rose
& threw herself into her father's arm-chair & ~~ther~~ sat in silence
listening for his tread, perhaps she might fall into abstracted
reverie & begin to recall former days, to remember her eldest
sister who died when she was a child, to think of the funeral –
day – of the ~~cold~~ rigid & lengthened corpse laid in its coffin on
the hall-table, of the servants pressing round to gaze on Miss
Harriet for the last time of the kiss that she herself was bidden

to give the corpse, of the feeling tha which then for the first time first gushed into her childish & volatile heart that Harriet had left her them for ever. She recollects the contrast that struck upon her mind of her dead & of her living sister, the tall girl of sixteen eighteen who had left school, who was privileged always to be in the drawing-room, when Mr & Mrs Kirkwall & Sir Frederic & Lady Fala came to pay their annual visit, who had her own dressing-room with her toilette table & her dressing case who used so kindly to come into the nursery sometimes after dinner & bring them all down into the parlour where she play would sing for them & play marches & waltzes on the piano – very lovely and a little awful did she then seem to the eye of Jane her superior stature, her handsome dress, her gold watch & chain – her powers of drawing & playing & reading French & Italian books, all tended to make her seem invest her with the character of a being of a superior order. With these reminiscences comes one of a rumour Jane used to hear whispered by the house-maid to the nurse that her sister was to be married to Mr Charles Kirkwall – & therewith steps in Charles' image, a tall young man, who in those days was no unfrequent visitor at the hall, he always attended Miss Moore in her walks & rides, often from the nursery window has Jane seen them both mounted on horseback & dashing down the avenue. she remembers her sister's figure as she bent over the neck of her beautiful mare Jessy, her long curls & veil & her purple habit streaming in the wind[58] & she remembers Charles too, his keen features & penetrating eye – always watching her sister Miss Moore. then from those forms of Life, from Harriet's mild & pleasing face as it was in health, never very blooming but lighted with hazel soft grey eyes of sweetest lustre, Jane's memory turns to the white, shrunk sightless corpse. She starts & a tear falls on her silk frock. ask her what she's crying for, because I'm so low-spirited with being alone", she will answer. Such is not Jane Moore's element, the inspiration of Twilight, solitude melancholy musing is alien from her hear nature Step into this great public assembly room full of Angrian Grandees, a public ball is given in remembrance celebration of the third anniversary of Independence[59] What light! what flashing of jewels! &

wearing of scarlet scarfs & plumes! what a tumultuous swell
of melody! it is from a single instrument & the air is one of
~~melody~~ triumph, It proceeds from that recess you cannot see
the grand – piano for the ring of illustrissima[60] crowding round
it, Listen! a voice electrically sweet & thrilling in its tones –
Angria's glorious Song of ~~Triump~~ Victory "Sound the Loud
Timbrel!"[61] Come nearer, lift up your eyes & look at the song-
stress You know her, plumed, robed in vermillion, with glowing
cheek & large blue eye eloquently telling what feelings the gales
of Angria breathe into her daughters – Jane Moore that feeling
will not last it will die away into oblivion as the echos of those
chords die away into silence ~~& t~~ that expression too will leave
your eye that flush your cheek, & you will look round & greet
with a careless laugh the first word of flattery uttered by that
Dandy at your elbow – yet your spirit can take a high tone it
can respond to an heroic call You are not all selfish vanity; all
empty show You are a handsome, generous, clever; flashy,
proud, overbearing woman.

[5]

About a week since I got a letter from Branwell[62] containing a
most exquisitely characteristic epistle from Northangerland to
his daughter – It is astonishing what a soothing and delightful
tone that letter seemed to speak – I lived on its contents for
days. in every pause of employment – it came chiming in like
some sweet bar of music – bringing with it agreeable thoughts
such as I had for many weeks been a stranger to – Some representing scenes such as might arise in consequence of that
unexpected letter some, unconnected with it referring to other
events, another set of feelings – these were not striking &
stirring scenes of incident – no they were tranquil & retired in
their character such as might every day be ~~seen~~ witnessed in the
inmost circles of highest society – A curtain seemed to rise and
discover to me the Duchess as she might appear when newly
risen, and lightly dressed for the morning – discovering her
father's letter in the contents of the mail which lies on her

breakfast-table – there seems nothing in such an idea as that – but the localities of the picture were so graphic – the room so distinct the clear fire – of morning – the window looking upon no object but a cold October sky except when you draw very near and look down on a terrace far beneath & at a still dizzier distance on a green court with a fountain and rows of stately limes – beyond a wide road a wider river and a vast metropolis – you feel it to be the Zamorna Palace for buildings on buildings embosomed piled round embosom this little verdant circle with its marble basin to receive the jet – and its grove of mellowing foliage – above fifty windows look upon the court admitting light into you know not what splendid and spacious chambers. The Duchess has read that letter – and she is following the steps of the writer – she knows not where – but it is with a vague idea that it is through no pleasant scenes – In strange situations her imagination places him – In the Inn of a sea-port Town sitting alone on a wet & gusty Autumn night – the wind bringing up the ceaseless roar of the sea – of the Atlantic to whose grim waves he will tomorrow commit himself in that Steamer[63] – hissing amongst a crowd of masts in the harbour – She looks from the window and there is the high roof and lordly front of Northangerland-House – towering like some great Theatre among above the streets of Adrianopolis – The Owner of that Pile is a homeless Man

Abbreviations

Barker	Juliet Barker, *The Brontës* (London: Weidenfeld & Nicolson, 1994)
BPM	Brontë Parsonage Museum
BST	*Brontë Society Transactions*
CBL	Margaret Smith (ed.), *The Letters of Charlotte Brontë* (3 vols.; Oxford: Clarendon Press, 1995–2004)
CBP	*The Poems of Charlotte Brontë*, ed. Victor A. Neufeldt (New York and London: Garland Publishing, 1985)
DVT	Francis Grose, *A Dictionary of the Vulgar Tongue* (London: C. Chappel, 1811)
EEW	Christine Alexander (ed.), *An Edition of the Early Writings of Charlotte Brontë* (Oxford: Basil Blackwell, vol. 1, 1987; vol. 2, parts i and ii, 1991)
Five Novelettes	Charlotte Brontë, *Five Novelettes: Passing Events, Julia, Mina Laury, Henry Hastings, Caroline Vernon*, ed. Winifred Gérin (London: The Folio Press, 1971)
Four Years Ago	Unpublished ms., dated 21 July 1837, whereabouts unknown, transcribed by C. W. Hatfield; Hatfield Transcription 10, BPM. Page references are to this typescript.
Gaskell	Elizabeth Gaskell, *The Life of Charlotte Brontë*, ed. Elisabeth Jay (Harmondsworth: Penguin, 1997)
Juvenilia	Juliet Barker (ed.), *Charlotte Brontë: Juvenilia 1829–1835* (Harmondsworth: Penguin, 1996)
Neufeldt	Victor A. Neufeldt (ed.), *The Works of Patrick Branwell Brontë*, 3 vols. (New York and London: Garland Publishing, 1999)

PPBB   Victor A. Neufeldt (ed.), *The Poems of Patrick Branwell Brontë* (New York and London: Garland Publishing, 1990)

OED   Oxford English Dictionary: www.oed.com

SHCBM   Thomas J. Wise and John A. Symington (eds.), *The Miscellaneous and Unpublished Writings of Charlotte and Patrick Branwell Brontë*, 2 vols. (Shakespeare Head edn., 1936 and 1938)

Notes

MINA LAURY

Untitled manuscript, signed 'C Brontë Jany 7th Haworth 1838', in the Robert H. Taylor Collection, Princeton University Library (Record ID 72190). Given the 'tentative title' of *Mina Laury* by Fannie E. Ratchford, in *Legends of Angria* (New Haven: Yale University Press, 1933).

1. *my last book*: The manuscript to which this refers has apparently not survived. *Four Years Ago*, dated 21 July 1837, ends with a description of the death of Zamorna's first wife at Douro Villa.

2. *dreary, wildered look of all without*: January 1838, when *Mina Laury* was written, was the coldest month ever recorded in England. 'In this month, the frost was so intense, that the principal rivers in England were completely frozen over,' writes John Mayhall, in his *Annals of Yorkshire* (1861), I, p. 455.

3. *newspaper*: From the beginnings of the Glass Town saga, the young Brontës were fascinated by newspapers. 'We take 2 and see three newspapers,' Charlotte writes in her youthful 'History of the Year' (1829); 'we take the Leeds Inteligencer [par]ty Tory and the Leeds Mercury Whig' (*Juvenilia*, p. 2). Many of the details of their childhood writings – from political disputes and parliamentary debates to accounts of exotic places – came from this early reading, and newspapers of different political persuasions were a prominent feature of their shared imaginary world.

4. *all's right with her*: Zenobia is happy because she is with Zamorna. She had loved him in youth, and remained passionately involved with him, even after his marriage. In a manuscript dated 31 October 1837, Branwell describes her continuing infatuation

with him, and the 'fixed freindship' between them (*[Angria and the Angrians] IV(j)*, Neufeldt, 3, p. 161).

5.   *Harlaw . . . comely and portly figure*: *Harlauw*: The Marquis of Harlaw, along with the Marquis of Ardrah, has been publishing 'vile and destable falsehoods' about Zamorna, as the latter puts it, in Northangerland's 'hired press' (*The Scrap Book*: *From the Verdopolitan Intelligencer, EEW*, 2.ii, p. 374). *comely and portly figure*: Zenobia is described in *Passing Events* (April 1836) as 'a woman who in her thirtieth year has waxed so imperially stout and high that she will not even leave her own saloons for the benefit of fresh air' (*Five Novelettes*, p. 50).

6.   *man mountain*: The name given to Gulliver in Lilliput, in Jonathan Swift's *Gulliver's Travels* (1726).

7.   *Lady Helen Percy*: Mother of Northangerland.

8.   *North Star . . . Hercules*: *North Star*: According to astrology, the stars have an almost omnipotent influence on men's destinies; Polaris, the Pole Star, which lies less than one degree from the Northern Celestial Pole, and so always lies north from an Earthbound observer's point of view, was thought to have been created by Zeus. Here, an ironic allusion to Northangerland and his influence over Zamorna. *Hector*: son of Priam, commander of the Trojan army in Homer's *Iliad*; a figure of military prowess. *Paris*, at the mercy of his feelings for women. When Paris was asked to judge between the rival claims of Hera, Athene and Aphrodite, each offered him a bribe: the first power, the second martial glory, and the third, the most beautiful of women; in choosing Aphrodite, he was enabled to seduce Helen, which led to the fall of Troy. *Sampson and Delilah*: Judges 16:4–21 tells how Delilah deprived Samson of his strength by shaving off his hair, and betrayed him to the Philistines. *Hercules*: Hercules was sold into slavery to the Lydian queen Omphale, who humiliated him by dressing him in women's clothes and forcing him to spin.

9.   *Bunyan's Giant Pope*: In John Bunyan's *Pilgrim's Progress Part I* (1678), Christian comes to a cave where 'two giants, Pope and Pagan, dwelt in old time, by whose power and tyranny the men whose bones, blood, ashes, etc., lay there, were cruelly put to death' (Roger Sharrock, ed., *Pilgrim's Progress* (Penguin, 1965), pp. 99–100).

10. *Much cry and little wool*: The reference is to the proverb 'A great cry and little wool, quoth the Devil when he sheared the hog' (James Howell, *Paroemiographia*, 1659). The proverb was clearly a favourite with Brontë: her *High Life in Verdopolis*

(March 1834) bears on its title page the motto 'Much cry and little wool, as St Nicholas said when he was shearing the Hog' (*EEW*, 2.ii, p. 3); 'I soon found out there was more cry than wool in the business', says Lucy Snowe, in Brontë's *Villette* (ch. 40).

11. *bitterest days of my life*: She is referring to the time, just over a year before, when Zamorna repudiated her, knowing that this would break her heart, in order to avenge himself on her father.

12. *Enara . . . Thornton*: Zamorna's allies in the battle for Angria.

13. *Mr Warner*: Warner Howard Warner, his Prime Minister.

14. *Ma belle . . . cruse-là*: My beauty! let me carry that jug! (French).

15. *suicide*: Edward Lytton Bulwer, in *England and the English* (1833), had argued against the prevailing notion that the English were a suicidal nation by producing statistics of suicides in London and in Paris to show that 'the French have, by *strict* calculation, been compelled to kill *their five to our one*' (*England and the English*, ed. Standish Meacham (Chicago, 1970), p. 56). The young Brontës, who could have found Bulwer's volume in Keighley Mechanics' Institute Library, were clearly much taken by this argument. In his *Historical Narrative of the War of Encroachment* (1833) Branwell had depicted a crisis in 'FrenchyLand', in which suicide became 'the one grand object which employed. the minds of every Frenchman' (Neufeldt, 1, pp. 365–8).

16. *raking*: Behaving like a rake, dissolutely. (*OED* does not cite this as a verb, but it is clearly what is meant.)

17. *sent to Coventry*: Cut off from social intercourse.

18. *Cirhala*: Zamorna's forces' final triumphant battle for Angria had taken place at Evesham, beside the Cirhala.

19. *western dandy . . . Take the bull by the horns*: *western dandy*: Zamorna, fictional son of the Duke of Wellington, is from Senegambia, to the west of Angria, a place modelled on Ireland, home of the actual Duke. *dandy*: Brontë probably knew that the Duke of Wellington, who once directed an engagement dressed in a white cravat, Hessian boots, leather pantaloons and a large cocked hat, had been called 'the Dandy' by his troops in the Peninsula. *genius of our land*: The distinctive character or spirit of our nation; Hartford, unlike Zamorna, is a native-born Angrian. *Take the bull by the horns*: Meet danger fearlessly.

20. *the end is not yet*: Refers in fact to the Gospels. Matthew 24:6: 'And ye shall hear of wars and rumours of wars: see that ye be not troubled: for all these things must come to pass, but the end is not yet.' Cf. also Mark 13:7 and Luke 21:9.

21. *Guanache . . . toast and water*: *Guanache*: Thus in the ms. 'Grenache', which is possibly intended, is a sweet wine, usually drunk with dessert, produced in the Languedoc-Roussillon region of France. *toast and water*: Toast soaked in water; used as a drink for invalids.

22. *Rivaulx*: Rievaulx Abbey, North Yorkshire; Brontë had copied an engraving of Gilpin's drawing, 'Cross of Rivaulx', on 23 June 1836 (Christine Alexander and Jane Sellars, *The Art of the Brontës* (Cambridge: Cambridge University Press, 1995), pp. 244–5).

23. *The Duchess herself gave it me*: When the first youthful love affair between Mina and Zamorna (then Marquis of Douro) had ended, the (fictional) Duchess of Wellington had sent for the heartbroken Mina Laury and shown her 'gentle attention and sympathetic kindness' (*Something About Arthur* (1833), *EEW*, 2.i, p. 40).

24. *daughter of a common soldier*: Mina is the daughter of Ned Laury, who first appears in the juvenilia as a body-snatcher and a poacher, and then as a retainer of the Duke of Wellington. For the early romance between the adolescent Zamorna and this 'low-born peasant's daughter', see *Something About Arthur* (1833), *EEW*, 2.i, pp. 7–40.

25. *Angria an independent kingdom*: Angria was proclaimed an independent kingdom, and Zamorna its king, by the Verdopolitan parliament in 1834. (See Patrick Branwell Brontë, *The Wool is Rising or the Angrian Adventurer: A Narrative of the Proceedings of the Foundation of the Kingdom of Angria*, in Neufeldt, 2, pp. 24–44.)

26. *Northangerland resigned the seals*: In 1835 Zamorna had denounced Northangerland for his treachery, demanded his 'seals of office' and dismissed him as Premier of Angria (*The Scrap Book: from the Verdopolitan Intelligencer*, in *EEW*, 2.ii, p. 376).

27. *triumph of . . . Restoration*: *triumph of*: Triumph over (*OED*, obs.). *Restoration*: The victorious return of Zamorna from exile, and his re-establishment as King of Angria.

28. *Ernest Fitz-Arthur*: Ernest Edward Wellesley, Baron Gordon, son of Zamorna by Lady Helen Victorine Gordon. His name signals that his parents either were not married, or that the marriage was not recognized; the prefix *Fitz* was usual in naming the illegitimate offspring of princes. After his mother's death Ernest was confided to the care of Mina Laury, who struggled to protect him during the civil wars, but he was murdered by Zamorna's enemies.

29. *Platonist*: Hartford is referring to the belief that Plato advocated non-sexual friendship between man and woman (derived from a misreading of a passage towards the end of his *Symposium*, in which he extols Socrates' loving but asexual interest in young men).

30. *western heart*: Mina is from Senegambia, to the west of Angria. 'Westerns', in the Angrian fictions, are passionate and imaginative.

31. *Ellibank ... St Cyprian*: *Ellibank*: Mina Laury, in her days of innocence, had worked for the Duchess of Wellington at her country estate of Mornington, in the hills of Ellibank. *St Cyprian*: A river on this estate; Brontë may well have taken the name from W. Harrison Ainsworth's popular *Rookwood* (1834), which contains a chapter entitled 'St Cyprian's Cell', describing a holy rural shrine to the saint (*Rookwood*, ch. 26). In *Mina Laury*, however, the name may have less elevated resonances; see below, ns. 36, 52.

32. *rowels*: Small stellar wheels or disks with sharp radial points and capable of rotation, forming the extremity of a spur. The repetition of 'dash' in this sentence suggests that Brontë may be remembering Sir Walter Scott's *Marmion* (1808), VI. X. iv: 'Lord Marmion turn'd, ... And dash'd the rowels in his steed'.

33. *shawled ... mackintosh cape*: *shawled*: Shawls worn over great-coats were much in demand as travelling wear for gentlemen in the 1830s. *mackintosh cape*: Waterproof garments were beginning to be widely used in the 1820s and 1830s. A 'newly invented Waterproof Beaver Hat' was advertised in the *Manchester Courier* in 1825. The mackintosh, made of Messrs Mackintosh & Co.'s Patent Waterproof milled beaver cloth appeared in 1836 (C. Willett Cunnington and Phillis Cunnington, *Handbook of English Costume in the Nineteenth Century* (London: Faber, 3rd edn., 1970, pp. 121, 142)).

34. *case*: Set.

35. *worshippers of Juggernaut*: Fanatical devotees of the Hindu god Juggernaut used to throw themselves to be crushed beneath the wheels of the enormous decorated car in which his image was carried.

36. *Cyprus or Cythera*: Both centres of the cult of Aphrodite, goddess of love.

37. *absurd extreme now contemplated*: Although duels were illegal, they were frequent amongst the upper classes both in actual life and in silver fork novels in the 1830s. A number of duels in the period are described in John Ashton, *When William IV was*

King (London: Chapman and Hall, 1906), pp. 303–10. Indeed, a handbook on their proper conduct, containing numerous accounts of recent duels – 'perused' (it is claimed on p. 3) 'with *great interest* by the Duke of Wellington' – had appeared in 1829 (Joseph Hamilton, *The Only Approved Guide Through All the Stages of a Quarrel* (London: Hatchard & Son, 1829)).

38. *doctors*: It was customary to have doctors in attendance at a duel.

39. *would not delay the business a moment*: A mark of Zamorna's fury: it was usual to fight a duel out of doors. Hamilton's 'Code of Honour' for duels stipulated that at least 24 hours should elapse between the challenge and the duel (*Only Approved Guide*, p. 18).

40. *Dr Cooper*: Sir Astley Poston Cooper (1768–1841), professor of comparative anatomy at the Royal College of Surgeons, had in 1828 become surgeon to the king. Branwell had chosen him as one of the chief men of his island at the founding of the 'Play of the Islanders' in November 1827 (Gaskell, p. 66).

41. *Flower*: Lord Richton's name is John Flower.

42. *without another word on either side*: In ' "O! let me be alone" he said', a manuscript poem preserved in the Brontë Parsonage Museum (undated, but apparently written, like *Mina Laury*, in January 1838), Brontë attempts a poetic rendering of Lord Hartford's delirious and despairing state of mind at this point (*CBP*, pp. 258–60).

43. *Her desk*: A portable repository for writing materials, letters, etc., with a sloping lid for writing on. A desk of this kind owned by Brontë is on display in the Brontë Parsonage Museum, Haworth.

44. *practice*: Arithmetical term for a method of performing multiplication, used in finding the value of a given number of articles at so many pounds, shillings and pence each.

45. *Necessity has no law*: Proverbial saying.

46. *the driving of Jehu the son of Nimshi*: 2 Kings 9:20: 'the driving is like the driving of Jehu the son of Nimshi; for he driveth furiously.'

47. *presently*: Here used in the now obsolete sense of 'instantly' or 'forthwith'.

48. *royal liberties*: The king's domain or property.

49. *Irving . . . Sneachiesland*: *Irving*: Edward Irving of the Church of Scotland, charismatic preacher on the second coming of Christ, was a controversial figure, who had drawn huge, fashionable

congregations during his time as minister of the Caledonian Church in Covent Garden, but fell into disrepute because of his charismatic beliefs; he remained, however, a firm favourite in *Fraser's Magazine*, to the early issues of which he had contributed. *Fraser's* carried a long obituary of him in January 1834. *Sneachiesland*: Associated with Scotland, as Senegambia is with Ireland.

50. *come, Esther . . . it shall be granted*: In the Old Testament book of Esther, Esther, Jewish wife of King Ahasuerus, pleads with her husband for her people, and he responds: 'What is thy petition, queen Esther? and it shall be granted thee: and what is thy request? and it shall be performed, even to the half of the kingdom' (Esther 7:2).

51. *Milesian*: Name given to the ancient Irish, because of the legend that two sons of Miledh, King of Spain, conquered the country in about 1300 BC and re-peopled it after exterminating the original inhabitants.

52. *Holy St Cyprian! . . . Mornington, 1829*: This poem, apparently written by Zamorna when he was Marquis of Douro and living on his father's country estate, speaks of his 'first passion' for and separation from Mina Laury, when she was a young peasant girl in Senegambia (see *Something About Arthur* (1833), *EEW*, 2.i, pp. 37–40). St Cyprian of Carthage was a third-century saint and martyr, and a figure of chastity. W. Harrison Ainsworth's *Rookwood* (1834) contains a 'Hymn to St Cyprian', sung in St Cyprian's cell by a dark-eyed, beautiful gipsy maid who, like Mina Laury, is faithful to her faithless lover. Ainsworth's 'Hymn', however, is a plea for the saint's intercession, quite different from this Byronically romantic lyric of secular sensibility. Indeed, the name 'Cyprian' – derived from the island of Cyprus, famous for the worship of Aprhrodite, goddess of love – in the context of Mina's story has a suggestiveness that is far from innocent. As her reference earlier in *Mina Laury* to 'an Angrian gentleman's dolly' suggests, Brontë was not ignorant of racy Regency slang. She can hardly have been unaware that 'Cyprian', in the early nineteenth century, denoted a fashionable courtesan.

53. *left-hand cousin*: To marry with the left hand is to contract a morganatic marriage; a child by the left hand is one born of such a marriage (*OED*).

54. *Low spirits . . . escape*: *Low spirits*, or 'Hypochondriasis' was seen as a disease in the early nineteenth century; the Brontë

family copy of Thomas J. Graham's *Modern Domestic Medicine* contains a section on the subject (p. 343). *the wicked ... escape*: Psalm 141:10: 'Let the wicked fall into their own nets, whilst that I withall escape.'

55.   *Apollo*: Represented in art as the perfection of youthful manhood.

56.   *For a long space of time, good-bye*: Brontë was about to return to school, and would have little opportunity to write before her next vacation.

STANCLIFFE'S HOTEL

Untitled manuscript in the Brontë Parsonage Museum, Haworth (BPM: Bon114). Given the title *Stancliffe's Hotel* in Christine Alexander, *The Early Writings of Charlotte Brontë* (Oxford: Basil Blackwell, 1983), p. 171.

1.   *exercised ... slang*: *exercised*: Conducted the service, expounded scripture (obsolete). *slang*: 'The special vocabulary or phraseology of a particular calling or profession' (*OED*); in this case, that of dissenting revivalism. The remark is apparently a comment on 'exercised'.

2.   *coolness ... starry skies*: *coolness*: 'abrupt' deleted in ms. immediately before this. *starry skies*: Louisa is romantically invoking Lord Byron's famous celebration of virtuous feminine beauty (1814): 'She walks in beauty, like the night / Of cloudless climes and starry skies'.

3.   *Richard, Marquis of Wellesley*: Louisa's elderly former husband, brother of the Duke of Wellington. He clearly has a weakness for 'rice-currie': he is portrayed in Branwell's *Historical Narrative of the War of Encroachment* (1833) at a dinner with an 'illustrious crowd' at the Duke of Wellington's table, 'peevishly' exclaiming 'Oh hold your filthy language realy I can not eat my rice curry in peace' (Neufeldt, 1, p. 401).

4.   *gouty chair and stool*: Special chair and stool used during an attack of gout.

5.   *bald elderly gentleman*: Alexander Percy, Earl of Northangerland, whose baldness is frequently mentioned in the Angrian mss. of this time. Louisa was formerly his mistress, and is the mother of his daughter, Caroline Vernon.

6.   *proof spirits ... silks*: *proof spirits*: Strong distilled alcoholic

liquor. *Hollands*: A grain spirit, or gin, manufactured in Holland; Branwell Brontë's Angrian mss. repeatedly portray Alexander Percy's heavy drinking. *pantaloons*: Tight pantaloons were the dandy fashion for evening wear. *silks*: silk stockings, or possibly silk knee-breeches, by the 1830s worn still only by the elderly (C. Willett Cunnington and Phillis Cunnington, *Handbook of English Costume in the Nineteenth Century* (London: Faber, 3rd edn., 1970, pp. 104–5, 45)). See *The Duke of Zamorna*, n. 38.

7.   *Countess's*: Lady Zenobia Ellrington's.

8.   *Dance*: Though now technically Marchioness of Wellesley, and previously Louisa Vernon, Louisa is sometimes referred to in the Angrian mss. as Louisa Dance. Presumably the Dance here referred to is a relative of her first husband, George Vernon, Lord Dance.

9.   *with you*: The ms. continues: 'I persisted, however, in excusing myself; and her ladyship, too urbane to shew displeasure at anything, allowed me to depart with no more severe reproach than what was conveyed in a gentle shake of the head. "How very odd," thought I, as I strolled away down the shrubbery, "that Louisa Dance should ever have had any charms for Lord Northangerland!" ' These two sentences, though not crossed out, seem to have been discarded in favour of a different version of events. The following sentence, which leads into the rest of the story, is inserted immediately afterwards in even smaller hand-writing.

10. *greatest man of his age*: Northangerland. The epithet signals Townshend's disaffection from Zamorna.

11. *adipose*: Fat. Apparently this is a comic substitution for 'coma-tose': Macara is not yet in command of language.

12. *indulgence of this kind*: The young Brontës would have been familiar with such descriptions of drug experiences. Thomas de Quincey's *Confessions of an English Opium-Eater* had appeared in 1822, and was much discussed and referred to thereafter in *Blackwood's Magazine*. In the course of one such discussion in 'Noctes Ambrosianae', James Hogg, 'the Ettrick Shepherd', offers a long and graphic description of taking five hundred drops of laudanum and sleeping from Monday to Friday (*Blackwood's Magazine* 14 (1823), pp. 485–6).

13. *frénétique ... Bromley*: *frénétique*: Frantic, frenzied (French). Louisa's use of French is an affectation of gentility; the *haut monde* practice of dropping French phrases into conversation was much portrayed in silver fork novels, often satirically: in Bulwer's *Pelham*, for instance, the hero's mother advises him to

'make very little use of French phrases; no vulgarity is more unpleasing' (ch. 26). *Ashworth*: As part of his attempt to undermine Zamorna before the rebellion of 26 June 1836, Northangerland had, as Branwell puts it, 'attracted popular attention by ridiculous Theology', delivering hell-fire sermons in disguise as 'Brother Ashworth' (*[Angria and the Angrians] III (c)*, Neufeldt, 2, p. 577). See *Passing Events, Five Novelettes*, pp. 53–4. Bromley: Methodist Minister in Verdopolis.

14. *news-room*: In the 1830s, a reading-room set aside for the reading of newspapers.

15. *fashionable paper*: The 'Fashionable Intelligence' or society gossip column of a newspaper was a popular feature of the silver fork novels of the 1820s and 1830s. Charlotte Brontë's *Four Years Ago* (1837) opens with Charles Townshend perusing the 'dust-dimmed paragraphs' of a 'Fashionable Intelligence' column of 'some four or five years back'.

16. *campaign of –33, the rebellion of –36*: The first was the Verdopolitan Union's campaign against the French, described by Branwell in his *Historical Narrative of the War of Encroachment* (1833) (Neufeldt, 1, pp. 365–405), the second the rising against the 'Parliament the Ministry and the Government troops' of Verdopolis under the command of Northangerland in June 1836 (described in Branwell's *[Angria and the Angrians] III (c)*, Neufeldt, 2, pp. 577–9).

17. *dress*: The more elaborate apparel proper to a public ceremony, a dinner or an evening party.

18. *market-fresh*: Slang for drunk, referring to 'that dubious degree of sobriety with which farmers too commonly return home from market' (1841; *OED*).

19. *Gentlemen in the soft and hard line*: Commercial travellers in different kinds of commodities. Cf. Charles Dickens, *Sketches by Boz* (1836), ch. 5: 'The man in the shop, perhaps, is in the baked "jemmy" line, or the fire-wood and hearth-stone line, or any other line which requires a floating capital of eighteen-pence or thereabouts.'

20. *in a gold chain*: Wearing a gold watch chain.

21. *Percy*: This is not Alexander Percy, Earl of Northangerland, who has withdrawn from public life, but his estranged son, Edward Percy, President of the Board of Trade, who is a woollen manufacturer and an astute businessman – as is revealed in the ensuing discussion of his driving a hard bargain over dyes.

22. *insults . . . the Czar*: *insults*: Brontë had written of the 'extreme

coldness' between Zamorna and Edward Percy, 'one of his ablest and highest ministers' in *The Scrap Book: Duke of Z and E Percy* in 1835 (*EEW*, 2.ii, pp. 360–1). The 'opportunity' here referred to presents itself later in *Stancliffe's Hotel*, when Percy is reported as saying 'he'll lie in bed all the day to-morrow' rather than rise to Zamorna's defence (p. 108). *the Czar*: A name for the Duke of Zamorna, indicative of his arrogance.

23. *Brandy and Water*: This appears to be Edward Percy's nickname; see *The Duke of Zamorna*, p. 107.

24. *screwed*: Forced the seller to lower his price.

25. *madder . . . barilla*: Vegetable substances used in dyeing. Chemical dyes did not appear until later in the century. *madder*: Root of the plant *Rubia tinctorum*, producing a reddish-purple dye. *indigo*: Substance obtained in the form of a blue powder from plants of the genus *Indigofera*, used as a blue dye. *logwood*: Heartwood of an American tree (*Haematoxylon Campechianum*) used in dyeing; so called from being imported in the form of logs. *barilla*: Maritime plant (*Salsola Soda*) which grows extensively in Spain, Sicily and the Canary Islands, dried and burned to produce an alkali used in making soap and soda.

26. *Angrian hue*: Red.

27. *Edwardston . . . Medina's kettle-drums*: Townshend is referring to the events following Zamorna's 'terrific defeat at Edwardston losing 18,000 men' in a battle against the assembled forces of Macterroglen (Jeremiah Simpson), Massena, Quashia and Sheik Abdulla Medina (Lord Jordan) on 27 June 1836. Zamorna, Branwell recounts, 'was taken alone and exhausted among the Warner Hills. then after detention and brutal insult from Simpson. Northangerland Bought him and had him conveyed to Verdopolis' (*[Angria and the Angrians] III (d)*, Neufeldt, 2, p. 602). *turbaned figure, with furred robes like a sultan*: Presumably Lord Jordan. In a manuscript written in 1837, Branwell had depicted him as a 'Statly and Haughty Turk . . . looking as lazy and sensual as an Ottoman D—l, all decked in Scarfs and Turban and Diamond hilted sabre with the three tailed Crescent born wavingly above his head' (*[Angria and the Angrians] IV(e)*, Neufeldt 3, p. 108).

28. *lavish the blunt . . . Genii dreams*: *lavish the blunt*: Fling money about; Lord Charles Wellesley, in *My Angria and the Angrians* (1834), speaks of 'that love of ostentatious pomp and flashy display which circulates through the veins of every Angrian as unceasingly as his blood' (*EEW*, 2.ii, p. 240). *Genii dreams*:

Comic reference to the origins of Angria in the Brontë children's Glass Town saga and their role as the Four Chief Genii therein.

29. *miracle of Cana . . . Moses*: *miracle of Cana*: In which Jesus turned water into wine (John 2:1–11). *Moses*: Apparently refers to Moses' miracles before Pharaoh (Exodus 7:9–21).

30. *Giaour*: Islamic term of abuse for Christians, and title of a poem by Lord Byron (1813). The above exchange is an example of 'dandified speaking', as *Fraser's* termed it in June 1838, citing (and mocking) a German writer on the subject:

> D. Whaiter, a cup of coffee, weak as a lady falling aswoon, and cool as a zephir.
> F. Whaiter, a cup of coffee, hot as hell, and strong as the devil.
> D. Pray, whaiter, what is the gentleman's name?
> F. Pray, whaiter, what is that lady's name? (*Fraser's Magazine* 17 June 1838, p. 693)

31. *endued . . . frock*: *endued*: Put on as a garment (*OED*); the word also has the sense of 'invest or endow with a spiritual gift', and carries a mock-heroic resonance here. *frock*: Frock-coat.

32. *sleeping like Moses amongst the flags on some river-side*: See Exodus 2:3.

33. *exertions . . . extirpate the savages*: Verdopolis had been founded on the expulsion of the Ashantees and the Negroes, and Zamorna's kingdom of Angria on his victory over the Ashantee, but the natives of these regions still remain unsubdued and their lands unexplored. Here, as throughout the Brontë juvenilia, they are stereotyped as 'savages'.

34. *leashes*: A leash is a set of three hounds.

35. *organ . . . cranium*: Sir William is here using the language of phrenology, the pseudo-science developed by Gall and Spurzheim at the end of the eighteenth century, which claimed to read character from the conformations of the skull. On the popularity of phrenology in the early nineteenth century England and the ways in which Brontë's fiction is 'permeated by its language and assumptions', see Sally Shuttleworth, *Charlotte Brontë and Victorian Psychology* (Cambridge University Press, 1996), ch. 4. Shuttleworth notes that The Keighley Mechanics Institute, used by the young Brontës, had acquired a *Manual of Phrenology* in 1837.

36. *cambric . . . huckaback*: *cambric*: A fine white linen. *huckaback*: A much rougher and stouter one.

37. *hells*: Gambling dens.

38. *perfect work*: Cf. James 1:4: 'Let patience have her perfect work.'

39. *Dutch capacity*: Dutch folk dress, still widely worn in the nine-teenth century, famously included baggy trousers, the original inspiration for knickerbockers or knickers. *Fraser's* speaks of the dandy fashion for 'puckering the trousers round the waist in large folds, until they "stand off" like those of a Dutch burgomaster' (*Fraser's* 15, February 1837, p. 237).

40. *branded brow ... wound*: *branded brow*: Cf. *Julia* (1837): 'it was Lord Hartford – I knew him by his military bearing, his mustachios – & the scar on his forehead' (*Five Novelettes*, p. 96). *wound*: In the duel with Zamorna described in *Mina Laury*.

41. *memorial*: Statement of facts forming the basis of or expressed in the form of a petition or remonstrance to a person in authority, a government, etc. (*OED*).

42. *fore-finger*: Cf. the description in *Julia* (June 1837) of a meeting between Charles Townshend and William Percy: 'I held out my hand, the officer put his fore-finger into it' (*Five Novelettes*, p. 105). *Fraser's Magazine* for May 1837 had carried a comic article on the 'new science' of 'Digitology', 'an easy means of ascertaining the characters and peculiarities of individuals, as exhibited in the usual mode of salutation': 'Some people dangle their hands into yours like the unwilling paw of a peaceable poodle; others stiffen the hand, and thrust four fingers into your palm, all smooth and wooden like a glover's last. Mr Doddle appears to have but one finger produceable; hard and bony it feels, like the handle of your tooth-brush on a frosty morning. Mr Trumpeter always holds out two fingers; I do the same; and it perplexes him not a little when the tips meet, and he fingers out the *da capo* of his own two to two too' ('Blue Friar Pleas-antries III: "A Few Hints for the Promulgation of a New Science", *Fraser's* 15, May 1837, pp. 571–2).

43. *full half hour to dress ... therein reflected*: *full half hour to dress*: The toilette was the great ritual of the dandy day; Beau Brummell famously spent well over two hours every morning on his appear-ance (Ellen Moers, *The Dandy: Brummell to Beerbohm* (Lincoln : University of Nebraska Press, 1978), pp. 32, 61). *therein reflected*: Brontë may well have been thinking of Daniel Maclise's famous satiric line drawing of Bulwer gazing at himself in a cheval glass, which appeared in one of the first copies of *Fraser's* to be taken in Haworth Parsonage ('Gallery of Literary Charac-ters', *Fraser's* 6, August 1832).

44. *for the bare life*: As if to save her life.
45. *Bochsa's harp*: Robert Nicolas Charles Bochsa (1789–1856), French composer and harp virtuoso, who did much to make the harp fashionable in the first half of the nineteenth century. His *New and improved method of instruction for the harp* was published in London in 1819. From 1822 to 1827, he was professor of harp at the Royal Academy of Music in London, until the scandal of his past as a convicted forger and possible bigamist brought about his dismissal. In the 1830s he played in London and the provinces with consistent success, and it is possible that the young Brontës heard him at this time. Charlotte Brontë refers to him in a manuscript of 1834 (*Corner Dishes: A Day Abroad*, *EEW*, ii.2, p. 110). For music in and around Haworth in the 1830s, see Barker, pp. 210–12.
46. *Simpson's hoof*: Its invasion by the troops of Zamorna's enemies, led by Jeremiah Simpson [Sir Jehu Macterroglen].
47. *a purple habit . . . her streaming veil*: Cf. Jane Eyre's first glimpse of Blanche Ingram: 'Her purple riding-habit almost swept the ground, her veil streamed long on the breeze; mingling with its transparent folds, and gleaming through them, shone rich raven ringlets' (*Jane Eyre*, ch. 17).
48. *comparison between eastern and western women*: Christine Alexander (*Early Writings of Charlotte Brontë*, p. 175) suggests that this is a reference to the Roe Head journal fragment, 'My compliments to the weather', but it seems unlikely that Brontë would expect her 'readers' to be familiar with this. It possibly refers to another Angrian manuscript now lost.
49. *I put my thumb to the side of my nose*: See *Henry Hastings*, n. 30.
50. *golden*: Her hair, as Townshend has noted, is 'of the true Angrian hue', i.e. red. This is possibly a joke about the 'reader''s (Branwell's) red hair.
51. *running*: Becoming.
52. *Turner Grey*: Jane, the native Angrian beauty, is singing of a native Angrian hero, George Turner Grey; and of Hartford and Warner, both members of old Angrian families. In an earlier novelette, Brontë tells of how George Turner Grey, squire of Ardsley in Angria, called his tenantry about him after the battle of Edwardston to make a last stand, giving them the motto, 'Ardsley to the van!' (*The Return of Zamorna*, December 1836, *SHCBM*, 2, pp. 301–6).
53. *Medina . . . Sir Jehu*: Sheik Abdulla Medina (Earl of Jordan) and

Sir Jehu Macterroglen (Jeremiah Simpson), two of the leaders of the forces massed against Zamorna.

54. *in form*: Formal; following established procedures.

55. *eye-glass*: By dandies 'it was . . . considered good breeding to be short-sighted and the exquisite's glass was in constant requisition' ('Dress, Dandies, Fashion &c.', *Fraser's* 15, February 1837, p. 237). Cf. Lord Richton's 'gold eye-glass set with brilliants' at the county ball in *The Duke of Zamorna*, p. 168.

56. *Cirhala . . . Evesham*: The battle of Evesham was the last great battle of the Angrian saga. Evesham on the river Cirhala had been fortified by Northangerland's revolutionary army, and was taken by General Thornton in the final, bloody battle of Zamorna's return to power.

57. *conflict won*: 'news of joy' deleted in ms.

58. *Who guards the martyr's grave*: 'Repose the martyred brave!' deleted in ms.

59. *No French! No Ardrahians!*: The French and the Verdopolitan troops under Ardrah had been allied with Northangerland against Zamorna.

60. *his son-in-law*: Zamorna.

61. *red*: 'Marked or characterized by blood or fire, or by violence suggestive of these' (*OED*); the modern sense of 'revolutionary', referring originally to the colour of a party badge, dates from 1848.

62. *ow'd worn-out rake*: Northangerland.

63. *flay*: Frighten. Cf. Charlotte Brontë, *Shirley*, ch. 5: 'Like as they're flayed wi' bogards.'

64. *by every lamp-post*: The suggestion is of impending insurrection. During the French Revolution, a popular cry of the revolutionists was 'A la lanterne!' ('Hang him from the lamp-post!').

65. *frogged dress coat*: Frogged coats were favourite dandy dress; cf. Hazlitt's contempt, in 'The Dandy School' (1827), for 'those who would persuade [John Bull] to build up his fame on frogged coats or on the embellishment of a snuff-box' (William Hazlitt, *Complete Works* (London, 1934), vol. 20, pp. 145–6).

66. *wet Quaker whom the spirit had not yet moved*: A 'wet Quaker' was one who did not follow the rules strictly. Cf. *Bentley's Miscellany* 4 (1838), p. 297: 'Who has not heard of . . . a wet Quaker? who *thees* and *yays*, wears no collar to his coat . . . but is in other respects . . . living that sort of life which, in England, is called that of a jolly dog.' It is customary in Quaker meetings to sit silent until moved by the spirit to speak.

67. *flew like chaff . . . sand of the desert*: Cf. Isaiah 40:24, 41:15–16.
68. *Sic transit etc.*: 'Sic transit gloria mundi' (Latin): so passes the glory of this world.
69. *dog-days*: The days about the time of the heliacal rising of the Dog-star (July–August), the hottest and most unwholesome period of the year, and one often seen as subject to malignant influences.
70. *Great Mogul*: Emperor of the Mohammedan-Tartar empire (1526–1707) in India. Like 'Czar', a dig at Zamorna's autocratic ways.
71. *four and twenty honey-pots all of a row*: Four and twenty is a favourite nursery rhyme number: e.g. 'Four and twenty black-birds baked in a pie', 'Four and twenty white bulls sat upon a stall', 'Four and twenty white horses on yonder hill', 'Four and twenty tailors went to kill a snail', 'Four and twenty taylors all on a row' (Iona and Peter Opie (eds.), *Oxford Dictionary of Nursery Rhymes* (Oxford: Clarendon Press, 1951), pp. 212, 401–2).
72. *that gaze*: The ms. here contains the following sentence: 'A lady stood by the sash of a large saloon at Stancliffe's.' The first three words are crossed out; the following sentence suggests that perhaps the intention was to cross out the whole.
73. *the couch*: 'her head' deleted in ms.
74. *piquing or soothing them*: Cf. *Jane Eyre*, ch. 16: 'I knew the pleasure of vexing and soothing him by turns.'
75. *slept . . . stoops*: Note change of tense; this is at once a narrative and a present scene.
76. *Sappho*: Greek lyric poetess of the seventh century BC, whose principal subject was love; used here to indicate any poetical woman.
77. *preferring*: Putting forward for consideration.
78. *Byron*: Lord Byron – both as a poet and as a cultural phenomenon – was one of the most potent influences on the Brontës' writings. Since early adolescence, Charlotte had been familiar not merely with his poetry and dramas but also with Moore's *Life of Lord Byron* (1830), which she recommended to her friend Ellen Nussey in 1834 (*CBL*, i, p. 131). Between 1833 and 1835 she had copied in pencil and in watercolour a number of the many engravings illustrating the poetry and life of Byron which were produced as 'embellishments' to the poet's works in these years (see Alexander and Sellars, *The Art of the Brontës*, pp. 16–20): her copies bear a distinct resemblance to her descriptions of Angrian charac-

ters and scenes. The developing figure of Zamorna is a markedly Byronic one: heroic, accomplished, magnetically sexually attractive, aristocratically careless of the world's opinion, and – by the time of *Mina Laury* – with a dark and sinful past. As Marquis of Douro, he had himself been a poet. In Branwell's *The Politics of Verdopolis* (1833) Sir Robert Pelham, a visiting Englishman and an early suitor of Mary Percy, finds her reading Byron. She shows him 'an exquisitly bound. little doudecimo. printed in a superlative stile upon. paper like Ivory . . . it was a volume of the poems of. Arthur Marquis of Douro.' She and Pelham agree that Douro's poems are better than Byron's', 'yet they are like each other' (Neufeldt, 1, pp. 350–1).

79. *[finger]*: Ms. reads 'figure'.
80. *[ready]*: Ms. reads 'red'.

THE DUKE OF ZAMORNA

The manuscript of *The Duke of Zamorna*, formerly in the Law Collection, has disappeared. The text given here is based on the transcript by Davidson Cook in the Brontë Parsonage Museum. (See Note on the Texts.)

1. *anecdotes . . . face to face*: *anecdotes*: Charles Townshend's musings here are evocative of Thomas Moore's account, well known to Charlotte Brontë, of the way in which the 'exaggerated stories' and 'strange anecdotes' of Byron's predecessor at Newstead wakened in his mind 'a sort of boyish admiration for singularities which he found thus elevated into matters of wonder and record' (Thomas Moore, *Life of Lord Byron* (1830), ch. 2). *face to face*: Cf. 1 Corinthians 13:12: 'For now we see through a glass, darkly; but then face to face.'

2. *Dorn . . . Lady Anne Vernon*: *Dorn*: Captain C. Dorn, leader of a regiment of Lancers in Percy's army in the rebellion of 1832 (*Letters from an Englishman Vol. IV*, Neufeldt, 1, p. 201). The character is undeveloped in the surviving writings of the Angrian saga. *Lady Anne Vernon*: Possibly a relative of Louisa Vernon's first husband, Lord George Vernon.

3. *terribly bad . . . vortices*: *terribly bad*: Cf. John Bud's description of the 'western aristocracy' in Branwell Brontë's *Life of Alexander Percy Vol I* (1834): 'All these men . . . lived in a first rate style kept up splendid establishments plunged headlong in play

and dissipation and in consequence grasped every penny they could lay their hands on and wrung without mercy all the savings of their harassed tenantry . . . of all persons whose names I have numerated there is not one now a[l]ive. No the short space of twenty years has swept them all from the earth and they have long heard their eternal sentence and entered on their eternal doom – their own deeds destroyed them and their own children hastened their end' (Neufeldt, 2, p. 113). *vortices*: A vortex is a situation into which persons or things are steadily drawn, or from which they cannot escape (*OED*).

4. *murderess*: As the letters that follow reveal, Augusta di Segovia had conspired to bring about the death of Edward Percy senior, father of her lover, the young Alexander Percy, so that the latter could come into his patrimony and repay his gambling debts.

5. *The hand is that of a lady*: Handwriting in the early nineteenth century carried distinctive cultural messages. As Brontë appears to have been sharply aware, there was a range of possible hands, each belonging to a particular social, occupational or gender group: 'ladies' hands', for example, were diminutive. In the course of the eighteenth century, there came to be increasing interest in handwriting as revelatory not merely of social standing but of the individual writer's character. The first full-length work on handwriting analysis, *The Art of Judging the Mind and Character of Men and Women from their Handwriting*, by the Frenchman Edouard Auguste Patrice Hocquart, appeared in French in 1812. Growing interest in this subject in the early nineteenth century meant that by the 1830s autograph collecting had become extremely popular (A. N. L. Munby, *The Cult of the Autograph Letter in England* (London: Athlone Press, 1962), p. 1). Brontë's interest in these questions is manifest in what follows. Percy's letter to 'Harry' is 'hastily written in a hand scarcely yet formed, almost that of a schoolboy'; the opera singer's misspelled epistle is in a 'female hand'. If Jeremiah Simpson's, 'much blotted and slurred', suggests drunkenness, Lord Caversham's 'almost illegible scrawl' is a mark of his aristocratic status. (Since clarity, above all, was required of counting-house clerks, it was unfashionable for a gentleman to write too legibly.) 'The clear mercantile strokes and turns' of Sir William Percy's letter are revelatory of 'what had once been the calling of the writer'; yet they are also quite distinctive: 'I knew the hand directly.' Later, in *Caroline Vernon*, Quashia's letter is 'a singularly folded epistle, directed in a large black autograph whose

terrible down-strokes, cross-dashes and circular flourishes seemed to defy all hands, mercantile, genteel and juvenile, that ever existed' (p. 334). In *The Professor* (written in 1846), the heroine, Frances' letter is addressed in 'a lady's clear, fine autograph'. 'I ... glanced at the small, neat, handwriting, not a bit like that of a mercantile man,' says Crimsworth, the narrator. 'They talk of affinities between the autograph and the character; what affinity was there here?' (*The Professor*, ch. 21).

6. *sinews*: The main strength, mainstay or chief supporting force, *of* something. Hence, money (as in the phrase, 'sinews of war').

7. *Adonis*: In classical mythology, a beautiful youth who was loved by Venus, and killed by a boar whilst hunting. Hence (usually ironically) any beautiful young man.

8. *men's evil actions ... write in water*: Cf. Shakespeare, *Henry VIII*, IV.ii. 51–2: 'Men's evil manners live in brass; their virtues/ We write in water.'

9. *little Harriet*: Harriet O'Connor, later to be seduced and abandoned by Alexander Percy. On 14 May 1838, two months before *The Duke of Zamorna* was written, Branwell had written a long dramatic monologue in which Harriet, on her deathbed, bewails the ruin to which her association with 'the Sultana' has led ('At dead of Midnight, drearily', Neufeldt, 3, pp. 223–31).

10. *cup play*: Drunken gambling.

11. *What's bred in the bone etc.*: The proverb continues 'will not out of the flesh'.

12. *'Of course ... our love'*: Neufeldt suspects that these lines are a quotation, but no source has been discovered (*CBP*, p. 376).

13. *our mutual friend Harry*: Harriet O'Connor. Branwell describes her as a girl, nicknamed 'Mr Harry', in his *Life of Alexander Percy Vol. II* (Neufeldt, 2, p. 153).

14. *Edward Percy*: Father of Alexander Percy, who is later to become Earl of Northangerland.

15. *take up my cross and follow him*: A blasphemous echo of Jesus' call to his disciples (Matthew 16:24). Pakenham is apparently trying to persuade the writer to elope with him.

16. *your pupil*: Alexander Percy, Augusta's 'pretty protégé', who is to become her husband.

17. *da Vega ... Pakenham's eldest daughter*: *da Vega*: Either Lope de Vega (1562–1635), founder of the Spanish drama and author of a number of plays, poems and romances; or Garcilasso de la Vega (1503–36), Spanish poet and friend of Boscan, mentioned by Byron in *Don Juan* 1, 95. *tassel gentle*: A 'tassel-gentle' is a

male falcon which can be owned only by a prince. The term 'tassel' is a corruption of 'tiercel', the male of the goshawk, so called because (like all male birds of prey) it is a tierce or third less than the female. Cf. *Romeo and Juliet*, II.ii.158–9: 'O for a falconer's voice / To lure this tassel-gentle back again!' *Pakenham's eldest daughter*: Lady Catherine Pakenham, who is to become Duchess of Wellington.

18. *These letters are all unconnected*: SHCBM adds here 'and I give them without arrangement.'

19. *young Duchess ... H. Montmorency*: *young Duchess*: The Duchess of Wellington, 'Pakenham's eldest daughter'. *drawing-room*: Formal reception by a king, queen or person of rank (in this case, presumably, the Duke of Wellington). *Mrs Alexander Percy*: Not Augusta di Segovia, who is by now dead, but Maria Henrietta Wharton, the 'Mary' of the following section, Percy's second wife. *H. Montmorency*: The writer is Montmorency's wife, the former Harriet O'Connor.

20. *Aura, veni*: Come, breeze (Latin). Thus Cepahalus, in Ovid's *The Art of Love* III, l. 698: '... mobilis aura, veni' ('Come, fickle breeze [to cool me]').

21. *The father disowns them*: The 'father' is Alexander Percy; the patient, Maria Henrietta, his second wife. Cf. Branwell Brontë, in a manuscript of 1836: 'his capricious temper hated the idea of looking on men as his children so he commissioned the hoary Bloodhound 'Sdeath to destroy them, but the villain only secreted them and Mary though filled with anguish could not speak against her God on earth She bore the sorrow in secret till she gave birth to a daughter and this he received as the image of its mother and his hope in years to come' (*[Angria and the Angrians] III (e)*, Neufeldt, 2, p. 660). The children are Edward, William, Henry and Mary Henrietta Percy. Henry meets an early death; the other three are all prominent in Charlotte's Angrian tales.

22. *decline*: Any disease in which the bodily strength gradually fails; used especially of tuberculosis.

23. *son and heir*: The future Duke of Zamorna.

24. *Gazemba ... that figure*: *Gazemba*: See Charlotte Brontë's poem, 'Review at Gazemba', dated 'July 7th 1838', two weeks before the completion of *The Duke of Zamorna* (CBP, pp. 262–5). *that figure*: Alexander Percy, future Earl of Northangerland.

25. *Lady Stuartville ... Countess of Arundel*: *Lady Stuartville*: Harriet, wife of Viscount Castlereagh; Christine Alexander conjectures that she is Montmorency's elder daughter (*EEW*, 2.ii,

p. 33 n. 55). *Lady Julia Thornton*: Lady Julia Thornton, originally Julia Wellesley, one of Zamorna's female cousins, of whom Lord Charles Wellesley remarks, 'Not one of them is better than she should be' (*The Scrap Book: A Late Occurrence*, *EEW*, 2.ii, p. 342). *Lady Maria Percy*: Wife of Edward Percy, formerly Maria Sneachie, a notorious coquette; her flirtation with Zamorna is described in Charlotte Brontë's *High Life in Verdopolis* (*EEW*, ii.2, pp. 49, 60). *Countess of Arundel*: Edith Sneachie, wife of Lord Frederick Lofty, the Earl of Arundel, whose 'hereditary pride' is noted in *High Life in Verdopolis*, *EEW*, ii.2, p. 14, and further discussed by Townshend when he meets her later in this story. All four of the just-mentioned ladies appear together, 'a splendid sight', in Charlotte Brontë's *My Angria and the Angrians*, *EEW*, ii.2, p. 255.

26. *evil genius . . . guardian angel*: *evil genius*: One of the two mutually opposed spirits (in Christian language *angels*) by whom every person was supposed to be attended throughout his life. Hence, a person who powerfully influences for good or evil the character, conduct or fortunes of another. *guardian angel*: An angel conceived as watching over or protecting a particular person or place.

27. *Lord Ellrington*: Alexander Percy has by now married Lady Zenobia Ellrington and taken her title.

28. *his endless limb*: Percy is portrayed throughout the juvenilia as very long-legged: in *Caroline Vernon* Quashia addresses him as 'Daddy-long-legs'.

29. *vice-president*: Ellrington and Douro are at this time leading members of a secret gambling and drinking club in Verdopolis, called the Elysium, or Paradise of Souls: Ellrington is its president and Douro its vice-president. (See Branwell Brontë, *Real Life in Verdopolis* (1833), Neufeldt, 1, p. 291.)

30. *the Drover . . . varying complexion*: *the Drover*: Subsequent to his early career as a pirate, Alexander Percy, Branwell tells, 'laid out thousands of his Gory gains in enormous stocks and set up an immense concern in Horses and Horned cattle, Travelling through the Different kingdoms of the Union attending all the Great Fairs . . . Percy of course became King and Emperor among all the Drovers' (*[Angria and the Angrians] III (e)*, (1836), Neufeldt, 2, p. 662). *varying complexion*: Zamorna's 'changeful cheek' is frequently remarked on in Brontë's descriptions of him. Cf. *Mina Laury*, p. 42.

31. *Milton's angels*: Cf. John Milton, *Paradise Lost*, II, ll. 557–61.

32. *my last work: Stancliffe's Hotel*, in which the Duke of Zamorna's visit to the ill and aged Northangerland forms a pivotal part of the plot.

33. *finishing boarding-school ... Brummell: finishing boarding-school*: Where young ladies learn the manners of polite society. *Brummell*: George Bryan Brummell, known as 'Beau Brummell' (1778–1840), famous dandy, wit and leader of fashion in London in the early years of the century; an intimate of the Prince Regent (later George IV). For the last fourteen years of his life he lived in poverty in France.

34. *viewless spirit of some sweet sound*: Byron, *Manfred* (1817), I.ii.53–7: 'Oh, that I were/ The viewless spirit of a lovely sound,/ A living voice, a breathing harmony,/ A bodiless enjoyment— born and dying/ With the blest tone which made me!'

35. *farmer person*: General Thornton.

36. *primitive peacock*: Possibly a reference to Northangerland's old-style dandy dress (see below, n. 38); the peacock is a type of ostentatious vanity and display. 'Primitive' seems here to have been chosen as much for its alliteration as for its meaning.

37. *Augean condition*: The stables of Augeas, the mythological king of Elis, in Greece, contained 3,000 oxen and had not been cleansed for 30 years. One of the labours of Hercules was to cleanse them.

38. *silks and smalls*: Northangerland's 'white tights and silks' are remarked upon in *Stancliffe's Hotel* (p. 69). *silks*: Apparently silk stockings; Northangerland is here being likened to an old-fashioned Regency 'buck', rather than a more up-to-date dandy in the Pelham mould. *smalls*: Not listed in *OED*; possibly a shortened form of 'smallclothes' or breeches; thus Dickens, *Pickwick Papers* (1836–7), ch. 15: 'what a difficult process it is to bow in green velvet smalls, and a tight jacket, and high-crowned hat; or in blue satin trunks and white silks.'

39. *deem*: Possibly a misprint, either in the ms. or the typescript, for 'demean'.

40. *in your custody*: Zamorna has become a kind of jailer to Louisa Vernon, since the end of her affair with Northangerland.

41. *Puritan*: Mocking or reproachful term for one who is or affects to be extremely strict, precise or scrupulous in religion or morals.

42. *Robert King Esqre*: Robert Patrick King, known familiarly as 'Sdeath, had been the 'valet rent-screwer and man of all work' of Alexander Percy's father. A figure of 'demoniacal malignity', he became the young Alexander's 'Great Mentor', his 'infallible

Oracle in all thoughts and actions' (Branwell Brontë, *Life of Alexander Percy I*, Neufeldt, 2, pp. 109, 110, 113).

43. *has no soul at all for music* ... *'The soldier's tear': has no soul for music*: On the young Alexander Percy's passion for music and his 'extraordinary musical genius', see Branwell Brontë, *Life of Alexander Percy I*, Neufeldt, 2, pp. 100, 124. *'Angels ever bright and fair'*: Aria from Handel's *Theodora* (1749). In a manuscript apparently written about a year earlier than this, Branwell describes the first meeting between Alexander Percy and Louisa Allen, who was to become Louisa Vernon. She is singing 'Angels ever bright and fair' at the Fidena Grand Musical Festival, and he, captivated, forcibly ejects the organist and accompanies her himself (*[Angria and the Angrians] IV(g)*, Neufeldt, 3, pp. 134–6). *'Thou wilt not leave my soul in Hell'*: Psalm 16:10. *'Hark 'tis the breeze of twilight calling'*: Song by Thomas Moore (1779–1852). *'The soldier's tear'*: Words by Thomas Haynes Bayly (1797–1829), music by George Alexander Lee (1802–1852). From the English musical *Sold for a Song* (1830). Its sentimental import is suggested by its closing lines: 'Go watch the foremost ranks / In danger's dark career, / Be sure the hand most daring there / Has wip'd away a tear.' Zamorna's susceptibility is akin to Byron's: 'I have not unfrequently ... seen the tears in his eyes while listening to "the Irish Melodies",' remarks Thomas Moore, in his *Letters and Journals of Lord Byron*, Vol. 2, p. 121.

44. *my own 19*[th]: Zamorna's regiment.

45. *Paul's epistles*: St Paul was famous for his injunctions that women be modest, silent and subservient to men; see, for example, 1 Timothy 2: 9–14.

46. *tormenting me to murder*: When Northangerland's rebellion against Zamorna ended in temporary victory, the latter was condemned to death but the sentence was commuted to exile, much to the fury of Louisa Vernon, who had been vociferous in her demands that he be put to death (*[Angria and the Angrians] III(d)*, Neufeldt, 2, p. 604).

47. *Shaver*: Northangerland's servant.

48. *I had forgot there was such an existence*: Brontë must have been aware that aristocrats in the Regency period usually acknowledged their illegitimate children, especially those borne by mistresses of higher social rank. William IV had sired ten children by the actress Mrs Jordan before his marriage to Adelaide; they were given the surname Fitzclarence and went to live with him

at court. The children of the mistress of the fifth Duke of Devon-
shire were brought up with his own. In *Jane Eyre*, the young
Adèle Varens, putative daughter of Rochester, is taken to live
with her father and provided with a good education.

49. *features are not ideal*: That is, they are taken from real life.

50. *Flower of Senegambia*: Harriet O'Connor, described by
Branwell's Lord Richton in 1837 as 'the beautiful but misguided
girl who lies in Fidena Minster a thousand miles from her ruined
Home' (*[Angria and the Angrians] IV(d)*, Neufeldt, 3, p. 158).

51. *haughty Rover*: Alexander Percy in his young days was a pirate,
known as the Rover, a name presumably taken from the cant
term 'rover': a pirate, a vagabond (*DVT*).

52. *what features . . . last night*: The 'not ideal' features of the statue
he has described.

53. *the Devil to pay*: Saying which refers to bargains with Satan, and
the inevitable payment to be made to him in the end.

54. *Blood and 'oons*: Blasphemous ejaculation, referring to Christ's
blood and wounds; *'oons!* Euphemistic abbreviation of *by God's
wounds* (variants: gadswoons, odsoons, zoons, zounds).

55. *helm . . . helm*: The word is being used in two different senses
here: first as a poetic and archaic term for a helmet; second as
the handle, tiller or wheel by which the rudder is managed in
ships, and hence, by extension, the position of control.

56. *organ-pipes*: Throat.

57. *Clytemnestra*: Wife of Agamemnon, King of Argos. On the return
of her husband to the Trojan War, she and her lover Aegisthus
murdered Agamemnon; she, in her turn, was murdered by
Orestes, Agamemnon's son.

58. *chilly, white and cold*: This phrase is in quotation marks, but
I have been unable to find a source for it.

59. 'AUGUSTA! . . . Without an echo die': Cf. ll.219–222 of
Branwell Brontë's 'Misery. Scene 1st', written in 1835, and sent
by him to the editor of *Blackwood's* in April 1836 as a specimen
of his work:

> 'Maria!' But the silence round
>   Would give him no reply,
> And straightway did that single sound
>   Without an echo die. (*PPBB*, p. 104)

60. *All this has been told you . . . Revenons à nos moutons*: *All this
has been told you*: Branwell had included a long, melodramatic

description of Augusta's death in his *Life of Alexander Percy Vol II*, written between 22 October and 17 November 1835 (Neufeldt, 2, pp. 173–8). *Revenons à nos moutons*: Let us return to the subject in hand (French); a typically affected, dandyish use of French. Cf. Pelham's friend Guloseton, writing to him from London: '*Mais revenons à nos moutons* – (a most pertinent phrase, by the by – oh! the French excel us in every thing, from the paramount science of cookery, to the little art of conversation).' (Edward Lytton Bulwer, *Pelham* (1828), ch. 70).

61. *calling of the writer*: Sir William Percy had begun his career as a clerk in his brother's counting house. Mercantile advice books in the early nineteenth century urged their readers to develop a straightforward 'Clerk-like Manner of Writing, fit for the Dextrous Dispatch of Business', without the dandyish flourishes used by gentlemen (Thornton, *Handwriting in America*, pp. 13–14).

62. *Selkirk ... Ascension Isle*: *Selkirk*: Alexander Selkirk (1676–1721), Scotsman from Largo, Fife, and the inspiration for Daniel Defoe's novel *Robinson Crusoe* (1719). While sailing with English privateers in 1704, he quarrelled with his captain and asked to be put ashore on Juan Fernandez, an uninhabited island off South America; he took with him a musket, a hatchet and a few utensils; there he survived alone for over four years before being rescued by another English ship, with which he sailed for two years before returning home. *Ascension Isle*: Remote island in the middle of the southern Atlantic, on which a British naval garrison had been established in 1815, when the exile of Napoleon to St Helena made it strategically significant. It was made part of the landscape of the Angrian saga when Branwell portrayed his 'Young Men' landing there on their original voyage to Africa (*The History of the Young Men*, Neufeldt, 1, p. 142). It was to Ascension Island that Zamorna was exiled after his defeat at Edwardston by Northangerland in 1836 (*[Angria and the Angrians] III(d)*, Neufeldt, 2, p. 602).

63. *Zamorna, Adrianopolis ... beasts of the field*: What Percy means here is not that the rest of Angria is literally uninhabited, but that it lacks people of fashion. For the dandy view of such figures as 'Mrs Chester' and 'Susan' and the boy who carries Townshend's carpet-bag, mentioned in his narrative, see Lytton Bulwer, *Pelham*, ch. 34:

> That tribe one never, indeed, considers as possessing a life separate from their services to us: beyond that purpose of existence, we

know not even if they exist. As Providence made the stars for the
benefit of earth, so it made servants for the use of gentlemen; and,
as neither stars not servants appear except when we want them, so
I suppose they are in a sort of suspense from being, except at those
important and happy moments.

64. *wounded deer ... mutual acquaintance*: *wounded deer*:
     The wounded deer was supposed to hide herself away until
     death:

> So wings the wounded Deer her headlong flight,
> Pierced by some ambush'd archer of the night,
> Shoots to the woodlands with her bounding fawn,
> And drops of blood bedew the conscious lawn;
> There hid in shades she shuns the cheerful day,
> Hangs o'er her young, and weeps her life away.
> > Erasmus Darwin, *The Botanic Garden* (1799),
> > > Part II, *The Loves of the Plants*,
> > > > Canto III, 263–8

     mutual acquaintance: The reference is to Jane Moore, their meet-
     ing with whom was recorded in *Stancliffe's Hotel*.
65. *chest padded ... grizzling locks curled*: Well-known dandy
     fashions. 'You are to be padded ... you are to wear stays ... you
     are to have a French valet who is to put your hair in papillottes
     [curl-papers]', says Caroline, who is attempting to turn her
     brother into a dandy, in Harriette Wilson's *Paris Lions and
     London Tigers* (1825).
66. *slough ... one too sublime to be named*: *slough*: The outer skin
     periodically cast or shed by a snake, adder, or similar reptile;
     used figuratively to mean a feature or quality which is thrown
     off. *one too sublime to be named*: Zamorna. Refers, apparently,
     to false gossip about Hartford and Mina Laury.
67. *eye-glass*: On the importance of the dandy eye-glass, see *Stan-
     cliffe's Hotel*, n. 55.
68. *Oh, waltz ... Not for worlds*: The waltz was introduced to
     England in 1811 (Adburgham, p. 8). Because it was a dance
     performed in triple time, by couples almost embracing, it was
     seen by many as indecent. Byron's *The Waltz: An Apostrophic
     Hymn* (1813) details the public intimacies it permitted.
69. *mulatto*: Perhaps simply a derogatory reference to Hartford's
     often-mentioned 'sunburnt' complexion, possibly a suggestion

NOTES   495

that he is of mixed race. Unlike Townshend and Sir William, he is Angrian born, descended from one of the country's oldest families; the hint may be that he counts amongst his ancestry some of its original inhabitants. Cf. *Henry Hastings* n. 86.

70. *people would say I wanted to marry you*: Jane Moore has already admitted this to the Thorntons, in *Stancliffe's Hotel* (p. 104).

71. *your Lordship shall be the lady*: Such play with gender roles recurs in Brontë's later novels. Rochester appears disguised as an old gipsy woman in *Jane Eyre*; Shirley calls herself 'Captain Keeldar' (*Shirley*, ch. 11); in *Villette*, Lucy Snowe appears as a man in the play on Madame Becke's fête day, and is 'haunted' by a young man dressed as a nun.

72. *Lord Lieutenant's*: Lord Stuartville, Earl of Castlereagh.

73. *Lancers*: A quadrille.

74. *Order of the Rising Sun*: The rising sun is the national symbol of Angria.

75. *Pooh*: Both typescript and *SHCBM* read *Poor*. I suspect a misreading of 'Pooh', an expletive which Percy uses later in this letter.

76. *all empty froth to the far-end*: Like a glass filled with froth, not beer.

77. *puts on character and acts a part at will*: Cf. the writer's own performance as William Clarke on his visit to Miss Moore in *Stancliffe's Hotel*.

78. *the organ of secretiveness*: Term taken from phrenology; see *Stancliffe's Hotel*, n. 35.

79. *tents of Kedar . . . living out of the world*: *tents of Kedar*: Kedar was son of Ishmael, and ancestor of a tribe of nomadic Arabs; the phrase means 'houses in the wilderness of this world': 'Woe is me, that I sojourn in Mesech, that I dwell in the tents of Kedar' (Psalm cxx:5). *living out of the world*: 'In the language of the Regency, "the world" meant the world of fashionable society, of privilege and politics, rank and talent' (Adburgham, *Silver Fork Society*, p. 5).

80. *His gallant lordship has no literary turn*: Townshend is, as he says in *Stancliffe's Hotel*, 'a popular author' in Angria.

81. *college-bred*: An ironic reference to Thornton's rough manner of speech.

82. *with all expedition*: Quickly.

83. *your all-but-father*: In his younger days, Townshend (then Lord Charles Wellesley) had been placed under the guardianship of

Thornton, and lived with him in Thornton Hotel and Girnington Hall (see Charlotte Brontë, *A Leaf from an Unopened Volume* (1833), *EEW*, ii.1, pp. 323–4).

84. *loud huzza of scorn*: Edwardston Hall is the country estate of Sir William Percy's brother, Edward. The antipathy between them is explained on p. 181.

85. *smacking . . . browns and stones*: *smacking*: Getting a move on. *Doverham*: Angrian equivalent of Dover. *collier*: Ship engaged in the carriage of coal. Cf. *Caroline Vernon*: 'getting on board a steamer and away all fizz and foam, down past Mouthton and coasting it along by Doverham'. *browns and stones*: Refers apparently, to the colours of the gig-driver's dress, 'stone' is a fashion shade of yellowish or brownish grey.

86. *Butter and brimstone . . . Brandy and Water*: *Butter and brimstone*: 'Fire and brimstone!' is the usual ejaculation (see *Twelfth Night*, II.v.56; *Othello* IV.i.245); the change perhaps emphasizes Edward's watered-down ridiculousness. *Brandy and Water*: Apparently a nickname for Percy.

87. *Tiger*: General Henri Fernando di Enara, Commander of Zamorna's Angrian forces.

88. *wild Salvator scenes*: The sublime and terrifying landscapes of Salvator Rosa (1615–73), with their jagged rocks and stormy skies, were enormously popular in the nineteenth century.

89. *family*: Enara's daughters' characters are not developed in any surviving Angrian manuscripts, but there is a glimpse of them in a manuscript fragment of Branwell's written in 1834: '3 little girls of. 5. 6 or 7. years old small and yellow in countenance. with wild black eyes and raven hair and faces of the most. strange elfish animation The necks and arms of the little savages were sunburnt to the last degree and they ran frightened round the room with the speed of 3 wild Rabbits.' (*[Angria and the Angrians] I(b)*, Neufeldt, 3, p. 251).

90. *elf-locks*: Tangled hair, superstitiously attributed to the agency of elves, especially Queen Mab, which it was supposed unlucky to disentangle.

91. *wine was sacré – it was not for heretics*: Enara and his family, being Spanish, are Roman Catholics: the child's naive belief that wine itself is sacred seems to be a dig at the doctrine of transubstantiation.

92. *lying at the wall*: Put on one side.

93. *Edward and I . . . our union*: In *The Wool is Rising* (1834) Branwell had described how the Percy brothers, disowned by

their father at birth, together began a wool-combing business, which rapidly became successful. 'Edward Percy now with the the audacity and keenness peculiar to himself [claimed] the whole management of the concern', and William, less thrusting and ruthless, became his oppressed and bullied subordinate (Neufeldt, 2, pp. 45–50). Charlotte was to draw upon and rework this material in her portrayal of William and Edward Crimsworth in the opening chapters of *The Professor*.

94. *Helen ... Cleopatra*: *Helen*: Helen of Troy, legendary beauty; daughter of Zeus and Leda, and wife of Menelaus, she eloped with Paris, and thus brought about the siege and destruction of Troy. *Cleopatra*: Queen of Egypt, joint ruler with and wife of her brother, Ptolemy Dionysius. In 48 BC she was ousted from the throne, but she captivated Julius Caesar, and in 47 BC. was reinstated by him. After Caesar's death Mark Antony fell in love with her, and repudiated his wife Octavia for her sake.

95. *one such woman*: It seems from the description here of a 'noble spirit and disastrous destiny' and a 'pale inspired face' that the dark-eyed object of Sir William's desire is Mina Laury, whose name on the letter later entrusted to him 'somehow made my hand tremble'. This is, apparently, the unrequited 'mad passion' for 'one of the most beautiful and celebrated women of her day' of which he tells Elizabeth Hastings in *Henry Hastings* (pp. 297–8).

96. *bamming ... soft line*: *bamming*: Imposing on your credulity; a favourite word in early issues of *Blackwood's*. *soft line*: Commercial term for the stock on hand of soft goods. Here comically used for a sentimental bit of writing.

97. *Victoria Delph ... Flower*: Victoria Delph is to recur in these tales as an object of masculine desire: see *Henry Hastings* n. 68. The bald-headed 'great earl' is Northangerland, the 'magnificent monarch', Zamorna, the 'poor lunatic of the name of Flower' is Sir John Flower, Viscount Richton. The stories alluded to here, if they were ever amongst the mss. of the Angrian saga, seem to have disappeared.

98. *three-legged stool, a fatted calf, or even the Marquis of Harlaw*: An incongruous series, the first an inanimate object, the second a dumb animal, and the third, by implication, even lower than the other two. *three-legged stool*: The champion in the old university disputations held during the admission of candidates to their degrees in Cambridge used to sit on a three-legged stool. *fatted calf*: See the parable of the prodigal son, Luke 15:30. *Marquis of*

Harlaw: Ally of Ardrah, and one of the leaders of the forces ranged against Zamorna.

99. *fair gentle ladye*: An invocation of the language of romance; thus, for example, Sir Walter Scott's *The Lay of the Last Minstrel* Canto 6, 23: 'Moor, moor the barge, ye gallant crew!/ And gentle ladye, deign to stay!'

100. *last person*: Because of his recent quarrel with Zamorna over Mina Laury. This is apparently also the reason for William Percy's 'hatred' of him.

101. *Hussars*: A light cavalry regiment; named after a body of light horsemen organized in Hungary in the fifteenth century.

102. *threw a challenge*: The traditional way of challenging to a duel was to throw down the gauntlet or glove; here, Hartford's throwing down of a calling-card ironically indicates that such heroic days are gone.

103. *charging pill*: A purgative.

104. *battle of Leyden*: Zamorna and his troops won a decisive victory over Quashia, Montmorency, Simpson and Lord Jordan at the battle of Leyden in 1837. Branwell describes the battle from the perspective of Henry Hastings, now defected from Zamorna's 19ᵗʰ and fighting on the other side, in *[Angria and the Angrians] IV(e)*, Neufeldt, 3, pp. 108–113.

105. *exhibit*: Administer.

106. *unkindest cut*: Cf. Shakespeare, Julius Caesar, III.ii.62.

107. *stranger to the country*: Sir William is from Senegambia; not, like Hartford (and Warner), a native of Angria.

108. *lust of the flesh . . . pride of life*: Cf. 1 John 2:16: 'For all that is in the world, the lust of the flesh, and the lust of the eyes, and the pride of life, is not of the Father, but is of the world.'

109. *down to hell along a path strewn with flowers*: Cf. Dryden's translation of Virgil's *Aeneid* (owned by the Brontë family), vi, ll.126–7: 'Smooth the descent and easy is the way / (The Gates of Hell stand open night and day).'

110. *bread of life . . . sour as vinegar*: John 6:35: 'And Jesus said unto them, I am the bread of life'. The similes which follow carry blasphemous echoes of the Bible. Christ on the cross is given 'vinegar to drink mingled with gall' (Matthew 27:34).

111. *vials of your wrath*: Cf. Revelation 16:1: 'And I heard a great voice out of the temple saying to the seven angels, Go your ways, and pour out the vials of the wrath of God upon the earth.'

112. *the changes continually rung in my ears*: To ring the changes

means to go through all the changes in ringing a peal of bells; here used figuratively to mean to go through all the possible variations of any process; to repeat the same words, statements, etc., in various ways.

113. *Cossack . . . Talleyrand*: *Cossack*: Warlike Turkish people now subject to Russia, occupying the parts north of the Black Sea. Though acknowledging the authority of the Tsar, they had a very strong tradition of independence, formulated in the saying: 'We do not bow to anybody, except the Tsar' (*My ne klanyaemsya nikomu, okromya Gosudarya*). *I'm a made man*: My success in life is assured (colloqu.). *Talleyrand*: Charles Maurice de Talleyrand-Perigord (1754–1838) was one of the most important diplomats in Europe during the late eighteenth and early nineteenth centuries, and famous for his deviousness, which was much discussed in *Fraser's Magazine*. (See, for example, his portrait in its 'Gallery of Literary Characters' *Fraser's* 7, January 1833, p. 80.) He had entered the Angrian saga in 1833, when Branwell tells he has been 'informed of the loss of 3 ships of the French Nation' at the hands of the pirate, Alexander Percy ('The Pirate', Neufeldt, 1, p. 242); he later that year appears in person in Branwell's *Historical Narrative of the War of Encroachment* (Neufeldt, 1, pp. 368–9), and is apparently friendly with Northangerland in Charlotte Brontë's *Four Years Ago* (p. 21). Sir William's parting shot makes flippant reference to the actual Talleyrand's recent death: he had died on 17 May 1838, and *The Duke of Zamorna* was written in July of that year.

HENRY HASTINGS

Untitled ms. in two parts, the first signed 'C Townshend Feby 24th 1839' and the second 'Charles Townshend – March 26th 1839', in the Widener Collection, Houghton Library, Harvard University. There appears to have been an intervening 'volume', now missing; see n. 95.

1. *wife . . . pecuniary endowment*: In the increasingly mobile society of early nineteenth-century England, the daughters of manufacturers, city merchants and bankers provided an important source of wealth for a cash-strapped and extravagant aristocracy. The heiress became an important figure in silver fork novels of the period, which acted, in their turn, as guidebooks to the elegant

lifestyle for those aspiring to enter it (see Adburgham, *Silver-Fork Society*, pp. 68–9).

2. *Miss Victoria Delph*: See *The Duke of Zamorna*, n. 97, and n. 68 below.

3. *advertisement . . . a metropolitan print*: *Fraser's Magazine* for April 1835 had printed a spoof 'matrimonial advertisement' which it claimed to have inserted in a newspaper:

> A young lady, just of age . . . of highly respectable family and connexions, determines rather to take a highly unfeminine step than be hurried into a match repugnant to her sensibility. She has a fortune, and considerable expectations. She hopes none but gentlemen of undoubted respectability will notice this; and that no one will harass an afflicted female by impertinent curiosity.
> Address (post paid) L. S., Twopenny Post Office, Maddox Street, Hanover Square.

The long article which followed detailed the various replies received ('April Fools; or, One Hundred Matrimonial Letters', *Fraser's Magazine* 11, April 1835, pp. 370–403).

4. *two horns of a hideous dilemma . . . raise the wind*: *two horns of a hideous dilemma*: Faced with two equally disagreeable alternatives; the 'horns' are each of the alternatives of a dilemma (in scholastic Latin *argumentum cornutum*), on which one is figured as liable to be caught or impaled. *raise the wind*: Cause the wind to blow; used figuratively to mean 'get hold of money'.

5. *Hymen with waving torch . . . African fair*: *Hymen with waving torch*: Greek god of marriage, traditionally represented as a youth carrying a torch and veil. *fascinating as a pheasant*: The point seems to lie in the alliteration. *apple of discord*: A cause of dispute; at the marriage of Thetis and Peleus, Discord (Eris) threw on the table a golden apple for the most beautiful of the goddesses present: Juno, Minerva and Venus each put in a claim. *African fair*: The ladies of the Verdopolitan Union, which is established in Africa.

6. *Regardez . . . commencer* (French): Attention now; we are going to begin.

7. *Megatherium*: Giant ground sloth of the genus *Megatherium*, known by fossil remains; hence, by extension, something of huge or ungainly proportions. There is probably also a suggestion of an antiquity verging on extinction. The enterprising youth of the country have removed from Verdopolis to the new city of

Adrianopolis, capital of Angria, whence Townshend is travelling. His coach stops at Zamorna in between.

8. *bolted*: Darted.

9. *19ᵗʰ*: Zamorna's regiment, 'the Terrible D-l's Own!' (*[Angria and the Angrians] IV(e)*, Neufeldt, 3, p. 110), in which the speaker's brother, Henry Hastings, had been a captain (though Hastings has by now deserted to the other side).

10. *parcel of blackguards*: Pack of criminal ruffians.

11. *to trop*: Thus in the ms. Possibly Townshend is trying to impress the stranger by dropping a French word into his conversation.

12. *Westwood ... as drunk as they could sit in their saddles*: Branwell routinely describes the troops on both sides as drinking heavily before battles. In a manuscript of 1837, he gives an account of the battle of Westwood, in which Zamorna and his troops routed Northangerland's allies Montmorency and Simpson, from the point of view of Hastings, who has defected from the 19ᵗʰ and is fighting on the other side. 'I filled the canteen with liquor,' he says of a moment at the height of the battle, 'and swigged till I forsook the beast for the ground and then vomiting violently I gained releif enough to mount once more' (*[Angria and the Angrians] IV(e)*, Neufeldt, 3, p. 111).

13. *Stuart March: Stuart*: Stuartville, in the province of Zamorna, near Edwardston, was the Angrian country seat of Lord and Lady Castlereagh. *March*: A tract of land between two properties.

14. *seven*: Angria has seven provinces, of which Zamorna is one.

15. *Adrahians ... Bloodhounds: Adrahians*: Followers of the Marquis of Ardrah, opponent of Zamorna. *Bloodhounds*: An infantry regiment in the Angrian army, described by Hastings in an earlier manuscript of Branwell's as 'a host of Dark whiskered and bearded warriors such looks of savage and relentless ferocity I never beheld before ... Their great Raven Banner bore in silver Blazonry the single emphatic syllable. "DEATH" at their head ... accompanied by 8 vast liver colored dew lapped. red eyed Bloodhounds held in leashes stood the second commander of the Army their Colonel Henry Fernando Enara' (*[Angria and the Angrians] I(d)*, December 1834, Neufeldt, 2, p. 299).

16. *condescend on particulars*: Legal and theological expression, meaning to specify or particularize, to mention particularly or by name.

17. *carriages roll in ... from the country*: In Verdopolis, as in England in the early nineteenth century, the town social season coincides with the parliamentary sessions, because most

aristocrats with country seats are in one way or another connected with parliament.

18. *cholera morbus*: Early nineteenth-century term for acute gastro-enteritis occurring in summer and autumn and marked by severe cramps, diarrhoea and vomiting. The Brontë family copy of Thomas J. Graham's *Modern Domestic Medicine* (1826) has an entry on cholera morbus, extensively annotated by Rev. Patrick Brontë, which perhaps contains a clue to the narrator's meaning here: the cause of cholera morbus, says Graham, 'has been generally considered to be an inordinate secretion of bile' (p. 233).

19. *House*: Parliament.

20. *skinning alive a poor eel ... Constitutionalists*: *skinning alive a poor eel*: Apparently a catchphrase. *Constitutionalists*: The faction led by John, Duke of Fidena, who have 'sworn to preserve inviolate Ancient Laws and institutions and Monarchy and Country from every assault and every foe' (Branwell Brontë, *[Angria and the Angrians] II (f)*, Neufeldt, 2, p. 529).

21. *specimen of a certain style*: The style is that of Branwell Brontë, whose manuscripts of 1836–8 are filled with similar descriptions of parliamentary altercations. The 'dear reader' who is addressed in the next sentence is likewise, most immediately, Branwell, who is invited to imagine the mocking figure of Charlotte's Townshend next time he tries to write thus.

22. *gent*: 'A *gent* is an individual of that genus for whom cheap stocks and flash garments, at alarmingly low prices, are ticketed all round Charing Cross ... A *gent* is he to whom the assiduous Boots proffers a pair of dirty slippers ... in which ... the party sits at ease at his tea, or brandy and water, exchanging facetiousness with, or extracting conversation from the waiter' (*Blackwood's Magazine* 45, May 1839, p. 684).

23. *young member*: Sir William Percy, long-legged like his father, returned from his mission to Paris.

24. *jew's-harp ... any sucking dove*: *jew's-harp*: Small lyre-shaped musical instrument held between the teeth and struck with the finger. *any sucking dove*: Cf. Bottom in *A Midsummer Night's Dream*, I.ii.100–101: 'I will aggravate my voice so that I will roar you as gently as any sucking dove.'

25. *identity*: Macara Lofty, opium addict.

26. *coronet embroidered in black hair*: Cf. the description in *Passing Events* (1836) of Zamorna's 'cambric handkerchief with a coronet wrought upon it in black-hair' (*Five Novelettes* p. 46).

27. *thoughts that breathe and words that burn*: 'Bright-eyed Fancy,

hov'ring o'er,/Scatters from her pictured urn/ Thoughts that breathe and words that burn' (Thomas Gray, *The Progress of Poesy* (1757), III. 3, ll.2–4).

28. *turtle*: Turtle dove.

29. *easy*: Graceful.

30. *putting his thumb to his nose-end*: Charles Mackay, in 'Popular Follies of Great Cities', describes how, in the early nineteenth century, it was 'thought the height of vulgar wit to answer all questions by placing the point of the thumb upon the tip of the nose, and twirling the fingers in the air. If one man wished to insult or annoy another, he had only to make use of this cabalistic [sic] sign in his face, and his object was accomplished.' (*Memoirs of Extraordinary Popular Delusions* (London, 1841), I, p. 337). (See also n. 163.)

31. *Every man to his mind ... it's no go*: *Every man to his mind*: 'Every man to his taste'. *corn*: Corn-whisky (US, early nineteenth century); here, apparently, a term for alcohol in general. *it's no go*: I can't go on.

32. *mysterious number of seven times*: Seven has long been considered a mystic number. Astrologers and alchemists recognized seven planets; there are seven days in creation; seven days in the week; seven graces; seven ages in the life of man. Here, the number has no 'mysterious' significance: it is simply an ironic indication of Hastings' immoderate drinking.

33. *muddy*: A rare usage, meaning not clear in mind, confused.

34. *Fidena school ... retreat ... 1833*: *Fidena school*: The Angrian Duke of Fidena was famous for his 'inflexible uprightness' and an 'integrity that death could not turn from the path of right', as well as for 'an air of reserve, of stiffness, which warns us that [he] ... lays emphasis on the forms of courts, the usages of high circles, and will brook no breach of them, however trivial, in those under his authority' (as Lord Charles Wellesley puts it, in Charlotte Brontë's *Corner Dishes: A Peep into a Picture Book* (1834), *EEW*, 2.ii, p. 89). *retreat ... 1833*: In his *Historical Narrative of the War of Encroachment* Branwell describes the strategic retreat of the Verdopolitan army before Massena, leader of the French forces, in 1833 (Neufeldt, 1, pp. 376–98).

35. *lying snug with Squire Warner ... Angrian Hills*: *lying snug with Squire Warner*: Branwell depicts Fidena, Richton and Colonel MacArthur going to dine with Warner in his country house whilst Massena is bearing down on Angria (Branwell Brontë, *Historical Narrative of the War of Encroachment*, Neufeldt, 1, pp. 382–3).

hiding from danger: Warner Howard Warner had been neutral (or, as Branwell wonderfully puts it, 'neuter') during the War of Encroachment against the French (ibid., p. 383). *marshes ... Angrian hills*: 'all around us lay flat elevated marshes and moorlands. untracked by pathways and. delugged with water. beyond and on their sides rose wet moorlands' (ibid., p. 393).

36. *stand to it*: Persist in affirming it.

37. *parlour in an old hall ... passport of fame*: Refers to a scene in an earlier novelette (an untitled manuscript known as *Julia*, dated 20 June 1837) in which Henry Hastings is portrayed 'at Girnington-Hall ... seated at Lady Thornton's tea-table between herself and Lady Maria Percy'; 'he spoke fast and eloquently – not very discreetly or correctly – but at every little slip the ladies laughed again and encouraged him to proceed' (*Five Novelettes*, p. 94). The memory here is clearly triggered by the narrator's conscious or unconscious perception of 'Wilson''s true identity.

38. *basilisk*: Fabulous reptile, hatched by a serpent from a cock's egg; its breath, and even its look, was reputed to be fatal.

39. *Soldan ... pledge him*: *Soldan*: Wilson clearly means Zamorna, referring to his tyrannical nature. A number of such epithets are applied to him in these last Angrian tales: 'the Czar', 'the Great Cham', 'that d—n—d Turk in the east'. *pledge him*: Drink to the toast which has been proposed.

40. *fair and poetic ... moonlight lane*: An intertextual joke, looking back to the opening of *Stancliffe's Hotel*.

41. *policeman ... sword-stick*: *policeman*: The Metropolitan Police Force had been established in London in 1829, when Sir Robert Peel was Home Secretary: it replaced a patchwork of private security agencies. In 1835 the Whig government extended the 'new police' to all corporate towns, and the County Police Act, allowing the establishment of county police forces, was passed in 1839. None of these measures was uncontroversial: it was feared in some quarters that the new police would act as agents of continental-style despotism. Brontë's portrayal of a new policeman in Zamorna's Angria suggests her awareness of such arguments. *dark blue uniform*: Police uniform, a dark blue swallow-tail coat, with metal buttons down the front and on the cuffs, and duck trousers. *sword-stick*: A hollow cane or walking-stick containing a steel blade which could be drawn or shot out and used as a sword.

42. *nearly ... former works*: *nearly*: Closely, carefully. *former*

works: I have been unable to find any references to James Ingham in Charlotte Brontë's surviving Angrian manuscripts, though in *Stancliffe's Hotel* Townshend wonders whether to visit 'my friend Tom Ingham's farm at the foot of Boulshill' (p. 76).

43. *no small shakes*: Comic reversal of 'no great shakes', meaning to be nothing extraordinary in ability or importance. The original phrase perhaps alludes to the shaking of dice.

44. *Go it . . . change for your notes*: *Go it*: Away with you (obs.). *play off*: Perpetrate. *change for your notes*: pay you out.

45. *ramrod*: Rigid, stiff, straight. A ramrod was a rod used for ramming down the charge of a muzzle-loading firearm.

46. *Gardiner . . . Wellesley*: For Gardiner, see *Stancliffe's Hotel*, p. 97 and for Wellesley, see n. 47. Jones and Collier are apparently other aliases adopted by Townshend in the course of his chameleon career.

47. *relations*: An ironic reference to the fact that the character of Charles Townshend was developed out of that of Lord Charles Albert Florian Wellesley, son of the Duke of Wellington and brother of Arthur Wellesley (who became the Duke of Zamorna).

48. *quill . . . testimonials*: *quill*: As his interlocutor well knows, Townshend is a writer. *character*: A character reference. *testimonials*: Townshend's negative reply to this question is an ironic dig at his interrogator, who is named as one of his character references in the matrimonial advertisement with which *Henry Hastings* opens.

49. *William Clarke*: Refers to his friendship with his interrogator, Sir William Percy. See *Stancliffe's Hotel*, pp. 90–100, for the jape they carry out disguised as 'Messrs Clarke and Gardiner'.

50. *branded*: Marked with infamy (*OED*). Seemingly refers to the disfiguring mark inflicted on a criminal's forehead (brow) by a branding iron, a practice dating back to Roman times and beyond. ' "Mistress", I suppose, is branded on my brow,' says Mina Laury bitterly in *Mina Laury* p. 51). In *Stancliffe's Hotel*, Hartford is described as having 'his branded brow corrugated over his eyes with the sour malignant look of a fiend' (p. 89).

51. *Turk in the east*: *Turk*: Zamorna. *east*: Angria is to the east of Verdopolis.

52. *bitterest enemy . . . spurned the Baron*: For Hartford's hostility to Sir William and his spurning by Zamorna's government, see *The Duke of Zamorna*, pp. 186–9.

53. *flashed upon their inward eye*: Typically sardonic use of romantic allusion; here, to William Wordsworth, 'Daffodils' (1804): 'For

oft, when on my couch I lie / In vacant or in pensive mood, / They flash upon that inward eye / Which is the bliss of solitude.'

54. *stinted*: Halted.

55. *folded*: Shut up in their folds.

56. *heaven above and earth beneath*: Cf. the Old Testament commandment against idolatry, Exodus 20:4: 'Thou shalt not make unto thee any graven image, or any likeness of any thing that is in heaven above, or that is in the earth beneath.'

57. *Cain-like wanderer*: Genesis 4:16: 'And Cain went out from the presence of the LORD, and dwelt in the land of Nod, on the east of Eden'. Nod, in Hebrew, means 'wandering'.

58. *Adams . . . Lord Hartford*: *Adams*: Colonel Adams, the superior officer for whose murder Hastings is being pursued. *Lord Hartford*: Hartford's hostility to Hastings is depicted in Charlotte Brontë's *Julia* (*Five Novelettes*, pp. 93–101). In a manuscript by Branwell, written in January 1837, Hastings explains it thus: 'My Commander thought it expedient that a farmers Son should not shame by his Advancements the pampered ignorents of Eastern Aristocracy' (*[Angria and the Angrians] IV(c)*, Neufeldt, 3, p. 17).

59. *slaves . . . apotheize*: *slaves*: Slavery had been abolished in the British West Indies on 1 August 1838. *seven years absence*: Presumably refers to a Verdopolitan law. *apotheize*: Apparently a misspelling of 'apotheosize', to elevate to, or as if to, the rank of a god; to deify, glorify.

60. *If we do . . . a wrong*: Byron, *Mazeppa* (1819) X, ll.418–22.

61. *broken by a court-martial*: Deprived of commission, warrant or rating by a court-martial.

62. *les trois maisons dans la bouche*: Three houses in the mouth (French). I cannot find the source of this phrase, which presumably derives its meaning from the expression '*gros comme une maison*' (as big as a house), and clearly refers to the fact that in the early nineteenth century false teeth were extremely cumbersome and uncomfortable.

63. *I'd lose . . . to obtain*: He is speaking of his passion for Mina Laury.

64. *Simpson . . . Macqueen*: Allies of Northangerland and enemies of Zamorna.

65. *Long gallop . . . hunter's fire*: Cf. Byron, *Mazeppa* (1819), XII, ll. 494–6: 'Their troop came hard upon our back, / With their long gallop, which can tire / The hounds deep hate, and hunter's fire.'

66. *tiger hunt . . . O'Shaughnessy*: *tiger hunt*: A hunt not of, but by, 'the Tiger', Henri Fernando di Enara, Commander-in-Chief of the Angrian forces, with Zamorna 'at his heels'. *O'Shaughnessy*: Ironic reference to the Senegambian, or Irish, origins of Arthur Adrian Augustus Wellesley, Duke of Zamorna.

67. *Phidias ... nose like Alexander the Great's*: *Phidias*: c. 500–c. 432 BC, one of the greatest sculptors of ancient Greece. *Paros*: An island in the Greek Cyclades, famous for its marble. *nose like Alexander the Great's*: Ancient paintings, sculptures and documents suggest that the Macedonian conqueror known as Alexander the Great was very handsome, with a straight nose, whose bridge was of the same height as the forehead.

68. *pale . . . Quakeress in grey . . . Victoria Delph*: *pale . . . Quakeress in grey*: Cf. Brontë's later heroines, Jane Eyre and Lucy Snowe. *Victoria Delph*: Angrian society belle, first introduced in *The Duke of Zamorna*. One of the heiresses named by Townshend in his opening matrimonial advertisement, she is described by Branwell in a manuscript dated 21 February 1839 – three days before the date at the end of this part of *Henry Hastings* – as 'the Great Heiress Miss Victoria Pelfe'. Branwell's name for her is apparently a comment on what is, for most Angrians, her most prominent characteristic, her wealth (*pelf* means wealth; it is also a dialect term for a good-for-nothing or worthless person); but, as he makes clear, her appearance, too, is well known in Angria: 'prints and caricatures have made the city acquainted with her figure . . . a very little girl with diminutive hands and feet a fair face a rather plump figure and an expression of petted caprice' (*[Angria and the Angrians] V(d)*, Neufeldt, 3, p. 264).

69. *omnigatherum*: *Omnium gatherum* is dog Latin for a gathering or collection of all sorts of persons and things, without regard to suitability or order. *Omnigatherum* was the alchemical antidote to the philosophers' stone: a tincture of omnigatherum was supposed to turn gold back into what it had been composed of before it had been turned into gold from something else. Brontë here seems to be jokingly compounding these two meanings.

70. *the chalice fate commends to her lips*: Cf. *Macbeth*, I.vii.10–12: '. . . this even-handed justice/ Commends the ingredients of our poison'd chalice/ To our own lips.'

71. *solitary and neglected . . . a moment before*: On page 33B of the manuscript, in the midst of William Percy's description of his pursuing ride with Lord Hartford, there is another draft of this passage:

herself solitary & neglected – there is no bitterness the human heart
ever knows like that of being alone & despised whilst around it
hundreds are loved & idolized – I think I should have spoken to
her but something suggested to me, let her drink the chalice fate
commends to her lips – every body has their own burden to bear –
Besides all at once I perceived that she was not quite ugly there was
something very lady-like in her form & her dress though exceedingly simple was graceful

72. *in my special behoof*: Especially for me.
73. *his songs were sung at public dinners and meetings*: When
Branwell began to use him as a narrator, Hastings was 'the Poet
of Angria', 'author' of a number of patriotic Angrian songs –
'Sound the loud Trumpet o'er Afric's bright sea', 'Shine on us,
God of Afric, shine' and 'Welcome heroes, to the War!' – all
written by Branwell in 1834 (*[Angria and the Angrians] I(a)*,
Neufeldt, 2, pp. 204, 206, 252); one of Branwell's mss. describes
the singing of the first two of these at the coronation of Zamorna
(*[Angria and the Angrians] I(a)*, Neufeldt, 2, pp. 204–7).
74. *The stillest time*: Here, apparently, Townshend resumes his
narration.
75. *character of Captain Hastings*: In December 1834, Branwell,
in the person of Lord Richton, had introduced Henry Hastings
as the new narrator of his continuing Angrian saga (*[Angria and
the Angrians] I(d)*, Neufeldt, 2, p. 278). In a series of Branwell's
mss. written between the beginning of 1835 and the end of 1837
Hastings gives an account of his first campaign as a young ensign,
records his meetings with the great and famous, and gives a
first-person account of the progress of the war. These writings
chart his rise in fame as a historian; in one, the Duchess of
Zamorna summons him to tell him 'what pleasure I derive from
reading your account of the Campaign and victories of my Husband' (*[Angria and the Angrians] I(e)*, Neufeldt, 2, p. 100). But
they chart, also, his hardening in battle, his bitterness at his
treatment by his jealous superiors (Richton and Warner and,
especially, Hartford), and his gradual degeneration into drunkenness. In October 1837 he is depicted 'drinking with a set of
Atrocious Debauchees who a few years ago had entered life
ambitious of distinction . . . broken from one military service and
a fugitive in another with a desperate heart and a constitution
that was yielding to his unchecked intemperance' (*[Angria and*

the Angrians] *IV(I)*, Neufeldt, 3, p. 147). Charlotte Brontë had portrayed Hastings for the first time in *Julia* (June, 1837), where Townshend muses uneasily over 'the last volume published by Captain Hastings, late of the 19ᵗʰ', and recalls the moment from which 'Henry Hastings may date his ruin', when as a dashing young man 'in the blaze of his fame' he incurred the hostility of Hartford on a visit to Girnington Hall (*Five Novelettes*, pp. 93–101); see above, n. 37.

76. *Beelzebub*: The devil.

77. *Pandemonium ... Armageddon*: *Pandemonium*: In Milton's *Paradise Lost*, the capital of Hell. *Armageddon*: In the Apocalypse, the site of the last great battle between the nations before the Day of Judgment (Revelation 16:16).

78. *St Nicholas*: Old Nick, or the Devil.

79. *Sir William Percy's diary*: After this, there is a cancelled passage in the ms.: 'The captain and his sister were sitting in the oak parlour at Massingham when a [illegible] came to the door.'

80. *sacred rage*: More usually a phrase describing poetic inspiration; e.g. Alexander Pope, *Windsor Forest* (1713), ll. 289–90: 'Here noble Surrey felt the sacred rage,/*Surrey*, the *Granville* of a former age.'

81. *Rookwood's Northern Magazine*: William Harrison Ainsworth's *Rookwood* had been published in 1834, and went through five editions in three years. Like *Henry Hastings*, it contains a sprinkling of flash slang (much noted by contemporaries). *Rookwood's Northern Magazine* appears to be an allusion to the monthly *Bentley's Miscellany*, of which the author of *Rookwood* was to become editor in March 1839; in February, when Brontë was writing the first part of *Henry Hastings*, Ainsworth's wildly successful Newgate novel, *Jack Sheppard*, was beginning to be serialized there. See Introduction, pp. xxi–xxii.

82. *besotted ... Tartarus*: *besotted*: Intellectually or morally stupefied (Cf. *Villette*, ch. 30: 'the besotted "lecture pieuse", drawled by a sleepy pupil'). *Bentley's Miscellany* specialized in half-comic, half-macabre Gothic tales whose excess of horror bordered on the parodic. *Leasehold Beck*: Two series of 'Tales and Legends' of horror and superstition associated with places (Scotland and the Isle of Wight) were being published in *Bentley's* through 1838. *Tartarus*: To the ancient Greeks, the lowest region of the world, as far below Earth as Earth is from Heaven; like Hell, a place of punishment for sinners.

83. *ghoul*: Evil spirit supposed (in Muslim countries) to rob graves and prey on human corpses. Sir William is still half inhabiting the world of his 'besotted tale'.

84. *tiger*: A slang term for a smartly liveried boy acting as groom or footman, who sometimes stood on a small platform behind the carriage; less strictly, an outdoor boy-servant. Brontë's interest in the word is evident in the play between its usual and its slang meanings in the exchange that follows here.

85. *pricked up*: Set upright.

86. *Creole*: Term for a person of European parentage born in the West Indies. In the early nineteenth century there was some controversy as to whether Creoles were of purely European stock. Hartford is descended from an old family of early Angrian settlers. In *The Duke of Zamorna*, Sir William terms him a 'mulatto' (p. 166); and in *Henry Hastings* Charles Townshend speaks of his 'swarthy skin' and 'air of a gigantic ourang-outang' (p. 283).

87. *train*: Track.

88. *Judge Jeffrey's*: George Jeffreys (1648–89), who became Lord Chief Justice of the King's Bench in 1683, was famous as the 'hanging judge'.

89. *how they were off for soap ... chickens*: *how they were off for soap*: A common urban catch-phrase of the early nineteenth century; it appears to mean 'What are you good for?' in the way of cash or anything else. *when brought to bay*: When, in the course of being hunted, unable to flee farther, the stag turns, faces the hounds and defends itself at close quarters. *chickens*: Firearms (slang); the term appears prominently at the end of a manuscript of Branwell's, finished the day before the first part of *Henry Hastings*: 'Zamorna had unconsciously plunged one hand into his waistcoat pocket and Percy smiling again asked "Chickens? – eh Arthur?" – delicately drawing forth a round mahogany head from his own pocket ... more quietly Percy had slipped one or two chickens into his waistcoat' (*[Angria and the Angrians] V(d)*, 23 February 1839, Neufeldt, 3, pp. 269–70).

90. *chance*: In case.

91. *petticoat perverseness*: One of a number of suggestions that there is something effeminate in Sir William's dandyishness.

92. *Lawrence ... beauty of life*: *Lawrence*: Sir Thomas Lawrence (1769–1830), fashionable romantic portrait painter, of whom Branwell's drawing-master, William Robinson, had been a pupil (Alexander and Sellars, *The Art of the Brontës*, pp. 73–4). *legendary lady ... beauty of life*: Refers to the fairytale, 'Sleeping

Beauty', translated by Robert Samber from Charles Perrault's *La Belle au Bois Dormant* (1697) in 1729. The princess, having pricked her finger when spinning, is shut up by enchantment in a castle where she sleeps for a hundred years, during which time an impenetrable wood grows up around. At last, she is woken by the kiss of a young prince, who marries her.

93. *drawing it mild*: Literally, in reference to beer. Here used figuratively, to mean being gentle; the opposite of 'coming it strong'.

94. *legs jammed into the body like a telescope*: The image, possibly suggested to Sir William by the horrid tale he has been reading, is reminiscent of grisly descriptions in early tales of terror in *Blackwood's*, such as were familiar to the Brontë children (see Robert Morrison and Chris Baldick, eds., *Tales of Terror from Blackwood's Magazine* (Oxford: Oxford University Press, 1995).

95. *My last volume . . . midnight loosed at noon*: *My last volume*: The volume here referred to has not survived; it apparently included a scene between Warner, Prime Minister of Angria, and Elizabeth Hastings regarding the fate of her brother. *midnight loosed at noon*: Cf. Amos 8:9: 'I will cause the sun to go down at noon, and I will darken the earth in the clear day'. I have been unable to find the source of this phrase. It is also quoted in a manuscript of Branwell's, dated three days before the completion of *Henry Hastings I* (*[Angria and the Angrians] V(d)*, 21 February 1839, in Neufeldt, 3, p. 267). As Branwell's narrator (Richton) stands watching the 'Majestic Countess Zenobia' standing over Victoria Pelfe 'with looks like "Midnight loosed at noon"', he is tapped on the arm by Charlotte's narrator, 'Charles Townshend Esqr', here making one of his very rare appearances in Branwell's later manuscripts (*[Angria and the Angrians] V(d)*, Neufeldt, 3, p. 267). Years later, Branwell quotes the same phrase in his '*and the weary are at rest*' (c. 1845): 'with raven locks as Symmons has it "like midnight loosed at noon"' (Neufeldt, 3, p. 432). Neufeldt suggests that Symmons may be Charles Symmons (1749–1826), poet and literary biographer, who published a life of Milton in 1806, but has been unable to find the phrase in this work.

96. *country rung with his name once*: As 'the Poet of Angria', author of some of its most stirring patriotic songs and historian of its battles, Hastings had 'heard his name mentioned in every street and saw it printed in every shop window' (Branwell Brontë, *[Angria and the Angrians] I(d)*, Neufeldt, 2, p. 331).

97. *take with*: Please.

98. *random ... breathing myself*: *random*: A rare usage, meaning living irregularly. Cf. *Villette*, ch. 37: '"Human Justice" rushed before me in novel guise, a red, random beldame with arms akimbo.' *breathing myself*: Giving myself a breathing space.

99. *they were nearer home than France*: Branwell's account of the return of Hastings as 'Wilson' tells of widespread rumours in Angria that Northangerland's old allies were regrouping themselves (*[Angria and the Angrians] V(d)*, Neufeldt, 3, pp. 251–9).

100. *Edward's slang ... Drover's daughter*: *Edward's slang*: Their brother, Edward Percy's, constant abuse of their father. *Drover's daughter*: Northangerland had, in his young days, been known as the Drover. See *The Duke of Zamorna*, n. 30.

101. *hypochondria dread ... fiend*: *hypochondria dread*: 'Hypochondria' in the early nineteenth century could mean either imaginary illness, or 'incurable despair' and 'melancholy forebodings'. See Shuttleworth, *Charlotte Brontë and Victorian Psychology*, p. 141. *fiend*: Since his first extended portrayal by Branwell in *The Pirate* (1833), Alexander Percy had appeared in the Angrian saga as an increasingly satanic figure: 'Alexander Rougue looked like Satan the prince of darkness Lord Northangerland looked like Lucifer Star of the Morning' writes Branwell in 1834 (*[Angria and the Angrians] I(c)*, Neufeldt, 2, p. 259).

102. *Cham, Chi Thaung-Gu ... turn out my fool*: *Cham, Chi Thaung-Gu*: Zamorna. Like his other nicknames, 'Czar' and 'soldan', this figures him as a despot; *Cham*: An obsolete form of Khan, applied to the rulers of the Tartars and Mongols, and to the emperor of China; *Chi Thaung-Gu*: Apparently a made-up name. *turn out my fool*: Put on my performance as a fool.

103. *Pelham*: Branwell Brontë, in *The Politics of Verdopolis* (November 1833) portrays the preparations for marriage between Mary Percy and Sir Robert Weaver Pelham, a rising young politician just arrived from England. This marriage never takes place. (Neufeldt 1, pp. 345–64).

104. *flay the world alive*: Thrash the world (slang). This section ends here, and the rest of the page is left blank. The next section, which begins on the next page of the ms., is much more neatly written, and divided into paragraphs.

105. *Major King*: 'John King, Major in the 19th infantry', who had been portrayed by Branwell, in a manuscript dated the month before this, writing to General Enara about his discovery of the return of Hastings and 'the landing from the french coast of one

or more of those Outlawed Rebels whom were prowling about Paris and who must intend some movement which it must be our duty to prevent' (*[Angria and the Angrians]* V(d), Neufeldt, 3, pp. 249–51).

106. *framed*: To shape one's course (obs.).

107. *Salvators ... Corregios*: All Italian painters of the High Renaissance: Salvator Rosa (1615–73), Annibale Carracci (1560–1609), Antonio Allegri Correggio (c. 1489–1534). In a manuscript 'list of painters whose works I wish to see', made when she was thirteen, Brontë had included 'Corregio' and 'Annibal Carracci' (Gaskell, p. 68). It is highly unlikely that she would by 1839 have seen any of these, but she could have known of them both from journal descriptions and through the prints and engravings which circulated widely amongst the educated classes in the early nineteenth century (see Alexander and Sellars, *The Art of the Brontës*, pp. 11–12).

108. *cheval mirror*: A free-standing mirror swung on a frame, of sufficient length to reflect the whole figure.

109. *first gentleman in Angria ... inexcusables*: *first gentleman of Angria*: Apparently refers to the fact that Hartford's is one of the oldest established families in Angria. *inexcusables*: Trousers, distinguished from breeches chiefly by covering the whole leg, and by not being shaped so as to fit tightly, began to come into fashion after the Napoleonic wars. From the end of the eighteenth century there had been a running joke in Britain to find 'delicate' synonyms for them – *inexpressibles* (1793), *indescribables* (1794), *etceteras* (1794), *unmentionables* (1823), *ineffables* (1823), *indispensables* (1828) (Richard W. Bailey, *Nineteenth-Century English* (Ann Arbor: University of Michigan Press, 1996), p. 187). In 1834, Branwell portrays S'Death 'habited in a respectable and veteran snuff coloured coat and unmentionable unmentionables' (*[Angria and the Angrians]* I(a), Neufeldt, 2, p. 218). *inexcusables* is clearly Charlotte's contribution to this series.

110. *Barras, Dupin and Bernadotte*: Northangerland's former French allies, modelled on actual French historical figures: Paul Barras (1755–1820), Robespierre's deputy and mentor to Napoleon; Charles Dupin (1784–1873), naval engineer, who spied for France in England; Jean-Baptiste Bernadotte (1763–1844), one of Napoleon's marshals. See *Caroline Vernon*, n. 109.

111. *Belcastro*: Apparently the new Colonel of Enara's 'Bloodhounds', now that Enara himself has become Secretary at War.

112. *Etrei*: Enara has become Earl of Etrei, apparently in recognition of his military service there.

113. *black bile ... court-insult*: *black bile*: Atrabilis, choler adust, or melancholy, the fourth of the 'humours' of early physiology. *court-insult*: An insult deserving of legal prosecution.

114. *Tuesday by the week*: 19 March 1839 fell on a Tuesday.

115. *corning ... Leyden*: *corning*: Giving a feed to. *Westwood ... Leyden*: Sites of two decisive battles of the Angrian civil war, in which Zamorna had triumphed over Northangerland's allies. In the latter, according to Branwell, over 11,000 men were killed (*[Angria and the Angrians] IV(e)*, Neufeldt, 3, pp. 108–12).

116. *drab*: Dull light brown or yellowish-brown.

117. *left hand nor the right*: Biblical phrase indicative of unswerving straightness of purpose, here ironically invoked. Thus Deuteronomy 5:32: 'Ye shall observe to do therefore as the Lord your God hath commanded you: ye shall not turn aside to the right hand or to the left.'

118. *Belial ... etceterorum*: *Belial*: In Milton's *Paradise Lost*, a prince of darkness. Brontë is probably thinking here of his description in Book II: 'A fairer person lost not Heav'n; he seemd / For dignity compos'd and high exploit: / But all was false and hollow; though his Tongue / Dropt Manna, and could make the worse appear / The better reason, to perplex and dash / Maturest Counsels' (Book II, ll. 110–15). *etceterorum*: In the early nineteenth century 'etcetera' spawned various whimsical nonce-words, such as etceterist, etceterize, etceteraly. Thus, two periodicals with which the young Brontës were familiar: 'to write critically, scientifically ... etceteraly' (*Blackwood's Magazine* 12, 1822, p. 56); 'He ... sowed his wild oats of course, soberized, etceterized' (*Fraser's Magazine* 3, 1831, p. 67).

119. *Judas*: Refers to Judas Iscariot, false disciple of Jesus.

120. *stand pepper*: Stay hostile. In allusive or proverbial expressions, pepper usually refers to the pungent or biting quality of pepper.

121. *tip King's evidence*: Turn to give evidence for the prosecution.

122. *stupid*: Obstinate, stubborn (northern dialect).

123. *come it very strong*: Are very severe.

124. *before and behind*: Cf. Revelation 4:6: 'round about the throne, were four beasts full of eyes before and behind.' The same text is invoked in *Villette*, ch. 21, where Lucy remarks of M. Paul: 'It was very much his habit to wear eyes before, behind, and on each side of him.'

125. *How are the mighty fallen*: 2 Samuel 1:19.

126. *chasing the rainbow*: It is fabled that if one reaches the spot where a rainbow touches the earth, one finds a pot of gold; hence, a rainbow-chaser is one who hopes for impossible things.

127. *kingdoms of the world and the glory of them*: Cf. the gospel account of Christ's temptation in the wilderness: 'The devil taketh him up into an exceedingly high mountain, and sheweth him all the kingdoms of the world, and the glory of them' (Matthew 4:8).

128. *Pygmalion*: Sculptor and king of Cyprus, who fell in love with his own marble statue of Aphrodite. When the goddess heard his prayers and gave life to the statue, he married it.

129. *medium*: Cf. Rochester to Jane, when she calls Thornfield 'a splendid mansion': 'The glamour of inexperience is over your eyes . . . and you see it through a charmed medium' (ch. 20).

130. *make off . . . emmet*: *make off*: Dispose of (obsolete). *emmet*: Emmets, or ants, were fabled for their industry.

131. *specimens of her accomplishments*: Presumably examples of her playing and her drawing, like the portfolio Jane shows to Rochester in *Jane Eyre*, ch. 13.

132. *settled*: Established in life.

133. *nightmare*: A female spirit or monster supposed to beset people and animals by night, settling upon them when they are asleep and producing a feeling of suffocation by its weight.

134. *artist's sketch*: Conventional instruction in drawing in the early nineteenth century, such as Brontë had received at Roe Head School, included much copying of 'picturesque' subjects such as this (Alexander and Sellars, *Art of the Brontës*, pp. 54–6; and for examples of such 'sketches' by Brontë, made in the 1830s, plates 81, 82, 96, 117, 126, 137, 140).

135. *draw in*: Not in OED. Apparently, slow down, contract her steps.

136. *your refusal to accept that silly little cross*: This incident presumably took place in the missing second 'volume'; see n. 95.

137. *most beautiful and celebrated women of her day*: See *The Duke of Zamorna*, p. 182.

138. *stamp of the hoof*: The devil was believed to fix his mark with his talon upon those who made a pact with him. Thus, Zamorna speaks of his friendship with the Duke of Fidena: 'every advance of intimacy which I make towards him oppresses him with precisely the same sensations that would affect a man who was in cordial league with the Prince of Darkness. He is afraid the mark of the horse-shoe will remain on his hand if I clasp it' (*The Scrap*

Book. From the 'Verdopolitan Intelligencer' (1835), *EEW*, 2.ii,
p. 371).

139. *RESURGAM*: (Latin): I shall rise again. Cf. *Jane Eyre*, ch. 9.

140. *suit him to a hair*: Edward Percy is known as a tight-fisted
businessman.

141. *I had placed my thumb to the side of my nose ... was off for
soap*: See notes 30 and 89.

142. *kettle of fish*: An awkward state of affairs.

143. *cut*: Made off (slang).

144. *Rosamund Wellesley*: Cousin of Zamorna who became his mistress, and was kept by him first at Fort Adrian and then at Scar
House, Ingleside, where shame led her to suicide. In *The Scrap
Book* (1835), Brontë portrays her being hissed by an Angrian
crowd loyal to Mary Percy (*EEW*, 2.ii., pp. 364–5).

145. *not wisely but too well*: Cf. *Othello* V. 2, 404: 'One that loved
not wisely but too well.'

146. *Art of Love*: An ironic reference to Ovid's *Ars Amatoria* (c. 1 BC).

147. *fairly*: By proper or lawful means, legitimately; opposed to
'foully'.

148. *mute allegories ... Christian*: In John Bunyan's *Pilgrim's Progress Part I* (1678), the Interpreter shows Christian a series of
enigmatic scenes – a picture of a man with the world behind his
back and the Bible in his hand; the sprinkling of water on a
parlour full of dust, to enable it to be swept; two children, figures
of Passion and of Patience; oil and water being cast on a fire; a
man hacking his way past guards into a beautiful palace; a man
in an iron cage; one waking from a dream of the Last Judgment
– and construes their allegorical meanings for him, 'that they
may be as a goad in thy sides, to prick thee forward in the way
thou must go' (Roger Sharrock, ed., *Pilgrim's Progress* (Penguin,
1965), pp. 60–69).

149. *old Dutch groups of ghosts ... they are dead*: Brontë is presumably here thinking of paintings such as Brueghel's *Children's
Games* or David Teniers the Younger's *Soldiers Playing Dice*.

150. *all things must have an end*: Apparently refers to the proverb 'All
good things must come to an end'.

151. *chartists*: Cartographers.

152. *read*: Possibly meaning 'administered a reprimand or a lecture'
(*OED*).

153. *piccaninny ... Tunis*: Having suppressed Northangerland's
rebellion, 'with a kingdom just recovering and only barly [sic]
recovering from a most terrible struggle with Armies outworn

and finances reduced to the last penny', Zamorna is turning his attention to exterminating the Ashantees and Negroes, as well as to 'the exploration of the interior' (Branwell Brontë, *[Angria and the Angrians]IV(j)* (15 December 1837), Neufeldt, 3, p. 177).

154. *deduce an inference*: Logical terms. In logic, to *deduce* is to draw a conclusion from something already known or assumed; an *inference* is the process of reasoning from something known or assumed to something else which follows from it.

155. *caps the globe*: Outdoes, surpasses. Originally, a northern dialect expression; hence, 'as they say in Angria', which is often associated with Yorkshire. Cf. *Jane Eyre*, ch. 32: ' "Well!" I exclaimed, using an expression of the district; "that caps the globe, however!" '

156. *Greville's*: 'Vernon' cancelled in ms.

157. *demi-rep . . . make hay while the sun shines*: *demi-rep*: Contraction of *demi-reputation*. A woman whom 'everybody knows to be what nobody calls her' (Henry Fielding, *Tom Jones* (1749), ch. 15). *make hay while the sun shines*: Take advantage of a favourable situation (proverbial).

158. *One down, and another come on*: Pugilistic slang.

159. *Nathaniel without guile*: Ironic invocation of John 1:47, in which Jesus commends Nathaniel as a man 'in whom there is no guile'.

160. *little fellows in blue dresses*: In the early nineteenth century boys up to the age of five or six were dressed as little girls.

161. *grandfather*: Northangerland.

162. *Spare the rod and spoil the child*: Old saying, derived from Proverbs 13:24.

163. *took a sight*: 'A vulgar action employed by street boys to denote incredulity, or contempt for authority, by placing the thumb against the nose and closing all the fingers except the little one, which is agitated in token of derision' (*OED*, qu. *Slang Dictionary*, 1860). *Fraser's Magazine* in September 1837 carried a line drawing of a boy 'putting his thumb upon his nose, and wagging his little finger, thus . . . a mode of expression which has since become as general in use as it is particular in provocation.' (*Fraser's* 16, September 1837, p. 357). (See also n. 30.)

164. *in the sullens*: In a state of gloomy ill-humour.

165. *De Lisle's pencil . . . Chantry's chisel*: *De Lisle's pencil*: Sir Edward De Lisle, friend of Zamorna and portrait painter in Glass Town and in Angria. *Chantry's chisel*: Sir Henry Chantry, sculptor in Glass Town and in Angria.

CAROLINE VERNON

Untitled ms. in two parts in the Widener Collection, Houghton Library, Harvard University. The numbering of the manuscript pages is not in Charlotte Brontë's, but in a later hand; volumes I and II have been reversed, so that Volume I is on nine sheets folded and gathered as described in n. 95, to form pp. 33–68 and Volume II on eight sheets folded to form pp. 1–32.

1.   *three moons . . . dirty work again*: The last page of the final volume of *Henry Hastings* is dated 'March 26th 1839'. *Caroline Vernon* was apparently begun in the summer of 1839, either when Charlotte Brontë returned from her employment as a governess with the Sidgwicks in mid-July, or – just possibly – before. The date given in the first chapter for the Earl and Countess's breakfast quarrel – '1st of July' – may be the actual date of composition, though the exhaustion Brontë describes in a letter to Ellen Nussey written the preceding day (*CBL* 1, pp. 193–4) makes this perhaps unlikely. The quotation is from Alexander Pope, *Epistle to Dr Arbuthnot* (1735), ll. 89–92: 'Who shames a Scribler? break one cobweb thro', / He spins the slight, self-pleasing thread anew: /Destroy his fib, or sophistry, in vain, / The creature's at his dirty work again.'

2.   *baby capital . . . a willow*: *baby capital*: Adrianopolis, newly built capital of the young kingdom of Angria, established five years before, and now growing rapidly as a result of the new state of peace. 'Taxes may double upon us but Adrianopolis is spreading new streets and Buildings round us,' Branwell had written in December 1838 (*[Angria and the Angrians] V(c)*, Neufeldt, 3, p. 246). *water-god*: Fabulous deity, supposed to dwell in or rule over water, often portrayed as crowned with reeds or rushes. *sedge*: A generic name for coarse, grassy, rush-like or flag-like plants growing in wet places. *willow*: Traditionally a symbol of grief for unrequited love or the loss of a mate (see, for example, *Othello*, IV. iii, ll. 28–59). To sit under a willow 'to eat a cold fowl and drink a bottle of ginger-beer' is characteristic of Charles Townshend's provocative anti-romanticism.

3.   *female . . . died twenty years ago*: Mary Henrietta Wharton was Northangerland's second wife: for an account of her unhappy married life and early death, see *The Duke of Zamorna*, pp. 139–44.

4. *notes of a tourist*: *tourist* was a relatively new word in the early
    nineteenth century, and was steadily acquiring negative conno-
    tations (see James Buzard, *The Beaten Track: European Tourism,
    Literature, and the Ways to Culture, 1800–1918* (Oxford:
    Clarendon Press, 1993), p. 1). Townshend's creator would have
    been sharply aware of what 'sold' in journals such as *Black-
    wood's* and *Fraser's*. 'Notes of a Traveller' – an account of a tour
    to France, written in long breathless sentences such as Towns-
    hend uses here – appeared in *Blackwood's Magazine* in May and
    July 1839.

5. *Angrian campaign . . . Earl hadn't rather*: These verses appear to
    be a comic commentary on Branwell's extensive descriptions, in
    his writings of 1834–8, of the wars and political disputes which
    ravaged Angria. *duke and a lord*: The Duke of Zamorna and
    Lord Ellrington, Earl of Northangerland. *shopkeeper militant*:
    Jeremiah Simpson, villainous associate of Northangerland, who
    'though moving in circles so Aristocratic was nothing more in
    rank than an Extensive and Fashionable Dealer in Linen Drapery
    &c in Wellingtons town whose splendid shop attracted a mob of
    titled purchasers' (Branwell Brontë, *The Life of Alexander Percy
    Vol II*, Neufeldt, 2, p. 171). In Branwell's account, Simpson
    extends his establishment to Verdopolis and gradually through
    money-lending gains power over many. He eventually becomes
    General Sir Jehu Macterroglen, and joins with Medina and Qua-
    shia in support of Northangerland's occupation of Angria. *King
    Boy and King Jack*: 'Boy's and Jack's Negroes' are prominent
    along with Quashia's Ashantees in Branwell's accounts of the
    battles against Zamorna of 1836–7. In a manuscript fragment
    dated 6 January 1837, he portrays Bingo and Quacco Camingo,
    their commanders, as 'King Boy' and 'King Jack', 'two elegant
    chaps', dressed up in waistcoats and sitting down to breakfast in
    Zamorna's Verdopolitan palace (*[Angria and the Angrians]
    IV(a)*, Neufeldt, 3, 5–9). *Holy Alliance*: The league formed by
    Russia, Austria, and Prussia in 1815 to regulate the affairs of
    Europe after the fall of what was known as the Holy Alliance;
    here, the term is used of the distinctly unholy alliance between
    Jeremiah Simpson and Boy's and Jack's Negroes. *prince finding
    brandy*: Quashia Quamina, leader of the Ashantees, usually por-
    trayed in Branwell's manuscripts in a state of intoxication. *man
    of his hands*: A man of valour, skill, or practical ability; Shake-
    speare, *Merry Wives of Windsor* (1598), I. iv. 27: 'He is as tall a
    man of his hands, as any is between this and his head.' *death . . .*

carriage: Possibly a reference to a song sung by the drunken Montmorency in one of Branwell's manuscripts of 1836:

> Sing Hey for Cock Robin in regular verse
> How he harnessed Old Dobbin one day to the hearse
> For a marvel had happened that could not be holpen
> His wifes mouth was shut! and the graves mouth was open

> ... A Lady was there and her face looked so fair
> That each look he cast on her dried up a tear
> Lord he said if its greivous a[n] old wife to bury
> Why sure the best cure is a new one to marry ...
> (*[Angria and the Angrians] III (d)*, Neufeldt, 2, p. 640)

bigamy cause: Apparently refers to a now-vanished Angrian story. *king versus laws*: In Branwell's account, the Marquis of Ardrah had introduced in the Verdopolitan parliament a 'Bill for the Reform of the Angrian Kingdom', proclaiming on 27 January 1836, 'That the King and Government of Angria have broken the Laws Resisted their execution and incited the Nation to revolt against their Authority' (*[Angria and the Angrians] I(e)*, Neufeldt, 2, p. 439). *short transportation*: Refers apparently to Zamorna's banishment from Angria in June 1836. *him and his father*: Zamorna and Northangerland, his father-in-law.

6. *growing corn ... Leyden ... Evesham*: *growing corn*: Thus Branwell, in December 1838, describes the regeneration of Angria after the civil war: 'Edwardston Hall has put forth 2 fresh wings instead of the old Demolished Centre Edwardston fields have waved with a second crop above the bones of its martyred soldiers In short the removal of Old things though Violent has given more room for the vigorous springing of the New' (*[Angria and the Angrians] V(c)*, Neufeldt, 3, p. 246–7). *Leyden ... Evesham*: Sites of great battles in the recent Angrian wars.

7. *improved ... pennons*: *improved*: Such improvements were frequent in the rapidly industrializing Pennines of Brontë's youth. *Has life no variety now*: Many in the England of the 1820s and '30s looked back to the time of the Napoleonic wars as a time of excitement now vanished. 'It was dull ... last season, very dull,' says Disraeli's Vivian Grey. 'If it wasn't for the General Election, we really must have a war for variety's sake. Peace gets quite a bore' (*Vivian Grey* (1826), Vol. II, ch. 10). *Love*: Traditionally

personified as Cupid, a winged boy. *pennons*: Banners; or, poetically, pinions or wings; Victory was portrayed in classical statuary as having great feathery wings.

8.   *nobleman . . . reformation*: *nobleman*: Duke of Zamorna, whose liaisons are always a subject of public gossip. *reformation*: In 1787 William Wilberforce had obtained a royal 'Proclamation for the Encouragement of Piety and Virtue, and for the Prevention and Punishing of Vice, Profaneness, and Immorality' and founded the Proclamation Society for what he called the 'reformation of manners', aimed especially at aristocratic vice, gambling, duelling and libertinism. The first decades of the nineteenth century saw a continuing campaign to promote morality and public decorum. By the late 1830s the scandals of the Regency were receding into the past, and it was generally felt that the morals of society had improved.

9.   *nightingales . . . faithless mate*: *nightingales*: Cf. Milton, *Comus*, ll. 234–5: 'Where the love-lorne Nightingale / Nightly to thee her sad Song mourneth well'. *turtle-doves . . . faithless mate*: Cf. Bewick's *History of British Birds*, of which Rev. Patrick Brontë owned a copy, and from which Charlotte, Branwell, Emily and Anne Brontë all copied wood engravings between 1828 and 1833: 'The note of the turtle-dove is singularly tender and plaintive . . . on which account this bird has been represented in all ages, as the most perfect emblem of connubial attachment and constancy.'

10.   *parched scroll . . . ex-president*: *parched scroll*: From 'That Day of Wrath, That Dreadful Day' a thirteenth-century hymn by Thomas de Celano depicting the Day of Judgment, translated by Walter Scott and included in *The Lay of the Last Minstrel* (1805), VI, xxxi.5–8: 'When, shrivelling like a parched scroll, / The flaming heavens together roll; / When louder yet, and yet more dread, / Swells the high trump that wakes the dead.' *ex-president*: A joking reference both to Northangerland's former positions of political power as Prime Minister of Angria, and briefly as Lord President of the republican Provisional Government in Verdopolis (Branwell Brontë, *[Angria and the Angrians] III(d)*, Neufeldt, 2, p. 601), and also to the fact that he had formerly been 'president' of the Verdopolitan drinking and gambling club, Elysium (see *The Duke of Zamorna*, n. 29). All of these glories are now past.

11.   *Is it hysterical*: Thomas J. Graham's *Modern Domestic Medicine* (1826) describes hysteria as a disturbance of the nervous system,

characterized by 'convulsive struggling', 'wild and irregular actions' and 'alternate fits of laughter, crying, and screaming', to which 'the female sex' is particularly prone. 'I mastered the rising hysteria, lifted up my head, and took a firm stand on the stool,' says Jane Eyre, of her public exposure as a liar at Lowood (*Jane Eyre*, ch. 7). 'My nerves disdained hysteria', says Lucy Snowe of her final, triumphant, confrontation with the Nun (*Villette*, ch. 39).

12. *Miss Delph*: See *Henry Hastings* n. 68. Victoria 'Pelfe' 's sobs and tears and 'trembling with fear and passion' when confronted by a furious Zenobia had been described in a manuscript of Branwell's a few months before this (*[Angria and the Angrians] V(d)*, 23 February 1839, in Neufeldt, 3, pp. 267–9).

13. *Furies*: Roman name for the Greek Erinyes, variously supposed to be the three daughters of Earth and of Night: Tisiphone (the Avenger of blood), Alecto (Implacable) and Megaera (Disputatious).

14. *make a hit*: Say something striking and effective.

15. *seventy and seven times*: A flippant allusion to Matthew 18:21–22: 'Then came Peter to him, and said, Lord, how oft shall my brother sin against me, and I forgive him? till seven times? And Jesus saith unto him, I say not unto thee, Until seven times: but, Until seventy times seven.'

16. *hay-tenters*: In Yorkshire dialect, one who minds or has charge of something, such as a machine, a flock or (as here) the hay.

17. *at the close of the day when the hamlet is still*: James Beattie, 'The Hermit', in *Poems on Several Occasions* (1776), 1.1.

18. *Daddy Long-legs . . . Sober*: *Daddy Long-legs*: Popular name for a spider. Possibly a slang term for an old buck, though I have not found it in any slang dictionary. Thackeray in *Pendennis* (1850) ch. 36 speaks of 'An old reprobate daddy long legs, who has never said his prayers (except perhaps in public) these fifty years: an old buck who still clings to as many of the habits of youth as his feeble grasp of health can hold by: who has given up the bottle, but sits with young fellows over it, and tells naughty stories upon toast and water.' *Daddy*: Old boy; a familiar address to an old man (*DVT*). *Long-legs*: Northangerland, the recipient of the letter, is throughout the Angrian saga represented as having very long legs. *Sober*: The writer is Quashia, Prince of the Ashantees, and formerly Northangerland's ally in his campaign against Zamorna, now living in exile in Boulogne. Despite this declaration, his letter – demanding that he be given Northangerland's

daughter, Caroline Vernon, in marriage – is a drunken, almost incoherent mishmash of malapropisms and garbled poetical and biblical phrases.

19. *bleached bones ... right hand and on my left*: *bleached bones*: Cf. Byron, *Childe Harold's Pilgrimage*, 88, ll. 951–2: 'Let their bleached bones, and blood's unbleaching stain, / Long mark the battle-field with hideous awe.' *burning souls*: Eighteenth-century poetic staple, indicative of a state of fervour. The phrase recurs in James Macpherson, *The Poems of Ossian*: '. . . let me meet him, O my father; I feel my burning soul!' (*Croma*); 'I will fight the king; I feel my burning soul! (*Carric-Thura*). An 1819 edition of *The Poems of Ossian* was owned by the Brontës, and loved by them as children, but Charlotte would have known that by 1839 their 'rant, bombast, and fustian' had made them 'the ridicule, not merely of our critics but some of our greatest living poets' (*Blackwood's Magazine* 45, November 1839, p. 693). Here, the fragmentariness, emotional vagueness and blurring of the boundaries between metaphor and reality characteristic of Ossian are being used to comic effect. *game-cocks, booted and spurred*: Cocks trained and equipped for fighting. *right hand and on my left*: In Matthew 20:21, the mother of Zebedee's children asks Jesus to 'Grant that these my two sons may sit, the one on thy right hand, and the other on the left, in thy kingdom.'

20. *Sai Too-Too ... Anamaboo*: *Sai Too-Too*: Sai Too Too Quamina, King of the Ashanteees, father of Quashia Quamina, who died in the Battle of Coomassie when Quashia was a child. The name derives from Sai Tootoo, an early eighteenth-century king of the Ashanti, of whom the Brontës may have read in an extended review of Edward Bowditch's *Mission from Cape Coast Castle to Ashantee*, which appeared in *Blackwood's Magazine* 5, 1819, pp. 175–83, 302–10 (Barker, 155). *Sambo Mungo Anamaboo*: The names given all confusedly evoke late eighteenth- and early nineteenth-century European interest in Africa. *Sambo*: A colloquial or humorous name given to a Negro in the early nineteenth century; more specifically a name given to one who is half mulatto, half Negro (from the Spanish *zambo*: bow-legged). *Mungo*: Mungo Park had gone to explore the Niger basin in 1797 under the auspices of the London-based Associ-ation for Promoting the Discovery of the Interior Parts of Africa, inaugurated in 1788. His enormously popular *Travels in the Interior Districts of Africa*, published in 1799, was in the library at Ponden House, from which the Brontës are thought to have

borrowed books; they would certainly have read of it in *Black-wood's Magazine*. *Anamaboo*: A place on the coast of Ghana; the 'king of Anamaboo' figures in the *Blackwood's* review of Edward Bowditch referred to above.

21. *What's the fun*: This phrase appears in quotation marks in the ms. It is the first remark made by Jingle in Dickens' *Pickwick Papers* (1837) ch. 2 – ' "What's the fun?" said a rather tall thin young man, in a green coat, emerging suddenly from the coach-yard' – and may have become a popular catchphrase.

22. *old Ocean himself trembles*: Cf. James Macpherson, 'Death', in *The Poems of Ossian*, ll. 318–19: 'Old ocean trembles; and fraternal shades/ To frighten'd Neptune seem a kind recess.'

23. *child of perdition . . . cab of Dove's dung*: *child of perdition*: One predestined to damnation. *cab of dove's dung*: See II Kings 6:25: 'And there was a great famine in Samaria: and, behold, they besieged it, until an ass's head was sold for fourscore pieces of silver, and the fourth part of a cab of dove's dung for five pieces of silver.' *cab*: (Hebrew: kab) a dry measure equal to 1.1600 quarts; while some believe the dove's dung referred to in this passage is literally the waste of the bird (pigeons' excrement has been eaten in times of desperate food shortage), others take it to be the bulb of the star of Bethlehem plant. Quashia's meaning, here as elsewhere, is obscure.

24. *sort of a mist . . . play's nearly played out*: *sort of a mist*: Cf. Townshend's description of his drunkenness in *Henry Hastings*, (p. 227). *hoyle*: Room (northern dialect), cf. *Shirley*, ch. 12: ' "as he'll enter through this hoyle" '. The word occurs in a manuscript of Branwell's, dated 20 October 1837, in the course of a description of Quashia and his cronies all blind drunk: ' "Theres a Hell ith Hoyle!" muttered Crofton in his slumbers' (*[Angria and the Angrians] IV(d)*, Neufeldt, 3, p. 153). *round-about . . . cloudiness*: He is drunk, and the room is spinning round him. *play's nearly played out*: Cf. *I Henry IV*, II.iv.467, 'Play out the play'. Brontë uses the phrase in *Jane Eyre*, ch. 19, where Rochester, dressed as a gipsy, says to Jane, 'Rise, Miss Eyre: leave me; "the play is played out" ' and in *Villette*, ch. 39, where Lucy says of her night at the fête, 'the play was not yet indeed quite played out'.

25. *foxes and holes . . . Scaramouch*: *foxes and holes*: Irreverently garbled invocation of Matthew 8:20: 'The foxes have holes, and the birds of the air have nests; but the Son of man hath not where to lay his head.' *toil and spin*: Similarly garbled reference to

Matthew 6: 28–9: 'Consider the lilies of the field, how they grow; they toil not, neither do they spin: And yet I say unto you, That even Solomon in all his glory was not arrayed like one of these.' *Scaramouch*: Stock figure in old Italian farce, introduced into England in the latter half of the seventeenth century. He was a braggart and a fool, usually dressed in a black Spanish costume like a don.

26. *prison house ... bridegroom waits*: *prison house*: Refers to Caroline's seclusion at Hawkscliffe. *bridegroom waits*: Another comically garbled scriptural reference; in Acts 7:56 the heavens open and 'the Son of man' appears 'standing on the right hand of God'; in the book of Revelation, the church is figured as the bride who waits for her bridegroom (Revelation 22:7).

27. *promised me another ... numb-scull*: *promised me another*: Quashia had several years before demanded the hand of Mary Henrietta Percy in return for his assistance to her father, then Lord Ellrington. See Branwell Brontë, *The Politics of Verdopolis* (1833), Neufeldt, 1, p. 355. In Charlotte Brontë's *Passing Events* (1836), Townshend tells of rumours that Northangerland has promised Quashia 'the hand of the Duchess of Zamorna' in return for his military assistance (*Five Novelettes*, p. 50). *like a lily drooping bowed her head and died*: John Gay, ''Twas when the seas were roaring', air from *The What D'Ye Call It* (1715), II.viii: 'All melancholy lying' ... Then like a Lilly drooping,/ She bow'd her Head, and dy'd.' *numb-scull*: Zamorna.

28. *A better lot is thine, fair maid*: Cf. the 'roundelay' from Sir Walter Scott, *Rokeby*, III, xviii, ll. 7–10: 'A weary lot is thine, fair maid,/ A weary lot is thine! /To pull the thorn thy brow to braid, /And press the rue for wine!' The phrase is echoed also by Branwell in a manuscript dated 4 February 1839 (*[Angria and the Angrians] V(d)*, Neufeldt, 3, p. 253): 'Another lot is thine my lad/ Another lot is thine'. A sumptuous edition of *Rokeby* and *The Vision of Don Roderick*, illustrated by Westall, had been presented to Charlotte on her departure from Roe Head School on 23 May 1838.

29. *I rejected her*: This is a lie. To Quashia's fury, Mary's father immediately reneged on his promise of her hand (Branwell Brontë, *The Politics of Verdopolis* (1833), Neufeldt, 1, p. 358).

30. *squire of high degree, Q in the corner*: *The Squire of Low Degree* is an early fourteenth-century metrical romance beginning with the lines 'It was a squire of low degree / That loved the King's daughter of Hungary.' *Q in the corner*: An old children's game,

like 'Puss in the corner'; also a colloquial expression for something not seen at first but subsequently brought to notice. The
expression probably originates in the French term, *queue*, meaning the thong to which seals are attached in the corner of legal
documents. *Fraser's Magazine* for June 1838 contains 'Reflections at an Evening Party. By Q in the Corner' ('Blue Friar
Pleasantries', xxiii, *Fraser's Magazine* 17, 1838, p. 677). Quashia
is playing on his own initial.

31. *Roman hand*: Italic cursive script, a version of which was 'very
fashionable amongst the fair sex' in the early nineteenth century
(J. Dunbar, *Principles of Penmanship* (1841), p. 33). Cf. Mal-
volio, of whom Brontë is clearly thinking here: 'I think we do
know the sweet Roman hand' (*Twelfth Night*, III.iv.29). The
Earl's comment, of course, is ironic; see *The Duke of Zamorna*,
n. 5.

32. *naught to me 'at I know on*: The rest of this page is left blank in
the ms.

33. *country*: Region.

34. *deep-mouthed bark of welcome . . . aclivity*: *deep-mouthed bark
of welcome*: Cf. Byron, *Don Juan* (1818), I, 123, ll. 977–8: ' 'Tis
sweet to hear the watch-dog's honest bark / Bay deep-mouth'd
welcome.' *aclivity*: Not in *OED*. A declivity is a downward slope
or inclination (of a hill, etc.); presumably, an aclivity is an upward
slope.

35. *put up*: Shut up (in its case).

36. *elegant extras*: A joking allusion to Vicesimus Knox's popular
Elegant Extracts in Verse (c. 1780) and *Elegant Extracts in Prose*
(1783), each of which had gone into at least fifteen editions
by 1839. 'It must be known to most of my Readers,' writes
Wordsworth in the third of his *Essays upon Epitaphs* (1810), 'as
it is circulated every where and in fact constitutes at this day
the poetical library of our Schools.' A manuscript of Branwell's
written in January 1837 is entitled *Elegant Extracts: the dying
effort of distraction ([Angria and the Angrians] IV(b)*, Neufeldt,
3, p. 10).

37. *planter's vade mecum*: The plantsman's manual. *vade mecum*: A
handbook or manual suitable for carrying about with one for
ready reference (Latin).

38. *croft . . . house*: *croft*: Small piece of agricultural land adjacent
to a dwelling. *bigging*: Northern dialect term for an outbuilding,
as distinguished from a house. *grange*: Country house with farm
buildings attached, usually the residence of a gentleman-farmer.

house: Living-room in a farmhouse which the family usually occupy. Cf. Jane Moore, in *Henry Hastings*: 'he was sitting in his kitchen – what they call the house' (p. 245).

39. *in a rope*: With a rope around its neck.

40. *poached . . . try for it*: *poached*: In early nineteenth-century England there were about three thousand gamekeepers, whose job was to supervise the breeding and preservation of game on large country estates. Their chief enemies were poachers: between 1827 and 1830, one seventh of all criminal convictions were under the Game Laws. *try for it*: Do something that will cause me to be brought to trial.

41. *dine . . . seldom later than three*: Another indication of Zamorna's rustic mode of life: the fashionable dined in the evening.

42. *omlets and patés*: Zamorna is mocking Northangerland's poor state of appetite; he can eat neither wholesome farmhouse fare nor fancy French food.

43. *Kashua*: Quashia.

44. *Douro the dandy*: In his days as Marquis of Douro, Zamorna had been a dandy. In a manuscript now known as *Four Years Ago*, written in July 1837, and describing a time four years earlier, Brontë's narrator Townshend had noted the 'rivalry' of the young Douro and the then Lord Ellrington 'regarding the cut of a coat or the model of a castor – I've seen them not unfrequently meet in a perfumers shop' (p. 15).

45. *Society . . . Vitality*: In March 1828 Charles Knight had joined with Henry Brougham to form the Society for the Diffusion of Useful Knowledge with the aim of producing cheap instructive literature for the working classes. The Society was to come to an end in 1846, but in the late 1830s it was successful enough to be satirized; thus, in the opening chapter of *Pickwick Papers* (1837), the aims of the newly founded Pickwick Club are comically described as 'the advancement of knowledge, and the diffusion of learning'. Here, Zamorna is pointing back to the days of the Earl's ascendancy. 'Vitality', meaning the essential energy of a nation, was a cornerstone of Northangerland's political philosophy, and a subject over which he and Zamorna had disagreed in the past. In a letter dated 12 September 1834, the exiled Alexander Percy had written to the Angrians of his fear that Zamorna would not 'give that VITALITY to the world which he is so gloriously qualified to give' (Branwell Brontë, *[Angria and the Angrians]* I *(b)*, Neufeldt, 2, p. 245). In Charlotte's 'Speech of His Grace the Duke of Zamorna at the Opening of the

First Angrian Parliament', dated 20 September 1834, Zamorna replies to this charge:

> He speaks of vitality. Many of you Angrians would neglect that word as being, to use a customary phrase, 'quite out of your line'. Some would laugh at it, and a few would ponder it deeply. I am of the last number. I pondered it and I comprehended it. Vitality is the errant light, the wandering sun, the latent, essential flame, which in turn has glowed and vanished on every empire that, since the fall of man, WAR has founded and SCIENCE polished ... Extinguished in Europe, it was kindled in Africa. There now Verdopolis sees it flicker and fade. Angria smiles in its earliest dawn and Percy has formed in his Titanic mind a scheme for making that dawn immortal. He would fain fix the fleeting, futile, but undying mystery – never before was an idea so sublime conceived by mortal intellect.'
> (Charlotte Brontë, *The Scrap Book, EEW,* 2.ii, pp. 305–6)

Here, in *Caroline Vernon*, five years later, Zamorna is taunting Northangerland with the loss of his once 'Titanic' power.

46. *Arthur Wellesley ... stick*: *Arthur Wellesley*: As in his earlier reference to 'Douro, the dandy', Northangerland is recalling the different phases of Zamorna's former existence by invoking his different names. *sticking the bills*: Posting up placards. *stick the whole concern*: Here, *stick* seems to be used in the northern dialect sense of to spoil in the execution.

47. *musical talent she ought to inherit*: Caroline's 'musical talent' is an inheritance from both her parents, who were brought together by music. On the young Alexander Percy's 'extraordinary musical genius', see Branwell Brontë, *Life of Alexander Percy I*, Neufeldt 2, p. 124. Louisa Vernon, as Louisa Allen, had been a famous singer, 'the Musical Star of the world'. 'Every Newspaper had spread her wonderful powers, every festival for months to come had hired her prescence,' says Townshend in a manuscript of Branwell's, in which he looks back to the moment of her meeting with Northangerland, when 'before all the assembled Nobility of Sneachies Land the proud and polished looking Blackguard stepped forth from their aristocratic throng assumed his place at the grand piano and accompanied Miss Allen' (*[Angria and the Angrians] IV(d)*, Neufeldt, 3, pp. 135–6).

48. *pencil-case: Chambers' Cyclopedia* (1741) describes a pencil-case as 'an instrument serving to inclose a pencil, and occasionally also used as a handle for holding it. It is usually four or five

inches long, and contrived so as the pencil may be slid up and down it by means of a spring and button' (*OED*).

49. *fitness of things*: Phrase extensively used in the eighteenth and early nineteenth centuries, with reference to the ethical theory of Samuel Clarke (1675–1729), in which the quality of moral rightness is defined as consisting in a 'fitness' to the relations inherent in the nature of things. The phrase was popularly and playfully used to mean 'what is fitting or appropriate'. Cf. Charlotte Brontë to her publisher (6 November 1852) on Lucy Snowe's name: 'A *cold* name she must have – partly – perhaps – on the "lucus a non lucendo" – principle – partly on that of the "fitness of things" ' (*CBL*, 3, p. 80).

50. *French society*: In *Four Years Ago* (21 July 1837) Brontë describes the French society which used to gather at Ellrington House, Northangerland's home in Verdopolis: 'The universal language of that house was French ... The French of Ellrington House were Revolutionists and infidels ... and certainly though polished and clever they were a very depraved set' (p. 19).

51. *passed current for*: Were generally accepted or received as (*OED*).

52. *Donna Julias ... Cecilias*: Loose Spanish and Italian women. Donna Julia seduces the youthful Don Juan in Byron's *Don Juan* Canto I (1819).

53. *exclusive*: High class; a term associated with the silver fork novel. Lady Charlotte Bury's *The Exclusives*, which included recognizable portraits of many fashionable figures, was published in 1830; it was well known enough for *Fraser's* to mock the 'Exclusiveites' along with the 'Pelhamites' in an early attack on the genre ('The Dominie's Legacy', *Fraser's* 1, April 1830, p. 318).

54. *where ignorance is bliss 'tis folly to be wise*: Thomas Gray, *Ode on a Distant Prospect of Eton College* (1742), ll. 99–100.

55. *Has sorrow thy young days shaded*: From Vol. 6 of Thomas Moore's enormously popular *Irish Melodies* (1808–34).

56. *wild-fire*: Wild-fire, will-o'-the-wisp, or *ignis fatuus* is a flame-like phosphorescence which appears flitting over marshy ground (due to the spontaneous combustion of the gases therein) and deluding people who attempt to follow it; hence, it is used as an image for any delusive aim or object. Cf. *Jane Eyre*, ch. 16: 'a secret love ... which ... must lead, *ignis fatuus*-like, into miry wilds whence there is no extrication'.

57. *Ellrington and Douro resuscitated*: Like the old days of their friendship, when Northangerland, newly married to Zenobia,

had assumed the title of Lord Ellrington, and Zamorna was Marquis of Douro.

58. *vapours*: Morbid depression of spirits, hypochondria or hysteria.

59. *Attendez un peu, Monsieur loves you jusqu'à folie*: Wait a little, Monsieur loves you to distraction (French).

60. *Non, avec tendresse, avec ivresse*: No, with tenderness, with rapture (French).

61. *C'est trop modeste*: That's too diffident.

62. *Ecoutez la fille . . . Northangerland*: Listen to the girl! He's a hard man. As for love, he hardly knows what it is. He looks on women as slaves. He amuses himself with their beauty for a moment, and then he abandons them. One must hate and avoid such a man and I hate him exceedingly – yes, I detest him. Alas, how different he is from my Alexander! Elise, remember my Alexander, the handsome Northangerland! (French).

63. *C'etait fort gentil*: He was very nice (French).

64. *Gentil! . . . cheveux chataignes*: Nice! Elise, he was an angel! I seem to see him in this very room, with his blue eyes, his face expressive of so much sweetness, and his marble brow surrounded by chestnut hair (French).

65. *Mais le Duc a des cheveux chataignes aussi*: But the Duke has chestnut hair too (French).

66. *Pas comme ceux de mon pre[cie]ux Percy*: Not like my precious Percy's (French).

67. *il sut apprecier mes talen[t]s*: He could appreciate my talents (French).

68. *Lord George*: Lord George Vernon, who was to become her first husband.

69. *less than him*: Smaller than he is.

70. *Miss Gordon*: Lady Helen Victorine Gordon, first wife of Zamorna when he was Marquis of Douro, and mother of the Ernest Fitz-Arthur whom Mina Laury struggled to protect (see *Mina Laury*, n. 28). Her longing for her absent husband and her early death in childbirth were portrayed by Brontë in a poem written in January 1836 ('But once again, but once again', Victor Neufeldt, ed., *The Poems of Charlotte Brontë: A New Text and Commentary* (New York: Garland, 1985), pp. 184–91).

71. *c'est finie*: This is finished (French).

72. *piano very well touched*: In the early nineteenth century, music was an essential part of a young lady's education, and one of the 'accomplishments' she was supposed to acquire. The invention of the upright piano in 1827 meant that even modest-sized houses

had room for a piano. Patrick Brontë bought a cottage piano – now
in the Brontë Parsonage Museum – for his children in late 1833
or 1834 (Barker, p. 212), and a quantity of their sheet music
(ranging from settings of Handel, Purcell, Rossini and Beethoven
to popular songs of the period) survives at Haworth Parsonage.

73. *Jim Crow*: Popular song in 1839. Thomas Dartmouth Rice had
popularized the black-faced minstrel on the American stage with
his 1828 caricature of a crippled plantation slave, dancing and
singing the words 'Weel about and turn about and do jus' so, /
Eb'ry time I weel about, I jump Jim Crow'. After touring American cities, Rice took his act to the Adelphi Theatre in London in
1836; it became, as *Fraser's* put it, 'the rage all over the town
. . . not only has the fashionable world crowded to the Adelphi
theatre under the sole attraction of this barbarism, but the fair
twirlers of Almack's have ordered it to be arranged as a quadrille
. . . so that beauty can "jump Jim Crow"' (*Fraser's* 15, May
1837, pp. 666–7). In December 1838, Thomas Rice returned to
the Adelphi with three further 'Jim Crow' plays, which played
throughout the following year.

74. *sheet of music . . . title-page*: There was a huge demand for sheet
music in the early nineteenth century, and publishers quickly
realized that an appealing cover image, often of a star performer,
would help to sell their musical scores. See Introduction, n. 38.

75. *mauvaise honte*: Painful shyness. Cf. Brontë to her friend Ellen
Nussey, written on 4 August 1839, at about the time she began
Caroline Vernon: 'at home you know Ellen I talk with ease and
am never shy – never weighed down and constrained by that
miserable mauvaise honte which torments & constrains me elsewhere' (*CBL*, 1, p. 198).

76. *of her age*: For her age.

77. *worked trousers*: White frilled or trimmed drawers, ornamented
with needlework, reaching to the ankles (or nearly so), worn by
little girls in the first half of the nineteenth century.

78. *megrims*: The term can mean either a sick headache (migraine),
'vapours', low spirits, or a fad or fancy; here it is perhaps a little
of both.

79. *fly*: Explode, burst out (slang).

80. *frocks*: Dr Johnson's *Dictionary* in 1755 defined a frock as 'A
kind of gown for children'; and the term was throughout the
nineteenth century applied chiefly to the garment worn by children and young girls. A gown was a dress with some pretension
to elegance, and was worn by grown women.

81. *Aladdin's lamp*: In the oriental tale, *Aladdin and the Wonderful Lamp*, included by Galland in his edition of *The Arabian Nights' Entertainments*, Aladdin, the son of a poor tailor, finds a lamp which possesses magical powers. Whenever he rubs it, a genie appears and grants his wish.

82. *reading Lord Byron has half turned my head*: The girl driven out of her mind by reading Byron was a stereotype of the period. 'Byromania' (as it was termed in 1812 by Byron's future wife, Annabella Milbanke) lasted well into the 1830s.

83. *Lord Edward Fitzgerald ... Moore*: Brontë would have been familiar with Fitzgerald from Thomas Moore's *Life of Byron* (1830), which quoted Byron's journal entry of 10 March 1814: 'If I had been a man [at the time of the Irish rebellion] I would have made an English Lord Edward Fitzgerald.' Fitzgerald (1763–98) was the twelfth child of the first Duke of Leinster and an officer in the British army, with whom he fought in the American War of Independence and journeyed through unexplored territory to Quebec. When he returned to Ireland, he became MP for Kildare, and visited Paris in 1792, staying with Thomas Paine. At a dinner of British residents there, he joined in a toast to the abolition of hereditary titles and was cashiered from the army as a result. Returning home, he joined the United Irishmen, who were seeking to establish an independent republic in Ireland, and whom he pledged to assist as commander in chief of their rebel army. On the eve of the rebellion of 1798 he was betrayed by an informer and arrested; he died of wounds sustained at his arrest. Moore's *Life of Lord Edward Fitzgerald* (1831) gives a graphic account of Fitzgerald's 'unconquered intrepidity, republicanism, and devotion to Ireland' (II, p. 183).

84. *Miss Martineau*: Harriet Martineau had proved herself an intrepid traveller whilst researching her *Society in America* (1838), which was reviewed at length in *Fraser's Magazine* in May 1839. There is an intriguing parallel between the reviewer's complaint that 'the authoress allows her judgment to be run away with by the exuberance of her fancy' (p. 571) and Charlotte Brontë's portrayal of the youthful Caroline Vernon; though 'Miss Martineau' 's 'visionary ... theories' of female independence and rational democracy are very different from Caroline's romantic dreams ('Practical Reasoning *Versus* Impractical Theories', *Fraser's* 19, May 1839, pp. 557–92).

85. *Alcibiades ... Alexander the Great*: Alcibiades: (450–04 BC),

Athenian statesman, friend and follower of Socrates, perhaps the most gifted Athenian of his generation. *Alexander the Great*: King of Macedonia (356–23 BC) who conquered Greece in 336 BC, Egypt in 331 BC and the Persian Empire in 328 BC, and founded Alexandria.

86. *Haephestion*: Macedonian nobleman (c. 357–24 BC), closest friend and lover of Alexander the Great.

87. *He is silly*: In *The Duke of Zamorna* Sir William Percy describes Arundel as 'displaying by far the finest head of the three councillors – but between ourselves, Townshend, I conceive, the least brains to furnish it' (p. 190).

88. *pirate . . . Jericho*: *pirate*: Alexander Percy's early career as a pirate is described in detail by Branwell Brontë in *The Pirate* (8 February 1833), Neufeldt, 1, pp. 240–49. *doddered*: Word used of old oaks (rarely other trees), apparently meaning having lost the top or branches through age and decay; hence, remaining as a decayed stump. Thus *Villette*, ch. 12: 'Nasturtiums clustered beautifully about the doddered orchard giants'. Here it is used by extension to mean decrepit with age. *kings up at Verdopolis*: The reigning monarchs of Africa, who had thrones in the Verdopolitan parliament, were at this point six in number: the four original kings of the Verdopolitan Union – Arthur, Duke of Wellington, King of Senegambia; William Edward Parry, King of Parrysland; John Ross, King of Rossland; Alexander Sneachie, King of Sneachiesland; and two others, Frederic Hume, King of the island of Fredericia, and James Hume, King of Menzies Isle. *Alexander*: Alexander Sneachie, King of Sneachiesland. *to Jericho*: As far away as possible.

89. *thread-paper and maypole style*: Thin and tall. A 'thread-paper' was a person of slender figure.

90. *unsnuffed*: The snuff is that portion of the wick of a candle which is partly consumed in the course of burning to give light, and has to be pinched or removed at intervals.

91. *Alhambra . . . Caliph*: *Alhambra*: The citadel and palace built at Granada by the Moorish kings in the thirteenth century; its name, meaning 'the red castle', comes from the Arabic. The Alhambra figured largely in romantic fantasies in the 1830s: in Disraeli's silver fork novel, *The Young Duke* (1831), the unbelievably wealthy hero constructs a replica of the Alhambra in nine acres off St James for his mistress. Washington Irving's enormously successful *Alhambra*, a collection of legends set in Moorish Spain, was published in London in 1832. *Caliph*: Title signifying

'successor of Mohammed', given to the chief civil and religious ruler in Muslim countries.

92. *inexpugnables*: Trousers; see *Henry Hastings*, n. 109. *inexpugnable*: Impregnable, invincible.

93. *My heart is wae*: Cf. 'Lord Maxwell's Goodnight', ll. 3–4, from *Minstrelsy of the Scottish Border* (1802): 'Adieu! fair Robert of Orchardstane, / My heart is wae for thee.'

94. *Paris or Fontainebleau*: In a manuscript written in 1837, Brontë had described Zamorna's view of the French women who used to gather at Ellrington House: 'The Ladies had qualities which the Marquis in his lofty purity looked upon as peculiarly revolting ... their manners he abhorred and this abhorrence he showed not by shrinking from their society or by declining their advances which some of them were willing enough to make *à un tres beau garçon* but by bluntly checking and abashing them at every opportunity that offered' (*Four Years Ago*, p. 20). The motif of the young Englishwoman whose sexual innocence is threatened by continental travel recurs in travel literature of the post-Napoleonic years: see James Buzard, *The Beaten Track: European Tourism, Literature, and the Ways to "Culture", 1800–1918* (Oxford: Oxford University Press, 1993), pp. 130–52.

95. *He had never been so stern and didactic before*: Brontë wrote two alternative endings to the first volume of *Caroline Vernon*. The passage given in the text, from 'His allusions to matrimony etc. too, confounded her' to the end of this chapter, seems, from manuscript evidence, to be the second of these. The first, and shorter, version reads as follows:

> She wanted to change the conversation, and so, by way of giving it another turn, she asked the Duke whether he would be so kind as to write to her sometimes when she was gone. He said, 'He did not know; he could not promise; his time was very much occupied.' Caroline was again silent. She thought the answer scarcely kind.
>
> 'Would he never write to her?' she said, after a pause.
>
> 'Perhaps he might sometimes. There was no impossibility in the case.'
>
> Again Miss Vernon was disappointed and saddened. His Grace was certainly displeased with her. He was not accustomed to speak so coldly, and instead of holding her hand, as he generally did when she walked with him, he had allowed her arm to drop, and barely suffered her to keep by his side.

'And won't you even think of me, my lord?' she said at last.

'I shall think of you when I hear your name, I suppose,' replied the Duke.

Caroline slackened her pace, and dropped behind. This was too bad. She had always thought herself a favourite; she found she was mistaken. Her guardian cared nothing about parting with her. The last night, when she had thought he would be kinder and fonder than ever, to treat her so coolly, so austerely! Her heart swelled, and a tear or two was forced into her eye.

'Now, child, where are you?' said the Duke, turning abruptly. She was only a pace or two behind him, and her handkerchief was at her eyes. 'What ails you?' continued his Grace, taking her hand from her face. 'A little touch of sentimentalism about leaving Hawkscliffe, eh? Come, come, all will be right to-morrow.'

'You don't know me,' said Miss Vernon. 'You think I'm pleased with all kinds of novelties, but I'm not.'

'Stuff! This little fit will go off soon.'

His Grace stood in the moonlight, and looked at Miss Vernon, and laughed. She turned away, feeling about as bitter a pang at that moment as she had ever known in her life. It was the anguish of discovering that her strongest and most genuine feelings were not appreciated, that a person whom she was disposed to care for intensely would not condescend to let her tell him how much she regarded him, would not stoop to understand her emotions, to enter into them or in the least degree return them. Stifling her sobs and dashing away her tears as well as she could, she would have hurried away to the house, but his Grace said,

'Caroline!'

She did not stop for the first call, nor answer it. He repeated,

'Caroline!'

The tone was not one to be disobeyed. Besides, she felt that if she parted from her guardian so, without a reconciliation, she would not sleep that night. So she returned to him. They were near a little bower with a seat in it. He took her there, and having sat himself down, he placed his ward beside him. He divided her hair from her forehead and, as he smoothed away her curls, said in a far different tone from what he had hitherto used, a tone that changed the whole idea of his character,

'What is all this little flutter about, Caroline? Tell me now.'

Miss Vernon's answer was plain truth at least.

'I'm sorry,' said she, 'that I'm going to part with you, and still more sorry that you don't care for parting with me.'

'Who told you that I did not care?' asked his Grace.

'You're so cold,' said she. 'You call me child, and look as if you despised me.'

It is probable that the Duke smiled at these words, though it was almost too dusk to see, for the moon pentetrated but faintly into the little bower.

'Come, Caroline,' he said, after a pause. 'You and I can't afford to quarrel, so we'll be friends again. Now, is all right?'

'I'm afraid you don't care for me,' persisted Miss Vernon, distrustfully.

'Hush, no more misunderstanding,' said the Duke. 'What is there to make you doubt whether I care for you now? Can you be nearer to me?'

All at once, Miss Vernon's fears were removed. She was satisfied. It was not the Duke's words, but his voice, that produced this happy change. There was something in its tone that assured her he did not now, at least, regard her as a mere child.

'Are you cold, Caroline?' he asked. 'Does the air feel damp?'

'No.'

'What are you looking at so earnestly, my little girl?'

'Only the sky. It seems so full of stars. I shall always remember this night. Oh, I can't bear to go away to-morrow – but I won't think of to-morrow.'

Just then, a voice was heard in the garden crying 'Miss Caroline! Miss Caroline!' It was Mademoiselle Touquet, who had been sent in search of the young lady.

Winifred Gérin and Christine Alexander both argue that this shorter ending is a second, and superior, draft. Gérin, in *Five Novelettes*, prints it as the tale's conclusion (following on from 'He had never been so stern and didactic before'), on the grounds that it is 'incomparably superior, and shows not only a greater sense of realities, but a refinement in taste' (*Five Novelettes*, p. 274). Alexander, too, prefers this version, because 'had Zamorna shown his true feelings for Caroline, as in Charlotte's first draft of this scene, their friendship would no longer have been innocent' (Alexander, *The Early Writings of Charlotte Brontë*, p. 198). Yet *Caroline Vernon* is rather more sardonic about 'morality' than this suggests, and the Caroline who wants 'to be dashing and to be very much admired', and who blushes 'red as fire' when her mother hints at her feelings for Zamorna, is from her first appearance not exactly a figure of innocence. The longer version given in the text here, with its ironic observation of Zamorna's and Caroline's differing embarrassments as he educates her in the ways of the world ('What he said . . . about the French ladies and the Italian men and women made her feel very queer'; 'Before the Duke answered this question, he took out a red silk handkerchief and blew his nose'), its mockery of romantic cliché ('Mr Percy was very poetical in his youth. Consequently, he must have been very much smitten with the stillness of the summer night'), its insertion of 'Mr Percy' as a silent eavesdropper on the latter part of the scene, and its comic final encounter between 'Mr Percy' and 'Mr Wellesley' picks up and develops these ironies in a sophisticated riposte to the sentimental morality of contemporary Gothic romance.

Moreover, an examination of the manuscript suggests that that which Gérin and Alexander prefer as a 'rewriting' is almost certainly Brontë's first draft. It is true that in the manuscript preserved in the Houghton Library the shorter ending given above ('She wanted to change the conversation . . . sent in search of the young lady') appears on the page now numbered 67, after the longer one ('His allusions to matrimony . . . turned laterally onto Mr Wellesley'), which is on pp. 63–6. But it is the shorter version which appears to have been written first. Brontë wrote – or 'printed' – each of the two surviving volumes of *Caroline Vernon* on sheets of paper folded in half and gathered into a single quire, so that the final page at the back of the 'book' is on the second half of the first sheet; thus, the final page of Volume I (a blank page numbered 68) at the back of the 'book' is on the second half of its first sheet, p. 33. (The page numbering is not in Brontë's, but in a subsequent hand; see Note on the Texts.) The shorter version of the ending is on the reverse of this, on the page numbered 67 (the second half of p. 34). In other words, it is an integral part of the original folded ms. 'book', and follows on quite easily from p. 62 ('He had never been so stern and didactic before'), though not from p. 66 ('turned laterally onto Mr Wellesley'). It is the so-called 'first draft' which seems to be the later addition. This is on a single sheet, folded like the rest to form four pages, but quite separate from the original 'book'. It seems that Brontë was dissatisfied with her original conclusion, and used another sheet of paper to write an alternative ending. This additional piece of paper has been inserted into the 'book', to follow on from p. 62, and numbered accordingly 63–6. The first ending, however, could not be scrapped without spoiling the 'book'; it remains on the page which has been numbered 67.

96. *Lalande ... St James*: Mistresses of Northangerland.

97. *read gross novels*: Cf. Brontë to her friend Ellen Nussey, 20 August 1840:

> I have got another bale of French books from Gomersal, containing upwards of 40 volumes – I have read about half – they are like the rest clever wicked sophistical and immoral – the best of it is, they give one a thorough idea of France and Paris – and are the best substitute for French Conversation I have met with. (*CBL*, 1, 226)

98. *wild-eyed charioteers ... handfuls*: *wild-eyed charioteers*: Percy Bysshe Shelley, *Prometheus Unbound* (1820), II.iv.130–2: 'I see cars drawn by rainbow-wingèd steeds / Which trample the dim winds: in each there stands / A wild-eyed charioteer urging their flight.' Shelley's *Complete Works* had been published for the first time in 1839; this allusion suggests that they must have reached the Parsonage very soon after this (see Edward Chitham, 'Emily Brontë and Shelley' in Edward Chitham and Tom Winnifrith, eds., *Brontë Facts and Brontë Problems* (London, 1983), p. 59). *gleaners of grapes in that vineyard*: Cf. Leviticus 19:10: 'Thou shalt not glean thy vineyard, neither shalt thou gather every grape of thy vineyard.' *vineyard of experience*: Cf. *Shirley*, ch. 7: 'at eighteen, the school of Experience is still to be entered, and her humbling, crushing, grinding, but yet purifying and invigorating lessons are yet to be learned'. *Boaz*: In the biblical book of Ruth, the widowed Ruth, a Moabitess, goes to live with her mother-in-law Naomi in Bethlehem, and asks to glean ears of corn in a field belonging to Boaz, Naomi's wealthy kinsman. She finds favour in the sight of Boaz, and he marries her (Ruth 2–4). *handfuls*: In the biblical account, Boaz commands his young men to 'let fall also some of the handfuls of purpose for her, and leave them, that she may glean them' (Ruth 2:16).

99. *broad and burning*: Possibly another allusion to Shelley: '... in the east / The broad and burning moon lingeringly rose / Between the black trunks of the crowded trees' ('The Sunset' (1816), ll. 17–19).

100. *clay in the hands of the potter ... polished vessel of grace*: *clay in the hands of the potter*: Isaiah 64:8: 'But now, O Lord, thou art our father; we are the clay, and thou our potter; and we all are the work of thy hand.' In Charlotte Brontë's *Corner Dishes*:

A Peep Into A Picture Book (1834), Lord Charles Wellesley describes Caroline's father, the young Alexander Percy, at the age of twenty-four: 'What a vessel to be moulded from the coarse clay of mortality! . . . And the vessel is without flaw, polished, fresh and bright from the last process of the maker' (*EEW*, 2.ii, p. 86). *polished vessel of grace*: An ironic mingling of the languages of religion and of fashion, each rather differently directed at young girls in this period. *polished*: Refined, cultured, elegant, according to the demands of the fashionable world. Cf. Northangerland's 'notion that it was necessary [Caroline] should go [to Paris] to acquire a perfect finish' (p. 389). *vessel of grace*: One chosen by the Lord. Thus, Mrs Chapone's *Letters on the Improvement of the Mind* (1773), on which the curriculum at Roe Head School was based: 'We know not whether . . . they might not prove . . . chosen vessels to promote the honour of God' (Vol. I, p. 93).

101. *Mr Percy was very poetical in his youth*: For an example of Alexander Percy's youthful poetry, see the lines addressed to his first wife, Augusta di Segovia, in Branwell Brontë's *Life of Alexander Percy*, Neufeldt, 2, pp. 137–9.

102. *Endymion*: In Greek mythology, a beautiful youth who, as he slept on Mount Latmus, so moved the cold heart of Selene the moon goddess that she came down and kissed him. Possibly another (ironic) allusion to Shelley; thus *Epipsychidion*, ll. 293–4: 'Illumining my slumbers, like the Moon / Waxing and waning o'er Endymion.'

103. *noiseless tenor of his way*: Cf. Thomas Gray, *Elegy Written in a Country Churchyard* (1751), ll. 75–6: 'Along the cool sequestered vale of life / They kept the noiseless tenor of their way.'

104. *Lucifer-match . . . his mother knew he was out*: *Lucifer-match*: Name of one of the earliest forms of matches tipped with a combustible substance and ignited by friction; such matches were in common use by 1839. *his mother knew he was out*: The catchphrase, 'Does your mother know you're out?' is, according to Eric Partridge, 'one of the three or four most remarkable of all British catch-phrases', 'sometimes jocular, sometimes sarcastic, but especially addressed derisively to someone displaying either an exceptional simplicity or a youthful conceit or presumption' (*A Dictionary of Catch-Phrases* 2nd, edn., London: Routledge, 1985). It seems to have been a new and popular saying in 1839. Brewer, in his *Dictionary of Phrase and Fable*, traces it to a comic poem published in the *Mirror* on 28 April 1838; and

OED cites *Bentley's Miscellany* for that year 'How's your mother? Does she know that you are out?' In December 1837, English and French versions of a song entitled 'Does your mother know you're out?' appeared in *Fraser's Magazine* (*Fraser's* 16, December 1837, p. 682).

105. *November, nearly December*: Probably the actual time at which the second volume of *Caroline Vernon* was begun. In the intervening months, Brontë, like her young heroine, had had her first independent holiday, going with Ellen Nussey to stay for five weeks at the seaside at Easton near Bridlington. Juliet Barker conjectures that this volume of *Caroline Vernon* may have been finished as late as spring 1840 (Barker, p. 896, n. 115). Certainly, Brontë would have had little time for writing in the final months of 1839; Tabby, the Parsonage servant, was ill in November and December, and Charlotte and Emily, the two sisters at home, were fully occupied with household duties and 'shirt-making and collar-stitching' for their brother, who departed to new employment on 1 January 1840 (*CBL*, I, pp. 206–7).

106. *merry as a grig*: Slang phrase alluding to the apparent liveliness of a grig, or young eel (*DVT*).

107. *paper caps ... lamp-posts*: Cf. Thomas Carlyle, *The French Revolution* (1837), ch. 2, 1:9: 'The Printers have come marching, Prudhomme's all in Paper-caps with Revolutions de Paris printed on them.' See *Stancliffe's Hotel*, n. 64.

108. *at Paris*: After the abdication of Napoleon in April 1814 and his expulsion to Elba, large numbers of the fashionable English began to revisit a Paris now filled with returning French diplomats, statesmen and aristocrats.

109. *the Dupins, the Barrases and the Bernadottes*: Leaders of the revolutionary and republican factions of Frenchyland in Branwell Brontë's *Historical Narrative of the War of Encroachment* (1833; Neufeldt, 1, pp. 366–7). They had allied with Northangerland against Zamorna in the civil war of 1836. See *Henry Hastings* n. 110.

110. *a triumph*: In ancient Rome, the entrance of a victorious commander with his army and spoils in solemn procession.

111. *men-monkeys*: French aristocrats. Large numbers of these who had fled the Revolution had lived in England during the Regency; they returned to Paris after Waterloo. A *man-monkey* is possibly a dandy; see *Stancliffe's Hotel*, p. 105, and *Henry Hastings*, p. 238.

112. *Hector Montmorency Esqre*: Like Alexander Percy, a native of Senegambia.

NOTES 541

113. *cette jolie petite fille à cheveux noirs*: That pretty little girl with black hair (French).

114. *gentleman of the west*: A Senegambian (or Irishman).

115. *Lord's Prayer written within the compass of a sixpence*: There was apparently a vogue for such things in the early nineteenth century. See the entry for *Buckinger's boot* in Hewson Clarke, *Lexicon Balatronicum: A Dictionary of Buckish Slang, University Wit, and Pickpocket Eloquence* (1811): 'Matthew Buckinger was born without hands and legs; notwithstanding which he drew coats of arms very neatly, and could write the Lord's Prayer within the compass of a shilling.' Robert Anderson, the Cumberland dialect poet (1770–1833), is reported by his biographer to have 'succeeded in writing by candle light, and without the aid of glasses, the Lord's Prayer, the Creed, the Ten Commandments, a psalm, and his name, upon a piece of paper the size of a sixpence' (*Anderson's Cumberland Ballads, with Notes Descriptive of the Manners and Customs of the Cumberland Peasantry; a Glossary of Local Words; and a Life of the Author* (Carlisle, n.d.), p. xii).

116. *Simon Pure*: The real man, the authentic article. The proverbial phrase derives from Susannah Centilivre's comedy, *A Bold Stroke for a Wife* (1718), in which Colonel Fainall, in order to win the consent of Obadiah Prim, the Quaker guardian of Anne Lovely, to his marriage with her impersonates Simon Pure, 'a quaking preacher'. As soon as he does so, the Quaker turns up and proves beyond doubt that he is the 'real Simon Pure'.

117. *the stoic of the woods, the man without a tear*: The popular *Gertrude of Wyoming* (1809) by Thomas Campbell (1777–1844), a poem in Spenserian stanzas, describes an impassive Oneida Indian chief as 'a stoic of the woods – a man without a tear' (Part I, l. 207).

118. *badger*: Refers to Denard's grey hairs.

119. *organ*: A protuberance, a swelling. Apparently a mocking reference to phrenology, which analysed character by measuring the size and shape of protuberances on the skull, from which it claimed to determine the size of the 'organs'. Thus, for example, *Shirley*, ch. 1: 'Davy, thou hast an enormous organ of wonder in thy cranium.' Here, with a debunking humour characteristic of these Angrian tales, the term is used not to designate a 'faculty', but of a mere bump on the head, caused by a collision with a door.

120. *a bob and two joeys*: A shilling and two fourpenny pieces, or

groats. Joeys were relatively new coins, issued for general circu-
lation in 1836. The name derived from Joseph Hume (1755–
1855), MP for Kilkenny, who recommended their coinage for
use in paying short cab-fares, instead of the more usual sixpence.
This was extremely unpopular with cab-drivers, who frequently
received only a groat where otherwise they would have received
a sixpence without any demand for change. As a result, they
named the coin a 'joey' in derision.

121. *large tom-cat . . . magnified*: *large tom-cat*: Cf. Charlotte Brontë's
earlier description of Zamorna in *The Scrap Book: Duke of Z
and E Percy* (1835), *EEW*, 2.ii, p. 366:

> Taking him on the whole he resembles nothing so much as an
> uncommonly large tortoise-shell tom-cat which I once had, a perfect
> wonder for fierceness, prowess and beauty. Its soft fine fur and
> singular feminine colour answer to his splendid locks and, for a
> man, most unique complexion. Herod was victorious amongst the
> race of cats, wherever he came would fight like a tiger, domineered
> over three or four dogs which I kept, killed rats as ferociously as
> Adrian does Negroes, attracted the admiration of every lady who
> saw him. An old maid of my acquaintance, indeed, once made an
> attempt to steal him. Now, reader, is not the parallel complete?
> I think you will answer in the affirmative.

magnified: Exaggerated. Cf. *Jane Eyre*, ch. 18: 'The ladies Lynn
and Ingram . . . nodded their two turbans at each other, and
held up their four hands in confronting gestures of surprise, or
mystery, or horror, according to the theme on which their gossip
ran, like a pair of magnified puppets.'

122. *taken out a furlough*: Taken leave of absence.

123. *jest was given for earnest and earnest for jest*: Cf. Shakespeare,
Richard III, V.i.22–4: 'That high All-Seer which I dallied with /
Hath turn'd my feigned prayer on my head, / And given in earnest
what I begg'd in jest.'

124. *rounded her periods like a blue*: *rounded*: Of periods, neatly
finished; well turned. *periods*: A sentence consisting of several
clauses, grammatically connected and rhetorically constructed;
hence, in plural, rhetorical or grammatical language (*OED*). *a
blue*: A learned lady, a blue-stocking.

125. *crowned . . . wandering star*: Cf. ll. 22–3 of Branwell Brontë's
'Sound the loud Trumpet o'er Afric's bright sea', the 'National
Song of Angria', written by Hastings for the coronation of

Zamorna in spring 1834: 'All ye proud mountains that shadow-ing afar/ Crown your blue brows with the wandering star.'

126. *her Siberia and not her Eden*: A place of exile, rather than a paradise. *Siberia*: The name of a region in Russia, used figura-tively to mean a cold, inhospitable place, or a place of banishment or imprisonment. *Eden*: The abode of Adam and Eve at their creation, used figuratively to mean a delightful abode or resting-place, a paradise.

127. *and no mistake . . . irreproachables*: *and no mistake*: Without a doubt. A recent saying in 1839; cf. *Pickwick Papers* (1837), ch. 26: ' "The action's going on, and no mistake," thought Sam.' *irreproachables*: Trousers; see *Henry Hastings*, no. 109.

128. *tower looking towards Lebanon*: An ironic echo of Song of Solomon 7:4: 'thy nose is as the tower of Lebanon which looketh toward Damascus'.

129. *little Flowers*: The children of John Richton, Baron Flower.

130. *She would go to him . . . pity her*: Cf. her mother's fantasies about Northangerland, p. 360–1 above: 'for if he would only be exceedingly savage, I might fall into great terror and faint, and then perhaps he would pity me afterwards.'

131. *direction*: . . . *wafer-stamp*: *direction*: Address. *wafer-stamp*: Wafer-seal, a small disk of flour mixed with gum and non-poisonous colouring matter, moistened and used for sealing let-ters, attaching papers, or receiving the impression of a seal; a wafer stamp, a hand-stamp for impressing a device on wafers. Zamorna's use of such a seal is a sign of his carelessless in writ-ing this letter. 'Never use a wafer; it is a nasty and unlady-like custom, and is allowable by tradespeople only, in the hurry of business,' advises the author of *Etiquette for the Ladies. Eighty Maxims on Dress, Manners, and Accomplishments* (4th edn., London, 1837).

132. *singular epistle that follows*: The following draft of the letter occurs first in the ms.:

My dear little Caroline
    You trusted to an unsafe plan when you left your letter at Wellesley House to wait for me till my coming there. The chances were ten to one that I might never have received it. And indeed, it was not put into my hands till many days after my arrival. Even then, I had no leisure to answer, as the first week or two of my stay in town brought continual and pressing calls on my attention. I am at present a little more disengaged, having contrived to get away

from Verdopolis in order to complete a small business transaction relative to an affair of some old houses which has for many years been pending between myself and Mr Warner. The matter is not one likely ever to be settled, because it only relates to a rental of some ten pounds per annum arising from a brace of tenements whose roofs are nearly off. However, it gives Mr Warner a pretext for demanding my presence at his place, Woodhouse Cliff, about twice a year, in order to survey the buildings and discuss afresh the disputed point of their value. Mr Warner, my little Caroline, wishes me to take them off his hands without requiring any repairs, and I am considerably too much a man of business to consent to any such arrangement. My young Ward will wonder what all this has to do with her

This is immediately followed by a second, finished version of the letter, which has been written with a different pen.

133. *somnambulists ... destruction*: Cf. Robert Macnish, *The Philosophy of Sleep* (1830), p. 160: 'To walk on the brink of house-tops, to scale precipices, and descend to the bottom of frightful ravines, are common exploits to the somnambulist; and he performs them with a facility far beyond the power of any man who is completely awake.' Rev. Patrick Brontë records his reading of this volume, held in Keighley Mechanics' Institute Library, in the margin of the Parsonage copy of Thomas J. Graham's *Domestic Medicine*.

134. *the devil to pay*: Popular saying, referring to bargains made with Satan, and the inevitable payment to be made to him in the end.

135. *shoulder knots ... shining emblems*: *shoulder knots*: Knots, at first of ribbons of the family colours, subsequently of lace, worn on the shoulder by some livery servants. *shining emblems*: Candlesticks; cf. Revelation 1:20: 'the seven candlesticks which thou sawest are the seven churches.'

136. *one of the most powerful men in Angria*: Mrs Warner's husband, Warner Howard Warner, Prime Minister of Angria.

137. *on the stretch*: Strained to the utmost. Cf. *Journal Fragment* 1 (4 February 1836): 'my mind relaxes from the stretch on which it has been for the last twelve hours' (p. 447).

138. *won't wash*: Will not bear investigation, stand the test, prove to be genuine. The first such colloquial usage given in *OED* is Charlotte Brontë's *Shirley* (1849), ch. 18: 'That willn't wash, Miss'. But the play with the phrase here suggests that it was a catchphrase of the 1830s.

139. *Mr Ferguson*: A fictional character, one invented as a substitute for the actual culprit. In the early nineteenth century, young men about town brought before the magistrates for bad behaviour would give the name of 'Ferguson' in place of their proper names. John Ashton, in his *Gossip in the First Decade of Queen Victoria's Reign* (London: Hurst and Blackett, 1903), pp. 7–8, gives an account of one such case, involving twisting the knockers off door-handles, reported in *The Times* on 10 July 1837. The invocation of the fictional 'Ferguson' led to the popular catchphrase, 'It's all very well, Mr Ferguson, but you can't do that, you mustn't go there, etc.' Thus, Gilbert à Beckett and Mark Lemon, *St George and the Dragon, in Two Acts* (1837), I. iii, ll. 10–12: 'I'll soon make it clear, /That, like Mister Ferguson, /You don't lodge here.'

140. *Blarney Mills*: Apparently an allusion to *blarney*, a slang term for flattering, wheedling speeches, or unabashed lying.

141. *her sister dead and herself his wife*: Marriage to a deceased wife's sister was not merely a violation of canon law, as set out in the Book of Common Prayer in 1662 and posted in parish churches. Four years before *Caroline Vernon* was written it had – controversially – become a violation of civil law. An Act of Parliament, introduced by Lord Lyndhurst to rectify anomalies in the marriage laws, ruled that all marriages with a deceased wife's sister – until then, permissable under civil law – that were contracted after 31 August 1835 were invalid. This aroused enormous feeling, partly about the right of the state to interfere in domestic matters, more crucially, perhaps, about the place of sexuality within the English family, conventionally portrayed as a haven of purity. The 'deceased wife's sister' became the focus for anxieties about jealousy, rivalry, triangular desire and the potential disruptive entry of sexuality into domestic tranquillity. Brontë's depiction of the first meeting between Caroline and Zamorna in *Julia* (29 June 1837) –

> 'You will make such a woman as your half-sister Mary I fancy – child, I could almost imagine it was her little hand that clasped mine so.' 'That's your wife – am I like your wife? when I'm old enough I'll marry you – I will, and I often tell mamma so – just to put her in a passion.' (*Five Novelettes*, p. 115)

– and her description in *Caroline Vernon* of Zamorna's reaction to 'the striking similarity of that grey silk dress, that pretty form and tiny slender foot to something that might be a hundred miles off at Wellesley House' suggests that she was well aware of the frisson surrounding this figure.

142. *image*: Statue.

143. *Mentor . . . garment of light*: *Mentor*: Friend of Ulysses, whose form Minerva assumed when she accompanied Telemachos in his search for his father. Hence, a wise and faithful guide. *garment of light*: Cf. Psalm 104:2: 'who coverest thyself with light as with a garment'.

144. *Fidena . . . Greatheart*: *Fidena*: Prince John Augustus Sneachie, Duke of Fidena, eldest son of the King of Sneachiesland, and one of Zamorna's most trusted friends, is noted for his moral uprightness. *Greatheart*: The Christian warrior who guides Christiana and her family to the Celestial City in Bunyan's *Pilgrim's Progress*, Part II.

145. *laurel crown . . . blue venom*: *laurel crown*: Worn by Apollo, god of the sun, with whom Zamorna is often associated (the rising sun is the symbol of Angria). *blue venom*: Brontë here seems to be recalling the description in Dryden's translation of Virgil's (70–19BC) *Aeneid* of serpents attacking Laocoon: 'The priest thus doubly chok'd, their crests divide,/ And tow'ring o'er his head in triumph ride./ With both his hands he labors at the knots;/His holy fillets the blue venom blots' (Book II, ll. 289–92). She seems, however, to have misremembered: it is not Calchas, the Greek soothsayer, who is being strangled here, but Laocoon, the Trojan priest. Branwell and his father, according to a note made by the latter, began reading the first six books of the *Aeneid* together in June 1839, just before *Caroline Vernon* was begun (John Lock and Canon W. T. Dixon, *A Man of Sorrow: The Life, Letters and Times of the Rev. Patrick Brontë* (London: Nelson, 1965), pp. 274–5).

146. *Turk . . . my harem*: Cf. Jane Eyre's later annoyance at Rochester's 'eastern allusion': 'I would not exchange this one little English girl for the grand Turk's whole seraglio; gazelle-eyes, houri forms and all!' (*Jane Eyre*, ch. 24). The Turk was a potent figure of lechery in the early nineteenth-century popular imagination. *The Lustful Turk*, one of the most popular works of nineteenth-century pornography, was published in 1828 (see Steven Marcus, *The Other Victorians: a study of sexuality and pornography in mid-nineteenth-century England* (London: Weidenfeld & Nicolson, 1966), p. 210). The harem was the part of a Muslim dwelling-house appropriated to the women,

constructed so as to secure the utmost and privacy. An object of great fascination in early nineteenth-century England, it figured largely in Byron's works (for example, *Don Juan, The Corsair, The Giaour, Sardanapalus*) and (just before the writing of *Caroline Vernon*) in Julia Pardoe's very successful *The City of the Sultan; and Domestic Manners of the Turks, in 1836* (London, 1837); Pardoe's *The Romance of the Harem*, a 'collection of Oriental Fictions', was published in 1839.

147. *Gehenna ... recesses: Gehenna*: The place of eternal torment; see Milton, *Paradise Lost*, Book I, l. 403. *recesses*: A favourite word in Gothic fictions, most markedly in those of Mrs Radcliffe. Here, Brontë makes explicit her ironic evocation of this still popular genre. See Introduction n. 34.

148. *Krooman ... Joliba: Krooman*: One of a negro tribe of Liberia and the adjacent coast, often employed as seamen. *Joliba*: Mali name for the River Niger, meaning 'riches of life'.

149. *Crede Zamorna*: Trust Zamorna (Latin). As Brontë would have known from Moore's *Life of Byron*, Byron's motto was 'Crede Byron'; like Byron, Zamorna is notorious for his sexual infidelities.

150. *King and Conqueror had been before me*: He is referring to the death of his mistress, Rosamund Wellesley, described in *Henry Hastings* p. 301–2.

151. *it did not linger long*: Cancelled in ms.: 'it did not tame his vehemence nor quell his passion'.

152. *The man beside her ... Zamorna*: Zamorna, as Caroline's guardian, has stood in a fatherly relation to her. Incest was a frequent theme in female Gothic fictions; see, for example, Ann Radcliffe, *The Italian* (1797), chs. 1, 4, 9. Here, familial feeling shifts into sexuality in a manner that is disturbing, erotic, thrilling, rather than terrifying.

153. *conscience was feeble opposed to passion*: Contrast *Jane Eyre*, ch. 27: 'conscience, turned tyrant, held passion by the throat'.

154. *passes shew*: Cf. *Hamlet* I .ii.85–6: 'But I have that within which passes show, /These but the trappings and the suits of woe.'

155. *Gazemba ... Arundel's: Gazemba*: Refers to the civil war, when Fort Gazemba on the banks of the Calabar was held by Zamorna's troops under General di Enara. *Arundel's*: Arundel is an ally of Zamorna's, here represented as hunting his defeated enemies, Northangerland's allies.

156. *I'd say it to the D—l's face*: 'Go to the Devil then' cancelled in the ms.

157. *boyish ardour*: 'and attachment' cancelled in the ms.

158. *tantalizations*: 'leaving her for months' cancelled in the ms. *tantalization*: Being tormented by the sight, show or promise of a desired thing which is kept out of reach, or removed or withheld when on the point of being grasped. In Greek mythology, Tantalus was plunged up to the chin in a river in Hades, with a tree hung with fruit just above his head. Whenever he tried to drink, the waters receded, and when he tried to eat, the fruit was out of reach. Cf. *Shirley*, ch. 8: 'Rose had no idea of tantalization, or she would have held him awhile in doubt.'

159. *Nathan ... fructified by it*: In II Samuel 12:1–7, the prophet Nathan comes to King David, who has made Bathsheba, wife of Uriah the Hittite, pregnant, sent her husband into 'the hottest battle' to be killed, and taken her as his wife. He tells David the parable of 'two men in one city; the one rich, and the other poor. The rich man had exceeding many flocks and herds: But the poor man had nothing, save one little ewe lamb, which he had bought and nourished up: and it grew up together with him, and with his children; it did eat of his own meat, and drank of his own cup, and lay in his bosom, and was unto him as a daughter. And there came a traveller unto the rich man, and he spared to take of his own flock and of his own herd, to dress for the wayfaring man that was come unto him; but took the poor man's lamb, and dressed it for the man that was come to him. And David's anger was greatly kindled against the man; and he said to Nathan, As the Lord liveth, the man that hath done this thing shall surely die: And he shall restore the lamb fourfold, because he did this thing, and because he had no pity. And Nathan said unto David, Thou art the man' (2 Sam 12:1–7). *fructified by it*: It has borne fruit in you. Cf. Anne Brontë, *Agnes Grey* (1847), ch. 23: 'And as for all the wisdom and goodness you have been trying to instil into me – that is all very right and proper, I dare say; and if I were some twenty years older, I might fructify by it.'

160. *Harriet O'Connor*: Mistress of Northangerland when he was Alexander Percy. Her miserable death was portrayed by Branwell in a long poem entitled 'At dead of Midnight, drearily', dated 14 May 1838 (Neufeldt, 3, pp. 223–31).

161. *horned cattle*: Cuckolds, traditionally said to wear horns on their brows.

162. *annihilation ... I shall live again*: *annihilation*: An idea developed by Lucretius (c. 99–55 BC) in his *De Rerum Natura*, Book I. Thus, for example, *The Nature of Things*, trans. Thomas Busby

(London: J. Rodwell, 1813): 'To their constituent seeds all things decay,/ Annihilation steals no part away' (Book I, ll. 258–9). The Brontës possibly knew this work in John Mason Good's slightly earlier translation, *The Nature of Things: a Didactic Poem translated from the Latin of Titus Lucretius Carus* (2 vols., London, 1805); there is a suggestive parallel between Good's rendering of Book I, ll. 52–3 – 'How nature all creates, sustains, matures, /And how, at length, dissolves' – and Emily Brontë's 'No Coward Soul is Mine' (1846): 'With wide-embracing love/ Thy spirit animates eternal years/Pervades and brood above,/ Changes, sustains, dissolves, creates and rears.' *I shall live again*: Possibly an ironic reference to the Brontës' early practice, as the 'Chief Genii' of Glass Town, of resurrecting those who had been killed in the course of their 'plays'. It was a custom Charlotte Brontë had revived in *The Return of Zamorna* (c. 24 December 1836) where she had restored to life Mary Percy, Duchess of Zamorna, whose death had been described at length by Branwell in a manuscript written between September and November of the same year (*[Angria and the Angrians] III(d)*, Neufeldt, 2, pp. 613–24).

163. *Moored . . . ruder it blow*: From Walter Scott, 'Boat Song', *The Lady of the Lake*, Canto II, xix.

THE ROE HEAD JOURNAL FRAGMENTS

Parts of the Roe Head Journal were published in *SHCBM* II, pp. 123–4, 255–7. They were first published in their entirety, edited by Christine Alexander, in Richard Dunn, ed., *Jane Eyre* (2nd edn., New York and London: Norton, 1991). The exact date of some fragments is uncertain: it is discussed in Christine Alexander, *The Early Writings of Charlotte Brontë* (Oxford: Basil Blackwell, 1983), ch. 19. I have adopted Alexander's ordering.

1. *Well here I am at Roe Head*: Miniature ms. diary fragment; Pierpoint Morgan Library MS MA 2696. '*Well here I am at Roe Head*' and '*Now as I have a little bit of time*' are both written on a single sheet of paper, 22 cm × 18.6 cm, folded to form four pages. The former, which is undated and was apparently written first, is on pp. 2 and 3 and continues halfway down p. 4. The latter, which is preceded by the date 'Friday afternoon – Feb 4th 1836', is on the remainder of p. 4. Brontë apparently then turned

back to the unused p. 1 and – possibly at a later date – wrote the fragment beginning 'Two gentlemen in earnest conversation'.

2. *stretch on which . . . the ark . . . boundless deluge*: *stretch on which*: The state of tension in which. *the ark . . . boundless deluge*: Cf. Genesis 7:17–18.

3. *as God was not in the wind . . . the still small voice*: 1 Kings 19:11–12: 'but the Lord was not in the wind: and after the wind an earthquake; but the Lord was not in the earthquake: And after the earthquake a fire; but the Lord was not in the fire: and after the fire a still small voice.'

4. *continent*: The Africa of the Angrian saga.

5. *like heath in the wilderness*: Cf. Jeremiah 48:6: 'Flee, save your lives, and be like the heath in the wilderness.'

6. *Adrianopolis . . . was not darkened*: *Adrianopolis*: In a manuscript apparently completed on 14 January, whilst Charlotte was still at home in Haworth for the Christmas holiday, Branwell had described the fall of 'youthful magnificent Adrianopolis', Zamorna's flight from the city, and the entry of the invaders (*[Angria and the Angrians] II(a)*, in Neufeldt, 2, p. 469). *was not darkened*: Cf. Ecclesiastes 12:3: 'In the day when . . . those that look out of the windows be darkened'.

7. *ottoman*: Cushioned seat like a sofa, but without back or arms, for sitting or reclining on.

8. *Quashia . . . queen of Angria's sanctuary*: Quashia is portrayed as lusting for Mary Percy on her first appearance in the Glass Town saga, in Branwell Brontë's *The Politics of Verdopolis* (1833). See *Caroline Vernon* n. 27.

9. *his sable hair . . . even in sleep*: This is the early nineteenth-century European stereotype of 'the savage', drunken, lecherous, degenerate, animalistic. Cf. the description of Africa in the young Brontës' copy of Goldsmith's *Grammar of General Geography* (1823): 'Man, in this quarter of the world, exists in a state of the lowest barbarism.'

10. *Friday afternoon – Feb 4th 1836*: This date, in a large, regular, sloping copper-plate hand, appears prominently in the middle of the page, before the beginning of [1b]. Alexander, noting 'the variations in the style of writing between the phrases "Friday afternoon" and "February 4th, 1836"' suggests that the two halves of the date could have been written at different times, and that 'February 4th, 1836' (a Thursday) refers to [1a] and 'Friday afternoon' to [1b], begun on the following day (Alexander, 'Some

New Findings in Brontë Bibliography', *Notes and Queries*, June 1983, p. 236).

11. *I can't enter into any continued narrative*: Cf. *Passing Events*, begun, apparently, a few months later, in April 1836, where the narrator Townshend declares, after several pages: 'Reader, as yet I have written nothing, I would fain fall into some regular strain of composition, but I cannot, my mind is like a prism full of colours but not of forms. A thousand tints are there, brilliant & varied, & if they would resolve into the shade of some flower or bird or gem, I could picture before you. I feel I could' (*Five Novelettes*, pp. 38–9).

12. *slight & pleasant sketch ... jotting it down*: Cf. Brontë's later heroine, Jane Eyre, 'sketching fancy vignettes, representing any scene that happened momentarily to shape itself in the ever-shifting kaleidoscope of imagination' (*Jane Eyre*, ch. 21).

13. *It seemed to me that the war was over*: Brontë seems here to be casting herself forward into an imagined future, in which the civil war which Branwell was currently depicting as devastating Angria has ended. But the 'festal rest' and triumph she imagines here are very different from the aftermath of Zamorna's defeat at Edwardston in the summer of 1836, as Branwell – and she herself – were to portray it in mss. written in late June of this year. See n. 17 below.

14. *Two gentlemen in earnest conversation*: This fragment, though apparently a continuation of [1b] begins on a new side. Just possibly, it was written much later, on the internal date (29 June) when Brontë had returned home from Roe Head for the summer holidays: its emphasis on the setting sun could figure the disastrous defeat of the Angrians at Edwardston. See n. 17 below.

15. *Italian articulation*: Margaret Smith speculates that Bronte may have begun to learn Italian from Margaret Wooler, said by her nephew to be 'a fine Italian scholar', as a pupil at Roe Head in 1832 (*CBL*, 1, p. 269n.). Now that she was, as a teacher, more in contact with Margaret Wooler, her interest had perhaps been renewed.

16. *Henrico*: Henri Fernando di Enara, Italian commander-in-chief of Zamorna's forces.

17. *fire-dyed banner ... 29th of June: fire-dyed banner*: The flag of Angria was red, and carried the kingdom's symbol of the rising sun. *29th of June*: The specificity of the date is intriguing. Late June 1836 was a momentous period in the history of Angria.

According to Branwell, Zamorna was defeated at the battle of Edwardston on 27 June 1836; he escaped to the Warner Hills, was recaptured in early July, and banished by Northangerland to the Ascension Isle (*[Angria and the Angrians] III(d)*, Neufeldt, 2, pp. 601–2). On 28 June 1836, Charlotte – now back at Haworth for the school holidays – completed a sketch referring to Zamorna's defeat at Edwardston ('It is all up!', printed as part of *Passing Events* in Gérin, pp. 72–82. For the dating of this ms., see Jos Bemelmans, 'Passing Events and Another Manuscript', *Brontë Society Transactions* 20: 3, 1991, pp. 121–5). It is possible that the following day she turned once again to the sheet of paper on which, at Roe Head, she had depicted a peaceful conclusion to the war, and added the passage beginning 'Two gentlemen in earnest conversation', with its suggestions of 'gathering darkness' and approaching doom.

18. *Memnon's wondrous statue*: The statue of Amenophobis III in Thebes was said to produce a sound like a musical note when first struck by the rays of the rising (not the setting) sun. Ancient Greeks thought that the statue represented King Memnon, and that the sound was his greeting to his mother Eos (see 'On the Musical Memnon', *Fraser's* 1, 1830, pp. 153–4).

19. *All this day . . . infernal world*: *All this day*: MS Bon 98 (8) BPM [11 August–14 October 1836]. Miniature / 11.1 × 18.6 cm. Dated at the beginning 'Friday August 11th' in miniscule hand and at the end 'October 14th 1836' in longhand; 11 August was a Thursday in 1836. *infernal world*: Angria. Nearly seven years later, on 1 May 1843, Brontë was to write to Branwell from school in Brussels: 'It is a curious metaphysical fact that always in the evening when I am in the great Dormitory alone – having no other company than a number of beds with white curtains I always recur as fanatically as ever to the old ideas the old faces & the old scenes in the world below' (*CBL*, 1, p. 317).

20. *Miss Lister . . . Cook . . . article and a substantive*: *Lister . . . Cook*: Pupils at Roe Head School; the 'clever – but refractory' Harriet Lister was the sister of Mrs Ingham, who was to employ Anne Brontë as a governess at Blake Hall, Mirfield; Miss Marriott was possibly a daughter of the original owners of Roe Head (*CBL*, 1, p. 158n.); Ellen Cook, aged eight, was the daughter of Thomas Cook, a banker and merchant in Dewsbury; her sister, Ann, aged ten, became a friend of Anne Brontë's whilst at the school (Barker, p. 884 n. 45). *article and a substantive*: A very basic parsing lesson. W. Pinnock, *A Comprehensive Grammar*

of the English Language (London: Poole & Edwards, 1830),
owned by Charlotte Brontë, contains successive chapters on the
Article – 'a word placed before substantives, to point them out,
and to show their signification; as "*A* palace, *an* envoy, *the* king"
(p. 42) and the Substantive – 'or NOUN . . . the name of any
thing that exists; as, house, man, thought' (p. 45).

21.	*Huddersfield . . . Heaton Lodge*: Roe Head School, situated in
the part of Mirfield known as Mirfield Moor, had expansive
views over the Calder valley to Huddersfield, and, in the distance,
of the road between Huddersfield and Leeds. *Hopton*: A hamlet
in the parish of Mirfield, 3½ miles NE of Huddersfield. *Heaton
Lodge*: In the parish of Kirkheaton, 3 miles from Huddersfield.

22.	*North . . . West . . . East*: Cf. Branwell's description of the geogra-
phy of Angria, apparently written, like this journal fragment, in
the autumn of 1836: 'in its general features very like England.
placed under the sky of Italy . . . Beginning westward from the
mouth of the Gambia . . . is a grand expanse of. Woodland and
cultivable champaign well watered diversified with hills and laid
out in a noble park like scenery . . . clothed with the Elms the
Oak. and the Ashes of England with the Myrtles the Cypress and
here and there the Olive of Italy. Always canopied by the divine
Southern Sky and now spotted with the Halls of Old England
. . . the Verdopolitan valley elevates the country into a table land
and beyond is the region which used to be called Soudan. Heath
towers over Heath hills beyond Hills ending at length in the huge
snow clad summits of the Branii Hills . . . so round Eastward to
the Calabar and the Etrei which flows among tropical palms and
African sands' (*Angria and the Angrians III (e)*, Neufeldt, 2,
pp. 653–4).

23.	*In the afternoon . . . oecumenical*: *In the afternoon*: This section
begins on the reverse side of the page. *Miss E—L—*: Ellen Lister.
trigonometrically oecumenical: Trigonometry is the branch of
mathematics which deals with the measurement of the sides and
angles of triangles, particularly with certain functions of their
angles or of angles in general. *oecumenical*: Or ecumenical.
Belonging to the whole world; universal, general, worldwide.
The intended meaning seems to be a combination of 'going off
at a tangent' and 'vaguely generalizing'.

24.	*abymé . . . Miss M—t*: *abymé*: Sunk into the abyss. *Miss L—and
Miss M—t*: Miss Lister and Miss Marriott.

25.	*unconnected scenes . . . very pleasing*: The image is evocative of
the 'dissolving views' that were popular in the 1830s. These were

pictures produced on a screen by a magic lantern, one picture being caused gradually to disappear while another gradually appeared (see Martin Meisel, *Realizations: Narrative, Pictorial and Theatrical Arts in Nineteenth-Century England* (Princeton: Princeton University Press, 1983), p. 38).

26. *opium . . . lady*: *opium*: Cf. the description which follows with that of Macara Lofty, unable to rouse himself from an opium trance, in *Stancliffe's Hotel*, pp. 70–2. *lady*: The ensuing description of the dark-haired beauty alone in 'a Gentleman's house', holding the light for the doctor who has apparently been treating a man wounded in battle, strongly suggests Mina Laury. See n. 28 below.

27. *Brandon . . . Locksley Esqr*: These characters do not occur in any known Angrian manuscript.

28. *Ryder . . . Lucy*: *Ryder*: Does not appear elsewhere in the surviving Angrian manuscripts; he seems to have been wounded in the 'Revolution' referred to a little later in this fragment. *Lucy*: This second female figure in the scene is apparently a young countrywoman in attendance upon the patient, whose 'melancholy brow' and 'faded bloom' seem to remind the doctor of the fading Mary Percy, Duchess of Zamorna. Lucy does not appear elsewhere in the surviving Angrian manuscripts, but the ensuing vignette, which depicts her 'at the door of a lone cottage' smiling at an approaching figure, suggests that an embryonic story attaches to her.

29. *panorama*: Cf. Townshend in *Passing Events* (April 1836): 'A Panorama is round me whose scenes shift before I can at all fix their features . . .' (*Five Novelettes*, p. 39); and in *Four Years Ago* (1837) : 'A man like me, unconnected disentangled has great advantages – how coolly he can gaze on the moving panorama of life which encircles him' (p. 41). The huge circular panoramas of the late eighteenth and early nineteenth century, in which hyper-realistic scenes of urban and rural landscapes and historical events (such as the Battle of Waterloo or Captain Ross's expedition to the Arctic) were displayed, became immensely popular. At the turn of the century, the 'moving panorama' was developed; in this, enormous canvases were wound from one spool to another, producing the illusion of constantly shifting scenes. Both kinds of panorama were taken on tour in the provinces, and the young Brontës, if they did not see them, would have read accounts of them in newspapers and periodicals. See Ralph Hyde, *Panoramania: The Art and*

Entertainment of the 'All-Embracing' View (London: Trefoil
Publications, 1988).

30. *dead & buried under the newly plotted sod*: Mary Percy, Duchess
of Zamorna, who, when Charlotte left Haworth, had been fading
to death at Alnwick because of Zamorna's repudiation of her.

31. ~~fiction~~ *vision . . . symmetrical figure*: ~~fiction~~ *vision*: Brontë was
to exploit the tension between the narrative and the visual that
is evident in this deletion in her later Angrian tales (see Introduction, p.xxxvi–xxxix). *whole country . . . reinstated*: A shorthand
reference to the wars which Branwell had described as ravaging
Angria throughout 1836 (see *[Angria and the Angrians] III(d)*,
Neufeldt, 2, pp. 605–9). *pictured . . . alarming distinctness*: 'If
you have ever been accustomed to such society Sir', Brontë was
later to write to Hartley Coleridge of her characters, 'you will be
aware how distinctly and vividly their forms and features fix
themselves on the retina of that "inward eye" which is said to be
"the bliss of solitude"' (*CBL*, 1, p. 240). The romantic rhetoric
of imagination as 'vision' acquires, in passages such as these, a
peculiar literalism. Indeed, the Brontë family copy of Lindley
Murray's *English Grammar* contains some suggestive evidence
of family opposition to the denigration of 'vision' as merely a
'figure of speech': Murray's definition of 'vision' as metaphor
('when, instead of relating something that is past, we use the
present tense, and describe it as actually passing before our eyes')
has been deleted by an unknown hand. *symmetrical figure*: Cf.
the description of Mina Laury in *Passing Events* (21 April 1836):
'a kind of military erectness in her form, so elegantly built, & in
the manner in which her neck sprung from her exquisite bust &
was placed with graceful uprightness on her falling shoulders'
(*Five Novelettes*, p. 43).

32. *impossible . . . flung itself across me*: Cf. Branwell's description
of Northangerland at his daughter's deathbed, written a month
before this journal fragment, on 19 September 1836: 'there was
a weight upon him as in a Nightmare and he felt as if he could
never speak again' (*[Angria and the Angrians] III(d)*, Neufeldt,
2, p. 620). In his *Modern Domestic Medicine* (1826), a copy of
which was owned by the Brontës, Thomas J. Graham describes
'Night-Mare' as 'a nervous affection, in which there is a violent
struggle and tremor, with a severe pressure on the chest' (p. 425).

33. *October 14th 1836 . . . I'm just going to write*: *October 14th 1836*:
Written in a copperplate script much larger than the print of the
rest. *I'm just going to write*: Miniature 11.3 × 18.6 cm. Bon 98

(7) BPM. No date is given on the ms. but it was evidently written during the period in which, according to Branwell, the Duchess of Zamorna was dying at Alnwick, deserted by her husband, i.e. in the early autumn of 1836.

34. *Wiggins . . . Bashan*: *Wiggins*: Charlotte had introduced 'Patrick Benjamin Wiggins', a caricature of Branwell, into the Angrian saga in May 1834 (*Corner Dishes: A Day Abroad, EEW*, 2.ii, pp. 108–115). In a slightly later manuscript, she portrays his contempt for his sisters – 'Charlotte Wiggins, Jane Wiggins and Anne Wiggins', 'miserable silly creatures not worth talking about' (*My Angria and the Angrians* (October 1834), *EEW*, 2.ii, p. 250). *scriblo-mania*: Thus in ms.; *scribblemania* or *scribbleomania* was apparently a contemporary term; thus Coleridge, 1792, qu. *OED*: 'I have never had the scribble-mania stronger on me'; *Scribbleomania*, a collection of doggerel verses cataloguing and criticizing contemporary writers of all kinds, by William Henry Ireland (1777–1835), the notorious forger of Shakespearean documents and plays, was published in 1815. *calves of Bashan*: Cf. Psalm 22:12–13: 'Many bulls have compassed me: strong bulls of Bashan have beset me round. They gaped upon me with their mouths, as a ravening and a roaring lion'. Bashan was a rich country beyond Jordan, with abundance of cattle; in Amos 4:1 the wealthy Israelites 'which oppress the poor, which crush the needy, which say to their masters, Bring, and let us drink' are addressed as 'kine of Bashan'.

35. *AC—k . . . E L—r . . . Miss W—er*: Ann Cook, a pupil at Roe Head who became a friend of Anne Brontë; Ellen Lister; Miss Wooler, the head teacher.

36. *Hohenlinden . . . Burial of Moore*: All poems lamenting death in battle. *Hohenlinden*: Thomas Campbell's (1777–1844) famous poem (1802) described the aftermath of the Battle of Hohenlinden (1800), during the Napoleonic wars, in which the French under General Jean Moureau defeated the Austrians. Campbell was one of the poets Brontë recommended to Ellen Nussey in a letter of 4 July 1834 (*CBL*, 1, p. 130). *Childe Harold*: Byron's *Childe Harold's Pilgrimage*, published 1812–18, with its evocative description of the eve of Waterloo, had long been a favourite of the Brontës; a copy bought by Branwell in May 1835 survives in Haworth Parsonage. *Flodden Field*: Possibly Scott's *Marmion*; *A Tale of Flodden Field* (1808), later extolled by Jane Eyre, as 'one of those genuine productions so often vouchsafed to the fortunate public of those days – the golden age of modern litera-

ture' (ch. 32), but more probably 'Flodden Field' by David Moir (1798–1851), which appeared in the *Literary Souvenir* for 1830, one of the three annuals from which the young Brontës copied engravings (Alexander and Sellars, *The Art of the Brontës* (Cambridge: Cambridge University Press, 1995), p. 15). As 'Delta', Moir regularly contributed poems and ballads to *Blackwood's Magazine* between 1820 and 1844, and seems to have been a particular favourite of Emily Brontë's (see Barker, p. 274, p. 889 n. 63). *Burial of Moore*: *The Burial of Sir John Moore after Corunna* (1817) by Charles Wolfe (1791–1823), a very well-known poem commemorating the death of Moore in the Battle of Corunna during the Napoleonic wars. Branwell quotes from it in his *Historical Narrative of the War of Encroachment*, written in 1833 (Neufeldt, 1, p. 384). Wolfe's *Remains*, published in 1829, are amongst the 'biographies' recommended to Ellen Nussey in Brontë's letter of 4 July 1834 (*CBL*, 1, p. 131). The longing expressed in this fragment is not simply to 'repose on' the Angrian dream, or to enter into its scenes, but for literary achievement, such as these works represent.

37. *Branwell ... killed the Duchess*: Branwell had written a long account of Mary Percy's death, as yet unseen by Charlotte, on 19 September (*[Angria and the Angrians] III(d)*, Neufeldt, 2, pp. 613–24).

38. *Zenobia's thoughts ... Ennerdale*: Zenobia, alienated from her husband, both because of his infidelities and because of his attempts to oust Zamorna, who had been her youthful love, has retreated to her country estate at Ennerdale. In a manuscript dated 31 October 1837 Branwell describes her there: 'To enter her Room and meet with statly silence and costly desolation to sit hours thinking with eyes abstractly fixed on wall or window to walk about chafing her haughty heart in silence such had long been Zenobias daily employment' (*[Angria and the Angrians] IV(j)*, Neufeldt, 3, p. 167). See *Mina Laury*, n. 4.

39. *feels unconsciously the power of*: Here, the fragment breaks off, half-way down the page; the remainder of the sheet is filled by the following, in a fainter ink:

> Look into thought & say what dost thou see
> Dive, be not fearful ~~plunge through the foam~~ how dark the waves flow
> Sink ~~in the waves~~ through the surge & bring pearls up to me
> Deeper aye deeper, the fairest lie low

I have dived I have sought them but ~~I find none to bring form~~ none
    have I found
In the gloom that closed o'er me no floated by
As I sunk through the void depths so black & profound
How dim died the sun & how far hung the sky

What had I given to hear the soft sweep
Of a breeze bearing life through that vast realm of death
Thoughts wear untroubled & dreams were asleep
The spirit lay dreadless & hopeless beneath

40. *My Compliments ... I wonder what it*: These words (the first
line of the ms.) are in large copperplate; the rest of the ms. is in
Brontë's characteristic tiny print. MS Bon 98 (6) BPM. Undated.
The 'I' with whom this fragment begins seems to be Charlotte
Brontë, 'calling up spirits' on an 'allegorical whim', but quickly
mutates into Townshend, sending out for porter to the public
house and sharing jokes about the Angrians.

41. *calling up spirits from the vasty deep*: Cf. *Henry IV Part I*
III.i.53–5:

    Glendower: I can call spirits from the vasty deep.
    Hotspur: Why, so can I, or so can any man;
      But will they come when you do call for them?

42. *jane*: Or *jean*. A twilled cotton cloth; a kind of fustian.

43. *John of the Highlands*: This appears in much larger print than
the rest of the ms. In Branwell Bronte's early *History of the
Young Men* (1830–31) and *Letters from an Englishman* (June
1831), the names of kings – Wellington, John, Crashey, etc. –
are written in capital letters (Neufeldt, 1, pp. 138–69, 181–9).
As the cancelled word in the speaker's next speech indicates,
Saunderson is an alias for Sneachie. This is apparently John
Sneachie, Duke of Fidena, eldest son of Alexander, King of
Sneachiesland.

44. *mull ... rappee*: *mull*: Scottish term for a snuff-box, originally
one in which tobacco could be ground to powder by a simple
mechanism. *rappee*: A coarse snuff made from the darker and
ranker tobacco leaves, and originally obtained by rasping a piece
of tobacco.

45. *March ... madder ... by his hilts*: *March ... madder*: Refers
apparently to the saying, 'Mad as a March hare', deriving from

the fact that in March, which is their rutting season, hares are wild and excitable. *fighting still*: In March 1837 Zamorna and his Angrian army are pursuing his foes westward; though tattered and 'vermined', they are to be victorious in a series of bloody battles at Leyden and Westwood and Evesham in the course of the next few months. *by his hilts*: An oath. Thus Byron, *Don Juan* (1823), XI. lvii: 'A modern Ancient Pistol by the hilts!' *hilts*: handles of swords or daggers.

46. *peace would soon be restored . . . East*: *peace would soon be restored*: The suggestion is that the Angrian army is so ragged already that such an oath has little force. *Wellesley Senr.*: Duke of Wellington. *East*: Angria. Neither 'John' nor the writer are Angrians: the former is from Sneachiesland in the north, and the latter, who seems to be Townshend, is from Senegambia in the west.

47. *soaking*: Drinking immoderately.

48. *Mr Sanderson spoke again*: There is a gap here, and what follows is written in a different ink, evidently a fortnight later. The 'I' here is once again Charlotte Brontë, recalling her 'little room' at Haworth and more doubtfully trying 'to summon around me the dim shadows of incidents long departed'.

49. *limited & dim*: Here there is a gap in the ms.

50. *rack*: Clouds, or a mass of cloud, driven before the wind in the upper air. Cf. *Villette*, ch. 42: 'a rack sails from the west'.

51. *I saw them . . . saloons*: Cf. Thomas de Quincey, in a passage from *Confessions of an English Opium Eater* (1822), reprinted in John A. Heraud's essay 'On Poetical Genius, Considered as a Creative Power', in *Fraser's* 1, February 1830, pp. 61–2: 'I know not whether my reader is aware that many children, perhaps most, have a power of painting, as it were, upon the darkness, all sorts of phantoms: in some, that power is simply a mechanic affection of the eye; others have a voluntary, or a semi-voluntary power to dismiss or to summon them . . . at night, when I lay awake in bed, vast processions passed along in mournful pomp; friezes of never-ending stories . . . a theatre seemed suddenly opened up and lighted within my brain, which presented nightly spectacles of more than earthly splendour.'

52. *different from . . . Senegambia's daughters*: The differences between Angrians and 'westerns' (or Senegambians) were to be much stressed in Charlotte Brontë's Angrian fictions of 1838 and 1839.

53. *Ann's*: Spelt thus in the ms. Probably Anne Brontë, noted for her docility; possibly Ann Cook, aged 10, who seems to have been

one pupil for whom Charlotte Brontë did care (see *CBL*, 1, p.181 n. 3, pp. 208–9 and n. 1).

54. *Jane Moore*: First appearance of the Angrian heroine, Jane Moore, in Charlotte Brontë's surviving Angrian writings. She is to figure largely in *Stancliffe's Hotel, The Duke of Zamorna* and *Henry Hastings*.

55. *forests of Kentucky*: Kentucky was famous for its fecundity. In her *Society in America* (1837), Harriet Martineau describes 'the off-hand air with which a dashing Kentuckian intimates to you the richness of the soil, saying, if you plant a nail at night 'twill come up a spike next morning'. (Vol. III, Part 3, Ch. 1, section 3).

56. *prairies*: Tracts of level or undulating unwooded grassland. The term is usually applied to the grassy plains of North America: its use here reflects the fact that Angria is a newly settled and non-European country.

57. *flash & glitter*: The Angrians are known for their love of show and display. See *Stancliffe's Hotel*, p. 84.

58. *long curls . . . streaming in the wind*: See the later description of Jane herself in *Stancliffe's Hotel*, p. 95.

59. *third anniversary of Independence*: Angria had been declared an independent kingdom by the Verdopolitan parliament in February 1834.

60. *illustrissima*: Feminization of the Italian *illustrissimo*, elite. One of a number of Italian words and references in these journal fragments, possibly reflecting the influence of Miss Wooler, a noted Italian scholar. See n. 15 above.

61. *sweet and thrilling . . . Sound the Loud Timbrel*: *sweet and thrilling*: For Jane Moore's 'thrilling' singing of patriotic Angrian songs, see *Stancliffe's Hotel* p. 105. *Sound the Loud Timbrel*: Charlotte Brontë is clearly here referring to 'Sound the loud Trumpet o'er Afric's bright sea', one of several patriotic anthems composed by Branwell's Henry Hastings, the 'Poet of Angria', two years earlier, and sung at Zamorna's coronation in 1834 (*[Angria and the Angrians] I(a)*, Neufeldt, 2, p. 204); all were transcribed by Branwell into a new manuscript volume on 9–10 March 1837, around the time of this Roe Head journal fragment (Neufeldt, 3, pp. 48–9). Neufeldt suggests a source for this song in 'Sound the loud timbrel o'er Egypt's dark sea', by Thomas Moore (1779–1852), a conjecture borne out by Charlotte's mistitling of it here (Victor A. Neufeldt, ed., *Poems of Patrick Branwell Brontë. A New Text and Commentary* (New

York and London: Garland Publishing, 1990), p. 413). See *Caroline Vernon*, n. 125.

62. *About a week since I got a letter from Branwell*: Miniature diary fragment; 11.3 × 18.4 cm. MS Bon 92 (1) BPM. No date; dated by Alexander c. October 1837. This date is disputed by Juliet Barker, who suggests that 'it must date from the autumn of 1835, before [Mary Percy's] divorce', because 'Northangerland's daughter was dead by 1836' (Barker, 884 n. 46). But in *The Return of Zamorna*, written in January 1837, Charlotte Brontë had resurrected Mary by claiming that the account of her death written by Branwell in the persona of Lord Richton was a politically expedient fiction (*SHCBM*, pp. 282–314). She is certainly living, and Zamorna's wife, in Charlotte's tales of 1838–9. Here, she is in Zamorna Palace, apparently restored to its former glories after the occupation of Adrianopolis. The 'soothing and delightful' feelings Charlotte speaks of here may well be a response to Branwell's acquiescence in Mary's return to life. Moreover, the reference to Northangerland's exile at the end of this fragment suggests that it was written in October 1837, after his flight from Verdopolis before the battle of Evesham. 'They say he lies in Moncays Isle beneath Equatorial suns wasting out that life which decay and sorrow and dissapointed Ambition is fast undermining' reports Branwell's narrator Henry Hastings in June 1837 (*[Angria and the Angrians] IV(e)*, Neufeldt, 3, p. 113).

63. *commit himself in that Steamer*: Northangerland seems to be writing to Mary to announce his return from exile. On 31 October 1837 Branwell depicts him returning, 'drooping and woeworn', to Zenobia at Ennerdale, after 'lingering out 3 quarters of a year in utter solitude' (*[Angria and the Angrians] IV(j)*, Neufeldt, 3, pp. 163–8).

Glossary

acumen: Quickness of penetration.

address (n.): (1) General bearing and manner of speaking (2) Dexterity, adroitness.

ad libitum: At one's pleasure; to the full extent of one's wishes, as much as one desires (Latin).

aërial: Ideal, delicate.

affection: State of mind.

agacerie: Allurement, coquetry (French).

aigrette: Spray of gems, worn on the head; the name derives from the tuft of the egret (French).

animal: Contemptuous or humorous term for a human being who is no better than a brute, or whose animal nature has the ascendancy over his reason.

answer (v.): Prove a success.

antediluvian: Primeval, antiquated.

articles: Each of the distinct charges, or counts, of an accusation or indictment.

ascent: Eminence (obsolete).

asseverate: Declare emphatically.

at fault: Puzzled, at a loss.

au clair de la lune: By moonlight (French).

au désespoir: To the point of despair (French).

bagman: A commercial traveller whose business it is to show samples and solicit orders on behalf of manufacturers etc. A somewhat depreciatory term.

bam (v.): To trick, to hoodwink (*DVT*).

ban: Sentence of outlawry.

bandeau: A headband.

bank-note: Promissory note given by a banker.

barouche: A four-wheeled carriage with a half-hood behind which can be raised or let down at pleasure, with a seat in front for the driver, and seats inside for two couples to sit facing each other.

bashaw: Grandee, from the earlier form of the Turkish title, Pasha.

baton: A staff or truncheon carried as the symbol of office, command or authority.

beau: Eighteenth-century term for a man who gives particular, or excessive, attention to fashion and social etiquette; an exquisite, a fop, a dandy.

beaver: Hat made of beaver fur, or some imitation of it.

beck: Northern English word for a brook or stream.

bergère: A large easy chair of a style fashionable in the eighteenth century, with canework sides and back, and a cushioned seat. (French).

bigging: A building, an edifice; also, an out-building as distinguished from a house (northern dialect).

billet: A short informal letter or note. *billet doux:* A love-letter (usually used jocularly).

blackguard: A shabby, mean fellow; a term said to be derived from the dirty ragged boys who blacked the boots of the soldiers in the Horse Guards (*DVT*).

blade: A gallant, a free-and-easy fellow; generally laudatory, sometimes good-naturedly contemptuous.

bleed (v., trans.): (1) To draw or let blood from (for medicinal purposes). (2) To draw or extort money from.

blethering: Foolishly voluble.

blister (v.): To apply irritants to the skin in order to relieve painful inflammation.

blond: A silk lace of two threads, twisted and formed in hexagonal meshes, originally made from unbleached silk. First made in 1745. Cf. *Jane Eyre*, ch. 25: 'I thought how I would carry down to you the square of unembroided blond I had myself prepared as covering for my low-born head.'

blow (v.): To flourish, bloom, grow to perfection.

blow-out: Colloquial for a lavish feast.

blue (n.): A learned woman, a blue-stocking.

blunt: Money (*DVT*).

boa: A snake-like coil of fur or feathers worn by women about the neck. The earliest usage in this sense cited in the *OED* is 1836; Charlotte Brontë was clearly familiar with the latest fashions.

bottom: Spirit poured into a glass before water is added. 'Bottom is a good familiar alehouse term and shows acquaintance with life and its usages', writes Branwell Brontë, in a manuscript of 1837 (*[Angria and the Angrians] IV(g)*, Neufeldt 3, p. 134).

bower: Poetic word for a lady's private apartment.

boudoir: A small elegantly furnished room, to which a lady could retire to be alone or to receive her intimate friends.

bound in: Hardened by.

bourne: The ultimate end or point to which something tends.

bravura (adj.): Dashingly executed.

brick-bats: Pieces of a brick, used as missiles.

brilliants: Diamonds of the finest cut and brilliancy.

buck: A debauched fellow; a dandy or fop. The former meaning was the prominent one in the eighteenth century, but by the early nineteenth century the latter meaning predominated.

buckish: Foppish.

bumper: A cup or glass filled to the brim (*DVT*).

cabinet: Small private apartment or boudoir, opening off a larger room.

camarade de vie: Companion in life (French).

camarade de voyage: Travelling companion (French).

canaille: A contemptuous name given to the populace, the rabble, the mob.

cap (v.): Puzzle (dialect).

capital (adj.): First-rate.

carbonardoed: Scored across and broiled.

carr-brake: Fen or bog surrounded by low growth.

case-bottle: A bottle, often square, made to fit into a case with others.

cashier: To dismiss from service.

castor: A hat, originally either of beavers fur, or intended to be taken as such.

causeway: A highway; usually a paved way, such as existed before the introduction of macadamization.

cavalier: Horseman.

c'est tout: That's all (French).

chain-shot: A kind of shot formed of two balls, or half-balls, connected by a chain, chiefly used in naval warfare to destroy masts, rigging and sails.

champaign: An expanse of level, open country.

charger: The horse of a military officer.

chaussure: Shoe (French).

cheep: To utter shrill feeble sounds like those of young birds, mice, bats, etc.

chevalier: A mounted soldier, a knight.

cher ami: Dear friend (French).

chit: Contemptuous term for a person considered as no better than a child. It was mostly, by the 1830s, used of girls or young women.

choky: Apt to choke one who tries to swallow it; harsh, dry and gritty (*OED*).

choler: Irascibility.

choleric: Inclined to wrath, irascible, hot-tempered.

chop-house: An inferior grade of eating-house, serving mutton-chops, beefsteaks and the like.

chuck: A familiar term of endearment.

clod-hopper: Country labourer.

coach: A large closed carriage with seats inside and several outside, used for the public conveyance of passengers.

cock: (1) A gallant fellow who fights with pluck, like a fighting-cock (*DVT*); (2) A conical heap of material such as hay in the field.

codger: Irreverent term for an old man (*DVT*).

commons: Daily fare.

con amore (Italian): With great pleasure, feelingly.

concatenation: Chain.

confounded: Damned, brought to perdition; applied by way of execration to any person or thing strongly objected to.

consumed: 'Confounded', as an expression of execration or dislike.

continuations: Gaiters continuous with 'shorts' or knee-breeches, as worn by bishops, deans, etc.

contumaciously: Stubbornly, perversely.

corned: Drunk (*DVT*). Hence *corn*: Drink.

corruption: The old Adam, fallen human nature.

countenance: Patronage, support.

cow-jobber: A cow dealer.

cover: Deceitfulness.

cozening: Cheating, deceitful, fraudulent.

crack (adj.): First class (slang).

cracks (n.): Lies.

croft: A small agricultural holding worked by a peasant tenant, usually adjacent to his house.

crotchet: A whimsical or perverse idea, at odds with common sense.

crusher: I have been unable to trace this word in any slang dictionary, though from context it appears to be a glass. In Branwell's *Angria and the Angrians III (d)*, Montmorency is portrayed in an inn 'leaning forward over the table and twirling a crusher between his fingers' (Neufeldt 2, p. 642).

cub: An undeveloped, uncouth, unpolished young person. After the young of the bear, which was fabled to be born in a shapeless condition and afterwards licked into shape by the mother.

curling-irons: Heated iron instrument for curling the hair.

cynosure: Centre of attraction and admiration.

czar: Supreme authority, from the title of the Russian emperor.

daddle: The hand or fist (*DVT*).

dandcr: Ruffled or angry temper (*OED* gives it as US slang 1831).

deaurate: Gilded, golden (obsolete.).

deep-mouthed: Having a deep or sonorous voice, especially of dogs.

desperado: A desperate or reckless man; one ready for any deed of lawlessness or violence.

de trop: Too much (French).

dial-plate: Sun-dial.

dickey with: All over with (early nineteenth-century slang; *DVT*).

diddling: Cheating (*DVT*).

dint: Stroke of thunder.

diplomatique: Diplomatic (French).

direfully: Dreadfully, terribly.

discussion: Investigation of the quality of an article of food etc. by consumption of it; humorous and colloquial. Cf. *Villette*, ch. 6: 'The small dainty messes Miss Marchmont's cook used to send up . . . to the discussion of which we could not bring half an appetite between us!'

disembarrassed from: Rid of, unhampered by.

dished: Slang term meaning cheated, or 'done for'; from the notion of meat being cooked and dished (*OED*).

dolly: A kept woman (early nineteenth-century slang).

done up: Exhausted. Cf. *Villette*, ch. 25: 'There is Lucy, too, looking quite done up.'

double (v.): To be duplicitous or evasive.

double-dyed: Deeply imbued or stained (with guilt etc.).

dragoon: Cavalry soldier.

drumly: Troubled, cloudy (often used literally of the sky).

duello: duel (obsolete).

éclat: (1) A scandal. (2) Celebrity, social distinction.

embayment: Bay-like recess (of a window).

en cavalier: Like a horseman (French).

en comité: Together (French).

ennuyé: Afflicted with weariness and dissatisfaction.

en passant: In passing (French).

enthusiast: One who feels with passionate intensity; the word carries suggestions of self-delusion.

enthusiastic: Passionate.

epaulette: An ornament worn on the shoulder as part of a military uniform.

era: A memorable or important date.

espièglerie: Roguishness (*OED*).

exies: Hysterics.

exordium: The introductory part of a discourse.

eye-glass: A lens of glass or crystal for assisting defective sight.

fairing: A present given at or brought from a fair.

famous: Splendid (colloquial, often ironic).

fatuitously: Foolishly.

feint: Pretence.

figurante: Ballet dancer.

fillet: A head-band.

fire-eater: One fond of quarrelling or fighting.

fire-flaught: Lightning.

frank: The superscribed signature of a person, e.g. a member of parliament, entitled to send letters post free.

frantic: Insane.

fricandeau: A slice of meat fried or stewed with sauce. *fricandeau de veau*: A slice of veal served thus (French).

frogged: Fastened or ornamented with frogs – ornamental spindle-shaped buttons which pass through a loop on the garment's opposite side. Usually used on a military coat or cloak.

front (n.): A man's detachable insert (usually starched) to simulate the front of a shirt.

front (v.): To face.

fructify: To bear fruit.

fudge: Stuff and nonsense (*DVT*).

furlough: Leave of absence, esp. a permit or licence given to a soldier (or more rarely, an official) to be absent from duty for a stated time.

furor: Fury, rage, madness.

gall: Bile, the bittter fluid secreted by the liver; more generally, bitterness.

garçon: Serving-man (French).

gig: A light two-wheeled one-horse carriage.

grin: To snarl, show the teeth (northern dialect).

give back: To retreat, fall back (obsolete).

glean: To strip (a field, vineyard, etc.) of the produce left by the regular gatherers.

go it: (1) To go along at great speed; to pursue one's action with

furious vigour; (2) to engage recklessly in dissipation (slang); (3)
Away with you! (obsolete).

grapery: A building, made mainly of glass, in which grapes are grown.

grass-plat: A small patch of grass.

greenhorn: A novice, one inexperienced in a trade. In buckish slang,
'a novice on the town, an undebauched young fellow, just initiated
into the society of bucks and blades' (*DVT*).

green room: Backstage room in which actors and actresses could
entertain friends before and after performances, so called because
the walls were once painted green to relieve them from the glare of
onstage lights.

gripe: The action of griping, clutching, grasping or seizing tenaciously,
especially with the hands, arms, claws and the like. Cf. *Villette*, ch.
21: 'This morning the pang of waking snatched me out of bed with
a hand like a giant's gripe.'

grizzle: To turn grey.

hackney coach: A four-wheeled coach, drawn by two horses, with
seats for six persons, kept for hire.

hackneyed to: Habituated to.

haver (n.): Foolish or senseless talk; nonsense (northern dialect).

hazing: Scolding.

heel-tap: The liquor left at the bottom of a glass after drinking.

hillo: Call used to hail a distant or occupied person; now, more often,
to express surprise at an unexpected meeting (*OED*).

horehound: Or hoarhound, a herb whose juice is used as a remedy for
coughs etc.

hotel: French term for a large private town mansion.

houri: One of the black-eyed virgins of the Muslim Paradise, possessed
of eternal youth and beauty; hence, any dark-eyed beauty.

house: The living-room in a farmhouse, which the family usually
occupy, as distinguished from the parlour, bedrooms, etc. (dialect).

howsumdever: Nevertheless (dialect).

humbug (n.) rubbish, deception, pretence; *humbug* (v.) To impose
upon, hoax, delude.

huzza: Said to have been originally the cry of the huzzars, or Hungarian
light horse; but by the early nineteenth century, 'the national shout
of the English, both civil and military' (*DVT*).

id est: That is (Latin).

inceding: Measured or stately in pace.

ings: Meadows, especially low-lying ones by the side of a river.

instanter: Immediately, forthwith, at once; an emphatic substitute for
instantly.

in deshabille: Partly undressed.

in statu quo: In the same state (Latin).

invincible: Insurmountable.

irid: The iris of the eye.

jackanapes: A pert, impertinent fellow, who assumes ridiculous airs (*DVT*).

jade: A term of reprobation applied to a woman.

jarvey: Early nineteenth-century term for a hackney-coachman.

jeans: Trousers made of coarse, twilled cotton cloth.

jeunes gens: Young people (French).

jilt: 'A tricking woman, who encourages the addresses of a man whom she means to deceive and abandon' (*DVT*).

jobation: A reproof, a talking to (*DVT*).

keckle: To laugh.

lèse-majesté: Any offence against the sovereign authority; treason (French).

letting down: A come-down.

levant (v.): To steal away, to abscond.

levee: A reception of visitors held by a prince or person of distinction.

lick: To thrash or beat (colloquial).

line: Commercial term for the stock on hand of a particular class of goods or goods of a particular design.

lo you!: Interjection used to direct attention to what is about to be said.

lucubration: The product of nocturnal study and meditation; hence, a literary work showing signs of careful elaboration. Used derisively to suggest the notion of something pedantic or over-elaborate.

macassar oil: A kind of hair oil much used in the nineteenth century, which the manufacturers (Rowland and Son) represented as made with ingredients from Makasar.

mackintosh: The waterproof material consisting of two or more layers of cloth cemented together with india-rubber invented by Charles Macintosh (1766–1843) had been patented in 1823. By the 1830s the word 'mackintosh' was being applied to garments.

magnate: A great or noble person.

magnifico: A great or noble person (originally an honorary title applied to any of the magnates of Venice).

make no bones of: To do something without scruple or hesitation.

man-of-war's man: A sailor.

mandarin: From Malay and Hindi, *mantra*, counsellor; name given by Portuguese colonists to officials at Macao. The word is used derisively for over-pompous officials.

maudlin: Weak or mawkish sentiment.

mauvais sujets: Bad lots (French).

meritricious: Alluring by false show; befitting a prostitute.

mess: A prepared dish, a serving of food. See *discussion* above.

midden-cock: A cock which lives on a dung-heap.

monitor: Something which provides guidance as to conduct, especially a person's conscience. Occasionally personified.

moreen: A coarse woollen fabric.

morning-gown: For men, an elaborate dressing-gown, worn before one was formally dressed, highly fashionable in the 1820s and 30s.

morocco: Made of a kind of fine flexible leather made originally in Morocco.

mort de ma vie!: Death of my life! (French). See *Henry V*, III. iv.11.

muck-midden: Dung-heap.

mulatto: A person having one white and one black parent, or, more generally, a person of mixed race resembling a mulatto.

mussulman: A Mohammedan.

myrmidons: A warlike race of men inhabiting ancient Thessaly, whom, according to the Homeric story, Achilles led to the siege of Troy (*Iliad* II. 684). In the early nineteenth century a cant term for the constable's assistants, watchmen, etc. (*DVT*).

nab (v.): Snatch or steal (*DVT*).

nabob: A person of high rank or great wealth; more specifically, one who returned from India with a large fortune acquired there.

nankeens: Trousers made of pale yellowish cloth.

negus: A mixture of wine and hot water, sweetened with sugar and flavoured.

Newmarket coat: A long close-fitting coat worn for riding.

nicher: To laugh like a neighing horse (Scottish and northern dialect).

n'importe: It doesn't matter (French).

nob: A person of high rank (*DVT*).

no go: An impasse. *it's no go*: It's impossible.

nolens volens: Whether willing or not, willy-nilly (*OED*).

noodle: A simpleton, a stupid or silly person.

nout: Obsolete form of 'nowt', a stupid, coarse or clumsy person (*OED*).

numb-scull: A stupid fellow (*DVT*).

objurgations: Reproaches.

onerous: Of the nature of a legal obligation.

ordinary (n.): An eating-house or tavern where public meals are provided at a fixed price.

outré: Eccentric, beyond the bounds of what is considered correct and proper (French).

packet: Short for *packet-boat*, meaning a vessel sailing at regular intervals between two ports for the conveyance of mail, goods and passengers.

palfrey: A small saddle-horse for ladies.

palter: To trifle.

pantaloons: A tight-fitting kind of trousers fastened with ribbons or buttons below the calf, which began to supersede knee-breeches late in the eighteenth century.

parle: A discussion, or, more specifically, a meeting to discuss terms of truce between enemies.

parvenu: Upstart.

passengers: Passers-by.

pastille: A small roll of aromatic paste which was burnt as a perfume.

pathétique: Pathetic (French).

pattens: Wooden-soled overshoes worn to raise the ordinary shoes out of mud or wet.

pavé: Paved street (French).

peach: To inform against an accomplice; to turn informer (*DVT*).

pea-surtout: Stout overcoat made of coarse cloth.

pelisse: Long outdoor coat for women, reaching to the ankles.

pennon: Flag or banner.

pet (n.): Temper (*DVT*).

petits soins: Small attentions or services (French).

petit souper: Light supper (French).

phaeton: A light four-wheeled open carriage, usually drawn by a pair of horses, and with one or two seats facing forwards.

philosophique: Philosophical (French).

phiz: Face (colloquial).

phrenzy: Wild folly, craziness.

piccaninny: A young child, an infant (orig. West Indian Creole, *DVT*).

piece-hall: An exchange where cloth is sold by the piece.

plantation: Wood of planted trees.

pluffing (n.): A strong puff or explosive emission of air, gas or smoke (as in the firing of gunpowder); hence, colloquially, shot of a musket.

pointer: A dog used by sportsmen in hunting game.

pose (v.): Puzzle.

post-chaise: A travelling carriage, seating two to four persons, hired from stage to stage.

postillion: One who rides the leading near horse of a team or pair drawing a coach or carriage when there is no coachman (*OED*).

preferment: Advancement or promotion in condition, status or position in life.

presence-chamber: The chamber in which a sovereign or other great personage receives guests.

prig (n.): Dandy, fop, coxcomb; also, a thief (*DVT*).

prig (v.): To steal (*DVT*).

prima donna: Principal female singer in an opera.

prime: To put gunpowder in the pan of an old-fashioned firearm; used figuratively of filling up with liquor, or of taking snuff.

protégé(e): One who is under the protection or care of another, especially of a person of superior position or influence.

phthisis: A progressive wasting disease; specifically, pulmonary consumption.

public (n.): Short for public-house.

pumps: Thin dress shoes.

push (n.): A determined effort.

quadrille: A square dance of French origin, usually performed by four couples (*OED*).

quality: A mental or moral attribute, trait or characteristic.

quartier: A neighbourhood, district (French).

quietus: Release from life, death.

quondam: Former.

raff: People of the lowest class, worthless.

ragout: Highly seasoned dish of stewed meat and vegetables.

rate: To scold, chide.

rattling: Lively.

ree: Excited, especially with drink; crazy, delirious.

reflect: Reflection.

refulgent: Radiant.

rencontre: Chance meeting.

repeater: A repeating watch, i.e. one which strikes (the last hour or quarter) again.

reverie (v.): To indulge in reveries or daydreams.

rhodomontade: Extravagant boasting.

riding habit: A riding-dress worn by ladies, consisting of a cloth skirt worn with a double-breasted tight-fitting jacket.

roquelaire: A cloak reaching to the knee worn by men during the eighteenth century and the early part of the nineteenth. Usually 'roquelaure'.

royal liberties: The domain or property of the king.

rum: Odd, strange, queer (slang).

sackless: Guileless, feeble-minded, dispirited.

sacré: Holy, sacred (French). Used also as a profane imprecation.

salmagundi: Dish composed of chopped meat, anchovies, eggs, apples and onions, with oil and condiments (*DVT*).

saloon: The reception room of a lady of fashion; hence, a gathering of notabilities at the house of such a lady.

salver: A tray used for handing refreshments or for presenting letters, visiting-cards, etc.

Saracen: A non-Christian, heathen or pagan; an unbeliever, infidel (obsolete).

satin paper: A fine writing paper.

savannah: A treeless plain; properly, one of those found in various parts of tropical America.

scrubs: Persons of little account or poor appearance (*DVT*).

scum: A worthless wretch (obsolete).

scunner: A stab of loathing.

seat: The country residence of a gentleman or nobleman.

second: One who acts as representative of a principal in a duel, carrying the challenge, arranging locality and loading weapons (*OED*).

self-gratulation: Self-congratulation (nineteenth century).

sheltie: Shetland pony.

shog: To go away, begone. Usually with *off*.

signify (v., intrans.): Matter.

slab: A small table hinged to the wall in the passage or hall of a house (*OED*).

slang: Cant language.

slap up: First rate (slang; first *OED* usage given is 1823).

slot-hounds: Sleuth-hounds.

sobriquet: A nickname.

soirée: An evening party or gathering (French).

solus: Alone (Latin).

sot (v.): Drink to excess.

sovereign (adj.): Of remedies etc., extremely efficacious or potent.

spang: A sudden and violent movement.

spark: Depreciatory term for a foppish young man, affecting smartness of dress and manners; 'a spruce, trim, or smart fellow' (*DVT*).

specific: A remedy.

spindle: Thin, feeble, as in 'spindle-shank'.

springes: Snares for catching small game.

sprung: Slightly drunk, tipsy (Partridge).

spunkie: Spirited, mettlesome.

spurt out: Burst out angrily.

stalled: Weary.

stanchions: Upright bars between the mullions of a window.

steam-packet: See *packet*.

stived up: Suffocated, deprived of fresh air.

stock: A stiff, close-fitting neckcloth, originally worn by the military.

strait: A narrow or tight place, a time of sore need, an awkward circumstance, a difficulty or fix. More commonally used in plural (*OED*).

stumps: Legs. *to stir one's stumps:* To get going (*DVT*).

sultana: The wife of a sultan; hence, any noble and imposing woman.

summat: A certain amount (dialect variant of *somewhat*).

summering: Meadows for the pasturing of cattle in summer.

surtout: A man's great-coat or overcoat.

swells: Smooth rounded hills, broad in proportion to their height.

syren: A fabulous monster, part woman, part bird, supposed to lure sailors to destruction by her enchanting singing. Hence, any alluring woman.

taper (adj.): Tapering.

termagant: A violent, quarrelsome woman; an outrageous scold (*DVT*).

throng: Crowded.

thrown by: Discarded.

tight: Neat in appearance; neatly and carefully dressed; trim, tidy, smart.

tights: Tight-fitting breeches, worn by men in the eighteenth and early nineteenth centuries; also, by the latter period, applied to skin-tight stockings worn by men.

toast and water: Toast soaked in water; used as a drink for invalids.

toilet, toilette: Toilet table; also, the process of dressing and grooming.

ton: Fashionable style.

tournure: Manner or bearing.

tout ensemble: Total effect (French).

trail: A collection of persons, drawn along by, or following in the wake of, another.

trim (adj.): Spruce (*DVT*).

turnspit: A man or boy whose office was to turn the spit. Used as a term of contempt.

twang: A ringing sound.

twit: Taunt.

turn-up: A boxing contest; hence, loosely, a fist-fight, a set-to.

turnspit: A boy or man whose office was to turn the spit. Used as a term of contempt.

unconscionable: Unreasonably excessive.

understrapper: An underling; an inferior (*DVT*).

valetudinarian: An invalid.

van: Foremost position.

vengeable: Very great, severe, strong, intense.

verjuice: The acid juice of green or unripe grapes, crab-apples or other sour fruit, expressed and formed into a liquor. The word was in the early nineteenth century used as an adjective to mean bitter or sour-looking.

victual: Article of food.

vinaigrette: A bottle of smelling-salts.

vis à vis: One or other of two persons facing, or situated opposite to, one another (French).

vitiated: Corrupted.

viznomy: Physiognomy (dialect).

voilà tout: That's all (French).

wae: Distressed, grieved, afflicted (dialect).

walt: Toss (dialect).

watering-place: A fashionable resort, either for drinking or bathing in the waters of a mineral spring, or for sea-bathing.

whiggish: Seditious, factious (slang).

whisht: Hush! (dialect).

wildered: Pathless, wild.

withdrawn: Gone away.

wrestle: To strive earnestly with God, in prayer.

Chronology of Angria

This chronology, based on Charlotte and Branwell Brontë's surviving manuscripts, offers a bare outline of the complicated history of Angria, from its foundation in 1834 until Charlotte's 'Farewell to Angria'. It is intended to assist the reader who wishes to understand how the tales in this volume relate to the 'Angrian saga' they shared.

I am indebted to Christine Alexander's *Early Writings of Charlotte Brontë* (Oxford: Basil Blackwell, 1983), and to Victor Neufeldt's edition of *The Works of Patrick Branwell Brontë*, 3 vols. (New York and London: Garland Publishing, 1999), which has at last made it possible to track in detail the interrelationship between the two collaborators in Angria.

1834 Arthur Wellesley, Marquis of Douro, having led the Verdopolitan forces to victory during the War of Encroachment against the united armies of the Ashantees, Arabs and French, is made Duke of Zamorna. Alexander Percy, his ally, becomes Earl of Northangerland. Zamorna demands his newly conquered territory from the Verdopolitan Parliament, and the kingdom of Angria is born, with Zamorna its King and Northangerland its Prime Minister. Zamorna's new wife, Mary Percy, daughter of Northangerland, is Queen. Charlotte's Angrian writings for this year chart the increasing dissension between Zamorna and Northangerland.

1835 Zamorna, in a speech in the Verdopolitan Parliament, accuses Northangerland of making league with his Verdopolitan, French and Ashantee enemies, Ardrah, Bernadotte and Quashia. He demands that unless Northangerland puts an end to his treachery, he must resign his seals of office as Prime Minister of Angria. Branwell, as 'Henry Hastings', records Northangerland's devastated reply, his subsequent departure from office and public denunciation. By June, however, there is an uneasy rapprochement between Northangerland and Zamorna. On 19 December Charlotte, on her Christmas holidays from Roe Head, completes a long poem, with a prose continuation, celebrating the extraordinary burgeoning of the children's youthful plays ('We wove a web in childhood', *Juvenilia*, pp. 261–9). On the same day, in Branwell's account, Angria is expelled from the Verdopolitan Union by Ardrah and his Reform Party. Zamorna and Northangerland now unite in defence of Angria.

1836 After a series of battles the Angrian forces are defeated, and Adrianopolis, the capital of Angria, falls. Zamorna and Northangerland flee the city. Northangerland begins once again to fraternize with Zamorna's arch-enemies, Quashia and Montmorency. By March, Branwell's Hastings reports that half of Angria is 'in possession of our foes'. There are preparations for further war all over Verdopolis. On 21–29 April, Charlotte, at home for the Easter holidays, and for the first time using the persona of Charles Townshend, writes a series of separate sketches relating to the events that Branwell had been chronicling: Zenobia quarrelling with her husband, who is about to join Zamorna's enemies; Zamorna's mistress, Mina Laury, entertaining his chiefs of staff in the hunting lodge which is her home; Northangerland disguised as 'Brother Ashworth' delivering a half-political, half-religious 'harangue' in a Wesleyan chapel, in an attempt to rouse the populace against Zamorna; Mary, Duchess of Zamorna, in Wellesley House in Verdopolis, longing for word from her husband, who has cast her off to punish her father; Townshend and William Percy catching a glimpse of the Duchess as she drives off to find her husband; and finally the meeting between Zamorna and his wife (*Five Novelettes*, pp. 35–72). During this year Northangerland becomes increasingly isolated and depressed, alienated both from Zamorna and his wife. His daughter Mary is dying of grief because of Zamorna's desertion of her. On 24–28 June Charlotte, now back at home, writes another Angrian sketch, in which Townshend, on the eve of the battle of Edwardston, reads the attacks on Zamorna in the Verdopolitan newspapers, attends the sale of Zamorna's confiscated property at his former home, Douro Villa, and in a few brief final sentences, describes the news reaching Verdopolis that Zamorna has been defeated at Edwardston – 'the Angrian army . . . ruined, the Angrian nation enslaved and the Angrian King disgraced!' (*Five Novelettes*, pp. 72–82; Jos Bemelmans, '*Passing Events* and Another Manuscript', *BST*, 20:3, 1991, pp. 121–5). In July Northangerland's troops storm Rivaulx, where Mina Laury is sheltering with

Zamorna's son, Ernest Fitz-Arthur and some of Zamorna's defeated followers. Hartford escorts them to Zamorna, where Fitz-Arthur is snatched. Mina Laury goes into exile with Zamorna. Northangerland by now is in league with Montmorency and Quashia. Between **August** and **October**, Angria is a devasted country, under the control of Northangerland's forces. Northangerland himself is in a state of 'miserable melancholy', 'ever tormented with the future' because of his daughter's decline, his wife Zenobia's alienation from him and the 'intrigues' of his various mistresses. Some of Zamorna's allies – including Fidena, Warner and his troops in the Warner Hills, and di Enara at Fort Gazemba – fight on; Ryder, the wounded man in Journal Fragment IIb, appears to be one of these. On **19 September** in Branwell's account, Mary, Duchess of Zamorna, dies at Alnwick. **October–December** Northangerland's wife Zenobia is living alone in the north; he, broken-hearted at the death of his daughter, is in Verdopolis amongst his 'impetuous and imperious' mistresses, whilst his army occupies devastated Angria. On **17 December** Warner Howard Warner, Zamorna's Angrian prime minister, rallies the 'warworn' Angrian troops gathered in the Olympian hills, with a stirring speech calling for vengeance for the death of Ernest Fitz-Arthur, Zamorna's son.

1837 January Charlotte, at home for Christmas in Haworth, and writing as Townshend, refutes propagandist reports of Mary's death. In the novelette now known as *The Return of Zamorna* she depicts the Duchess of Zamorna revived by news of her husband's return (*SHCBM*, 2, pp. 281–314). **January–June** Northangerland's retreating allies are routed by forces loyal to Zamorna, first at Leyden, then at Westwood, and finally in June at Evesham. Northangerland himself has gone into exile, where he stays for many months. **29 June** Charlotte, at home for the summer holidays, writes the novelette now known as *Julia*, another series of sketches related to the events that Branwell has been chronicling. In one scene Townshend recalls Hastings, 'two years ago . . . in the blaze of his fame', in Lady Julia Thornton's drawing-room; in another, Zamorna, sickened with battle, thinks longingly of Mary, and is interrupted by the child Caroline Vernon, whose mother Louisa is a prisoner of his. ' "You will make such a woman as your half-sister Mary," ' he tells her; ' "child, I could almost imagine it was her little hand that clasped mine so" ' (*Five Novelettes*, pp. 85–121). **30 June** Zamorna is victorious at the battle of Evesham, the last major battle of the war. **12 July** Branwell portrays Hastings descending into debt and drunkenness, having killed his superior officer and deserted to

Zamorna's enemies. 21 **July** Charlotte finishes another novelette, now known as *Four Years Ago*, in which she looks back on the early relationship between Northangerland and Zamorna, when they were Ellrington and Douro, and recalls the brief life of Zamorna's previous wife, Marian (ms. untraced; Hatfield Transcription 10, BPM).

1838 There is now peace in Angria. Zamorna's enemies are scattered; Northangerland has returned to his wife and his country seat.

1839 January–February Branwell tells of Hastings' return to Angria from Paris in disguise as 'Wilson', and of the attempt he makes on the Duke of Zamorna's life. On **21–23 February** in Branwell's account Zamorna holds a reception for the Angrian aristocracy, and confounds his allies by inviting their enemy, Northangerland. An angry crowd gathers outside, threatening to break the palace windows because of his presence there. Zamorna and Northangerland leave together. The bond between them is apparently an unbreakable one.

Principal Characters

Many Angrian characters have a number of different names, titles or pseudonyms. Thus Alexander Percy is Lord Ellrington and Earl of Northangerland; he is also known by his early nicknames of Rogue, the Pirate and the Drover. I have listed each character under the name they are most often given in these tales. Those only mentioned once or twice are identified in the notes.

Ardrah Arthur, Prince of Parrysland and Marquis of Ardrah, Lord High Admiral of the Verdopolitan Navy, editor of *The Northern Review* and a deadly enemy of Zamorna.

Arundel, Earl of Viscount Frederick Lofty, friend of Zamorna, a popular field-marshal in the Angrian army, Governor of the Angrian province of Arundel and Grand Chevalier of Angria. Brother of Macara Lofty and married to Edith Sneachie.

Ashworth The Duke of Northangerland, disguised as a Methodist preacher.

Augusta See Segovia, Augusta Maria di.

Castlereagh, Frederick Stuart Early friend of Zamorna, who becomes Earl of Stuartville and a general in the Angrian army. A noted fop.

Caversham, Lord One of the few aristocrats amongst Alexander Percy's early, reprobate associates. His father was murdered by Alexander Percy in a duel at Percy Hall.

Delph, Victoria A famous heiress.

Denard, Sir John Uncle to Louisa Vernon, and an early associate of Northangerland.

Ellrington, Paulina Louisiada Castilian wife of Lord Henry Ellrington and mother of Zenobia Ellrington.

Ellrington, Lady Zenobia Only daughter of the Earl of Ellrington, an imposing dark beauty and blue-stocking. Her childhood friendship with Zamorna led to passionate love on her part. When this was unreciprocated, she became the wife of Northangerland, giving him the title Lord Ellrington.

Enara, General Henri Fernando di Nicknamed 'The Tiger'. Italian ally of Zamorna, Lord Lieutenant of the Province of Etrei and Commander-in-chief of the Angrian army. He becomes Earl of Etrei in return for his services during the civil war.

Fidena, Duke of Prince John Augustus Sneachie, son and heir of the King of Sneachiesland. Unswervingly loyal to Zamorna, he plays a prominent part in the campaign against the Ashantees. A morally upright, reserved and conservative character; his virtues, says Lord Charles Wellesley, 'seem of that high and holy order which almost exempt their possessor from sympathy with mankind' (*Corner Dishes: A Peep into a Picture Book* (1834), *EEW* 2.ii, p. 90).

Flower See Richton, Viscount.

Harlaw, Marquis of Originally Edward Tut Ross, son of John King of Rossland; ally of Ardrah against Zamorna in the Angrian civil wars.

Hartford, Lord Edward Angrian landowner and member of one of the oldest Angrian families. General in Zamorna's army.

Hastings, Captain Henry Angrian soldier and writer; poet and historian of Angria, author of its national anthems. A pseudonym much used by Branwell.

Hastings, Elizabeth Sister of Captain Henry Hastings and companion to Jane Moore.

Jordan John Julian di Segovia, Earl of Jordan, Lord Lieutenant of the province of Douro and profligate brother of Augusta di Segovia. As Sheik Abdulla Medina, he was an ally of MacTerroglen in the occupation of Angria.

King, Robert A malignant and evil figure, otherwise known as S'Death; mentor, agent and familiar of Northangerland.

Kirkwall, Sir John Angrian squire and member of parliament. General in the Angrian army. His son, Charles Kirkwall, was to marry Jane Moore's elder sister Harriet, who died.

Lofty, Macara Younger brother of Frederick, Viscount Lofty, Earl of Arundel. Once a member of the Verdopolitan Government under Ardrah, he is by the time of these tales a rather disreputable character, an associate of Charles Townshend and lover of Louisa Vernon.

MacTerroglen, Sir Jehu Originally Jeremiah Simpson, shopkeeper and money-lender, an early associate of Alexander Percy. Later, as MacTerroglen, he becomes leader of the forces massed against Zamorna during Northangerland's rebellion.

Massena Commander of the French forces against Verdopolis; later he joins with Ardrah and Northangerland against Zamorna.

Moore, Jane Angrian beauty, known as 'the Rose of Zamorna'; daughter of a noted Angrian barrister.

Montmorency, Hector Matthias Mirabeau Companion of Alexander Percy in his early dissipations, he later becomes a Verdopolitan banker and nobleman. An ally of Ardrah and subsequently of Northangerland in their campaigns against Zamorna. His heavy drinking and 'towring ferocious ill-nature' are much portrayed by Branwell. At the time of these tales he is living in exile in Paris.

Northangerland, Duke of See Percy, Alexander.

O'Connor, Arthur One of 'Rogue' Percy's early associates in his days as a cattle dealer, who becomes a colonel in his rebel army.

O'Connor, Harriet Sister of Arthur O'Connor and subject of several poems by Branwell, as well as of a song sung by Caroline Vernon in *The Duke of Zamorna*. She was to be seduced by Percy, married (unhappily) to Montmorency and thereafter to elope with Percy. When the latter deserted her she died alone and in exile in Fidena.

Percy, Alexander, Duke of Northangerland Variously known as Rogue, Alexander Percy, Ellrington and Northangerland. Introduced to the Angrian saga by Branwell, as a pirate named Rogue (or as Branwell spells it, Rougue). His first wife was the dissolute Augusta di Segovia; his second was Maria Henrietta Wharton, who died young, partly of consumption and partly of grief at his banishment of her sons. Heartbroken by her death, he became an atheist, a pirate, a compulsive gambler, a rapacious cattle-dealer (the Drover), and the seducer and betrayer of countless women. Lady Zenobia Ellrington became his third wife. His closest bond throughout is with Zamorna, whom he helped to make King of Angria, and whose first Prime Minister he became, but against whom he subsequently conspired. Northangerland was the name adopted by Branwell as a pseudonym when he published twelve poems in the *Halifax Guardian* in the years between 1841–7.

Percy, Edward Elder son of Northangerland, rejected at birth by his father. He becomes a leading industrialist in Angria and Angrian Minister for Trade.

Percy, Mary See Zamorna, Duchess of.

Percy, Lady Mary Alexander Percy's wife and mother of his children William, Edward, Henry and Mary Henrietta (Duchess of Zamorna).

Percy, Lady Helen Mother of Alexander Percy.

Percy, Sir William Youngest son of Northangerland. Like his brother Edward, rejected at birth by his father. A complex, subtle and changing character, he rises to the rank of lieutenant general in the Angrian army and is sent on a diplomatic mission to find and capture Henry Hastings.

Quashia Quashia Quamina, son of Sai Too Too, King of the Ashantee tribe of native Africans. He was captured as a child and adopted by the Duke of Wellington, and thus became the adopted brother of Zamorna. He became the enemy of Zamorna and the Angrians, conspiring with Northangerland and invading Angria with Ardrah and MacTerroglen.

Richton, Viscount Sir John Flower, Verdopolitan Ambassador to Angria; renowned as a scholar and historian. One of the group of aristocrats faithful to Zamorna. A pseudonym used by Branwell in his writings of 1831–4.

Rosier, Edward A Frenchman; valet to the Duke of Zamorna.

Rowley, Hannah Housekeeper at Townshend's lodgings in Verdopolis.

S'Death See King, Robert.

Segovia, Augusta Maria di Profligate, beautiful Italian, who became the first wife of Alexander Percy; she plotted to kill Percy's father and was herself poisoned by her accomplices. Elder sister and guardian of Lord Jordan.

Shaver, James Northangerland's manservant.

Steighton, Major George Vernon's steward and minion of the young Alexander Percy. He becomes steward of the Earl of Northangerland's Ellrington estates.

Stuartville See Castlereagh, Frederick Stuart.

Surena Surena Ellrington, younger brother of Zenobia, who keeps a linen-draper's shop in Verdopolis, where Townshend lodges with him.

Thornton, General Wilson or Wilkin Ally of Zamorna and eventually Commander-in-Chief of Angria's army. A bluff Angrian farmer who speaks with a strong Yorkshire accent, he is married to Lady Julia Wellesley.

Thornton, Lady Julia See Wellesley, Julia.

Townshend, Charles Originally Lord Charles Wellesley, younger son of the Duke of Wellington and brother of Arthur, Marquis of Douro. As Charles Townshend, dandy, author and young man about town, he is the principal narrator of the late novelettes.

Vernon, Caroline Illegitimate daughter of Louisa Vernon and the Earl of Northangerland; half-sister to the Duchess of Zamorna.

Vernon, Louisa Also known as Louisa Dance. She first appears in the Angrian mss. as Louisa Allan, an opera-singer, who married (1) 'the dashing fashionable Lord George Vernon', also known as Lord Dance and (2) Richard, Marquis of Wellesley, uncle of Zamorna. After the latter's death, she became mistress of Northangerland, and bore him a daughter, Caroline Vernon. But when Northangerland refused, during the civil war, to execute the defeated Zamorna, she left him and became mistress of Macara Lofty. Later, she became a kind of prisoner of Zamorna.

Warner, Warner Howard, Esquire Head of an old family of settlers in Angria and landlord of the Hastings family. He becomes Zamorna's Home Secretary, and succeeds Northangerland as Prime Minister. A slight and slenderly formed, effeminate-looking man, he is pious, upright and hard-working.

Wellesley, Julia Zamorna's cousin; married to General Thornton.

Wellesley, Richard Marquis of Elder brother of the Duke of Wellington, modelled on the real-life Duke's elder brother. Elderly husband of Louisa Vernon.

Wellesley, Rosamund Cousin of Zamorna, who became his mistress, and committed suicide.

Zamorna, Duchess of Formerly Mary Henrietta Percy, daughter of Northangerland and wife of the Duke of Zamorna. Caroline Vernon is her illegitimate half-sister.

Zamorna, Duke of Born (c. 1812) Arthur Augustus Adrian Wellesley, Marquis of Douro, eldest son of the Duke of Wellington. Awarded the kingdom of Angria in 1834 for his fighting on behalf of the Verdopolitan Union against the Ashantees and the French. Briefly exiled to the Ascension Isle after Northangerland's rebellion, but returns and retakes his kingdom.

Zenobia See Ellrington, Zenobia.

Places

The children's 'plays' were originally set in a fictionalized Africa. The romantic pastoral landscapes and natural fertility of Angria and the harshness of the Etrei portrayed in these novelettes reflect the dual presentation of Africa in travel writing of the time, both as rich in natural resources and as a wasteland inhabited by savages. But in most respects this 'Africa' is quite European (see *Journal Fragments*, n. 22).

The Verdopolitan Union consisted of a number of kingdoms, each with its own capital. Angria lay to the east, Senegambia to the west. Frenchy's land, with its capital Paris, was on an island east of Angria. Verdopolis is the old capital of the Verdopolitan Union, Adrianopolis the centre of Angrian society. The commercial city of Zamorna is midway between. In the valley of the Olympian outside Zamorna lie the country estates of the Angrian aristocracy – Girnington Hall, Edwardston Hall, Hartford Hall; further away in the north, beyond the Olympian Hills, is the home of Warner Howard Warner and his tenants, the Hastings family. Hawkscliffe Forest and the Lodge of the Cross of Rivaulx are halfway between Verdopolis and Adrianopolis.

Adrianopolis Magnificent and rapidly growing capital of Angria, built at the foundation of the kingdom in 1834, on the river Calabar, 150 miles from Verdopolis. The 'Great Move' from Verdopolis to Adrianopolis is described in Charlotte Brontë's *My Angria and the Angrians* (1834).

Alnwick Country residence of the Percy family, about fifty miles west of Verdopolis; named after the actual Northumberland seat of the Percys.

Angria Large, fertile and largely unpopulated land with a landscape like that of Yorkshire, to the east of Verdopolis. It originally belonged to the Ashantees and its first European settlers were from Yorkshire and Lancashire. It was given to Zamorna as his kingdom in 1834, in acknowledgement of his defence of the Verdopolitan Union against the French and the Ashantees.

Arno River near Hawkscliffe.

Arundel A rural province of Angria.

Boulshill A hill near Pendleton, home of Henry and Elizabeth Hastings. There is a Boulsworth Hill, near Haworth.

Calabar The 'wide, bright ocean-like' river on which Adrianopolis is situated, whose source is in 'burning and desolate and hostile Africa' (Neufeldt 2, p. 233).

Cirhala The river in Angria on which Evesham is situated.

Dongola Fort and city at the mouth of the Etrei, scene of a hideous massacre by Quashia and his Ashantees in 1834.

Doverham Port on the west coast of Angria, the closest point to Calais in Branwell Brontë's Frenchyland.

Edwardston Chief manufacturing town in Angria, in Zamorna province. Site of battle at which Zamorna is defeated in 1836.

Edwardston Hall Edward Percy's country estate.

Ellrington House The imposing mansion in Ellrington Square, Verdopolis, purchased by Northangerland on his marriage to Zenobia.

Etrei Large desert province of Angria, whose capital is Dongola. Also, the river which runs through this province, marking the boundary between Angria and the Ashantees.

Evesham City on the river Cirhala in Angria, which had been fortified by Northangerland's revolutionary army, and was taken by General Thornton in the final battle of Zamorna's return to power.

Fidena Capital city of Sneachiesland, 300 miles from Verdopolis.

Flower House The residence of Lord Richton.

Fort Adrian 'A strong dark mansion' on the east bank of the Calabar, 'at a distance much resembling a fortified castle', belonging to the Duke of Zamorna (*EEW* ii.2, p. 330).

Freetown City in Sneachiesland.

Gazemba Frontier town on the east bank of the Calabar, in the midst of the African desert. Centre for Zamorna's military operations against the Ashantees. It is here that he reviews his troops before the battle of Evesham.

Girnington Hall General Thornton's country house in Angria.

Guadima River on which the city of Verdopolis is built.

Hartford Hall Home of the Hartford family in Angria.

Hawkscliffe Zamorna's Angrian country estate in the north of the province of Zamorna at the foot of the Sydenham hills.

Kirkham Lodge Home of the Moore family in Angria.

Leyden Small town in Angria, site of a battle in which Zamorna and his allies roundly defeat Northangerland's forces.

Mornington Country estate of the Duke of Wellington (the name is taken from one of the titles of the actual Wellesley family).

Northangerland House Northangerland's house in Adrianopolis.

Olympian River in Angria, in the valley of which are the country houses of the Angrian gentry. .

Pendleton Native village of the Hastings family in the Warner hills in Angria.

Rivaulx Hunting lodge about five miles from Hawkscliffe, on the edge of the royal forest.

St Cyprian River on the Duke of Wellington's Mornington estate in Senegambia.

Selden House Country home of Northangerland, situated in Rossland.

Senegambia Or 'the west'. Westernmost kingdom of the Verdopolitan Union, originally settled by the Irish. Birthplace of Zamorna, Mary Percy and Mina Laury.

Sneachiesland One of the kingdoms of the Verdopolitan Union, ruled by Alexander Sneachie, and akin to the Scottish Highlands.

Stancliffe's Hotel Principal inn in Zamorna.

Sydenham Hills A long moorland range of hills near Hawkscliffe in Angria.

Verdopolis Originally Glass Town, 'the old capital' of the Verdopolitan Union.

Waterloo Palace Residence of the Duke of Wellington in Verdopolis.

Wellesley House Home of the Duke of Wellington's family in Verdopolis.

Woodhouse Cliff A country house near Freetown belonging to the Warner family. The name was probably derived from Woodhouse Grove Academy, near Bradford, where Rev. Patrick Brontë had been employed as school examiner in 1812, and where he had met his wife Maria Branwell.

Zamorna A province in the west of Angria, and also the capital of that province, an industrial town with 'mercantile suburbs' on the banks of the Olympian.

Zamorna Palace Home of the Duke of Zamorna in Adrianopolis.

THE STORY OF PENGUIN CLASSICS

Before 1946 ...'Classics' are mainly the domain of academics and students, without readable editions for everyone else. This all changes when a little-known classicist, E. V. Rieu, presents Penguin founder Allen Lane with the translation of Homer's *Odyssey* that he has been working on and reading to his wife Nelly in his spare time.

1946 *The Odyssey* becomes the first Penguin Classic published, and promptly sells three million copies. Suddenly, classic books are no longer for the privileged few.

1950s Rieu, now series editor, turns to professional writers for the best modern, readable translations, including Dorothy L. Sayers's *Inferno* and Robert Graves's *The Twelve Caesars*, which revives the salacious original.

1960s The Classics are given the distinctive black jackets that have remained a constant throughout the series's various looks. Rieu retires in 1964, hailing the Penguin Classics list as 'the greatest educative force of the 20th century'.

1970s A new generation of translators arrives to swell the Penguin Classics ranks, and the list grows to encompass more philosophy, religion, science, history and politics.

1980s The Penguin American Library joins the Classics stable, with titles such as *The Last of the Mohicans* safeguarded. Penguin Classics now offers the most comprehensive library of world literature available.

1990s The launch of Penguin Audiobooks brings the classics to a listening audience for the first time, and in 1999 the launch of the Penguin Classics website takes them online to a larger global readership than ever before.

The 21st Century Penguin Classics are rejacketed for the first time in nearly twenty years. This world famous series now consists of more than 1300 titles, making the widest range of the best books ever written available to millions – and constantly redefining the meaning of what makes a 'classic'.

The Odyssey continues ...

The best books ever written

PENGUIN 🐧 CLASSICS

SINCE 1946

Find out more at www.penguinclassics.com

PENGUIN CLASSICS

EMMA   JANE AUSTEN

'I never have been in love; it is not my way, or my nature; and I do not think I ever shall'

Beautiful, clever, rich – and single – Emma Woodhouse is perfectly content with her life and sees no need for either love or marriage. Nothing, however, delights her more than interfering in the romantic lives of others. But when she ignores the warnings of her good friend Mr Knightley and attempts to arrange a suitable match for her protégée Harriet Smith, her carefully laid plans soon unravel and have consequences that she never expected. With its imperfect but charming heroine and its witty and subtle exploration of relationships, *Emma* is often seen as Jane Austen's most flawless work.

This edition includes a new chronology and additional suggestions for further reading.

'A masterpiece . . . the fusing of moral consideration and human drama achieves perfect pitch' Carol Shields

'These modern editions are to be strongly recommended for their scrupulous texts, informative notes and helpful introductions' Brian Southam, The Jane Austen Society

Edited with an introduction and notes by Fiona Stafford

PENGUIN CLASSICS

LADY SUSAN / THE WATSONS / SANDITON
JANE AUSTEN

'She has poured forth her tender tale of love in vain and exposed herself forever to the contempt of the whole world'

These three short works show Jane Austen experimenting with a variety of different literary styles, from melodrama to satire, and exploring a range of social classes and settings. The early epistolary novel *Lady Susan* depicts an unscrupulous coquette, toying with the affections of several men. In contrast, *The Watsons* is a delightful fragment, whose spirited heroine, Emma Watson, finds her marriage opportunities restricted by poverty and pride. Written in the last months of her life, the uncompleted novel *Sanditon* is set in a newly established seaside resort, with a glorious cast of hypochondriacs and speculators, and shows the author contemplating a changing society with a mixture of scepticism and amusement.

Margaret Drabble's introduction examines these three works in the context of Jane Austen's major novels and her life, and discusses the social background of her fiction. This edition features a new chronology.

'In it [*Sanditon*] she exploits her greatest gifts, her management of dialogue and her skill with monologue. The book feels open and modern . . . as vigorous and inventive as her earlier work' Carol Shields

Edited with an introduction and notes by Margaret Drabble

PENGUIN CLASSICS

MANSFIELD PARK   JANE AUSTEN

'We have all been more or less to blame ... everyone of us, excepting Fanny'

Taken from the poverty of her parents' home, Fanny Price is brought up with her rich cousins at Mansfield Park, acutely aware of her humble rank and with only her cousin Edmund as an ally. During her uncle's absence in Antigua, Mary Crawford and her brother Henry arrive in the neighbourhood, bringing with them London glamour and a reckless taste for flirtation. As her female cousins vie for Henry's attention, and even Edmund falls for Mary's dazzling charms, only Fanny remains doubtful about their influence and finds herself more isolated than ever. A subtle examination of social position and moral integrity, *Mansfield Park* is one of Jane Austen's most profound works.

This edition is based, for the first time since its original publication, on the first edition of 1814. It includes a new chronology, additional suggestions for further reading and the original Penguin Classics introduction by Tony Tanner.

'These modern editions are to be strongly recommended for their scrupulous texts, informative notes and helpful introductions'
Brian Southam, the Jane Austen Society

Edited with an introduction by Kathryn Sutherland

PENGUIN CLASSICS

NORTHANGER ABBEY   JANE AUSTEN

'What have you been judging from? . . . Dearest Miss Morland, what ideas have you been admitting?'

During an eventful season at Bath, young, naive Catherine Morland experiences fashionable society for the first time. She is delighted with her new acquaintances: flirtatious Isabella, who introduces Catherine to the joys of Gothic romances, and sophisticated Henry and Eleanor Tilney, who invite her to their father's house, Northanger Abbey. There, influenced by novels of horror and intrigue, Catherine comes to imagine terrible crimes committed by General Tilney, risking the loss of Henry's affection, and must learn the difference between fiction and reality, false friends and true. With its broad comedy and irrepressible heroine, *Northanger Abbey* is the most youthful and optimistic of Jane Austen's works.

This edition is based on the first edition of 1818, and includes a new chronology and additional suggestions for further reading.

'These modern editions are to be strongly recommended for their scrupulous texts, informative notes and helpful introductions'
Brian Southam, the Jane Austen Society

Edited with an introduction by Marilyn Butler

PENGUIN CLASSICS

PERSUASION   JANE AUSTEN

'She had been forced into prudence in her youth, she learned romance as she grew older'

At twenty-seven, Anne Elliot is no longer young and has few romantic prospects. Eight years earlier, she had been persuaded by her friend Lady Russell to break off her engagement to Frederick Wentworth, a handsome naval captain with neither fortune nor rank. What happens when they encounter each other again is movingly told in Jane Austen's last completed novel. Set in the fashionable societies of Lyme Regis and Bath, *Persuasion* is a brilliant satire of vanity and pretension, but, above all, it is a love story tinged with the heartache of missed opportunities.

In her introduction, Gillian Beer discusses Austen's portrayal of the double-edged nature of persuasion and the clash between old and new worlds. This edition also includes a new chronology and full textual notes.

'These modern editions are to be strongly recommended for their scrupulous texts, informative notes and helpful introductions'
Brian Southam, The Jane Austen Society

Edited with an introduction and notes by Gillian Beer

PENGUIN CLASSICS

SENSE AND SENSIBILITY   JANE AUSTEN

'The more I know of the world the more am I convinced that I shall never see a man whom I can really love. I require so much!'

Marianne Dashwood wears her heart on her sleeve, and when she falls in love with the dashing but unsuitable John Willoughby she ignores her sister Elinor's warning that her impulsive behaviour leaves her open to gossip and innuendo. Meanwhile Elinor, always sensitive to social convention, is struggling to conceal her own romantic disappointment, even from those closest to her. Through their parallel experience of love – and its threatened loss – the sisters learn that sense must mix with sensibility if they are to find personal happiness in a society where status and money govern the rules of love.

This edition also includes explanatory notes, textual variants between first and second edition, and Tony Tanner's introduction to the original Penguin Classics edition.

'These modern editions are to be strongly recommended for their scrupulous texts, informative notes and helpful introductions'
Brian Southam, The Jane Austen Society

Edited with an introduction by Ros Ballaster

PENGUIN CLASSICS

MOLL FLANDERS   DANIEL DEFOE

'I grew as impudent a Thief, and as dexterous as ever *Moll Cut-Purse* was'

Born and abandoned in Newgate Prison, Moll Flanders is forced to make her own way in life. She duly embarks on a career that includes husband-hunting, incest, bigamy, prostitution and pick-pocketing, until her crimes eventually catch up with her. One of the earliest and most vivid female narrators in the history of the English novel, Moll recounts her adventures with irresistible wit and candour – and enough guile that the reader is left uncertain whether she is ultimately a redeemed sinner or a successful opportunist.

Based on the first edition of 1722, this volume includes a chronology, notes on currency, and maps of London and Virginia in the late seventeenth century.

Edited with an introduction and notes by David Blewett

PENGUIN CLASSICS

JANE EYRE CHARLOTTE BRONTË

'I am no bird and no net ensnares me. I am a free human being with an independent will'

Having endured humiliation and loneliness in the home of her heartless Aunt Reed, and the harsh regime of Lowood, a charity boarding school, the orphaned Jane Eyre survives her childhood unbroken in spirit and integrity. When she takes up a post as a governess at Thornfield Hall, she also finds love with her employer, the dark and sardonic Mr Rochester. But her discovery of Rochester's terrible secret forces Jane to follow her own moral convictions, even if it means giving up her chance of happiness. Although many were shocked by its depiction of a woman's bold and passionate search for independence and love on her own terms, *Jane Eyre* was an immediate success when it appeared in 1847 and remains one of the most popular of all English novels.

In his introduction, Michael Mason discusses the literary critical history of *Jane Eyre*. This edition includes suggestions for further reading, notes and a new chronology.

'The masterwork of a great genius' William Makepeace Thackeray

Edited with an introduction and notes by Michael Mason